"I hear ther

house," Jonathar

his voice.

"Yeah, isn't that cool?" Bruce replied.

"No, it's not cool. It's stupid," Jonathan said firmly. "Because there isn't going to be a party at my house."

"Unfortunately, I think it's too late to cancel now," Bruce said, meeting Jonathan's gaze evenly. "Half the school is already planning to come."

"What exactly do you think you're doing?" Jonathan asked. "What gives you the right to use my house?"

"Don't you want to fit in, Cain?" Bruce challenged him. "Any *normal* guy would be psyched to have the bash of the season."

Jonathan's eyes glittered, but Bruce's words seemed to have hit home. "Fine, have it your way," he relented. "The party's on."

"Cool! I knew you'd come around!" Bruce enthused.

But Jonathan wasn't smiling. "Just one thing," he added ominously. "Don't blame me for anything that happens on Friday night." Then he turned around and pushed his way out of the cafeteria.

DANCE OF DEATH

Written by
Kate William

Created by
FRANCINE PASCAL

BANTAM BOOKS
NEW YORK • TORONTO • LONDON • SYDNEY • AUCKLAND

DANCE OF DEATH
A BANTAM BOOK : 0 553 50460 6

Originally published in USA by Bantam Books

First publication in Great Britain

PRINTING HISTORY
Bantam edition published 1997

Conceived by Francine Pascal

Produced by Daniel Weiss Associates, Inc,
33 West 17th Street, New York, NY 10011

Cover photo by Oliver Hunter

Bantam Books are published by Transworld Publishers Ltd,
61–63 Uxbridge Road, Ealing, London W5 5SA,
in Australia by Transworld Publishers (Australia) Pty Ltd,
15–25 Helles Avenue, Moorebank, NSW 2170,
and in New Zealand by Transworld Publishers (NZ) Ltd,
3 William Pickering Drive, Albany, Auckland.

Printed and bound in Great Britain by
Cox & Wyman Ltd, Reading, Berkshire.

To Chris Kaller, Johnny's friend

Chapter 1

Sixteen-year-old Jessica Wakefield stared into Jonathan Cain's eyes. She and Jonathan were standing in the shadowy foyer of his crumbling mansion on Saturday night, and she was still reeling from the intensity of his kiss. His whispered words were echoing in her mind. *You shouldn't have come here,* he'd said. *It may have been the biggest mistake of your life.*

A mixture of pain and confusion stabbed at Jessica's heart. Just when she'd been sure Jonathan would confess his love, he had frozen up again. She studied the contours of Jonathan's beautiful pale face, searching for a clue to his behavior. But his features were shrouded in darkness, and the light from three long red candles in a wall sconce cast eerie, flickering shadows across his cheek. "Jessica,

I'm telling you," Jonathan repeated. "You shouldn't have come."

"But aren't you glad I'm here?" Jessica asked in a low voice. "Don't you like being with me?" She flipped her long blond hair over her shoulders and stared at him directly, a challenge in her blue-green eyes.

Jonathan's gaze traveled down her face, lingering on the rounded neckline of her blue silk dress. "It's not that," he said, putting out a hand and caressing the soft curve of her neck. Jessica shivered at the featherlight touch of his fingers. He pulled away from her suddenly. His fingers trembling slightly, he grabbed a glass of red wine from the side table. Closing his eyes, he lifted the crystal goblet and drank from it greedily.

Jessica's eyes widened as he downed the glass in one gulp. It was as if he were trying to quench an unquenchable thirst. *A thirst for me,* she thought in satisfaction.

Jonathan turned to face her with dark, smoldering eyes. "Jessica, I'm telling you, leave before it's too late," he insisted, his voice low and urgent. The wine had stained his already deep red lips, and his fathomless blue eyes glowed with a strange luminescence. Jessica felt as though his gaze were burning a hole into her, as though he were trying to send her an unspoken message.

A strangely exhilarating chill traveled up her spine. Every nerve ending in her body was alive and tingling. She'd had this giddy feeling ever since Jonathan Cain moved to Sweet Valley a short time before. He was a senior transfer with a cool, distant air and an almost magnetic aura. With his reserved manner and haunted-looking eyes, he seemed like a tortured soul—and Jessica had found herself irresistibly drawn to him. Jonathan was tall and lanky, with smooth white skin and a gorgeous face that looked as though it had been chiseled from marble. His face was framed by long, wavy black hair, and his piercing blue eyes stood out in the paleness of his face, giving him a stark, dramatic look.

"Too late for what?" Jessica returned in a low, husky voice.

Jonathan's eyes narrowed, and a look of torment passed over his features. He twisted his fingers, causing the ring he wore on his middle finger to glint in the light of the flickering candles. Jessica eyed the solid ring with curiosity. It was an ornate wooden band with an onyx-and-silver inlay. *What does it mean?* she wondered. *Where did he get it, and why does he wear it all the time?*

Everything about Jonathan was a mystery. He had seemed to appear out of nowhere. Mr. Cooper, the principal, had introduced Jonathan to the student body at an assembly and had provided almost all the information Jessica knew. Apparently Jonathan had been living abroad before he moved to Sweet Valley. According to Mr. Cooper, he'd attended schools all over Europe—in Sweden, England, and even Greece. Now he was living all alone in Sweet Valley in this desolate old mansion. Jessica's eyes narrowed. He didn't seem to have a real home or parents. *Who is Jonathan Cain?* she wondered.

But there was nothing Jessica liked better than a mystery. The moment she'd caught sight of Jonathan in the auditorium, she knew instinctively that he was the one for her. And the more she saw of him, the surer she became. Everything about him appealed to her. Jonathan wore black jeans and a black leather jacket. And he drove a big Harley, a beautiful black motorcycle with silver stripes. Jonathan was definitely her kind of guy—dark, dangerous, and mysterious.

Jessica had turned on the charm full force, but up until a few moments ago, Jonathan had resisted all her advances. She had deliberately parked next to him at school, and she had slipped him notes in French class. She had even jumped on the back of his motorcycle one afternoon at the mall, forcing him to give her a ride home. Most boys turned to jelly the minute Jessica turned her blue-green eyes on them, but Jonathan had remained as cold and unyielding as a boulder. In fact, he'd pushed her away at every turn.

Jessica couldn't understand why he'd been resisting her. She was sure he shared her feelings. And she was sure he felt the electric current that sizzled between them.

Jonathan looked at her with pleading eyes. "Jessica, please don't make me do something I'll regret." His words were barely a whisper.

Jessica responded in the same low tone. "Don't worry, you won't regret it."

Jonathan's jaw clenched. "Jessica, what did I tell you in my note in French class?" he asked.

Jessica smiled. "You said you ate little girls like me for breakfast."

"And what did I tell you last night?" Jonathan demanded.

Jessica recalled the experience vividly. She had gotten home late to discover that her new kitten, Jasmine, had disappeared. Terrified that something had happened to her pet, Jessica had run out to hunt for her. She had finally found the kitten stuck in a neighbor's tree, mewling in fear. Then Jonathan had suddenly appeared out of the darkness. Jasmine had reacted as if she had seen a ghost. Yowling and hissing, she had clawed wildly at the tree bark. After Jessica retrieved her,

Jasmine had even tried to scratch Jonathan's face. But even stranger than Jasmine's behavior had been Jonathan's words, which seemed to be engraved in her mind. "You said, 'Beware of predators,'" Jessica recalled. "'They come in all shapes and sizes.'"

Jonathan looked anguished. "Isn't that enough for you?"

Jessica smiled coyly. "I like a challenge," she said softly. "And I like predators."

"Jessica, this isn't a game," Jonathan told her. He pulled the front door open, and a gust of wind shot through the opening. "Please go before it's too late."

Jessica shivered as the blast of cold air hit her bare neck and whipped through her thin silk dress. She wrapped her arms around her body, hesitating. She couldn't bear to give up now—she was so close. Jonathan was clearly interested in her. Jessica didn't know why he'd been fighting his feelings for her, but she intended to find out. Standing on her tiptoes, she captured his lips with hers. His kiss was salty and sweet at the same time and tasted faintly of red wine. She felt him resist for a moment, but then he returned the kiss with a strength that left her breathless.

Jonathan pulled back abruptly and looked at her with fire in his eyes. "Fine, have it your way," he muttered. Jessica's heart pounded as he slammed the door shut and blew out the candles, roughly pulling her toward him in the darkness.

"Todd!" Elizabeth gasped, pulling abruptly out of Joey Mason's embrace in the foyer of the Wakefield house. Elizabeth could feel the blood rush to her cheeks as she faced her boyfriend. Todd Wilkins was standing squarely in the doorway, his hands on his hips.

"Elizabeth," Todd answered wryly.

Elizabeth studied his expression, her heart sounding a drumroll in her chest. Her boyfriend's face was a calm mask, but hurt and anger were flickering in his deep brown eyes.

"Uh—I—I—" Elizabeth stammered, searching desperately for an explanation. She had spent a month the summer before as a counselor at Camp Echo Mountain, a performing-arts camp in the mountains of Montana. Todd had been away at basketball camp outside of Los Angeles. Despite her best intentions, she had found herself irresistibly drawn to Joey Mason, the drama counselor, and they'd had a secret fling.

Her affair with Joey had thrown her into confusion, but when Elizabeth came back to Sweet Valley, she'd made a firm decision. Her summer romance was just that—a summer romance. She was still in love with Todd, and there was no reason for him to know anything about her little fling with Joey. Joey had been planning to go to Yale in the fall, and she had thought she would never see him again. But things had gotten unexpectedly complicated. Joey had sent her a letter with the news that he had decided to go to UCLA instead and wanted to resume his relationship with her.

Elizabeth drew a ragged breath and composed herself. "Todd, this is Joey. He's a friend from—"

"Save it, Elizabeth," Todd interrupted. Then he wheeled around and slammed the door behind him.

Elizabeth stared at the door, her mouth gaping.

"I guess you're still with Todd," Joey said dryly.

Elizabeth looked at him in surprise. She had almost forgotten he was there. "I'll be right back," she told Joey. Flinging the door open, she raced out and sprinted down the driveway after Todd.

"Todd!" Elizabeth called.

"What do you want?" Todd barked. He was standing at the edge of the driveway, his face contorted in rage.

"Would you just talk to me?" Elizabeth called, running toward him. But Todd backed away and jumped into his black BMW.

Elizabeth pounded on the driver's-side window. Todd waved her away and revved the engine.

Undaunted, Elizabeth pounded harder. "Just hear me out!" she yelled. Giving her a dirty look, Todd rolled down the window.

"Would you mind letting me leave?" he snarled at her.

"I just want to explain," Elizabeth said.

"Well, I don't want an explanation," Todd said angrily. "I've heard enough lies from you."

Elizabeth winced, but she didn't back down. "Fine, we'll talk later! But right now we've got to help Jessica!" she implored desperately.

Todd gunned the engine. "Get your *other* boyfriend to help," he said.

Then he screeched off into the night, leaving a wake of dust in his trail.

Elizabeth stared at the retreating taillights of Todd's BMW, blinking back tears. Now she'd really blown it. Even if she told him that she and Joey were just friends, he'd never believe her. Winston Egbert and Aaron Dallas had also been counselors at Camp Echo Mountain. They were two of Todd's best friends, and she was sure they were suspicious of her and Joey's relationship at camp. Elizabeth sighed. *Was a summer fling worth it?* she wondered. *Is Joey important enough to me to be worth losing Todd?*

Then Elizabeth shook her head. She couldn't think about that now. There were more pressing matters at hand. She had just heard a broadcast on the radio with the news that a young blond woman had been murdered that evening near Secca Lake. And her twin sister, Jessica, had disappeared. Elizabeth was terrified that the murdered girl might be Jessica.

Frantic after hearing the news, Elizabeth had run to the phone and called Todd, begging him to come help her look for her sister. He had assured her he would be right over to pick her up. But before Todd had arrived, Joey had shown up on her doorstep. And now they were losing time. Even if Jessica was OK, she was still out there somewhere. And so was the murderer.

Hit again with a feeling of panic, Elizabeth raced up the driveway and charged through the front door. Joey was pacing around the foyer.

He turned to face her as she came flying in. "What did you tell him?" Joey asked.

"Nothing," Elizabeth said, shaking her head. "But it doesn't matter now." She yanked her coat from the closet and grabbed Joey's hand. "Come on," she said urgently. "We've got to go!"

"Where?" Joey asked as she led him out the front door.

"We've got to find out who the dead girl is," Elizabeth explained, pulling Joey down the driveway.

"What?" Joey asked, baffled. "The dead girl?"

Elizabeth pulled open the passenger-side door of Joey's Land Rover. "Get in," she said. "I'll explain on the way."

Joey jumped into the driver's seat and started the car.

"A girl was murdered earlier this evening at Secca Lake," Elizabeth explained as they sped down Calico Drive. "Take a right at the stop sign and go straight till you get to the light. And hurry!"

Joey looked at her with concern in his green eyes. "Did you know the girl?"

"I'm scared it might be—" Elizabeth got choked up as she tried to get out the words. Taking a deep breath, she forced herself to speak. "I'm scared it might be Jessica," she whispered.

Joey's eyes filled with alarm. "Jessica! What makes you think it could be Jessica?" The light turned green, and Joey hit the gas pedal, flying down the road.

Elizabeth started to cry. "Because she found the body in the trash when Jasmine was in the tree. She's the one who could have witnessed the murder! And she has blond hair and blue eyes!"

"Whoa! Slow down," Joey said, laying a comforting hand over hers. "Now start at the beginning."

Elizabeth pulled a tissue out of her purse and

wiped her eyes. Drawing a shaky breath, she tried to compose herself. "A week ago a boy named Dean Maddingly from Big Mesa High was murdered at the Dairi Burger. They found him in the Dumpster behind the restaurant. His body was drained of blood." A chill traveled down Elizabeth's spine at the thought of it.

Joey nodded. "Go on," he said.

"Jessica found the body," Elizabeth said.

"In the Dumpster?" Joey interrupted.

Elizabeth nodded. "She lost one of a pair of diamond earrings that our grandmother gave her, and she and Lila were sifting through the trash looking for it. But instead she found the . . . the body. And there was a kitten in a tree as well. The police think the kitten witnessed the murder, because she was yowling her lungs out. Jessica adopted her. Her name's Jasmine." Elizabeth peered into the steady evening traffic. "Here, take this ramp onto the highway."

Joey took the ramp and whizzed onto the freeway. The stormy ocean came into view. The waves crashed wildly against the shore, echoing the turbulence in Elizabeth's heart. Cutting smoothly across the four lanes of traffic, Joey moved into the left lane and put his foot hard on the accelerator.

Elizabeth took a deep breath and continued her story. "Tonight Jessica and I were supposed to hang out and watch movies, but she disappeared. Then I heard this report on the radio that a girl was killed this evening—a young blond girl." Elizabeth's lips quivered as she forced out the words.

Joey squeezed her hand. "Elizabeth, I'm sure it's not your sister, but I'm going to take you there as fast as I can to find out."

Elizabeth squeezed his hand in return. Leaning back into the seat, she watched the ocean in the distance. A cold knot of fear seized her stomach at the thought of what lay ahead. *Jessica,* she whispered in her mind. *Jessica, please be OK.*

Enid Rollins shut off the car's headlights and cut her speed as she turned the corner. "Forrest Lane," she whispered to herself. Forrest Lane was Jonathan's block. It was a long, winding street in a desolate area on the outskirts of Sweet Valley.

I can't believe people actually live here, Enid thought as she took in the run-down houses and overgrown lots. A tremor of fear made her catch her breath. The street was completely deserted, and she could barely see in the dim light of the streetlamp.

Suddenly a big, ugly rat poked its head out of a storm drain and slithered across the road.

"Huh?" Enid slammed on the brakes. *A rat!* The rodent scampered into an open field on her left. Enid squinted as she watched the rat disappear in the high weeds. *What else is in there?* she wondered. *Poisonous spiders? Rattlesnakes?* Then her mind flashed to the radio broadcast she had heard earlier. The body of a girl had been found at Secca Lake—drained of all her blood. Enid shuddered. What if the murderer was out there?

I've got to get out of here! Enid flipped on the lights and shifted the car into reverse. Her heart beating wildly, she backed down the street and turned the corner onto Maple Lane. Enid shifted back into first gear and drove rapidly down the street. She heaved a sigh of relief as she reached the crowded intersection.

The light turned green, but Enid hesitated. After all, she had come all this way to see Jonathan. She had gotten so close. Did she really want to back out now? A car honked loudly behind her, and Enid crossed the intersection, turning into a side street. She pulled to a stop and considered her course of action.

You're overreacting, she told herself. *You let yourself get spooked by a dark street and a little rodent.* After all, Jonathan lived on Forrest Lane. It couldn't be that dangerous. There was no reason to think the murderer would be there. He could be anywhere in Sweet Valley. The important thing was to be inside. Enid was sure that Jonathan would calm her fears when she told him about the murder. He would be impressed that she had risked her life to come see him, and he would take her in his arms and comfort her. . . .

That's it, Enid decided. She wasn't going to let a radio broadcast scare her. But she had to make her move soon. The longer she waited outside in the dark, the more frightened she was going to become.

Putting her foot on the gas, she accelerated and drove slowly down the block. The street wasn't lit at all, and Enid had to squint in the darkness as she drove. She swung the car carefully around the corner and continued down the next block. When she reached the corner of Jonathan's street, she pulled the blue hatchback to a stop. *Time to make your move,* Enid told herself, her heart beginning to thump loudly in her chest.

But Enid hesitated again before continuing down the block. Usually she was pretty shy around guys. Unlike a lot of the girls in the junior class, Enid almost never chased after boys, which she normally considered a ditzy thing to do. Guys usually liked her for her intelligence and her sense of humor. Her relationships tended to start off as friendships and blossom into something more. But Jonathan wasn't the aggressive type. He kept to himself most of the time and didn't seem particularly impressed by any of the girls at Sweet Valley High. If Enid wanted him, she was going to have to make the first move.

And she did want him. At the first sight of Jonathan Cain, Enid had realized she'd found her soul mate. Everything about him mesmerized her: the way he walked, the way he talked, the deep, soulful look in his eyes. . . .

But Jonathan hadn't even noticed she was alive. She had tried to catch his eye in the hall a number of times, but he had just walked right by her. So Enid had undergone a transformation. She had performed a complete body and personality make-over on herself.

Enid smiled as she thought of her metamorphosis. The old Enid had been boring and conservative, with curly reddish brown hair and a nondescript manner of dressing. The new Enid was hip and sophisticated. After a trip to the beauty salon, she'd been transformed into a new woman. Her curly hair had been dyed and chemically straightened. Now it was jet black and fell fine and straight over her shoulders. Her nails were long and pointed, and her eyebrows were thin and arched. Thick black eyeliner and blue-black lipstick provided a stark contrast to the pale foundation that she'd smoothed over her face.

The old Enid had been invisible. She was always

hiding behind a book or behind a computer. She was the type to get lost in the crowd. The new Enid could compete with the most popular girls in Sweet Valley—even Lila Fowler and Jessica Wakefield.

The old Enid had spent most of her time in Elizabeth Wakefield's shadow, following along inconspicuously as Elizabeth led her perfect life. But now all that had changed. Enid was her own woman, and she wasn't even friends with Elizabeth anymore.

Enid gritted her teeth as she remembered the reason for the new chasm between her and her former best friend. *Maria Slater.* When Elizabeth was at camp last summer, she had rekindled her friendship with Maria, who had been a good friend of Elizabeth's in grade school before Maria's family moved away to New York. It was bad enough that Maria had gone to summer camp with Elizabeth, but now she'd moved back to Sweet Valley for good. As soon as Maria came back into her life, Elizabeth had dropped Enid like a hot potato.

Enid scowled. Obviously Elizabeth preferred star material to average Enid Rollins. Maria had created quite a stir when she returned to Sweet Valley. She had been a child actress until the age of twelve and still had the presence of a movie star. She was tall and statuesque, with short-cropped curly dark brown hair, smooth ebony skin, and wide-set deep brown eyes. Elizabeth and Maria were always sharing stories about camp and making private jokes. Elizabeth used to be a supportive friend, but now she was trying to become Enid's nagging conscience. Not only did she disapprove of Enid's interest in Jonathan, but she hated her new look as well.

That figures, Enid thought as she stared out at the desolate street. Elizabeth Wakefield was too conservative for her, anyway. The cool gothic crowd was more her type. Jonathan's somber style of dressing had started a craze at Sweet Valley, and now a lot of girls in the junior class were dressing in the gothic style, wearing dramatic black clothes, dark lipstick, and thick black eyeliner. As soon as Enid had adopted her new look, Lynne Henry, Julie Porter, and Jennifer Mitchell had welcomed her into their fold, and Enid had made a whole new set of friends.

Enid adjusted the rearview mirror and studied her reflection. Pulling out a tube of Midnight Blue lipstick from her bag, she carefully outlined her lips. Then she blotted her lips on a piece of tissue and sucked in her cheeks, admiring the shadows under her cheekbones. She was breathtaking. With her dramatic makeup and strong bone structure, she looked glamorous and sophisticated—like a movie star. *I'm perfect for Jonathan,* she told herself with a smile. *What am I waiting for?*

With renewed confidence, Enid restarted the engine and coasted down the block, pulling to a stop in front of Jonathan's house. Enid shook her head as she took in the forlorn old mansion. If she hadn't followed Jonathan home the week before and seen him enter the house with her own eyes, she wouldn't have believed anybody lived there. The dark house was crumbling and neglected, with peeling gray paint and cracked windows. Several towers and gables poked up from the roof, creating the effect of an abandoned fortress from the Middle Ages. The front porch sagged dangerously to one side, and the yard was overgrown with tall weeds.

The last time Enid had been there, she'd peered through a window. She had been shocked to find the inside as run-down and neglected as the outside. Fraying carpets covered the wooden floors, and a few pieces of musty old furniture stood in the living room. The rest of the furniture was covered with white sheets, as if the house were for sale. Enid's heart went out to Jonathan. She couldn't imagine living in that ghost house. From what she had seen, it looked as though Jonathan lived alone. The only vehicle parked in the driveway had been Jonathan's Harley, and she hadn't seen anybody else in the house. *He must be lonely,* Enid thought.

Well, he won't be lonely for much longer, she decided, lifting an elegant heel out of the car and stepping onto the pavement. But as soon as her foot hit the asphalt, she caught sight of another car parked farther down the street. Enid's eyes narrowed suspiciously. The street had been completely deserted a few minutes ago. Enid squinted into the darkness and tried to make out the vehicle. It was the Wakefield twins' Jeep.

Jessica, Enid thought with dismay, ducking back into her car. She knew Elizabeth couldn't be there. Elizabeth hated Jonathan—she'd made her feelings about him clear enough. She wouldn't stop telling Enid to keep away from him. But how did Jessica know where Jonathan lived? Enid was the only one who knew where his house was—because she had followed him home one day after school.

Enid tapped her long fingernails on the steering wheel. Was Jonathan interested in Jessica? Had he invited her over? A tidal wave of jealousy crashed over her, and the street blurred in front of her. Were Jonathan and Jessica dating? *They can't be, they can't be, they can't be,* Enid told herself. They couldn't be going out. Enid closed her eyes and took a deep breath. There had to be another explanation.

Then her conversation at the Dairi Burger with

Jessica came back to her, and Enid swore under her breath. She knew exactly how Jessica had gotten the information—from Enid herself. On Friday afternoon Enid had been sitting alone at the Dairi Burger, feeling completely dejected. Jessica had joined her. She had acted completely sympathetic, and Enid had spilled her guts. She had told Jessica all about her crush on Jonathan and about following him home. "Does Jonathan live near you?" Jessica had asked innocently. "Are you sure you had the right house?" Enid should have known Jessica was being nice to her only because she wanted more information about Jonathan. Typical.

Enid felt like kicking herself. She never should have revealed Jonathan's address to Jessica. She should have known that conniving, scheming Jessica Wakefield would try to get him herself.

I wish I'd never met either Wakefield, Enid thought angrily. *They're both totally self-centered.*

Chapter 2

"So, are you going to show me around?" Jessica asked, pulling back from Jonathan. Her lips felt raw and bruised from his rough kiss.

"I suppose so," Jonathan said, taking her hand and leading her down the hall.

But Jessica pulled her hand out of his grasp. Since she had him now, she decided it was time to be coy. She didn't want to be *too* easy to get—it wasn't her usual style. Jessica Wakefield never ran after the guys she wanted. She usually had full control of every situation, playing it cool until the guy she had her eye on fell head over heels in love with her.

Jessica squinted in the darkness. "Don't you have any lights in this place?" she asked.

"I think it's important to conserve energy, don't

you?" Jonathan asked with an ironic smile. A pile of burning embers glowed red in the fireplace. Jonathan placed a few logs on the fire and tossed a handful of kindling wood on top of them. Then he crumpled up a piece of newspaper and threw it in as well. The flames licked hungrily at the edges of the paper, and the fire burst into a riot of orange and red.

Jessica took in the interior of the mansion with amazement. She couldn't believe someone actually lived there. It looked like the set of a horror movie. The walls were peeling, and there were holes in the floorboards. She ran her finger down a crooked crack in the wall, causing tiny shards of plaster to fall to the floor. Stained, fraying carpets covered the floors, and white sheets were draped over most of the furniture. Jessica peeked under one of the sheets and saw a majestic grand piano. *Wow,* she thought, *this mansion must have been something before it went to pieces.* Jessica hit a few notes randomly, then draped the sheet back over it. The only furniture that wasn't covered was a green couch with torn upholstery and a broken armchair in the corner.

"You're like a cat, aren't you?" Jonathan asked, watching as she investigated the room. "Curious."

Jessica gave him a flirtatious smile. "And *yes,* I know what happened to the curious cat. Don't worry, I'm just checking out my surroundings."

"I wouldn't get too comfortable if I were you," Jonathan said. "Remember, you're still in foreign territory." His tone was light, but his forehead was creased, and something flickered in his eyes for a moment. Then it was gone.

"I think *barren* is a better word for it," Jessica replied. "Any reason you haven't bothered uncovering the furniture?" She smiled at him mischievously. "So you can make a quick getaway?"

Jonathan's eyes glittered strangely. "Something like that."

Jessica put her hands on her hips. "No, really."

Jonathan shrugged. "I just haven't gotten around to it."

Jessica turned to take a seat on the couch. She brushed off the sagging cushion before sitting down, coughing as a cloud of dust flew into the air. "Ick!" she exclaimed, waving the dust away wildly with both hands.

Jonathan watched her with crossed arms, looking amused.

Jessica walked across the room and perched on the arm of the chair. "You could use a few decorating tips from my mother," she said. "She's an interior decorator."

"I could use your mother for a few other things as well," Jonathan replied. "Like disciplining you."

He looked at her oddly. "Does anyone know you're here?"

Jessica shook her head, her heart racing with excitement. Her mother wasn't the problem—her sister was. Elizabeth would kill her if she knew Jessica was there. Jonathan had cornered Elizabeth one day in the *Oracle* office and warned her to keep Jessica away from him. Elizabeth hadn't liked Jonathan from the start, but after that she had lost it. Elizabeth had made Jessica promise that she wouldn't see Jonathan anymore, so Jessica had been forced to sneak out that evening.

Jessica sighed inwardly. Sometimes Elizabeth acted more like her mother than her mother did. Even though the twins were identical in appearance, from their long golden blond hair to their sparkling blue-green eyes to their slim, athletic figures, they couldn't be more different in character. Elizabeth was thoughtful and cautious; Jessica was impetuous and careless. Elizabeth planned things in advance; Jessica acted on impulse. Elizabeth saved up to buy; Jessica spent on credit.

Their lifestyles reflected the differences in their personalities. Elizabeth had a serious and conscientious nature. She was a straight-A student with high ambitions to be a writer someday. As a staff writer for the *Oracle,* the school newspaper, Elizabeth wrote a weekly column called "Personal

Profiles." Jessica, on the other hand, lived for the moment. She was cocaptain of the cheerleading squad and an active member of Pi Beta Alpha, the most exclusive sorority at Sweet Valley High. While Elizabeth spent much of her spare time alone at her desk or curled up with a book, Jessica could usually be found in the center of the crowd, either on the beach or at the mall.

Jessica shivered as she looked around the drafty old house. It wasn't just that the house was badly decorated—it didn't even look lived in. The few lamps in the room were coated with layers of dust, and the sheets draped over the furniture gave the house a ghostly appearance. The only signs of life were the crackling fire in the fireplace and a bottle of red wine sitting on the coffee table.

She shook off her eerie feeling and walked to the fire, warming her hands.

Jonathan poured a glass of blood-red wine into a glass. "I would offer you some, but you're underage," he said. "And unfortunately I don't have any lemonade."

"Do you have any milk?" Jessica asked sarcastically, turning around to face him.

Jonathan smiled a little bashfully. "Sorry, I didn't mean to patronize you."

"You're underage too, you know," Jessica pointed out.

Jonathan took a sip of the wine. "Not exactly," he said, the mysterious tone returning to his voice.

Jessica's eyes narrowed. Jonathan was only a senior in high school—he *couldn't* be twenty-one. Maybe he'd lost a few years traveling around the world. Maybe he really *was* much older. That would explain why he seemed so much more sophisticated than the other guys at Sweet Valley High.

"How old *are* you?" Jessica asked.

Jonathan paused, as if he was considering something. "I'm older than the stars," he responded finally, a cryptic tone in his voice.

Jessica rolled her eyes, but she dropped the subject. In any case, he was older than she was, and the thought excited her. She loved older men.

"Actually, I'd like a glass of water," Jessica said. "If you don't mind."

Jonathan gave her a twisted smile. "I think I can manage that."

She followed Jonathan down a narrow passageway lined with bookshelves. She ran her fingers along the old books as they walked down the hall, drawing a line in the dust on the spines. She flicked the dust from her fingers as they reached the kitchen. "Oh, boy," she breathed as she took in the room. It was completely barren except for a big sink and an antique stove. But the stove was lying on its side in the middle of the floor.

Jonathan ducked under a swaying lamp and reached around the stove. Turning on the faucet, he filled a glass with water.

"You know, the stove works better when it's standing upright," Jessica said as Jonathan handed her the glass.

Jonathan hit the side of his head, a glint in his eyes. "So *that's* why all my pots and pans have been sliding to the floor. I knew there was something wrong."

Jessica laughed. She took a sip of water as she scanned the cruddy old room. The linoleum floor was warped and stained, and the bottom of the stove was worn through with rust. There were no cabinets, and there was no refrigerator. She looked at Jonathan in amazement. "What in the world do you eat here?" she asked.

Jonathan cocked his head at her. "I told you already."

Jessica nodded. "I know, you eat little girls for breakfast." She set down her glass of water on the stove and gave him a flirtatious smile. "That must get a little boring. Girls like me can be tough to digest."

Jonathan shook his head. "No, they're sweet—thick and sweet." He smiled, but the smile didn't reach his eyes. Jessica smiled back, but a sudden chill coursed through her veins.

Feeling suddenly nervous, Jessica walked back into the living room and stood in front of the fire. A huge portrait hung over the mantelpiece. The guy in the painting looked exactly like Jonathan, but the portrait was obviously very old. Jessica studied it curiously. The picture had an ornate gold frame and a black background. It reminded Jessica of one of the old paintings in the Louvre museum. The young man in the picture looked serious and dignified. He was wearing a black riding coat with a high turned-up collar, an ivory ascot around his neck, and highly polished black boots. But despite the difference in style, the resemblance to Jonathan was uncanny.

"Do you like art?" Jonathan asked, appearing suddenly in the doorway.

Jessica jumped, but she didn't want him to see that she was shaken up. "Of course. And I particularly like this painting. Who's that? A relative of yours?" she asked.

"You ask too many questions," Jonathan said, coming up behind her. He wrapped his arms around her and brought his moist lips to her neck. Jessica closed her eyes and shivered in delight. As his lips sucked at her neck, Jessica felt the blood rush to her ears. She felt his heart beating in time with her heart, and the heady sensation made her dizzy. Her head whirled, and she felt as if she were about to lose consciousness.

Jonathan groaned, almost a strangled cry. Then he wrenched his lips from her neck and turned her around.

Jessica stared into Jonathan's blue eyes. They were so dark they looked almost black. His skin was flushed bright red—not its usual pale white. Jessica felt light-headed. *It must be because of the heat of the fire,* she thought.

Jessica swayed, and Jonathan caught her, wrapping his arms tightly around her. Then he nibbled at her lips, biting softly, playfully. Jessica groaned with pleasure. Finally he caught her lips with his. When he kissed her, she lost all sense of time and place. She felt as though she were falling through a thousand lifetimes.

"I want to belong to you," Jessica whispered.

"That's it, Joey!" Elizabeth exclaimed, pointing to a placid dark lake in the distance.

Joey exited the highway and followed the road to the edge of Secca Lake. The road was blocked off to traffic, and Elizabeth could see the lights of several police cars and ambulances blinking in the distance. The area was swarming with TV news teams and curious onlookers.

Elizabeth felt faint with terror. "I feel sick," she murmured.

Joey put an arm around her shoulder. "Hey, Liz, don't worry," he said, trying to calm her down.

But Elizabeth shrugged his arm off. Another news bulletin had come over the radio, and she wanted to hear it. "Shhh! Listen!" she hissed.

"Again, we repeat tonight's breaking story. The body of a young woman was found near Secca Lake this evening. The cause of the death was exsanguination—the draining of the blood."

The blood drained from Elizabeth's face at the thought of it. "The body has still not been identified," continued the broadcast. "But the police believe the case may be linked to the recent murder of Big Mesa High School student Dean Maddingly, whose body was found exactly one week ago at the Dairi Burger. The latest victim is similar in appearance to the first one—a young Caucasian in her late teens with blond hair and blue eyes."

Elizabeth moaned and leaned her head against the headrest. "What if it's Jessica?" she whispered.

"Come on, Elizabeth," Joey reassured her. "Of course it's not Jessica. A million girls fit that description. Especially in California."

"Well, I'm going to find out," Elizabeth said with determination. She pulled open the door and jumped out.

"Elizabeth!" Joey protested. "You can't get through! The area is blocked off."

Elizabeth's blue-green eyes glittered as she faced Joey. "Joey, my twin is in trouble. I can feel it," she said.

Joey nodded. "OK, then, let's go."

They leaped out of the car and pushed past the DO NOT CROSS police tapes.

"Hey! Get back here!" a police officer yelled.

One of the paramedics tried to grab her, but Elizabeth wriggled out of his hold. The reporters and police officers crowding the path caused her panic to grow. Adrenaline was flowing through her body.

"Joey! This way!" Elizabeth yelled, weaving her way through the line of police cars. But Joey didn't appear, and Elizabeth turned, looking wildly through the crowd. He wasn't anywhere to be seen. Elizabeth shrugged and kept going. "Jessica! Jessica!" she yelled hysterically, running right into the arms of an officer.

"No, my name is Officer Gordon," he said. "And I think you'd better come with me, young lady."

Elizabeth backed up and gulped as she looked up into the stern eyes of the police officer.

Enid was brooding in her car outside Jonathan's house. She kept turning the engine on and off, trying to get herself to go home.

She knew she didn't stand a chance competing against Jessica, but Enid felt paralyzed—she couldn't stop staring at the house.

A fire was flickering inside, sending leaping shadows against the windows. Enid imagined what was going on in the house. She envisioned Jonathan pulling Jessica into his arms, and Jessica smiling up at him with her Doublemint Twin smile. Seething with jealousy and frustration, Enid clenched her fingers on her forearm. Suddenly she jerked back in pain, realizing that she had raked her long, sharp fingernails along her bare arm.

Enid stared at the four even traces carved into her skin. *Maybe it's a sign,* she thought, *a sign that the new Enid is out for blood.* Maybe it meant that she should fight to get what she wanted. Enid traced a finger along a tender pink scratch, her eyes narrowing. Maybe she should barge into the house and ruin their evening. *Jonathan will take one look at me and realize that* I'm *the one he truly loves.*

Enid leaned back against the seat and closed her eyes. Was she going crazy? Maybe everybody was right. Maybe she really *was* losing it. Ever since Jonathan had cast his spell on her, her entire life had fallen to pieces. She wasn't speaking to Elizabeth, and her grades were plummeting. The previous day some annoying, busybody guidance counselor named Mrs. Green had called her mother to issue a "progress warning." Her mother had grounded her indefinitely—until her grades and her attitude picked up.

Enid shook her head. Nobody understood what she was going through. Nobody understood her love for Jonathan. Her mother said she had turned into a "freak-show queen," and Elizabeth said she was in the grip of an obsession that was spinning out of control. Enid's lips turned down in a scowl. They were both totally condescending. She wasn't going through some kind of juvenile phase. She was experiencing the most important change of her life, finally becoming the person she was always meant to be.

Enid knew Jonathan would understand her. She sensed it instinctively. A lot of the students at school wondered why Jonathan had come all the way to Sweet Valley from Europe, but Enid knew why. He had come to be with her. She could feel it deep inside. It was as though their souls had been searching for each other for years—and they had found each other at last. His presence at school soothed her. Even if they didn't speak, she felt his presence in the halls, in the cafeteria, in study hall. And when she had come home from school that day, she'd had an eerie sense that he was beckoning to her. She could feel him calling to her across town. The pull was irresistible. She had to go to him.

Desperate to see him, Enid had slipped past her mother and sneaked out of the house that evening. If her mother caught her now, she'd probably disown her. But that didn't matter. *I would risk anything to be with Jonathan,* Enid realized with sudden clarity. A tear came to her eye and she brushed it away, slumping her head against the seat. She clenched her hands into fists and choked back a sob. She had taken such care in dressing that evening. And she had gone to so much trouble to get out of the house. But now Jonathan was with Jessica instead of her. Enid was risking her mother's trust for nothing.

"Enid, go home," she told herself. She turned the engine on again and gave the house one last look. But then she shut the motor off again. It was as if an unseen force were holding her where she was.

I have to see what's going on in there, she decided finally. *I have to see it with my own eyes.*

Wiping her eyes with her fists, she pushed the car door open and stepped out soundlessly. She clicked the door shut, shivering in the cool night air. Her short black dress and sheer black nylons provided little protection from the elements.

Wrapping her arms around her body, she stepped gingerly onto the wet lawn. The trees cast spooky shadows on the crumbling brick walls of the mansion, and the cracked windows gaped at her ominously from the second floor. She shuddered with fear as she made her way through the tall weeds surrounding the house.

Feeling her way along the building, she crept to the long bay window of the living room. She hated herself for what she was doing, but she couldn't help it. She had to find out if Jonathan and Jessica were together.

Long curtains blocked her view, and the flickering fire sent bursts of light along them. Keeping low, Enid inched to the middle of the window and peered between the curtains. She saw two figures silhouetted by the light of the fire, locked in an embrace. At the sight of their passionate kiss, Enid wanted to die. But she stared, transfixed by the image. Jonathan grabbed a handful of Jessica's hair and crushed her even closer to him. Jessica wrapped her arms tighter around his neck, kissing him wildly the whole time. Then he picked her up in his arms and carried her across the room. The couple disappeared from sight.

Enid whimpered and gazed at the flickering fire. Then she laid her forehead against the cold glass of the window and closed her eyes in pain.

With her palm flat against the brick building, she slowly sank to the ground below the window. Enid crouched on the ground and wrapped her arms around her body. She had never felt more desperate in her entire life.

"I'm in charge of security here," Officer Gordon said to Elizabeth, flashing his badge at her. "You could get a big fine for crossing those police lines, young lady," he said sternly.

"I know, and I'm sorry. It's just that—" Elizabeth began.

But Officer Gordon interrupted her. "I don't care what your story is." He held a hand forehead high. "I've had it up to here with excuses. The reporters have to get through—they're holding the presses for this story. The medical staff has to get through—they want to run some tests on the body. The public has to get through—they want to see the murder victim with their own eyes." Officer Gordon shook his head in disgust. "There's been a murder, and all anybody cares about is publicity. A human life has been taken, and everybody's interest is sensationalistic. I have *had* it." Taking Elizabeth by the shoulders, he steered her back to the police line.

"Liz!" Joey exclaimed as he caught sight of her. He was standing right in front of the yellow tape, an anxious look on his face. "I thought I'd lost you."

"I think you'd better keep an eye on her, young man," Officer Gordon told Joey.

"Don't worry, I'll keep her out of trouble," Joey said, slinging an arm around Elizabeth's shoulders.

But Elizabeth pushed his arm away. She faced the police officer squarely, her eyes flashing with Wakefield determination. "I'm not going anywhere," she said firmly. "I don't care what other people have told you. I have to see who that girl is."

The police officer sighed. "And what makes you an exception?" he asked skeptically.

"Sorry, sir. She's just a little worked up," Joey said apologetically.

Elizabeth shot him a look. "I am *not* worked up. You see, Officer, I think I know who the girl is. I think she might be my . . . my sister." Voicing her fears out loud caused tears to spring to her eyes, and Elizabeth blinked them back desperately. She didn't want the police officer to think she was hysterical. And Joey wasn't helping matters.

The officer looked at her in concern. "Why do you think it's your sister?"

Elizabeth burst out sobbing. "Because she disappeared tonight, sometime before the murder."

"What does she look like?" Officer Gordon asked.

"She looks just like me!" Elizabeth exclaimed, sniffling. "We're twins!" She pulled a tissue out of her pocket and dabbed at her eyes.

"Do you know how many girls in California fit your general description?" Officer Gordon asked.

Joey nodded. "That's what I told her."

Elizabeth gritted her teeth. She felt like socking him. It was bad enough that the police officer wasn't taking her seriously. She didn't need Joey undermining her at every turn.

"Do you know how many calls we've received this evening from hysterical parents?" Officer Gordon went on. "If I let everyone through who knew somebody with blond hair and blue eyes, we'd have a mob on our hands. I'm sorry, but you're just going to have to go home and wait for the radio report like everybody else."

"But Jessica's the one who found the body last week!" Elizabeth insisted.

"Jessica Wakefield?" Officer Gordon asked, his interest piqued. "The girl whose picture was in the paper?"

Elizabeth nodded. "I'm Elizabeth Wakefield. Jessica's my sister." She tried to catch her breath, but a sob caught in her throat.

"Shhh . . . OK, calm down," Officer Gordon said. He looked at her carefully while she brushed away her tears. "You think the murderer might have had a motive to get rid of your sister?"

Elizabeth could feel her throat constricting as he put her fears into words. She swallowed hard and nodded.

"OK, come with me," the police officer said, lifting the yellow plastic tape and leading them back through. Elizabeth shot Joey a victorious glance and held her chin high. Joey winced and followed docilely after her.

But then the gravity of the situation hit Elizabeth again as they walked down the dirt path toward Secca Lake. With each step her panic mounted. This wasn't about proving something to Officer Gordon and Joey. They didn't matter. This was about Jessica—her only sister, her twin. If something happened to Jessica, Elizabeth wouldn't be able to go on. She couldn't live in this world without her other half. Elizabeth clutched the hem of her shirt, her whole body constricted in fear.

The lights of an ambulance stood blinking in the distance, and paramedics were clustered around a body on a stretcher.

Elizabeth's heart leaped into her throat. The body was laid out with a sheet thrown over it. "Joey!" she whispered hoarsely, grabbing for him.

"I'm here, Liz," he said, folding a strong hand around hers. Elizabeth grasped his hand tightly, digging her fingers into his palm.

"This is Elizabeth Wakefield," Officer Gordon said as they joined the paramedics. "She might be able to identify the body."

A man nodded and lifted the sheet off the body.

Elizabeth gasped as the victim came into view. The girl looked ghastly. It was obvious that she had been drained of blood. Her face was so white it was almost blue. Her eyelids were translucent, and her lips were pale and cracked—like two faded petals. The only sign of color was an ugly bluish bite mark that stood out in stark relief on her pallid neck.

It wasn't Jessica. Relief flooded Elizabeth's mind and body. Despite the girl's ghostly pallor, she resembled someone Elizabeth vaguely knew from Palisades High. Elizabeth tried to place the girl. She thought she had seen her at a basketball game before, but she couldn't remember the girl's name.

As she looked down at the poor teenage girl, Elizabeth couldn't help shuddering. *What if that had been my sister?* she thought in horror. She couldn't even bear to imagine the sensations she would have felt. A wave of nausea welled up inside her from just the thought.

"Elizabeth," Joey said softly by her side.

Elizabeth put out a shaky hand and touched his arm. "It's not Jessica," she said, her voice trembling with emotion.

Then, overcome with emotion, she collapsed.

"I'll take care of her," she heard Joey said. Then she felt herself being lifted into his arms and carried down the path.

"We can't do this," Jonathan whispered raggedly as he stopped for air.

"I can," Jessica replied, her blue-green eyes sparkling mischievously in the light of the fire.

Jonathan pulled away from Jessica and held her at arm's length. "*I* can't do this. I can't get involved with you."

Jessica crossed her arms across her chest and smiled up at him. "Why? Do I scare you?" she asked. "Are you scared you're going to lose yourself in me?"

Jonathan nodded and leaned against the mantel. "Yes," he answered, avoiding her gaze. "You scare me."

Jessica looked up at him with solemn eyes. "I promise I won't make you uncover the furniture.

Or turn the stove upright." She danced around the room with her arms spread wide, feeling giddy. "We'll keep the room just the way it is." Dizzy, Jessica collapsed into the armchair. She curled her legs underneath her and gave him a coy smile.

But Jonathan wasn't laughing. His eyes were dead serious.

"Hmpf," Jessica pouted, tapping the arm of the chair. "You're spoiling all the fun."

"I'm sorry," Jonathan said, hanging his head. "But believe me, it's better this way."

"Why do you keep saying that?" Jessica asked in frustration. "Why are you . . . *resisting* me? What is your *problem*?"

Jonathan's face clouded over. "Jessica, I can't go into it, but just trust me. This can't be."

"Jonathan, please, tell me what the problem is," she begged him.

Jonathan shook his head silently for several moments. When he finally spoke, his voice was laden with pain. "Jessica, there are things you don't know about me. To get involved with me would only lead to disaster."

"Well, I don't think you have the right to make that decision alone," Jessica said, her tone light. She smiled at him, letting the dimple in her left cheek deepen. "I can choose for myself. And I've decided that *I'm* not afraid to take a risk."

Jonathan's lips trembled with emotion. "It's not a right. It's a desire."

Jessica mind clicked rapidly. Maybe Jonathan wasn't afraid of hurting her. Maybe he was afraid of getting hurt *himself*. At camp the summer before, Jessica had gotten involved with a boy named Paul Mathis. Paul had put up serious resistance to Jessica because he'd been badly hurt by his last girlfriend, and Jessica had had to fight to get him. "It's because of another girl, isn't it?" Jessica guessed. "You've been badly hurt in the past, and you don't trust women anymore."

But Jonathan shook his head. "No, not exactly. *I* haven't been the one who got hurt."

Jessica jumped up. "Then you have a girlfriend somewhere! In Europe! You're engaged!"

Jonathan shook his head and knelt down in front of the fire, shifting the logs with an iron poker. His ring glinted in the light of the fire, and Jessica looked at it suspiciously. "You're already married! You have an entire family in Europe, and you've left them all behind. You . . . you—" She snapped her fingers, searching for a plausible explanation for his behavior. "You're in some kind of trouble, and you don't want to endanger them. You're . . . you're in the witness protection program, and you have to stay hidden from the bad guys so they don't find your family."

A smile twitched Jonathan's lips. "You have a very active imagination."

Jessica put her hands on her hips. "What's her name?" she demanded.

"Jessica, it has nothing to do with other women. It has to do with *me,*" Jonathan insisted, standing up and leaning the hot poker against the wall.

Jessica sighed. Why was he being so difficult? She paced across the room, causing the floorboards to creak. Maybe he really was much older than she was. Maybe he wanted a woman his own age. Jessica walked over to the fireplace and looked straight into his eyes. "Is it because you think you're too old for me? Do you think I'm not ready for a mature relationship?" She was standing just inches away from him, and she could feel the heat emanating from his body. It was as though there were a tangible emotional stream between them. Jessica leaned forward, drinking it in.

Jonathan shook his head quickly and took a step back, breaking the spell. "No, you're . . . uh . . . *more* mature than most girls I've known." His voice was shaky.

Jessica stamped her foot. "Then what is it?" she burst out. "Why can't you get involved with me?"

"Jessica, I've said more than I should say. I can't say any more," Jonathan said quietly.

She stared into his deep blue eyes, but they

stared back at her implacably. Jonathan's smooth face was set, and Jessica could see he wasn't going to give her any more information. She blinked, feeling hot tears come to her eyes. No matter what she did, she couldn't seem to make him change his mind. For the first time in her life, her charm had failed her.

Not wanting him to see her sob with frustration, she ran to the door. Jonathan followed her with long, even strides.

Her hand on the knob, she turned to face him with burning eyes. "I know you'll give in eventually, Jonathan Cain."

Jonathan shook his head.

"No matter what you think is haunting you, you won't be able to resist me in the long run," Jessica predicted. "There's something undeniable between us."

Then she slammed the door behind her, tears cascading down her face.

Enid flattened herself against the wall as Jessica came barreling out of Jonathan's house, wiping tears away from her eyes.

She stood perfectly still and held her breath as Jessica rushed past her. But Jessica didn't seem to notice her at all. She had an expression of anguish on her face.

"Well, looks like that didn't work out too well," Enid said with a small smile. She experienced a gratifying sense of victory. Maybe next time Jessica would think twice before she tried to butt in where she didn't belong.

But then the image of Jessica and Jonathan returned to her in full force, and her feeling of triumph disappeared. *It's not fair,* she thought angrily. Why shouldn't *she* experience something like that for once? Enid was sick and tired of sitting back and watching the rest of the world have exciting romances. She deserved Jonathan's love as much as anyone else—even more.

Enid considered her plan of action. Part of her wanted to go home. She felt wounded that Jonathan had been with Jessica—he had betrayed her. *But then,* she reasoned, *it's possible that Jessica forced herself on Jonathan. He probably didn't want to hurt her feelings*. And he had obviously rejected her in the end. *No,* Enid decided, *I won't run away*. That's what she would have done in the past. The old Enid—the mousy girl with frizzy reddish brown hair—would have crept home to lick her wounds by herself. The new Enid—the one with jet black hair and blue-black lipstick—was going to take control of her life.

Enid contemplated her ruby-colored clawlike fingernails, deep in thought. Jessica and Elizabeth got their own way because they fought for it. And they stopped at nothing to get what they wanted.

It's time for me to show my fangs too, Enid thought as she flexed her fingers. *It's time to say good-bye to Ms. Nice Guy.*

Enid listened carefully as Jessica gunned the engine of the Jeep and went roaring down the street. As the sounds of the car faded away into the distance, Enid crept up the porch steps. Her foot slipped into a gaping hole in one of the steps, and she grabbed the railing for balance. Steadying herself, she nudged open the unlocked front door. She took a deep breath, and then she slipped into the house.

"What a relief!" Elizabeth exclaimed, letting her head fall against the seat as Joey pulled up to the Wakefields' house. She took off her seat belt and stretched her neck, feeling the tension melting out of her body. She still couldn't quite believe that Jessica was OK. Her twin radar didn't usually send false alarms.

"Now your troubles are over and we can concentrate on *us,*" Joey said, cutting the engine. He folded his hands behind his neck and gave her a lazy, sexy smile.

Elizabeth sat up with a start. She had been so worried about Jessica that she had forgotten all about Todd. But now that Jessica was no longer an immediate concern, she realized that she had a *huge* mess on her hands. What in the world was she going to do about Joey? How was she going to explain things to Todd?

Elizabeth could feel Joey's eyes on her, and she returned his smile weakly. His gaze was so intense that her stomach fluttered. She looked away quickly, fidgeting with her bag as she considered her options. She should tell Joey right away that she couldn't get involved with him. Then she could tell Todd that Joey was just a good friend from camp. Elizabeth bit her lip worriedly. That plan could backfire. If Todd asked Aaron or Winston, they would be sure to voice their suspicions.

"You sure know how to show a guy an exciting evening," Joey said in a low voice, unbuckling his seat belt and moving closer to her. He slipped his arms around Elizabeth's waist and nuzzled her hair. Elizabeth closed her eyes and wrapped her arms around his neck. Joey hugged her tightly, and Elizabeth sighed. *A hug is OK, right?* she told herself. *A hug is innocent.* Elizabeth sighed and breathed in his scent. It felt so good to be with Joey again—to feel his strong arms around her and to inhale his clean, rugged smell.

But then Joey lifted her chin toward him, leaning in to kiss her. Elizabeth stiffened and turned her face away from his.

Joey pulled back quickly, looking hurt. "Hey, just trying to comfort you," he said, sounding slightly defensive. "I'm not the vampire who sucked that girl's blood."

Elizabeth shivered at the memory of the drained body. "I know, and I'm sorry," she replied quickly. "I'm just confused about Todd."

"I don't know why you're so upset about some little high-school junior," Joey scoffed with a superior tone in his voice. "His biggest worry is probably finding a date for the prom." Then he gently ran his hand down her cheek. "Elizabeth, you're too much of a woman for a high-school guy."

Elizabeth jerked away from his touch. She didn't like this new, cool side of Joey. She wasn't impressed with his swaggering. In fact, he was beginning to remind her of Bruce Patman, the richest and most arrogant boy at Sweet Valley High. Joey had the same kind of sexy appeal as Bruce, and Elizabeth wasn't about to fall for it. "Well, sometimes high-school guys are appropriate for high-school girls," she pointed out, pursing her lips.

"Sometimes," Joey said, "but in this case, I know one high-school girl who is *perfect* for one college guy."

Elizabeth gave him a halfhearted smile.

"Seriously," Joey said, taking her hand. "Please don't stay with Todd out of misguided loyalty."

"I don't know *what* I want," Elizabeth confessed. "For the last few weeks I've been nothing but confused."

"Well, let me help you figure it out," Joey said, with a rakish glint in his eyes that made her heart flutter. He lifted her chin again and kissed her—a delicious, gentle kiss. Elizabeth closed her eyes and gave in to the moment.

Finally Elizabeth pulled back, feeling more confused than ever. "I'd better go in. It's been a long night."

"Tonight didn't go exactly as I'd planned," Joey said. "I was thinking maybe a movie, not a murder."

Despite the tension, Elizabeth had to laugh.

Joey tried to kiss her again, but Elizabeth pulled away. "I've got a lot of thinking to do," she explained.

"Don't take too long," he said suavely.

Joey's arrogant tone made the hair rise on the back of Elizabeth's neck. He was already acting like some big man on campus, and he'd barely started college. "Look, Joey," Elizabeth said harshly. "I'm my own person, and at the moment I'm committed to Todd. I'll do something about that *if* and *when* I want to. If you don't have time to wait, then you're free to go back to UCLA and find some sorority girl."

As soon as the words had left her mouth, she regretted them.

Joey looked stunned at her outburst. "Elizabeth, I'm sorry. I didn't mean it the way it came out."

Elizabeth's face flushed. "It's OK, Joey. I'm sorry too. I didn't mean to attack you. I guess it's just all the pressure of this evening. . . ." Her voice trailed off.

"Yeah, really, this was quite an evening," Joey said. "Murder, intrigue, a tangled romance—it sounds like the plot of a Hollywood movie."

Elizabeth sighed. "I just hope there aren't any more unexpected plot twists," she said.

Jessica screeched to a stop in the Wakefields' driveway. All she wanted to do was sneak inside and drown her sorrows in a huge dish of ice cream: rocky road, piled high with whipped cream and drenched with chocolate syrup. Then she would bury herself under her covers and go into hibernation for a week. Maybe a year.

No such luck. As soon as she was out of the car, Elizabeth came barreling out of a Land Rover toward her.

Jessica did a double take. Joey Mason was sitting in the front seat. *Where did he come from?* she wondered. Were he and Elizabeth dating again? Was Elizabeth cheating on Todd?

"Thank goodness you're alive!" Elizabeth yelled, running up to her and smothering her in a bear hug.

Jessica felt as though she were suffocating. She couldn't breathe, and her rib cage felt as if it were about to crack. "Liz!" she complained, wriggling out of her sister's grip. "What's this—" Jessica started to ask, but before she could get her question out, Elizabeth was lecturing her.

"How dare you sneak out like that? How dare you? Of all the rotten, selfish things to do!" Elizabeth's aquamarine eyes were flashing with anger, and she pointed an accusing finger at her twin. "You let me believe we were going to watch movies together. But I should have known better. I should have known that you had an ulterior motive, that you were just baiting me so you could sneak out and see that *greaseball.*" Elizabeth's eyes narrowed. "Well, you went too far this time, Jessica. I was out of my mind with fear."

Jessica looked at Elizabeth carefully. Was her sister going over the edge? "Elizabeth, what in the world are you talking about?" she asked.

"As if you didn't know!" Elizabeth huffed. Then she turned her back and marched away.

Jessica was baffled. Why was her twin so worried? And what was she doing with Joey Mason?

Chapter 4

Enid closed the door quietly behind her and leaned back against it, her heart thumping loudly in her chest. The foyer of Jonathan's mansion was pitch black, and she blinked as her eyes slowly adjusted. Enid drew a silent breath, her whole body trembling. A marble shelf jutted out from the wall, and she put a hand on it to steady herself.

Enid saw herself reflected in the antique oval mirror that hung above the shelf. A jagged crack ran down the front of the mirror, making her face look distorted. Her green eyes stared back at her, enormous and luminous in her pale face.

Enid turned away from the twisted image, feeling spooked again. With its high ceilings and marble floor, the foyer was cool and airy, and the house was as silent as a tomb. A long, narrow corridor stretched out before her. Holding her breath, Enid tiptoed down the long hall, her footsteps as quiet as those of a mouse.

"Who's there?" Jonathan called from the other room.

Enid jumped. How could he have heard her? She had made practically no sound at all.

All of a sudden Enid saw how foolish she was. She had no business sneaking into this guy's house. How could she possibly explain it to him? How could she put into words the irresistible pull she had felt that evening? And how could she justify creeping into the house instead of knocking?

Enid turned quickly and headed for the door, but suddenly Jonathan was standing beside her.

Enid sucked in her breath when she saw him. The color was high in his face, and his blue eyes glowed with a piercing light. His eyes were so fevered that he looked deranged. *Maybe this wasn't such a good idea after all,* she thought, taking a step backward.

"You're Enid Rollins," Jonathan said abruptly.

Enid nodded, her tongue caught in her throat. How did he know her name? Had he been watching her the way she'd been watching him? Did he feel the bond between them too?

"I—m-my car broke down," Enid stammered, feeling her face flush.

"Well, why don't you just warm up for a minute and then we'll take a look at it?" Jonathan asked, his voice as smooth as silk.

Enid hesitated. Her eyes darted around the drafty old house, and a chill ran through her. It looked as though Jonathan really did live by himself. Now that she was all alone in the big house with him, she realized that he was truly a stranger. She didn't know anything about him. *It is kind of weird for a high-school boy to be living alone in a big mansion in the middle of nowhere,* Enid thought. He could be dangerous after all. And nobody knew where she was. Maybe she should leave before she got into trouble.

Then she pictured Jessica's usual smug face. She could hear Jessica bragging to her friends about going to Jonathan's house by herself. She thought about the way Jessica had manipulated her in the Dairi Burger, and her blood started boiling again. If Enid left, Jessica would have Jonathan all to herself. No, this was Enid's chance to take a risk. This was her chance to become someone special at Sweet Valley High. After all, if Jessica hadn't been afraid to come there all alone, then she shouldn't be either.

"I was just having some wine," Jonathan said. His voice was strange and throaty. "Would you like some?"

Enid shook her head, feeling mesmerized. She stared at his glass of wine. The dark liquid swirled in the delicate crystal goblet.

"It matches your fingernails," Jonathan said.

Enid looked down at her ruby red nails and nodded.

"The color of blood," Jonathan said. He laughed strangely, guiding her to a chair near the fireplace.

But before she could sit down, Jonathan grabbed her in his arms and pressed his lips on hers. He kissed her with an urgency she had never experienced. Enid gasped, feeling as if she were being consumed. His lips devoured her hungrily, and his body crushed hers in his grasp. She wrapped her arms around his neck and returned the kiss with the same ardor. She could smell the animal scent of his neck and feel the tense muscles in his back. Enid closed her eyes and lost herself in his embrace. This was the moment she had been waiting for all her life.

Suddenly Jonathan pulled back and stared at her with wild eyes. Without saying a word, he picked her up as if she weighed no more than a feather and sat down in an armchair with her on his lap.

"Jonathan, I don't know if this is such a good idea," Enid whispered.

"Shhh," Jonathan said, putting a finger on her lips. "Don't say anything. Just close your eyes and feel the sensation." Entranced by his soothing tone, Enid shut her eyes and obeyed.

"Just feel the sensation," Jonathan repeated in a barely audible voice. He dropped light kisses on her eyelids, her cheeks, her lips. Then he traced a burning trail of kisses down her neck. Brushing her hair off her shoulders, Jonathan closed his warm lips around the side of her throat. Enid moaned as she felt a sharp sting. The sensation was exquisite: intense pain and a searing pleasure mixed into one.

Enid sat in tense anticipation as he teased her with his lips, sucking so gently that she could barely feel the pressure. She squirmed in frustration and clawed at his back, silently begging for more. Then she felt his lips clamp down on her skin, and she moaned softly. Enid's muscles relaxed as he sucked hungrily at her neck. The blood whirled in her veins, blotting out the world around her. All she could hear was a roaring in her ears and the beating of their two hearts together. It was a communion that she had never imagined possible.

"Jonathan," Enid gasped. "Don't stop." Closing her eyes, she lost herself in the liquid fire running through her and the pulsing of their hearts. She felt her body get lighter and lighter and the world get whiter and whiter. Enid swooned in ecstasy as the whiteness turned into blackness.

"Here, kitty!" Jessica called late Saturday night, throwing a piece of popcorn on the living room rug of the Wakefield house. Jasmine ran after it and swatted at it. The popcorn kernel bounced away, and the little white-and-gray kitten dived under the table after it, getting tangled up in the phone cord as she batted the kernel around.

Jasmine meowed loudly, thumping her tail angrily on the rug. Jessica got up to help her, but Jasmine charged away from her, freeing herself in the process. Then she ran in a series of rapid little circles and jumped straight up in the air.

Jessica and Elizabeth laughed.

"Psycho kitty," Jessica said.

Jessica cast a sidelong glance at her sister. *At least Liz is laughing again,* Jessica thought. *Maybe she's already forgotten that she was mad at me.*

But Elizabeth caught her look. "Don't think I'm not mad anymore, Jess," she said, crossing her arms across her chest. "Because I'm more than mad. I'm *furious.*"

"Liz, I can explain everything," Jessica said. She hopped up quickly. "I'm just going to get some ice cream, OK?" Jessica hurried down the hall to the kitchen before her sister could protest. She had to come up with an excuse fast. She grabbed a container of rocky road ice cream from the freezer and spooned out two big scoops. Her mind was clicking as she added whipped cream and maraschino cherries to both bowls.

Tucking a bottle of chocolate syrup under her arm, she carried the two bowls out to the living room. As she walked into the room Elizabeth tapped her foot impatiently.

"Let's have it," Elizabeth said, taking a bowl from her hand. "And it'd better be good."

Jessica sat down cross-legged on the rug, her back propped against an armchair. She squeezed a generous amount of chocolate syrup on the ice cream, then dipped her spoon in. "Mmm, delicious," she said.

"Jess . . . ," Elizabeth said in a warning tone.

"Liz, you know I'd never sneak out on you," Jessica said, turning an innocent gaze on her. Elizabeth rolled her eyes and took a bite of ice cream.

"I just went out to pick up a pint of ice cream for our movie," Jessica explained.

Just then Jasmine sneaked under Jessica's arm and stuck her head in the bowl of ice cream. "Jas!" Jessica exclaimed, picking up the kitten and cradling her in her lap. "You have to wait till I'm finished," she admonished her.

"We already have ice cream," Elizabeth pointed out.

"I know, but we don't have Strawberry Scream, Casey's latest flavor," Jessica said, stroking the kitten's fur. "I thought it would be perfect for the Hitchcock movies. You know, the movie would probably be scary, and it might make us scream. Get it? Scream, scream?"

Elizabeth laughed. "I didn't rent a Hitchcock movie, I rented two *Bogart* movies. But I gotta hand it to you for trying."

Jessica looked at her twin, indignant. "Well, if you're not going to believe me no matter what I say, I might as well stop talking." She folded her arms and pouted.

"Sorry," Elizabeth said, a slight smirk crossing her features. "Please go on."

"The car broke down on Valley Crest Highway," Jessica explained. "Remember how the engine died last week in the school parking lot?"

Elizabeth still looked skeptical, but she nodded.

"Well, the same thing happened tonight," Jessica continued. "The car just stopped, right outside Casey's. Some guys tried to fix it, but I finally had to call AAA. They took forever to come." Jessica wiped her hands on a napkin and crumpled it into a ball, then threw it on the rug. Jasmine jumped out of her lap and ran after it, hitting it with her paws.

"What was wrong with the Jeep?" Elizabeth asked. She finished the rest of her ice cream and set the bowl down on the coffee table. Jasmine batted the ball against Elizabeth's legs and charged after it. Elizabeth picked up the ball and threw it across the room. Jasmine meowed and zoomed away in pursuit.

Jessica shrugged. "Some kind of engine problem. I think a cable connection to the battery came loose. They had to tighten it." Jessica stood up quickly and rubbed her hands together. "So why don't we put on a video?" she suggested. "It's not that late. We can still watch one of the movies."

But Elizabeth would not be distracted. "Don't you think you're kind of overdressed for Casey's?" she asked.

"What? This old thing?" Jessica asked, waving a dismissive hand at her blue silk dress.

Elizabeth lifted an eyebrow but didn't say anything else.

Jessica breathed a sigh of relief. Clearly Elizabeth didn't buy any of it, but at least she'd stopped asking questions. The important thing was to steer her twin clear of any discussion about Jonathan. Jessica picked up one of the videos on the coffee table and inserted it into the VCR before Elizabeth could say another word. Then she grabbed the remote control and fell into an armchair. She pointed the remote at the TV and pressed play.

Elizabeth curled up on the couch and tucked her feet underneath her. "What a night," she said, blowing a hair out of her face. "I could use a little relaxation."

Suddenly Jessica remembered that Elizabeth had had a busy night herself—with Joey Mason. Jessica pressed the pause button and turned to face her sister. She had been so worried about covering her own tracks that she had completely forgotten that Elizabeth had some explaining of her own to do. "You can say that again," Jessica said with a grin. "Looks like tall, dark, and *Joey* came back into your life."

Elizabeth sighed. "Looks like it," she said. She stood up and grabbed an afghan from the wooden chest in the corner. Shaking it out, she settled back down on the couch and threw the blanket over her.

"So, c'mon, Liz, give," Jessica said, waving an encouraging hand. "What's going on with you and Joey?"

"That's a good question," Elizabeth said, a worried expression on her face. Jasmine jumped up on the couch and snuggled into Elizabeth's lap. Elizabeth scratched behind her ears, and the kitten purred contentedly.

"Have you decided to dump old Toddie?"

Jessica pressed. She swung her legs up over one side of the chair.

"I haven't decided anything," Elizabeth said with a sigh. She told Jessica the whole story, from Joey's letter to his unexpected arrival to Todd's untimely appearance. "But actually, I guess there's really no dilemma," Elizabeth finished. "Todd's not talking to me anyway."

"He'll get over it," Jessica predicted. She made a kissing sound and called the cat to her. Jasmine jumped to the floor and then leaped onto Jessica's lap.

"But I just don't know what to do," Elizabeth wailed, kicking the blanket off and sitting up suddenly. "I'm in love with Todd, and I'm attracted to Joey."

"So what's the problem?" Jessica asked, rubbing the kitten's neck.

Elizabeth looked at her in shock. "What's the *problem?* I have to choose between them, *that's* the problem."

Jessica shrugged. "Just date them both at the same time."

Exasperated, Elizabeth closed her eyes. "OK, I think we should drop this subject."

Just then Jessica heard the sound of a key turning in the lock.

Elizabeth held up a finger to her lips. "Shhh . . .

Mom and Dad are home." She waved a hand at the TV. "Turn the movie on."

Jessica pressed the pause button once more, and the film suddenly came back to life.

"Hi, girls!" Ned Wakefield called out in a booming voice.

"Wow, Dad, don't you look dashing!" Elizabeth said. Mr. Wakefield was wearing a navy blue double-breasted blazer and a deep maroon tie.

"We've been to a little café theater," Mr. Wakefield explained.

"Your father can still be a romantic old fool when he's in the mood," Alice Wakefield added as she walked into the room. She was wearing an elegant fitted winter-white suit, and her blond hair was swept up in a chignon. Her blue eyes were sparkling, and her cheeks were flushed pink with excitement. She swayed a bit as she crossed the room.

Mr. Wakefield put an arm around her waist. "I think you had too much fun tonight."

"I think it was the bottle of wine with dinner that did it!" Mrs. Wakefield giggled, her tone giddy.

Jessica shot Elizabeth a look. She hated it when her parents acted as though they had just started dating, especially in front of them.

"How was your evening, girls?" Mr. Wakefield asked.

Jessica yawned. "Fine," she said.

"Nothing special," Elizabeth added.

"You girls are getting old," Mr. Wakefield joked. "Looks like there's more action with the old folks."

"Yep," Jessica agreed.

She and Elizabeth glanced at each other. Jessica didn't know why, but an eerie premonition hit her. Somehow she didn't think the action was going to stop now. The story of Jessica and Jonathan was far from over.

A young man stared out his window at the dark night. The sweet taste of blood was fresh on his lips, but he hungered for more. He clenched his fist in frustration. He longed to join the night and find a few moments of oblivion again, a few moments in which he could forget himself and drown in the taste of another human being.

But he'd already gone too far that day. If he wasn't careful, the police would come after him. Another town would try to hunt him down. Another wild mob would chase after him with torches. He'd lost control again that night. He was getting greedy. *But I was lucky,* he consoled himself. It could have been much, much worse.

The image of a young girl appeared before him like a vision. She was pure and full of life, with smooth, rosy skin and long golden hair. Her lips were full and red like a rosebud, and her neck was long and graceful like a swan's. His blood pounded through his veins at the thought of her.

He knew she loved him, and he loved her as well. He loved her more than she could possibly understand. And he longed to show her his love, to love her in his way, in the most intense way there was.

The young man closed his eyes and tried to force the image from his mind. But she danced before his mind even more vividly, her lips curved in a gently mocking smile, her eyes bright and sparkling. Her scent, the perfume of young, sweet female flesh, returned to him as if she were present.

The young man moaned in anguish and stared out at the starry sky in despair. The moon hung low over the horizon. This was where he belonged. He belonged to the night, like the moon and the stars. He had no place in her world. She was a being of light and sunshine. He was a creature of darkness and despair.

The young man clenched his jaw and cursed his fate. Why had he been given this twisted nature—the desire to love and the need to kill?

As the young man gazed out at the silent night, he made a firm resolve. This time his desire would outweigh his need. His love would outweigh everything. But he would have to be very, very careful.

Chapter 5

"Huh?" Enid murmured as the jangling of the phone broke into her dreams Sunday morning. She was buried under her covers. The phone rang again, and Enid struggled to open her eyes. Her body was warm and heavy, and her eyelids felt as though they weighed two tons each.

Finally she gave up. With her eyes closed, she reached for the receiver and dragged it into bed with her.

"Mmm-hmmm?" Enid said into the phone.

"Good morning!" Elizabeth exclaimed, chirpy as usual.

Enid groaned. Elizabeth was always bounding with energy in the morning.

"Mmm," Enid responded, snuggling more deeply under the covers.

"Enid, are you OK?" Elizabeth asked.

"Someone glued my eyes shut," Enid mumbled.

"Do you want to call me back?" Elizabeth asked.

"No, just a minute, I think I've got a pair of pliers here." Enid pushed back the covers and forced her eyes open. Her body felt leaden. Dragging herself out of the covers with an effort, she slid out of bed and made her way groggily to the bathroom.

Enid turned on the faucet and splashed cold water on her face. She raised her tired eyes to the mirror and jumped at the sight that stared back at her. Her face was wan, and her lips looked as though they were on fire. They were raw and swollen and had turned an almost scarlet color. Then she remembered. *Last night with Jonathan.* Turning her neck slightly, she fingered the reddish purple bruise on her neck. It was sore.

Enid squinted into the mirror, trying to piece together the events of the evening. The last thing she remembered was being on Jonathan's lap in the armchair, lost in the delicious sensation of his lips. *How did I get home?* Enid shook her head hard. She couldn't remember driving, or taking off her makeup, or putting on her nightshirt. It was as if the whole night had been lost in a fog.

Oh, well, Enid said to herself with a secret

smile. *That's what love is. Oblivion. It's like being drunk without drinking anything.* She trotted back to bed with her arms wrapped around herself. She felt as if she were about to burst with happiness.

Enid climbed back into bed and picked up the receiver, sitting up cross-legged. "OK, that's better," she said into the mouthpiece.

"What's wrong? Late night out?" Elizabeth asked.

Enid opened her mouth to tell Elizabeth about her daring adventure of the night before. She was dying to share her new experience with someone. But then she stopped herself. She knew Elizabeth wouldn't understand. Not only did Elizabeth despise Jonathan, but she thought Enid's interest in him was a ridiculous crush. The last thing she needed was for Elizabeth to stomp on her one moment of happiness.

Elizabeth used to be such an understanding friend, Enid thought. *Now she's completely judgmental.* And she wasn't her best friend anymore, anyway. She was Maria's best friend.

"Enid, you there?" Elizabeth asked.

"Oh, sorry, yeah, I was just . . . thinking," Enid replied, kicking the sheets into place and burrowing underneath them. She cradled the receiver against her shoulder. She longed to return to sleep, to dream of her evening again and again and again.

"So what did you do last night?" Elizabeth repeated, a bit impatiently.

"Oh, I just watched a late movie on TV," Enid said.

"Well, I was calling to see if you want to get together to make cookies tomorrow. You know, like we used to," Elizabeth said. Enid thought she detected a slightly wistful tone in her voice. "We could make our favorite—chocolate chip pan cookies."

Enid brightened. Maybe Elizabeth was trying to reestablish their friendship after all. Monday was a school holiday, and Enid didn't have anything planned.

"Maria's going to come over in the morning to help me with the shopping, and then we thought you might want to join us later," Elizabeth continued.

Enid felt a fresh wave of alienation. "No, sorry, I'm busy," she said curtly.

"Oh," Elizabeth said, the disappointment plain in her voice.

"Listen, I've got to go," Enid said. "I've got a lot of stuff to do today. I'll see you in school on Tuesday."

"See you on Tuesday," Elizabeth echoed, her voice slightly bewildered.

Enid hung up abruptly. She knew she was widening the rift, but she was sick of the way

Elizabeth was treating her. Suddenly she was hit with a feeling of loss and jealousy, a feeling so strong it threatened to overwhelm her. But then she forced the thought away. She had new friends now. Lynne and Julie would be thrilled to hear about her evening.

Elizabeth doesn't matter anyway, Enid thought. *Jonathan's what really counts.* She fingered her swollen, tender lips and her raw, bruised neck. She thought of his hungry kisses, his passionate embrace, and the pulsing energy of his lips on her throat.

It was the most wonderful night of my life, Enid thought as she lay down and closed her eyes. *Jonathan and I are finally, truly in love.*

"Yum," Elizabeth murmured on Monday afternoon in the sunny yellow Wakefield kitchen, popping a chunk of chocolate chip cookie dough into her mouth.

"Elizabeth!" Maria protested. "If you keep eating all the dough, we're not going to have enough to make the cookies." With that, she stuck a spoon into the batter and licked it clean. "Well, it *is* really good," she enthused.

Elizabeth laughed. "Maria, you're one to talk!" She bent over and checked the oven. "OK, I think we're ready to go. Now let's get those cookies in there before we both totally lose control."

Maria laid a buttered square pan on the kitchen counter, and the girls spread the batter thickly into the pan. Elizabeth slid it into the oven and set the timer.

"That smells delicious," Elizabeth said as the warm aroma of baking cookies filled the air. Then her expression turned serious. "Cookies will do me good. I need something to cheer me up."

"The Joey-Todd dilemma getting you down?" Maria asked sympathetically.

Elizabeth nodded and hopped up onto a stool, propping her chin on her folded hands. "I just don't know what to do," she said despairingly. "Todd won't even talk to me."

"Have you tried calling him?" Maria asked pointedly.

Elizabeth shook her head, slightly abashed.

"Girl, the problem is *you,*" Maria said in a matter-of-fact tone. "Todd will listen to you if you call him."

"But I don't know what to tell him," Elizabeth wailed.

Maria raised an eyebrow. "Are you thinking of making up some story about you and Joey?"

Elizabeth groaned. "Maria, do you always have to be so moral about everything?" she complained.

"Me?" Maria protested. "*You're* the one who's

always being accused of being on a moral high horse."

Elizabeth sighed. "I know. I don't know what's gotten into me."

Maria shook her head. "Well, it's not about morality, anyway. It's about self-respect."

Elizabeth silently digested Maria's advice. She knew Maria was right, but she didn't feel ready to confront Todd with the truth. "Maybe I'll talk it over with Jessica," she said with a small grin.

Maria laughed. "She'll tell you what you want to hear."

"Yeah, Jessica has no qualms about making up a story," Elizabeth said. "You should have heard the whopper she came up with on Saturday night."

"I'm all ears," Maria said, leaning back against the counter and crossing her legs.

"She said she went out to get a special flavor of ice cream—Strawberry Scream—because it was appropriate for the movie we were going to watch." The corners of Elizabeth's mouth turned up. "She was wearing a blue silk dress."

Maria laughed. "Well, you've got to hand it to her for trying." But then her expression turned serious. "Jessica was lucky," she said. "She was lucky another girl with blond hair and blue eyes was the victim of the week."

"I know," Elizabeth said, the terror of the night

returning to her. "It was weird. I was so scared. It was as if I knew that Jessica was in terrible danger."

"I'm sure you were just being a paranoid twin sister," Maria assured her.

Elizabeth nodded, but inside she didn't agree. She couldn't quite shake the feeling of menace. It was as though a red light were flashing a danger signal. She wanted to keep Jessica chained in her room until the feeling passed. Elizabeth sighed. *This must be what it feels like to be a mother.*

"But there is something strange in the air," Maria said.

"That's for sure," Elizabeth agreed. Everything seemed to be changing. And Elizabeth never liked it when her world was rocked.

Monday night Todd lay on his bed methodically throwing an orange Nerf basketball in the air. He was in a catatonic state. He had no energy, and he had barely moved for two days. Without Elizabeth, his life seemed to have no purpose.

He thought of that horrible instant when he had caught Elizabeth in the arms of another guy. The pain of the moment came back to him as strong as it had been that night—the numbing shock, the desperate disbelief, the stabbing pain. It was as if he'd been whacked in the stomach with a soccer ball. The moment kept returning to him again and again, constantly catching him by surprise. He couldn't seem to digest it, to make sense of it. *Liz, how could you do this to me?*

After seeing Elizabeth in the arms of that guy from camp, Todd had driven around for hours. He had raced like a madman up the coastal highway, trying to escape the painful feeling of betrayal, the agonizing feeling of loss. He had cruised along the ocean on the way back, the top of his car down and the wind whipping at his hair. Then he had woven his way around the winding streets of Sweet Valley, saying good-bye to all the memories that the town evoked for him. He'd driven late into the night, and finally he'd worn himself out. Returning home, he'd fallen into a blank sleep. When he woke up, he'd felt completely empty—bewildered, betrayed, and empty.

He reached over and opened the drawer of his nightstand, pulling out the letter that Elizabeth had sent him from camp. He fingered the pale pink envelope with her initials monogrammed on it. Reaching inside, he drew out the color photos she had sent him. In one picture she was standing on a dock in front of a boat, her golden blond hair in a high ponytail and a white visor on her head. She looked exuberant and healthy in a bright blue CAMP ECHO MOUNTAIN T-shirt. In another, she and Maria were standing in front of a big gnarled tree, their arms wrapped around each other and big smiles on their faces.

Todd threw the photos down in disgust. No wonder Elizabeth had written so rarely. She'd promised to write every other day and ended up writing him *once*—once in a whole month. And no wonder she'd looked so happy. She'd been busy with another guy.

Then a horrible thought struck Todd. Todd had missed Elizabeth so much that he had paid her a surprise visit at camp. He wondered if she'd already been involved with Joey when he visited her. Now he remembered that she had been walking with Joey from the dock when he showed up in the parking lot. And she'd been wearing a little orange bikini—a bikini that was more likely to belong to Jessica than Elizabeth. Todd slammed down his fist in anger. What a fool he'd been! How could he have been so naive?

Todd picked up the pictures and ripped them into little pieces. It would have been bad enough to know that Elizabeth had fallen in love with another guy. But this was much worse. She'd lied to him and cheated on him. She'd showed no respect for him at all, and she'd made a fool of him in front of Winston and Aaron.

Todd's anger sent a burst of adrenaline coursing through his body. He kicked at the pieces on the floor, grinding them with his heel as if to make them disappear. *I'll never trust her again,* he vowed to himself.

This is what I get for all my affection, all my devotion, all my trust, Todd thought with rage as he pulled on a pair of blue sweatpants over his shorts. *This is what I get for being a loyal boyfriend. A slap in the face.*

It's true that nice guys finish last, Todd mused as he yanked a white T-shirt over his head. He shoved a baseball cap on his head and grabbed his high-top sneakers.

Well, I've had enough of being a nice guy. His eyes steely with determination, Todd laced up his sneakers and picked up his basketball. No more sitting around feeling sorry for himself. No more pain and self-pity. From now on, he was looking out for number one.

Chapter 6

"Well, you look like the Bride of Frankenstein this morning," Jessica said in a chipper voice as she steered the Jeep down Valley Crest Highway on Tuesday morning.

"Thanks for the support, Jess," Elizabeth said wryly, rubbing a hand across her tired eyes. She flipped down the mirror and studied her appearance. Her face was pale and drawn, and she had dark circles under her eyes. She tucked a few stray blond hairs back into her headband and slapped her cheeks, trying to get some color in her face. "Ugh," she groaned, flipping the mirror back up. "It's useless."

"Maybe you should join the gothic group," Jessica suggested. "That way you could patch up your friendship with Enid and get a new look, all at the same time. All you need is some black lipstick and matching nail polish."

"Jess, do you mind?" Elizabeth said sharply. "I feel bad enough as it is."

"Hey, chill out," Jessica responded, a defensive note in her voice. "I was just kidding around."

"Sorry," Elizabeth said. "I'm just a little out of sorts today."

Jessica shrugged and turned on the radio.

"Out of sorts" is an understatement, Elizabeth thought. *I'm not out of sorts. I'm a total wreck.* She had barely slept since Saturday night, and now she had to face Todd in school. Plus she was worried about her sister. She was sure Jessica had sneaked out to be with Jonathan Saturday night, and she knew her twin wouldn't keep her promise to tell her if she went to see him in the future.

Elizabeth chewed on her lower lip. Jonathan was bad news—she could feel it in her bones. And both Jessica and Enid were under his spell. But Jessica wouldn't listen to her, and Enid wouldn't talk to her. Elizabeth sighed and rested her head against the seat. She had to take things one step at a time. And step one was Todd.

The car screeched to a stop, and Elizabeth's eyes flew open. They were in the parking lot of Sweet Valley High, parked as usual next to Jonathan's black motorcycle. Elizabeth shook her head in disgust but didn't bother saying anything.

"See you later, Liz!" Jessica said, jumping out of the car and running across the parking lot. She obviously wanted to catch Jonathan before classes started. The only time Jessica ran into school was when she was running after some guy.

Elizabeth trudged across the parking lot after her twin. She couldn't figure out her own feelings. After she'd gotten Joey's letter, she hadn't been able to stop thinking about him. But now that Joey had shown up in Sweet Valley, she couldn't stop thinking about Todd. The pained look on Todd's face came back to her. She could see his expression clearly: the hurt in his eyes, the shock in his face. Elizabeth was hit with a pang of self-loathing. How could she have cheated on Todd? How could she have lied to him? How could she hurt him like this?

That's it, Elizabeth decided suddenly. She was going to come clean to Todd. It was obvious that sneaking around hadn't gotten her anywhere. She was going to tell him the whole truth and ask him to forgive her. And if he wouldn't have her back, then that was the price she'd have to pay. Maria was right. Maybe she'd lose Todd, but at least she'd have her self-respect back.

Feeling a new sense of determination, Elizabeth swung through the door of Sweet Valley High. The corridors were crowded with students talking in loud groups and grabbing books from their lockers. Weaving her way through the crowd, Elizabeth turned the corner and glanced around the hall for Todd.

Elizabeth's heart skipped a beat when she saw him at his locker. Taking a deep breath, she smoothed her hair around her headband and approached him.

"Todd," she said, her voice cracking.

Todd turned to face her, and Elizabeth's eyes widened. He looked worse than she did. He was dressed all in black and was wearing a black baseball cap pulled low over his forehead. His strong jaw was covered with a three-day growth of stubble, and his brown eyes looked a little wild.

"What?" Todd asked rudely.

Elizabeth looked at him imploringly. "Can we talk?" she asked.

Todd slammed his locker door shut and turned away. "I never want to speak to you again," he replied. Then he stomped off, leaving Elizabeth staring after him. A tear trickled down her cheek, and she wiped it angrily away.

"What were Martin Luther King Jr.'s major accomplishments?" Jessica asked Lila frantically as they walked down the hall together to their first-period history class. They had a big test in Mr. Jaworski's class covering the civil rights movement, and Jessica hadn't prepared. She'd been grilling Lila for the past fifteen minutes.

Lila rolled her eyes. "Oh, come on, Jessica, you must know *something* about history."

"I can only think of the 'I Have a Dream' speech," Jessica said desperately.

"The boycott of public buses in Alabama in 1956 to protest racial segregation and the voter registration drive in the mid-1960s," Lila recited.

"What was the name of that big Supreme Court ruling that said the separate-but-equal doctrine was unconstitutional?" Jessica asked.

"Jessica, why don't I just lend you my brain during the test?" Lila asked in an irritated tone.

"Lila, please," Jessica implored. "I need your help. This is a *huge* test. If I fail this, I'm doomed."

"OK, OK, it was the *Brown versus Board of Education* case in—"

Suddenly the crackling of the PA system interrupted them.

"Hey, maybe Chrome Dome has something to tell you about the civil rights movement," Lila said, referring to Mr. Cooper, the bald-headed principal.

"May I have your attention, please!" the principal's voice boomed over the loudspeaker system. "All students please go immediately to the auditorium for a special assembly. First-period classes are canceled today."

"Saved by the bell!" Jessica exclaimed happily.

"You can say that again!" Lila said. "Now you can study and leave me alone."

Jessica looked at Lila as though she were nuts. "Study? But now we won't have class."

Lila sighed. "Come on, let's go see what ol' Chrome Dome has to say."

"I never thought I'd be happy to go to an assembly," Jessica said as they made their way down the hall with a throng of students. "But anything's better than history class."

"Bo says history is very important. Especially if you want to be a diplomat," Lila asserted.

Jessica cringed at the mention of Lila's boyfriend. At camp, Lila had gotten involved with a wealthy boy from Washington, D.C., named Beauregard Creighton III. She and Bo were now having a long-distance relationship, and Lila talked about him nonstop.

Lila got a dreamy look on her face. "We talked for hours this weekend. We recited French poetry together on the phone." Lila sighed. "It was *so* romantic."

"Bleah," Jessica said, making a face. "Lila, you're really turning into a sap."

Jessica pushed open the doors of the auditorium

and searched for a seat. "There," she said, pointing to a row of empty seats in the back.

"'*Il pleure dans mon coeur / Comme il pleut sur la ville,*'" Lila recited, walking up the steps as if she were in a trance. "'It's crying in my heart / Like it's raining in the city.' Isn't that beautiful? It's Verlaine."

"That's really beautiful," Jessica said flatly, pushing Lila down into a seat. She climbed up onto her own seat and searched the crowded room for Jonathan.

"Jess!" Amy Sutton called from the front of the auditorium. She was standing with a tall blond girl that Jessica didn't recognize.

"C'mon up!" Jessica called, scanning the crowd. Jonathan was nowhere to be seen.

"Hi!" Amy said a few minutes later, slightly panting. "This is my cousin Katrina. She's visiting for a few weeks from San Francisco."

Katrina flashed a wide smile. She was an attractive girl with warm brown eyes and a smattering of freckles across her cheeks. "Hi," she said.

"Hey, nice to meet you," Jessica said. "I'm Jessica, and this is Lila." Lila was gazing dreamily into space. "Don't mind her—she's been transported by French poetry."

Lila snorted. "You simply don't understand *anything* about French culture."

"Well, I know something about French kisses," Jessica responded.

"From Jonathan, you mean?" Lila asked. She poked Amy in the side, and they both laughed.

"As a matter of fact, yes," Jessica said. "You won't *believe* what happened this weekend." She was thrilled that Katrina was there. She loved to have an audience when she had a story to tell—and the more the merrier. Jessica cleared her throat. "I went over to Jonathan's on Saturday night," she began.

"Oh, yeah?" Amy asked with a strange smirk. "How was it?" Lila giggled slightly.

"Jonathan made a fire. It was very *hot*," Jessica replied.

"Who's Jonathan?" Katrina asked.

"He's a gorgeous new guy in school," Jessica explained. "He's older than we are, and he lives alone."

"He looks like one of the creatures of the night," Lila put in.

"But I hear he gives great hickeys," Amy added, sending Lila into a fit of laughter. Jessica glared at them, annoyed to have her moment ruined. "What's going on?" she asked.

"Just a little something that you don't know . . . ," Amy said in an irritating singsong voice.

"You planning to tell me?" Jessica asked.

"Shhh!" Lila said as Mr. Cooper, the principal,

walked onstage. "Chrome Dome has arrived."

"Hmpf," Jessica pouted.

Elizabeth tapped her foot impatiently as Mr. Cooper stepped up to the microphone. She was sitting with Maria in the front of the auditorium, and she felt listless. For the first time in ages, she had no interest in school. She just wanted to crawl back into bed and hide from the world.

"Thank you all for convening here this morning," Mr. Cooper began in a serious voice.

"You'd think we were in a court of law," Maria whispered.

Elizabeth grumbled something incoherent and slouched down in her seat. Sometimes school was unbearable.

"As you probably know, Jean Hartley from Palisades High was murdered this weekend at Secca Lake," Mr. Cooper announced.

A murmur went through the crowd, and Elizabeth sat up straighter. She had been sure she recognized the girl from Palisades. Now she could place her. Jean had been a cheerleader, and she had led the squad in the last Palisades-SVH basketball game. The picture of her leaping and shouting on the sidelines stood out vividly in Elizabeth's mind. And then the image of the girl's still, drained body flashed in front of her eyes. An eerie chill rippled through Elizabeth as the two images juxtaposed horribly in her mind.

"The police believe there is a pattern to the crimes, and they are now searching for a serial killer," Mr. Cooper was saying. "In both cases, the murder victims were teens with blond hair and blue eyes who had been drained of their blood."

For a moment the auditorium was completely silent, then the room erupted into chaos. The din was deafening as everybody started talking at once.

A sudden, instinctive fear seized Elizabeth's heart with ice-cold fingers. Jean Hartley was a blond junior and a cheerleader, just like Jessica. She glanced wildly around the auditorium for her sister.

"Maria, do you see Jessica anywhere?" Elizabeth asked frantically.

Maria laid a comforting hand over hers. "Up there," she said, pointing to a back row. Elizabeth twisted around to look, breathing a sigh of relief when she caught sight of her sister. She wished she could lock Jessica up until the murderer was apprehended.

"Attention, please!" Mr. Cooper yelled, rapping on the mike. The room quieted down. "I don't mean to alarm you, but the situation is extremely serious. Our number-one priority at Sweet Valley High is your safety. Therefore, I have spoken with the city council, and we've all decided that an emergency curfew is hereby in effect until the murderer is apprehended. No one under eighteen is allowed out after ten o'clock at night."

Groans erupted in the auditorium, but Elizabeth was thrilled.

"Oh, great," Maria moaned. "Sweet Valley is becoming a prison."

Elizabeth looked at her with shining eyes. "I know. Isn't it great?"

"A curfew! I can't believe it!" Amy exclaimed in indignation as they walked out of the auditorium. "The only time Katrina is in town, Chrome Dome helps make us prisoners in our own homes."

"You'd think we were living through a plague in the Middle Ages," Lila muttered in disgust.

"It is kind of like a quarantine," Katrina agreed.

"This is absolutely ridiculous!" Jessica put in. "There is no way I'm going to pay attention to that curfew. Especially not now that Jonathan and I are a couple."

Lila gave Amy a sidelong glance, and they both giggled.

"Well, see you later, Jess," Lila said as they turned the corner. "We've got study hall."

Jessica stopped and put a hand on her hip. "Do you *mind* telling me what's going on?" she asked, her eyes glinting angrily.

Lila looked at Amy with questioning eyes. Amy lifted her shoulders indecisively.

"I *demand* that you tell me what this is about," Jessica insisted.

"OK," Amy said with a sigh. "But you're not going to like it."

"I'm sure I can handle it," Jessica said, tapping a foot impatiently.

"Well, Amy and I ran into Enid at the mall on Sunday," Lila began.

"Enid was trying on a black tube dress at Bibi's," Amy put in.

"*Pouring* on a tube dress is more like it," Lila said with a smirk.

Jessica stamped her foot impatiently. "Would you get to the point?" she asked.

"Well, let's just say that Enid was looking a little lovesick," Lila said.

Jessica rolled her eyes. "So tell me something I don't know," she said sarcastically. "The drip has a crush on Jonathan."

Amy laughed. "And it looks like Jonathan has a crush on the drip."

Jessica narrowed her eyes. "What are you talking about?"

"Enid had a hickey on her neck," Lila explained. "From Jonathan."

Jessica gasped. "*What?*" she exclaimed. She

pictured Jonathan kissing Enid the way he had kissed her, and she felt sick. She imagined him touching Enid's chalky cheeks and kissing her messy red lips. She saw him pushing back her thin black hair and sucking at her neck. Jessica felt dizzy all of a sudden. The image of Jonathan and Enid together was revolting. No, it was more than revolting. It was grotesque. It wasn't possible. Jessica shook her head. "I don't believe it."

Amy shrugged. "Go check it out for yourself."

"See you later," Lila said, waving as they walked away.

Jessica turned and marched down the hall, her blood boiling. Had she been outdone by the drip? She stalked down the corridor, heading for the vacant lockers near the back door where she could be alone. *That little vamp,* Jessica thought angrily, her hands curled into tight balls at her sides. Just because Enid had a new, glamorous look, she thought she could compete with Jessica Wakefield. *And Enid isn't just competing with me,* Jessica thought, her fury mounting. *She's trying to steal Jonathan!*

Jessica turned a corner and punched a locker in rage, the sound reverberating in the empty corridor. If the story was true, Enid was going to be sorry. Jessica didn't know how she was going to do it, but she'd get her revenge. Enid Rollins would rue the day she'd first set eyes on Jonathan Cain.

But then Jessica stopped and leaned against a locker, feeling suddenly weak. The full weight of Jonathan's betrayal suddenly hit her, and her knees buckled. Jessica slid to the floor and pulled her knees to her chest, wrapping her arms around them. She thought of the intense look in Jonathan's eyes on Saturday night, of the tender way he had held her, and of his passionate, hungry kisses. . . .

Jessica didn't know why he was resisting her, but one thing was sure—Jonathan was in love with her. "Jonathan, how could you betray me like that?" Jessica whispered. "How you could betray our love?" A tear slid slowly down her cheek.

Chapter 7

Todd turned up the collar of his black leather jacket and swaggered slowly into the cafeteria on Tuesday at lunchtime, imitating Jonathan's walk. He was wearing black jeans and a black denim shirt with a white T-shirt underneath. His face was unshaven, and he'd dyed his hair black. Todd's new look gave him a sense of fresh confidence. The old, sappy, sentimental Todd was gone, and the new, tough Todd was here. He and Elizabeth were through for good, and he was ready to get crazy.

He spotted Ken, Bruce, and Winston sitting at a table in the corner.

"Hey, guys," Todd said, approaching the table.

Bruce whistled softly. "Lookin' good, baby," he said, holding up a hand.

Todd grinned and slapped his hand.

The guys were all dressed in the gothic look. Bruce and Ken were wearing black jeans and matching T-shirts, and they both looked dark and self-contained. Winston, on the other hand, still looked like his goofy self. He was wearing a black tuxedo jacket over black jeans and a wide, painfully bright green tie.

Todd swung his leg over a chair and hunched over the table. "This place needs some action," he muttered. He pulled out his lunch bag and fished inside it for his sandwich.

"You can say that again," Bruce agreed, gulping down his soda. "Ever since that curfew was imposed, this place has become boresville."

"This curfew is the worst," Ken put in, drenching a handful of fries in ketchup and stuffing them in his mouth.

"I kind of like it," Winston put in. "It gives me an excuse to stay inside and catch up on old movies." He pulled a big red apple out of his lunch bag and polished it on his jeans.

Bruce gave him a withering look. "Can it, Egbert," he said.

"I saw this great old Audrey Hepburn movie last night," Winston went on, waving his apple in the air. "With Humphrey Bogart. It was called *Sabrina*." He smiled at them and crunched loudly into his apple.

Ken and Bruce groaned. "You're a hopeless geek," Bruce despaired. He picked up his fork and stirred the soggy brown vegetable mess on his tray, looking at it suspiciously. "What's this supposed to be, anyway?" he asked.

Winston studied the platter. "I think it's chop suey," he decided.

"*Slop* suey is more like it," Bruce commented.

Todd drummed his fingers on the table and looked at the guys through narrowed eyes. "Things at SVH need to get exciting," he said, his eyes intense. "I say we stir things up a bit." Todd picked up his chicken sandwich and took a big bite.

"I second the motion," Bruce agreed emphatically.

"You guys are right," Ken agreed, downing the rest of his milk. "We need a plan for fun." He crumpled up the empty carton and threw it on his tray.

Just then Jonathan walked into the cafeteria and caused a small commotion. A bunch of girls from the gothic table let out whistles and catcalls, and a dozen pairs of girls' eyes followed his path as he headed to the lunch line.

"And I think the plan just walked in," Bruce said.

Ken's blue eyes glinted. "I heard a rumor that Jonathan lives alone," he said.

Todd got the idea. "Perfect for a huge bash," he added.

The guys laughed and high-fived each other.

Bruce stood up and shouted across the cafeteria, "Jonathan!" Jonathan turned slowly in line and caught his gaze. "Over here!" Bruce called, waving. Jonathan nodded and turned back to the line.

"What do you think happened to his parents?" Winston asked, sitting back and loosening his tie. He rubbed his neck and stretched.

"I heard they were living in Europe," Ken said.

"I heard he doesn't have any parents," Bruce said with a laugh.

"It doesn't matter," Todd said. "The important thing is that they're not around."

Todd was psyched. This party would be the perfect opportunity for him to make his first public appearance. He couldn't wait to show Elizabeth the *new* Todd Wilkins, the one who didn't need her at all.

Jessica stormed across the cafeteria to Enid's table, where she was sitting with the gothic girls. Enid was wearing a black cotton miniskirt and a cropped leather jacket. Her jet black hair fell like a mop over her shoulders, and a silver skull-and-crossbones pendant swung from her neck.

Jessica slammed her tray down on the table and

took a seat next to her. "Who do you think you are?" she demanded.

Enid turned to her, a cat-that-ate-the-canary grin plastered on her face.

"I beg your pardon?" she asked slyly. Enid's superior look made Jessica rage inwardly. She wanted nothing more than to swat the smile off End's grotesquely pale face.

Jessica forced her voice to remain calm. "I know about the stories you've been telling," she informed Enid.

Enid grinned wickedly and shook her hair over her shoulder. A long skeleton bounced from her left ear. Then she pushed away her collar to reveal a purple hickey. "They're not stories," Enid said with a gleeful smile.

Jessica felt the blood drain from her face. "So you've got a hickey. Big deal."

"A hickey from Jonathan," Enid said, fingering the bruise on her neck lovingly.

"Oh, right," Jessica scoffed. She resisted the urge to pull Enid's fingers away from her neck.

"You don't believe me?" Enid asked softly.

Jessica shook her head and leaned in close. "Prove it," she challenged.

Enid leaned back and crossed her legs. Her blue-black lips forming an O, she took a long draw on her lemonade.

Jessica drummed her fingers impatiently on the tabletop.

"Well, I went over to Jonathan's on Saturday night," Enid began.

"*I* was with Jonathan on Saturday night," Jessica interrupted triumphantly.

Enid gave her a small smile. "I believe it was after you left."

Jessica's eyes narrowed.

"Jonathan was drinking wine—red wine from a crystal goblet, and the house was completely dark except for a fire in the hearth." Enid got a faraway look in her eyes as she recited her story, making it look as if she were possessed. "All the furniture was covered except for an old sofa and a broken-down armchair. Jonathan started kissing me, and then he pulled me onto his lap in the armchair." Enid's green eyes glinted strangely. "And then he kissed my neck. But it wasn't really a kiss. It was this intense pressure. It felt like something I've never experienced—as if our hearts were joined."

An eerie chill went through Jessica as Enid described her evening with Jonathan. It was as if she were describing *Jessica's* experience exactly.

"And then—"

But Jessica jumped up and cut her off before she was finished. She couldn't stand to hear another word. "Don't you dare try to compete with me," Jessica hissed. "I'm warning you, you'll regret it." She gave Enid a withering look and stomped off.

But Enid's eerie laughter rang in her ears.

Todd watched in awe as Jonathan sauntered slowly across the cafeteria toward them. Half the girls in the cafeteria were staring at him openly, and a lot of the guys were looking at him with admiration as well. *He has some kind of aura,* Todd thought admiringly. Jonathan Cain had coolness down to a science.

"Hi, guys," Jonathan said as he approached their table, his voice impassive as usual. A cup of steaming black coffee was in his hand.

"Jonathan!" Bruce exclaimed. "Why don't you join us?"

Jonathan shrugged and sat down at the table, placing his cup of coffee in front of him.

"You're not having lunch today?" Bruce asked.

"I didn't have time to make anything this morning," Jonathan explained, lifting the black coffee to his lips.

"Do you want some of my fries?" Ken offered.

Jonathan shook his head. "Not hungry," he muttered.

Todd stared at Jonathan in fascination. He was the kind of guy that girls were wild about. They loved the aloof, bad-boy type. Jonathan walked by them without a second glance, and they fell madly in love with him. He had barely spoken to anyone since he'd been at Sweet Valley High, and he already had a fan club.

Todd glanced surreptitiously at the gothic girls' table. Lynne Henry and Julie Porter were staring at Jonathan's back. Enid Rollins looked as though she might swoon.

Todd shook his head in amazement. No girl had ever fallen for him like that. *I'm too nice and too clean-cut—that's the problem.* Girls liked him, but they didn't drop at his feet. *That's all about to change, starting now,* he decided. From that moment on, he'd emulate Jonathan. He'd copy his every gesture and his every word. Soon he would be as cool and collected as Jonathan Cain, and Elizabeth would regret the day she'd set foot in Camp Echo Mountain.

Bruce's strained voice broke into his reverie. "Look, Jonathan, it's a great idea," he was saying.

"What's a great idea?" Todd asked.

Bruce looked at him in surprise. "Haven't you been sitting right here?"

"The *party* is a great idea," Winston explained.

"Well, it's not an option," Jonathan said shortly. "I'm not going to be around this weekend. I'm going to the mountains to get away from this place for a while."

"So we'll have it next Friday," Bruce insisted.

"Yeah, that'd be perfect," Ken agreed. "It's the night of the Big Mesa game. We'll all be psyched up to go out."

"There's a curfew in effect," Jonathan pointed out.

"Who cares?" Bruce countered. "It'll add an element of danger."

Jonathan got a dark look in his blue eyes. "I don't need any more danger in my life," he said under his breath. Then he got up and walked away without a backward glance.

Jessica stalked across the parking lot after school. She was steaming mad and determined to confront Jonathan. She had parked next to Jonathan that morning, and his motorcycle was still sitting beside the Jeep. Its silver stripes gleamed in the slanting rays of the late afternoon sun.

Jessica paced around the parking lot, her heels tracing a line in the gravel. Ever since she had confronted Enid at lunch, she had barely been able to see straight. Was it possible that Jonathan had been with another girl—and on the same night he'd been with her? Had she been outdone by Enid Rollins, of all people?

Jessica gave a stone a vicious kick, tears coming to her eyes. It wasn't possible. She knew Jonathan's feelings for her were genuine. She could see it in the look in his eyes, and she could feel it in the passion of his kiss.

Then a thought struck her. Enid had said that she was with Jonathan on Saturday night after Jessica left. How did Enid know Jessica had been with Jonathan? Had he told her, or had she been watching from her car? Maybe she had spied on them from the window the whole time. Maybe she had simply recounted Jessica's experience as if it were her own.

That's it, Jessica thought, feeling a bit calmer. Enid had made the whole thing up. She was simply jealous. She was mad at Jessica for winning Jonathan's affection, and she was bent on getting revenge. She'd gotten the hickey from some other guy.

But a nagging detail still bothered her. Enid had described her kiss with Jonathan in minute detail. She had said that he kissed her neck and that it felt as though their hearts were joining. How could she have known that?

Jessica punched the side of the Jeep, her fury mounting again. Suddenly she heard the sound of a motorcycle roar to life. She whirled around. Jonathan was seated calmly on his bike, wearing his usual black jeans and a black leather jacket.

Jessica faced Jonathan with glittering eyes. "Turn off the bike," she said.

Jonathan cut the engine, and a lock of black hair fell across his forehead. "What is it, Jessica?" he asked. His face was impassive, but his eyes looked pained.

"I've heard rumors about you and Enid Rollins," Jessica said. "Are they true?"

"It doesn't matter if they are," Jonathan said, brushing the hair out of his face.

Tears sprang to Jessica's eyes. She had been sure he would deny it. She had been *desperate* for him to deny it. "What do you mean, it doesn't matter?"

"A relationship between you and me would never work out," Jonathan responded in an even voice. "I already told you that."

But Jessica wasn't one to back down so easily. "I dare you to look me in the eye and tell me you don't have strong feelings for me," she challenged him.

"No problem," Jonathan said coolly. He looked her straight in the eye. "I don't—" he began. But then his voice wavered. His eyes locked on hers, causing Jessica's heart to flutter. Then he looked away quickly. "I've got to go, Jessica," he said quietly. He revved the engine and backed out of his spot.

Jessica drew a long, shaky breath, leaning back against the Jeep for support, as he peeled out of the parking lot. Her face was burning, and her nerves felt raw and exposed. Jessica didn't know what was happening to her. She'd never felt so desperate for anyone before. She wasn't used to feeling so out of control with a guy—and the feeling scared her.

When she turned around, Enid was staring at her hatefully from across the parking lot. Jessica smiled smugly as she caught Enid's eye. Then she waved merrily and shook her hair, imitating Enid's gesture from lunch.

Elizabeth ripped her "Personal Profiles" column out of the printer on Thursday afternoon at the *Oracle* office. She scanned the article in dismay. The column was due the next day, but it was in no shape to be published. Of all the difficult assignments she'd had in the past, this was the worst. This week's column for the *Oracle* featured Jonathan Cain. Olivia Davidson had come up with the idea the week before, and the whole staff had been enthusiastic about it. Elizabeth had hedged at the time, and she had hoped they would forget about it. But a few days later Mr. Collins, the *Oracle* advisor and Elizabeth's favorite English teacher, had given her the assignment. When Elizabeth had protested, he suggested she see it as a challenge. "Journalists have to be objective," he had said. "You have to learn to put all your personal feelings aside."

Elizabeth read through the piece again. "'Mystery man comes to Sweet Valley High . . . lived in Europe and studied abroad . . . aced Mr. Russo's advanced chemistry unit exam without taking the class . . . knows more about modern cultures of Eastern Europe than Ms. Jacobi does . . . equals Todd Wilkins on the basketball court . . .'"

Elizabeth sighed. The piece was just a bunch of conjecture strung together into incoherent sentences. Her strongest source of information had been Caroline Pearce, who had a notorious reputation as the class gossip. Even though Elizabeth had agreed to write the column, she hadn't been able to bring herself to interview Jonathan Cain. Just being in his presence gave her the creeps.

Elizabeth chewed on a fingernail and stared at the article. Then she crumpled up the page and threw it into the trash can.

"Well, you certainly look like the troubled artist," Maria said, pulling up a chair next to her. Maria shared Elizabeth's interest in journalism, and she had taken a position as a staff writer on the *Oracle*.

"Troubled, yes. Artist, no," Elizabeth responded. "I don't know why I think I can be a writer. I can barely get out a coherent sentence." Elizabeth sighed and held her head in her hands.

"Maybe the subject matter is the problem," Maria suggested.

"That's definitely *part* of the problem," Elizabeth conceded. The last person in the world she wanted to write about was Jonathan Cain. He had already cast a spell on most of the girls in the junior class, and Elizabeth's column would only add to his fame. But Elizabeth knew that wasn't the only problem. She was so upset about Todd that she could barely concentrate on anything at all.

"And the rest is you," Maria guessed, pulling her legs up cross-legged on the chair.

Elizabeth looked at her good friend in dismay. "Maria, I'm at my wit's end. I got up all my courage to come clean with Todd, and he won't even look at me." She raked a finger through her tangled hair. "Joey's been calling every night, but I won't take his calls. I have to speak to Todd first."

Maria nodded and gave her an encouraging smile. "You're on the right track, Liz."

Elizabeth threw her hands in the air. "I *was* on the right track, but Todd won't talk to me. I give up."

"Where is he now?" Maria asked, a gleam in her deep brown eyes.

Elizabeth sighed. "Probably at basketball practice."

"Well, why don't you go find him?" Maria suggested.

"It's no use, that's why," Elizabeth said. She propped her elbows on the table and rested her chin on her hands dejectedly. "I've been trying to talk to him for days. He won't give me the time of day."

"Then corner him," Maria urged. "Remember, he doesn't have to say anything. He just has to listen."

Elizabeth nodded in determination. "You're right. I'm going to find him right now." She jumped up and grabbed her backpack. Then she stopped. "But what about the column?"

But Maria was already sitting at the computer. She waved her away with a flip of her wrist. "Don't worry about it," she said. "I can write sentences."

"Maria, are you sure?" Elizabeth asked.

Maria shooed her away. "Now would you get out of here?"

Elizabeth flashed her a grateful smile and hurried out of the room. She glanced at her watch as the door shut behind her. It was five o'clock. Todd would just be getting out of basketball practice. If she hurried, she could still catch him.

Throwing her backpack over her left shoulder, she ran down the long corridor to the gym. Pulling open the heavy doors, she poked her head inside.

The gym was empty. Elizabeth's heart sank. She had missed him.

Maybe he's still in the locker room, Elizabeth thought, desperate to speak to him while she still had the courage. She walked quickly across the hardwood floor of the gym, her steps echoing in the vast, empty space. She ducked under the aluminum bleachers and hurried toward the boys' locker room.

As she reached the door she heard the sounds of male voices inside. *They're still here!* she thought with renewed hope, swinging through the door of the locker room. The room was humid, and a faint smell of chlorine hung in the air.

A chorus of shouts greeted her arrival. The guys hooted and hollered, letting out whistles and catcalls. Elizabeth gasped and clapped her hand over her mouth. She had been so upset that she hadn't thought twice about walking into the guys' locker room. The boys were all gathered by the lockers in various states of undress. Jason Mann was walking out of the shower with a white towel wrapped around his waist. A.J. Morgan was reaching into a high locker, clad only in a pair of red polka-dot boxer shorts. Keith Webster was sitting on the bench in sweatpants, pulling on a pair of high-tops.

Elizabeth took a step back, her face flaming at the commotion that ensued.

"Hey, Liz, c'mon in!" A.J. yelled, giving her a big, goofy grin. He looked ridiculous standing on the bench in his polka-dot boxer shorts, and Elizabeth fought back a smile.

"Did you want a shower?" Jason asked. "I'm almost done with my towel."

Terrified that he was going to offer her the towel, Elizabeth held up a hand and shook her head frantically. The boys burst out laughing. "I . . . I was just looking for Todd," she said, backing out quickly.

"He's already gone," A.J. informed her, grabbing a bundle of clothes from his locker and jumping to the ground.

"OK, thanks," Elizabeth said, practically running out of the room.

As she flew out of the locker room, she slammed into yet another basketball player, Tom Hackett.

"Oh, sorry!" Elizabeth exclaimed, recoiling from the shock.

"I didn't expect to find *you* coming out of the boys' locker room," he said, a teasing grin on his face. It looked as though he'd had a strenuous workout. Tom's face was red, and his T-shirt was drenched in sweat. He had a water bottle tucked under his arm and a towel slung around his shoulders.

"I was looking for Todd," Elizabeth explained, her face flushing again.

"He took off right after practice," Tom said, pulling the towel off his shoulders and mopping his face with it. "He went somewhere with Bruce."

"Thanks," Elizabeth said, perplexed. Usually Todd thought Bruce was a jerk.

Elizabeth hurried out of the building, her cheeks still burning. What in the world had gotten into her? How could she have barged into the boys' locker room without thinking? But a small smile tugged at the corners of her lips as she thought of A.J. in his boxer shorts. She couldn't wait to tell Enid. Her friend would think it was hilarious.

But then her mood sobered again. Enid didn't want to have anything to do with her. Elizabeth trudged across the football field, hit with a wave of nostalgia. She felt as though she had lost her two best friends. *I have lost my two best friends*, she realized sadly. *And it's my own fault.* She'd cheated on Todd, and she'd been neglecting Enid. They both felt they'd been replaced. Elizabeth sighed. She didn't want a new boyfriend, and as much as she liked Maria, she didn't want a new best friend, either. She wanted Todd and Enid back.

Elizabeth thought of all the time she had spent with Enid—all the hours they spent talking on the phone, going to movies, hanging out at the Dairi Burger. And she remembered how her days used to be filled with Todd, how they would eat lunch together and walk down the halls together and take late night drives to Miller's Point together. . . .

A tear trickled down Elizabeth's cheek. She missed them. Sweet Valley wasn't the same anymore.

Chapter 8

"Hey, man, ready to rule the school?" Bruce asked Todd as they walked into the halls of Sweet Valley High on Monday morning.

"You got it," Todd returned with a grin. He was glad he and Bruce were hanging out again. Sometimes Bruce acted a little too arrogant, but for the most part he was a really cool guy.

Todd and Bruce were both dressed in the hip gothic style. Todd was wearing black jeans and his black leather jacket, and his dyed black hair was slicked back. Bruce had on a black tuxedo jacket and a narrow red tie. Todd swaggered down the hall next to Bruce, aware of all the attention they were getting.

A bunch of sophomore girls stopped and stared as they passed by.

"Lookin' good!" a girl yelled. Somebody else let out an appreciative whistle.

Todd didn't crack a smile. In fact, he pretended not to notice. But he loved the way girls were staring at him. *This is the proof that I'm over Elizabeth,* he thought. He never would have enjoyed all this attention if he still cared for her.

Bruce rubbed his hands together. "We've gotta start getting the word out about Jonathan's party on Friday," he said.

"I'm not sure if we should do that," Todd said worriedly. "Jonathan didn't actually say we could have a party at his place."

Bruce shrugged. "I don't think he's going to have a choice."

"Hold it a sec. I've gotta get a few books," Todd said as they approached his locker. Bruce slouched against the wall as Todd spun the combination lock.

"Hey, Todd, like the look," a low female voice said.

Todd turned to find Katrina standing by the locker. She was smiling up at him flirtatiously, her large brown eyes warm and inviting.

"Hey, you going to the party on Friday?" Bruce asked her.

"What party?" Katrina asked.

"Jonathan's having a party on Friday night," Todd explained, getting into the spirit of things.

Bruce grinned at him, and Todd smiled back. He felt just a twinge of guilt over the fact that Jonathan had never actually *agreed* to the party.

"I'm going if you're going," Katrina said, batting her eyelashes at him.

"I'll be there," Todd said, giving her a cool smile. He was *definitely* enjoying being single.

"Here's a typo," Maria said, pointing to the page proofs laid out before them. It was Tuesday afternoon, and Maria and Elizabeth were at the *Oracle* office, proofreading the latest edition of the paper. Maria was lying flat on her stomach on the carpet, propped up on her elbows. Elizabeth sat cross-legged next to her.

Elizabeth circled the error with a thick red pencil. Penny Ayala had written an editorial about the new gothic look and had typed in *ghastly* instead of *ghostly*. "'The gothic group has created a new ghastly look,'" Elizabeth read aloud, and laughed. "I think the typo is a lot more appropriate."

Maria joined in her laughter. "I agree one hundred percent. I can't believe what's happening to the junior class. The guys have become Jonathan look-alikes and the girls all resemble Morticia Addams."

"All because of that new creep," Elizabeth put in. "He's created a revolution." She shook her head.

"I'm telling you, this guy has a weird power."

"Oh, lighten up, Liz," Maria protested, pulling herself up to a sitting position. "It's just a fad. Things like this happen all the time." She propped herself against the back of a desk, crossing her long legs in front of her.

"Nothing has been the same since he came to town," Elizabeth insisted, standing up and pacing the carpet. "Half the kids in the junior class are mindless copies of him, and both Jessica and Enid are under his power. Not to mention the fact that the first murder occurred two days before he came to Sweet Valley High."

Maria looked at her in astonishment. "You can't blame Jonathan for the actions of a serial killer!" she exclaimed.

Elizabeth shrugged. "Believe me, Maria, this guy's bad news."

"But Liz, he hasn't done anything," Maria insisted. "I don't think you're being rational about this."

"Maria, I know you're the voice of reason, but in this case I think I'm right," Elizabeth maintained. "There's something spooky about that guy."

"Ghostly," Maria put in.

"Ghastly," Elizabeth corrected.

They both laughed.

"Well, it's good to hear you laughing again,"

Maria said. "Did you work things out with Todd last week?"

"Not exactly," Elizabeth said, folding up the page proofs. "He wasn't there."

"He wasn't at practice?" Maria asked. She stood up and stretched her arms above her head.

"No, he wasn't in the locker room," Elizabeth said wryly.

Maria wheeled around and looked at her in shock. "Are you telling me you walked right into the boys' locker room?"

Elizabeth nodded. "And you should have seen A.J. Morgan's red polka-dot boxers." Supporting herself with the palms of her hand, she hopped up on a desk.

Maria burst out laughing. "Liz, you are in a bad way," she said. "We are going to resolve your dilemma here and now."

"I just can't seem to make a decision," Elizabeth said, swinging her legs. "Everything's whirling around in my brain."

"Why don't you try writing down how you feel?" Maria suggested.

Elizabeth nodded. "That's a good idea," she agreed. Writing always helped her work out her feelings.

"OK, why don't we take these page proofs to the back, where we have more privacy?" Maria suggested with a wink.

The girls headed to the back of the office and pulled two office chairs into a secluded corner. Whipping out a piece of paper, Maria drew a straight line down the center and labeled one side *Todd* and the other side *Joey*. "All right, go to it," she said, rubbing her hands together. "Pros and cons of each."

Elizabeth looked at Maria helplessly. "I don't know where to begin," she said.

"First category: strength of character," Maria stated.

"Well, I don't even have to think about that one," Elizabeth said. "Joey wins in that column hands down. He does exactly what he believes in. He was all set to go to Yale, one of the best colleges in the country, when he realized that he was trying to please his parents, not himself. Todd, on the other hand, has become a Jonathan wanna-be." Elizabeth put a check in Joey's column.

"Next category: artistic ability," Maria said.

Elizabeth added another check to Joey's column, thinking of Joey's talented direction of the camp play.

Maria rested her chin on her hand, reflecting. "How about something that affects you—like the way they treat you?" she suggested.

Elizabeth bit her lip. It looked as if Joey scored in that category as well. He was practically fawning over her. He'd been calling her every day, and he'd sent her a bouquet of fresh flowers the night before. Todd, on the other hand, wouldn't even speak to her.

Half an hour later, Elizabeth scanned the list. Joey had won in almost every area: strength of character, artistic ability, humor, wit, maturity, and sensitivity. Todd had come out on top in a few minor categories: intelligence, athletic ability, and history with Elizabeth.

"Well, looks like the results are in," Maria said, adding up the checks.

Elizabeth nodded resolutely. She and Todd were through. Officially.

"Are you relieved?" Maria asked.

Elizabeth nodded again. "Completely. Now the decision has been made, and there's nothing else to it." But a small voice inside her head disagreed. She was hit with such a wave of sadness that it threatened to overwhelm her.

"Listen, I've got to get home," Maria said, pushing back her chair and jumping up. "I promised my mother I'd go grocery shopping."

"OK, I'll talk to you later," Elizabeth said. Maria threw her backpack over her shoulder and waved on her way out.

After Maria was gone, Elizabeth studied the pros-and-cons list again. One category jumped out at her: history with Elizabeth. She stared at it, fixated. She and Todd had been dating for ages. He had been her first boyfriend, and she had always thought he would be her last. Elizabeth bit her lip. Maybe history wasn't such a minor category after all.

When she got home that afternoon, Elizabeth marched into the house and climbed up the steps two at a time. She was going to call Joey. She wanted to make a date with him before she changed her mind. And besides, if Todd was going to be such a jerk, she might as well not torture herself over her decision. She had tried to be honest with Todd, but he'd lost his chance.

Elizabeth threw her book bag on her velvet chaise longue and flopped down on the bed. Pulling her hair back into a ponytail, she picked up the receiver from the bedside table and punched in Joey's number. Elizabeth twirled the cord around her fingers nervously as the phone rang. Maybe Joey wasn't interested in her anymore. Maybe he was angry that she hadn't thanked him for the flowers. Maybe she *wanted* him to be angry with her.

Joey picked up on the third ring, and Elizabeth's voice caught in her throat.

"Hello?" he asked again. His voice was low and sexy on the phone. It was the voice of a man, not a boy. A thrill surged through Elizabeth.

"Uh, Joey?" Elizabeth asked nervously.

"Elizabeth!" Joey exclaimed. "I've been dreaming of hearing your voice."

Elizabeth's heart skipped a beat. "I wanted to thank you for the flowers," she said. "They're really beautiful."

"Beautiful flowers for a—" But then Joey stopped in midsentence, laughing. "Sorry, I was about to throw out a cliché. I'm just so glad you called. I discovered the most romantic spot in California, and I want to take you there."

"OK," Elizabeth agreed quickly.

"OK? Great!" Joey exclaimed. "When? How about now?"

Elizabeth hesitated for a moment. It all seemed so sudden. But then she decided that seeing Joey immediately was probably the best thing to do. After all, Jessica always said the best way to get over one relationship was to start another. Maybe going somewhere new with Joey would take her mind off her memories of Todd.

"Sure, I guess that's OK," Elizabeth said.

"I'll be there in half an hour," Joey said.

"See you soon," Elizabeth responded. She put down the phone and stared at the receiver. *Am I doing the right thing? Am I ready to lose Todd forever?*

• • •

Jonathan paced nervously around his living room on Tuesday night. Ever since Sweet Valley had imposed a curfew, he'd been feeling extremely edgy. The streets were deserted now at night. Nobody went out after ten o'clock.

He had thought his weekend alone in the mountains would help quench his thirst. He had hoped he would forget his insatiable appetite. He had spent the entire weekend alone, camping out and catching wild animals. He had thought that communing with nature would help fulfill his instinctual needs. But now that he had come back to Sweet Valley, everything was exactly the same.

He craved the sensation of a girl's soft skin and hair.

Immediately his mind turned to Jessica. Her face hovered before him like a glowing light. She radiated all the power of sunshine. She was lively and sparkling, like a summer day, and her bright smile warmed his troubled soul. He ached to have her in his arms, to feel the softness of her body, to taste the salty sweetness of her skin, to start kissing her neck—

He clenched his fists, forcing the image away. He couldn't let Jessica be in his life—she was too important to him.

Jonathan prowled across the room like a panther,

turning off all the lamps. He walked over to the mantel and blew out the flickering wicks in the candelabra. His keen eyes adjusted immediately to the dim light, and he breathed in the darkness of the room. Jonathan twisted the wooden ring on his middle finger. It was a relief to be out of the glaring light, to return to the soothing darkness.

Jonathan stood before the portrait above the mantel, studying the image. A memory flashed before him, a memory that seemed to belong to another lifetime. The face of the guy in the picture faded into the image of a young man in a small fishing village.

The young man is sitting on a jutting rock overlooking the Baltic Sea. An older man with a tanned, weathered face is at his side, a fishing rod in his hand. Then the two are gathered around a crude wooden table with a stocky woman and a beautiful young girl, a platter of freshly steamed fish in front of them. The family scene dissolves into a funeral procession. A long line of people dressed in black are walking solemnly along a dirt road. A tall woman with a black veil over her face approaches the young man. Her eyes are glowing with a strange yellow light. The young man stares, mesmerized, into the woman's eyes.

The eyes in the portrait stared back at Jonathan.

Blinking, Jonathan tore himself away from the magnetic pull of the image. Shaking his head hard, he pulled himself out of his reverie. He picked up a glass of red wine and drank it in one gulp. But the wine only fed his hunger—his hunger for a time gone by, his hunger for a girl he couldn't have.

Jonathan pulled back the heavy ivory damask curtains and gazed out at the midnight blue sky. He longed to go out into the night. *You cannot,* a voice in his head told him. *It's too risky.* Jonathan paced back across the room, his longing eating away at him.

He picked up the phone impulsively and dialed Jessica's number. *I just want to hear her voice,* he told himself. But he hung up on the second ring. He was fooling himself. She was sure to come over.

Picking up the phone again, he sifted through some scraps of paper until he found the one he wanted. A phone number was scrawled next to the name of a girl: Enid Rollins. If he saw Enid, maybe his desire for Jessica would be pushed away. Holding the receiver between his neck and shoulder, he quickly dialed the number.

"Hello?" came a girl's breathless voice.

"Enid, it's Jonathan," he said.

"Jonathan!" Enid breathed.

"I was wondering if you'd like to come over," Jonathan said.

"I'd love to," Enid said, practically purring. "I'll be there in fifteen minutes."

Enid hurried up the mossy path that led to Jonathan's house, her heart soaring in excitement. She couldn't believe that Jonathan had actually called her. He really wanted to have a relationship with her. He had finally seen what she had known all along—that they were soul mates, that they were meant for each other.

Enid skipped up the front steps, carefully avoiding the hole in the third step. She paused before knocking, taking a moment to compose herself. Pulling out a compact from her purse, she quickly checked her makeup. She fluffed up her hair and smoothed down her short black tube dress. Then she lifted her hand to the ornate brass knocker on the door. But suddenly the door opened.

"Oh!" Enid exclaimed in surprise.

"Come in," Jonathan said, holding the door wide open. As Enid walked in past him, her heart began to pound in her chest again. The house was shrouded in darkness. She blinked and tried to adjust to the lack of light as she made her way down the hall.

"Jonathan, I'm so glad you called," Enid said, turning around. Then she jumped. Jonathan was standing right behind her, his hands reaching to her neck.

She gasped, looking up at him in fear.

"Oh, sorry," Jonathan said smoothly. "I didn't mean to scare you. I just wanted to take your coat."

Enid laughed nervously. "Oh," she said, wriggling out of her black rain slicker. Jonathan took it from her and hung it in the coat closet.

"So, what did you do this weekend?" Enid asked, trying to make conversation. Suddenly she felt very uncomfortable, as if Jonathan were a total stranger. *He is a total stranger,* she reminded herself. *I know almost nothing about him.*

"Nothing much," Jonathan said, pulling her into his arms and kissing her roughly. Enid kissed him back, but then she pushed him away. She didn't want Jonathan to think she was some kind of sex toy. She wanted him to learn who she *really* was, who she was inside.

Enid swallowed. "Don't you think we should get to know each other first?" she asked nervously.

"We *are* getting to know each other," Jonathan said, pulling her toward him again.

Enid resisted with more force this time, placing her palms on his chest and pushing him away. Jonathan dropped his arms, a cold glint in his eyes.

Enid turned away and walked into the living

room. Jonathan followed close behind. "So how come you're living alone?" Enid asked.

Jonathan looked at her with a tortured expression on his face. "Enid, I've missed you so much this weekend. Can't we just be together for a while and then talk afterward?" he implored.

Enid's resolve melted instantly. She blinked and mentally pinched herself, feeling as though she were in a daze. *Did I actually hear right? Did Jonathan actually say that he missed me terribly?* These were the words she had heard in her dreams. Enid nodded, unable to speak.

Jonathan pulled her down next to him on the couch and captured her lips with his, kissing her with an intensity that left her breathless. Then he buried his face in her neck. Enid closed her eyes and moaned. With Jonathan's lips on her face and neck, Enid felt herself traveling to that mystical place where Jonathan's kisses took her.

She felt a reckless sense of danger, but she didn't care. The important thing was that *she* was the one he wanted.

Jessica paced back and forth in her bedroom, literally biting her nails. She hadn't spoken to Jonathan since the previous Tuesday. After she had found out about Enid, she had made a firm resolution that she wouldn't call him anymore. She had decided that she had been making herself too available. She had been sure Jonathan would crack and call her. But he hadn't. She had stared at the phone all week, willing it to ring. But it had just stared back at her, silent. She felt like strangling it with its own cord. *Ring!* she commanded it. *Ring!* Nothing. Silence.

Jessica growled in frustration and plopped down on the bed, drawing her knees to her chest. She had overheard Bruce saying that Jonathan was going to the mountains for the weekend. Even though Jonathan had told her he couldn't get involved with her, Jessica had been sure he would change his mind. She had been sure he wouldn't be able to resist her for long. A tiny part of her had hoped that he would invite her to go away with him for the weekend. *Where did he go?* Jessica pondered. *And why did he go away all alone?* She wondered for the hundredth time if he had a girlfriend somewhere. Maybe they had spent a romantic weekend together hiking in the Rocky Mountains. Or maybe he had taken a flight to Europe to go skiing with her in the Swiss Alps. Jessica rocked back and forth, twisting her hands together. She pictured him with a dark-haired beauty from Greece, swimming in a mountain stream. The thought was unbearable. She stood up suddenly, forcing the image from her mind.

Jessica walked the length of her room, kicking clothes out of her way. She felt as though the walls of her room were closing in on her. The weekend had been interminable. It was bad enough waiting for Jonathan to call, but it was even worse knowing he *couldn't* call. Jessica had thought about Jonathan all her waking hours, and she had dreamed about him at night. Jessica gnawed on a nail and picked up the phone for the tenth time. She'd never, ever been so desperate for a guy.

Jessica hung up the phone and looked at the calendar on the wall. A full week had gone by. She couldn't hold out any longer. She picked up the receiver again and punched in Jonathan's number. The phone rang and rang. Jessica fell back onto her bed and drummed her fingers on the covers, waiting with bated breath while the phone jangled in her ear.

Jonathan answered on the tenth ring. "Yes?" he asked. He sounded unlike himself. His voice was thick and distant.

"It's Jessica," she said softly, her voice almost a whisper.

"I can't talk right now," Jonathan said abruptly. "This is a . . . a bad time."

Jessica's face fell. "Are you sick?" she pressed.

"You could say that," Jonathan answered cryptically.

As Jessica digested the information she was hit with an idea. She sat up suddenly, her eyes lighting up. "OK, I guess I'll see you tomorrow, then," she said.

Jessica hung up the phone and stared at it, her mind clicking away. A grin crossed her features as she formed a brilliant plan.

Jasmine meowed and pranced into the room with her tail held high.

"You like the idea too, huh?" Jessica said, scooping up the furry little kitten. She waltzed around the room with Jasmine in her arms, anticipating the evening. "I could have danced all night, I could have danced all night," she sang under her breath. Suddenly she tripped over a pile of clothes and went flying across the room. Jasmine sprang out of her arms with a yowl.

"Is something wrong?" Elizabeth asked, popping her head in.

"No, nothing," Jessica said with a smile from the floor. "Jasmine and I were just having a moment."

Jasmine protested with a sharp *Mrrw!* and bolted out the door, scrambling through Elizabeth's legs.

Elizabeth's eyes narrowed. "Why are you happy all of a sudden?"

Jessica pulled herself up to a sitting position. "I can't believe this!" she said, throwing up her hands. "I can't even smile without making you suspicious."

Elizabeth crossed her legs at the ankles and leaned against the doorway. "Well, you've been moping for days," she pointed out. "It seems a little strange that you should have such a sudden mood change—right after you were talking on the phone."

"Do you mind leaving before you make me entirely miserable again?" Jessica asked.

"Jessica, who were you talking to?" Elizabeth pressed.

"It's none of your business," Jessica responded, standing up and heading into the bathroom.

She was sick of Elizabeth's acting like the love police. Elizabeth had no right to lecture her on matters of the heart. After all, her high-and-mighty sister was no one to talk—she was dating two guys at the same time! "And please shut the door when you leave."

"My pleasure!" Elizabeth retorted, slamming the door behind her.

Chapter 9

"For you, *mademoiselle,*" Joey said with a low bow as Elizabeth answered the door. He whipped out a bouquet of wildflowers from behind his back.

Elizabeth flushed at his gallantry. "Joey, they're beautiful," she said. "Wildflowers are my favorite." She breathed in the fragrant aroma of the fresh bouquet. "Where did you ever find them?"

"From a field, of course," Joey said with a grin. He put out an arm for Elizabeth to take. "And now I am going to escort you to the most romantic spot in southern California."

Elizabeth took his arm and walked by his side to the car. She knew she should be thrilled with all the attention, but for some reason she was completely unaffected. In fact, she felt almost irritated. She didn't feel like holding on to Joey's arm, and she felt oppressed by his presence.

Joey held open the passenger-side door as Elizabeth stepped in, shutting it carefully behind her. Then he slipped into the driver's seat and started the engine.

"Where are we going?" Elizabeth asked as they cruised down Calico Drive.

"It's a surprise," Joey said, his green eyes mischievous. He flipped on the radio and turned the knob adeptly, stopping at a classical-music station. The soothing sounds of a Vivaldi symphony wafted through the air. Elizabeth leaned her head back against the headrest and tried to relax.

Joey turned onto Valley Crest Highway and headed straight for the ocean. "We're going to take the scenic route," he said.

Elizabeth studied his features as he maneuvered the car. Joey was even more handsome than he had been at camp. Instead of shorts and a T-shirt, he was dressed in khaki pants and a green cotton button-down shirt. His curly light brown hair had grown longer, and a slight stubble darkened his strong jaw. *What is wrong with me?* Elizabeth wondered. *Why am I not attracted to him? Am I really so fickle?*

Within minutes they were driving alongside the ocean. It was a windy night, and the ocean rolled with foamy dark waves. A light fog blew across the sea, creating a vaporous mist that sifted across the crashing breakers. Elizabeth stared longingly at the ocean, feeling wistful. The scene reminded her of something out of a nineteenth-century English novel. It was the perfect setting for romance. *Too bad the characters are wrong,* she thought.

Joey leaned over and squeezed her hand. "I'm so glad you called," he said. "I didn't know if I could wait any longer for a decision."

"Everything's over between me and Todd," Elizabeth said. Her voice sounded wooden even to her own ears.

"Did you break up with him?" Joey asked.

"Well, not in so many words," Elizabeth said. "I . . . oh, it's just—" She stumbled on her words and faltered.

Joey put a hand over hers. "Don't worry about it. You're with me and that's all that counts."

Elizabeth opened her mouth to protest. She felt a surge of anger at being shut up. She wanted to tell Joey the whole story. She wanted to tell him about her attempts to talk to Todd, about her talks with Maria, about her confusion and uncertainty. *But then,* she thought, *he's probably right.* Talking about Todd the whole night wouldn't help her to get over him.

"I went to this great frat party at Sigma Chi last night," Joey said.

"On a Monday night?" Elizabeth asked in surprise.

"At college, there are parties *every* night," Joey said with a slightly condescending laugh.

Elizabeth bristled at his tone. She and Jessica had spent a week at Sweet Valley University visiting their brother, Steven, and she'd been completely turned off by the whole Greek scene. Joey didn't seem like the same guy she'd known at camp. At camp he'd been quietly authoritative. He'd managed to pull off a complicated dramatic production without ever raising his voice. He was talented and gorgeous but completely humble at the same time. That's what Elizabeth had found so attractive about him. Now he seemed just the opposite: immature and full of himself.

"Yeah, I'm thinking of rushing Sigma Chi next semester," Joey said.

Elizabeth looked at him in surprise. Joey wasn't the type to join a frat. "I thought you were going to join the drama club and try out for some plays."

Joey shrugged. "I don't know. I might bag that and just hang out for a while. I've been too serious for too long. I worked so hard to get into a good school. I think it's time for me to take it easy and spend some time on myself—and on *you*, of course." He smiled at her and winked.

Elizabeth tried to smile back, but she didn't

achieve much more than a grimace. Turning her head, she looked out at the view. They were turning off Ocean Crest Road onto a small, winding road in Sweet Valley's posh hill area. *If Joey wants to be a frat guy, that's his business,* Elizabeth admonished herself. *I'm probably being too judgmental.* Joey had the right to enjoy himself for a while. He'd been a serious actor all through high school, and he deserved a break. He had just started college, after all. He probably had to explore lots of things before he decided what he really wanted to do.

Suddenly Elizabeth recognized the route Joey was taking. Her heart plummeted as he climbed the twisting road that led to Miller's Point. Miller's Point was a popular parking spot overlooking Sweet Valley, and she and Todd had spent countless romantic evenings there.

Joey pulled into an empty spot in the grassy lot and cut the lights. Sweet Valley twinkled like a jewel far below them. A light mist blew across the rooftops of the houses in the valley, making the town seem enchanted. "Well, *mademoiselle,*" he said with a sweep of his head, indicating the vista, "isn't it romantic?"

Elizabeth squirmed in her seat and swallowed hard. "It's . . . it's beautiful, Joey," she said, barely managing to get out the words.

Joey smiled and took her hand, his green eyes dancing with pleasure. "I was so excited when I found this spot. The minute I saw it, I thought of you. I was dying to tell you about it, but I wanted it to be a surprise. I knew you'd love it."

Elizabeth gulped. Getting over Todd wouldn't be as easy as she'd hoped.

"Yes!" Jessica exclaimed from her bedroom window as she watched Elizabeth and Joey walk down the driveway together. "Freedom!" As soon as the car faded out of sight, Jessica sprang into action. She dove into the shower. When she was done, she pulled on a pair of soft, faded jeans and a pink cotton sweater. Then she applied her makeup with care and brushed her golden hair with strong strokes. After quickly flipping her head upside down, then right side up, she watched in satisfaction as her silky hair fell in fluffy waves around her shoulders. Jessica smiled at her reflection in the mirror. She looked lovely. Her complexion was clear and rosy, and her eyes were bright and sparkling.

Time to put my plan into action, Jessica thought as she skipped down the steps.

Jessica found Mrs. Wakefield in the kitchen, standing by the stove, stirring a pot of spaghetti sauce with a wooden spoon.

"Hi, Mom!" Jessica said brightly, reaching into the refrigerator and pulling out a variety of vegetables.

"Honey, I'm just fixing dinner," Mrs. Wakefield said.

"I know," Jessica said. "But Amy's sick, and I told her I'd bring her some chicken soup." She dumped an armful of vegetables on the kitchen counter and reached for the cutting board. After setting a green pepper in the center of the board, she whacked it with a sharp knife.

Mrs. Wakefield looked at her in concern. "It's almost eight o'clock," she said worriedly. "Are you sure you'll get back by ten o'clock?"

"Of course," Jessica said, throwing the slices of pepper into a glass bowl.

"I don't know, Jessica," Mrs. Wakefield said. "I don't like the idea of you driving around alone in the dark. Why don't I take you?"

"Actually, I'm going to pick Lila up on the way, so I won't be alone." She chopped up an onion deftly and added it to the bowl. Tears sprang to her eyes, and Jessica wiped them away with the back of her sleeve.

"I guess it's OK," Mrs. Wakefield said, reaching into the refrigerator and pulling out half a chicken. "Let me help you. The faster you get this cooked, the faster you'll be back."

Jessica flashed her mother a grateful smile. "You're the best, Mom."

Forty-five minutes later, a pot of homemade chicken soup with fresh vegetables and chunks of potato was simmering on the stove. Jessica hummed to herself as she stirred the broth. Cooking was a truly loving act for her. She hoped Jonathan would appreciate it.

She dipped a spoon in the broth and blew on it, bringing it to her mouth. "Mmm," she murmured.

"Here, why don't you use this?" Mrs. Wakefield said, handing her a thermos. Grabbing a big ladle from the counter, Jessica carefully filled up the container. Then she kissed her mother on the cheek and pulled on a denim jacket.

"See you later, Mom," she said. "And don't worry!"

Humming with anticipation, Jessica headed out the door with the thermos.

There wasn't a guy alive who could resist a real-life Florence Nightingale.

"Jonathan," Enid murmured dreamily, leaning back against Jonathan's strong chest. They were sitting on the rug on the floor, directly in front of the fire. Jonathan's arms were wrapped tightly around her, and his hungry lips were on her neck. The heat of the fire and the heat of his body filled

Enid with a languorous pleasure. She felt giddy and light-headed as he slowly sucked at the skin on her neck.

Suddenly a sharp knocking on the door jolted her out of paradise.

Enid felt Jonathan tense up, and she opened her heavy eyelids. The knocking repeated itself. Enid groaned. She knew instantly that it was Jessica at the door.

"What a magnificent view!" Joey breathed as he gazed out at the charming town. He turned to Elizabeth with a smile. "Do you remember how beautiful the mountains of Montana were?" Joey got a wistful look on his face. "I can still see the green lake sparkling in the moonlight and the snowcapped mountains rising up behind it."

Elizabeth nodded, but the image evoked nothing for her. All she saw was a grassy knoll and a couple of cars parked nearby. She didn't feel nostalgic and imaginative. She felt plodding and tired. She just wanted to go home and curl up with a book—all alone.

"You know, being here with you makes me feel like we're back at camp again," Joey said. He touched her hand softly.

"Me too," Elizabeth murmured. But she didn't share his sentiments. Camp Echo Mountain seemed like a lifetime away. She didn't feel as though they were back at camp. She knew exactly where she was. She was at Miller's Point, where she and Todd had spent many blissful, romantic hours. Elizabeth bit her lip nervously. Maybe she should just tell Joey that coming there was a bad idea, that this place held too many memories for her.

Joey turned to face her and stared into her eyes, running a finger down her cheek. Elizabeth swallowed nervously. She couldn't bring herself to do it. After all, Joey had gone to so much trouble to bring her to this spot. He had been so excited about surprising her. And Elizabeth hadn't said anything. Now it was too late.

Joey put a hand on her back and brought his lips to hers, his kiss long and sweet.

Elizabeth closed her eyes and tried to concentrate on Joey, but her mind kept wandering back to times with Todd. Fragments of conversations came back to her—"I never thought I'd find someone like you"; "We're meant for each other"; "Elizabeth, we'll be together forever."

A montage of images flashed through her mind: she and Todd running on the beach with Prince Albert, the Wakefields' golden retriever; she and Todd sharing a chocolate shake at the Dairi Burger; cheering Todd on from the bleachers as he ran across the basketball court. . . .

"Oh, Elizabeth, you're so beautiful," Joey said, running a hand through her silky blond hair.

Elizabeth swallowed hard and gave Joey a crooked smile. *What am I supposed to say to that? 'Oh, Joey, you're so handsome?'*

Suddenly a wave of guilt washed over Elizabeth. She had been unfaithful to Todd with Joey at camp, and now she was being unfaithful to Joey in her mind.

To assuage her guilty feelings, she wrapped her arms around Joey's neck and kissed him passionately. "Mmm," Joey responded, his hand tightening on her hip.

Elizabeth closed her eyes and tried to get into the moment. She concentrated on the feel of Joey's muscular arms and the soft pressure of his lips.

From now on, she would think of Miller's Point as *their* place. *I couldn't be happier,* she told herself. *Really.*

Chapter 10

"Come on, Jonathan, answer," Jessica muttered under her breath as she waited at his door. She lifted the brass knocker again and rapped it hard three times. Jessica pressed her ear to the wood, listening for the sounds of his footsteps. She thought she detected some movement in the house. It sounded as if one of the floorboards were squeaking.

"Jonathan, I know you're in there," she said to the door. She banged the thermos repeatedly against the peeling painted surface, determined to make Jonathan answer. She didn't care how sick he was, and she didn't care if he didn't want to see her. She *had* to see him.

Jessica tapped a foot on the stoop impatiently as she considered her next move. Finally she decided she would have to walk in. After all, maybe Jonathan was too sick to get out of bed. He would be thrilled that she had brought him soup. She would stay by his bedside day and night and nurse him through his illness. Jessica unscrewed the cap of the thermos to see if the soup was still hot. She dipped a finger in the broth and brought it to her mouth. *Mmm, perfect,* she thought in satisfaction.

Jessica lifted her hand to the doorknob, but then she distinctly heard the sounds of his familiar quiet footsteps coming down the hall.

Jonathan opened the door a crack. "Jessica!" he exclaimed in a whisper.

Jessica proudly held out her thermos of homemade chicken soup. "A Jessica a day keeps the doctor away!" she exclaimed.

But Jonathan's odd expression made her heart sink. His lips were red and bruised, and his face was flushed an unnatural color.

"Jonathan, what's wrong?" Jessica asked warily, dropping her hand to her side.

Jonathan swallowed uncomfortably. "Nothing. I'm just not feeling very well."

"Jonathan, who is it?" came a groggy female voice.

"It's nothing!" Jonathan called into the hallway.

Jessica took a step back, feeling as if she had

been stabbed in the heart. "Nothing?" she echoed. Jonathan's face clouded over in pain, and he wouldn't meet her eyes.

Just then Enid appeared behind him. She looked like some kind of freakish vision. Her straight black hair was in wild disarray, and her cheeks were flushed scarlet. She looked straight at Jessica, a glazed look in her eyes. Then her lips curled up in an evil smile.

Jessica looked from Enid to Jonathan, unable to believe her eyes. "You really *are* sick, aren't you?" she spat out. Then she lifted her arm in the air and threw the thermos at Jonathan with all her might. The cap flew off, and the container hit him squarely in the chest. Steaming soup splashed all over his shirt. Jessica flinched as she saw Jonathan jump in pain. She had forgotten the thermos was open. Bitter tears stung her eyes, and she turned and ran down the walkway.

"Hey, are you OK?" Enid exclaimed in concern as hot soup cascaded down Jonathan's chest. She leaned down and scooped up the empty thermos.

"I'm fine," Jonathan said. He seemed oblivious to the steaming soup dripping down his white shirt and onto his skin. He stared fixedly at the walkway, watching as Jessica climbed into the Jeep.

"Here, let me clean you up," Enid said, reaching for his shirt.

Jonathan swatted her hand away. "I told you, I'm fine," he said through clenched teeth. He looked at her with unseeing eyes.

Enid's heart hurt at Jonathan's expression. His eyes were full of longing and anguish. He never looked at her the way he had looked at Jessica. With Enid, Jonathan was always cool and in control. She never made the impact on him that Jessica had. Enid would be blind not to see the love for Jessica in his eyes.

I'll make *him forget her,* she vowed. If Jonathan was capable of such deep feelings, there was no reason he couldn't direct them toward Enid. He just didn't know her well enough. But when he learned who she really was, he would forget that Jessica Wakefield had ever existed.

Enid moved to kiss him again, but he pushed her gently away.

Enid recoiled as if she'd been slapped. "Sorry," she said, gripping the iron bars of the railing behind her. Her face burned in humiliation.

"I think you'd better go," Jonathan said softly.

"But Jonathan, you're hurt," Enid said softly, gazing into his eyes. She was desperate to forge a connection again. She couldn't leave him like that. She couldn't leave him with Jessica Wakefield on his mind. But Jonathan didn't see her at all.

"Please," Jonathan said shortly.

Choking back a sob, Enid ran down the steps.

Jonathan sat huddled by the fire after Enid left, letting the heat dry his wet shirt. The bright flames of the fire reminded him of the daggers that had shot out of Jessica's eyes. Jessica had more sides to her than he had realized. The more he got to know her, the more she intrigued him. She was warm and caring and feisty and spirited at the same time.

Jonathan closed his eyes in agony, filled with self-loathing. He ripped off his shirt and threw it into the fireplace. The fire blazed into a brilliant display of orange and red flames. Jonathan looked at his bare chest, savoring the pain of the burns. Bright red welts stood out on his pale skin, and a few spots on his stomach were beginning to blister.

I deserve more than a few burns, Jonathan thought in disgust. He watched the flames lick at his shirt and slowly devour it. He wished he could disappear with it into the heat of the blaze. The last thing he wanted to do was hurt Jessica.

Jonathan thought of the bright look in her blue-green eyes as she'd held out the thermos toward him. The gesture touched him deeply. She had driven all the way to his house just to bring him some homemade soup. She was like a guardian angel who had appeared on his doorstep to save him.

And she did save me, Jonathan realized. *She saved me from myself—this time at least.* Jessica had shown up just in the nick of time. Enid didn't realize it, but she should be grateful to Jessica. Very grateful.

At ten o'clock sharp, Elizabeth walked through the front door of the Wakefield house. She had used the curfew as an excuse to cut short her date with Joey. Sighing, she hung up her coat in the closet and trudged up the steps. *What happened to the magic of last summer?* she wondered. Maybe a summer romance could be magical for only a short time. Or maybe Joey had changed. Or maybe she truly loved Todd after all.

Suddenly she heard a low whimpering sound. Elizabeth stopped with her hand on the banister, listening closely. It sounded like crying, and it was coming from Jessica's room.

Sprinting up the steps, she ran down the hall and rapped on her sister's door. "Jess?" she asked.

"I'm not here!" Jessica croaked out between sobs.

Elizabeth pushed open the door. "Jess! What happened?"

"Nothing happened!" Jessica exclaimed. "What makes you think something happened?" She was walking agitatedly around the room, a big blue box of tissues tucked underneath her arm. She was wearing a pink nightshirt, and her hair was wild and tangled. Her eyes were swollen, and red blotches stood out on her pale face.

Elizabeth sucked in her breath as she surveyed the chaos of the room. It looked as though Jessica had been on the warpath. Jessica's room was always a mess, but now it was a disaster zone. Her clothes were strewn everywhere—on the bed, on the night table, even on the desk. CDs were scattered across the bed, and a few ripped T-shirts lay on the floor.

Elizabeth picked up the shirts in concern. "Are you tearing your heart out?" she asked.

"Something like that," Jessica said, pacing around the room like a caged tiger. She looked as though she were about to explode.

"Tell me what happened," Elizabeth coaxed.

"Look, it's nothing," Jessica said. "Jonathan said he was sick, so I made him some soup. And I brought it over to him as a surprise. And then—" Jessica's lips quivered. A few tears ran down her cheek, and she brushed them away angrily. Pulling a tissue out of the box, she blew her nose loudly.

"And then?" Elizabeth coaxed.

"He was with Enid Rollins," Jessica finished.

"With Enid?" Elizabeth asked in wonder. She knew Enid had a crush on Jonathan, but she'd thought Jonathan was interested in Jessica.

"Enid Rollins!" Jessica said, her fury mounting again. She kicked at a pile of clothes and paced around the room. "The drip! He chose the drip over me!"

"Jessica, she's not a—" Elizabeth began, but then she stopped herself. She had instinctively started to defend Enid, but this clearly wasn't the time. Jessica was in terrible pain, and she needed her twin's support. "Oh, Jess, that's horrible," Elizabeth said.

"I know," Jessica said, her eyes filling with tears again. She flopped down on the bed and burst out sobbing.

Elizabeth sat down on the edge of the bed and rubbed her sister's back. "Shhh, it's OK," she said soothingly. "It's going to be OK."

As Jessica's sobs got quieter Elizabeth silently fumed. She hadn't trusted Jonathan Cain before, and this just confirmed her suspicions. He was only going to hurt Jessica. She didn't know exactly what he was out to do, but she was sure it was something dangerous.

Chapter 11

"Hey, guys, we heard about the party on Friday night at Jonathan's," Lynne Henry said, stopping at Todd and Bruce's table at lunch on Wednesday. She was standing with Julie Porter and sophomore Jennifer Mitchell. They were all decked out in gothic attire. Lynne had on black jeans and a black T-shirt, which gave her long frame a fashionable gaunt look. Jennifer was wearing a black leather miniskirt, a white T-shirt, and thigh-high suede boots. Julie was sporting a man's tuxedo jacket with a cream lace camisole underneath.

"It's all anybody's been talking about all week," Julie added.

"Is he really having a party despite the curfew?" Jennifer asked.

Todd nodded. "That's right," he said smoothly.

Lynne pushed back a lock of black hair from her eyes. "We've got a few questions about the party," she said.

"Well, you've come to the right place," Todd said, putting on his new macho act. "Have a seat, girls." He patted the places on either side of him. Lynne and Jennifer sat down next to Todd, and Julie took a seat next to Bruce. Bruce winked at Todd from across the table.

Todd scanned the crowded cafeteria as the girls got settled, wondering if Elizabeth could see him. Lynne and Jennifer were both very attractive girls. Lynne was tall and willowy, with beautiful green eyes and high cheekbones. Her normally short light brown hair had been dyed black, which made her look even more striking than usual. Jennifer had the face of an angel, with china blue eyes and a cleft chin. She had dyed her hair a rich sable color, which gave her an almost impish look.

Todd smoothed his black hair back over his forehead, feeling triumphant. Elizabeth was sure to regret her actions when she saw all the attention he was attracting.

He leaned back and folded his hands behind his head. "So, what can I do for you? You can just call me Mr. Info." But before he could get his sentence out, they were firing questions at him.

"What time is the party?" Lynne asked.

"Should we bring anything?" Julie wondered.

"Is it formal?" Jennifer asked.

"What should we wear?"

"I'm so excited!"

"Whoa!" Todd protested, raising a hand. "One question at a time." The girls laughed.

"Sorry," Lynne said. "We're just so psyched about it. We've all been cooped up at home ever since the curfew was imposed."

"The party's at eight sharp," Bruce explained calmly. "It's casual. Wear whatever you want."

"And just bring yourselves," Todd added. He picked up his milk carton and took a big gulp.

Suddenly Jonathan appeared at the table, an angry glint in his dark blue eyes.

"Uh . . . Jonathan," Todd said nervously, attempting a half wave. The milk carton flipped out of his hand and bounced across the table. A stream of milk poured out and spilled over the edge onto his new black jeans. Todd grabbed the carton and righted it.

"We were just talking about you," Jennifer said, giving Jonathan a flirtatious smile.

"Is that so?" Jonathan asked, shifting his gaze from Todd to Jennifer.

Todd groaned underneath his breath and grabbed a napkin. He mopped up the trail of milk on the table and rubbed at the splotch on his jeans, carefully averting his eyes as he did so. He was glad Bruce was there to handle Jonathan.

"I hear there's a party this weekend at my house," Jonathan said, a slightly wry tone to his voice.

"Yeah, isn't that cool?" Bruce said gruffly.

"No, it's not cool. It's stupid," Jonathan said firmly. "Because there *isn't* going to be a party at my house."

"Unfortunately, I think it's too late to cancel now," Bruce said, meeting Jonathan's look evenly. "Half the school is already planning to come."

Todd fidgeted nervously in his seat. Even though he'd known Bruce Patman for years, Bruce's gall never ceased to amaze him.

"What exactly do you think you're doing?" Jonathan asked Bruce in a tightly controlled voice. "What gives you the right to use my house?"

"Don't you want to fit in, Cain?" Bruce challenged him. "Any *normal* guy would be psyched to have the bash of the season."

Jonathan's eyes glittered, but Bruce's words seemed to have hit home. "Fine, have it your way," he relented. "The party's on."

"Cool! I knew you'd come around!" Bruce enthused.

But Jonathan wasn't smiling. "Just one thing," he added, his tone ominous. "Don't blame me for anything that happens on Friday night." Then he turned around and pushed his way out of the cafeteria.

Elizabeth rushed into the cafeteria, determined to make another attempt to communicate with Enid. She couldn't let this situation go on any longer. If Enid continued to see Jonathan Cain, something horrible was going to happen. Elizabeth could feel it in her bones.

She scanned the cafeteria quickly for the gothic girls. She caught sight of them at the far side of the room and hurried toward the table.

Then she stopped short. It wasn't Enid's table. Some of the gothic girls were sitting with Todd and Bruce. Lynne Henry and Jennifer Mitchell were on either side of Todd, and Julie Porter was sitting next to Bruce.

Todd was at the center of the group, and all eyes were turned to him. He was sitting back confidently, running his fingers through his grotesquely colored hair. Elizabeth felt sick as she watched him preen. Todd said something, and the girls laughed. Lynne leaned in close and whispered something in his ear.

Elizabeth backed away quickly, feeling a slow wrenching in her gut. It obviously hadn't taken Todd too long to recover from their breakup. Every time Elizabeth had seen him that week, Todd had been surrounded by a group of girls.

Elizabeth looked wildly around the crowded room, desperate to sit down before Todd caught sight of her. Then she spotted the back of Enid's straight black mop. Enid was sitting alone at a table in the corner, a magazine spread out in front of her.

Elizabeth rushed across the room. "Hi, Enid," she said, giving her a friendly smile.

"Hi, Liz," Enid responded shortly. Elizabeth tried not to recoil at Enid's gruesome appearance. She was wearing a black miniskirt and a white skull-and-crossbones T-shirt. Purple lipstick coated her lips, and a thick line of matching eyeliner rimmed her green eyes.

"Do you mind if I join you?" Elizabeth asked.

Enid shrugged and took a sip of her soda.

Elizabeth put her lunch down and took a seat on the other side of the long table, pretending not to notice Enid's aloof air.

"So, what are you reading?" Elizabeth asked brightly.

Enid showed her the cover of *Biker*, an unspoken challenge in her eyes. A voluptuous woman in a green string bikini was draped over the body of a gleaming black motorcycle. "Babes on Wheels," the caption read.

Elizabeth's eyes widened. "Oh, neat," she said lamely.

Enid snorted. "What? Did you come over here to give me a lecture? Do you think I should be reading *Jeep Journal* instead? Would that live up to your high standards?"

Elizabeth winced at her angry words, but she refused to let Enid shut her out. She had to make one more effort to get through to her.

"Listen, Enid, I know you're mad at me, but I still consider you my best friend," Elizabeth said, her tone almost desperate. "I care about you more than you realize, and I don't want to see you get hurt."

Enid sighed. "Would you get to the point?" she said rudely. "I have some important reading to do."

Elizabeth took a deep breath. "Look, I know about you and Jonathan," she blurted out. "Jessica told me all about it. I just don't understand why neither you nor Jessica can see what a jerk he is."

Enid's eyes blazed. "Is that what you came over here to tell me?"

"Enid, would you just hear me out?" Elizabeth implored.

Enid drummed two long black fingernails on the table. "Fine," she said curtly. "Say what you have to say."

"Look, I don't know why, but I have this feeling about Jonathan. I really think he's bad news." Elizabeth paused. "I'm worried about you and Jessica."

"Well, thanks for the concern, but you're going to have to come up with a better reason than *that*," Enid said, her tone slightly sarcastic.

Elizabeth looked at her with imploring eyes. "Can't you see what he's doing to the whole school?" she asked. "He's becoming a cult figure, and he's got everybody under his spell. Half the kids in school are dressing in black and dyeing their hair and imitating everything he does."

"Oh, Liz, you're just too uptight," Enid scoffed.

Elizabeth clenched her jaw, but she ignored the barb. "He even told me himself he was trouble," she confided. "He came into the *Oracle* office one day last week and gave me a warning. He told me to keep Jessica away from him if I wanted to protect her."

Enid laughed a hollow laugh. "You're so naive. Jonathan was probably just sick of being bothered by Jessica." She crossed her legs and let a hand flutter in the air in a sophisticated gesture. "Apparently she won't leave him alone. I'm sure she told you what happened last night."

Elizabeth stared into Enid's eyes, trying desperately to make a connection. But Enid's painted eyes stared back at her like glittering green marbles.

Elizabeth sighed deeply. Obviously nothing she said would change Enid's mind. She couldn't reach her at all. The girl sitting across from her was a total stranger. The Enid Elizabeth knew was a sweet, supportive, caring girl. This completely new person obviously cared only about impressing Jonathan Cain. She never used to be so callous. Or so competitive. "Enid," Elizabeth began, "it's like you're under some sort of *spell—*"

"Elizabeth, why don't you go back to your new best friend?" Enid interrupted rudely. "You simply can't understand the trials of true love."

"Fine, I will," Elizabeth said, finally fed up. She grabbed her bag from the table and walked away quickly. Hot tears stung her eyes as she crossed the cafeteria. First she'd lost Todd, and now she'd lost Enid. Her whole life was falling apart.

Thank goodness for Joey, Elizabeth thought. He was the only constant she had at the moment. Everybody else was going insane around her.

Wednesday evening Jessica lay on her bed in the dark. She stared up at the ceiling, her mood blacker than the night. She was completely and utterly depressed. She didn't know when she'd ever felt worse in her life. Jessica sighed deeply. *I'm humiliated* and *lonely,* she thought. *Some combination.*

The image of Enid with her bruised lips and wild hair came back to her again and again. Jessica couldn't quite digest it.

"Jonathan belongs to me," Jessica muttered into the empty room. "He belongs only to me." But then she pictured Jonathan kissing Enid's red lips and tangling his fingers in her black hair. She stiffened her arms at her sides, feeling physically sick.

Jessica closed her eyes and tried to force the image of Enid and Jonathan from her mind, but it kept returning to her. She envisioned Jonathan holding Enid in his arms, pulling her onto his lap in the armchair, sucking gently at her neck. A knife twisted slowly in Jessica's heart.

Jessica flopped onto her stomach and rested her chin on her palms. She felt empty and hollow inside. It had been one thing when Jonathan was resisting her. Jessica had been sure Jonathan was hiding some deep, dark secret that would explain everything. She could even handle the idea that he had a girlfriend somewhere. But this was unbearable. To have been outdone by *Enid Rollins!* It was unthinkable.

Wanting some sympathy, Jessica called for the cat. At least Jasmine was a loyal companion. She would comfort her. But the cat didn't come to her as usual.

"Jasmine!" Jessica called again. She listened for the quiet patter of the kitten's paws, but no sound came.

"Here, kitty, kitty!" Jessica yelled.

Again there was no response from Jasmine.

"Arghh," Jessica muttered, heaving herself off the bed to go search for the cat. She flipped on the overhead light and blinked in the glare.

"Jasmine!" Jessica cried, kneeling on the carpet and peeking underneath the bed. Clothes and CDs were scattered on the floor, but there was no sign of Jasmine. Pulling herself back to her feet, Jessica yanked open the closet door and peeked into the laundry hamper. Jasmine wasn't in there.

She must be downstairs, Jessica decided. "Sweetie! Kitty!" she called as she trudged downstairs and began to search the den and the dining room. But Jasmine wasn't in those rooms either. "Jasmine," Jessica called to the cat, "where are you hiding? C'mon out, Jas."

Nothing, Jessica thought. *I hope she didn't get shut into a closet by mistake.*

Jessica headed for the living room. Lying down flat on her stomach, she lifted the skirt of the sofa and peeked underneath. No Jasmine.

Hmmm, Jessica thought in consternation. *Where would I hide if I were a tiny ball of fur?* Then it hit her. She must be in the kitchen. One day the week before, Jasmine had managed to climb up on top of the high kitchen cabinets. She had gotten stuck and cried plaintively until Jessica retrieved her. Jessica hurried down the hall and hoisted herself up onto the stove. Standing on tiptoe, she peered over the top of the cabinets—and promptly sneezed. There was nothing up there but dust.

Jessica jumped down and crossed the kitchen tiles, racking her brain to remember any other of Jasmine's favorite hiding places. As she passed the sliding glass doors that led out to the pool, a cool breeze wafted in.

"Oh, no!" Jessica exclaimed, stopping short. Somebody had left the doors open. Jasmine must have gotten out. Suddenly she was hit with a sense of déjà vu, and her mouth went dry. Jessica grabbed the back of a chair for support. She didn't know why, but she had an eerie sense of foreboding—that something truly terrible had happened.

She remembered the last time that Jasmine had gotten out. Jessica had desperately searched the neighborhood and had finally found her in a tree in the Beckwiths' yard. Disjointed scenes flashed before her mind like a sequence in a dream: Jessica running across the neighborhood lawns in the dark, Jasmine clawing and hissing high up in the tree, and then Jonathan's uncanny appearance. He had stepped out noiselessly from behind a tree, and then, when Jessica turned her back to speak to her sister, he was gone. He had appeared out of nowhere and had disappeared the same way. Jasmine had yowled and hissed that evening, just as she had done the night of the murder at the Dairi Burger. The cat had sensed danger. Jessica was sure of it. The serial killer could have been in the neighborhood that evening! *Good thing Jonathan was nearby that evening,* Jessica thought. *Who knows what might have happened otherwise?*

A cold knot of fear formed in her stomach. Where was Jasmine this time? Had she stumbled upon another murder?

Grabbing her denim jacket from the kitchen chair, Jessica charged outside.

"Here, kitty! Here, kitty, kitty!" she called frantically.

Jessica flipped on the patio lights and scanned the backyard desperately, her sense of panic mounting. Jasmine could be anywhere. She could have climbed the fence and run out to the street. She could be lost somewhere in any neighborhood of Sweet Valley. She could even have gotten hit by a car. Jessica's chest tightened, and she hurried across the patio, looking under the side tables and chaise longue.

"Jasmine!" she yelled, cupping her hands around her mouth while running around the pool. The cat was nowhere to be seen. Tears came to Jessica's eyes, and she shuffled through the grass, looking up at the branches of the trees. She made her way around the perimeter of the fence, beginning to despair. Her kitten was so tiny and helpless. Anything could have happened to her.

Suddenly she glimpsed a little bundle of fur curled up by the corner of the fence.

"Jasmine!" Jessica breathed, trembling in relief. "There you are!" Running alongside the shrubbery, she hurried toward the cat. "Now, don't worry, kitty, we're going to take you inside and give you some yummy cat food," Jessica said, her voice soft and soothing. "Your favorite kind of crunchy dry cat food—the kind you eat every single day."

She reached out her arms to scoop her up, but suddenly she stopped and gasped in horror. The cat was dead. Jessica let out a bloodcurdling scream and backed into a tree. She grasped the trunk for support, trembling uncontrollably.

"Jas," Jessica choked out, bringing a shaking hand to her mouth as she took in the horrible vision before her. The cat's yellow eyes were wide and staring, and her previously cute, full face was drawn. It looked as though she had been hollowed out, sucked dry . . . *or drained of blood,* Jessica realized in horror. Jasmine's head was so shrunken that it resembled a hunter's trophy, and all that remained of her body was a white and gray fur pelt.

Jessica fell to her knees and cradled Jasmine's tiny, broken body in her arms, sobbing uncontrollably.

The young man stood under the shadows of some tall trees, watching Jessica weep over the cat. He flinched at the pain he had caused her.

She huddled with the cat's body on the patio, crying hysterically. Her beautiful blond hair fell like a curtain over the poor creature. "Oh, Jas, oh, Jas," she gasped between sobs, her breath coming out in short spurts. The man longed to run over and join her, to take her in his arms and comfort her—but he could not. It was too dangerous, for him and for her.

The bitter taste of sour blood stung his palate, and his hunger still gnawed at him relentlessly. The kitten was nothing. It was a mere appetizer. It hadn't even taken the edge off his terrible craving. He shrank back into the darkness, feeling like an abomination. He never should have come there. He should have known what would happen.

The young man leaned against the tree, wracked with pain. He wished he could undo the last hour. He wished he had never met the young woman crying over her kitten in her beautifully landscaped yard. He wished he'd had the strength to stay away. But his wishes meant nothing now.

Why am I so weak? the young man wondered as he turned and disappeared into the night.

"Hey, Jess!" Elizabeth called, poking a head out the sliding glass door. "Do you want to make steamed veggies for dinner?"

Jessica shook her head, and a sob escaped her throat. She was huddled with Jasmine in her lap, shaking all over.

Elizabeth's eyes widened. She yanked open the glass door and sprinted across the patio. "What happened?" she cried.

Jessica pointed at the cat in her lap, unable to form any words. Tears cascaded down her cheeks in a steady stream.

"What's wrong? Is Jasmine sick?" Elizabeth asked, kneeling down next to her.

Jessica shook her head, her sobs increasing.

Elizabeth recoiled in horror when she realized the cat was dead. There was almost nothing left to her but a pile of fur. "Oh!" she exclaimed, clapping a hand over her mouth. A wave of nausea threatened to overwhelm her. Closing her eyes, Elizabeth fought down the feeling. Jessica needed her now.

Elizabeth hunched down next to Jessica and took her sister in her arms. Jessica cried uncontrollably on her shoulder. Her shoulders heaved, and wrenching sobs came from her. "Shhh, it's OK, it's OK," Elizabeth murmured. She felt as if they were repeating the night before, and she blamed Jonathan for everything. She had never seen her sister in so much pain.

Poor Jasmine, Elizabeth thought sadly. The kitten had been so cute and playful. It had been fun to have another pet in the house. And Jasmine had had a personality of her own, sweet and mischievous. A tear came to her eye, and Elizabeth wiped it away quickly. She couldn't go to pieces as well.

Elizabeth's eyes narrowed as she stroked her sister's hair. Was this someone's idea of a sick joke? Or was it possible that Jasmine's death was the work of the serial killer?

The second possibility made Elizabeth suddenly nervous. If the murderer had killed Jasmine, then he was probably still lurking around somewhere. And Elizabeth was sure he would prefer to take the twins as his victims rather than an innocent little animal. A knot of fear twisted her stomach. Maybe the cat was a decoy. Maybe the serial killer had wanted to lure the twins outside.

Elizabeth's mind flashed to the headlines of the next day's edition of the *Sweet Valley News*: "Blond Twins Next Victims in Chain of Serial Killings. Cause of Death: Exsanguination." She shuddered, and her tongue went dry.

"Jess." Elizabeth nudged her sister. "Why don't we go inside? It might be dangerous out here." She jumped up quickly, entirely spooked.

Jessica stood up with the cat in her arms, a bit calmer now. She sniffled and rubbed her red-rimmed eyes. "What should we do with Jasmine?" she asked.

Elizabeth bit her lip. "I don't know," she admitted. "We can't tell Mom and Dad what happened."

Jessica agreed. "They would freak out with worry."

"Why don't we say Jasmine ran away?" Elizabeth suggested.

Jessica nodded and sniffed. "I wish she *had* run away," she said in a small, bitter voice.

"C'mon, Jess," Elizabeth said, slinging an arm around her shoulder. "Let's hide Jasmine for now and go in the house." Elizabeth's number-one concern at the moment was getting herself and her twin inside.

They walked around to the side of the house, where the shrubbery was thickest. Kneeling down, Jessica carefully placed the cat deep in the bushes. Casting one last long look at her beloved pet, Jessica walked steadily away.

"I'm glad there's a curfew," Elizabeth declared as soon as they were safely in the house. "No one should be wandering around until the killer is caught." She latched the glass doors firmly and shut the blinds.

Jessica sat down hard in a kitchen chair. "We're going to have to break curfew on Friday for the party," she pointed out. She pulled a napkin out of the holder on the table and began shredding it into little pieces.

"What party?" Elizabeth asked.

Jessica stared at her sister in shock. "Elizabeth, do you live in a box? You must be the only person in school that hasn't heard about Jonathan's party."

"Jonathan's having a party?" Elizabeth asked in alarm. She swept the pile of ripped-up paper into her palm and carried it to the garbage can. Stepping on the lever, she threw the pieces in the trash and wiped off her hands.

"It's going to be the bash of the season," Jessica said. "You have to come."

Elizabeth looked at Jessica in surprise. "I can't believe that you actually want me to go to a party at Jonathan's after the terrible way he's treated you." No matter how well she thought she knew her sister, Jessica still managed to surprise her. Elizabeth couldn't fathom how Jessica could still have a crush on Jonathan. And she couldn't believe that Jessica was still planning to break the curfew after what had happened to Jasmine that evening.

"Anything for love," Jessica responded flatly.

Something in Jessica's voice made Elizabeth shudder. Jessica didn't sound like herself at all. *This obviously isn't one of her usual crushes,* Elizabeth thought. *I've never seen her this . . . hypnotized over a guy.* It was as though Jessica were under Jonathan's spell.

Elizabeth crossed her arms over her chest, trying to think of a good reason why her twin wouldn't be able to go to the party. "How are you planning to get around Mom and Dad?" she asked.

Jessica shrugged. "I'll find a way. Maybe they'll go out that night."

Elizabeth glared at her twin. "Well, I completely disapprove. Don't even *think* about asking me to cover for you."

Jessica gave her a knowing smile. "I won't. Because you'll be coming with me."

Elizabeth sighed. Her twin had her over a barrel. Jessica was clearly not going to change her mind. And that meant that Elizabeth had to go to the party as well. *Somebody* had to watch out for her sister.

Chapter 12

"Hey, do you need a lift?" Joey asked on Thursday afternoon, leaning out the window of his Land Rover. He was parked near the front steps of Sweet Valley High.

"Joey!" Elizabeth exclaimed. For once she was happy to see him. Besides Maria, Joey was the only sane person she knew at the moment. She was estranged from both Enid and Todd, and Jessica had her own problems. Even though her feelings for Joey were ambiguous, Elizabeth appreciated the fact that he was stable. At least she could talk to him.

Joey reached over and pushed open the passenger-side door. A wrapped package with a big silver bow sat on the seat.

"What's this?" Elizabeth asked excitedly. She

picked up the package and ducked into the car, pulling the door shut behind her.

Joey grinned. "Just a little souvenir," he said. He gunned the engine and pulled out of the parking lot.

Elizabeth's face flushed with pleasure as she untied the silver ribbon and ripped off the bright blue wrapping paper. After watching girls fawn over Todd all week, it was nice to have somebody show her some attention for a change. Elizabeth lifted the tissue paper and pulled out her gift. It was a white baseball cap with CAMP ECHO MOUNTAIN printed over the brim.

"Oh, this is great, Joey!" Elizabeth exclaimed, delighted. She pulled her hair out of her ponytail holder and put the cap on. It was a perfect fit.

"You like it?" Joey asked.

"I love it," Elizabeth affirmed.

Joey cast a glance at her. "You look very sexy in that hat," he said.

"I'm not supposed to look sexy," Elizabeth protested. "I'm supposed to look tough."

"Tough and sexy," Joey amended as he started up the car. "It's a lethal combination."

Elizabeth smiled and leaned back in the seat as Joey began to drive down the street. She was glad to relax for a few minutes. She rolled down the window and watched the familiar sights of the town go by. It was a balmy afternoon, and the wind caressed her face with a light touch. Then she noticed that they were on River Crest Road, which led to downtown Sweet Valley.

"Hey, this isn't the right way to my house," Elizabeth pointed out.

"That's because I'm not taking you home," Joey said. "I've got another great find to show you."

"Oh, really?" Elizabeth asked, her eyes sparkling in excitement. "What is it?"

"Well, I don't want to give it away, but believe me, you're going to love this place," Joey said. "It's got wooden booths and an old-fashioned counter. Not to mention a real jukebox."

Uh-oh, Elizabeth thought, her heart plummeting. It sounded suspiciously familiar.

Elizabeth watched with a sinking feeling as Joey turned onto Lakeview Drive and cruised down the tree-lined road. *Right, then left,* Elizabeth thought. Joey took a right at the corner, then an immediate left onto Bayside Drive. He slowed down at a stop sign and pointed to the restaurant ahead.

"Look! There it is! The Dairi Burger!" Joey said, waving at the red neon sign that lit up the popular teenage hangout.

Elizabeth sighed and tucked a lock of hair back under her cap.

Joey turned into the crowded parking lot and

pulled adeptly into one of the only free spots. "Isn't it great?" he enthused. "Just like a real fifties joint. Supposedly they've got great burgers and shakes."

Elizabeth just couldn't bring herself to burst his bubble, even though she was sure she had mentioned the Dairi Burger to him before. *He must have forgotten I told him that this is where Jessica found . . . the first body,* she thought with a shudder. She followed him warily to the door, praying that Todd wouldn't be there.

Joey held open the heavy wooden door and ushered her in. Elizabeth was dismayed to find that the restaurant was hopping. Ever since the night of the murder, things had been relatively quiet in Sweet Valley. But obviously everybody was getting a little antsy. A group of kids was crowded around the jukebox, and bleeps and pings sounded from the game room. Elizabeth scanned the restaurant quickly. Bruce Patman was sitting with Winston Egbert and Aaron Dallas in a booth. Amy was perched on a stool at the counter with her cousin Katrina. Enid and the gothic girls were talking in low voices at a square table, looking cool and indifferent in their black attire. But she didn't see Todd anywhere.

Elizabeth breathed a sigh of relief. She prayed that Todd wouldn't show up. It was bad enough that she had started dating someone else while they were still going out. She didn't have to throw it in his face.

"Let's sit back there, Joey," Elizabeth said, pointing to an empty booth in the back. She pulled her cap low over her forehead and wove her way through the crowd, careful not to make eye contact with anyone.

"I get the feeling you know this place," Joey said once they were seated.

"Well, it's kind of a hangout around here," Elizabeth admitted. "I think I've even mentioned it to you before. This is where Jessica found the . . ." Her voice trailed off. "Never mind," she finished lamely.

Joey's face fell. "So I guess I didn't surprise you."

"Of course you did," Elizabeth reassured him. "I had no idea you were going to show up at school. And I had no idea you were going to bring me a gift."

Just then the waitress appeared at their table, an order pad in her hand.

"You do the honors," Joey said.

"OK, we'll have two strawberry shakes and an order of fries," Elizabeth said.

After the waitress was gone, Elizabeth slouched low in her seat. She flashed Joey a nervous smile.

Joey took her hand. "I feel like I don't get to see you at all anymore."

"Things have been a bit crazy lately," Elizabeth agreed.

"Do you want to do something tomorrow night?" Joey asked. "I'd love to go to a movie. There's a great Greta Garbo film playing at the revival theater."

Elizabeth bit her lip. Friday night was Jonathan's big bash. She had no desire to go to the party, but she had to keep an eye on Jessica. She knew Joey wouldn't understand. He'd already lectured her once. He'd told her that he thought she was an overprotective older sister, even if she was only four minutes older than her twin, and that she should let Jessica lead her own life.

And besides, even if she insisted on going to the party, she was sure Joey would want to come along. There was no way Elizabeth could bring him to the party and flaunt her affair in front of everyone. Aaron and Winston would recognize Joey from camp, and Todd would be publicly humiliated. But Joey wouldn't understand that either, especially since she'd already admitted to him that Todd was flaunting his attraction to other girls. Joey would think she was ashamed of him and that she didn't want her friends to see them together. Elizabeth sighed. She felt trapped.

"So what do you say?" Joey asked.

"Joey, I'm really sorry, but I promised Jessica

I'd go to a movie," Elizabeth said. "And I don't want to let her down. She's been so upset lately." Elizabeth could feel the blood rushing to her cheeks. She wasn't used to lying.

"That's OK. I understand," Joey said. "Maybe we can do something Sunday night."

"That's a great idea," Elizabeth said, taking Joey's hand in hers across the table. "I'd love to."

"Hi, Liz!" came a girl's voice. Elizabeth looked up, cringing at the sound of the familiar voice and quickly dropping Joey's hand. Caroline Pearce was standing at the booth, and she was eyeing Joey with open curiosity. Elizabeth shook her head. That girl could smell the scent of gossip a mile away.

"Hi, I'm Caroline," she said to Joey, her green eyes dancing.

"Joey," he said, shaking her hand.

Elizabeth sat perfectly still, chanting a silent mantra to herself. *Please, Caroline, don't mention the party . . . don't mention the party . . . don't mention the—*

"Aren't you excited about the party tomorrow night?" Caroline asked with a toss of her red hair. "Jessica won't shut up about it." Elizabeth's heart sank into the floorboards.

"Uh, yeah," Elizabeth muttered.

"Well, see you tomorrow!" Caroline waved as she headed off.

Joey glared at Elizabeth. "I think I just lost my appetite," he said gruffly. He stood up abruptly and stalked across the room toward the exit.

"Joey, wait!" Elizabeth called. But he was already out the door.

Elizabeth blew out her breath in frustration and leaned back in the booth. *Figures*, she thought with a sigh. *That's what I get for lying!*

"My poor kitten!" Jessica exclaimed sadly, digging her shovel into the fresh earth and throwing a mount of dirt aside. It was late Thursday afternoon, and the twins were in the backyard digging Jasmine's grave.

Elizabeth gave her sister a sympathetic look. "It's such a shame," she said sadly. "She was such a sweet cat." She dug her spade deep into the ground and scooped out a pile of dirt.

"What time is it?" Jessica asked. She wiped her forehead with the back of her hand, leaving a smudge of dirt on her skin.

Elizabeth looked at her watch nervously. "It's almost six o'clock." Their parents would be home any minute. "Jess, we'd better hurry," she warned.

Jessica nodded her head and threw out a last shovelful of earth. Then she picked Jasmine up from the ground and laid her solemnly in the grave. "Bye, Jas," she said sadly, a tear trickling down her cheek.

A tremor of fear passed through Elizabeth's body as she saw the tiny animal lying in the earth. Shuddering, she threw a mound of dirt back on the grave. "What a horrendous thing," Elizabeth said softly. "She was just an innocent animal."

Jessica wiped away her tears, her eyes burning with anger. "How could anyone do such a thing to a poor, defenseless kitten?" she said. Jessica pushed some dirt back into the grave with the back of her shovel.

Elizabeth shook her head. "I have no idea."

"Whoever it is, he is very, very sick," Jessica said.

"That's for sure," Elizabeth agreed.

Jessica got a pensive look on her face. "I remember when the police showed up at the Dairi Burger when Dean Maddingly was murdered. They said Jasmine was the only witness to the crime," she recalled.

"And now all the traces of the crime are gone," Elizabeth said with a shiver.

Just then they heard the sound of a car pulling up in the driveway.

"Oh, no!" Elizabeth exclaimed. "We've got to hurry!" They quickly threw the last bits of dirt on the grave.

Jessica patted down the grave furiously with her shovel, trying to make the ground level.

"Hi, kids!" Mrs. Wakefield yelled cheerily, walking around to the backyard. "I heard your voices from the driveway." But her expression changed immediately to one of concern when she took in the scene before her.

"Girls, what happened?" she asked.

Elizabeth was tongue-tied. She stared at Jessica helplessly.

"Jasmine was hit by a car," Jessica said sadly.

"Oh, no!" Mrs. Wakefield exclaimed, clapping her hand to her mouth. "The poor creature!" She came over and put a comforting arm around the girls' shoulders.

"Do you know who did it?" she asked.

Elizabeth was silent, but Jessica shook her head firmly. She looked at her mother with sorrow-filled eyes. "It was a hit-and-run."

Chapter 13

"Maria, I'm so glad you came," Elizabeth said to her friend in the corner of the room at Jonathan's mansion. It was Friday night, and the party was in full swing. The boys had gone all out. They had moved all the furniture against the walls and had set out a long table with fruit punch and chips. A CD player was hooked up to giant speakers, and rock music was blasting. The boys had even hung up helium balloons, draped streamers over the table, and placed flickering candles in all the corners of the room. The party was obviously a huge success. The enormous living room was jammed with students from the junior and senior classes. Music bounced against the walls, and the din of kids' voices rose above it as they joked and laughed.

Maria widened her eyes in mock astonishment. "You think I'd let you come to this gig alone?" She shook her head firmly. "No way. We're in this together. Besides, I've felt as cooped-up lately because of the curfew as everyone else in here."

Elizabeth smiled gratefully. When Elizabeth had asked Maria if she was planning to attend the party, Maria had said there was no way she was setting foot in Jonathan's mansion. But when she heard that Elizabeth was going there to keep an eye on her sister, she'd changed her mind. "I'm coming to keep an eye on *you*," she had declared.

A fifties number came on, and a few couples started to do some swing dancing. Winston Egbert tried to spin around the floor on his heel, drawing shouts of laughter. Aaron Dallas picked up Jennifer Mitchell and swung her high in the air, and a crowd formed around them, hooting and hollering. Suddenly Tony Esteban grabbed the black hat Bruce Patman was wearing and ran through the crowd. Bruce and a bunch of laughing senior guys came charging after him. The guys dove on Tony, knocking Aaron and Jennifer over. They all collapsed into a pile of arms and legs, laughing hysterically.

Elizabeth shook her head, feeling completely removed from the action. "I've never seen a party with this kind of wild energy," she said. "You'd think we'd all been locked up or something."

"Well, we *have* sort of been locked up," Maria said.

"It's more than that, though," Elizabeth said thoughtfully. "Everybody's so enamored with Jonathan that this has become the social event of the season." Elizabeth's eyes narrowed, and she shivered. "There's a weird sort of group mentality in the air—almost like a mob. It's scary."

Maria gave her a look. "You're letting your imagination run away with you."

"But look how everybody's dressed," Elizabeth insisted, waving a hand at the kids around them. "Almost everybody's in formal attire. It's like this is a major event." Most of the girls had on cocktail outfits or black velvet dresses. Some of them were wearing long dresses and heels. Even the guys were clad in pants and shirts that were nicer than the ones they usually wore.

"Well, we fit in perfectly," Maria said with a laugh.

"You can say that again," Elizabeth agreed. Jessica had freaked out when Elizabeth had tried to attend in faded blue jeans and a soft teal sweater. Her twin had forced her to put on a long light blue dress that would have been more appropriate for a prom. Maria fit in even better, wearing a short black dress, a red headband, and funky silver earrings. *Maria always looks good in any situation,* Elizabeth thought in admiration. *I guess she learned that from her years in Hollywood and New York.*

"Well, maybe this way we'll blend in and won't have to talk to anyone," Maria said.

Elizabeth slouched against the wall. "To hear us, you'd think we were at a morgue, not a party." Her hair fell forward onto her forehead, and she pushed it back.

Maria laughed. "Well, it does sort of have that funeral feel. This mansion is *spooky*. Maybe we need some food to raise our spirits. I'll go get something from the refreshment table for us, OK?"

Elizabeth nodded. *Maria is right,* she thought, looking around. Even though the air was thick with excitement, the party had a solemn atmosphere. Despite the boys' attempts at a festive environment, there was no getting around the fact that Jonathan's dusty old house was creepy. The wind whistled through cracked windowpanes, and tree branches cast strange shadows on the long ivory curtains. Long, tapered white candles flickered from the corners, shrouding the place in an eerie yellow light.

Elizabeth glanced around the crowded room, wondering if she were crazy. She was obviously the only one who thought the house was eerie.

Kids were laughing and joking in groups, and the middle of the floor was packed with enthusiastic dancers. The gothic group seemed to be holding court by the refreshment table. A group of hangers-on swarmed around Lynne, Julie, and Bruce, who were all dressed in their signature black.

I wonder why Todd's not with them, Elizabeth thought.

Her eyes roamed the crowd on the dance floor. Winston and Maria Santelli were locked in an embrace as they swayed to a slow song. Elizabeth's mouth turned up in a slight smile as she noticed Winston's attire. He looked goofier than ever. He was wearing an oversized tuxedo jacket and a big orange bow tie. Aaron and Jennifer were dancing next to them. Jessica was safely on the dance floor as well. She was deep in conversation with Amy and Lila, and they were barely moving to the music. *That's typical,* Elizabeth thought with a smile. *They have no interest in dancing tonight. They just want to be seen.*

Then Elizabeth caught sight of Todd and caught her breath.

He was dancing with Amy's cousin Katrina. They were close together, moving easily to the soft music. Todd's arms were wrapped around Katrina's slender waist, and her head rested on his broad shoulder. Elizabeth watched in pain as Todd took her hand and whirled her around the floor. Katrina spun around gracefully and turned her laughing brown eyes to him. Then Todd whispered something into her ear. Katrina blushed and snuggled in closer to him.

Elizabeth thought she was going to be sick. If the party had been bad before, now it had become unbearable. Elizabeth wrenched her eyes away from the happy couple, feeling more miserable than ever. A wave of loneliness washed over her, and she longed for the feel of Joey's comforting arms. She wished she had let him come to the party. After all, Todd wasn't sparing a thought for *her* feelings.

But it's too late now, Elizabeth thought in despair. She'd blown everything with Joey. He would probably never speak to her again.

Elizabeth shrank into the corner, wishing she could melt into the peeling wall. In fact, she wished she could go home. But she had to keep an eye on Jessica. Elizabeth sighed. It was going to be a long night.

Enid sat huddled in the dilapidated armchair in the corner beside an ornate candleabra. She felt worse than she had in her whole life. Jonathan had completely ignored her since she'd arrived, and he'd been staring meaningfully at Jessica the whole evening.

Bitter tears came to her eyes, and Enid blinked them back. She'd been dreaming about this party all week. She had been sure that she and Jonathan would become an official couple that night. She had thought they would spend the whole night dancing together in the center of the dance floor. She had envisioned Jonathan kissing her passionately in front of the whole school. She'd imagined the admiring expressions on all the girls' faces and the appreciative looks of the guys. The gothic girls would drop dead with envy, and Jessica Wakefield would realize she had met her match. For once Enid Rollins would be someone important.

Enid had spent hours dressing for the occasion. She was wearing a fitted black velvet dress with tiny spaghetti straps that left her shoulders bare. Her makeup was done to perfection. She was wearing deep red lipstick and glamorous purple eyeliner, and her face was covered with pale foundation. Her green eyes shone luminously in the stark contours of her face. Enid knew she looked stunning—and all of her new friends had agreed.

But Jonathan had barely even noticed her. He hadn't even given her a second glance when she walked in. "Hi, Jonathan," she had said in her sexiest voice. But he had looked right through her. Then she had tried to catch him by the refreshment table, but he had muttered some excuse and slipped away.

Plus Elizabeth wasn't even *trying* to speak to her anymore. She had marched right by Enid with her chin held high when she arrived. Now she and Maria Slater were giggling together in the corner, happy as clams in their own private universe. Enid scowled. All Elizabeth cared about was Maria and Todd or Joey or whatever.

Out of the corner of her eye, she saw Jessica whispering to Jonathan by the fireplace. Enid jumped up and quickly threaded her way through the crowd on the dance floor. Inching her way surreptitiously along the wall, she sneaked up close to hear what Jessica was saying.

"Meet me upstairs," Jessica whispered to Jonathan, and he nodded.

Enid leaned back against the wall and closed her eyes, feeling a terrible twisting pain deep inside her.

As soon as Jonathan walked away Jessica scanned the dim room for her sister. Elizabeth had been sticking to her like glue all night. The only way Jessica had been able to lose her was by standing in the middle of the dance floor. But even then Jessica could feel the unrelenting gaze of her twin's watchful eyes on her.

Finally Jessica spotted Elizabeth through the throng of enthusiastic dancers. She was deep in conversation with Maria in the far corner. Making sure Elizabeth wasn't watching, Jessica flattened herself against the wall and inched her way to the hallway. Suddenly Elizabeth looked up. Jessica froze in the doorway as Elizabeth's eyes darted around the room. But then Aaron knocked into her by mistake on his way to the refreshment table, and Elizabeth turned in his direction. As Aaron apologized to Elizabeth, Jessica scampered out of the room.

Her cheeks flushed with excitement, Jessica crept down the hall and tiptoed up the long, winding staircase. The staircase wheezed in protest, and the wooden stairs creaked with each step. Holding her breath, Jessica kept to the right of the stairs and forced herself to take slow, tiny steps. The staircase seemed to go on forever. She bit her lip, expecting Elizabeth to appear at any moment at the foot of the stairs.

She breathed a sigh of relief as she reached the second floor. A dark, narrow hall led to a series of rooms. Jessica shivered. The upstairs was as creepy as the downstairs. A faded wine-colored Persian carpet covered the floor, and dusty old oil paintings hung crookedly on the wall.

Jessica crept down the hall and peeked into an ominously dark square room. It was completely empty except for a tall standing mirror and a giant armoire. A boarded-up window stared at her blindly from the far wall. Jessica backed out quickly and headed for the neighboring room.

The next room was pitch black and as quiet as a tomb. There were no windows at all. Jessica groped along the wall for a light switch, but nothing was there. Squinting, she peered into the darkness. An oil lamp sat on a low table, next to a box of matches. Kneeling down, Jessica struck a match and held it to the wick. The oil lamp sent up a low orange flame. Jessica glanced around the room. *This must be Jonathan's room,* she thought in satisfaction. A huge walnut four-poster bed stood in the middle of the room, and a rickety old desk was propped against the wall. An enormous antique chest sat against the opposite wall. The chest was approximately the same length as the bed. *You could probably fit twenty blankets in that old chest,* Jessica thought, eyeing it with curiosity.

Jessica sat down on the edge of the king-size bed, sinking into the soft mattress. A cloud of dust rose into the air, and Jessica stifled a cough. She crossed and uncrossed her legs, her heart pounding in anticipation. *Jonathan, where are you?* she wondered.

Just then all the lights in the house went off. Even the wick of the oil lamp flickered and extinguished. A chorus of gleeful shouts sounded, and joyous screams wafted up the stairs. "Party!" someone yelled.

Jessica's lips curved into a smile in the darkness. She didn't mind waiting for Jonathan in the dark. She couldn't wait to feel the sudden, surprising touch of his hand on her arm in the black room. He knew exactly where to find her, and she knew, deep inside, that he was on his way. Jessica was sure that this was the night Jonathan finally was going to admit his love.

Chapter 14

Elizabeth's heart leaped to her throat as the electricity cut off, all the candles suddenly blew out, and the room was thrown into darkness. A spontaneous cheer went through the air, and the place erupted into chaos. Couples took advantage of the darkness to dance intimately and to make out in the corners. Wild laughter wafted through the air as kids searched for friends and bumped into each other.

Although everyone else at the party seemed to be enjoying the total darkness, Elizabeth was terrified.

All she wanted to do was find Jessica and get out of there.

Elizabeth elbowed her way frantically through the crowd. "Jessica!" she shouted. Excited voices swirled around her, and bodies blocked her way. A paper cup came flying through the air and hit her on the shoulder. Elizabeth jumped as cold fruit punch dripped down her sleeve. Wiping the sticky liquid off her arm, she headed for the fireplace, where she had seen Jessica last.

"Jessica!" she yelled, cupping her hands around her mouth. She tripped over a couple on the floor and fell to the ground on top of them. "Oh, sorry!" she gasped, scrambling up and rushing to the fireplace. It was deserted. Elizabeth's heart plunged.

Elizabeth looked wildly around the room, squinting in the darkness. There was no sign of her twin anywhere. Her panic mounting, she ran to the dance floor and joined the wild frenzy of students.

"Hey, Liz, wanna dance?" Winston yelled, grabbing her and whirling her around.

Elizabeth pulled out of his arms and fled. She dodged a few couples and ran smack into a broad chest. She yelped and recoiled in pain.

"Do you mind watching where you're going?" came an angry voice.

"Todd!" Elizabeth breathed in relief.

"See ya," Todd muttered, turning away quickly.

"Todd! Wait!" Elizabeth yelled, latching onto his arm.

"What do *you* want?" Todd asked, shaking her hand off angrily. Elizabeth could see his jaw clench in the darkness.

"Todd, I need your help," Elizabeth pleaded.

Todd let out a snort and turned his head.

"We've got to get the lights on," Elizabeth implored desperately. Her voice quavered, and hot tears sprang to her eyes. "Please, you've got to help me."

"Get someone else to help," Todd said in a curt voice, not looking at her.

Elizabeth gasped. "But there's no one else," she sobbed. "No one will help me."

Todd turned back and paused a moment, considering. His face seemed to soften as he took in her panicked expression.

"Sure, I'll help you," he said softly. "Let's go." He took her hand and led her through the crowd.

Jonathan moved noiselessly up the steps, fresh life coursing through his veins. His body felt full and satiated, and now he just wanted a few minutes to hold Jessica in peace. If he could touch her satiny skin and feel her soft hair against his cheek, maybe he'd be whole in a way he hadn't been for a long, long time.

He walked into the bedroom and felt his heart leap as he saw her. Jessica looked like a vision, sitting on the edge of the bed. Her blond hair formed a golden halo in the dim light of the room, and her aquamarine eyes twinkled in the darkness. He could see the outline of her full pink lips, and he longed to kiss them.

"Jessica," Jonathan said softly, sitting down beside her.

"I knew you'd come," Jessica whispered. "I knew you wouldn't be able to resist me forever."

A pang of guilt tore at Jonathan's heart, and he looked down in his lap, twisting the ring on his finger nervously. "Jessica, I'm sorry about Enid," he said, his voice deep and throaty. "I was just trying to push you away. I thought she would help me to forget you." He looked deep in her eyes. "I never meant to hurt you."

But Jessica pressed a finger to his lips. "Shhh," she whispered. "I know." Then she wrapped her arms around his shoulders and buried her face in his neck. Jonathan circled her waist with his hands, breathing in her delicate scent. Jessica pressed her lips to the side of his neck and sucked lightly at his skin.

Jonathan's grip tightened as he enjoyed the delicious sensation. *Does she know the truth?* he wondered. *No, there's no way she could possibly have guessed.*

"Oh, Jessica," he whispered. "I want to be with you forever."

• • •

"Todd, I found it!" Elizabeth exclaimed as her eyes lit on a gray metal fuse box on the wall of the basement. The fuse box glimmered dully in the light of the flickering candle she was holding. Cupping her palm around the candle flame, she ducked under a low pipe and hurried across the cellar.

"Great!" Todd said, popping his head out of the doorway to the storage room. "I'll be right there." He shut the thick steel door carefully behind him and made his way across the crowded floor.

This basement is like some labyrinth from the underworld, Elizabeth thought, suppressing a shudder. Old pieces of furniture were scattered about the cement floor, most of them lying on their sides. Big iron pipes were suspended along the low ceiling, and a trail of water ran around the edges of the room like a moat.

Elizabeth flipped open the fuse box. Rows and rows of red and green switches stared out at her. Elizabeth bit her lip. She knew a little bit about electrical matters and she was familiar with fuse boxes, but this wiring was odd. She had never seen anything like it. She had no idea which switch controlled the electricity in which room.

Todd came up behind her and studied the fuse box.

"Do you know which ones we should turn on?" Elizabeth asked nervously.

"Of course," Todd said, reaching an arm around her and confidently flipping a few switches. "This one and this one." The heat of Todd's body close to hers made Elizabeth's stomach flutter. She wished she could just turn around and collapse in his arms.

"And *voilà*," Todd said, waving a hand. Nothing happened. "Hmmm," he said, stroking his chin and studying the system. "This must be it." He hit a few green switches. Something sizzled in the air ominously.

"Todd! Turn that off! I think something's going to explode," Elizabeth warned.

Todd quickly flipped the green switches back to the off position.

"I've just never seen anything like this," Todd admitted, squinting in the darkness. Elizabeth fidgeted next to him, beginning to despair.

"This must be it," Todd said finally. "The red switches!" He flipped two red circuit breakers on the right, and the electricity blazed on, flooding the basement with light.

A collective moan came from the first floor.

"Party's over!" Elizabeth heard Bruce Patman yell.

The sounds of grumbling and shuffling came from upstairs.

Then a hush fell over the group, and Elizabeth froze. Why were they so quiet? What was going on up there? She thought she heard a few audible gasps. Then somebody screamed. A knot of cold fear clenched in her gut.

"Todd, let's go—now!" Elizabeth exclaimed, grabbing his hand and pulling him across the room.

"What's the hurry?" Todd asked.

"Something's happened up there!" Elizabeth said. She could feel the panic closing in on her. The blood was pounding in her ears, and her whole body was trembling. Terrified, Elizabeth dodged her way through the maze of furniture. Then she flew up the cement steps, Todd close behind her.

Elizabeth rushed down the hall and stopped in the archway of the living room, her breath coming in small pants. Panicked, she scanned the room for her sister. The kids were all gathered together in some kind of circle, but she didn't see Jessica among them.

Her eyes stopped at the center of the room, and she gasped, feeling the world spin.

A girl was lying motionless on the floor on her stomach, pale as a ghost.

"Nooo!" Elizabeth yelled, letting out a primal scream. "Jessica!" she cried. She pushed through

the crowd brutally and ran to the middle of the room. Tears cascading down her face, she knelt down and turned the girl over.

It wasn't Jessica. It was Katrina.

And she was dead.

Elizabeth screamed again, her body shuddering violently in shock and relief. Katrina's face was as white as a sheet, and a large blue wound showed on her neck. The serial killer had been in the house—Katrina had been drained of blood. Around her, she heard the vague, distant echo of other screams.

Then Elizabeth's knees buckled under her, and the world went black.

SWEET VALLEY HIGH™

Bantam Books in the Sweet Valley High series.

Ask your bookseller for the books you have missed.

1. DOUBLE LOVE
2. SECRETS
3. PLAYING WITH FIRE
4. POWER PLAY
5. ALL NIGHT LONG
6. DANGEROUS LOVE
7. DEAR SISTER
8. HEARTBREAKER
9. RACING HEARTS
10. WRONG KIND OF GIRL
11. TOO GOOD TO BE TRUE
12. WHEN LOVE DIES
13. KIDNAPPED
14. DECEPTIONS
15. PROMISES
18. HEAD OVER HEELS
23. SAY GOODBYE
24. MEMORIES
26. HOSTAGE
30. JEALOUS LIES
32. THE NEW JESSICA
36. LAST CHANCE
44. PRETENCES
54. TWO-BOY WEEKEND
63. THE NEW ELIZABETH
67. THE PARENT PLOT
74. THE PERFECT GIRL
75. AMY'S TRUE LOVE
76. MISS TEEN SWEET VALLEY
77. CHEATING TO WIN
80. THE GIRL THEY BOTH LOVED
82. KIDNAPPED BY THE CULT!
83. STEVEN'S BRIDE
84. STOLEN DIARY
86. JESSICA AGAINST BRUCE
87. MY BEST FRIEND'S BOYFRIEND
89. ELIZABETH BETRAYED
90. DON'T GO HOME WITH JOHN
91. IN LOVE WITH A PRINCE
92. SHE'S NOT WHAT SHE SEEMS
93. STEPSISTERS
94. ARE WE IN LOVE?

SWEET VALLEY HIGH™

PROM THRILLER MINI-SERIES

Thriller: A NIGHT TO REMEMBER

95. THE MORNING AFTER
97. THE VERDICT
98. THE WEDDING
99. BEWARE THE BABYSITTER
100. THE EVIL TWIN

ROMANCE TRILOGY

101. THE BOYFRIEND WAR
102. ALMOST MARRIED
103. OPERATION LOVE MATCH

HORROR IN LONDON MINI-SERIES

104. LOVE AND DEATH IN LONDON
105. A DATE WITH A WEREWOLF
106. BEWARE THE WOLFMAN

LOVE AND LIES MINI-SERIES

107. JESSICA'S SECRET LOVE
108. LEFT AT THE ALTAR!
109. DOUBLECROSSED
110. DEATH THREAT
111. A DEADLY CHRISTMAS

WINNERS AND LOSERS MINI-SERIES

112. JESSICA QUITS THE SQUAD
113. THE POM-POM WARS
114. 'V' FOR VICTORY

DESERT ADVENTURE MINI-SERIES

115. THE TREASURE OF DEATH VALLEY
116. NIGHTMARE IN DEATH VALLEY

LOVING AMBITIONS MINI-SERIES

117. JESSICA THE GENIUS
118. COLLEGE WEEKEND
119. JESSICA'S OLDER GUY

RIVALRIES MINI-SERIES

120. IN LOVE WITH THE ENEMY
121. THE HIGH-SCHOOL WAR
122. A KISS BEFORE DYING

CAMP ECHO MINI-SERIES

123. ELIZABETH'S RIVAL
124. MEET ME AT MIDNIGHT
125. CAMP KILLER

DARK SHADOWS MINI-SERIES

126. TALL, DARK, AND DEADLY
127. DANCE OF DEATH

THRILLER EDITIONS

MURDER IN PARADISE
MURDER ON THE LINE

SWEET VALLEY HIGH SUPER STARS

BRUCE'S STORY
TODD'S STORY

SUPER EDITIONS

A KILLER ON BOARD
ELIZABETH'S DIARY
JESSICA'S DIARY
PERFECT SUMMER
RETURN OF THE EVIL TWIN
SPRING FEVER
STRANGER IN THE HOUSE

SPECIAL EDITIONS

THE WAKEFIELD LEGACY
THE WAKEFIELDS OF SWEET VALLEY

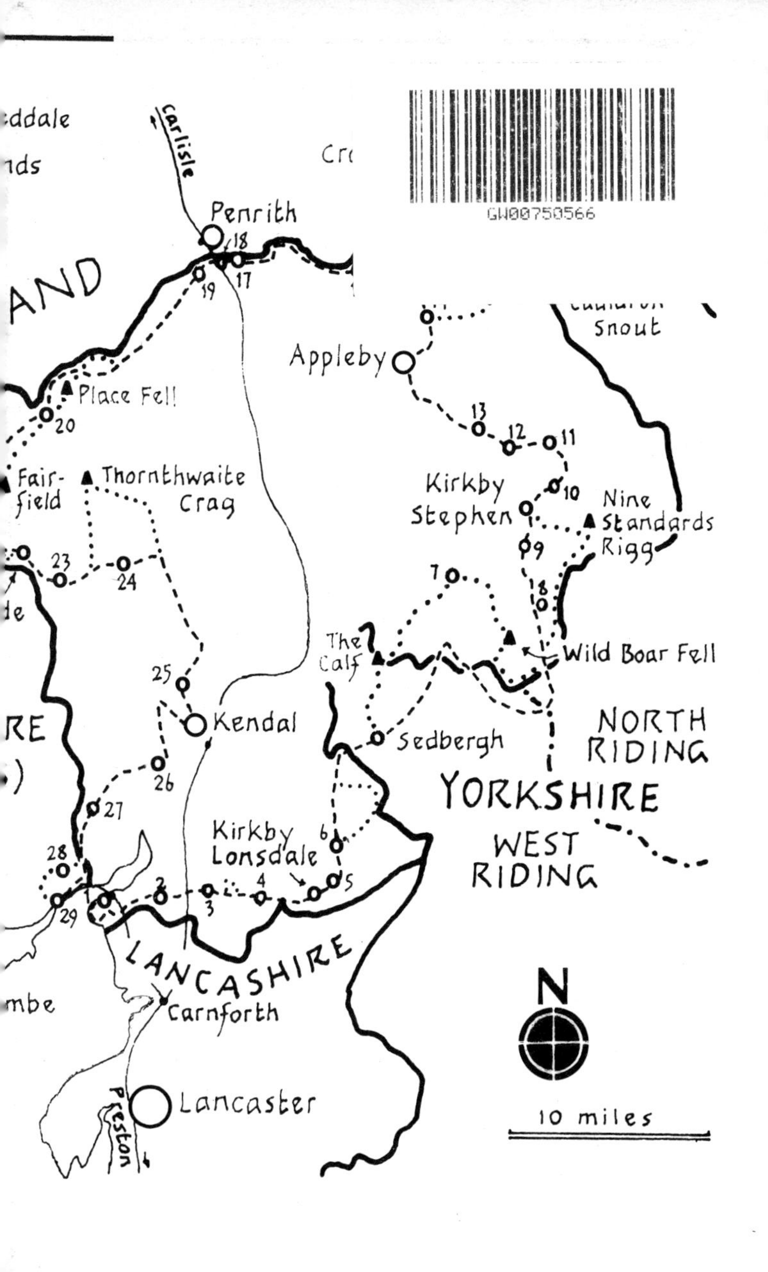

Carlisle
Penrith
18
17
19
AND
Cr
GW00750566
Snout
Appleby
Place Fell
20
13
12
11
Fair-
field
Thornthwaite
Crag
Kirkby
Stephen
10
Nine
Standards
Rigg
9
23
24
7
8
The
Calf
Wild Boar Fell
25
Kendal
NORTH
RIDING
Sedbergh
RE
26
YORKSHIRE
27
Kirkby
Lonsdale
6
WEST
RIDING
28
2
4
5
29
3
LANCASHIRE
N
Carnforth
Lancaster
Preston
10 miles

Middleton Hall

THE WESTMORLAND HERITAGE WALK

by
Mark Richards
and
Christopher Wright

CICERONE PRESS
MILNTHORPE, CUMBRIA, ENGLAND.

ISBN 0902363 94 8
First Published 1987

Nine Standards Rigg.

CONTENTS

About the Authors

Since his youth, when summer holidays were spent on a fell farm near Kirkby Lonsdale, Mark Richards developed a deep love of Westmorland. In his early twenties he made sorties into the hills with the guides of Alfred Wainwright in his pocket, stepping out his routes. Encouraged by him he produced a guide to the *Cotswold Way* which was followed by his guides to the *North Cornwall Coast Path* and *Through Welsh Border Country following Offa's Dyke Path.* He has illustrated a series of Penguin footpath guides by Hugh Westacott and has contributed articles and illustrations to the *Climber & Rambler* and *Great Outdoors* magazines. He has produced for Cicerone Press *High Peak Walks, White Peak Walks: The Northern Dales,* and *White Peak Walks: The Southern Dales.*

Christopher Wright was initiated to the Lake District as a teenager on family cycling and walking holidays and for the last twenty years he has lived and worked in Westmorland, exploring all corners of the county for work and pleasure. When still a teenager he made a solo trek of the Pennine Way and in his early twenties Constable & Company published his *Guide to the Pennine Way* which has become a classic best-seller. This was followed by contributions to *No Through Road* and *Classic Walks* and to the *Climber & Rambler* magazine. His other books, also by Constable, include guides to the *Pilgrim's Way and North Downs Way, Offa's Dyke Path* and *Pembrokeshire Coast Path.* A keen long-distance walker, mountaineer and skier, he lives within a stone's throw of this walk which he has helped to create.

Both authors have a close affinity with the high fells and verdant dales of Westmorland and it is the bedrock upon which this walk was inspired.

Cross Fell and Little Dun Fell from Milburn.

Introduction

Westmorland was described by Daniel Defoe as 'the wildest, most barren and frightful of any (county) that I have ever passed over in England of even in Wales itself; the west side of which borders on Cumberland is indeed bounded by a chain of almost impassable mountains'.

Isolated from the rest of northern England for hundreds of years - it was frontier territory disputed periodically between the Scots and English from the time of the Roman conquest to the 17c - for a long period Westmorland bordered with Scotland. Eamont Bridge near Penrith and Dunmail Raise near Grasmere marked the crossings of the boundary, with the 'almost impassable mountains' of the Lake District to the W and the wild wall of the Pennines to the E.

Westmerians - both locally born and bred, and offcomers who have adopted the place as their home - have long regarded their county as having the finest landscape in all England. If the lakes and peaks and crags and wooded valleys of the Lake District on the western side of the county did not attract all the attention the rest of the county's landscape would be better known and appreciated. Between the Lakes and the Pennines Westmorland is largely a rolling county of wide-open limestone and sandstone fells, bleak peat moorlands and rich agricultural farmland in the valleys of the Kent and Eden.

Westmorland may no longer exist in the eyes of Whitehall, but the 'lost county' is not so easily erased, and it is our intention to encourage a caring respect for all the precious landscapes that grace old Westmorland. What better way to appreciate the landscape and traditions than by making a walking tour around the former county boundary?

This county walk explores the beautiful bounds of Westmorland and is, in common with the majority of other unofficial long-distance walks, the product of enthusiasts. It exists merely as a concept in the confines of this one guide and has no official status, nor needs it. That others may accept the challenge, whether keeping to the authors' chosen steps or by adopting different objectives, is a matter purely for the individual.

This guide is presented by the authors in appreciation for so many days delighting in the invigoration of Westmorland's visual, historical and natural riches and the warm welcome of its people. Within this guide walkers may still see Westmorland as a living heritage, and by

Pike O'Blisco from South Gully, Pike O'Stickle.

marshalling their energies walk the high divide of its boundary and delve into its sequestered dales, from which will most surely come a genuine pleasure and enduring affection for this very special corner of Cumbria.

Arnside Point.

The Principles of the Route

Westmorland is very much a county for walking on the grand scale and any walking route is only an expression of the range and scope of walking potential, rather than an offering of a narrow threadway. This route is our own idea, but it enables variations to be made by the individual to suite his own tastes.

The former county only had a very tenuous hold of the coastline, at the estuary of the River Kent in the furthermost reaches of Morecambe Bay, and we feel it convenient to start at sea-level before walking to the high fells. We start at Arnside and follow an anti-clockwise course around the county only venturing slightly outside the boundary into neighbouring Lancashire, Yorkshire and Cumberland to use convenient rights-of-way where otherwise trespass or impracticability would result in our meanderings.

Where appropriate we have introduced alternatives for High Level or Low Level routes. It is appreciated that parts of the route - the Howgills, the Pennines and the Lakeland fells - attract low cloud and inclement weather at certain times of the year and an alternative to the high tops justifies a Low Level variation on such occasions. Our route is a walk for all seasons, and a sensible application of being prepared for the worst of the elements should not detract from the pleasure of the walk we offer.

We have divided the route of our walk around Westmorland into ten sections. These sections equate to physical features of the journey rather than lengths of a day's walk, though perchance some of the sections can be easily walked in a day. The first and the last are two examples, though sections in excess of 15 miles may be too much for some to accomplish in a day.

Each section is introduced by a bird's eye perspective of the route to be followed and is accompanied by a sectional profile (marked in miles, cumulative from Arnside) allowing the reader to see at a glance how much ascent and descent is involved on the route. Each section is then divided into detailed sketch-maps showing important features of the way to be followed and places en-route. A key is given on page 13. These maps are at a scale of 2¼" for 1 mile, and contours and heights are given in feet. Where metric heights are given these are taken from the Ordnance Survey 1:10,000 series maps: there may be no direct conversion between the imperial and metric figures as the metric heights are the result of more accurate survey methods.

Walkers will, however, need to carry Ordnance Survey maps to aid navigation and plan for escape routes in emergencies or to find places for accommodation, and to add pleasure to the journey by enabling the identification of features off our route. You will need the following OS 1:50,000 scale Landranger (Second Series) maps:

97 Kendal to Morecambe
98 Wensleydale & Upper Wharfdale
91 Appleby-in-Westmorland area
90 Penrith, Keswick & Ambleside area

By sheer good fortune rather than by judicious planning the route from Arnside around the county to its end at Grange-over-Sands is exactly 200 miles! This measurement has been checked by both of us using the High Level Route where it occurs, so this magical figure should not deter anyone from taking a short cut!

Cross Fell from Little Dun Fell.

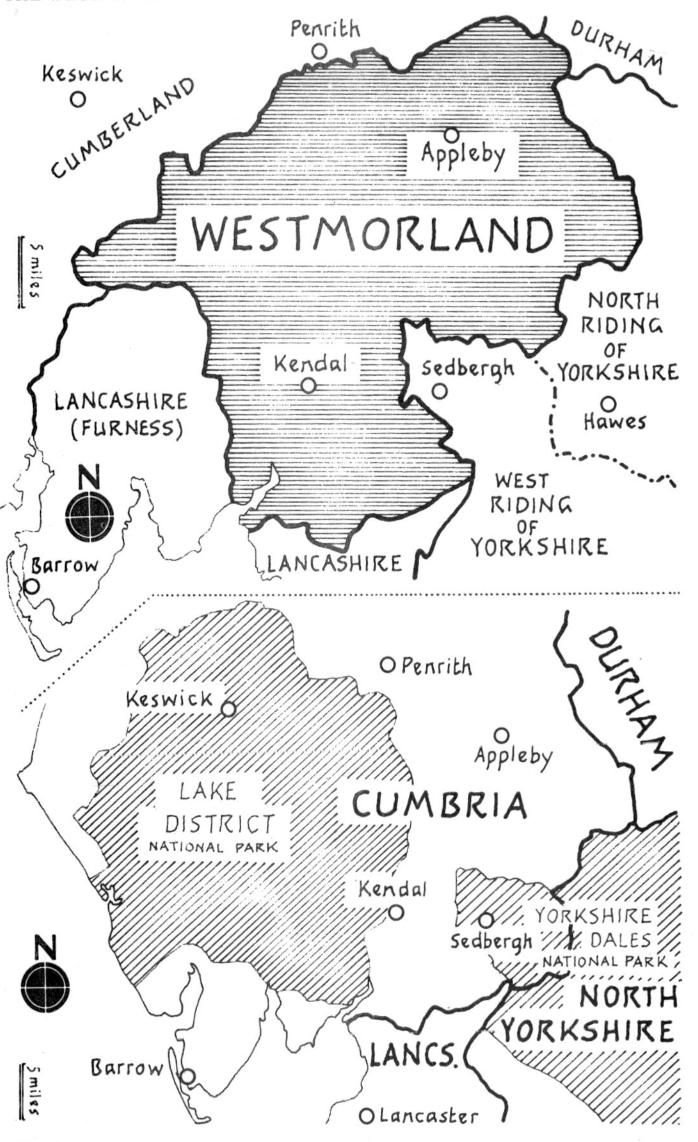
Penrith
DURHAM
Keswick
CUMBERLAND
Appleby
WESTMORLAND
5 miles
NORTH RIDING OF YORKSHIRE
Kendal
Sedbergh
LANCASHIRE (FURNESS)
Hawes
N
WEST RIDING OF YORKSHIRE
Barrow
LANCASHIRE
Penrith
DURHAM
Keswick
Appleby
LAKE DISTRICT NATIONAL PARK
CUMBRIA
Kendal
YORKSHIRE DALES NATIONAL PARK
Sedbergh
N
NORTH YORKSHIRE
LANCS.
Barrow
5 miles
Lancaster

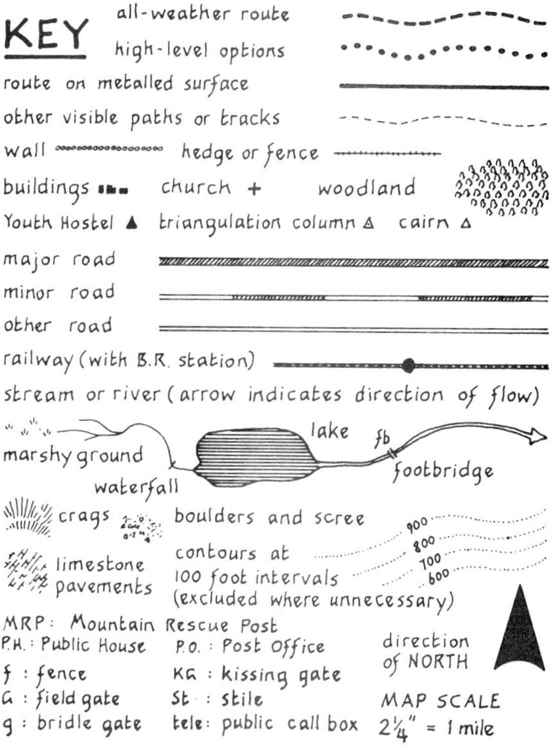

KEY

all-weather route
high-level options
route on metalled surface
other visible paths or tracks
wall
hedge or fence
buildings
church +
woodland
Youth Hostel ▲
triangulation column △
cairn △
major road
minor road
other road
railway (with B.R. station)
stream or river (arrow indicates direction of flow)
marshy ground
waterfall
lake
fb
footbridge
crags
boulders and scree
limestone pavements
contours at 100 foot intervals (excluded where unnecessary)
900
800
700
600

MRP: Mountain Rescue Post
P.H.: Public House
P.O.: Post Office
f: fence
KG: kissing gate
G: field gate
St: stile
g: bridle gate
tele: public call box

direction of NORTH

MAP SCALE 2¼" = 1 mile

The bold intersecting lines across the route near the margin show the angle and extent of overlap on the succeeding map, while the small arrows outside the margin indicate points of entry and exit.

The numbers in the margin locate the northings and eastings (grid lines) on Ordnance Survey maps.

The gradient profile facing each map is graduated in miles with 100 foot vertical scaling.

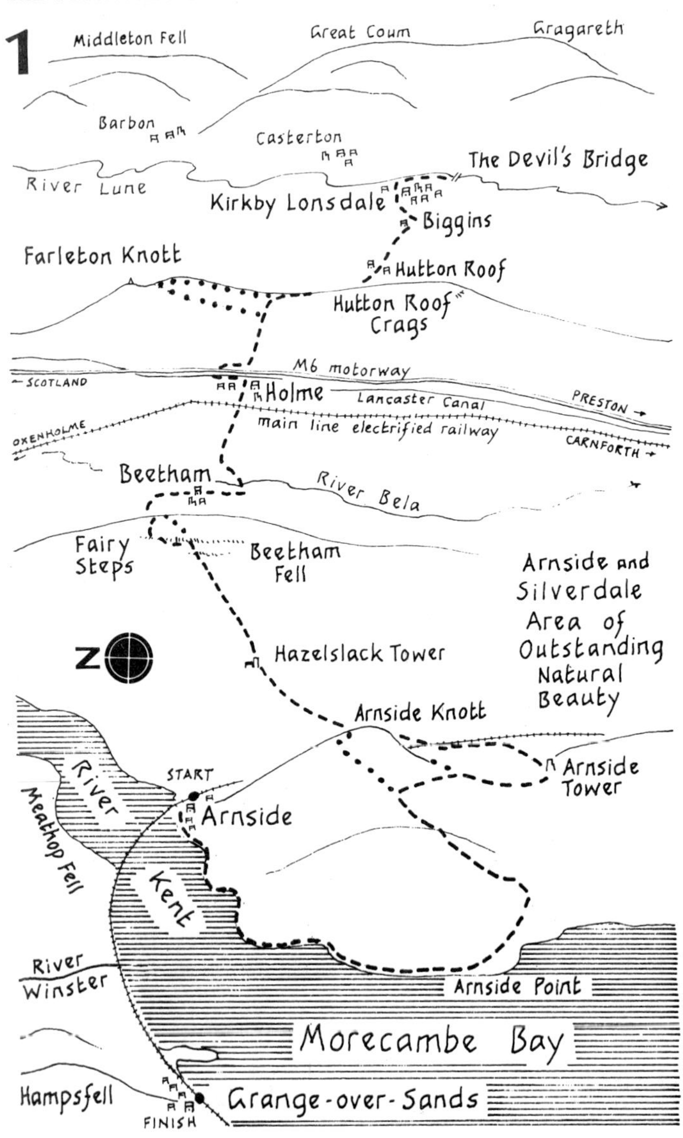
1
Middleton Fell
Great Coum
Gragareth
Barbon
Casterton
The Devil's Bridge
River Lune
Kirkby Lonsdale
Biggins
Farleton Knott
Hutton Roof
Hutton Roof Crags
M6 motorway
SCOTLAND
Holme
Lancaster Canal
PRESTON
OXENHOLME
main line electrified railway
CARNFORTH
Beetham
River Bela
Fairy Steps
Beetham Fell
Arnside and Silverdale Area of Outstanding Natural Beauty
Hazelslack Tower
Arnside Knott
Arnside Tower
START
Arnside
River Kent
Meathop Fell
River Winster
Arnside Point
Morecambe Bay
Hampsfell
Grange-over-Sands
FINISH

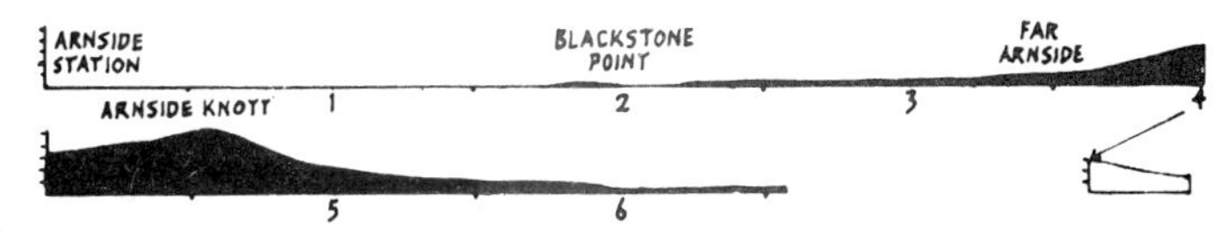

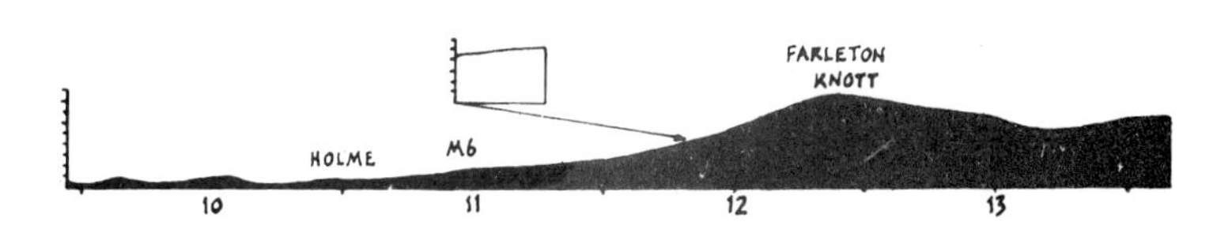

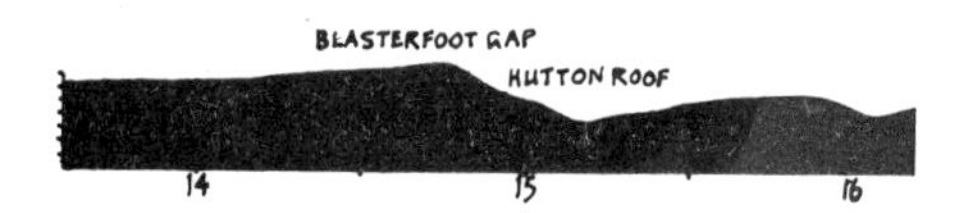

HIGH BIGGINS
KIRKBY LONSDALE
DEVIL'S BRIDGE
16
17
18

1. Arnside to Kirkby Lonsdale

The first stage of our journey is characterised by the ascent of two carboniferous limestone hills and the views they give over Morecambe Bay on the one hand and the southern parts of Westmorland extending up to the central Lake District fells on the other.

The great expanse of Morecambe Bay is best viewed from Arnside Knott. The mudflats and exposed sands stretch round from Morecambe across to Cartmel Sands and they support the biggest population of wintering birds in Britain. The saltmarshes fringing the bay are an integral part of the areas intertidal system and provide valuable high tide roosts for the birds. Morecambe Bay is a National Nature Reserve of international status.

The hills of Arnside Knott and Farleton Knott are geographically and ecologically similar. They have loose and fissured limestone pavements which provide a wide range of habitats for flora and fauna. All stages in the transition from bare limestone pavements to limestone grassland are represented and they are particularly notable for their quality of rare flowers, ferns, plants, butterflies and even a rare tree. The area around Arnside, in Westmorland, and neighbouring Silverdale, in Lancashire, is an Area of Outstanding Natural Beauty.

Our route from the estuary of the River Kent to the sylvan pastures of the River Lune passes not only over limestone hills but through woodland and agricultural land for a distance of 18 miles/29 kilometres. It is relatively easy going and there is a range of accommodation available at both Arnside and Kirkby Lonsdale, though nothing much between.

Map 1.1

We start our walk around Westmorland at Arnside. Why Arnside? Well, you've got to start somewhere and there are two reasons for choosing Arnside. Westmorland's major river, the Kent, flows into the sea at Arnside at the only place where the county has a coastline, and there is an aesthetic pleasure is starting any journey from sea level. A second reason is that there is good access to Arnside by rail via Carnforth from Lancaster off the London Euston - Glasgow Central line, and our walk ends at Grange-over-Sands railway station, the next stop along the line on the opposite side of the Kent estuary.

Arnside is Westmorland's seaside resort, but it was once a port, as the construction of the promenade and jetty testifies. Even as late as

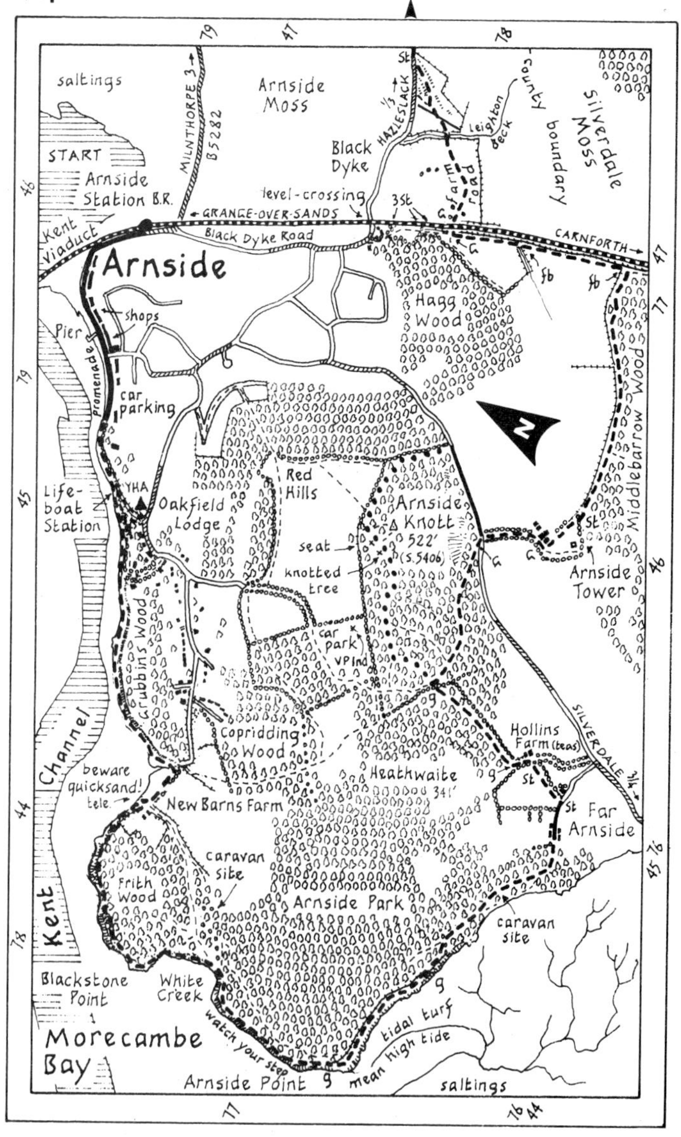
saltings
Arnside Moss
START
Arnside Station B.R.
MILNTHORPE 3
B5282
Black Dyke
HAZLESLACK
level-crossing
GRANGE-OVER-SANDS
Black Dyke Road
CARNFORTH
Kent viaduct
Arnside
shops
Pier
Promenade
car parking
Hagg Wood
Leighton Beck
farm road
County boundary
Silverdale Moss
Middlebarrow Wood
Red Hills
YHA
Oakfield Lodge
Life-boat Station
Arnside Knott 522' (S.5406)
seat
knotted tree
car park
VP Ind
Arnside Tower
Grubbins Wood
Copridding Wood
Heathwaite 341'
Hollins Farm (teas)
SILVERDALE
Far Arnside
Channel
beware quicksand!
tele
New Barns Farm
caravan site
Frith Wood
Arnside Park
Kent
Blackstone Point
White Creek
Morecambe Bay
watch your step
tidal turf
mean high tide
Arnside Point
saltings

1805 five vessels of nearly 100 tons each used upstream Milnthorpe as a port, but coast-wise trade ceased with the coming of the railways. The Kent is crossed by a 50-arch viaduct, 522yds/477m long, carrying the Furness Railway over the spot where people either forded or were ferried over in earlier times. The viaduct was completed in 1857. It is dangerous to swim or paddle in the vicinity of the viaduct because of quicksand and strong undertows in tidal currents.

From the railway station follow the promenade and when the road ends a path continues along the shoreline past the sailing club and inshore lifeboat station to New Barns Bay. At High Water this route is impractical so go inland past the youth hostel. Beware of quicksand if taking the short cut across the creek at New Barns Bay. Around Frith Wood and Blackstone Point the path runs along the top of low cliffs through trees and in parts beyond White Creek towards Arnside Point it is very close to the cliff edge. (At low water a route along the sands all the way to the caravan site at Far Arnside is feasible.) Beyond the second gate you pass through a (second) caravan park and navigation is straightforward. From Hollins Farm a good path climbs up to Arnside Knott.

Arnside Knott, 522ft/159m, is a local beauty spot, owned by the National Trust, with a fine view from its top. (A viewpoint indicator on the open hillside above the car park is just off our route, but it can easily be visited.) The limestone hill has rocky outcrops, open heath and grassland and a mosaic of dense scrub and natural woodland of oak, ash, hazel, birch, yew, beech, hawthorn and buckthorn, and there are some rare Lancastrian whitebeam.

There are many uncommon and rare flowers on the limestone grassland and on the south-eastern screes, including the Teesdale violet, fly orchid and dark-red helleborine. However, the Knott is noted for its rare butterflies, the sheltered grassland and heath providing the southern-most habitat in Britain for the Scotch argus butterfly and other uncommon species including the Duke of Burgundy, high-brown fritillary, the northern brown argus and the pearl-bordered fritillary.

A nature trail runs through the woodland and open ground of the Knott; leaflets are available at the newsagents in Arnside.

At a gate in a wall on the edge of the Knott a turn R on a main path (called Saul's Drive, a bridleway) is a short cut down to the Arnside-Silverdale road, but this misses out an important first panorama across the Kent estuary. Instead, at the gate go ahead, steeply upwards, on a main path, with its superior views. A diversion can be made to the viewpoint indicator, but it is not worth visiting the OS column on the summit of the Knott as the view from the top is blocked off by trees.

Arnside Tower

The path descends N slightly to a wall and here you turn E and then SE on another major path, soon reaching the Arnside-Silverdale road on the outskirts of Arnside. Turn R along the Silverdale road then take a turn L to Arnside Tower.

Arnside Tower is a ruined pele tower, the remains of a house once belonging to the Stanley's. Like those pele towers at Beetham, Sizergh and Levens - all S of Kendal - and Kentmere and Burneside, N of Kendal (both of which we will see later in our journey) - it was built *c.*14c, soon after the disastrous raid by the Scots under Robert the Bruce. It was burnt in 1602, probably repaired in the mid-17c, dismantled in the late 17c and is now ruinous.

Pele towers of the district consisted of a small square tower with very thick walls, a vaulted store-room on the ground floor, a narrow-windowed chamber above, and a room above that. Arnside Tower measures about 50ftx30ft/15mx9m and is five storeys high, but no floors are left and the SE tower has collapsed. It stands in a beautiful situation, but it is overshadowed by the attractions of the woods on Arnside Knott.

Beyond Arnside Tower is a stile into Middlebarrow Wood. Climb this. (Just below it on the farm track is a more obvious gate, but this is not the way for us.) Our path runs along and just inside the edge of the wood, then alongside the railway line. Where the route passes under the railway a signpost directs you along a farm track, supposedly marshalled by a fierce bull. Note that the right-of-way diverts off the farm road beyond Leighton Beck, along a bank, to reach a stile on Black Dyke Road, a few yards beyond the farm road gateway exit.

Map 1.2

Signposted paths run close to Carr Bank Road and behind a caravan site then the route turns R on a minor road to Hazelslack. Hazelslack Tower is another pele tower of the late 14c. Originally four storeys high it is partially demolished. At the road T junction go across on a signposted track to Fairy Steps through Underlaid Wood, a delightful mixed woodland on the limestone bedrock.

Fairy Steps are a notable natural feature enhanced by man and a local beauty spot. Two tiers of limestone escarpments rear up out of the woodland and the way between them is by a narrow cleft in the rocks, made into a staircase. The lower of the two flights of steps is broad and commodious but the upper tier is a narrow passage: walkers with too-wide rucksacks will need to turn L below the low cliffs of Whin Scar to reach the main Beetham Fell-Slackhead path and turn R. If you can squeeze through the upper tier without touching the

Fairy Steps

Map 1.2

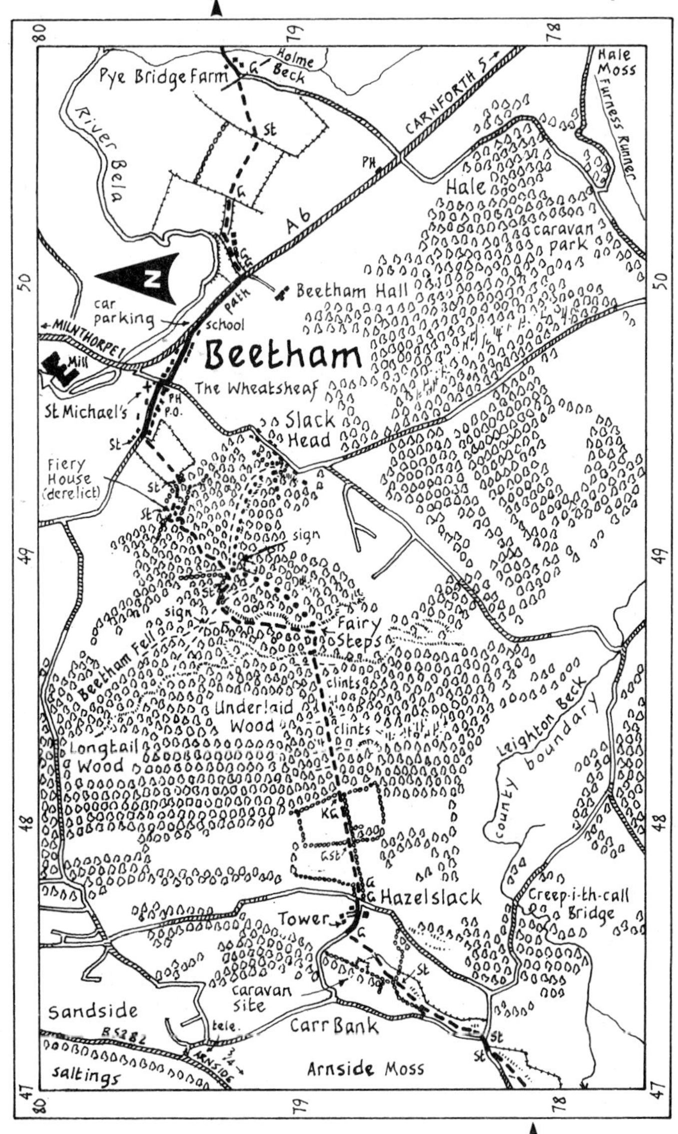

Pye Bridge Farm
Holme Beck
River Bela
CARNFORTH 5
Hale Moss
Furness Runner
PH
Hale
caravan park
A6
Beetham Hall
car parking
MILNTHORPE 1
school
path
Mill
Beetham
The Wheatsheaf
St. Michael's
PH
P.O.
Slack Head
Fiery House (derelict)
sign
Beetham Fell
Fairy Steps
clints
Underlaid Wood
Longtail Wood
Leighton Beck
county boundary
KG
Hazelslack
Tower
Creep-i-th-call Bridge
caravan site
Sandside
Carr Bank
B5282
tele.
ARNSIDE 3/4
saltings
Arnside Moss

side, and make a wish at the same time, the fairies will grant it. It is said that Fairy Steps lies on an ancient coffin route between Arnside and Beetham. There being no consecrated ground at Arnside the dead had to be buried at Beetham, but why they had to be brought this way is a mystery. The upper tier of the Whin Scar commands a widespread view of the great estuary of the Kent: with the backcloth of the peaks of Lakeland and the scene is as lovely as that of any of the Lakes.

The way beyond the upper tier of Fairy Steps leads to a broad path through the mature conifers of Whin Scar Plantation to a signpost at a junction with the Beetham Fell-Slackhead path. The path R to Slackhead is the more popular, but we think that the footpath leading directly ahead to the village of Beetham is preferable, though at first it is a little overgrown and indistinct as it swings round the derelict cottage (Fiery House) in the wood. As you reach the edge of the wood you can see the path across the field to Beetham. At the lane turn R, entering the village by Church Street.

Beetham is a small close-knit village, but off the busy A6, with the parish church of St. Michael's & All Saints at the village crossroads.

St. Michael's is a large church dating probably from 12c, with early Norman features though many times restored and now in partly mixed styles of Gothic. The S aisle was added *c.*1200 and widened in the 15c when the N aisle was added. The church was restored and a S porch added in 1873-74. There are a variety of Perpendicular windows with medieval glass, one of which incorporates a portrait of Henry IV. The NW window depicts St. Lioba, d.799, and St. Osyth, a notable lady killed by the Danes in 7c. An early-20c martyrs' window in the N aisle shows Charles I flanked by St. Oswald and St. Alban.

On display in the S aisle is a Bible of Edward VI date (*c.*1540), believed to be the first English Bible to be used in the church. Two much-deffaced effigies, damaged in Cromwell's time, show a man and his wife, he in armour she in a cloak. There is some doubt as to whether they are Sir Thomas Beetham or Sir Robert Mydleton and their respective wives. Dame Clara Butt, the singer, was married in the church in 1900, with Ivor Novello as a pageboy.

Just across the road and the River Bela, with access through Henry Cook's Waterhouse Paper Mills, is the **Heron Corn Mill**. The mill served the village and was constructed beside an ususual natural weir on the river. The mill has been fully restored and has exhibits showing the history of the mill and the milling process. The mill is open from April to the end of September, daily except Mondays, 1100-1215 and 1400-1700.

From the crossroads in the centre of Beetham village go ahead opposite The Wheatsheaf down the village street to its junction with the main road

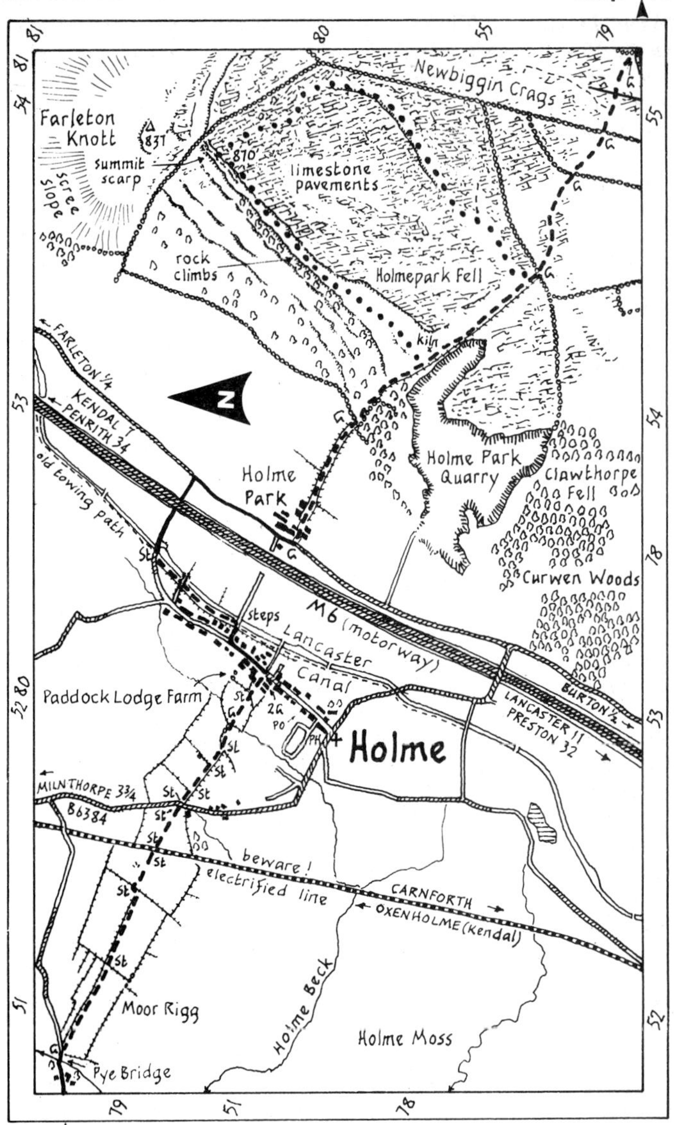
Newbiggin Crags
Farleton Knott
837
870
summit scarp
scree slope
limestone pavements
rock climbs
Holmepark Fell
kiln
FARLETON ¼
KENDAL 7
PENRITH 34
old towing path
Holme Park
Holme Park Quarry
Clawthorpe Fell
Curwen Woods
steps
M6 (motorway)
Lancaster Canal
Paddock Lodge Farm
PO
PH
Holme
BURTON ½
LANCASTER 11
PRESTON 32
MILNTHORPE 3¾
B6384
beware! electrified line
CARNFORTH
OXENHOLME (Kendal)
Holme Beck
Holme Moss
Moor Rigg
Pye Bridge

A6 and the Victoria Memorial School, built 1904. A footway runs alongside the A6 and just before Beetham Hall (farm) cross over and pass around some farm buildings and through fields to Pye Bridge Farm. The stile (more correctly a fence) on the approach to Pye Bridge Farm is not immediately obvious over the crest of the hill, and it is topped by a strand of barbed wire.

Map 1.3

From Pye Bridge to Holme navigation is quite straightforward. Beware of trains as you cross the London Euston - Glasgow Central railway line - they run at 90mph on this straight, level stretch. Cross the B6384 and go straight ahead into the village of Holme. The farmyard of Paddock Lodge Farm in the village street is guarded by dogs.

Holme is a straggling and unattractive village with appendages of modern housing estates off its main street, which itself is festooned by overhead wires and cables. Its growth dates from the construction of the Lancaster-Kendal Canal. More recent growth came about when the Bela River prisoner-of-war camp became an open prison (on the B6384 towards Milnthorpe, now closed), and houses were built in the village to accommodate prison staff. The cold and harsh Holy Trinity Church was built in 1839 and restored in 1902. The old National School was founded in 1840.

An Act of Parliament was secured in 1792 for making a canal from Kendal to Westhoughton in Lancashire. The length between Preston and Lancaster was opened in 1797 and the length between Tewitfield, N of Lancaster, and Kendal was opened on 18 June 1819. Most of the bridges on this section were constructed *c.* 1816 to the designs of John Rennie. Two sailing packets for passengers drawn by horses were subsequently based on the canal, which went at the rate of 4mph. The Swift Sailing Packet Boat Company brought the first express packet boat 'The Water Witch' onto the canal, which commenced sailing between Preston and Lancaster on 20 May 1833 and between Kendal and Preston on 9 July 1833. It went at a speed of 10mph, there being no locks to retard progress. A second express boat, the 'Swiftsure' joined the service in 1834, subsequently joined by two others in 1835, the 'Swallow' and the 'Crewdson', later renamed 'Water Witch II'.

When the railway reached Kendal in 1846 the canal packet boats ceased, but cargoes of coal and chemicals continued to go to Kendal for the gas works and Wakefield's gunpowder works until 1939, when the Westmorland section was closed because of leakages. By 1944 all commercial traffic N of Lancaster ceased. The section from Kendal to Hincaster has since been drained, but the remainder of the waterway

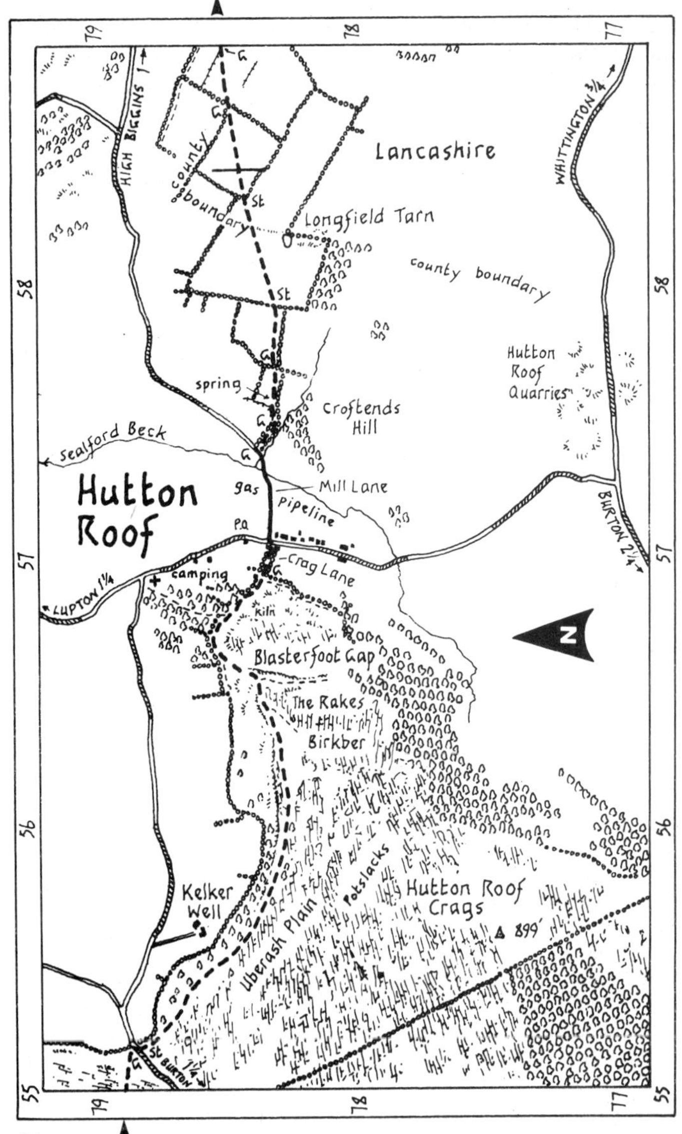
Lancashire
county boundary
Longfield Tarn
county boundary
HIGH BIGGINS 1
WHITTINGTON 3/4
Hutton Roof Quarries
spring
Croftends Hill
Sealford Beck
Hutton Roof
gas Pipeline
Mill Lane
P.O.
Crag Lane
camping
LUPTON 1 1/4
BURTON 2 1/4
Kiln
Blasterfoot Gap
The Rakes
Birkber
Potslacks
Hutton Roof Crags
Kelker Well
Uberash Plain
899'
BURTON 1 1/4
N

southwards to Tewitfield is no longer navigable because of the culverting of the canal by the M6 motorway and its associated road diversions. This section of the M6 motorway was opened on 23 October 1970 by the then Minister of Transport, Mr. Peyton.

Turn L in Holme's village street and take the second lane on the R: this was the former road to Holme Park and the A6070 before the motorway came. Go down steps beside Holme Park Bridge to the canal towpath and follow the canal N for a short way to the next road and turn R to pass under the M6 to the A6070 junction. Turn R again, S, then L at Holme Park to take the bridleway over Farleton Fell. The route of the bridleway is straightforward, passing through gates to reach the Clawthorpe-Hutton Roof road. However, a diversion is justified to the summit of Farleton Knott, 870ft/265m. The diversion strikes off the bridleway beside a long-disused limekiln, giving a gradual climb on turf between the limestone escarpments and leading easily to the top.

The ascent is through an area of rough limestone country, a gently shelving plateau dipping to the E with its scarp slope having prominent scars and screes towering above the M6 motorway. The limestone pavement complex on the plateau is not as good as that on Hutton Roof Crags to the SE because it has been greatly despoiled by the removal of surface stones for ornamental rockery gardens and much of the pavement has been ruined. The view from the top is more extensive than that from Arnside Knott, and gives a clearer view of the Middleton Fells beyond Kirkby Lonsdale.

From the top a route can be made through the limestone pavements at first SE and then SW, rejoining the bridleway at a gate in the wall. Turn L and pass through three more gates to reach the Clawthorpe-Hutton Roof lane.

Map 1.4

From the Clawthorpe-Hutton Roof lane a clear path runs through limestone outcrops, bracken and gorse through Uberash Plain across the flank of Hutton Roof Crags. A descent off the ridge of Birkber leads down to Blasterfoot Gap and an old limekiln and into the hamlet of Hutton Roof by way of Crag Lane, crossing the route of the Thirlmere-Manchester aqueduct.

Hutton Roof is a grey straggling hamlet dominated by the barren limestone crags that carry its name. It boasts a post office/store, but no pub, and its church stands outside on the N side.

St. John's was built in 1881-2 in the Perpendicular style to the designs of Paley & Austin. In the church and in the SE corner of the churchyard there are memorials to a one-time vicar, Theodore Hardy DSO MC VC. A former schoolmaster, he came to Hutton Roof in

1913, aged 50. He was vicar for five years, but for much of the time he was in France as chaplain to the troops, effecting many courageous rescues of dying and wounded from the battlefields.

At the opposite end of the village, next to Hutton Roof Hall, the former Wesleyan chapel, 1850, has its date on a scroll carved in relief with 'God is Love'. An inscribed tablet says that during the War of 1939-45 the chapel was used as HQ for the Hutton Roof Section of the Westmorland Home Guard. The chapel is now a private garage.

Take Mill Lane directly E from Hutton Roof, crossing the route of a North Sea natural gas pipeline. The plate on a concrete post saying simply 'Gas. Size 42' indicates the diameter of the pipe in inches. It carries gas from Frigg near Aberdeen to NW England. Pass under the Carlisle-Preston 400Kv electricity cables and over Sealford Beck by a bridge whose foundation stone was laid on 12 August 1867. A litle way beyond the bridge a signposted path crosses fields frequented by lively Friesian bullocks and cows. Longfield Tarn stands on the Westmorland/Lancashire county boundary. There is a low bank - possibly the line of an old wall - along the county boundary and the path to the stile and through the next field to a gate is in Lancashire.

Map 1.5

Our route through the fields is straightforward, but there is little evidence of a worn path on the ground. The path emerges onto Pit Lane by the driveway to Biggins House Farm then goes down the lane to Biggins, a hamlet divided into High and Low Biggins. The path leaves the road at Biggins Lodge Farm and passes through a wood called The Hynings to reach Low Biggins, where you turn L to the main A65 Kendal-Skipton road.

Cross the A65 and go straight ahead down Biggins Road opposite, past the school, turning R at the T-junction with the B6446 Old Kendal Road and at Abbot Hall bend R down New Road to the Market Square in the centre of Kirkby Lonsdale. (Abbot Hall is a charming example of a Westmorland yeoman's house. It is a much-altered 16c-17c house with typical mullioned windows of that period. Mr. Abbot was the first owner.)

Kirkby Lonsdale is a delightful country town of dark grey stone houses built on a high bank overlooking a bend of the River Lune. Its main attractions are the parish church, old buildings and streets, its 'Ruskin's View' overlooking the River Lune, and the Devil's Bridge.

On Thursday - Market Day - it bustles with activity as farmers and their families from scattered communities in the Lune valley converge for business. A 'Victorian Weekend' is held usually in September and

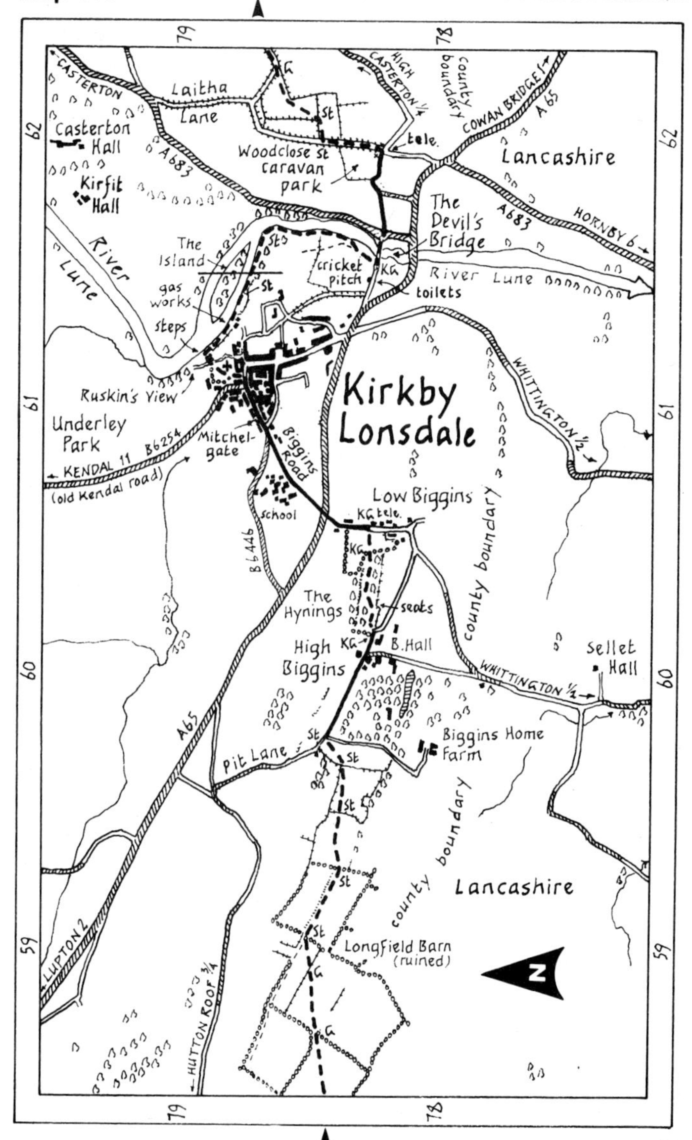
CASTERTON
Laitha Lane
Casterton Hall
Kirfit Hall
A683
Woodclose St caravan park
HIGH CASTERTON ¼
county boundary
COWAN BRIDGE 5
A65
tele.
Lancashire
The Devil's Bridge
A683
HORNBY 6
River Lune
The Island
gas works
steps
cricket pitch
KG
River Lune
toilets
Ruskin's View
Kirkby Lonsdale
WHITTINGTON ½
Underley Park
KENDAL 11 B6254
(old Kendal road)
Mitchel-gate
Biggins Road
Low Biggins
KG tele.
school
county boundary
B6446
The Hynings
seats
High Biggins
B.Hall
Sellet Hall
WHITTINGTON ½
A65
Pit Lane
St
Biggins Home Farm
county boundary
Lancashire
LUPTON 2
Longfield Barn (ruined)
HUTTON ROOF 3¼
N
79
78
62
61
60
59

is an event full of pageantry and fun when traders, residents and visitors 'dress-up'. The Lunesdale Show is held here in August.

The views over this area of the Lune are very pleasant: Ruskin was particularly enthusiastic about them and Turner painted a prospect from the churchyard. Charlotte Bronte was educated nearby and was less enthusiastic: the town featured as 'Lowton' in 'Jane Eyre'.

A Town Trail

We have devised a Town Trail for Kirkby Lonsdale as an extension of our route, which takes us through the town and the start of the next stage of our journey. As Kirkby Lonsdale is likely to be the termination of your first day's walk (15miles/24km from Arnside) the Town Trail can be easily accomplished as an evening stroll to ease off any stiff legs after a bath and dinner. We will begin our Town Trail from the Market Square.

Kirkby Lonsdale has been a market town since 1227 but its prosperity led to the creation of a 'new' **Market Square** in 1832. Except on market days the square is dominated, unfortunately, by parked cars. The **Market Cross**, an octagonal shelter in the Tudor Gothic style, was erected in 1905 and was presented to the town by the Rev. J.W.Davies DD, vicar of Kirkby Lonsdale from 1889-1908. Small houses, now shops, line the S side of the square, while the E side is occupied by the **Savings Bank,** 1847, by Thompson & Webster of Kendal. It has two pairs of Doric pillasters to its porch. On the W side is the **Royal Hotel** with a porch of Ionic columns. Once the 'Rose & Crown' it was reconstructed after a fire in 1820. The widowed Queen Adelaide stayed here once overnight in 1840 and appeared to the crowd on the small balcony over the entrance.

Go N beyond the square into narrow **Main Street,** possibly the finest street in the town. Not only the Victorian shops but the buildings and the ginnels and yards between them are interesting - Chapel Lane on the L and Salt Pie Lane on the R.

At the end turn L into **Market Street.** Main Street, Market Street and Mitchelgate were once the main road through the town from Lancashire and Yorkshire to the Lake District until 1932 when the A65 bypass was built. At the corner of Main Street and Market Street is the former **Market House,** its original ground floor arcade now filled by shop windows except for the central, gated, entrance. Designed by Miles Thompson of Kendal it was built in 1854 by public subscription as a Mechanic's Institute, library and county court, as well as a market hall, which runs back behind the shops. In **Mitchelgate,** at the corner of the cobbled Church Street, stands the 17c **Sun**

Hotel whose projecting upper floors are supported on Doric pillars of limestone. Turn into **Church Street** and through the wrought iron gates and arch and into the churchyard.

The church of **St. Mary the Virgin** stands near the site of a Saxon church, but the oldest parts of the present structure date from *c.*1115. It has an impressive Norman interior, with three lovely arches and columns on the N side of the nave, the diamond patterning of the columns being a fine example of the style current between 1096-1130 and imitating that of Durham cathedral. The corresponding arcading on the S side is less inspiring, and dates from *c.*1180. This decoration suggests plans for an ambitious church. The aisles are wider than the nave, which makes it look very narrow. In 1866 the Romanesque S porch was added when the church was 'restored' but the church's interior still presents a most impressive early Norman display. The door to the embattled W tower is boldly Norman, recessed in four orders and much enriched with zig-zag and other ornament, and there are two other reconstructed Norman doors, and a Norman window in the S aisle. The chancel was fitted with stalls in the restoration of 1619 and the charming six sided pulpit dates from the same century.

There are many interesting 18c table tombs in the churchyard. On the E side are two to the Burrow family, early and mid-18c; Rowland Taylor, 1716; Dorothy Cartwright, 1742, and John Dent, 1709. On the S side are those of Thomas Newby, 1775; Richard Turner, 1790, and Christopher Preston, 1763. To the W of the church are table tombs to Thomas Tiffin, 1787, and Edward Theobalds, 1818, while an obelisk of 1821 commemorates five women who died in the fire which destroyed the Rose & Crown in 1820. It was erected by voluntary contributions and has an inscription in a panel on one side and biblical texts on another.

Take the path next to the church tower and walk N through the churchyard to the octagonal gazebo, then follow along **Fisherty Brow** to **Ruskin's View** which is marked by a plaque on the wall. Turner painted his famous picture of the landscape described by Ruskin in his 'Fors Clavigera' as 'one of the loveliest scenes in England'. The gazebo was built in the corner of the churchyard at the turn of the 18c to enable visitors to benefit from the views: it was there when Turner painted the view. The sylvan banks of the river lead down to meadows, and in the middle distance the villages of Barbon and Casterton are hidden by trees. The view upstream also provides a glimpse of Underley Hall on the edge of the woods: it is a Jacobean style mansion built in 1825-8 by the Kendal architect George Webster for Alexander Nowel MP who had earlier (1811-25) lived in a large house he had built in Fairbank, near the parish church. Underley Hall was one of the first great houses of the Jacobean revival, one of Webster's finest surviving works, and the first house of this size to be built in Westmorland since Levens Hall. The house was altered and enlarged in 1872 by Paley & Austin for the Earl of Bective who created a farm estate and built an elaborate Gothic bridge over the Lune. The house is now a college. On the distant skyline is Brownthwaite with its cairn and to the R Gragareth and Ingleborough.

Turn back towards the churchyard. At the gazebo a steep flight of 85 steps - **Radical Steps** - lead down to the river. If you go down these steps you can take a footpath on the R bank and pass the Old Mill House on the way downstream towards Devil's Bridge.

However, our Town Trail goes to Devil's Bridge by continuing through the town. Take the path on the L through the churchyard to its SE corner, which leads through a ginnel to cobbled **Swinemarket** where the medieval market cross now stands. From the 13c or 14c this cross stood at the junction of Main Street and Mill Brow but it was moved here in 1822 to make more room for traffic.

On the L is steep **Mill Brow,** aptly named as no fewer than seven waterwheels were once sited along it. They were powered by a stream now chanelled underground, which rises at Beck Head and flows under Market Street. The single storey, 19c, mill toll house or weigh house is on the corner of Mill Brow and Swinemarket and the mills down the hill were the industrial heart of the town. There was a tanyard and a corn mill, a bark and a saw mill, a bone mill and even a snuff mill. Latterly some changed to making calico and horse blankets, and some have now been converted into houses: Mill Brow House, now flats, was built in 1811 as a workhouse but was condemned by the Poor Law Commissioners and changed into a hostel in 1910. The old coach road came up Mill Brow from Devil's Bridge on its way to Kendal and 'Cock' (extra) horses were attached at the bottom to haul coaches up the hill; hence Cocking Yard. It is said that Bonnie Prince Charlie came along Mill Brow during the '45 Rebellion.

From **Swinemarket** cross over diagonally L into **Horsemarket** with its cobbled forecourts and row of late-18c workers' cottages on the L. Continue along **Back Lane** in a SE direction. Salt Pie Lane comes in from the R and then further along, after passing through another small square, Jingling Lane also comes in from the R. This unusual name is derived from the sounds of water running in a stone drain beneath it. You can turn up **Jingling Lane** to get back to the Market Square.

Back Lane continues SE. Go under a bridge, beyond the cricket field to the old road, **Bridge Brow,** and turn L to the beautiful **Devil's Bridge.**

It is uncertain when **Devil's Bridge** was built, but it was repaired in 1272, although the present structure is 15c. It has three splendidly ribbed round arches, the central one 40ft/12m above the river, simple and graceful. On the SE corner of the bridge is the so-called Plague Stone of 1633, with an eroded inscription which calls on all who cross to 'Feare God, Honer the King'.

The road over Devil's Bridge was closed to traffic when **Stanley Bridge** was built downstream in 1932 to carry the town's bypass. The Devil's Bridge is a popular spot, with ice cream and hot dog vendors in attendance, and picnickers in **Jubilee Park,** and paddlers and swimmers in the river. The park was laid out in 1936 and the wrought iron gates were made by Jonty Wilson for the Coronation in 1953. Jonty was Kirkby's well-known blacksmith, historian and broadcaster, the last of a long line of family blacksmiths who served the town for more than 200 years. His smithy was in Fairbank. He died in 1982 aged 82 and a hooping plate from one of the cart wheels he used to make stands in the park in his memory.

Erratic on Farlton Fell.

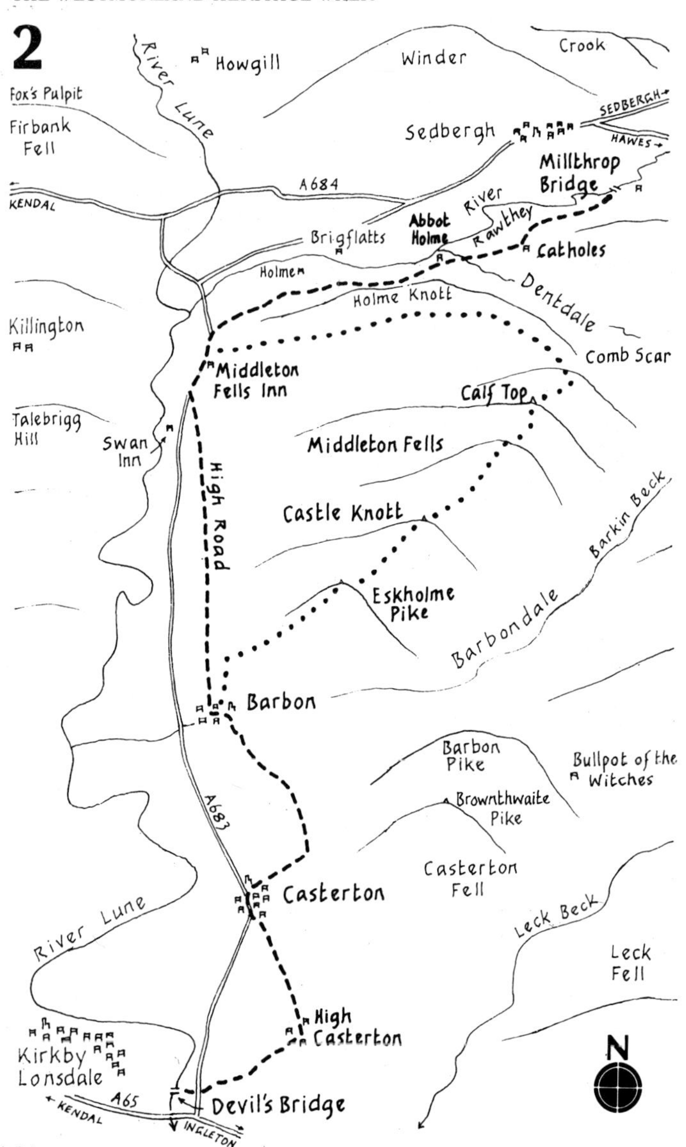
2
Howgill
River Lune
Winder
Crook
Fox's Pulpit
Firbank Fell
Sedbergh
SEDBERGH
HAWES
Millthrop Bridge
A684
KENDAL
River Rawthey
Abbot Holme
Brigflatts
Catholes
Holme
Dentdale
Holme Knott
Killington
Comb Scar
Middleton Fells Inn
Calf Top
Talebrigg Hill
Swan Inn
Middleton Fells
High Road
Barkin Beck
Castle Knott
Eskholme Pike
Barbondale
Barbon
Barbon Pike
Bullpot of the Witches
Brownthwaite Pike
A683
Casterton Fell
Casterton
River Lune
Leck Beck
Leck Fell
High Casterton
Kirkby Lonsdale
N
A65
KENDAL
Devil's Bridge
INGLETON

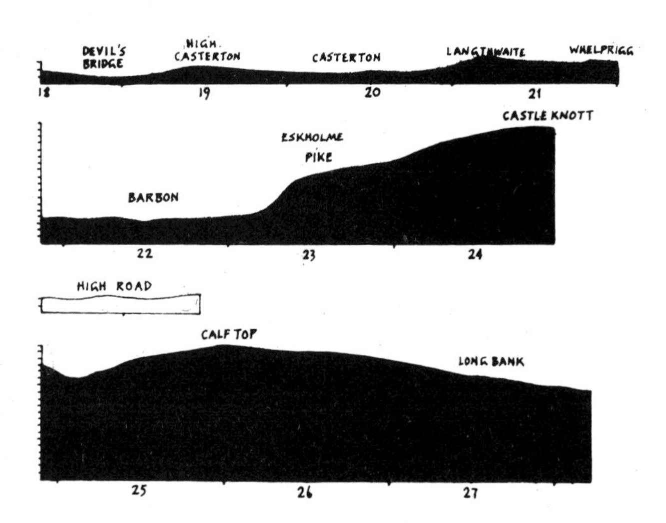
DEVIL'S BRIDGE
HIGH CASTERTON
CASTERTON
LANGTHWAITE
WHELPRIGG
18
19
20
21
CASTLE KNOTT
ESKHOLME PIKE
BARBON
22
23
24
HIGH ROAD
CALF TOP
LONG BANK
25
26
27

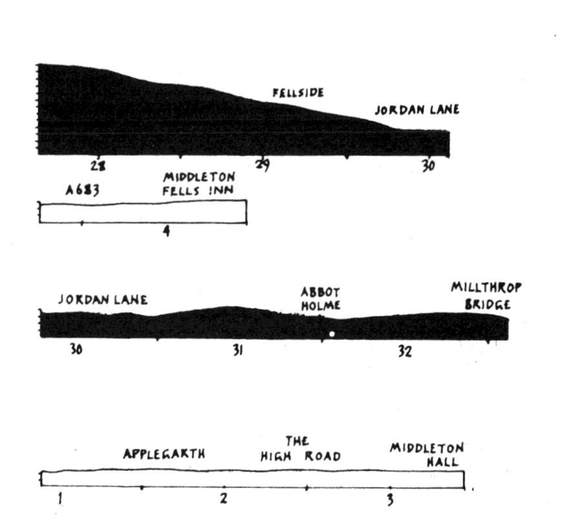
FELLSIDE
JORDAN LANE
28
29
30
A683
MIDDLETON FELLS INN
4
JORDAN LANE
ABBOT HOLME
MILLTHROP BRIDGE
30
31
32
APPLEGARTH
THE HIGH ROAD
MIDDLETON HALL
1
2
3

2. Kirkby Lonsdale to Sedbergh

Lunesdale is a beautiful valley. The middle section, where it runs between the fells, is perhaps the best known as it is followed by the main London-Glasgow railway line and M6 motorway, but fortunately the road engineers have not despoiled the wooded valley further downstream by their works, as was once planned in the 1950's.

The River Lune rises on the N flanks of the Howgill Fells near Newbiggin-on-Lune and flows westwards to Tebay. Here it is deflected southwards through the Tebay gorge, past Sedbergh and Kirkby Lonsdale, then south-westerly into Lancashire to Lancaster and the sea.

Unfortunately the banks of the Lune carry few public footpaths and we have to take an alternative line to Sedbergh. We have devised High Level and Low Level options for several parts of our walk, and the first occurs on this stretch. At Barbon, just N of Kirkby Lonsdale, our Low Level Route follows a course parallel the the Lune, while the High Level option takes us over the Middleton Fells which flank the valley on its E side.

From Kirkby Lonsdale to Sedbergh by the High Level Route is a distance of 15 miles/24km. It is a steep pull up to Calf Top from Barbon and there is no path visible on the ground but the traverse of the Middleton Fells alongside the county boundary wall is straightforward. The Low Level Route goes along a minor country lane from Barbon to Middleton for a distance of about 4 miles/6.4km, against the 8 miles/12.8km of the High Level Route between the same two points.

Map 2.1

From the Devil's Bridge at Kirkby Lonsdale cross the A683 Lancaster-Sedbergh road to the road opposite which leads to High Casterton. At a junction (TCB and caravan park) turn L along green Laitha Lane. Although signposted 'Bridleway to Colliers Lane' this track, and its E spur to Cragg House Hotel, is in fact a Road Used as a Public Path (RUPP). Turn R through a squeeze stile and cross fields to High Casterton. (Laitha Lane is not used in its entirety as it becomes narrow and is inclined to be overgrown and muddy.)

Turn N along the village street, passing a lovely rock garden, to a cross-roads. Turn L down Colliers Lane then R on an intricate little route through paddocks and small fields: go to the L of three bungalows ahead to

The Devil's Bridge, Kirkby Lonsdale

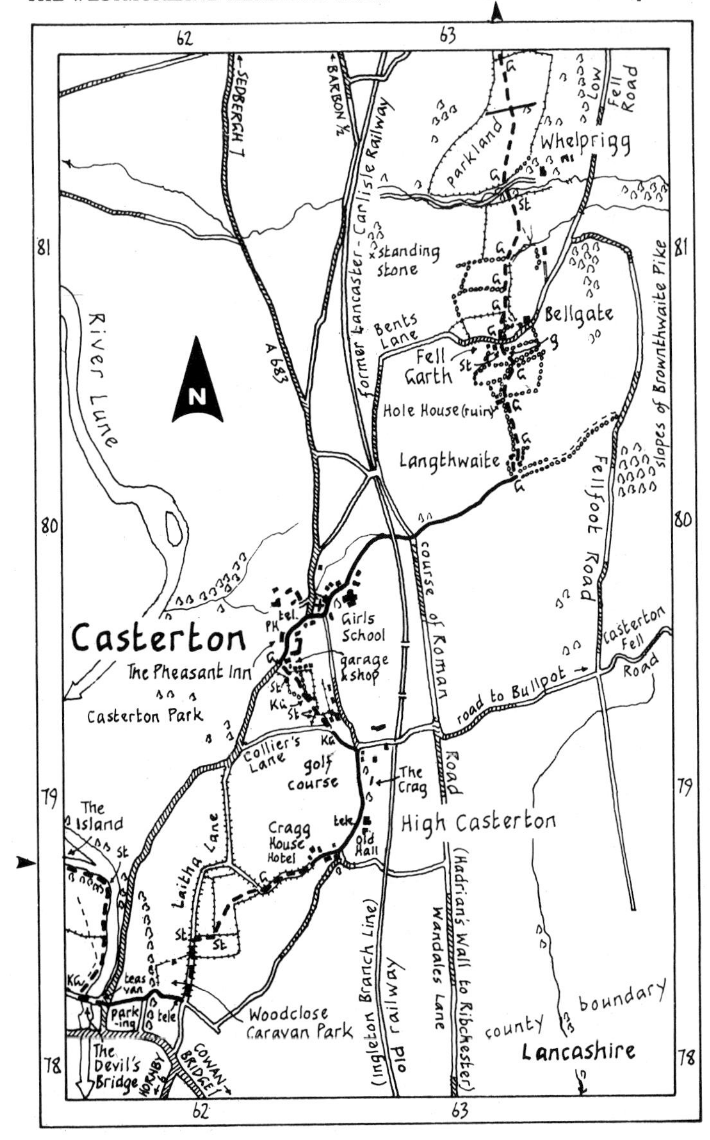
62
63
SEDBERGH 7
BARBON ½
Former Lancaster - Carlisle Railway
parkland
Whelprigg
Low Fell Road
St
standing stone
81
River Lune
A 683
Bents Lane
Bellgate
Fell Garth
St
N
Hole House (ruin)
Langthwaite
slopes of Brownthwaite Pike
Fellfoot Road
80
course of Roman Road
Casterton
tel.
PH
Girls School
garage & shop
The Pheasant Inn
Casterton Fell Road
road to Bullpot
Casterton Park
St
KG
Collier's Lane
golf course
The Crag
79
The Island
St
Laitha Lane
Cragg House Hotel
tele
Old Hall
High Casterton
(Hadrian's Wall to Ribchester)
Wandales Lane
(Ingleton Branch Line)
old railway
St
teas van
KG
Park-ing
tele
Woodclose Caravan Park
county boundary
Lancashire
78
The Devil's Bridge
HORNBY
COWAN BRIDGE

a squeeze stile to emerge on the A683 by Town End Garage. Turn R past the Pheasant Inn then R again into the centre of Casterton to its church and girl's school.

Casterton is an attractive village mostly of grey limestone houses standing above the Lune and is noted chiefly for its girl's school.

The Rev. William Carus Wilson, vicar of Tunstall, Lancashire, founded a school for clergymen's daughters in 1823 at Cowan Bridge (just down the road, in Lancashire) to which the Bronte sisters went. Charlotte spent 12 unhappy months of her education at Cowan Bridge in 1824-5. She never forgot how wretched she had been and she refers to her experiences in 'Jane Eyre'. The school moved to Casterton in 1833, where Wilson founded a bigger school, still performing its original purpose.

The Rev. Wilson also paid for the building in 1831-3 of the church of **Holy Trinity** for the use of the school. It is a bleak, unattractive, barn-like building, but it has the attractions of stained glass in the chancel and two W windows designed in 1897-9 by Henry Holliday (1839-1927), a friend of Burne-Jones and Holman Hunt. Paintings on the walls are by Holliday in 1894 and James Clark *c.* 1905-10. The Rev. Wilson, who died in 1859, is remembered by a Gothic tablet. On Sundays during term time the girls from Casterton School supplement the congregation and make a pretty sight in their bright blue uniforms and straw boaters.

Go away from Casterton church NE with the Girls School on your R and pass under the track of the former Lancaster-Carlisle railway.

The Lancaster & Carlisle Railway Company - later part of the London & North Western Railway - obtained an Act of Parliament in 1857 and built a railway up the Lune valley from Clapham to Lowgill, which was opened in 1861. Originally seen as providing a through route to Scotland via Shap it never functioned as a trunk route except when diversions from the Settle-Carlisle line were necessary. The line was closed in 1964.

Just beyond the railway bridge you come to a crossroads of Wandles Lane. This lane was a Roman road, the main artery from Manchester via Ribchester to Hadrian's Wall at Carlisle, passing through the Lune gorge.

From the Roman road go ahead, E, on a track to Langthwaite Farm, and just before the farmhouse turn N through fields past the ruins of Hole House to reach Bents Lane. Cross this road, go through more fields and then woodland bounding the driveway to Whelprigg, a mansion built in 1834 in the Jacobean style. The route across the parkland of Whelprigg is not easily defined on the ground, but continue in a northerly direction to the field corner and thus towards Barbon.

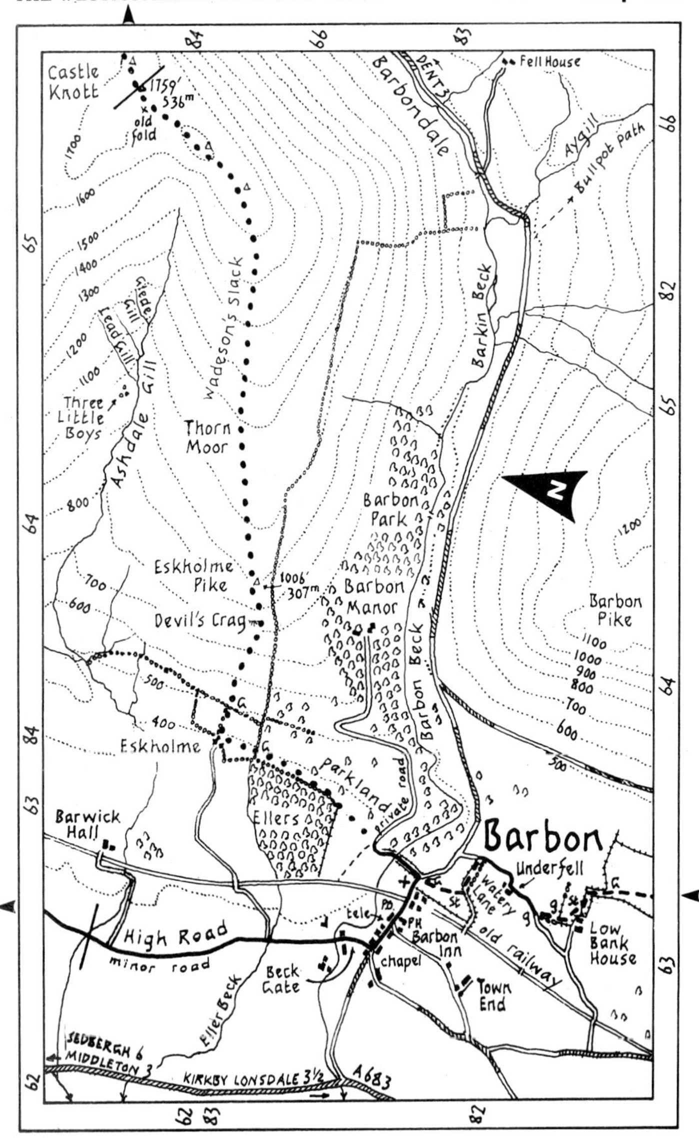
Castle Knott
1759'
536m
old fold
Fell House
DENT 3
Barbondale
Aygill
Bullpot path
Barkin Beck
Wadeson's Slack
Glede Gill
Lead Gill
Three Little Boys
Ashdale Gill
Thorn Moor
Barbon Park
Eskholme Pike
1006'
307m
Barbon Manor
Devil's Crag
Barbon Pike
Barbon Beck
Eskholme
Parkland
private road
Ellers
Barwick Hall
Barbon
Underfell
Watery Lane
old railway
Low Bank House
High Road
minor road
Barbon Inn
chapel
Beck Gate
Town End
Eller Beck
SEDBERGH 6
MIDDLETON 3
KIRKBY LONSDALE 3½
A683

Map 2.2

Emerging from the Whelprigg parkland our route does not go through the farmyard of Low Bank House but keeps to its E side, passing through two squeeze stiles occupied by gates. Follow the lane N but before reaching a T-junction turn L down a track (Watery Lane) then R across a field to emerge at the church on the E side of Barbon village.

Barbon is a scattering of houses, many whitewashed, where the Barbon Beck tumbles down the delightful Barbondale to meet the Lune.

St. Barthomew's church stands on the site of a pre-Reformation chapel. A church was built in 1600, demolished and rebuilt in 1814, then demolished and rebuilt again in 1893. It is an unpretentious but lovely church in the Perpendicular style. The E window is of clear glass so that Crag Hill (2239ft/682m) can be seen, giving meaning to Psalm 121 - 'I will lift up my eyes to the hills.' The font cover, lectern, organ case and chancel screen were all made in the village. The font of the 1814 chapel stands at the W end. The lychgate was built in 1915.

Wonderfully sited in the woods above Barbondale, and seen from our path on our approach to the village, is the Victorian Gothic mansion of **Barbon Manor**, built in 1862-3 by E.M.Barry. It is approached by a long winding drive from beside the church: this has been used since 1958 for motorcycle sprint hill-climbs, and they are still held in July each year.

At Barbon we provide a choice of routes - a High Level Route and a Low Level Route. Throughout this walk around Westmorland we regard the Low Level Routes as alternatives to the High Level Routes, to be used in bad weather or if time is short for you to reach your destination. Only by following the High Level Routes do we feel that the full flavour of Westmorland be appreciated. The two routes join up on the A683 just N of the Middleton Fells Inn: the Low Level Route takes *c.* 1¼ hours, the High Level Route *c.* 2¾ hours. A description of the High Level Route begins below while that for the Low Level Route begins on Page 43. The divergence of both routes starts on Map 2.2.

High Level Route

At the crossing of the Barbon Beck we make the transition from the Carboniferous limestone of the Lune valley to the Coniston Grits, of which the Middleton Fells are largely composed.

Take the private road/public footpath N of Barbon church towards Barbon Manor but at the first hairpin bend of the driveway strike N across

Map 2.3

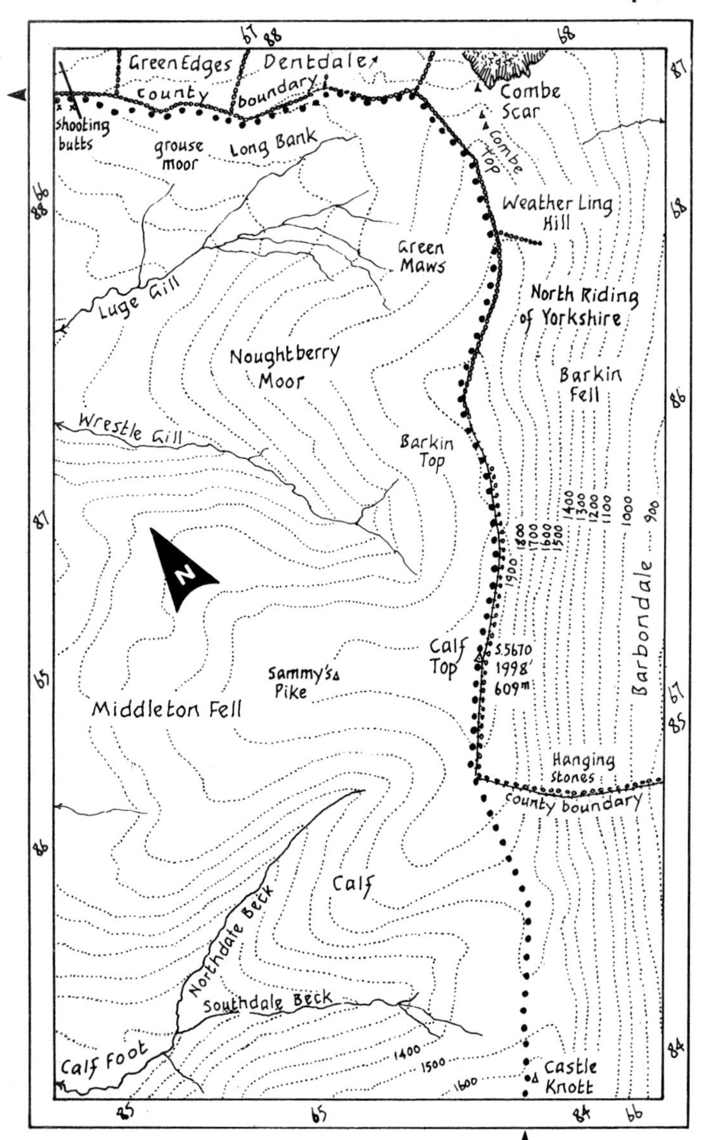

Green Edges
Dentdale
county boundary
shooting butts
grouse moor
Long Bank
Combe Scar
Combe Top
Weather Ling Hill
Green Maws
Luge Gill
North Riding of Yorkshire
Noughtberry Moor
Barkin Fell
Wrestle Gill
Barkin Top
Calf Top
S.5670
1998'
609m
Sammy's Pike
Middleton Fell
Barbondale
Hanging Stones
county boundary
Calf
Northdale Beck
Southdale Beck
Calf Foot
Castle Knott

the parkland to the E edge of Ellers (wood) and almost to the farmyard of Eskholme. Here turn R along the broken wall, and follow a right-of-way up the fellside to a gate (fixed: it has to be climbed).

The path strikes up the fellside, steeply at first to Devil's Crag (the only outcrop of any substance on the Middleton Fells, and this of Bannisdale Slate) and Eskholme Pike (1006ft/307m), a fine viewpoint for the Lune valley. A thin path follows the ridge called Wadeson's Slack, passing two cairns (at 490m and 510m) before reaching a third on Castle Knott (1759ft/536m) where Killington Lake and the M6 motorway come into view.

(High Level Route continues on Map 2.3)

Low Level Route

From Barbon church go down into the village, across the line of the former railway (now hardly noticeable, with bungalows on the site of the former station and station yard), past the Barbon Inn and down the main street, past the P.O. to the old Wesleyan chapel, 1888. A lane opposite, called Beckgate, leads down to an old pack-horse bridge over the Barbon Beck. This road is the ambitiously named 'High Road': the continuation of the Roman road from Casterton is the A683, just to the W, and this road is probably post-Roman to avoid turnpike tolls on the major road. It serves a number of farms and is narrow, with a green strip down its centre in parts, and is tarmacadamed all the way. (If a right-of-way had been created - whether public footpath or bridleway - along the old railway line when it was closed in 1964, a much better Low Level Route would be available between Barbon and Sedbergh.)

(Low Level Route continues on Map 2.4)

Map 2.3

High Level Route

This section is straightforward, even in mist.

From the cairn on Castle Knott (1759ft/536m) go NE along the ridge to a wall corner. This wall coming up from Barbondale is the County Boundary (with Yorkshire) and we follow it throughout whilst on this map. This wall also marks the boundary of the Yorkshire Dales National Park.

The OS bench mark on Calf Top (1998ft/609m) (not to be confused with The Calf in the Howgills) marks the highest point of the Middleton Fells. It is about 1½ hours walk from Barbon to here, and another 1¼ hours descent to the A683. Sammy's Pike is a prominent cairn on a spur of Middleton Fell which from the ascent of the Castle Knott ridge may be mistaken for the Calf Top cairn.

Land Rover/tractor tracks lead away from Calf Top and we follow these

Map 2.4

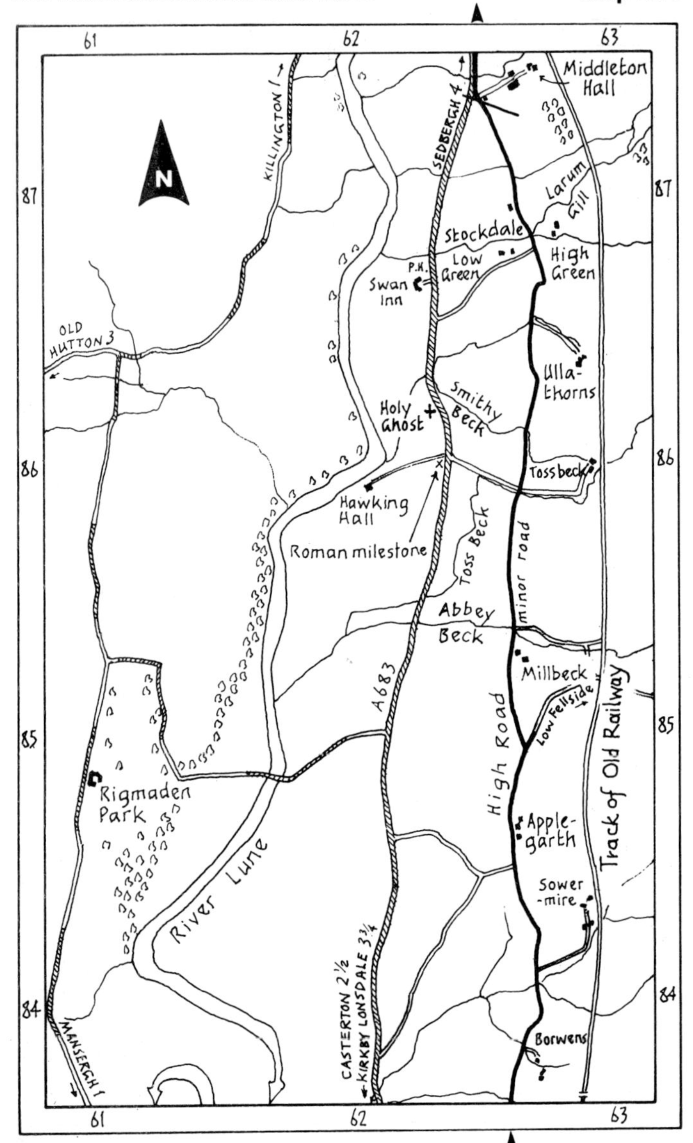

61
62
63
Middleton Hall
KILLINGTON 1
SEDBERGH 4
N
87
Larum Gill
Stockdale
High Green
P.H.
Low Green
Swan Inn
OLD HUTTON 3
Ulla-thorns
Smithy Beck
Holy Ghost
86
Tossbeck
Hawking Hall
Toss Beck
minor road
Roman milestone
Abbey Beck
Millbeck
A683
Low Fellside
85
High Road
Track of Old Railway
Rigmaden Park
Apple-garth
River Lune
Sower-mire
84
CASTERTON 2 1/2
KIRKBY LONSDALE 3 3/4
MANSERGH 1
Borwens

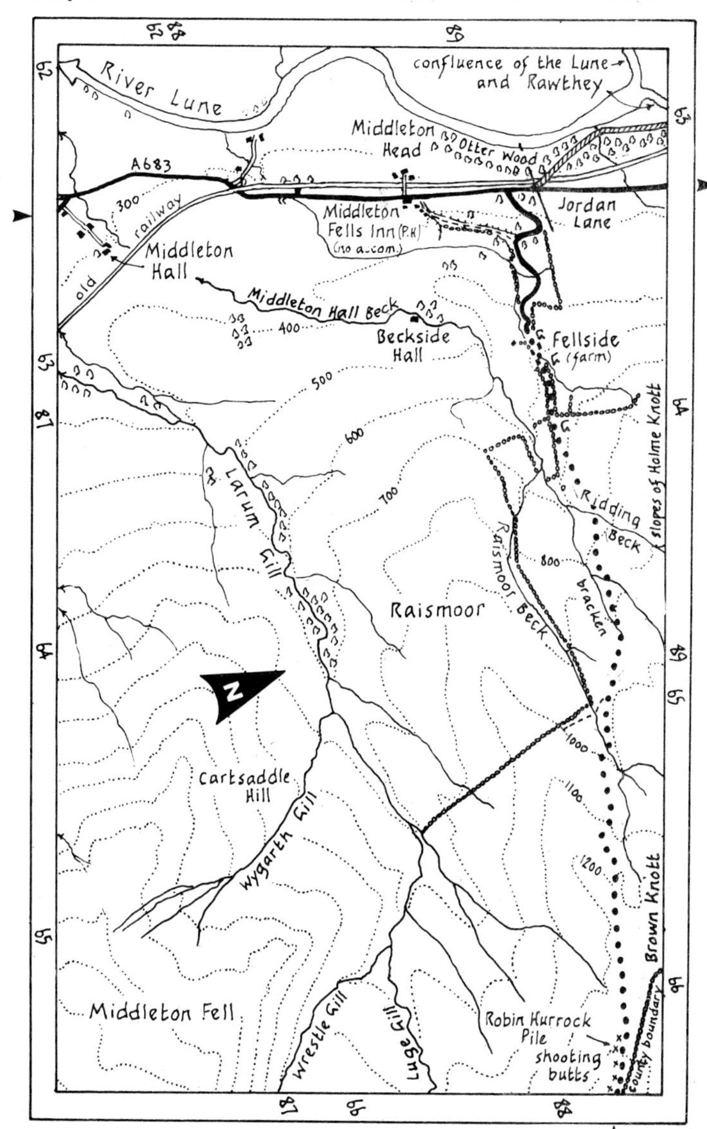

River Lune
confluence of the Lune and Rawthey
Middleton Head
Otter Wood
A683
300
old railway
Middleton Hall
Middleton Fells Inn (P.H.) (no accom.)
Jordan Lane
Middleton Hall Beck
400
Beckside Hall
Fellside (farm)
500
600
700
800
Larum Gill
Ridding Beck
slopes of Holme Knott
Raismoor
Raismoor Beck
bracken
1000
1100
1200
Cartsaddle Hill
Wygarth Gill
Brown Knott
Middleton Fell
Wrestle Gill
Luge Gill
Robin Hurrock Pile
shooting butts
county boundary
N

alongside the county boundary wall. The cairns above Combe Scar mark viewpoints over Barbondale and Dentdale but there is no access over or through the wall to this spot to enjoy the full view.

The moorland here is the first of only two stretches along our route where grouse shooting takes place: the other is in the area of Tarn Sike near Dufton.

(High Level Route continues on Map 2.5)

Map 2.4

Low Level Route

The route follows the 'High Road' all the way to Middleton Hall. It is tarmacadamed but very little used, nowadays only serving the dozen or so farms along the way.

A lane on the L leads to the isolated church of the **Holy Ghost, Middleton,** which although beside the A683 is a long way away from the scattered community it serves. It was rebuilt in 1878-9 in the Perpendicular style, but has little of interest.

Just S of the church, beside the approach to Hawking Hall, is a Roman milestone. A cylindrical stone shaft, 5ft 6ins/1.7m high, 1ft 6ins/460mm in diameter, it is inscribed M.P.L.III. Does this mean 53 miles from Carlisle?: the inscription has been renewed. The milestone was discovered nearby in 1836 and erected on the present spot.

Middleton Hall is the largest farm on this stretch of the Lune. Its medieval curtain wall is a scheduled ancient monument, and is accessible to the public for viewing. Wide doorways lead into a spacious courtyard of a fine 15c house on a H-shaped plan.

At Middleton Hall the 'High Road' joins the A683 and we follow this towards Sedbergh.

(Low Level Route continues on Map 2.5)

Map 2.5

Low Level Route

The 'High Road' meets the A683 just N of Middleton Hall and we follow the main road under the railway bridge (beware of oncoming traffic at the bends here) to the Middleton Fells Inn (no accommodation, but bar snacks and hot meals all day, presumably only during licensed hours). The High Level Route comes down to the main road just beyond the Inn.

High Level Route

The Land Rover/tractor track serving the grouse shooting butts is followed all the way down to Fellside (farm). Its tarmacadamed track bends down to the main road A683 just to the N of the Middleton Fells Inn.

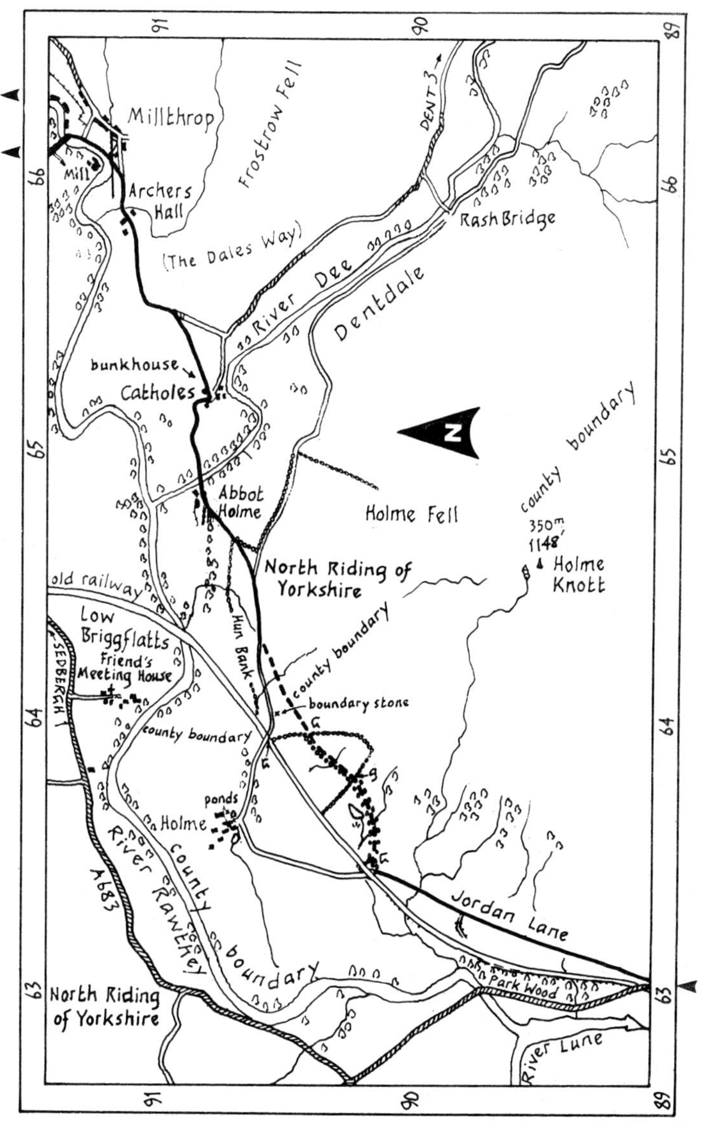
Millthrop
Mill
Archers Hall
Frostrow Fell
DENT 3
(The Dales Way)
River Dee
Rash Bridge
Dentdale
bunkhouse
Catholes
Abbot Holme
Holme Fell
county boundary
350m
1148'
Holme Knott
North Riding of Yorkshire
old railway
Low Briggflatts
Friend's Meeting House
SEDBERGH 1
Hun Bank
county boundary
boundary stone
county boundary
ponds
Holme
River Rawthey
A683
county boundary
Jordan Lane
Park Wood
North Riding of Yorkshire
River Lune
91
90
89
66
65
64
63

(If you need refreshment and if it is still 'opening time' you can branch off the fellside access road along a narrow strip of common land - occasionally occupied by travelling people - to reach the Middleton Fells Inn directly.)

Combined Route

Continue N along the A683, but where it bears L continue ahead on Jordan Lane, a sunken tarmacadamed lane contouring round the fellside towards Millthrop and Dentdale.

(Combined Route continues on Map 2.6)

Map 2.6

Follow Jordan Lane until it passes under the disused railway line, (here the route of the Roman road is lost) then go through a gate on the R to take a path between and alongside broken walls and on to the open fellside. Here we pass out of Westmorland and into Yorkshire.

The path meets an unenclosed minor road (a continuation of Jordan Lane via Holme to Dentdale) and we follow this for a short way before branching off L to Abbot Holme and the fine 17c single-arched Abbot Holme Bridge over the River Dee close to its confluence with the River Rawthey. The lane climbs up to Catholes (where there is good bunkhouse accommodation) and soon joins the main Dentdale road. Turn L and follow the road down into Millthrop, past Archers Hall (1681, for Richard and Isabella Hebblethwaite). The 17c two-arched Millthrop Bridge takes you over the River Rawthey and so into Sedbergh.

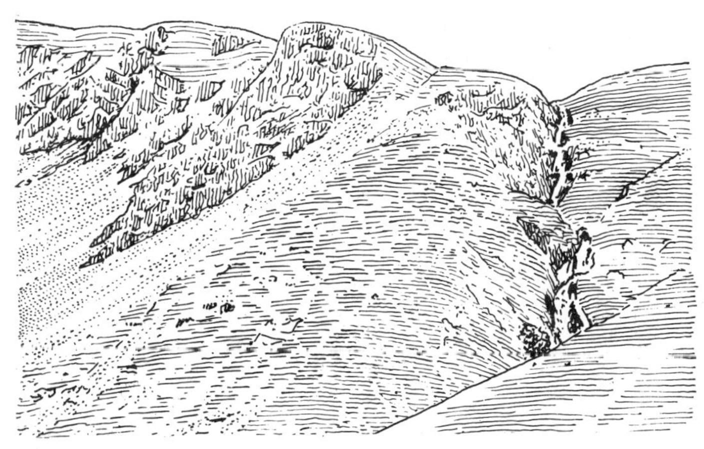

Cautley Spout and Crag.

Shippon in Grisedale.

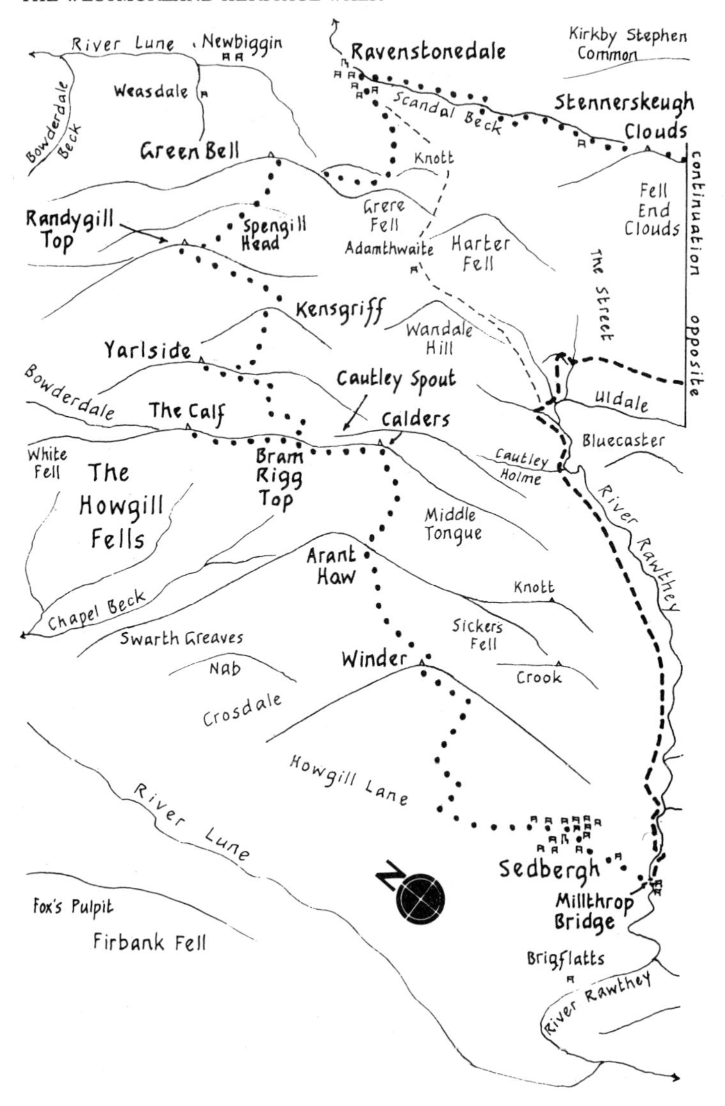
River Lune
Newbiggin
Ravenstonedale
Kirkby Stephen Common
Weasdale
Bowderdale Beck
Scandal Beck
Stennerskeugh Clouds
Green Bell
Knott
continuation opposite
Fell End Clouds
Randygill Top
Spengill Head
Grere Fell
Adamthwaite
Harter Fell
The Street
Kensgriff
Wandale Hill
Yarlside
Cautley Spout
Bowderdale
The Calf
Calders
Uldale
Bluecaster
White Fell
The Howgill Fells
Bram Rigg Top
Cautley Holme
River Rawthey
Middle Tongue
Arant Haw
Knott
Chapel Beck
Swarth Greaves
Sickers Fell
Nab
Winder
Crook
Crosdale
Howgill Lane
River Lune
Sedbergh
Millthrop Bridge
Fox's Pulpit
Firbank Fell
Brigflatts
River Rawthey

3

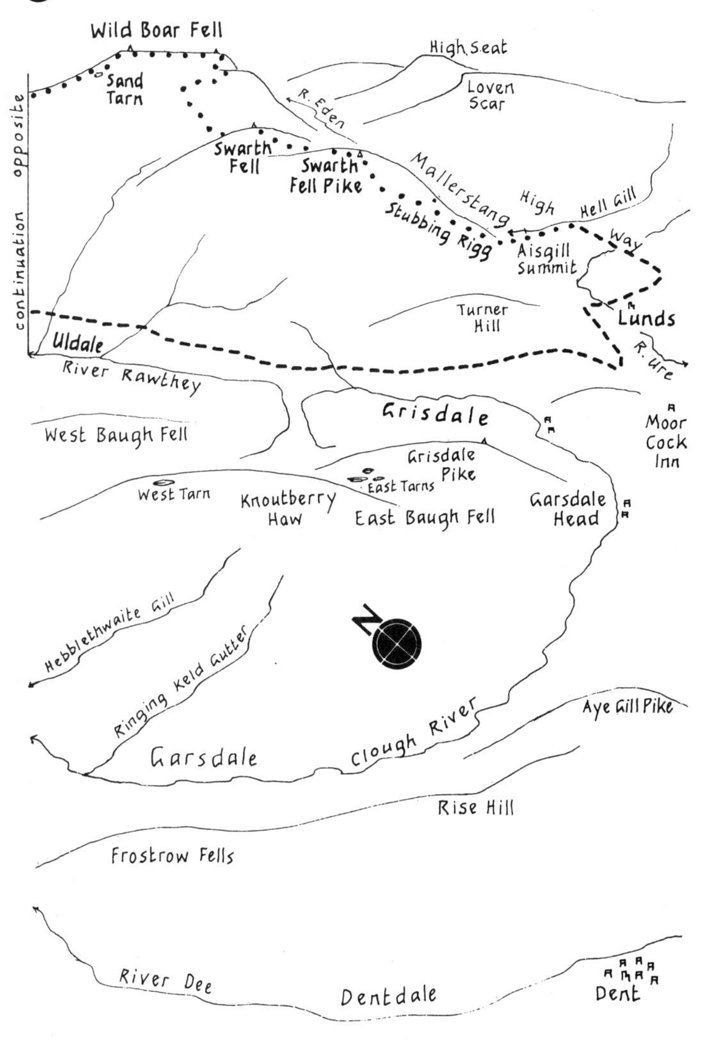
Wild Boar Fell
Sand Tarn
High Seat
Loven Scar
R. Eden
Swarth Fell
Swarth Fell Pike
Mallerstang
Stubbing Rigg
High
Hell Gill
Way
Aisgill Summit
continuation opposite
Turner Hill
Lunds
Uldale
R. Ure
River Rawthey
Grisdale
Moor Cock Inn
West Baugh Fell
Grisdale Pike
West Tarn
East Tarns
Knoutberry Haw
East Baugh Fell
Garsdale Head
Hebblethwaite Gill
Ringing Keld Gutter
N
Clough River
Aye Gill Pike
Garsdale
Rise Hill
Frostrow Fells
River Dee
Dentdale
Dent

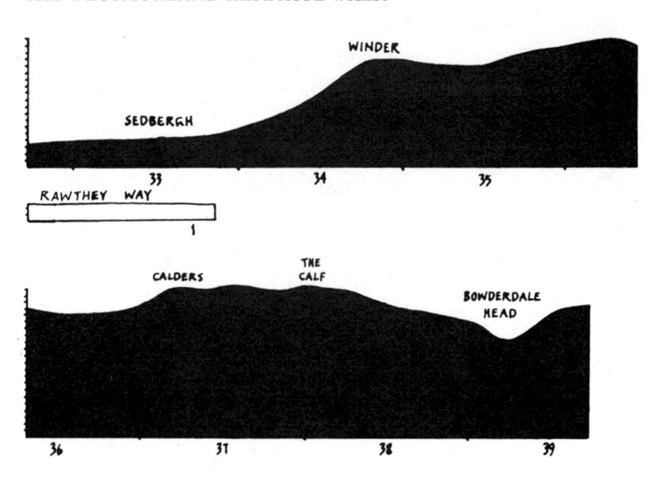
WINDER
SEDBERGH
33
34
35
RAWTHEY WAY
1
THE CALF
CALDERS
BOWDERDALE HEAD
36
37
38
39

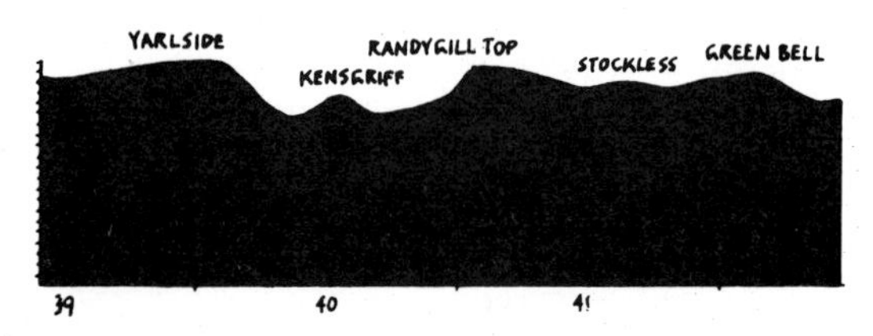
YARLSIDE
RANDYGILL TOP
KENSGRIFF
STOCKLESS
GREEN BELL
39
40
41

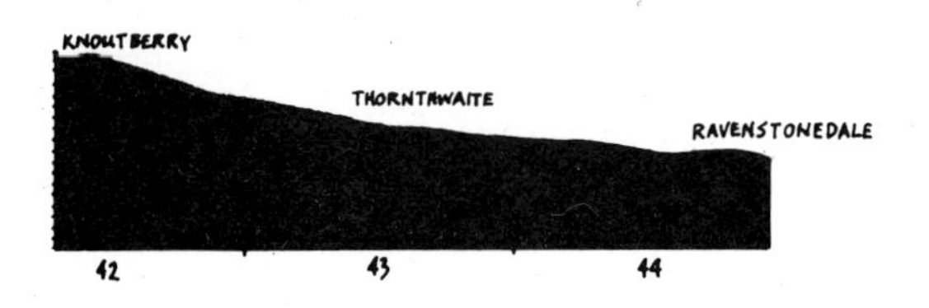
KNOUTBERRY
THORNTHWAITE
RAVENSTONEDALE
42
43
44

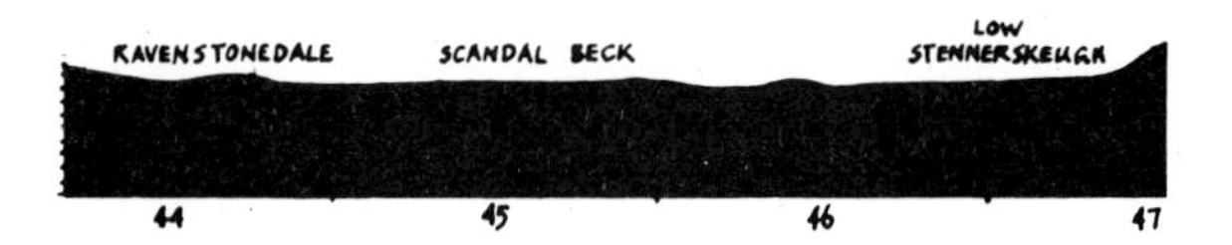
RAVENSTONEDALE
SCANDAL BECK
LOW STENNERSKEUGH
44
45
46
47

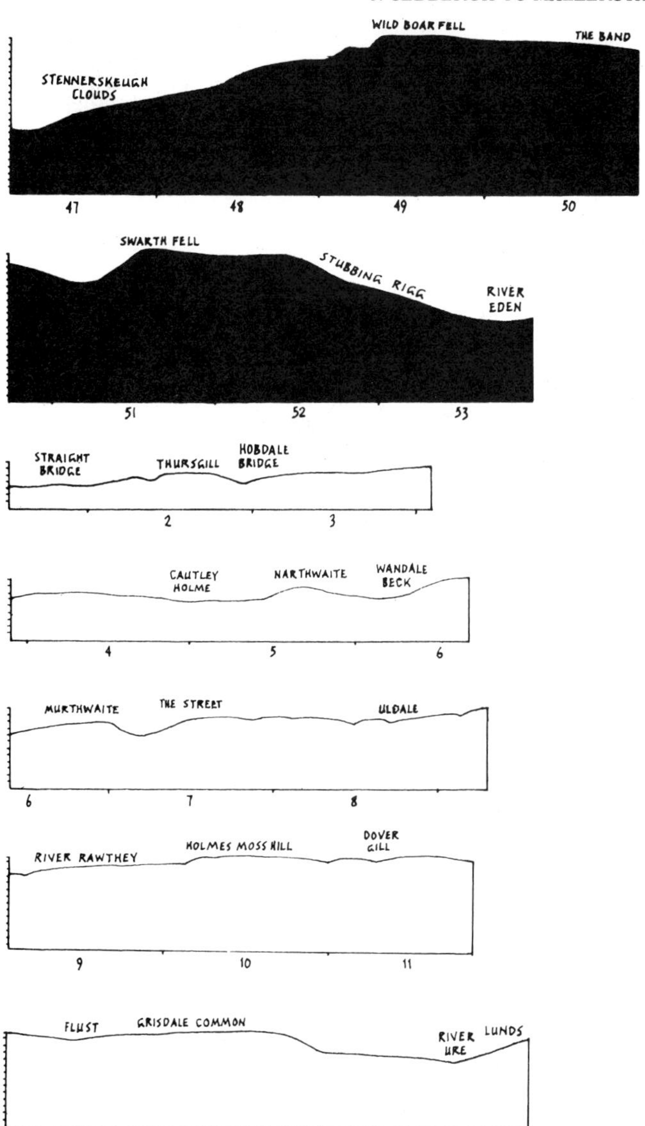
WILD BOAR FELL
THE BAND
STENNERSKEUGH CLOUDS
47
48
49
50
SWARTH FELL
STUBBING RIGG
RIVER EDEN
51
52
53
STRAIGHT BRIDGE
THURSGILL
HOBDALE BRIDGE
2
3
CAUTLEY HOLME
NARTHWAITE
WANDALE BECK
4
5
6
MURTHWAITE
THE STREET
ULDALE
6
7
8
RIVER RAWTHEY
HOLMES MOSS HILL
DOVER GILL
9
10
11
FLUST
GRISDALE COMMON
RIVER URE
LUNDS
12
13
14

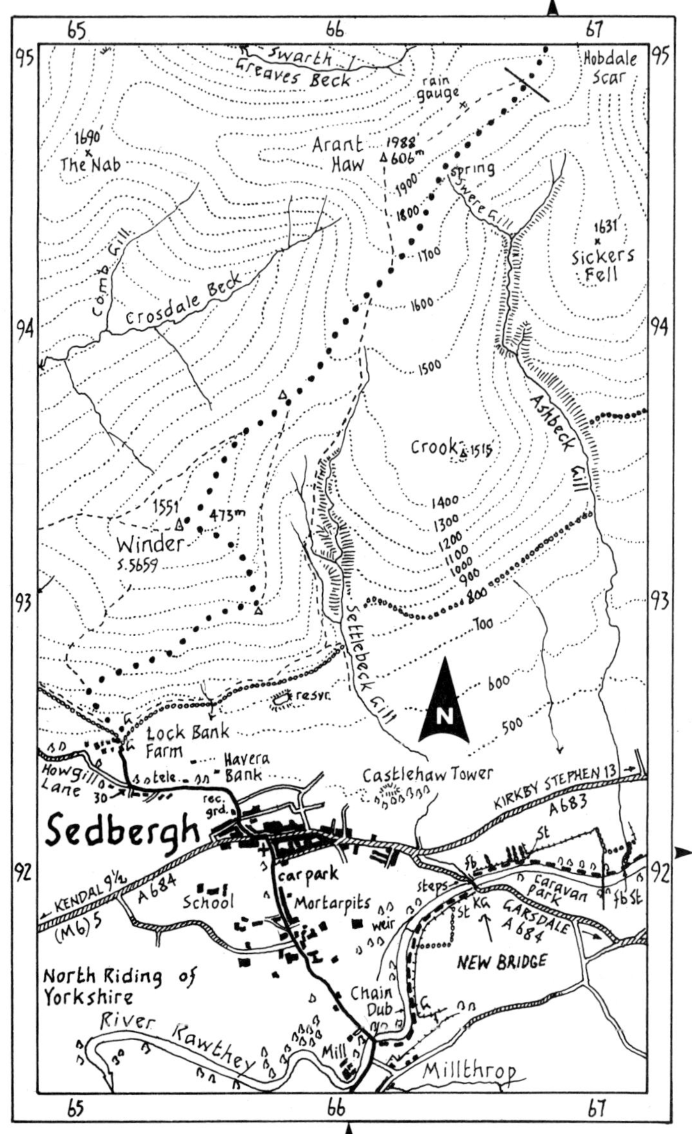
65
66
67
95
94
93
92
Swarth
Greaves Beck
rain gauge
Hobdale Scar
1690'
The Nab
Arant Haw
1988'
606m
spring
1900
1800
1700
Swere Gill
1631'
Sickers Fell
Comb Gill
Crosdale Beck
1600
1500
Ashbeck Gill
Crook
1515
1551'
473m
Winder
S.5659
1400
1300
1200
1100
1000
900
800
700
Settlebeck Gill
600
500
resvr.
N
Lock Bank Farm
Havera Bank
Howgill Lane
tele.
30
rec. grd.
Castlehaw Tower
KIRKBY STEPHEN 13
A683
Sedbergh
St
carpark
fb
steps
Caravan Park
fb St
KENDAL 9½
A684
School
Mortarpits
(M6) 5
weir
St
KG
GARSDALE
A 684
NEW BRIDGE
North Riding of Yorkshire
Chain Dub
River Rawthey
Mill
Millthrop

3. Sedbergh to Mallerstang

In order for us to get the best out of our circuit of Westmorland we find it necessary from time to time to cross over the boundary into another county. We have touched into Lancashire already and here at Sedbergh we make an entry into Yorkshire. The Howgills above Sedbergh are some gem rolling, grassy fells of Coniston Grit that Westmorland shares with Yorkshire and which form the Yorkshire Dales National Park's north-west frontier. We have to pass through Sedbergh to get into the Howgills and Westmorland again (or alternatively take a low-level route towards Mallerstang).

The **High Level Route** from the River Rawthey at Sedbergh to the River Eden at the head of Mallerstang is a distance of 20 miles/32km, with very little opportunity for accommodation beyond the village of Ravenstonedale (11 miles/17.7km from Sedbergh). From Ravenstonedale to Kirkby Stephen, the next suitable place for accommodation, is a distance of 22 miles/35.4km, which involves a traverse of the high fells on both sides of the Mallerstang valley.

The **Low Level Route** from the River Rawthey at Sedbergh to Lunds on the River Ure at the head of Wensleydale is a distance of 14 miles/22.5km. Accommodation may be available at the Moorcock Inn, but check in advance.

Map 3.1

Sedbergh was in Yorkshire until it was annexed by Cumbria in the boundary revisions in 1974. In 1986 there was serious talk that the parishes of Sedbergh, Dentdale and Garsdale wanted to go back into Yorkshire because they felt they hadn't had any benefit from being in Cumbria!

Sedbergh nestles below the Howgills where the River Clough in Garsdale and the River Dee in Dentdale flow into the River Rawthey just before the Rawthey flows into the Lune. It is a small market town, but famous for its public (private) school. Millthrop stands on its outskirts at the crossing of the Rawthey, and it is at Millthrop where our second High Level and Low Level options occur. Either may be combined with a Town Trail through Sedbergh itself, and this is described before we continue on our journey. As Sedbergh could easily be the termination of your second day's walk (15 miles/24km from Kirkby Lonsdale) the Town Trail can be easily accomplished as an evening stroll. Indeed, there may not be enough time for the Town

Trail the following morning as it is a long day's walk to accommodation in Mallerstang, and you will need all the time available, particularly if you intend to take the High Level Route.

A Sedbergh Town Trail

Sedbergh School stands on your L as you enter the town from the S. It was founded as a chantry school in *c.*1525 by Roger Lupton, a native of Howgill, who became the Provost of Eton. No original buildings remain, but the oldest building is the 'old grammar school' on Back Lane. A number of the school buildings were designed by Paley & Austin and built between 1879-97 by John Laing, the founder of the world-famous construction firm, who was born in Carlisle and lived in Sedbergh for some time.

At the bottom of **Loftus Hill** (the road from Millthrop), N of the free car park (toilets) at the junction where **Back Lane** turns off R, is the Sedbergh School Library, 1716. This is the oldest remaining school building, and was originally the Old Grammar School. Its classical style was considerably in advance of local architecture at the time it was built.

Opposite the end of **Back Lane** is a narrow path running alongside and giving access into the churchyard, although the main gate is further up **Loftus Lane** in the corner of the diminutive **Market Place.**

St. Andrew's is typical of a number of churches in northern England where the nave and chancel have no separation such as an arch and where the aisles run the whole length of the nave. Although largely 13c it retains evidence of some earlier building, with a Norman N doorway, some simple Norman arcading and traces of 12c windows. The W tower is 15c Perpendicular and the rest of the exterior is mainly Perpendicular.

Coming out of the main gate of the churchyard you enter the **Market Place** at the junction of Loftus Lane, Market Street and Finkle Street. A grant of a weekly market in Sedbergh was first made by Lady Alice de Stavely of Sedbergh Manor in 1251, and a market has been held on this spot ever since. (Market Day is Wednesday.) The Market Place was probably always small, but its size was reduced twice during the last century: in 1858 a public shelter and reading room was built by the Rev. J.H.Evans, headmaster of Sedbergh School, and in 1897 Finkle Street was widened by demolishing the buildings alongside the churchyard as part of Queen Victoria's Diamond Jubilee celebrations: a drinking fountain erected in 1897 commemorates the event. Today only a few stalls can occupy the Market Place, the overflow being accommodated in the Joss Lane car park, at the E end of Market Street. During the last century the Lancaster-Newcastle stage-coach halted in the Market Place outside the 'Kings Arms', now a grocer's shop.

Turn R with the main flow of traffic into one-way **Main Street.** This is one of the oldest streets in the town and has a variety of buildings and yards. On the R No.35 is a small shop with an overhanging upper storey. From the mid-17c onwards stone replaced timber as the primary building material and consequently few timber-framed buildings survive in this area. This building, dating from early 17c, but much altered since, is one of the few remaining.

Further along Main Street, on the S side, opposite the Bull Hotel, turn R down **Weaver's Yard,** a narrow alley opening out into a small cobbled yard. The first weaving looms in Sedbergh were set up in this yard, hence its name. From the yard the 17c external chimney breasts on the back of the adjoining premises can be seen: Bonnie Prince Charlie, the Young Pretender, is said to have hidden in this chimney before escaping in disguise with the pack horses taking away the woollen goods produced in the yard during his retreat in 1745.

Still further along Main Street, and still on the S side, opposite the National Westminster Bank, 1826, turn R into **Davis Yard,** the entrance to which is via a passage through the lower storey of No.55. At one time this yard had a toll gate across it, and a small charge was made to anyone wishing to go through the yard.

At the junction of Main Street with **Joss Lane,** on the N side, is the **United Reform Church,** built in 1828 and enlarged in 1871. A frequent preacher in this church was John Laing. At the **Joss Lane** car park (TCB, toilets) and having pedestrian access to it, is the **Yorkshire Dales National Park Information Centre,** in a building formerly called Sedbergh Manor. Opposite the Information Centre, on the S side of Main Street, is a narrow cobbled yard known as **The Folly,** or Folly Yard. Stone-built cottages on both sides retain the 'lived-in' atmosphere which the other yards have largely lost.

Retrace your steps along Main Street to the Market Place then go up **Howgill Lane,** beside the Golden Lion. Highfield Villas, 1883, are probably the oldest surviving buildings locally constructed from reinforced concrete. Boys from Sedbergh School were lodged in these villas (one of which is now the Masonic Hall) from 1915-27 when they moved to new accommodation to the SE of the town.

This is the end of our Town Trail and it ideally places us for the start of our High Level Route over the Howgills. (The start of the Low Level Route on Map 3.1 is described on Page 58.)

High Level Route

There is a good path up to Calders on the High Level Route. The way on to The Calf is across a plateau and there is no path beyond the Bowderdale path: navigation can be difficult in mist or low cloud, but the grass and turf provide pleasant conditions underfoot.

Go up Howgill Lane and just past the TCB and 30mph signs take the lane up to Lock Bank Farm and pass through the steel gate in the farmyard and on to the open fell.

The path going E along the fell wall to Settlebeck Gill then up the stream to its source is the more direct way of gaining the Arant How ridge, but the prettiest and easiest way is up Winder, on an obvious broad grassy path through the heather. From the gate then, bear L then R and at the first cairn go L more steeply uphill to the OS bench mark on Winder (1551ft/473m).

From Winder bear NE along the ridge, meeting a second cairn at a slight depression between Winder and Arant How. Continue in the same direction, passing just below the summit ridge of the fell. The summit cairn of Arant How (1978ft/605m on OS 1:10,000 scale maps, but 606m on the Landranger map) may be reached by a short diversion, but from the top follow the crest slightly E of NE passing a rain gauge to regain the main path. The main path goes just below the ridge, passing the spring of Swere Gill Well.

This path, from Lock Bank Farm, is the main route of ascent for The Calf, the highest fell in the Howgills, and is safe in mist.
(High Level Route continues on Map 3.2)

Low Level Route

The valley of the River Rawthey is signposted 'The Rawthey Way' and is a grand route beside the river into the hills.

From Millthrop do not cross Millthrop Bridge over the Rawthey but continue up the true L bank of the river to the bridge carrying the A684 Sedbergh-Hawes road over the river. Rawthey Bridge was built in 1822 after the original 16c bridge was partially destroyed by floods. Cross the bridge and continue upstream on the opposite bank, the true R bank.
(Low Level Route continues on Map 3.8)

Map 3.2

High Level Route

There is a slight descent as the path takes to the NW flank of the Arant How ridge, then a fence appears on your R and a sheepfold on your L. The ridge called Rowantree Grains is now followed, dividing the headwaters of Bram Rigg Beck and Hobdale Beck: it is fairly narrow and exposed to winds. The path is broad and well-defined and turns the fence corner and

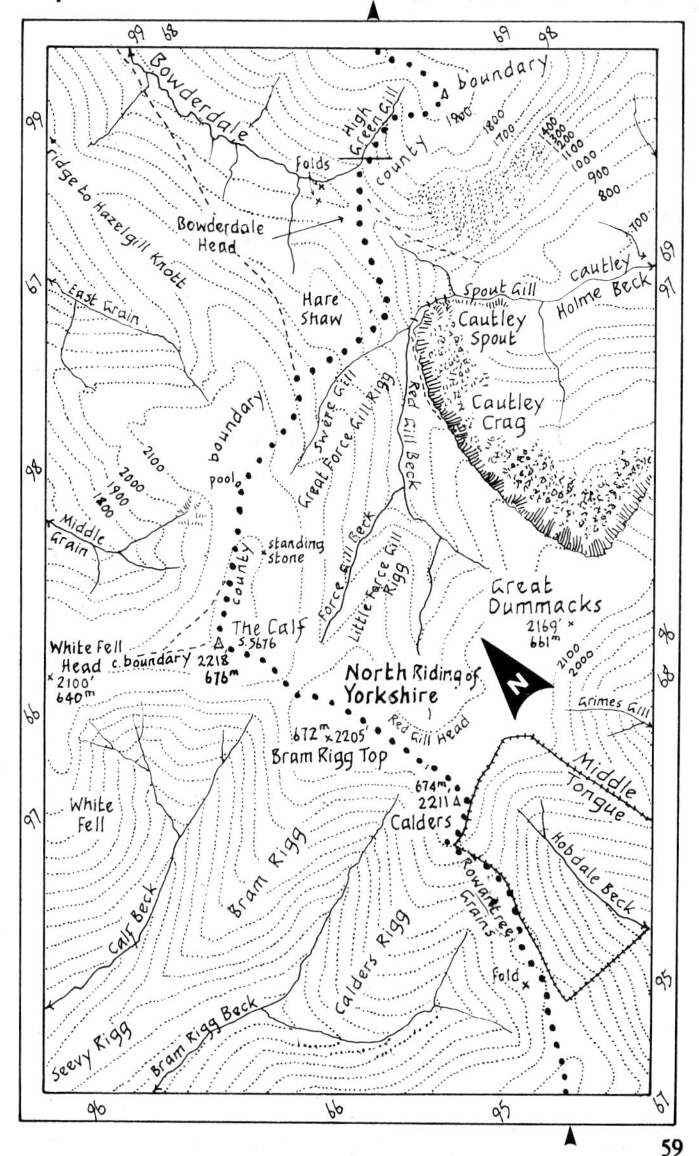
Bowderdale
High Green Gill
boundary
county
Folds
ridge to Hazelgill Knott
Bowderdale Head
Hare Shaw
Spout Gill
Cautley Holme Beck
Cautley Spout
Cautley Crag
East Grain
boundary
Swere Gill
Great Force Gill Rigg
Red Gill Beck
pool
Middle Grain
standing stone
county
Force Gill Beck
Little Force Gill Rigg
Great Dummacks
2169' × 661m
The Calf
S.5676
2218
676m
White Fell Head
× 2100'
640m
c. boundary
North Riding of Yorkshire
N
Grimes Gill
672m × 2205'
Bram Rigg Top
Red Gill Head
674m
2211
Calders
Middle Tongue
White Fell
Bram Rigg
Rowantree Grains
Hobdale Beck
Calf Beck
Calders Rigg
Fold
Bram Rigg Beck
Seevy Rigg

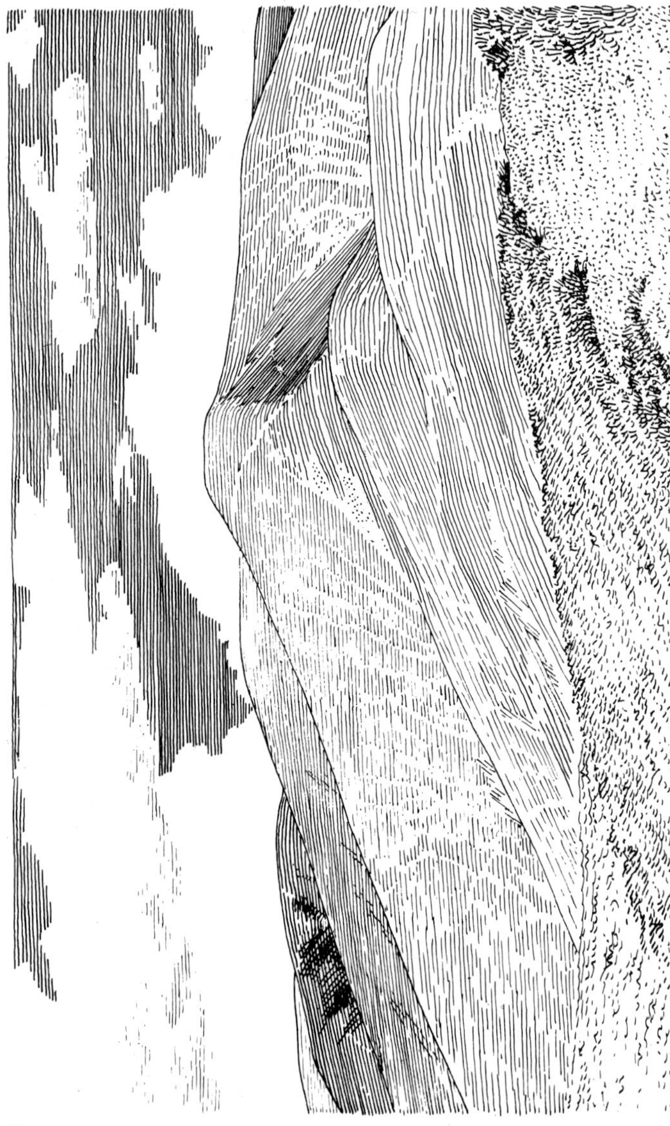

Calders from Arant How, Howgill Fells

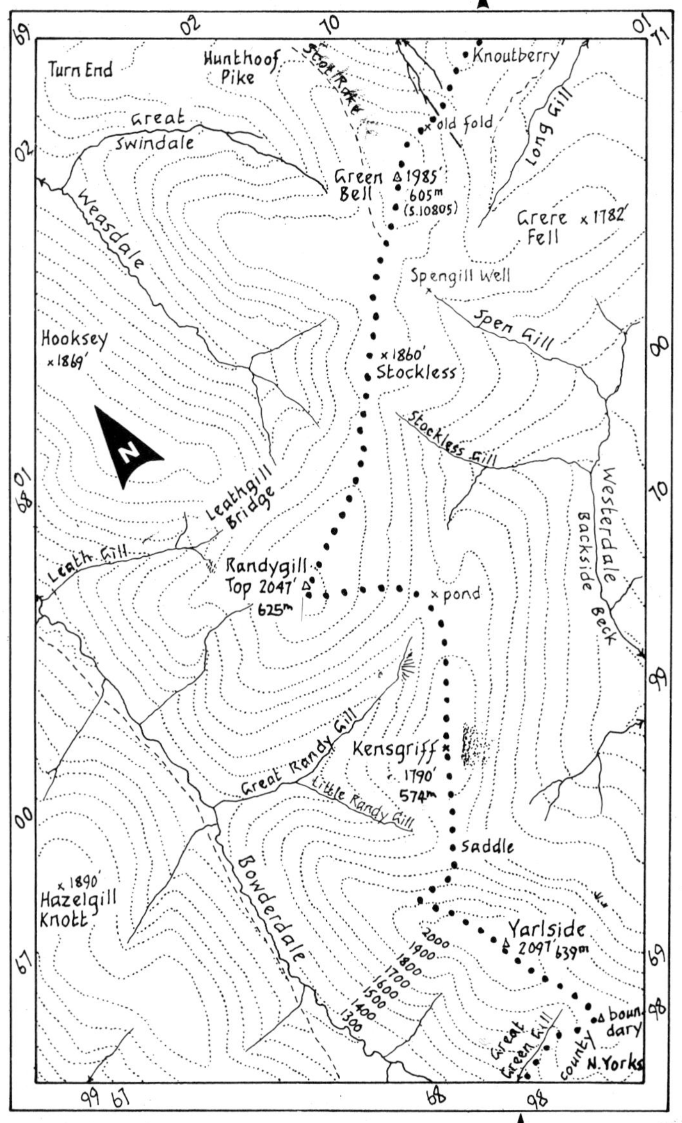
Turn End
Hunthoof Pike
Knoutberry
old fold
Long Gill
Great Swindale
Green Bell
1985'
605m
(S.10805)
Grere Fell
1782'
Weasdale
Spengill Well
Spen Gill
Hooksey
1869'
1860'
Stockless
Stockless Gill
N
Leathgill Bridge
Westerdale
Backside Beck
Leath Gill
Randygill Top 2047'
625m
pond
Great Randy Gill
Kensgriff
1790'
574m
Little Randy Gill
Saddle
1890'
Hazelgill Knott
Bowderdale
Yarlside
2097' 639m
2000
1900
1800
1700
1600
1500
1400
1300
Great Green Gill
boundary
county
N. Yorks
69
02
70
01
71
00
68
99
67
98

soon visits the pile of stones on the top of Calders (2211ft/674m).

The mile between Calders and The Calf is a broad flat plateau, with only a slight ascent to the latter summit. The path is indistinct because of broad areas of spongy ground, and in mist and bad weather a compass bearing is advisable. The path skirts to the E of Bram Rigg Top (2205ft/672m) but its summit is not easily distinguished. If you go off-course it will be useful to be reminded that the ground to the W falls more steeply than the ground to the E. If you need an escape route a descent NE to the headwaters of the Red Gill Beck is on safe ground, leads you in the direction of our route, and should bring you below cloud base level. However, be wary of going too far E because the plateau of Great Dummacks (2169ft/663m) falls away suddenly into Cautley Crags.

The OS column on The Calf (2218ft/676m) is the only feature of an otherwise barren plateau. It stands on the Westmorland/Yorkshire county boundary, but there is no wall, fence or other markers to indicate the boundary.

From The Calf the clear but narrow Bowderdale path is followed NE across the broad ridge, and as this turns N and goes more steeply downhill we branch off R over pathless steep ground above Swere Gill, a feeder of Red Gill Beck, to view Cautley Spout. At Cautley Crag the older mudstones and volcanics are laid bare by complex folding and the waterfall is an impressive sight as it cascades down the northern rim of the crags.

We are aiming for Yarlside, whose flanks appear formidably steep from Bowderdale Head (1414ft/431m). The steep screes on the S flank suggest a line of ascent up High Green Gill, the head stream of the Bowderdale Beck, and to the small cairn on the subsidiary summit. Bowderdale Head is on the county boundary and here we leave the Yorkshire Dales National Park. *(High Level Route continues on Map 3.3)*

Map 3.3
High Level Route

The Yarlside ridge runs S-N and the only path over its top (2097ft/639m) is made by sheep. In mist or low cloud be careful not to go too far down its northern side: the descent to the saddle between Yarlside and Kensgriff is steep, very steep, and is best taken on a diagonal line. In poor visibility it would be best to take a bearing from Yarlside's summit to the saddle, or alternatively to Kensgriff's top.

There is a stiff climb up to Kensgriff on a faint path. The imperial OS maps give Kensgriff a height of 1790ft, which when converted equals 545m. The new metric survey has elevated the fell to 574m, which when converted equals 1883ft. Another faint path goes up to Randygill Top (2047ft/625m on OS 1:10,000 map but 624m on Landranger map) after a

Map 3.4

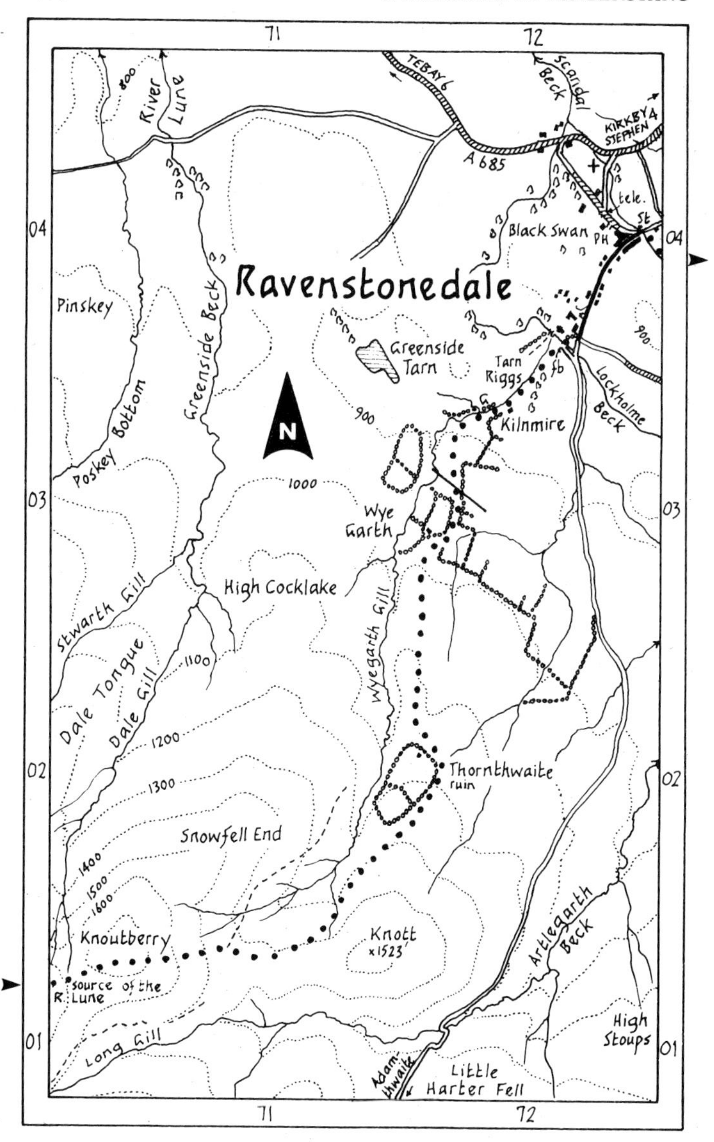

71
72
TEBAY 6
Scandal Beck
KIRKBY STEPHEN 4
800
River Lune
A 685
tele.
Black Swan
PH
St
04
Ravenstonedale
Pinskey
Greenside Beck
Greenside Tarn
Tarn Riggs
fb
900
Lockholme Beck
Poskey Bottom
Kilnmire
1000
03
Wye Garth
High Cocklake
Stwarth Gill
Dale Tongue
Dale Gill
1100
Wyegarth Gill
1200
02
Thornthwaite ruin
1300
Snowfell End
1400
1500
1600
Knoutberry
Knott
x1523
Artlegarth Beck
source of the R. Lune
High Stoups
01
Long Gill
Adamthwaite
Little Harter Fell

marshy patch on the broad saddle between the two tops. Tracks along the contour lines of Randygill Top are made by sheep, and one conveniently provides a short-cut towards Stockless.

Randygill Top provides an excellent viewpoint at the heart of the Howgills, and from there it is mostly downhill, with only a gradual climb up to the OS column on Green Bell. A faint path follows the crest of a broad ridge over Stockless (1860ft/568m) then heads direct for the top of Green Bell (1985ft/605m).

From Green Bell our route descends to the remains of a sheepfold - the only rudimentary means of shelter since leaving the sheepfolds at Bowderdale Head. The depression provides the source of the River Lune and beyond we go on to Knoutberry.

(High Level Route continues on Map 3.4)

Map 3.4

High Level Route

The descent from Knoutberry follows obvious sheep tracks around the headwaters of Wyegarth Gill and the isolated Thornthwaite (ruin). An improving track leads down to Kilnmire and the farm road meets the highway at Lockholme Beck.

Cross over the old bridge, now closed to traffic, and go up into Ravenstonedale by its old main street.

(High Level Route continues on Map 3.5)

Map 3.5

Ravenstonedale is the very epitome of a Westmorland settlement - a delightful, compact, stone-built village nestling in a fold of the hills and moors. It has two hotels - the Black Swan and the King's Head -and two chapels, but its pride is the parish church.

St. Oswald's was rebuilt in 1744 on the site of an earlier foundation. The earlier church had a separate bell-tower, resting on pillars, from which hung a 'refuge bell': if anyone guilty of a crime punishable by death escaped to Ravenstonedale and managed to toll the bell he was free from arrest by the King's officers. The privilege was abolished in the reign of James I in the early 17c. The bell-tower stood on the N side of the church, and apart from it, but in 1738 it had fallen down, so a new tower was built at the W end of the present church.

The church's interior has several unusual features. Box pews are arranged college-wise, so that the two halves of the congregation face each other, N and S. Few churches in the country are arranged in this way: it was a Georgian (Protestant) fashion. The oak for the pews came from Lowther Castle (near Eamont Bridge): some of the panel-

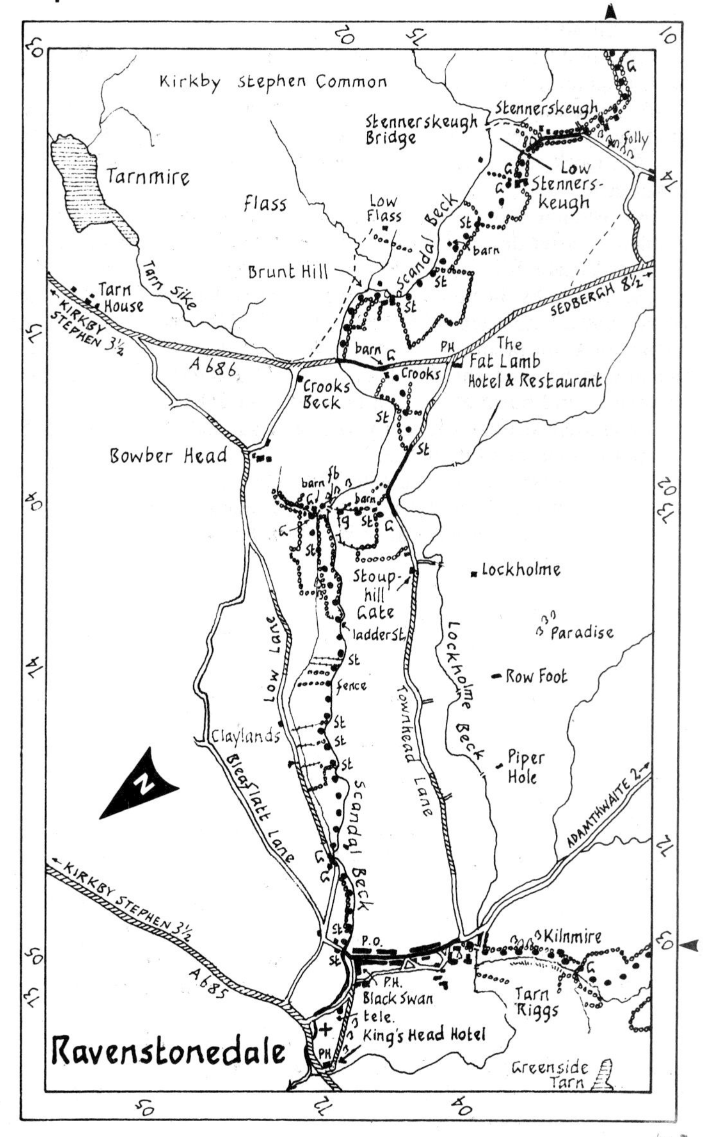
Kirkby Stephen Common
Tarnmire
Flass
Low Flass
Stennerskeugh Bridge
Stennerskeugh
Folly
Low Stennerskeugh
Scandal Beck
barn
Brunt Hill
Tarn Sike
Tarn House
KIRKBY STEPHEN 3½
SEDBERGH 8½
A 686
PH
The Fat Lamb Hotel & Restaurant
Crooks
Crooks Beck
Bowber Head
barn
fb
Stouphill Gate
ladder St
Lockholme
Paradise
Row Foot
Lockholme Beck
Low Lane
fence
Claylands
Bleaflatt Lane
Townhead Lane
Piper Hole
ADAMTHWAITE 2
N
KIRKBY STEPHEN 3½
A685
P.O.
Kilnmire
P.H.
Black Swan
tele.
King's Head Hotel
Tarn Riggs
Ravenstonedale
Greenside Tarn

ling is Elizabethan.

In the middle of the nave, on the N side, is a three-decker pulpit, with a sounding board. Royal Arms of George II hang on the S wall. A 1610 hourglass, a tuning fork for the choir and a pitch pipe for starting hymns are on display in a case under the gallery. A painted wooden clock face dated 1719, from the old church, stands in the tower aisle.

An E window is particularly interesting as it commemorates the last woman to suffer death in England in the cause of the Protestant faith. She was Elizabeth Gaunt, daughter of Anthony Fothergill of Brownber, sentenced by the notorious Judge Jefferies. William Penn was one of the crowd who attended her execution. In 1683 she had provided refuge for a conspirator of the Rye House Plot, but two years later he denounced her and she was tried at the Old Bailey, found guilty, sentenced, and burnt at Tyburn on 4 October 1685.

The churchyard has a lovely yew tree, a sundial of 1700 by the S porch and a curious tombstone:

> 1786. Here lies a wife Mary Metcalf
> Where I was born, or when, it matters not
> To whom related, or by whom begot.

High Level Route

The Scandal Beck flows down from Wild Boar Fell and our route from Ravenstonedale follows it to its source.

From the T-junction in the village street turn E along Bleaflatt Lane and once over the beck climb a stile and follow the true R bank of the stream, keeping to the edge of the meadows. You come to a ladder stile in a somewhat terminal state and beyond this the right-of-way aims diagonally to a fence stile beyond a copse, crosses an open ditch and proceeds to a gate in a walled lane, there turning R, then through the next gate and passes round a barn to a strong footbridge. The whole stretch just described would be greatly improved for the benefit of all interested parties if the way could continue down the pasture directly to the barn. The footpath rises from the footbridge to another barn before joining Townhead Lane. Follow the lane for a short way then go across two fields L aiming for Crooks Barn on the A686 Sedbergh-Kirkby Stephen road, just N of the Fat Lamb hotel and restaurant.

Go N along the main road for a short way then turn off alongside a wall on the R, following the L bank of Scandal Beck past Brunt Hill and through fields to Skennerskeugh.

(High Level Route continues on Map 3.6)

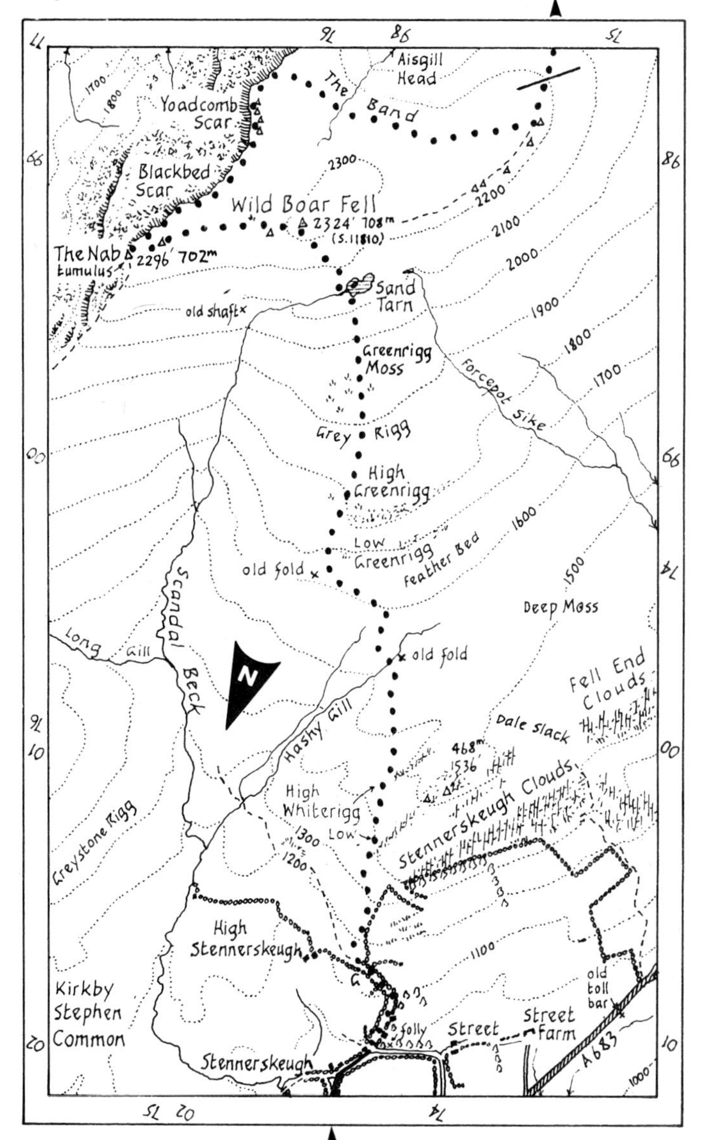
Aisgill Head
The Band
Yoadcomb Scar
Blackbed Scar
Wild Boar Fell
2324' 708m
(S.11810)
The Nab
2296' 702m
tumulus
Sand Tarn
old shaft
Greenrigg Moss
Forcepot Sike
Grey Rigg
High Greenrigg
Low Greenrigg
Feather Bed
old fold
Deep Moss
Scandal Beck
Long Gill
N
old fold
Hasky Gill
Fell End Clouds
Dale Slack
468m
1536'
High Whiterigg
Low
Stennerskeugh Clouds
Greystone Rigg
High Stennerskeugh
Kirkby Stephen Common
old toll bar
Street Farm
Street
folly
Stennerskeugh
A683
2300
2200
2100
2000
1900
1800
1700
1600
1500
1300
1200
1100
1000

Map 3.6
High Level Route

At Stennerskeugh you cross the famous Dent Fault which raises the Carboniferous limestone high above the Ordovician and Silurian rocks. **The Clouds**, otherwise known as Stennerskeugh and Fell End Clouds, dominate the scene on the approach to Wild Boar Fell. The limestone pavements form one of three best examples of this feature in Westmorland - we have already seen the other two - being of interest geologically but also having an outstanding flora, including many rare and uncommon plants.

Most of The Clouds is common land, heavily grazed by sheep and fell ponies, which restricts the growth of the plants to inaccessible grikes in the pavements, on scars and in areas of scree. Ash and ivy are most abundant in the grikes, although hawthorn, rowan, sycamore, raspberry and stone bramble also occur. Part of the area has been excluded from grazing and a small woodland of ash, sycamore, rowan, Scot's pine and sessile oak has developed.

Seventeen species of fern have been found by the botanists on the pavement of The Clouds, including the scarce rigid buckler-fern, holly fern, which is extremely uncommon in northern England, and two other uncommon species, limestone fern and green spleenwort. Almost as many herbs have been found, including the uncommon narrow-leaved bitter-cress, lily-of-the-valley, limestone bedstraw and spring sandwort. On the heavily grazed limestone grassland around the pavements is found the rare bird's-foot sedge, mountain everlasting, fairy flax, wild thyme, spring sandwort, eyebright, heath bedstraw and slender bedstraw. Tormentil, heather and bilberry grow on the acid grasslands away from the limestone outcrops.

Above Stennerskeugh Clouds the Great Scar Limestone gives way to grits at Low Whiterigg and High Whiterigg then to younger limestones above the source of Hashy Gill where shakeholes have been formed. At Low Greenrigg and High Greenrigg are outcrops of the millstone grit layers, which also cap Wild Boar Fell and neighbouring Swarth Fell.

Skennerskeugh is a delightful settlement off the main road. Go up the track between walls and at the fell gate turn R through an area of shakeholes and follow the wall on the obvious ascending track heading S, which disappears beyond the sheepfold in Hashy Gill. Aim for the second sheepfold on Low Greenrigg and then there is a steady pull up over the shoulder of High Greenrigg across boggy Greenrigg Moss to Sand Tarn, the source of Scandal Beck. Cross at its outlet. Dilligent searching hereabouts will reveal partially complete millstones: we are at the level of the millstone

Map 3.7

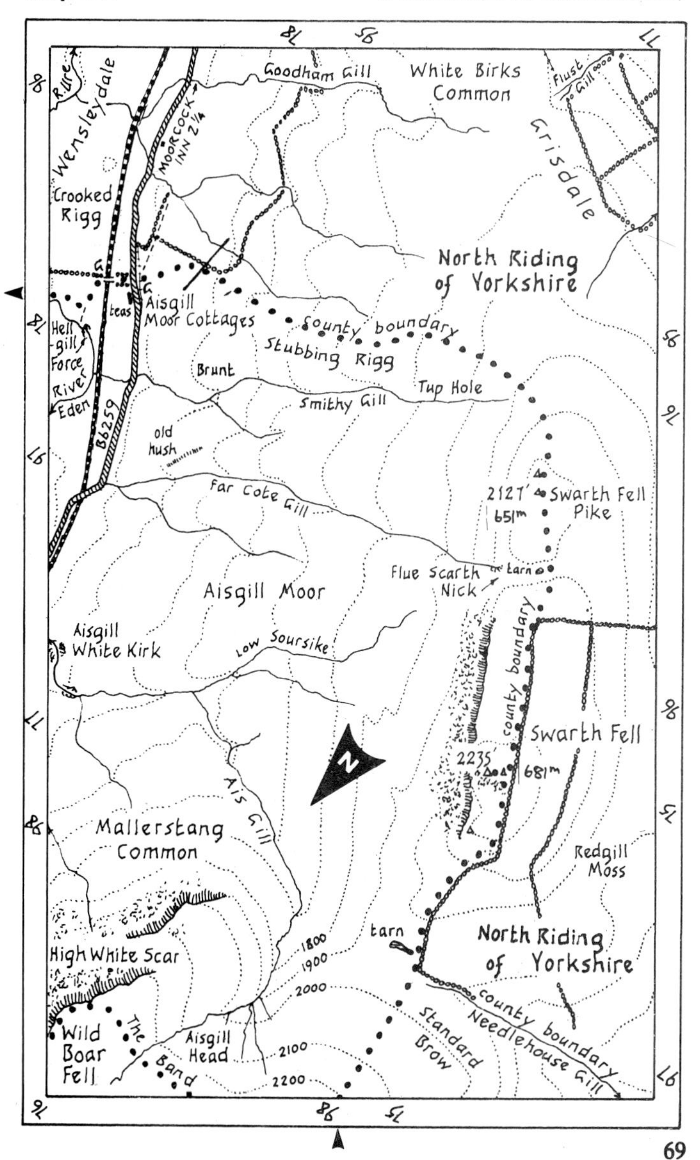
Goodham Gill
White Birks Common
Flust Gill
Grisdale
Wensleydale
MOORCOCK INN 2¼
Crooked Rigg
North Riding of Yorkshire
Aisgill Moor Cottages
teas
county boundary
Stubbing Rigg
Hell-gill Force
River Eden
Brunt
Tup Hole
Smithy Gill
B6259
old hush
Far Cote Gill
2127'
651m
Swarth Fell Pike
Flue Scarth Nick
tarn
Aisgill Moor
Aisgill White Kirk
Low Soursike
county boundary
Swarth Fell
2235'
681m
N
Ais Gill
Mallerstang Common
Redgill Moss
1800
1900
2000
2100
2200
tarn
North Riding of Yorkshire
High White Scar
Wild Boar Fell
The Band
Aisgill Head
Standard Brow
county boundary
Needlehouse Gill
78
95
77
96
97
98
75

Map 3.8

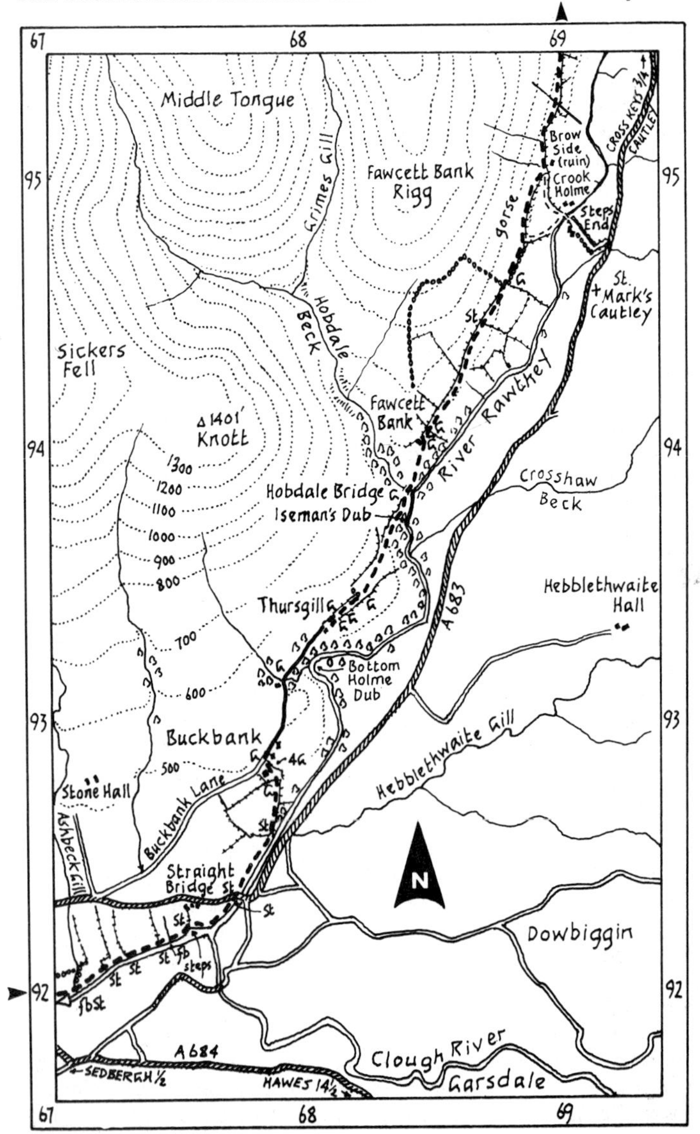

67
68
69
Middle Tongue
Grimes Gill
Fawcett Bank Rigg
gorse
Brow Side (ruin)
Crook Holme
Steps End
CROSS KEYS 3/4
CAUTLEY
95
St. Mark's Cautley
Hobdale Beck
Sickers Fell
River Rawthey
Fawcett Bank
1401' Knott
94
1300
1200
1100
1000
900
800
700
600
500
Hobdale Bridge
Iseman's Dub
Crosshaw Beck
Thursgill
Hebblethwaite Hall
Bottom Holme Dub
A683
93
Buckbank
Hebblethwaite Gill
Stone Hall
Buckbank Lane
Ashbeck Gill
Straight Bridge
N
Dowbiggin
steps
92
fb St
A684
SEDBERGH 1/2
HAWES 14 1/2
Clough River
Garsdale

grit, above the level of the Skennerskeugh limestone.

It is now a straightforward climb directly to the OS column on the top of Wild Boar Fell (2324ft/708m). A tour of the summit plateau is in order, and a cairned path can be followed southward to Standard Brow, but our route runs E to examine the tumulus on The Nab (2296ft/702m) and the fine escarpment overlooking Mallerstang before continuing across The Band to reach Standard Brow.

(High Level Route continues on Map 3.7)

Map 3.7

High Level Route

There are no navigational problems on this stretch.

It is downhill all the way from Wild Boar Fell (obviously, since this is the highest point!). At Standard Brow we meet a wall at a corner beside a tarn: the county boundary comes up Needlehouse Gill and we follow it alongside the wall over Swarth Fell (2235ft/681m) and leave the wall at another corner (though still following the county boundary) past another tiny tarn over Swarth Fell Pike (2127ft/651m).

We trend eastwards from here, still following the line of the county boundary, down to Aisgill Moor Cottages on the B6259 road in the upper part of the Mallerstang valley.

(High Level Route continues on Map 4.1)

Map 3.8

Low Level Route

The Rawthey Way keeps to the bank of the river and soon meets the A683 Sedbergh-Kirkby Stephen road. Cross over the road by the 17c single arched, high and narrow Straight Bridge and continue along the bank of the river through the next field, then alongside the next field to Buckbank Lane. Follow the lane from Buckbank to Thursgill.

There are no navigational problems as our route continues at this level above the river, a lovely walk below the flanks of the Howgills.

Across the valley, on the main road, is St. Mark's Church, Cautley. Designed by William Butterfield, it was built in the Decorated Gothic style in 1847.

(Low Level Route continues on Map 3.9)

Map 3.9

Low Level Route

Our path continues as before at a general level above the Rawthey, curving into the coombe of the Cautley Holme Beck and giving a view of Cautley Spout. Having crossed a footbridge we join the path that goes L up to

Map 3.9

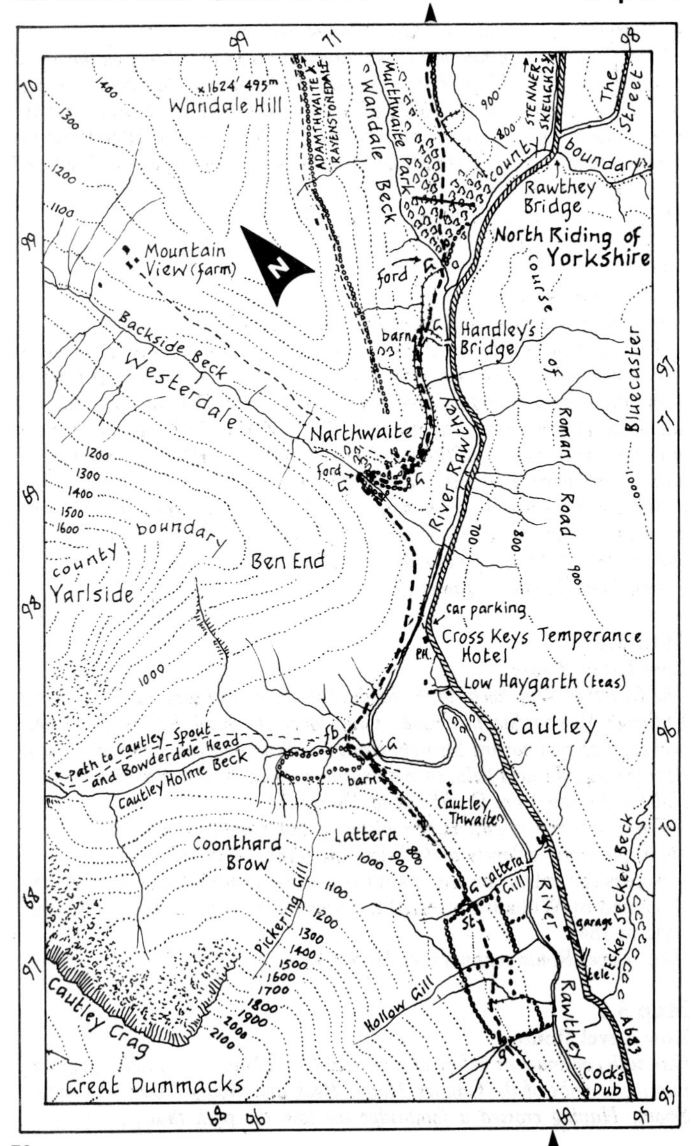
Wandale Hill
x1624' 495m
ADAMTHWAITE RAVENSTONEDALE
Wandale Beck
Murthwaite Park
STENNER-SKEUGH
The Street
county boundary
Rawthey Bridge
North Riding of Yorkshire
Mountain View (farm)
ford
barn
Handley's Bridge
course of Roman Road
Bluecaster
Backside Beck
Westerdale
Narthwaite
ford
River Rawthey
boundary
county
Ben End
Yarlside
car parking
Cross Keys Temperance Hotel
P.H.
Low Haygarth (teas)
Cautley
path to Cautley Spout and Bowderdale Head
fb
Cautley Holme Beck
barn
Cautley Thwaite
Coonthard Brow
Lattera
Pickering Gill
Lattera Gill
River Rawthey
garage
Ecker Secket Beck
tele.
Hollow Gill
A683
Cautley Crag
Great Dummacks
Cock's Dub

Cautley Spout and Bowderdale Head (where you can join the High Level Route on Map 3.2), but we turn R on it towards the Cross Keys hotel. This temperance hotel was built in 1732 and is owned by the National Trust. We do not cross the footbridge over the Rawthey to the Cross Keys but carry on to ford the Backside Beck and climb up to Narthwaite.

Follow the Narthwaite farm road, but just short of its descent to Handley's Bridge, by a barn, take the path through the pasture to a fixed gate and a ford of the Wandale Beck. A problem is likely to exist here in wet weather: the beck may flood and prevent a crossing. If this is the case you will have to cross Handley's Bridge, go up the main road to Rawthey Bridge (crossing the county boundary back into Westmorland) and turn R and up The Street to the Uldale turn-off.

Having crossed the Wandale Beck you enter the woodland of Murthwaite Park and go up the spur to the farm.

The Rawthey flows in a valley of Silurian rocks and the Howgills on your left hand side are formed of the younger, overlying Brathay Flags and Coniston Grits, except where complex faulting has laid bare the mudstones and volcanics at Cautley Crag. The valley, and its continuation north-easterly followed by the line of the A683 road towards Kirkby Stephen, is on the line of the famous Dent Fault, which raises up older rocks on the right hand side.

On the line of the fault, between the Rawthey and the Wandale Beck, at Murthwaite, a spur of boulder clay and mudstones occurs, a sole deposit of glacial drift in this valley standing on the Silurian shales. It supports an ancient Pennine oakwood, scarce in this area. Down by the two streams on the wettest and most base rich soils are strips of ash, wych elm, bird cherry and alder woodland. Oak, ash and hazel occupy the slopes above, with sessile oak, and higher up the slopes, on drier land, birch and hazel are more extensive.

(Low Level Route continues on Map 3.10)

Map 3.10

Low Level Route

The continuation of the Rawthey Way is without accommodation for a long way: walkers may either camp at Murthwaite or possibly near Green Slack before crossing over to Lunds or the Moorcock inn at the head of Wensleydale.

The old zig-zag path down to the main road is called Sally Brow and is an interesting feature, and its continuation opposite, up a long narrow pasture, is a RUPP leading to The Street, a minor road crossing the fell above and parallel to the main road A683. The Street is of Roman origin, but it is 'lost' after crossing the Rawthey on its way down the valley.

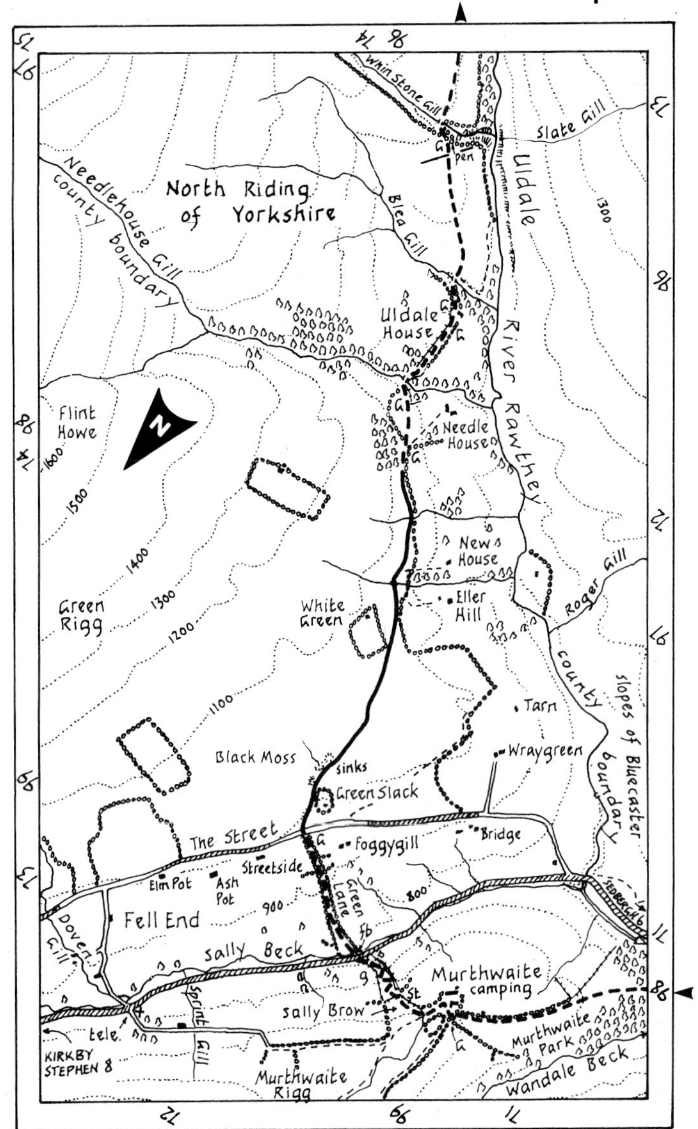
Whin Stone Gill
Slate Gill
pen
Uldale
North Riding
of Yorkshire
Needlehouse Gill
county boundary
Blea Gill
1300
Uldale
House
River Rawthey
Flint
Howe
N
Needle
House
1600
1500
1400
News
House
Roger Gill
Eller
Hill
Green
Rigg
1300
White
Green
1200
county boundary
1100
Tarn
slopes of Bluecaster
Black Moss
sinks
Wraygreen
Green Slack
The Street
Foggygill
Bridge
Streetside
Elm Pot
Ash
Pot
Green
Lane
800
Fell End
900
Doven Gill
fb
Sally Beck
Murthwaite
camping
St
Sprint Gill
Sally Brow
tele
KIRKBY
STEPHEN 8
Murthwaite
Park
Wandale Beck
Murthwaite
Rigg
SEDBERGH 6

Although there is a footpath off The Street via Tarn, Eller Hill and Needlehouse we feel that the direct way via an old drove road up the upper valley of the Rawthey (Uldale) to Grisdale is more practical and not without interest. (This is the first and only time you will find us recommending a road in preference to a parallel convenient footpath.) From Fell End, on The Street, pass round Green Slack Outward Bound Centre on a lane over Black Moss past several shakeholes to Needlehouse, where the lane stops. A track continues through the gate and enters Yorkshire and the Yorkshire Dales National Park again at the crossing of Needlehouse Gill and continues to Uldale House. (Uldale House was built as an inn in 1828, but never used as such as a projected road, which was to be served by the inn, was never built beyond Needlehouse Gill and the county boundary.) After Blea Gill continue on the old drove road - sadly for horsemen downgraded to a footpath now that we are into 'old' Yorkshire -to a sheepfold by the wall ahead at Whin Stone Gill.

(Low Level Route continues on Map 3.11)

Map 3.11

Low Level Route

From Whin Stone Gill the right-of-way takes a direct line to the gate in the wall on Holmes Moss Hill. However, we prefer a lower line following a shepherd's path to the enclosures and barn where the River Rawthey cuts a gorge through the limestone band. The path rises up the bank to the gate in the wall to meet the right-of-way.

From the gate in the wall on Holmes Moss Hill there is no path on the ground contouring to the line of sinkholes, but one materialises approaching Dover Gill. We start the descent of Grisdale to enclosed land and follow the wall on the edge of Grisdale Common. The OS have decided to call this valley and scattered settlement Grisedale, according to their 1:50,000 scale Landranger map.

(Low Level Route continues on Map 3.12)

Map 3.12

Low Level Route

Our path keeps alongside a wall on the edge of Grisdale Common, passing an old limekiln and a line of shakeholes. Although there is a footpath crossing the Swarth Fell ridge between Ewe Hill and Turner Hill the continuation of the old drove road via South Lunds Pasture is clearer in poor visibility and may be of value in reaching the public telephone on the B6259 or the Moorcock Inn (B&B) at the junction of the B6259 and the A684. Where the old drove road passes through a gate in the wall S of Turner Hill it becomes a bridleway again as far as the B6259.

Map 3.11

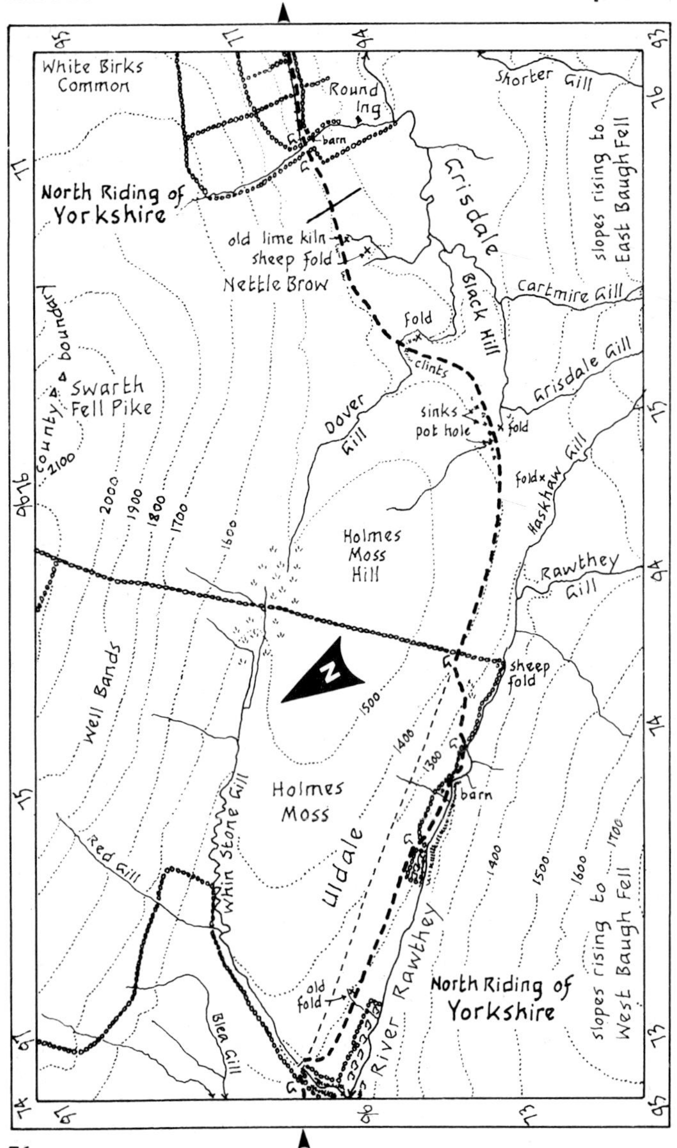

White Birks Common
Round Ing
barn
North Riding of Yorkshire
Grisdale
Shorter Gill
slopes rising to East Baugh Fell
old lime kiln
sheep fold
Nettle Brow
Black Hill
Cartmire Gill
fold
clints
Grisdale Gill
county boundary
Swarth Fell Pike
2100
2000
1900
1800
1700
1600
Dover Gill
sinks
pot hole
fold
Haskhaw Gill
fold
Holmes Moss Hill
Rawthey Gill
sheep fold
Well Bands
1500
1400
1300
barn
Holmes Moss
Whin Stone Gill
Red Gill
Uldale
River Rawthey
1400
1500
1600
1700
slopes rising to West Baugh Fell
old fold
Blea Gill
North Riding of Yorkshire

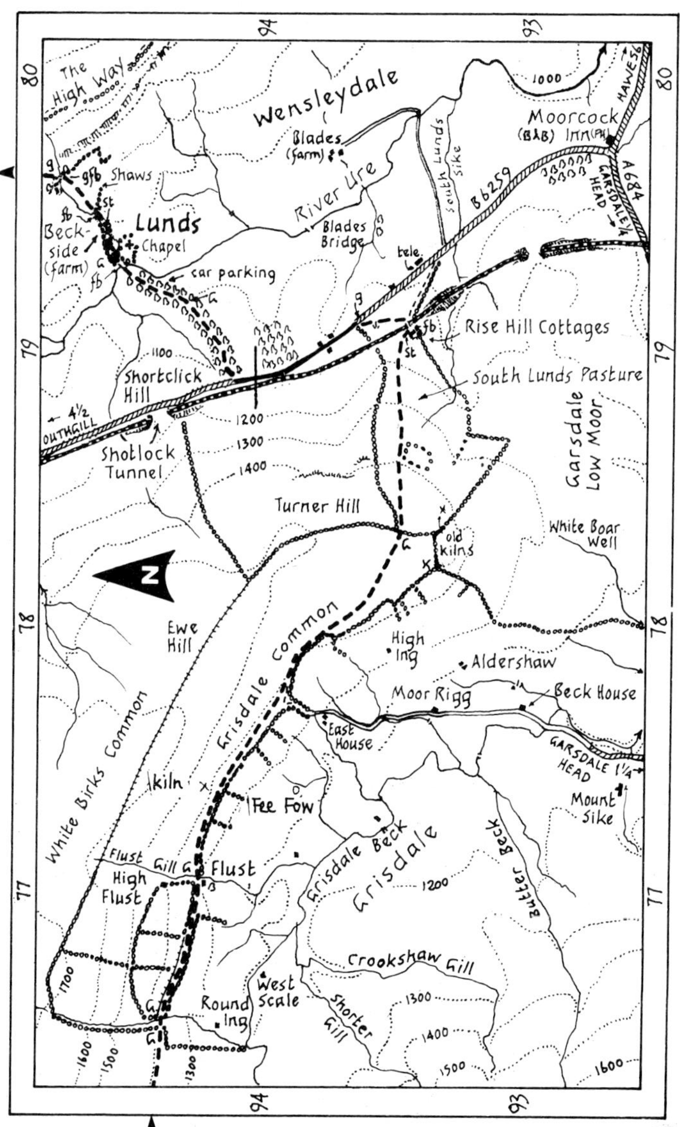
The High Way
Wensleydale
Blades (farm)
River Ure
Blades Bridge
South Lunds Sike
Moorcock (B&B) Inn (PH)
HAWES 6
A684
GARSDALE HEAD 1/4
B6259
1000
Shaws
Lunds
Beck-side (farm)
Chapel
car parking
tele
Rise Hill Cottages
South Lunds Pasture
1100
Shortclick Hill
4½ OUTHGILL
Shotlock Tunnel
1200
1300
1400
Turner Hill
Garsdale Low Moor
White Boar Well
old kilns
Ewe Hill
Grisdale Common
High Ing
Aldershaw
Moor Rigg
Beck House
East House
GARSDALE HEAD 1¼
White Birks Common
kiln
Fee Fow
Mount Sike
Grisdale Beck
Grisdale
Butter Beck
Flust Gill
Flust
High Flust
Crookshaw Gill
West Scale
Round Ing
Shorter Gill
1700
1600
1500
1300
1400
1500
1600
80
79
78
77
94
93

We cross the Settle-Carlisle railway line (constructed by the Midland Railway Company and opened on 1 May 1876) by a footbridge (turn R for the TCB or the Moorcock) and then L down to the B6259 Moorcock-Mallerstang road. Go along the road for a short way, then take the driveway on the R, fringed by trees, down to Lunds.
(Low Level Route continues on Map 4.1)

Wharton Hall Gatehouse.

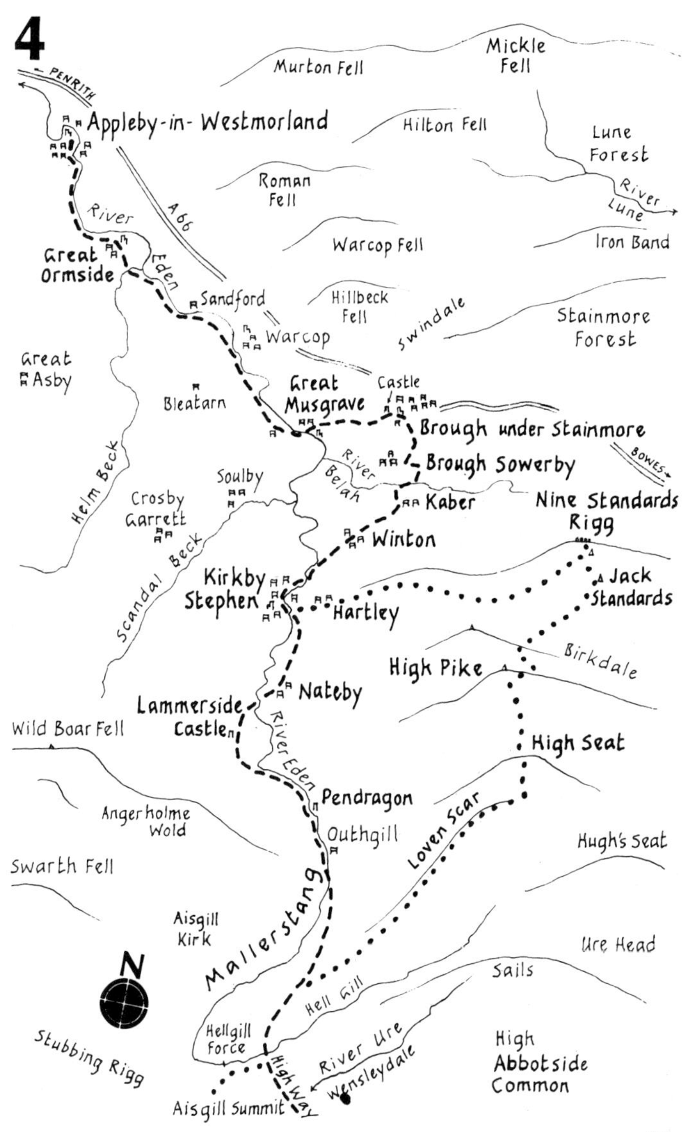
4
PENRITH
Appleby-in-Westmorland
Murton Fell
Mickle Fell
Hilton Fell
Lune Forest
Roman Fell
River Lune
River Eden
A66
Warcop Fell
Iron Band
Great Ormside
Sandford
Hillbeck Fell
Swindale
Stainmore Forest
Warcop
Great Asby
Bleatarn
Great Musgrave
Castle
Brough under Stainmore
Brough Sowerby
BOWES
River Belah
Soulby
Crosby Garrett
Kaber
Nine Standards Rigg
Helm Beck
Winton
Scandal Beck
Kirkby Stephen
Jack Standards
Hartley
Birkdale
High Pike
Nateby
Lammerside Castle
Wild Boar Fell
High Seat
River Eden
Pendragon
Angerholme Wold
Loven Scar
Outhgill
Swarth Fell
Hugh's Seat
Aisgill Kirk
Mallerstang
Ure Head
N
Sails
Hell Gill
Hellgill Force
Stubbing Rigg
High Abbotside Common
River Ure
Wensleydale
High Way
Aisgill Summit

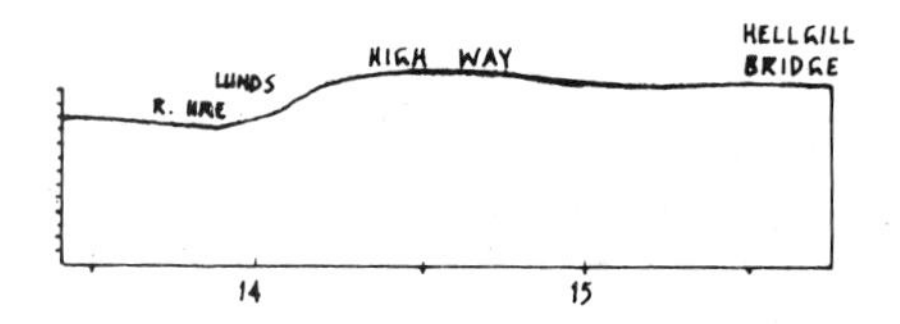
HELLGILL
BRIDGE
HIGH WAY
LUNDS
R. URE
14
15

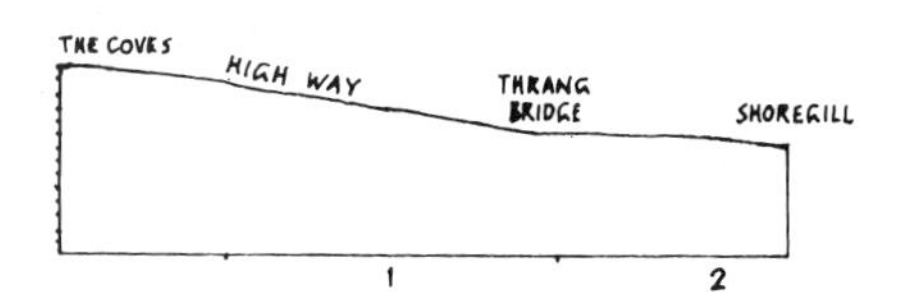
THE COVES
HIGH WAY
THRANG
BRIDGE
SHOREGILL
1
2

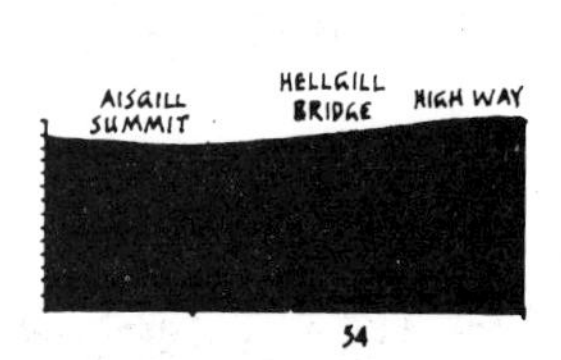
AISGILL
SUMMIT
HELLGILL
BRIDGE
HIGH WAY
54

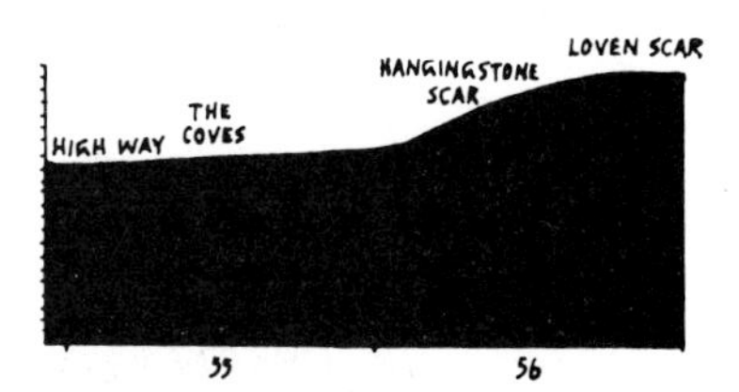
LOVEN SCAR
HANGINGSTONE
SCAR
THE
COVES
HIGH WAY
55
56

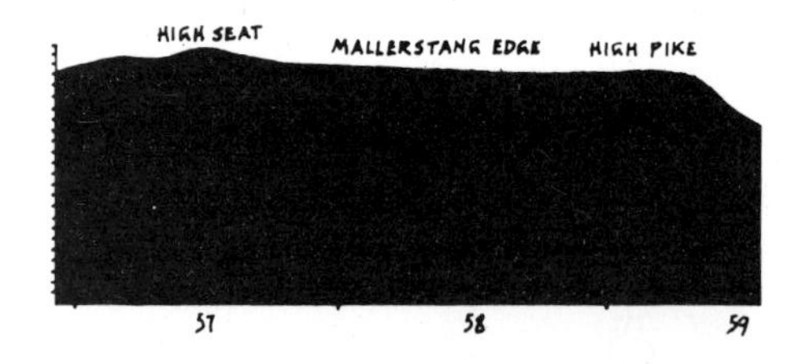
HIGH SEAT
MALLERSTANG EDGE
HIGH PIKE
57
58
59

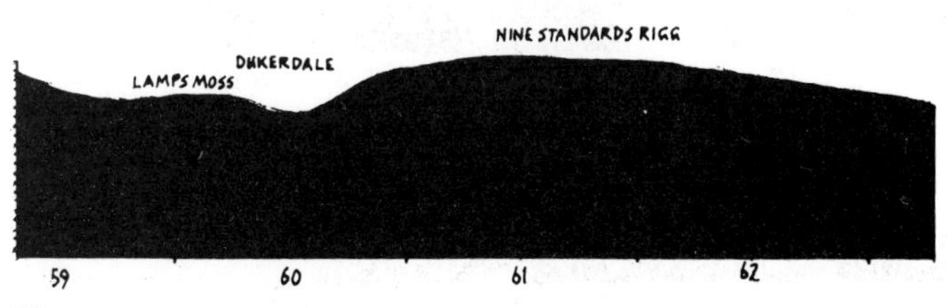
NINE STANDARDS RIGG
DUKERDALE
LAMPS MOSS
59
60
61
62

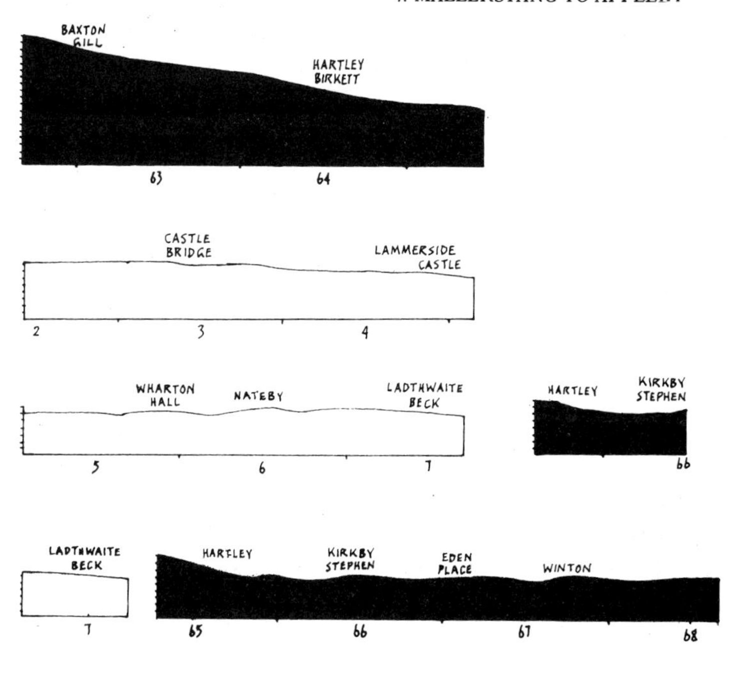
BAXTON GILL
HARTLEY BIRKETT
63
64
CASTLE BRIDGE
LAMMERSIDE CASTLE
2
3
4
WHARTON HALL
NATEBY
LADTHWAITE BECK
5
6
7
HARTLEY
KIRKBY STEPHEN
66
LADTHWAITE BECK
7
HARTLEY
KIRKBY STEPHEN
EDEN PLACE
WINTON
65
66
67
68

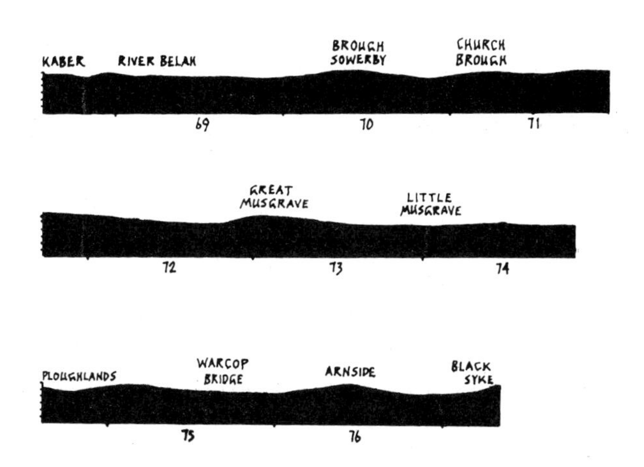
KABER
RIVER BELAH
BROUGH SOWERBY
CHURCH BROUGH
69
70
71
GREAT MUSGRAVE
LITTLE MUSGRAVE
72
73
74
PLOUGHLANDS
WARCOP BRIDGE
ARNSIDE
BLACK SYKE
75
76

4. Mallerstang to Appleby

The River Eden rises above Mallerstang Common on Black Fell Moss (2257ft/688m) and flows NW for 67 miles/108km through Kirkby Stephen and Appleby to Carlisle and the Solway. It is a clean river providing good fishing for salmon, trout, and grayling and it flows through a different kind of country to the Lake District and the moors we have just trod: the area of the Eden valley has only half the rainfall of the mountains to the W and its rich green agricultural land is suited to cultivation and stock rearing. The villages of the Eden valley are largely of New Red Sandstone with roofs slated with sandstone or millstone, giving the buildings a sturdy heavy look.

A strategic route since early times between the Scottish borders and York, the Eden valley was fortified by the Romans and later the Normans at Brough, Appleby, Brougham, Penrith and Carlisle. Our route passes the castles at the first three places and also passes the castles of Pendragon and Lammerside in Mallerstang.

On the border with Westmorland and Yorkshire, where our High Level Route runs, once stood a stone pillar - Lady's Pillar - which had been erected in 1664 by Lady Anne Clifford to perpetuate the memory of Sir Hugh de Morville. Sir Hugh had participated in the murder of Thomas a Becket, Archbishop of Canterbury, for which crime Sir Hugh suffered forfeiture of his estates. Today only Hugh's Seat perpetuates that memory.

Coal, copper and lead were mined in Mallerstang and smelted on the spot for many centuries, but by 1884 the lead and copper were largely exhausted. Today all signs of the smelt mills have disappeared and there are only a few signs of old coal pits on the moorlands.

The **High Level Route** from Aisgill Summit, over High Seat, High Pike and Nine Standards Rigg follows the same geological sequence as over Wild Boar Fell and Swarth Fell: alternating layers of Great Scar Limestone with younger limestones and millstone grits and other grits. The distance to Kirkby Stephen is 13 miles/21km.

The **Low Level Route** from Lunds follows the line of the Carboniferous limestones down to Kirkby Stephen keeping close to the banks of the Eden, a distance of 10 miles/16km.

Kirkby Stephen is a good place to stop for accommodation as the next suitable place down the Eden is at Appleby, a distance of 15 miles /24km. Our route through Kirkby Stephen, Winton and Kaber is along the edge of the Carboniferous Limestones and the Lower

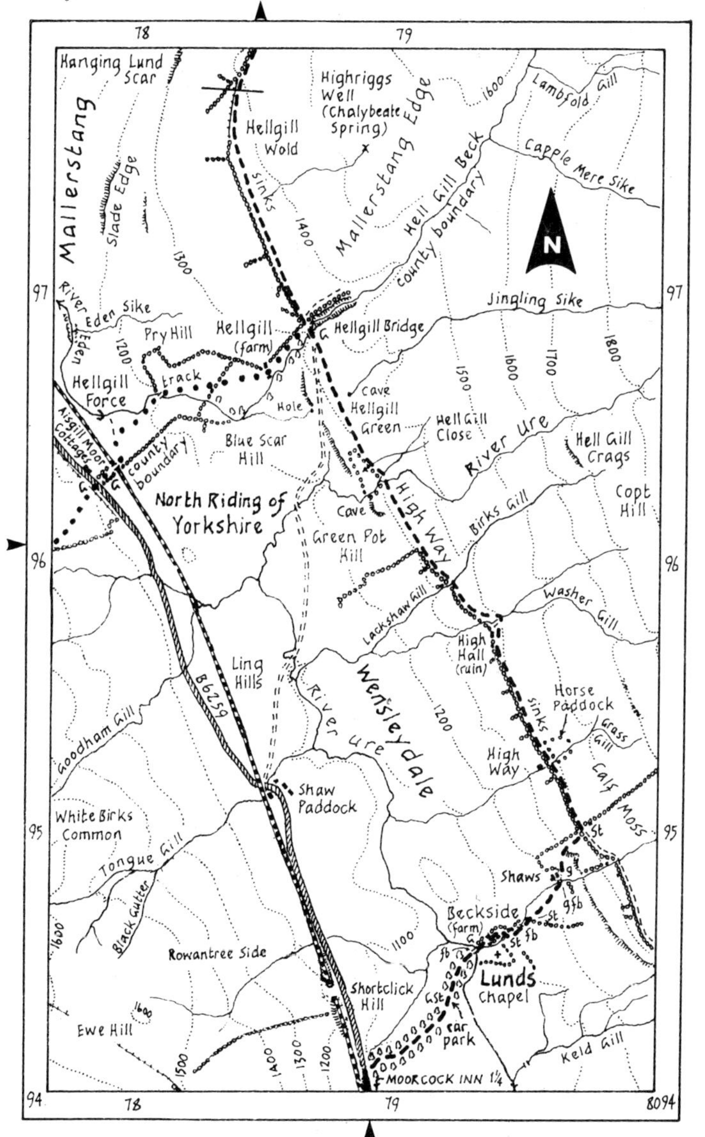
Hanging Lund Scar
Mallerstang
Slade Edge
Highriggs Well (Chalybeate Spring)
Hellgill Wold
sinks
Mallerstang Edge
Hell Gill Beck
county boundary
Lambfold Gill
Capple Mere Sike
N
River Eden
Eden Sike
Pry Hill
Hellgill (farm)
Hellgill Bridge
Jingling Sike
track
Hellgill Force
Hole
Cave
Hellgill Green
Hell Gill Close
River Ure
Hell Gill Crags
Aisgill Moor Cottages
Blue Scar Hill
North Riding of Yorkshire
Cave
High Way
Birks Gill
Copt Hill
Green Pot Hill
Lackshaw Gill
Washer Gill
High Hall (ruin)
Ling Hills
B6259
River Ure
Wensleydale
Horse Paddock
Grass Gill
Goodham Gill
High Way
Calf Moss
Shaw Paddock
White Birks Common
Tongue Gill
Shaws
Black Gutter
Beckside (farm)
Rowantree Side
Lunds Chapel
Shortclick Hill
car park
Ewe Hill
Keld Gill
MOORCOCK INN 1¼
78
79
80
97
96
95
94
1100
1200
1300
1400
1500
1600
1700
1800

Permian (Penrith) sandstone. Brough Sowerby stands on a cap of sandstone but the remaining distance down the Eden valley is on a layer of boulder clay with alluvial gravels in the valleys between the glacial hillocks.

Map 4.1

Low Level Route

From the B6259 Moorcock-Kirkby Stephen road go down the tree-lined drive to Lunds and the crossing of the River Ure in Wensleydale. Climb up to Shaws (former youth hostel, but still shown on current Landranger maps) to the High Way, an ancient right-of-way traversing high above Wensleydale and Mallerstang.

The route is straightforward beyond Shaws, following the High Way alongside a wall contouring across the fellside. It crosses the infant River Ure and enters Westmorland again at Hell Gill Bridge. Here the High Level Route joins from the L.

The High Way runs past several areas of shakeholes and caves. At Hell Gill Green the Jingling Sike disappears down Jingling Sike Cave, flows underground beneath The High Way and emerges at Jingling Hole some 150yds/m away and 50ft/15m down the fellside. At the county boundary the Hell Gill Beck cuts through the limestone in an impressive gorge. The gorge has been formed on the surface and shows no signs of collapse or underground development: it is an excellent example of surface river erosion in limestone where cave formation is only on a restricted scale.

(Low Level Route continues below as the Common Route)

High Level Route

From Aisgill Moor Cottages on the county boundary beside the B6259, go up the farm track to Hellgill Farm, making a short detour to view the superb waterfall of Hellgill Force, where the infant River Eden falls over a limestone scar.

Follow the track up to the farm and The High Way at Hell Gill Bridge. Here the Low Level Route joins from the R.

(High Level Route continues below as the Common Route)

Common Route

The High Level and Low Level routes run together along The High Way to where the wall ends above Hanging Lund Scar.

(Route continues on Map 4.2)

Map 4.2

High Level Route

At Hanging Lund Scar and the wall end the High Level Route leaves The High Way. The line of ascent from The High Way to the Raven's Nest (landslip) is rather arbitrary, there being no path on the ground. The end of the wall and a group of six shakeholes and potholes called collectively The Coves fix a start point and the escarpment of Hangingstone Scar is the objective.

Hangingstone and High Loven Scars are the highlights of this way to High Seat. The Three Men of Mallerstang may have some historical connections with some people who once lived in the valley below where the River Eden begins its delightful journey to the Solway.
(High Level Route continues on Map 4.3)

Low Level Route

Follow The High Way diagonally down the fellside to Thrang Bridge on the B6259 Moorcock-Kirkby Stephen road. Cross the road and the infant River Eden and follow the L bank of the river downstream to Shoregill. Shoregill is opposite Outhgill, and a footpath from the farm access bridge runs beside the river to give access to the hamlet on the main valley road.
(Low Level Route continues on Map 4.6)

Outhgill is a scattered community containing Mallerstang's church, a chapel and a few farms and cottages. The church of **St. Mary's** has a foundation of *c.* 1131 but the present single-cell structure is mostly of 1663 when it was largely repaired by Lady Anne Clifford. An inscription (renewed) in Roman capitals over the S porch records that she did it 'after it had layne ruinous and decayed some 50 or 60 years'. The small, octagonal font and the Royal coat-of-arms in the chancel also date from 1663. A panelled polygonal pulpit is of 1798 and a bread cupboard next to the S door was for 'Middleton's Charity. 1784'. The N windows and S door date from 1768 when the chapel was restored. Further restorations were done in 1879 and 1909. Lady Anne endowed the chapel with lands she owned at Cautley near Sedbergh, requiring the Curate or Reader to teach the children of the dale to read and write English in the chapel. The key to the church may be obtained from Pendragon House, opposite the church gate, or from the village Post Office.

In the beck N of St. Mary's, opposite Pendragon House, is the remains of an old water-powered paddle wheel. In the village is the **Wesleyan Chapel** of 1878.

Map 4.2

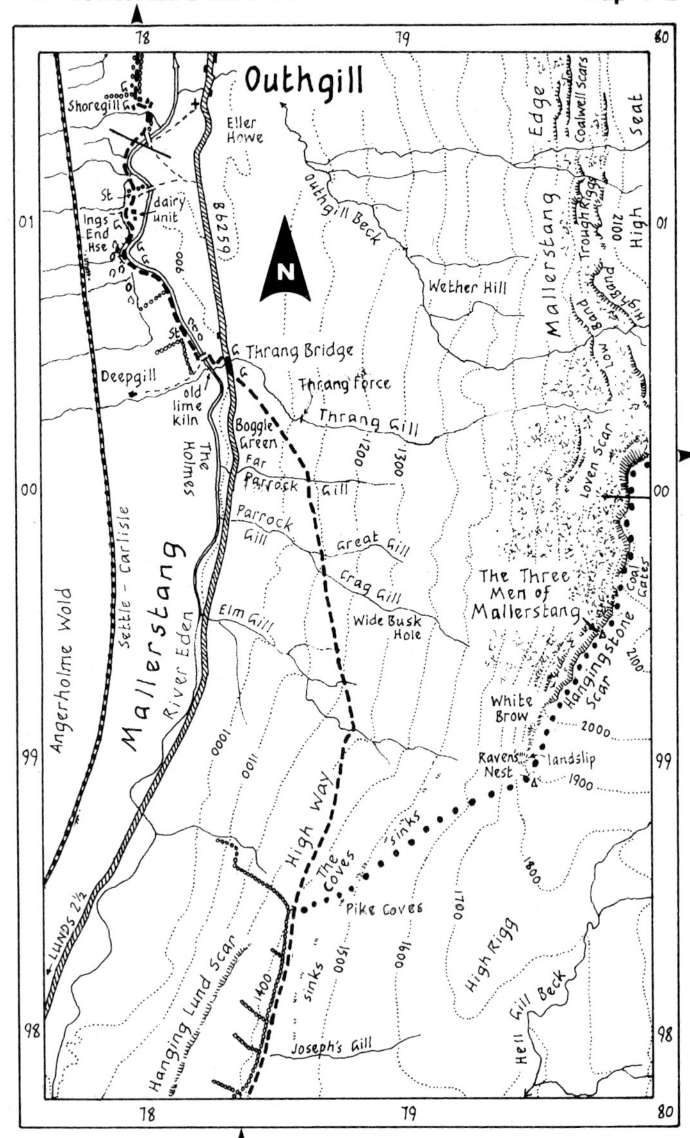
Outhgill
Shoregill
Eller Howe
St
dairy unit
Ings End Hse
B6259
Outhgill Beck
Edge
Coalwell Scars
Seat
Trough Rigg
High
Mallerstang
Wether Hill
High Band
Band
Low
Thrang Bridge
Deepgill
Thrang Force
old lime kiln
Thrang Gill
Boggle Green
The Holmes
Far Parrock Gill
Loven Scar
Parrock Gill
Great Gill
Crag Gill
The Three Men of Mallerstang
Coal Gates
Settle - Carlisle
Angerholme Wold
Mallerstang
River Eden
Elm Gill
Wide Busk Hole
Hangingstone Scar
White Brow
Raven's Nest
landslip
High Way
sinks
The Coves
Pike Coves
LUNDS 2½
High Rigg
Hanging Lund Scar
Hell Gill Beck
Joseph's Gill

Loven Scar, Mallerstang Edge

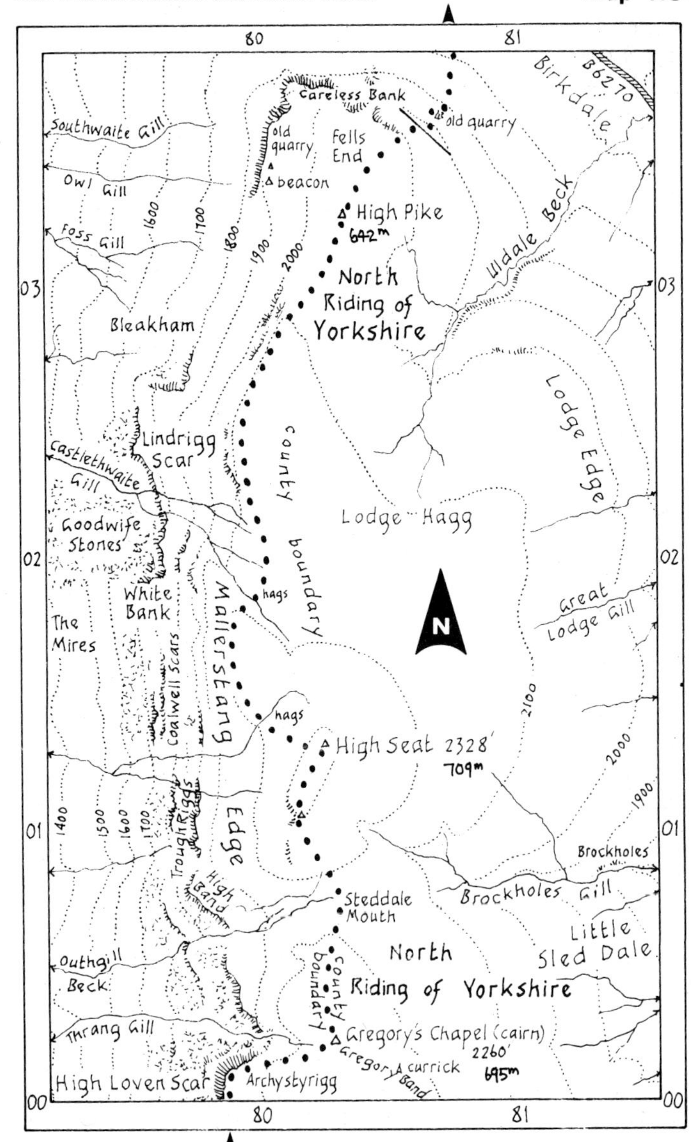
80
81
B6270
Birkdale
Careless Bank
old quarry
old quarry
Fells End
Southwaite Gill
Owl Gill
beacon
High Pike
642m
Foss Gill
1600
1700
1800
1900
2000
Uldale Beck
03
North Riding of Yorkshire
Bleakham
Lodge Edge
Lindrigg Scar
Castlethwaite Gill
county boundary
Lodge Hagg
Goodwife Stones
02
hags
White Bank
The Mires
Mallerstang
Great Lodge Gill
N
Coalwell Scars
hags
2100
High Seat 2328'
709m
2000
1900
1400
1500
1600
1700
Trough Riggs
Edge
01
Brockholes
High Band
Steddale Mouth
Brockholes Gill
Little Sled Dale
Outhgill Beck
North Riding of Yorkshire
county boundary
Thrang Gill
Gregory's Chapel (cairn)
2260'
695m
Gregory Band
currick
High Loven Scar
Archystyrigg
00

Map 4.3
High Level Route

What path there is tends quite naturally to follow Mallerstang Edge, meeting the county boundary with Yorkshire at Gregory's Chapel. (Who was Gregory? Possibly a shepherd - he made a fine cairn.) The imperial OS maps give Gregory's Chapel a height of 2260ft, which when converted gives 689m. The new metric survey 1:10,000 map has elevated the fell to 695m, which when converted equals 2280ft. Follow the watershed N to High Seat (2328ft/709m). Although higher by only a metre (4ft) High Seat challenges the more impressive Wild Boar Fell across the valley.

The High Seat-High Pike plateau, of gritstones and shales with mainly acidic soils, has a number of residual peat hags which shows that the plateau ground was once covered with a deep layer of blanket mire, which has since been lost by erosion. Recolonisation with mat grass, wavy hair grass and sheep's fescue has taken place, and dwarf ling and crowberry attest to the windy conditions experienced on these fells.

From the northernmost of the two cairns on High Seat's top go slightly W then N along Mallerstang Edge, crossing the peat hags at the sources of feeders for Outhgill Beck and Castlethwaite Gill, then go slightly E of N, still keeping the steeper ground to your L, down to the cairn on High Pike (2106ft/642m) and soon down to the B6270 Kirkby Stephen-Keld road. *(High Level Route continues on Map 4.4)*

Map 4.4
High Level Route

The direct line from the B6270 Kirkby Stephen-Keld road to Jack Standards along the county boundary is fraught with bogs. The prudent and more interesting line - the one followed by the public bridleway - keeps to the edge of the limestone pavement slightly W of N and gives you the opportunity of examining the strange canyon at the head of High Dukerdale, just over its enclosing wall. Our line then goes NE straight up to Jack Standards then N across peat hags and juicy bogs to Nine Standards Rigg (2170ft/662m).

The upland immediately N of the B6270 is a complete contrast to the gritstone country to the S of it. The limestone pavement flanking Lamps Moss and the craggy limestone glen of High Dukerdale is the habitat of certain flowers that are rare in northern England and is also the home of some interesting birds.

The limestone pavement is rather open and has a number of shake-holes and sinkholes while the hummocky turf of the sward between is crowned with lichens. This sward is the nesting habitat of probably

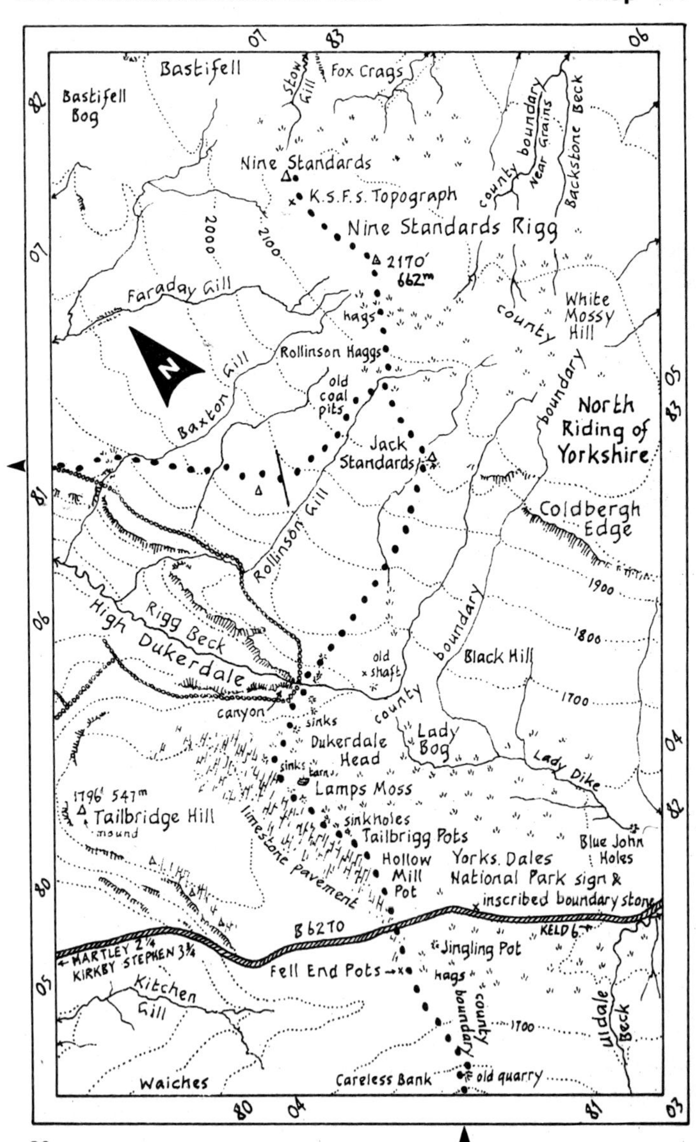

Bastifell
Bastifell Bog
Stow Gill
Fox Crags
Nine Standards
K.S.F.S. Topograph
Nine Standards Rigg
2170'
662m
2000
2100
county boundary
Near Grains
Backstone Beck
Faraday Gill
hags
Rollinson Haggs
White Mossy Hill
county boundary
Baxton Gill
old coal pits
Jack Standards
North Riding of Yorkshire
Rollinson Gill
Coldbergh Edge
1900
1800
Rigg Beck
High Dukerdale
county boundary
old shaft
Black Hill
1700
canyon
sinks
Dukerdale Head
Lady Bog
Lady Dike
sinks
tarn
Lamps Moss
1796' 547m
Tailbridge Hill
mound
limestone Pavement
sinkholes
Tailbrigg Pots
Hollow Mill Pot
Yorks. Dales National Park sign & inscribed boundary stone
Blue John Holes
B6270
KELD 6
MARTLEY 2¼
KIRKBY STEPHEN 3¾
Jingling Pot
Fell End Pots
hags
county boundary
1700
Kitchen Gill
Uldale Beck
Waiches
Careless Bank
old quarry

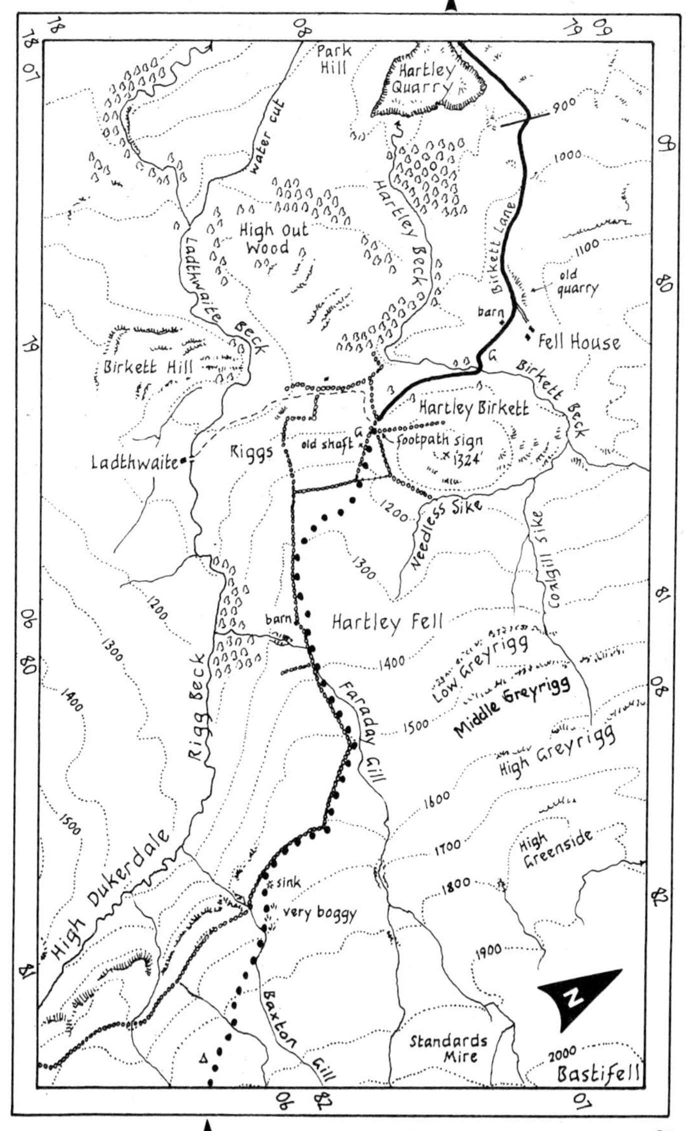
Park Hill
Hartley Quarry
water cut
900
1000
Hartley Beck
Birkett Lane
High Out Wood
1100
old quarry
Ladthwaite Beck
barn
Fell House
Birkett Hill
Birkett Beck
Hartley Birkett
footpath sign
Ladthwaite
Riggs
old shaft
1324'
Needless Sike
1200
1300
Coalgill Sike
barn
Hartley Fell
Low Greyrigg
1400
Rigg Beck
Middle Greyrigg
Faraday Gill
1500
High Greyrigg
1600
High Dukerdale
1700
High Greenside
sink
1800
very boggy
1900
N
Baxton Gill
Standards Mire
2000
Bastifell

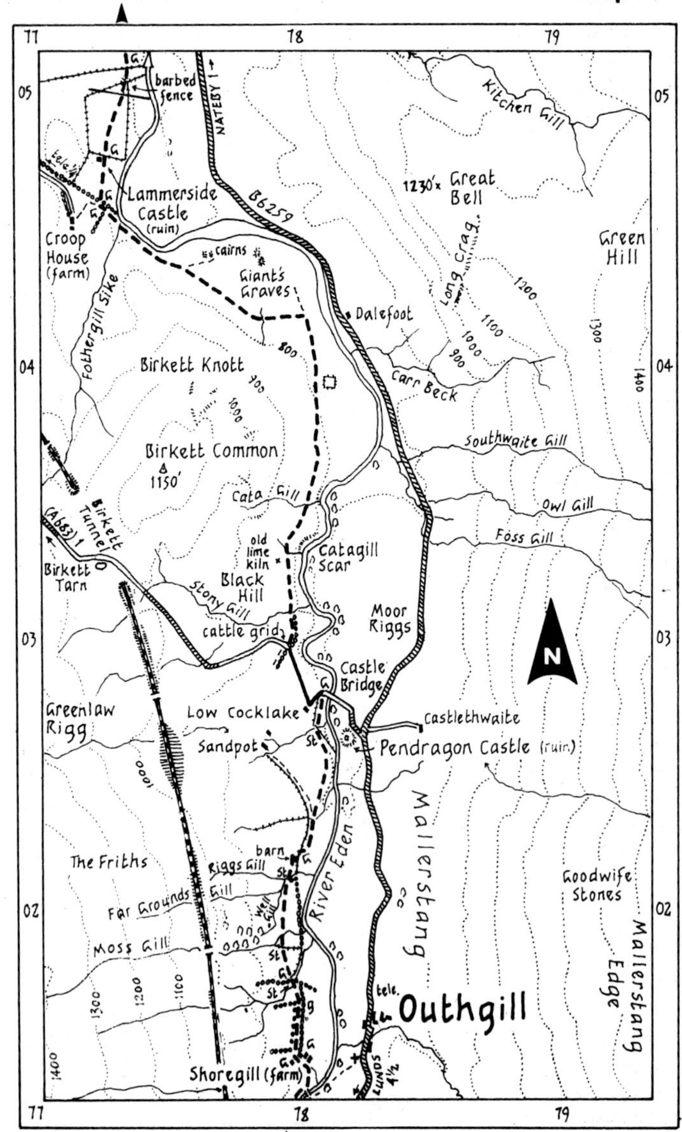
barbed fence
NATEBY 1
Kitchen Gill
Lammerside Castle (ruin)
B6259
1230' Great Bell
Croop House (farm)
cairns
Giant's Graves
Long Crag
Green Hill
Dalefoot
Fothergill Sike
800
1200
1100
1000
900
1300
Birkett Knott
Carr Beck
1400
Southwaite Gill
Birkett Common
1150'
Cata Gill
Owl Gill
Birkett Tunnel
(A683)
Foss Gill
old lime kiln
Catagill Scar
Birkett Tarn
Black Hill
Stony Gill
Moor Riggs
cattle grid
N
Castle Bridge
Greenlaw Rigg
Low Cocklake
Castlethwaite
Sandpot
Pendragon Castle (ruin)
Mallerstang
River Eden
barn
The Friths
Riggs Gill
Goodwife Stones
Far Grounds Gill
Well Gill
Moss Gill
Mallerstang Edge
tele.
Outhgill
Shoregill (farm)
LUNDS 4½
77
78
79
05
04
03
02

the densest population of golden plover now breeding in Great Britain, and there are also dunlin breeding here in an unusual habitat. In some years the population of nesting lapwings also reaches a high level while ring ouzels breed regularly in the shelter of the potholes and shafts. In High Dukerdale can be found bird's-eye primrose, alpine cinquefoil and horseshoe vetch.

The NW top of Nine Standards (2162ft/659m) with its huge cairns of mysterious origin is a turning point as it is the easternmost point on our boundary walk. Between the two summit cairns is a topograph erected by the Kirkby Stephen Fell Search Team describing the superb view of the curving Eden valley, the Lakeland fells and the Pennine ridge. Backtrack to the bogs between Nine Standards Rigg and Jack Standards and descend W and N on a bridleway to the High Dukerdale boundary wall. Where the path meets Baxton Gill it negotiates an area of spongy bog.
(High Level Route continues on Map 4.5)

Map 4.5
High Level Route

After the Baxton Gill bog it is a straightforward descent along the wall over Hartley Fell, joining a road at Hartley Birkett and descending past Hartley Quarry down Birkett Lane.

On the stretch between Nine Standards and Kirkby Stephen you are likely to be in the company of walkers on Wainwright's Coast-to-Coast Walk, though the majority of those met will be going on a W-E route.
(High Level Route continues on Map 4.7)

Map 4.6
Low Level Route

Beyond the second stile after Shoregill, at Moss Gill, the route is undefined across Far Grounds Gill, Well Gill and Riggs Gill. We found it easier to go through the gate beside the barn, alongside a fence, across the next gill and along the top of the Eden floodbank opposite Pendragon Castle to a stile by the next gill, crossing the tiny meadow frequented by a donkey and caravan enclosures to reach the Birkett Common road at Castle Bridge.

Castle Bridge is said to have been built by Lady Anne Clifford. Its single segmented arch spans *c.*30ft/9.1m: the underside of the arch shows the original width to have been *c.*4ft/1.2m, since widened to *c.*12ft/3.6m.

There is no access to Pendragon Castle, but none should be needed. Though shrouded by trees from our path beside the river it is easily seen from the road.

Pendragon Castle was traditionally the stronghold of Uther Pendragon, who was supposed to have been the father of the renowned King Arthur of the Round Table. Pendragon died here in 520 by treachery and poison, and was buried at Stonehenge on Salisbury Plain.

While he was still a Prince, Pendragon almost succeeded in expelling the Saxons from this part of the Kingdom of Cumbria. There is no reason to disbelieve the tradition that King Arthur was born in Westmorland, a fact that is supported by the existence at Eamont Bridge (qv) of King Arthur's Round Table where, so they say, King Arthur's Knights were based and where Sir Lancelot slew Tarquin. Nor is there any reason to doubt the legend that when King Arthur was dying he was taken by boat up Ullswater into the shelter of the mountains accompanied on his last voyage by three queens.

A local legend has it that deep beneath the foundation of the castle lies hidden a great treasure ever since the days of Merlin, the great Arthurian bard. In the reign of Henry II the castle was the home of Sir Hugh de Morville, at the time Justice of Cumberland, one of the knights who murdered Thomas a Becket in Canterbury Cathedral on 29 December 1170.

The castle was almost certainly a late-Norman pele tower of 12c. There are records that it was burnt down by the Scots in 1340, restored by the Cliffords *c.* 1360-70, and destroyed again by the Scots in 1541. It was again restored by Lady Anne in 1660 and finally dismantled in 1685 by her successor, who could find no use for it.

Up the farm lane from Pendragon is Castlethwaite, a satisfying group of three farmhouses, dated 1664, 1688 and 1732, and their associated byres and granaries.

Follow the Birkett Common road round the hairpin bend and steeply uphill for a short way and at the cattle grid follow the muddy RUPP along the flank of Birkett Common, passing the Giant's Graves (pillow mounds) and then alongside the bank of the River Eden to Lammerside Castle.

Lammerside Castle is another pele tower, but 14c and oblong. The surviving remains originally formed part of the building's central core, with barrel-vaulted ground floor rooms. It is reputed to have been the home of the de Quertons (the Whartons) before they moved to Wharton Hall (qv).

The bridleway passing Lammerside Castle is hindered where a new enclosure (cultivated field) is bounded by barbed wire, and no stile or gate has yet been erected.

(Low Level Route continues on Map 4.7)

Map 4.7

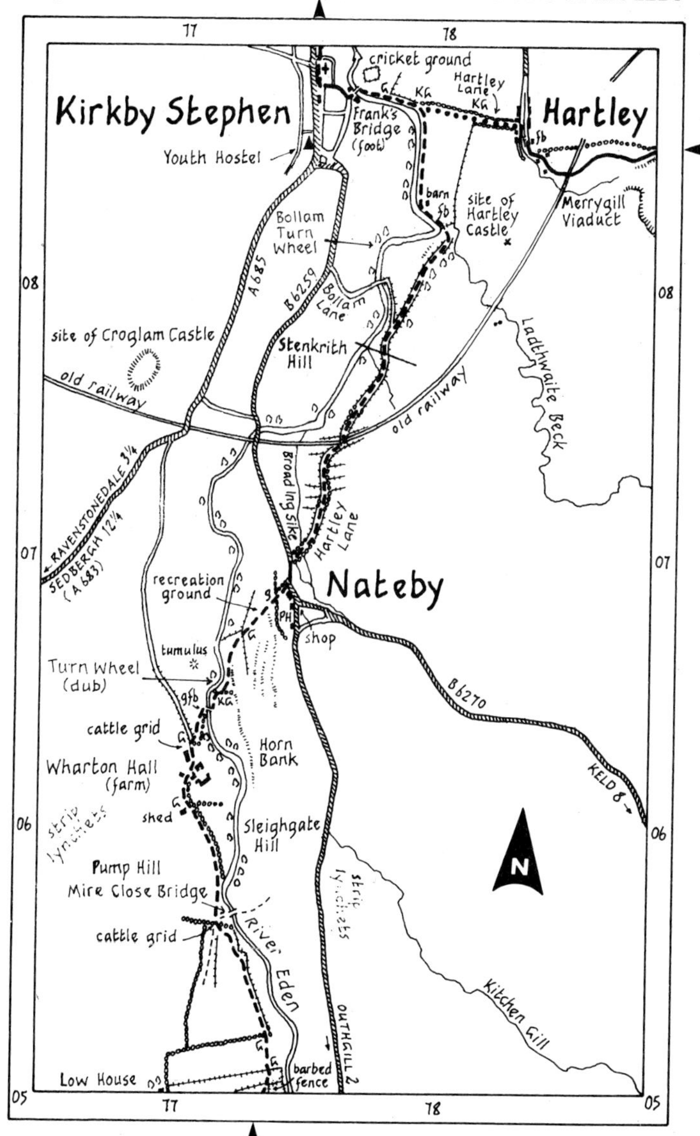
77
78
cricket ground
Kirkby Stephen
Hartley Lane
KG
Hartley
Frank's Bridge (foot)
fb
Youth Hostel
barn
fb
site of Hartley Castle
Merrygill Viaduct
Bollam Turn Wheel
A685
B6259
Bollam Lane
08
site of Croglam Castle
Stenkrith Hill
Ladthwaite Beck
old railway
old railway
Broad Ing Sike
Hartley Lane
RAVENSTONEDALE 3¼
SEDBERGH 12¼ (A683)
07
recreation ground
Nateby
PH
shop
tumulus
Turn Wheel (dub)
gfb
KG
B6270
cattle grid
Horn Bank
Wharton Hall (farm)
KELD 8
strip lynchets
shed
Sleighgate Hill
06
Pump Hill
Mire Close Bridge
strip lynchets
N
cattle grid
River Eden
Kitchen Gill
OUTHGILL 2
barbed fence
Low House
05

Map 4.7
High Level Route

Our path descends past the massive Hartley Quarry, under the 9-arch Merrygill Viaduct that carried the Durham and Lancashire railway and down into Hartley village. As you descend to the level at the S end of the hamlet take the path on the L marked by white railings and cross the beck and go up the other side. The lane to the L - private road, public footpath - leads to Hartley Castle, while the lane running R leads into the village.

Hartley is a lovely little village with limes and silver birches beside the beck, a little bridge and a few houses, but spoilt by all the traffic going to and from the nearby quarry.

Hartley Castle is now a farm but it contains fragments of the castle walls and part of the vaulted cellar to the former kitchen. Sir Andrew de Harcla, 1st Earl of Carlisle (the highest title of nobility of his time) lived in Harcla (or Hartley) Castle from *c.*1260-1323. He became Sheriff of Cumberland, Warden of the Western Marches and Keeper of Carlisle Castle. In 1315 he successfully held Carlisle in a siege from Robert the Bruce, who was determined to capture it as it had been commanded by his father from 1295-7. Bruce was fresh from his victory over the English at Bannockburn in 1314, but he could not capture Carlisle from Sir Andrew. Harcla quelled the dangerous rebellion of the King's cousin, the Earl of Lancaster, at Boroughbridge in 1322. Also in 1322, as Warden of the Western Marches, he was charged with negotiating for peace with Robert the Bruce but the terms, misconstrued by Edward II as treacherous, resulted in Sir Andrew being committed without trial to Carlisle Castle. On the orders of the King he was hung, drawn and quartered on 3 March 1325. His estates were forfeited to the Crown.

The estates came to be held through marriage by the Musgraves who owned Bewley Castle and large properties in Cumberland. Sir Thomas de Musgrave was granted a licence in 1359 by Edward III to rebuild the castle, and he was followed by Sir Richard, who is reputed to have killed the last wild boar on Wild Boar Fell. The Musgraves were buried in Kirkby Stephen church. Their successors demolished the castle in the 18c and used some of the stones to built a new manor house at Edenhall near Penrith.

From Hartley take the signposted path (Hartley Lane) between buildings W to Kirkby Stephen, crossing the River Eden by Frank's Bridge, a narrow 17c footbridge with two arches, up the wiend called Stoneshoot and into the town's Market Place.

(Route continues as the Common Route on Map 4.8)

Low Level Route

Having negotiated the barbed wire at Lammerside the route to Wharton Hall is clear.

Wharton Hall is a large house of courtyard plan, with Welsh slate roofs and projecting stone chimneys. It was formerly the stately home of the Whartons. Thomas, 1st Lord Wharton, b1495, was distinguished in the border wars. He was Captain of Carlisle Castle from 1534-37 and also Deputy Warden of the Western Marches. In 1540 he built his Great Hall here, 68ft x 27ft/21m x 8m, and substantial parts of the hall and kitchen survive today. In 1542 with Sir William Musgrave of Hartley Castle he repelled a large Scottish army at Solway Moss. In 1545, with Lord Dacre, he sacked Dumfries, and for this and other services he was created Baron Wharton. In 1559 Thomas built an embattled gatehouse to his hall, three storeys high. This is virtually intact, although lacking roof and floors. It has the Wharton coat-of-arms and date on the outside. Thomas founded Kirkby Stephen grammar school in 1566 and died in 1568. He is buried at Heelaugh.

At the cattle grid on the farm access to Wharton Hall bear R to the River Eden and cross it by a footbridge and continue up to Nateby, emerging on to the B6259 at the N end of the village beside the Methodist Church, 1875. Go N up the B6259 towards Kirkby Stephen and at the rise, where the road has been straightened out, take the green lane (a RUPP called Hartley Lane) on the R. Before it turns to cross the river continue ahead, then keep to the R bank of the river, cross Frank's Bridge and go up the wiend called Stoneshoot and into Kirkby Stephen's Market Place.
(Route continues as the Common Route on Map 4.8)

Map 4.8

In the Eden valley in the vicinity of Kirkby Stephen there is a change in the use of building materials from limestone to red sandstone. In Kirkby Stephen itself, however, the houses are chiefly built of brockram or breccia, consisting of small pieces of limestone fused with sandstone, creating a perfect transition. It is this material that is quarried from Hartley Quarry.

Kirkby Stephen is an important market town where the valley of the Eden broadens out after the river leaves the confines of the Mallerstang valley. It is a town with a wide main street, spacious squares and narrow passages. There are a few Georgian house, a quaint market hall and a noble church.

The town is a favourite stopping-off place for trans-Pennine travellers, particularly for those from Tyneside to Blackpool. There was

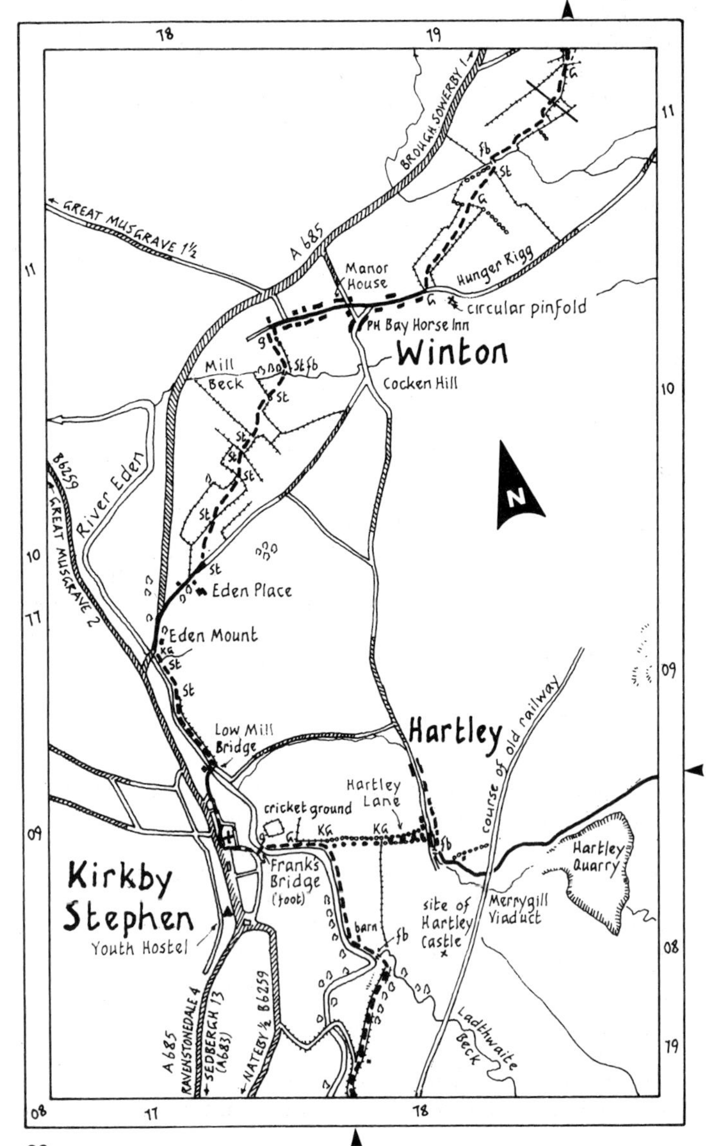
BROUGH SOWERBY 1
GREAT MUSGRAVE 1½
A 685
Manor House
Hunger Rigg
circular pinfold
PH Bay Horse Inn
Winton
Mill Beck
Cocken Hill
River Eden
B6259
GREAT MUSGRAVE 2
Eden Place
Eden Mount
Low Mill Bridge
Hartley
course of old railway
Hartley Lane
cricket ground
Frank's Bridge (foot)
Hartley Quarry
Kirkby Stephen
Youth Hostel
site of Hartley Castle
Merrygill Viaduct
barn
Ladthwaite Beck
RAVENSTONEDALE 4
SEDBERGH 13 (A683)
NATEBY ½ B6259

much local concern when the Primrose coach company decided, in the summer of 1984, to suspend its 30-minute 'tea-break' stop in the town, a tradition that local tea and gift-shop owners had become accustomed to over many years. The decision was prompted by proposals to introduce double yellow lines and parking charges in the town.

The wide, long main street is derived from its market origins. The **Market Place** once accommodated the Butter Market. On its N side, as a screen between the Market Place and the churchyard, are **The Cloisters,** 1810, by George Gibson, with eight unfluted Roman Doric columns, the central four standing forward of the rest and supporting a triangular pediment with bellcote.

St. Stephen's is a Norman church of 1170 on Saxon foundations. In 1220 a new cathedral-like nave was built in the Early English style. The tower was once central between N and S transepts, but it fell down and a very impressive three-storey Perpendicular tower was built *c.*1550 at its W end. It is one of the most graceful in Westmorland and after Kendal it is one of the largest parish churches in the country. It has magnificent early-13c arcades under a modern clerestorey and 16c roofs. The church is rightly called 'The Cathedral of the Dales'.

The church has two chapels to the two local families - the Musgraves and the Whartons. The Musgrave Chapel in the S aisle was founded by Sir Thomas de Musgrave, d.1376, and he lies in a red sandstone tomb with a cross in relief, behind the altar rail in the SE corner. Sir Richard de Musgrave, d.1409, has a fine altar tomb of him wearing jousting armour, with hip belt, and his feet on a lion. Another Sir Richard de Musgrave, grandson of the former Richard, who died in 1464, lies with his wife and son in a plain tomb under an arch in the S wall. Round the tomb is carved, in Latin: 'Here lies Richard Musgrave Knt near Elizabeth his wife and Thomas their son and heir who died on 9 November 1464 on whose soul have mercy, Amen'. The blue shield with six golden rings is the Musgrave coat-of-arms.

The Wharton Chapel in the N aisle has the rather battered stone figure of Thomas, first Lord Wharton, and his two wives. He is a knight in a plain suit of armour, his feet on a beast and his head on a tilting helmet. His wives wear French caps and gowns with tight bodices and full skirts. On his L is his first wife, Eleanor Stapleton, daughter of Sir Brian Stapleton of Wighill. On his R is Anne Talbot, daughter of George, Earl of Shrewshury. Two sons and two daughters kneel on the sides of their handsome tomb.

The former **Methodist Chapel,** 1889, at the other end of Main

Street, is now a youth hostel: YHA members voted it 'Hostel of the Year' in 1984. Nearby, at the junction of the B6259 Nateby road, is the former **Temperance Hall,** 1856, with a statue of Temperance and huge Grotesque lettering on its main elevation.

Kirkby Stephen is principally a market town serving the community in the upper Eden valley, but it has one interesting manufacturing industry. Heredities claim to be the world's largest creator of cold cast bronzes which are internationally famous, particularly their charming wildlife figures. The factory at Crossfield Mill, in Hobsons Lane on the N side of the town, is open all the year round, Monday-Friday, 0900-1700, and you can see the entire process of manufacture.

The High Level and Low Level Routes unite at Kirkby Stephen and run together until beyond Appleby.

From the Market Place take the wiend on the W side of the churchyard through to the Hartley road and follow this down to Low Mill Bridge, another 17c two-arched bridge over the River Eden. Cross over and keep to the R bank of the river to the next bridge, the A685 Tebay-Brough road. Turn R then R again on Kirkbank Lane, the road towards Winton.

Just beyond Eden Place on Kirkbank Lane turn off L for paths to the W end of Winton's single village street. Care is needed to maintain the course as there is little sign of a path on the ground, although stiles mark its course across the fields and the crossing of Mill Beck.

Winton is a delightful hamlet of neat sandstone cottages and a green at its crossroads. Like Hartley, Winton is a spring-line settlement, with dry limestone above it and well-watered fertile sandstone below. The village followed the ancient two-field system of agriculture, best exhibited on the fields N of the village between the River Eden and the River Belah. Long, thin strips of medieval ox-ploughed open fields were enclosed piecemeal in 17c or early-18c.

As you go down the village street the farm cottages on the R were the original 17c manor house and as you come to the crossroads the successor **Manor House** stands on the L. This splendid six-bay house of three storeys was built in 1726. It was once a school of the kind described by Dickens in 'Nicholas Nickleby'. Also at the crossroads, on the green is the old **Winton School.** A school was founded here by public subscription in 1659 but the present building was erected in 1862. The school closed in 1981 and became a Milk Marketing Board artificial insemination centre in 1983.

Continue E through the village past a small Methodist chapel to the **Baptist Chapel,** 1863, built at the expense of Mr. Isaac Ebdell, yeoman, which is one of only four Baptist chapels in old Westmorland.

Wild Boar Fell from Brough Castle

Map 4.9

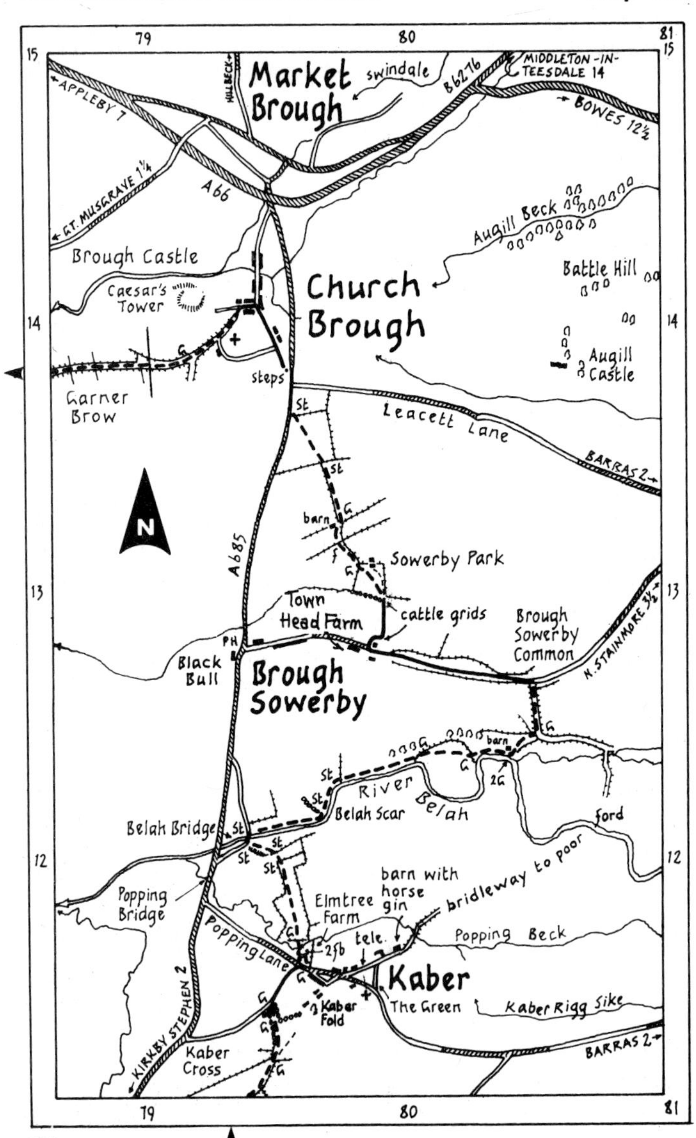

79
80
81
15
14
13
12
Market Brough
swindale
B6276
MIDDLETON-IN-TEESDALE 14
BOWES 12½
APPLEBY 7
HILLBECK
GT. MUSGRAVE 1¼
A66
Augill Beck
Brough Castle
Caesar's Tower
Church Brough
Battle Hill
Augill Castle
steps
Garner Brow
St
Leacett Lane
BARRAS 2
N
barn
Sowerby Park
A685
Town Head Farm
cattle grids
Brough Sowerby Common
N. STAINMORE 3½
PH
Black Bull
Brough Sowerby
barn
River Belah
Belah Scar
Belah Bridge
ford
2G
bridleway to poor
barn with horse gin
Elmtree Farm
Popping Bridge
Popping Lane
Popping Beck
tele.
Kaber
Kaber Fold
The Green
Kaber Rigg Sike
KIRKBY STEPHEN 2
Kaber Cross
BARRAS 2

The wide Fell Lane leading out of the village up Hunger Rigg was the 'outgang' - the way out from the 'inbye' land to the rough fell grazings. Originally the outgang may have been a funnel-like tongue of fell-land reaching down into the village, which enabled stock to be driven from the fell to the farms more easily. Similar examples can be seen at Kaber and Brough Sowerby. Here, at Winton, a circular stone cattle pinfold, of 18c or 19c date, is strategically placed in the mouth of the funnel.

Having passed through Winton to the pinfold just as the road rises up Hunger Rigg take the footpath signposted to Kaber, which continues in the general NE direction as before, through fields, to Kaber.

Map 4.9

Kaber is a small hamlet with a large common on its E side - a larger example of an outgang than Winton's - with an isolated Primitive Methodist Chapel of 1891 on the village green. Nelson House, 1774, on the N side of the green, used to be an inn. Next to Nelson House is the diminutive village school, rebuilt in 1802. It has a tablet on its wall taken from the earlier building with an inscription recording that on 7 March 1793 Anthony Morland, a yeoman of Rookby, to the SE of the village, left £50 to the school. The money was used to buy a field called Sandwath 'the yearly income of which is to be paid to the master thereof yearly for ever'.

Kaber has its place in history through the Kaber Rigg Plot, a plot in 1663 against Charles II by the inhabitants of Kirkby Stephen under the command of Captain Robert Atkinson, a native of Winton. Parliament had passed a series of penal measures against Nonconformists and Atkinson was approached by Insurrectionists of Yorkshire and Durham to lead a revolt to secure the return of religious tolerance. The rising was nipped in the bud, Atkinson was convicted of treason at Appleby Assizes in 1664 and executed, with three others, at Appleby Castle.

The direct line from Kaber to Church Brough is unfortunately the busy A685, and we want to avoid that. The direct way of getting there by public rights-of-way is to go via Brough Sowerby Common, but this bridleway is hampered by an unfordable River Belah (unfordable by walkers, but passable by horses). From Elm Tree Farm at Kaber walkers had better take the public footpath over Popping Beck to Belah Bridge (carrying a bypassed section of the A685), and along the bank of the river on the opposite side. At Brough Sowerby Common turn W down the unenclosed outgang towards Brough Sowerby village, but before you get into the village proper, near Town Head Farm, take the access to Sowerby Park and then by path NW to Church Brough.

Modern roadworks to provide Market Brough with a bypass of the A66 Scotch Corner-Penrith road have resulted also in a bypass for the A685 for Church Brough, and our route crosses over the main road and into the now quiet village street.

Brough consists of two settlements - Market Brough and Church Brough - indicating their original functions, today collectively called Brough-under-Stainmore. Market Brough is a little further to the N, at the junction of the A685 and the old A66 but is now more isolated from Church Brough as a result of the new A66 bypass.

The natural way from Carlisle to York is southwards via the Eden valley to Appleby and Brough, then over the Pennines by Stainmore to the Yorkshire plain. The Romans probably built their road along the line of an existing British road: the modern A66 still follows it, except for recent (1980's) improvements. The Romans chose the brow of a steep escarpment to built a fort in order to command this important gateway and called it **Verterae** and they occupied it for 300 years. Little remains: the Normans built a castle on its site, using its stones.

The imposing ruins of the Norman **Brough Castle** dominate the village. The castle was built shortly after 1092, perhaps 1095, at the time of William Rufus's acquisition of N Westmorland and part of Cumberland: it was a frontier castle, for NW Cumberland was still then part of Scotland. The great keep is at the western end of the bailey and its foundations and sizeable portions of the bailey walls are of the original 11c structure.

In 1174 the castle was breached and taken by William the Lion of Scotland. The castle was repaired in 1204 when it was granted by King John to Robert de Vipont, ancestor of the Cliffords. During the Scottish wars Brough Castle was repeatedly under attack but although Robert the Bruce's forces, after their victory at Bannockburn, burned the town in 1314 and again in 1319, the castle was undamaged.

The 9th Lord Clifford, who held Brough Castle during the Wars of the Roses, was a Lancastrian and because of his persecutions of the Yorkists was nicknamed 'Bloody Clifford' and 'The Butcher'. Shakespeare places him as an outspoken supporter of Henry VI (Henry VI, Part III). He was killed in action, reputedly by an arrow in his throat, in 1461, and the castle was taken by Warwick the King-maker. The Tudors restored the castle to the Cliffords and Henry, son of the 9th Lord Clifford, came back to Brough.

The castle was accidentally set on fire in 1521 and remained a ruin until 1659 when Anne Clifford, Countess Dowager of Pembroke,

Dorset and Montgomery, and restorer of so many Clifford castles and village churches, began the work of repair. Much extra work was done including the rebuilding of a tower in the SE corner, now called Clifford Tower.In 1666 there was another fire and the castle was no longer used. By the end of the century masonry was being removed for building material elsewhere and the remains were allowed to become ruinous. In 1923 the castle was handed over by the owner, Lord Hothfield, to the Commissioners of HM Works for conservation. It is now in the care of English Heritage (the Department of the Environment) and is open to the public during the usual hours.

From the **Castle** return to **The Square.** The first building on the L, Church Hill, is a cruck house (a medieval roof construction). At the far end of The Square, facing the maypole (where the market cross once stood) is a building that used to be the Green Tree Inn, while in the centre of the S side of The Square is Banks Farm, which used to be the Pack Horse Inn: both inns dated from the coaching days.

From the W end of **The Square** *go S on a lane past Wiend House to the parish church from which the village gets its name, and enter by its N porch.*

St. Michael's church was built *c.*1150 but, like most other buildings of that period in this area, was much damaged by raiding Scots. The church was under royal patronage from the reign of Richard Coeur de Lion to that of Edward III: it then became under the patronage of Queen's College, Oxford.

The sloping floor of the nave is a medieval feature and was to allow worshippers at the rear of the church a greater degree of participation in the service. The roof of the nave is of Tudor oak, the Norman original no doubt being destroyed by the Scots. Late in the 14c the nave was extended to form a N aisle and 7 arcades were built into the N nave wall. The fine three-storey W tower was added in 1513 by Blenkinsop of nearby Hellbeck and its bells, given to the church by John Brunskill, a yeoman of Stainmore, were the subject of a poem by Southey entitled 'Brough Bells'.

Next to the sandstone pulpit, dated 1624, on the S side of the nave is a memorial slab on the floor with the following interesting inscription: HERE LYE GABRIELL VINCENT STEWARD TO THE R H ANNE CLIFFORD COVNTESS DOWAGER OF PEMBROOKE DORSETT AND MONTGOMERY. AND CHIEF DIRECTOR OF ALL HER BVILDINGS IN THE NORTH WHO DYED IN THE ROMAN TOWER OF BROVGH CASTLE LIKE A GOOD CHRISTIAN THE 12 OF FFEBRVARY 1665 1666. LOOKING FOR THE SECOND COMMINGE OF OVR SAVIOVR IESVS CHRIST.

Map 4.10

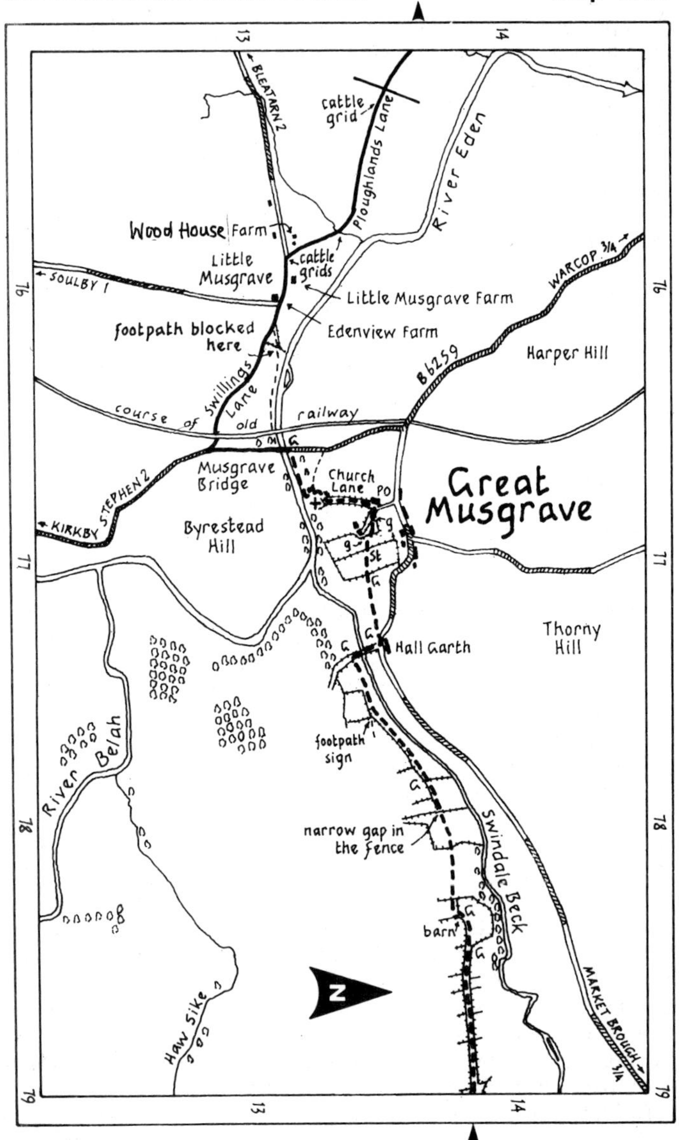
BLEATARN 2
cattle grid
Ploughlands Lane
River Eden
Wood House Farm
Little Musgrave
cattle grids
SOULBY 1
Little Musgrave Farm
WARCOP 3/4
footpath blocked here
Edenview Farm
Swillings Lane
B6259
Harper Hill
course of old railway
Musgrave Bridge
Church Lane
PO
Great Musgrave
STEPHEN 2
KIRKBY
Byrestead Hill
St
Hall Garth
Thorny Hill
footpath sign
River Belah
narrow gap in the fence
Swindale Beck
barn
N
MARKET BROUGH 3/4
Haw Sike

In the churchyard to the S of the chancel is the tomb to members of the Walton family of Helbeck. It commemorates William, d.30 August 1807, aged 70, and Elizabeth his wife d.9 August 1807, aged 72, and their son William, d.25 November 1841, aged 76, and Eleanor his wife, d.26 March 1862, aged 74. It is constructed in sandstone with an elaborately carved panel between pilasters decorated with classical urns in low relief to its two main sides: the panel on the N has Christ with an angel, that on the S has a body on a bed surrounded by mourners with death in attendance.

Leave **St. Michael's** *churchyard by its northern gate and turn L on the lane that goes W towards Great Musgrave.*

Map 4.10

The track from Church Brough ends at a barn but thereafter the bridleway is poorly marked as it runs beside the Swindale Beck to the bridge at Hall Garth. A path then runs across fields and into Great Musgrave. On the hillside on the descent from Brough, and on the hill between Hall Garth and the village are **lynchetts;** Bronze Age cultivation terraces. They are some of the finest examples in the country.

Great Musgrave was granted to Peter de Musgrave by King Stephen in the 1100's along with other lands, but the family lived elsewhere and there are no signs that they developed or defended the village.

Great Musgrave stands on a knoll above the confluence of the Swindale Beck with the River Eden and close to the River Belah, but instead of occupying the high point the church stands hard beside the River Eden. We reach the church by taking a path, Church Lane, S from the village post office.

St. Theobald's is the third church built on this site. The present church was built in 1845 at a cost of £550 to replace one which stood even closer to the river: when the Eden was in spate the church was flooded pew deep. (In a great flood in 1822 a pack horse bridge over the Eden near the church was washed away: all other bridges over the Eden were also destroyed, with the exception of the bridge at Warcop.) Inside the communion rail at the S end is a beautiful brass engraving set into a large flagstone in the floor. It is a 13½" high figure of Thomas Ouds, a monk of 1502, with an inscription on his chest, and him in a praying posture. The monument originally had the four evangelists, one at each corner, but only one now remains - that of the lion of St. Mark, bottom L. The church has a plain, whitewashed interior, and is uninteresting. The Rushbearing Ceremony is still kept here, being held nowadays on the first Saturday in July.

In 1856 the directors of the Stockton & Darlington Railway visited

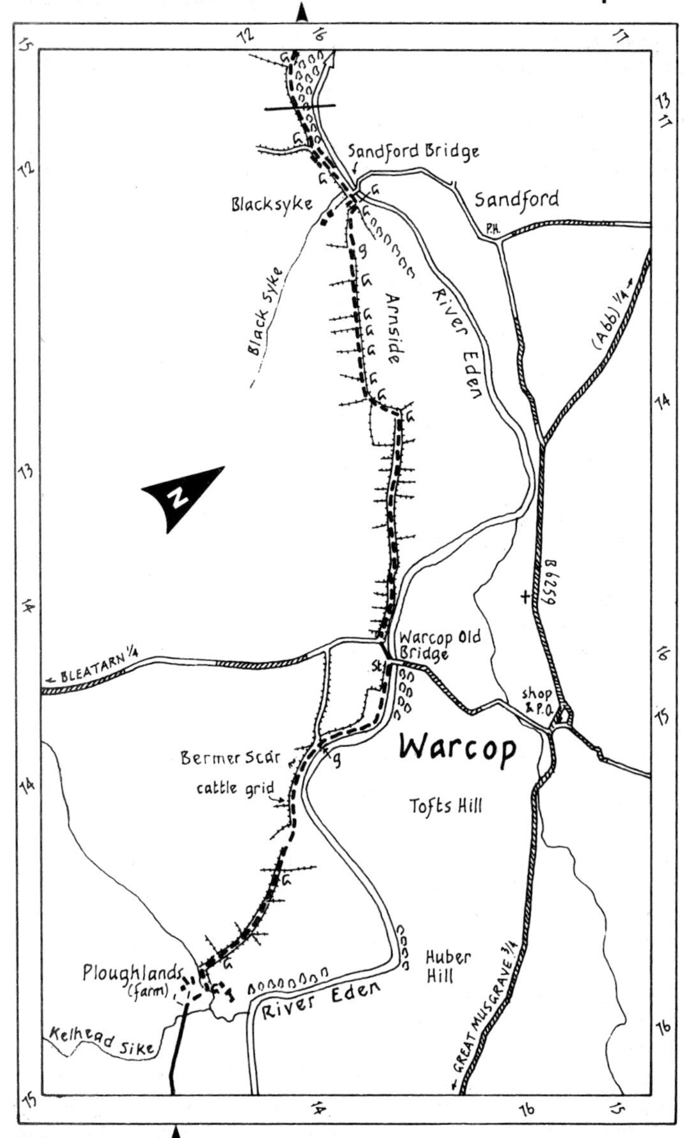
Sandford Bridge
Sandford
Blacksyke
P.H.
Black Syke
Arnside
River Eden
(Abb) 1/4
B6259
Warcop Old Bridge
← BLEATARN 1/4
shop & P.O.
Warcop
Bermer Scar
cattle grid
Tofts Hill
Huber Hill
Ploughlands (farm)
River Eden
Kelhead Sike
← GREAT MUSGRAVE 3/4

Brough in response to a deputation from Westmorland who had offered to help with the cost if the company built a line from Barnard Castle to Penrith via Brough. They met with such total opposition from the local landowners and the parish council that the line was routed through Kirkby Stephen instead. The Eden Valley Railway was opened in 1862 and a station was provided at Musgrave: it was called 'Musgrave for Brough' and wagonettes met trains to take goods and passengers to Brough. The line extended from Penrith to Keswick and Workington to carry coke from the Durham coalfield to the iron and steel industry on the W coast. With improvements in the making of coke from West Cumberland coal freight traffic declined quickly after 1910 and passenger traffic declined in the mid-1950's. The line was closed on 22 January 1962.

From Great Musgrave's church of St. Theobald's take the footpath beside the river to Musgrave Bridge carrying the B6259 Warcop-Kirkby Stephen road.

Regrettably the path continuing on the opposite bank of the Eden is blocked at the Little Musgrave end, and for the time being you have to go L down the B6259 then R along the road, called Swillings Lane, to Little Musgrave. The path from the bridge is used by fishermen and one would expect that they, as much as anyone, would make better use of it: a simple stile in the hedge would suffice in order to get into the sunken lane.

On the W side of Little Musgrave hamlet turn R between Little Musgrave Farm and Wood House Farm on Ploughlands Lane.

Map 4.11

Care is needed at Ploughlands where the route is obscure though passable. A farm track takes the path to a bend in the river, and where the track bears L at Bermer Scar continue along the river bank to Warcop Old Bridge.

Warcop

The 16c **Warcop Old Bridge** over the Eden is one of the finest in Westmorland. It has three segmental arches, each spanning 25ft/7.6m. The 10ft/3m wide roadway has polygonal refuges above the cutwaters. It is said that the bridge is the only one over the Eden to have withstood the floods of 1622. The bridge is believed to be the second oldest in Westmorland, after the Devil's Bridge at Kirkby Lonsdale. It was strengthened and repaired in March 1987 at a cost of £70,000.

The village lies a little to the N of the river, and on your way there you pass some of the amenities of Victorian social life - the Temperance Hall, 1865 and 1910; the Reading Room, 1877; and the Wesleyan

Map 4.12

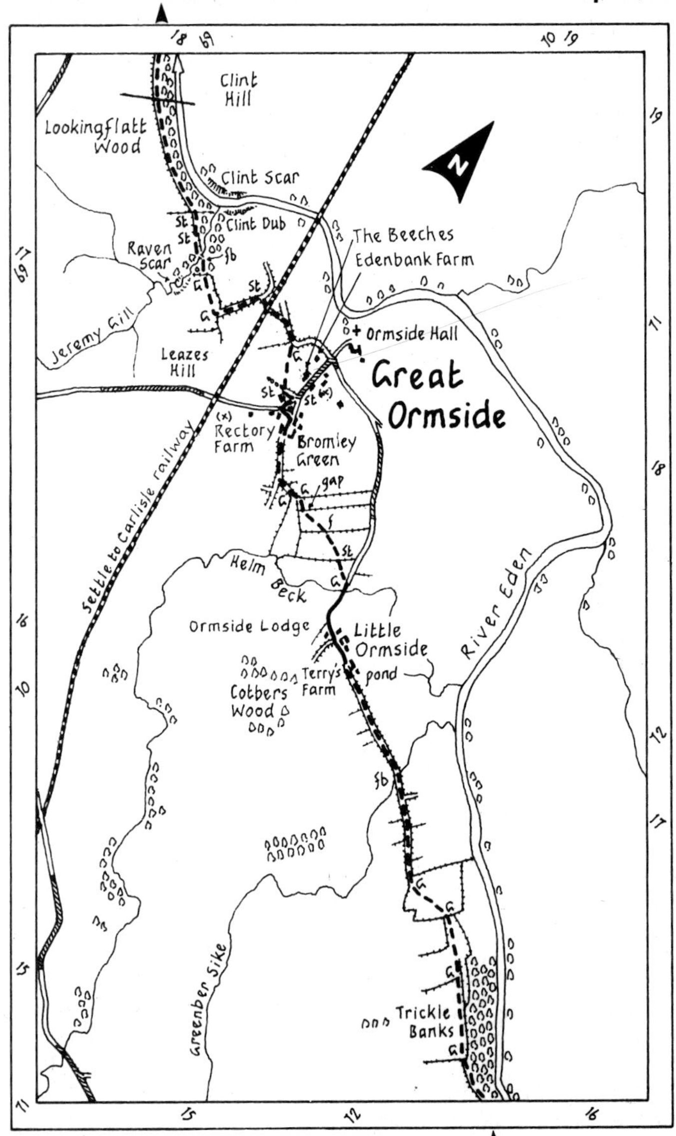
Clint Hill
Lookingflatt Wood
Clint Scar
Clint Dub
Raven Scar
fb
St
G
The Beeches
Edenbank Farm
Jeremy Gill
Leazes Hill
Ormside Hall
Great Ormside
Rectory Farm
Bromley Green
gap
Settle to Carlisle railway
Helm Beck
Ormside Lodge
Little Ormside
Terry's Farm
pond
Cotbers Wood
River Eden
Greenber Sike
Trickle Banks

Chapel, 1872. Nearby stands a tall maypole on five steps which were originally the base of an ancient cross. The maypole has a pheasant weathervane on top.

Among the cluster of houses on the N side of the village - if you can call the maypole its centre - is The Charnley Arms, formerly The Railway Inn, from the days of the Eden Valley Railway. Opposite the pub is the only remaining smithy in the village: originally there were three. It is surmounted by a lovely weathervane of a man ploughing behind two horses. The school and church stand aside from the village on its NW side.

St. Columba's is a squat sandstone church, with an odd turret tower at its W end and a massive buttress beside its S door. The N wall is Norman, but the church is mostly Perpendicular or Early English, though it was rebuilt in 1855. It has a large chancel, and there are numbered panelled box pews in the nave dating from 1716. Rushbearing takes place each year on St. Peter's Day - 29 June. This pre-Elizabethan practice had a less-ceremonial aspect when the church had an earthen floor: the rushes were gathered each summer and laid over the earth and the old rushes were burned.

Warcop today is the home of the military, though you will see very little of their presence in the village. Warcop Hall on the N side of the village is the administrative centre and barracks of their camp: the tank training ranges are seen from the A66.

From Warcop Old Bridge follow the road beside the Eden for a short way and then take to the farm track beside the river, but where this forks after a short distance do not keep to the river towards Langford but bear L (ahead) on the bridleway direct to Blacksyke and Sandford Bridge at Sandford. Keep to the Blacksyke lane then go R on a bridleway along the fringe of a wood in the same general NW direction as before towards Little Ormside.

Map 4.12

The bridleway to Little Ormside is straightforward, becoming clearer towards and beyond the crossing of the Greenber Sike. Just past the bridge over the Helm Beck the path goes through some small enclosures to a lane at Bromley Green and into Great Ormside.

Great Ormside is gathered around a triangular village green. A medieval preaching cross stood on the green, but it was destroyed during the Commonwealth, and shortly afterwards a sycamore sapling replaced it. The tree is now mature and has displaced the five large stone steps of the cross-base. The grey stone church is on a hill beside the Eden and beyond the village: the way to it is through the yard of a farm, formerly Ormside Hall.

The **Church of St. James** dates from the late 11c and has a short square tower with a gabled roof added in 12c, with small windows on its S and W sides and massive angle buttresses, giving it a strong, defensive appearance. The oak roof of the nave is 17c. The N aisle has two semi-circular arches and contains the Hilton Chapel, used for many years as the village school. The arms of the Hiltons in the chapel are dated 1723, but the chapel is earlier than this. There is no stained glass, but there is a fascinating hagioscope or leper-squint between the vestry and the chancel altar rail.

Ormside is famous for the Ormside Cup, the richest piece of Anglo-Saxon metalwork ever discovered. It is a silver-gilt and jewelled bowl and was found in the churchyard in 1823. It is now in York museum. Orm must have been a Viking and the cup was probably part of his booty from a raid on York: there is no other explanation as to how this rich treasure came to be in Ormside. Some Viking weapons were also found here in 1899 and are displayed in Carlisle museum.

Ormside Hall is a large house, its late-14c/early-15c S wing constucted of large sandstone blocks with quoins and the main hall block rebuilt *c.* 1683 using coursed, squared rubble. A range of outbuildings and barns flank the courtyard, including a late-18c/early-19c threshing barn on the W side.

Directly opposite Bromley Green Farm, 1687, a stile takes the path across a field to a gate to a farm track (which can also be reached from Ormside church) which passes under the Carlisle-Settle railway line. (The railway viaduct over the River Eden was built in 1870-75 with ten stone arches and was designed by the engineer J.C.Crossley.) Turn L then R to get back to the line of the river. Having crossed a footbridge over Jeremy Gill look for a kink in the fence where the path crosses from the field into the woodland above the river. The path runs along the upper fringe of Lookingflatt Wood as the river swings N towards Appleby.

Map 4.13

The path runs out of Lookingflatt Wood and into Wormrigg Wood and in doing so it descends to the level of the river. It clings to the water's edge and is liable to be dangerous in times of flood.

The path turns up into a lane at the foot of the knoll on which stands Appleby Castle. There is no access to the castle from here, nor is there a continuation of a riverside path into Appleby itself. (A turn R takes you down to the Eden where a footbridge, Jubilee Bridge, crosses the river and gives a pleasing view of Bongate Mill.)

Go up the lane L to the B6260 Appleby-Tebay road and turn R on this

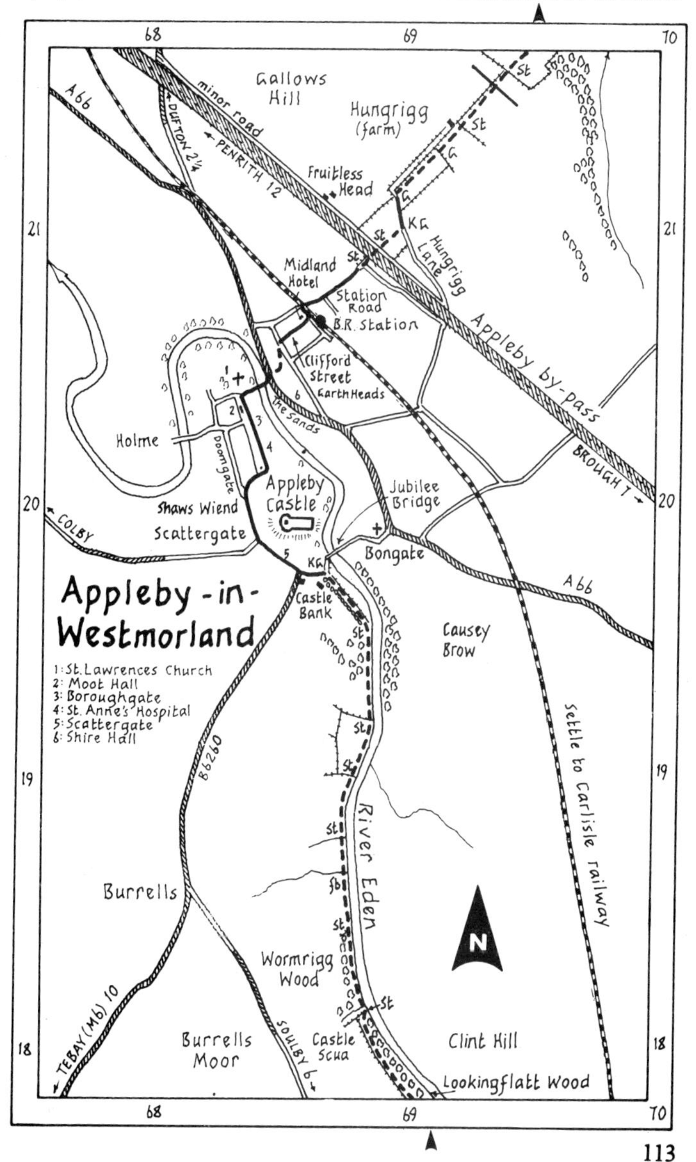
68
69
70
Gallows Hill
Hungrigg (farm)
minor road
DUFTON 2¼
PENRITH 12
A66
Fruitless Head
St
G
KG
Hungrigg Lane
Midland Hotel
Station Road
B.R. Station
Appleby by-pass
Clifford Street
Earth Heads
The Sands
Holme
Doomgate
Appleby Castle
Jubilee Bridge
BROUGH 7
Shaws Wiend
Scattergate
COLBY
Bongate
Castle Bank
Causey Brow
Appleby-in-Westmorland
1: St. Lawrences Church
2: Moot Hall
3: Boroughgate
4: St. Anne's Hospital
5: Scattergate
6: Shire Hall
B6260
Settle to Carlisle railway
River Eden
fb
Burrells
Wormrigg Wood
N
TEBAY (M6) 10
SOULBY 6
Burrells Moor
Castle Scua
Clint Hill
Lookingflatt Wood
21
20
19
18

and follow it into the town past Scattergate Green and up to the gates of Appleby Castle.

Appleby stands in the mid-valley area of the River Eden, a neat and unspoiled market town, strategically placed within a protective loop of the river with a castle on a hill protecting its open flank. Appleby was in Scottish hands until William Rufus advanced to Carlisle in 1092. William granted the lands to Ranulph de Meschines who built large earthwork defences of the motte and bailey type and laid out the town in 1110. The form of his town was basically a wide tree-lined avenue and market place separating the castle from the church, the one on the hill and the other on the riverside meadows.

Henry II granted Appleby the status of a borough in 1179 and it became the county town of Westmorland: it was re-named Appleby-in-Westmorland in 1974 when the 'lost county' was absorbed into Cumbria.

Appleby Castle is a splendid building, standing above the town, surrounded by a high wall and two outer and an inner bailey. The Keep, known as Caesar's Tower, is 12c, square with four turrets. The curtain wall is late 12c and a semi-circular tower to the N was built in 13c, as was the W part of the main house.

The castle belonged to the Viponts before it went to the Cliffords in late 13c. The E part of the main house was built in 1454. The house was partly dismantled in 1648 but was restored by Lady Anne in 1651-3. The castle remained with the Cliffords until the death of Lady Anne in 1675. It then went to her son-in-law, the Earl of Thanet, who built the stately domestic range to the castle in the Classical manner in 1686-8 with stones taken from the castles at Brough and Brougham. Inside there is a double-height hall, grand but intimate, dominated by the famous 'Great Picture', a huge triptych commissioned by Lady Anne in 1646 to commemorate the final reversion of the Clifford estates to her after long dispute. It shows her at 15 and at 56, with her parents, brothers and husbands and it illustrates, through elaborate heraldry, her genealogy. It is a marvellous monument of self-importance.

The castle is now owned by Fergusons, the tractor manufacturers. Although it is a private residence the keep and grounds are open to the public in summer.

In the grounds is a Rare Breeds Survival Trust Centre with a good collection of rare and endangered species of waterfowl, owls, ravens and British farm animals. In the Castle Park is a quadrangular stable block around a courtyard built by Lady Anne in 1652 and now divided into three dwellings, while in a copse to the NE of the former stable

block, on a bank above the river, is Lady Anne's Bee-house, built about the same time.
(Castle and Grounds open: Easter weekend and then May Day weekend until 30 September. Daily 1030-1700. Charge for admission. Free car park. Cafe.)

From the castle gate the main street, **Boroughgate,** (the street of the burgesses) runs down to the church. The broad street is fringed by trees and wide grass verges, and flanked by some decent, substantial 18c and 19c buildings. The length of the street is marked by a **High Cross** and a **Low Cross:** the **High Cross** is a stone Tuscan column, erected in 17c and inscribed 'Retain your Loyalty. Preserve your Rights' and topped by a windvane added in 1836. The **Low Cross** is identical, but supposed to be an 18c copy.

On the descent of **Boroughgate,** a little way down from the **High Cross** on the R, is **St. Anne's Hospital,** a charming group of twelve low sandstone cottages round a cobbled quandrangle with a small chapel in a corner founded by Lady Anne as almshouses in 1651. On the front above the archway is a panel and brass plate with the Clifford arms and inscription 'This Alms House was founded and begun to be built in the year 1631, and was finished and endowed for the yearly maintenance of a Mother, a Reader and twelve sisters for ever in 1653 by Anne Baronesse Clifford, Cumberland and Vesey, Lady of the Hon. of Skipton in Craven, and Countesse Dowager of Prembroke, Dorsett and Montgomery'.

Where **Boroughgate** widens out to form a market place the **Moot Hall** occupies an island site. Built in 1596 this whitewashed sandstone two-storey building is where the burghers used to assemble for a 'mote', a meeting to transact the business of the town. The Mayor and Town Council still meet in the building, while the Tourist Information Centre occupies the ground floor.

At the far end of the market place is the **Low Cross** and at the bottom of the hill is the church, screened by the **Cloisters.** The original was built and paid for by Bishop Smith in the mid-17c as a 'convenient and descent market' principally for the sale of buter, which was sold at the Low Cross in the open air. The Cloisters were rebuilt in 1811, by Sir Robert Smirke. It has seven pointed arches with a battlemented parapet containing the Appleby arms and date. At each end of the arcade is a square two-storeyed pavilion with machiolated parapet.

Go through the **Cloisters** to **St. Lawrence's** church. The oldest fabric of the church is *c.*1150 - the lower part of the tower - but the church has been burned and rebuilt several times since, having suffered damage from Border raids, and was restored by Lady Anne in 1654-5. Externally the style is predominantly 15c Perpendicular but internally it is predominantly 14c Decorated. It is built of coursed rubble and has lead roofs. The nave has castellated clerestory and the castellated W tower has a clock of 1699. An archway at the entrance to the 14c SW porch shows dog-toothed moulding and is of re-used 12c masonry. The church was restored again in 1861-2 and again in 1960. The church has a particularly fine and important organ brought from Carlisle Cathedral in 1674 and dating probably from 1571. The organ-case was reconstructed in 1836 using much old material.

Lady Anne Clifford was a legend in the North of England; she was independent, generous and fiercely loyal to the Crown. She was born in 1590 in Skipton Castle, daughter and heiress of George, Third Earl of Cumberland and 13th Lord Clifford. When 19 she married Richard, Third Earl of Dorset, with whom she lived at Knowle in Kent, bearing five of his children. She was left a widow at 34 and when aged 40 she married Philip, Fourth Earl of Pembroke. She was related by birth and marriage to an extraordinary number of powerful families. Her mother was the daughter of the Earl of Bedford and her aunt was the Countess of Warwick. Among other families with whom she was related were the Bouchiers, Cecils, Coniers, Devereaux, Dudleys, Howards, Lowthers, Percys, Russells, Scropes, Stanleys, Sydneys, Talbots and Whartons. Her eldest daughter and heiress married the Earl of Thanet and her second daughter married the Earl of Coventry.

By the will of her father the vast estates passed through the male Clifford line before reverting to the Countess and it was not until the deaths of her uncle and cousins, the fourth and fifth Earls of Cumberland respectively, that she entered into her inheritance in 1643. She was nearly 60 before she took possession, but between 1650-60 she restored her castles at Pendragon, Brough, Appleby, Brougham, Skipton and Barden, restored or rebuilt all the churches on her estates, founded the almshouses of St. Anne in Appleby, and assisted many of her retainers and tenants in building or restoring their properties. Lady Anne Clifford, Countess of Pembroke, Dorset and Montgomery, died on 22 March 1676, aged 86, and is buried in a splendid marble tomb in the church of St. Lawrence, next to the tomb of her mother, whom she had most tenderly loved. Lady Anne's monument has no effigy, but it has the family arms of the Cliffords with 24 shields. Beside her in a tomb surmounted by a beautiful effigy carved in alabaster is the tomb of her mother, Margaret Russell, Countess of Cumberland (d.1616), the widow of George Clifford, the

Third Earl, who was champion to Elizabeth I. The 'Life of Lady Anne Clifford' has been written by Dr. C.G.Williamson.

Not only does Appleby have a famous daughter, Lady Anne, but it also has a famous son, one John Robinson. Born in Appleby in 1727 he later lived at the White House, 1756, in Boroughgate, and became Freeman of Appleby, Alderman and Mayor, and then Member of Parliament for Westmorland during 1764-74. He was the first agent of Lord Lonsdale and then the political factotum of Lord North, whom he entertained in Appleby. In 1788 he was appointed by William Pitt the Younger as Secretary to the Treasury and Surveyor General of HM Woods & Forests. When Secretary to the Treasury, and accused of bribery in Lord North's unpopular government, he was 'named' in the House of Commons by Sheridan in the words: 'I could name him as soon as I could say Jack Robinson'.

Appleby has flourished as a prosperous market town for the vale of Eden for centuries. Local herds, feeding from the rich pasture in the valley, caused the Express Creameries to be established in the town in 1931 to process the locally produced milk. The factory became the first creamery to use bulk rail tanks for milk transport. Milk from the Eden valley herds was transported at nights in insulated tanks to arrive on London's doorstep in prime condition. In 1958 this service stopped and since 1959 Eden Vale cottage cheese, yoghurt, butter and cheese have been produced here.

Appleby is also famous for its annual **New Fair.** Each year in the third week of June gypsies and horse dealers come from all over Britain to buy and sell and haggle over horses. Based on Fair Hill, formerly Gallows Hill, the horse fair spreads into the town: horses are washed in the Eden on The Sands, groomed, and driven up and down the streets to show off their prowess. There is pandemonium in Appleby during New Fair and the grass verges of all the country lanes round about are occupied by the travelling people and their horses.

Leave Appleby by crossing St. Lawrence's Bridge (rebuilt in 1889 in the Georgian style) over the Eden to the old A66 at The Sands. Cross over the broad street diagonally L to an alleyway that leads up to Clifford Street and the Midland Hotel beside Appleby's railway station.

St. Lawrence's church bells were rung in 1866 when the news came through that the Bill to build a railway from Settle to Carlisle had received the Royal Assent. When the line was finished and opened on 1 May 1876 (and a station built at Appleby - Appleby West) the Midland Railway had its own route to Scotland high across the wild country of the Pennines by viaduct and tunnel. This magnificent and useful monument of Victorian engineering has recently been the subject of a public inquiry into British Rail's proposals to close it down. Ironically the line has had more use since BR's intentions were announced! Dales Rail and special excursion trains have carried thousands of passengers since the 'Save Settle-Carlisle' campaign was introduced. (At the present time - Spring 1987 - it looks as though the line might be saved. But who knows what mischief lurks in the official mind - Ed.)

It was on Appleby West station that Eric Treacy, Bishop of Wakefield, died in 1976 whilst photographing trains. It was an appropriate place, as well as an appropriate way, for the 'Railway Bishop' to go. A plaque has been erected to commemorate him.

The segmental arched wrought iron lattice footbridge over the railway tracks is of mid-late 19c and came here in 1901 from Mansfield station (now Mansfield Parkway, on the Nottingham-Sheffield line). Its fluted cast iron columns with acanthus capitals support the stairways. The span was reconstructed after damage in 1902.

Go L and under the railway arch on to Station Road (or cross the railway line by the footbridge at the station) and then go across the new A66 Appleby Bypass. (There is no footbridge: you take your life in your hands as you dash across.) The line of the bypass hereabouts runs along the line of the Roman road that went from Verterae (Brough) to Bravoniacum (Kirkby Thore).

When you reach the Hungrigg Farm track turn L and at a gate turn R on a path that runs parallel to the track, past the farm and down to the Frith Beck. From the fields on the approach to Hungrigg Farm material was excavated in 1980-81 for the construction of embankments on the Appleby Bypass.

Brougham Castle.

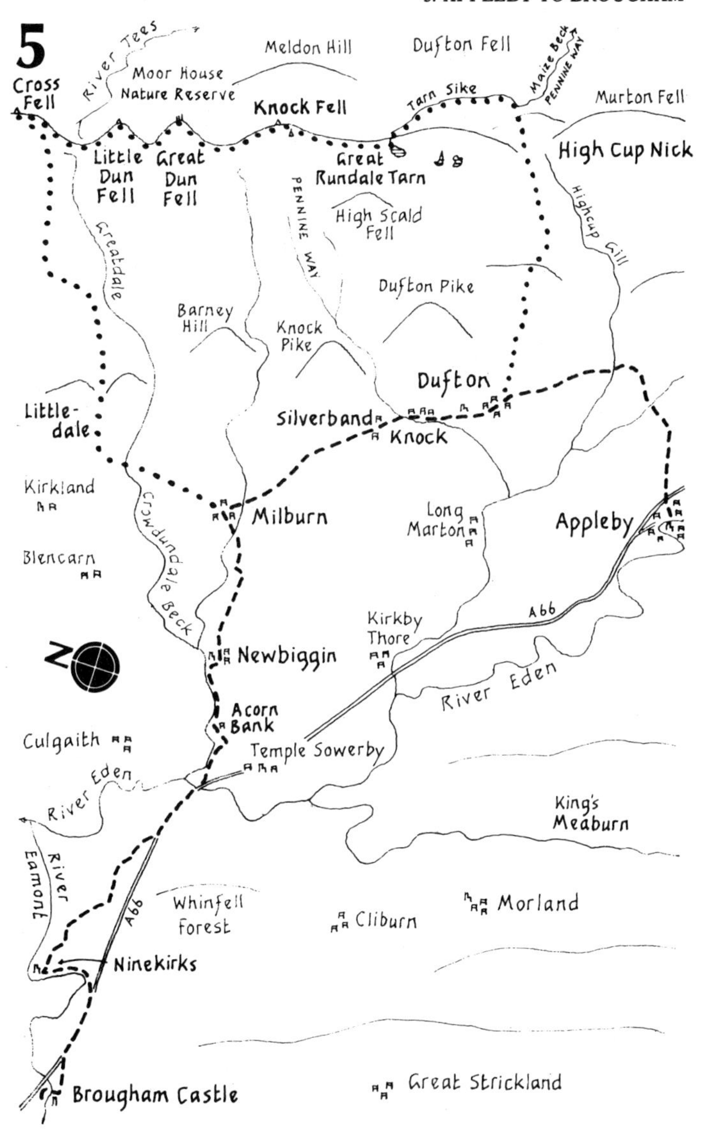
5
Cross Fell
River Tees
Moor House Nature Reserve
Meldon Hill
Dufton Fell
Maize Beck
PENNINE WAY
Murton Fell
Knock Fell
Tarn Sike
Little Dun Fell
Great Dun Fell
Great Rundale Tarn
High Cup Nick
PENNINE WAY
High Scald Fell
Highcup Gill
Greatdale
Dufton Pike
Barney Hill
Knock Pike
Dufton
Little-dale
Silverband
Knock
Kirkland
Milburn
Long Marton
Appleby
Crowdundale Beck
Blencarn
Kirkby Thore
A66
Newbiggin
River Eden
Acorn Bank
Culgaith
Temple Sowerby
River Eden
King's Meaburn
River Eamont
Whinfell Forest
A66
Cliburn
Morland
Ninekirks
Great Strickland
Brougham Castle

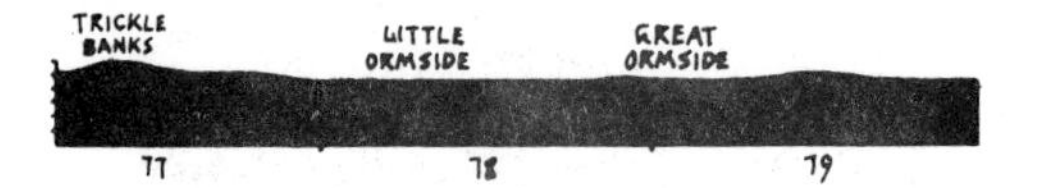
TRICKLE BANKS
LITTLE ORMSIDE
GREAT ORMSIDE
77
78
79

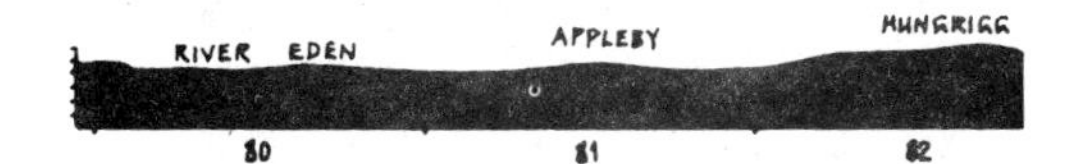
RIVER EDEN
APPLEBY
HUNGRIGG
80
81
82

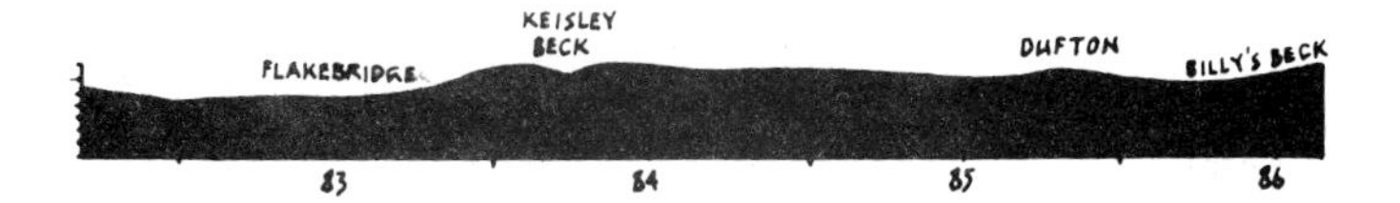
FLAKEBRIDGE
KEISLEY BECK
DUFTON
BILLY'S BECK
83
84
85
86

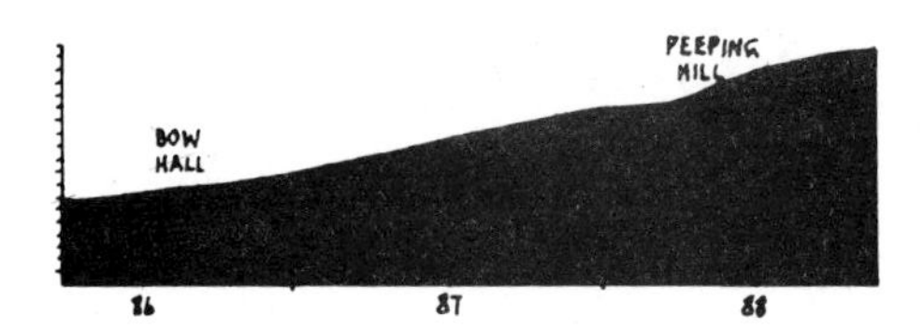
BOW HALL
PEEPING HILL
86
87
88

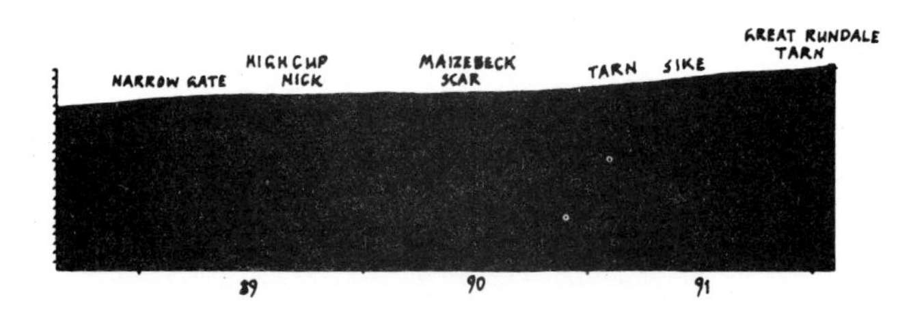
NARROW GATE
HIGH CUP NICK
MAIZEBECK SCAR
TARN SIKE
GREAT RUNDALE TARN
89
90
91

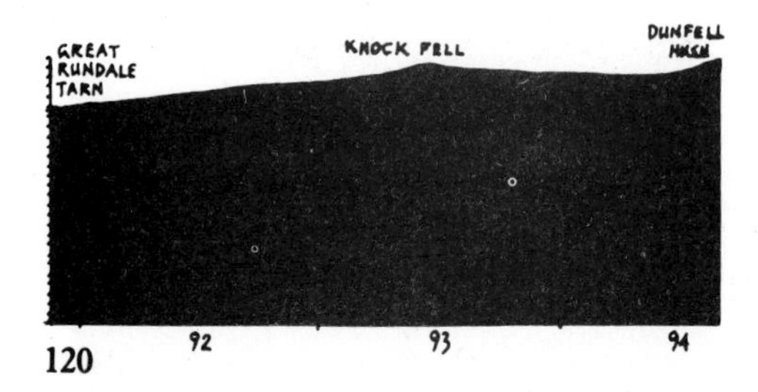
GREAT RUNDALE TARN
KNOCK FELL
DUNFELL HUSH
92
93
94

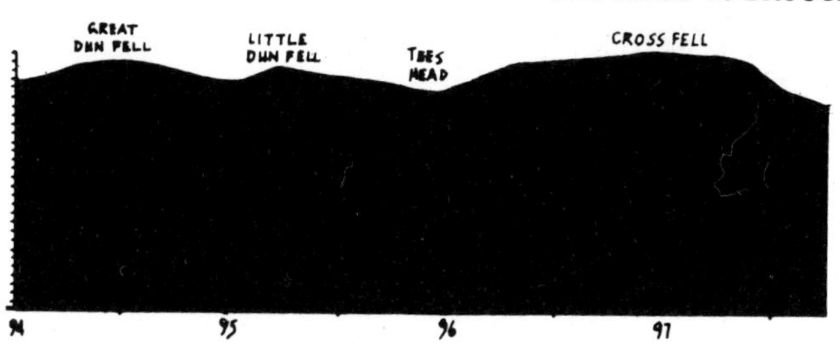
GREAT DUN FELL
LITTLE DUN FELL
TEES HEAD
CROSS FELL
94
95
96
97

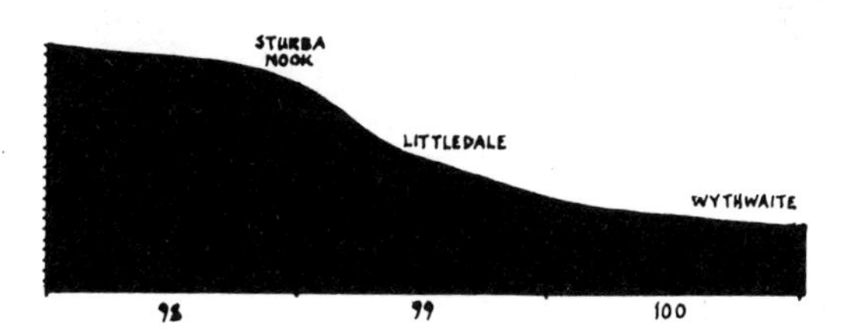
STURBA NOOK
LITTLEDALE
WYTHWAITE
98
99
100

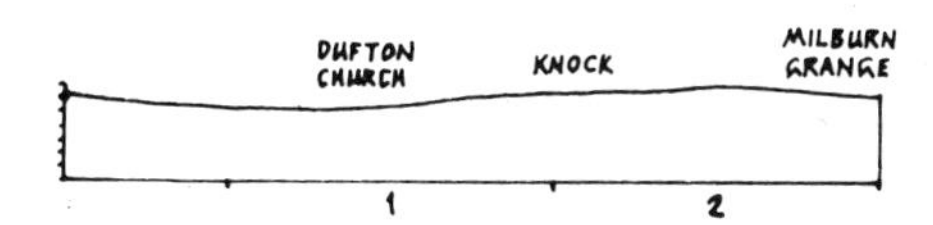
DUFTON CHURCH
KNOCK
MILBURN GRANGE
1
2

MILBURN GRANGE
STANK BECK
3
CROWDUNDLE BECK
MILBURN
101
102

GILLFOOT BRIDGE
NEWBIGGIN
ACORN BANK
103
104
105

EDEN BRIDGE
WOODSIDE
106
107

Low Cross and St. Lawrence's Appleby in Westmorland

5. Appleby to Brougham

On our journey down the Eden from Brough to Appleby the high wall of the Pennines has dominated our views. From Appleby we climb up to the top of these high hills on the High Level Route while the Low Level Route keeps below the foothills. We then join the course of the Eden again and follow it to the county boundary just beyond Brougham at Eamont Bridge.

Those parts of the common route - ie. between Appleby and Dufton and between Milburn and Brougham - and the **Low Level Route** from Dufton to Milburn, are entirely on the Triassic St. Bees Sandstone. Below the sandstones are Permian Eden Shales and in these shales are beds of gypsum and anhydrite which outcrop on the surface on the line of the river. These beds of gypsum and anhydrite - in the area bounded by a line drawn through Dufton, Knock, Milburn, Newbiggin, Kirkby Thore, Long Marton and Dufton - have been mined on the surface and underground by British Gypsum since 1880. Their plaster mill and plaster board works at Kirkby Thore is the biggest of its kind in the world. 4000 tonnes of plaster are produced each week and 67 miles/108km of plaster board are produced every day. Over 100 outgoing vehicles carry some 1800 tonnes of plaster and plaster board daily to building sites and depots throughout the country.

The **High Level Route** from Dufton to the tops of the Pennines and back down to Milburn passes through very complex geological strata. The Milburn Fault through Dufton and Milburn marks the transition from the St. Bees Sandstone (Triassic) to the Skiddaw Slates, then the Crowdundale Fault reveals the Carboniferous limestones. The Knock Pike Fault allowed intrusive volcanics to cap the limestone in places, illustrated very clearly in the prominent conical hills of Knock Pike, Dufton Pike and Murton Pike and other, unnamed hills along the same fault line, as well as at High Cup Scar. The limestone layer is capped by sandstones of the Millstone Grit Series: although the top of Knock Fell is a limestone plateau its higher neighbours to the N - Great Dun Fell, Little Dun Fell and Cross Fell - are all topped by sandstones.

From Appleby to Dufton is a distance of about 4.5 miles/7.2km. The **High Level Route** from Dufton to Milburn is about 17 miles/27km while the **Low Level Route** alternative between these two places is about 3.5 miles/5.6km (see further comments under Map

Map 5.1

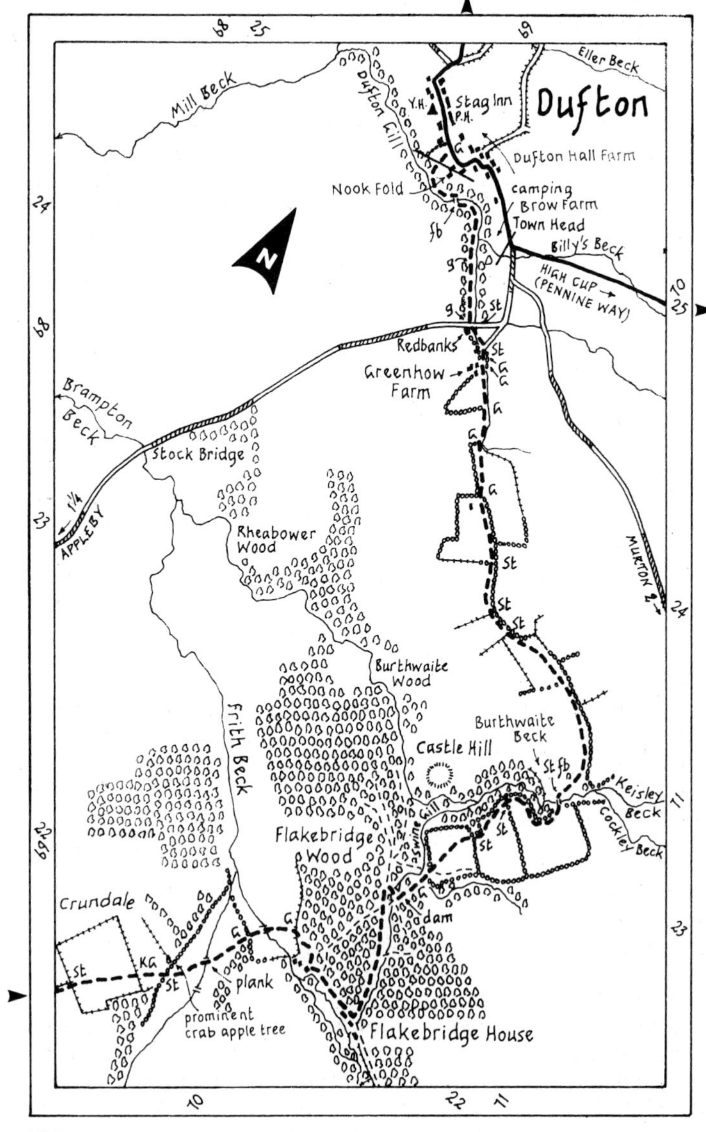
Dufton
Stag Inn
P.H.
Y.H.
Eller Beck
Mill Beck
Dufton Gill
Dufton Hall Farm
Nook Fold
camping
Brow Farm
Town Head
Billy's Beck
HIGH CUP
(PENNINE WAY)
Redbanks
Greenhow
Farm
Brampton
Beck
Stock Bridge
APPLEBY
Rheabower
Wood
MURTON
Burthwaite
Wood
Burthwaite
Beck
Castle Hill
Frith Beck
Keisley
Beck
Cockley
Beck
Swine Gill
Flakebridge
Wood
dam
Crundale
plank
prominent
crab apple tree
Flakebridge House

5.1). The distance between Milburn and Eamont Bridge is about 10.5 miles/17km.

The walker may be faced with logistical problems of accommodation (and transport) on this section of our journey round Westmorland. Fifteen miles/24km from Kirkby Stephen to Appleby is a good walk, but if it were stretched to Dufton (about 20 miles/32km) you would be better placed for the next day. Then you could do the **High Level Route** and return to Dufton, then the next day take the **Low Level Route** to Milburn and on to Eamont Bridge, a distance of about 14 miles/22.5km.

Map 5.1

The crossing of the Frith Beck is by one of the crudest plank footbridges ever seen, but the crossing of Murton Beck is much better. From Flakebridge Mill a path goes directly up the hillside through Flakebridge Wood, but it is easier to go a little way upstream on the track to Flakebridge House and then take the right-of-way diagonally up the wooded hillside, alongside Swine Gill, turning off at a little damed mill pool (cross the dam) out into the open, through three walled fields and down to the crossing of Burthwaite Beck by a decent footbridge below the confluence of Keisley Beck and Cockley Beck.

The path now swings NW towards Dufton, crossing the lane at Greenhow to Redbanks on the Dufton-Brampton road. Then go down Dufton Gill, a delightful place which is managed by the Woodland Trust. A footbridge crosses the beck and the path climbs up into the village green at Dufton.

Dufton has a very pleasant oblong green with trees and a red sandstone and cast iron fountain given by the London Lead Company in the late-19c. A quotation (attributed to Ovid) is carved on the top of the incised stucco column rising from the centre of the basin: FONS ERAT INLIMIS, NITIDIS ARGENTEUS UNDIS QUEM NEQUE PASTORES, NESQUE PASTAE MONTE CAPELLAE INFICIENT. ALIUDVE PECUS QUEM NULLA VOLUCRIS NEC FERA PERTURBAT. NEC LAPSUS AB ARBORE RAMUS. which freely translated says: 'The fountain is clear, silver with glittering waves which neither the shepherds nor the feeding mountain goats taint. Nor even the cattle nor any bird or wild animal disturbs it. Nor a fallen branch from a tree.'

Red standstone buildings stand around the green and include the Primitive Methodist church, 1905, a Conservative & Unionist club, 1911, and an old Wesleyan chapel, now a private house - note the carved sandstone figure, now unfortunately painted white, of Wesley

Map 5.2

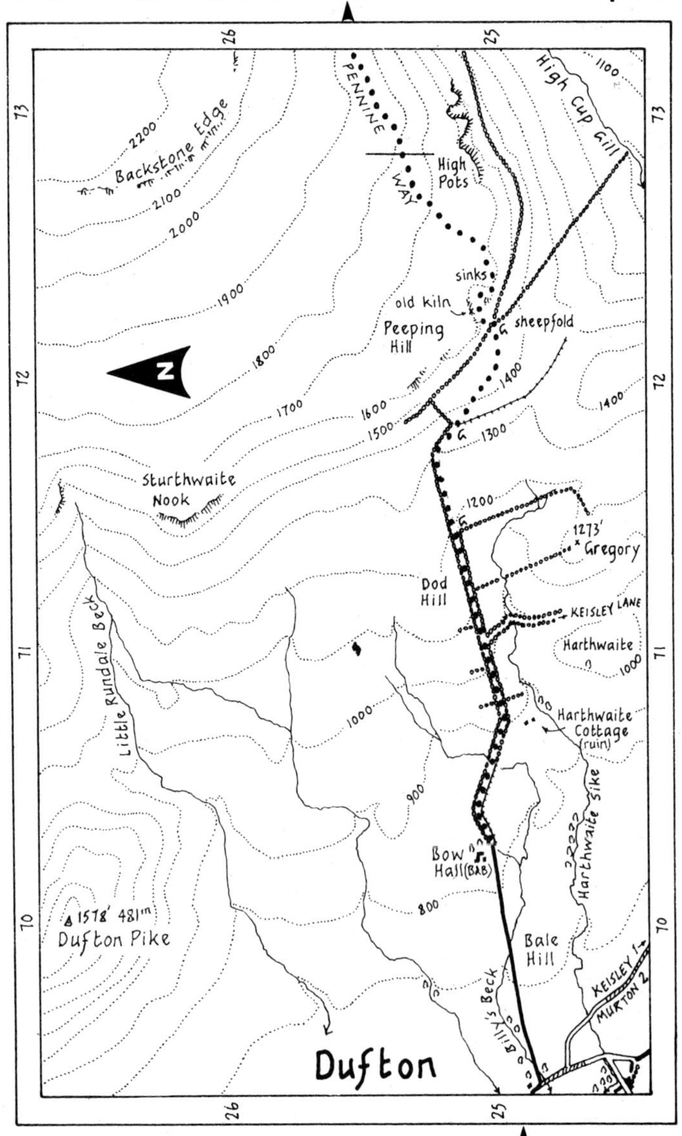

26
25
73
72
71
70
High Cup Gill
1100
PENNINE WAY
High Pots
Backstone Edge
2200
2100
2000
1900
1800
1700
1600
1500
1400
1300
1200
1000
900
800
sinks
old kiln
Peeping Hill
sheepfold
G
Sturthwaite Nook
1273'
Gregory
Dod Hill
KEISLEY LANE
Harthwaite
Harthwaite Cottage (ruin)
Little Rundale Beck
Harthwaite Sike
Bow Hall (B&B)
▲1578' 481m
Dufton Pike
Bale Hill
Billy's Beck
KEISLEY 1
MURTON 2
Dufton

(with a broken nose) in a niche halfway up the wall. The old white-washed village school at the W end of the green is now converted into a dwelling.

Dufton is well-known to Pennine Way-farers for a welcome rest in the youth hostel after a crossing of the Pennine 'backbone' - whether going N or S. We join and follow the Pennine Way for a short distance outside Dufton as from here we have our fourth High Level/Low Level option. The **High Level Route** goes along the Pennine Way as far as High Cup Nick, and starts on Map 5.2, while the **Low Level Route** continues on Map 5.7.

The **High Level Route** from Dufton to Milburn is a distance of about 17 miles/27km and in good conditions should take about 6.45 hours. Be warned that there is no footpath from the Maize Beck footbridge to the summit of Knock Pike and the ground underfoot presents some of the toughest, roughest going so far (but it won't be worse than this). By contrast the **Low Level Route** from Dufton to Murton takes about 1.40 hours and is mostly on roads.

Map 5.2
High Level Route

For those who have savoured the delights of the Pennine Way this stage will be familiar territory, as we follow the Pennine Way over the scarp slope of the Pennines to High Cup Nick and the Maize Beck.

From Dufton's village green take the road SE to Town Head and then the road to Bow Hall (signposted Pennine Way). A motorable track continues for another mile to a gate (with advance advertisements for accommodation in Dufton for Pennine Way walkers coming over from Teesdale). The track continues, now suitable for only off-road vehicles, to Peeping Hill.

On the ascent you notice three unusual hills to the N - Dufton Pike (1578ft/481m), Knock Pike (1306ft/398m) and Burney Hill (1400ft/427m). These conical foothills of the Pennine chain are of limestone, but a volcanic intrusion - the Whin Sill - lying laterally along a bedding plane has capped and protected the vulnerable, normally easily-eroded limestone. The volcanic intrusion is best seen at High Cup, where it rims the cliffs of a long glaciated side valley of the Eden.

The High Cup Scar is striking in the complete evenness of its upper rim of crags, which extend in a horseshoe round the dale-head. Weathering of the vertical structure of the cliffs has produced pinnacles and needles standing out from the cliffs and great fallen blocks on the screes below. The Whin Sill is overlaid by horizontal beds of limestone and provides the source of several streams: the spring of

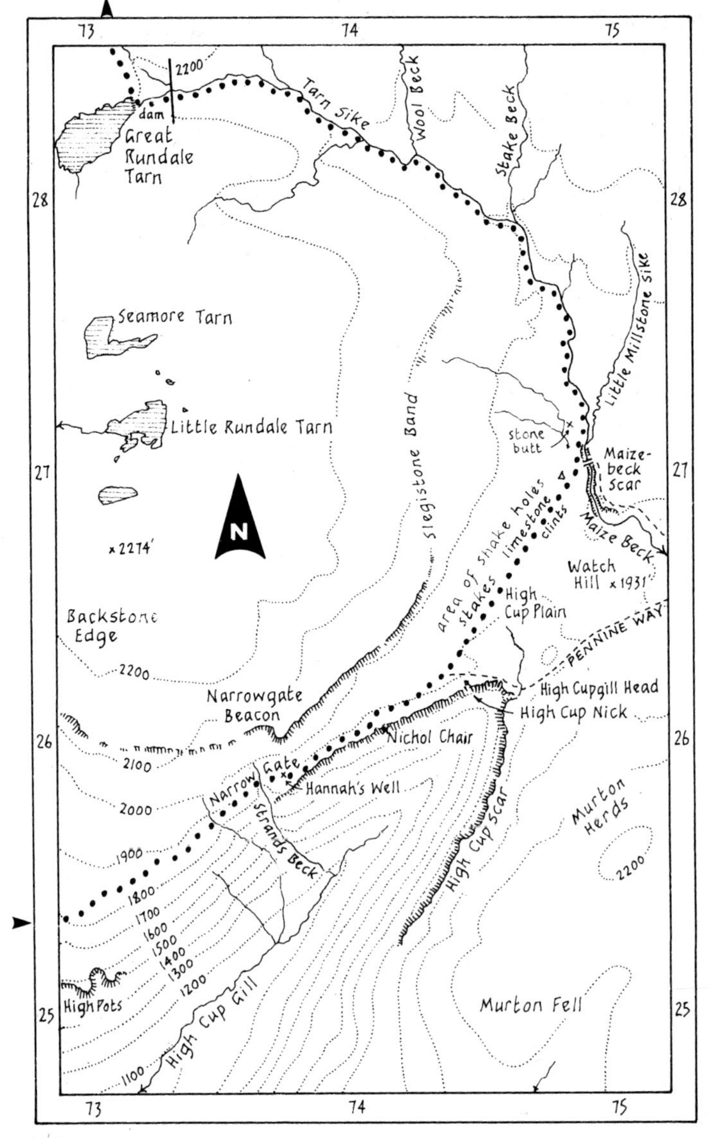
Great Rundale Tarn
dam
2200
Tarn Sike
Wool Beck
Stake Beck
Little Millstone Sike
Seamore Tarn
Little Rundale Tarn
Slegistone Band
stone butt
Maize-beck Scar
Maize Beck
area of shake holes
limestone clints
stakes
x2274'
Watch Hill x1931'
High Cup Plain
Backstone Edge
PENNINE WAY
2200
High Cupgill Head
High Cup Nick
Narrowgate Beacon
Nichol Chair
2100
Narrow Gate
Hannah's Well
2000
Strands Beck
High Cup Scar
Murton Herds
1900
1800
1700
1600
1500
1400
1300
1200
2200
High Pots
High Cup Gill
Murton Fell
1100
73
74
75
28
27
26
25

Hannah's Well is the largest. The acid and calcareous conditions at High Cup Scar support several interesting plants, including the rare clustered alpine saxifrage at its only location in the Pennines.
(High Level Route continues on Map 5.3)

Map 5.3

High Level Route

From High Cup Nick we had thought of taking you NW over the boggy plateau to visit Seamore Tarn and Little and Great Rundale Tarns, but we thought better of it. Practicable only in dry weather and good visibility, there would be only a few occasions when this could be a pleasant excursion.

Instead we have played safe by taking you first NE along the line of the limestone clints to the footbridge over Maize Beck (do not cross) then along the positive navigational aid of Tarn Sike, following it to its major source, the outlet of Great Rundale Tarn. You should be reaching the Maize Beck footbridge about 1.30 hours after leaving Dufton. There is rudimentary shelter inside a square stone-built shooting butt about 200m N of the footbridge. The faint trod on the W bank of Tarn Sike is made by sheep and used by the occasional grouse-shooter: if you can find it, use it, and you should reach the outlet of Great Rundale Tarn 45 minutes after leaving the footbridge.

The brown peaty waters of Maize Beck rush through a deep limestone ravine, its horizontal black rocks polished smooth by the waters. In the shelter of the ravine grows bird cherry and rock whitebeam and plants such as alpine cinquefoil, alpine meadow grass, northern bedstraw and the pink hairy stonecrop.
(High Level Route continues on Map 5.4)

Map 5.4

High Level Route

From the dam of Great Rundale Tarn take a compass bearing NW (337°) to the cairn on the top of Knock Fell (2604ft/794m). There is no path (as yet?). You won't be able to follow a direct line because of the peat groughs and bogs that bar the way. This is tough going, but in good conditions it should take you 45 minutes from the tarn to the fell top.

Apart from the ubiquitous red grouse this peat moorland supports considerable breeding populations of interesting birds. Ring ouzel and wheatear are well represented but wading birds are numerous and several species nest on these Pennine fells at record elevations in Great Britain - for example, redshank (2400ft/731m), snipe (2600ft/792m), curlew (2600ft/792m), and lapwing (2900ft/883m). Golden plover and dunlin breed within a short distance of the summit cairn on Cross Fell

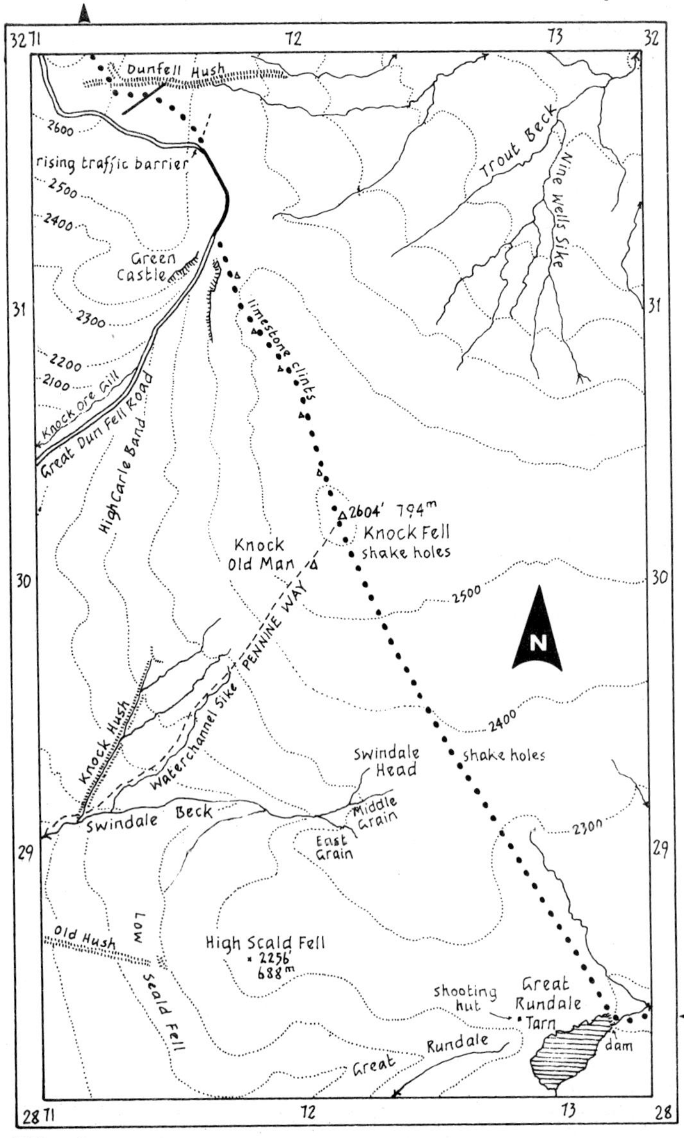

Dunfell Hush
2600
rising traffic barrier
2500
2400
Green Castle
2300
2200
2100
Knock Ore Gill
Great Dun Fell Road
High Carle Band
limestone clints
2604' 794m
Knock Fell
shake holes
Knock Old Man
PENNINE WAY
2500
Trout Beck
Nine Wells Sike
Knock Hush
Waterchannel Sike
2400
shake holes
Swindale Head
Swindale Beck
Middle Grain
East Grain
2300
Old Hush
Low
Scald Fell
High Scald Fell
2256' 688m
shooting hut
Great Rundale Tarn
dam
Rundale
Great
N
32 71
72
73
32
31
30
29
28 71
28

(2930ft/893m).

The main cairn on Knock Fell is on the western edge of a flat limestone plateau and the terrain changes: dry stony slopes and close cropped turf, a short relief.

At Knock Fell the Pennine Way comes up from Dufton on its way to Alston, and we follow this route - and the Pennine Way-farers - as far as Cross Fell. The route from Knock Fell is now well-defined with occasional cairns as far as the private road coming up from Knock. The popularity of the Pennine Way is shown by the broad path where thousands of footsteps have tried to avoid the boggy bits. Follow the road to the traffic barrier then continue NW across the head of Dunfell Hush to Great Dun Fell. (30 minutes from Knock Fell.)

(High Level Route continues on Map 5.5)

Map 5.5

High Level Route

Great Dun Fell is occupied by a Civil Aviation Authority radar station. Following a decision by the Secretary of State in 1984 the CAA commenced building a new radar station in the autumn of 1985 beside the old one. A novel feature is a huge golf-ball-like radome to protect the sensitive radar from the elements.

The radar station is also a meteorological station, and its records show that wide extremes of weather are encountered on these Pennine fells: snow falls on about 123 days per year and lies for about 152 days; for 265 days the fell is shrouded in cloud or hill fog, and the rainfall is 105″/2667mm per annum. The highest wind speed recorded is 116 knots, and there are on average 165 days of gales. The lowest temperature recorded has been −7.2°C and the highest +24.6°C (1983).

The path crosses Great Dun Fell (2780ft/847m) and continues in the same direction over Little Dun Fell (2761ft/842m) to Tees Head. This saddle (at 2532ft/772m) holds the source of the River Tees and the infant river and Crowdundale Beck mark the former Westmorland boundary with Cumberland. The descent to Tees head passes through the worst boggy stretch on the whole of our route.

We cannot continue on our way without venturing outside Westmorland to visit Cross Fell (2930ft/893m), the highest point of the Pennines. Our path, and the Pennine Way, negotiates its southern screes and crosses its grassy plateau to the OS column on its summit. (45 mins from Great Dun Fell.)

We have already seen, at High Cup Nick, that where the volcanic magma has broken through the earth's crust it has sometimes forced its way horizontally along the bedding plane of the sedimentary rocks. In subsequent erosion this rock has protected the softer rocks below

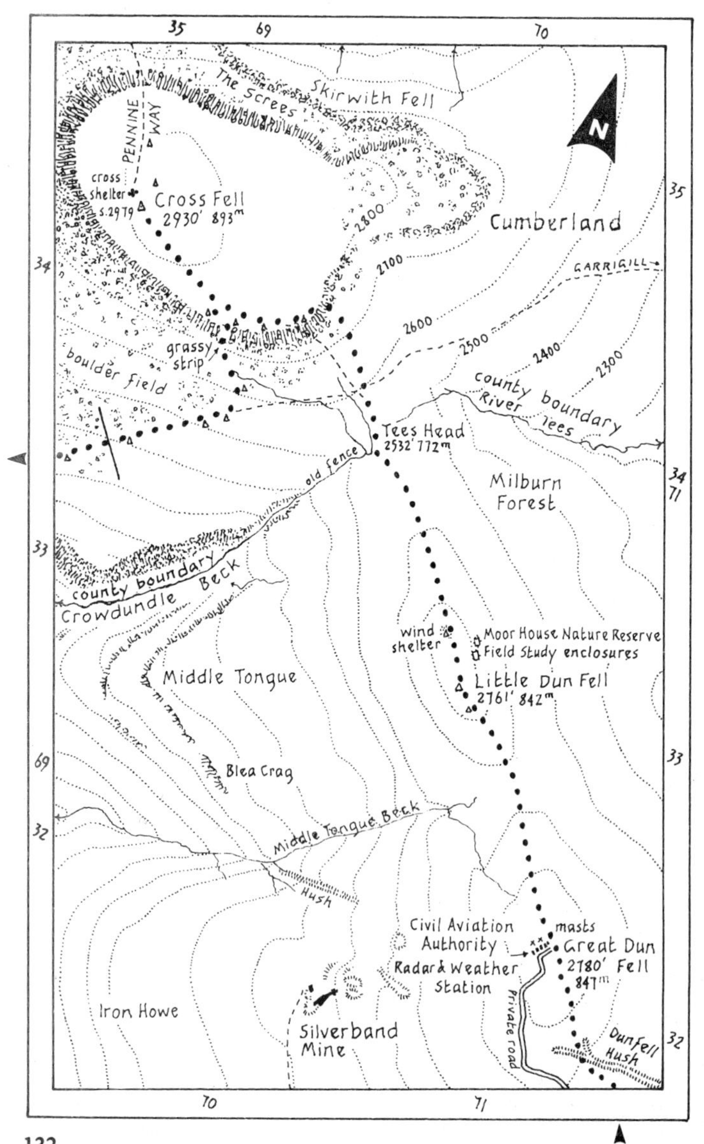
The Screes
Skirwith Fell
PENNINE WAY
N
cross shelter
S.2979
Cross Fell
2930' 893m
2800
Cumberland
2100
GARRIGILL
2600
2500
2400
2300
grassy strip
boulder field
county boundary
River Tees
Tees Head
2532' 772m
old fence
Milburn Forest
county boundary
Crowdundle Beck
wind shelter
Moor House Nature Reserve
Field Study enclosures
Middle Tongue
Little Dun Fell
2761' 842m
Blea Crag
Middle Tongue Beck
Hush
Civil Aviation Authority
Radar & Weather Station
masts
Great Dun Fell
2780'
847m
Private road
Iron Howe
Silverband Mine
Dunfell Hush

while all around rocks crumble away. The result at Cross Fell is a steep-faced hill with a large summit plateau: the volcanic rock in this instance is part of the Whin Sill, which supports Hadrian's Wall to the NE.

The summit plateau of Cross Fell is an arctic tundra and the freeze-thaw process has produced finely developed polygonal-shaped hummocks of soil and large scale patterns of stones. Mosses and lichens predominate but in spring can be seen the rare alpine foxtail and rare alpine forget-me-not, as well as the starry saxifrage, spring gentian and vernal sandwort.

Cross Fell was described in 1747 as 'a mountain that is generally ten months bury'd in snow, and eleven in cloud'. The fell has long been known as the source of the Helm Wind, a violent wind generated by strong southerlies scouring over the mountain range. The air stream behaves rather like a torrent of water pouring over a weir. While air further W might be calm a furious wind can be damaging buildings, trees and crops below the western escarpment. The effects of the wind are rarely felt W of the River Eden.

Retrace your steps from the summit of Cross Fell to the rim of the plateau and by some cairns - not those marking your ascent - find a grassy shelf past further cairns leading to the bridleway that crosses from Blencarn to Garrigill. Go SW down the cairned route.

(High Level Route continues on Map 5.6)

Map 5.6
High Level Route

The bridleway makes a good gradual descent, although the route is faint. The wind shelter near Sturba Nook (1986ft/605m) is a good viewpoint for the Eden valley. There is a sharp descent over Wildboar Scar and the route continues open and clear down Littledale, leading to a gate and sheep-pens at the end of the intake lane above the ruin of Wyethwaite. (1.15 hours from Cross Fell.) The gates are awkward to open/climb and the lane is muddy.

The right-of-way from Wyethwaite runs S through a broken gateway and alongside a broken wall to the crossing of the Crowdundale Beck, and we cross back into Westmorland.

(High Level Route continues on Map 5.8)

Map 5.7
Low Level Route

From Dufton the Pennine Way route is followed as far as Coatsike Farm, but bear off L beside a new bungalow on a signposted path towards Dufton church. This land is partially overgrown and in high summer it may be

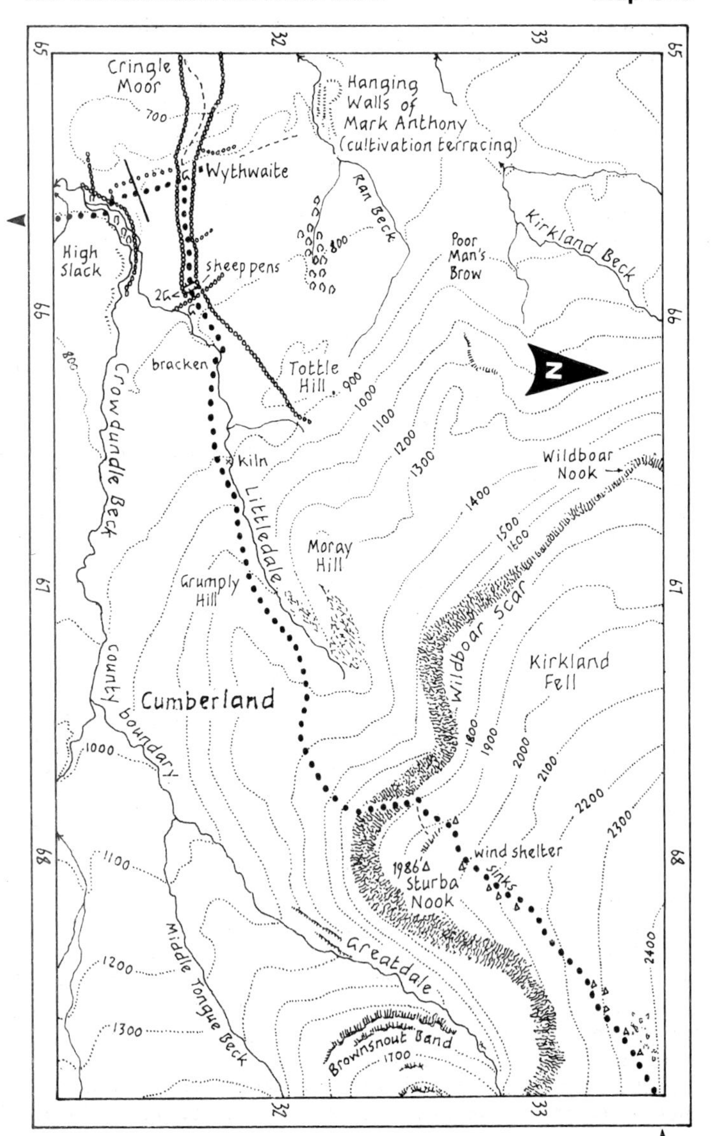

Cringle Moor
Hanging Walls of Mark Anthony (cultivation terracing)
Wythwaite
High Slack
Ran Beck
Kirkland Beck
Poor Man's Brow
sheep pens
bracken
Tottle Hill
Crowdundle Beck
Kiln
Wildboar Nook
Littledale
Moray Hill
Grumply Hill
Wildboar Scar
Kirkland Fell
County boundary
Cumberland
wind shelter
Sinks
Sturba Nook
Greatdale
Middle Tongue Beck
Brownsnout Band
N

preferable to follow the Dufton-Knock road as far as the church.

The church of **St. Cuthbert** is isolated and is shared between the villages of Dufton and Knock. It is a plain church with a gallery and was rebuilt in 1784 and the W tower added. It was thoroughly 'restored' in 1853.

Apart from the diversion to Dufton church and the crossing of Swindale Beck the route is obliged to follow the road through Knock and Silverband to Milburn Grange.

Knock is a delightfully compact little village with its strong stone cottages standing close to the road. The approach from Dufton is via an awkward narrow right-angled bend. The narrow road is flanked by massive thick walls from stones gathered in the neighbouring fields. Probably **Knock** and neighbouring **Silverband** accommodated the miners who worked lead and other ores from the fellsides above. The private road up to Great Dunn Fell gives access to the Silverband Mine, where veins of barytes are excavated by opencast methods. Until about 20 years ago the minerals were transported down the fellside by aerial ropeway to be processed at Silverband: the haulage and storage depot occupies its site.

(Low Level Route continues on Map 5.8)

Map 5.8

High Level Route

The right-of-way from the re-crossing of the county boundary at the Crowdundale Beck to the Milburn intake lane is not marked on the ground. The crossing of the beck is awkward - you have to wade - and would be difficult and dangerous in times of flood. The way southwards on the opposite bank is through rough and boggy ground: the driest land is alongside the wall. A good gate in the wall at some sheep-pens gives access to higher, firmer, ground but the three stiles on the right-of-way towards Milburn have had their steps removed and the netting fence topped with barbed wire.

Low Level Route

At Milburn Grange turn R and pass between the farm buildings and then L through fields to High Slakes and on a good track on the edge of Milburn Beck. Cross the beck by the bridge carrying the track to Howgill Castle (which cannot be seen from the path), turn L and pass through gates beside new farm buildings (muddy with slurry) and continue in the same direction as before into the village of Milburn.

Milburn is the most northerly village in Westmorland and one of the most attractive. It is rectangular in plan with its 18c and 19c houses

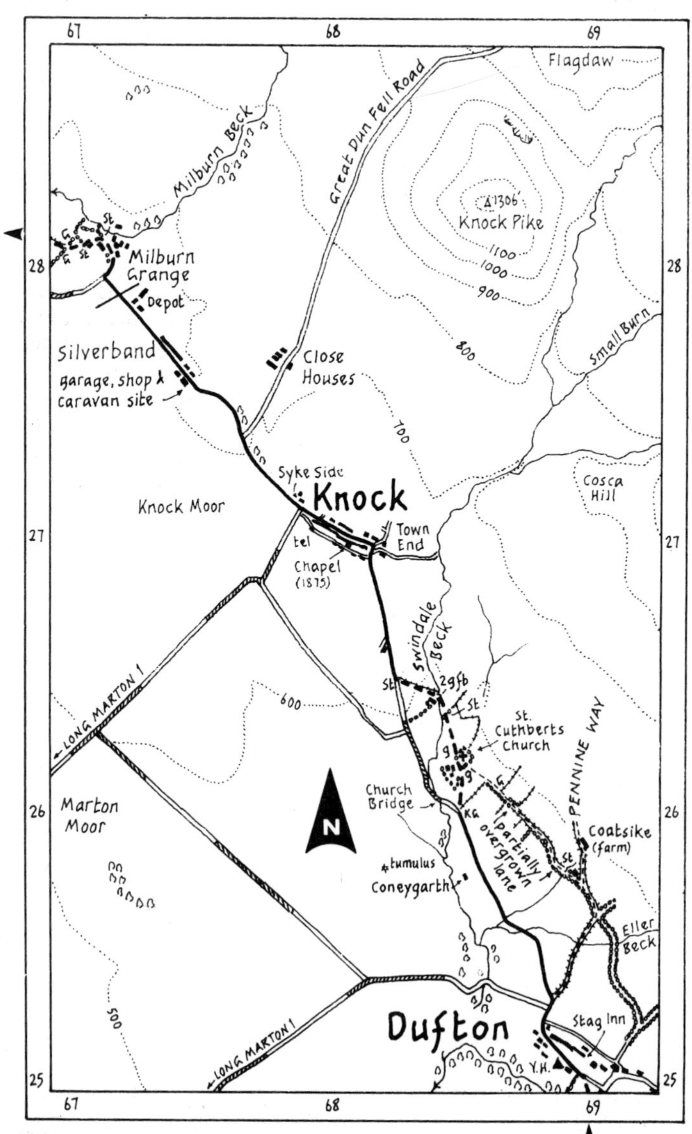

67
68
69
Flagdaw
Great Dun Fell Road
Milburn Beck
1306
Knock Pike
1100
1000
900
800
700
600
500
Milburn Grange
Depot
Silverband
garage, shop & caravan site
Close Houses
Small Burn
Syke Side
Knock
Knock Moor
Cosca Hill
Town End
tel
Chapel (1875)
Swindale Beck
St. Cuthberts Church
PENNINE WAY
LONG MARTON 1
Church Bridge
partially overgrown lane
Coatsike (farm)
tumulus
Coneygarth
Marton Moor
Eller Beck
N
Dufton
Stag Inn
Y.H.
28
27
26
25

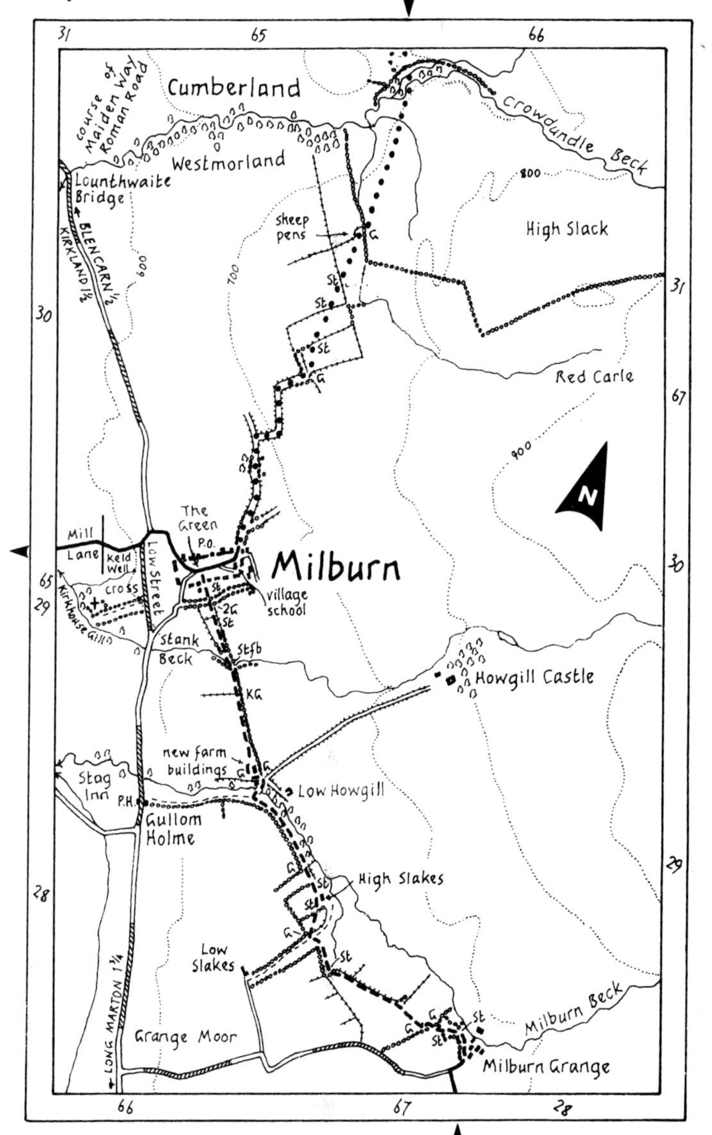
Cumberland
course of Maiden Way Roman Road
Westmorland
Lounthwaite Bridge
BLENCARN ½
KIRKLAND 1½
Crowdundle Beck
800
High Slack
sheep pens
G
St
700
600
30
31
Red Carle
67
900
N
The Green
P.O.
Mill Lane
Keld Well
Low Street
Milburn
village school
cross
Kirkhouse Gill
2G
Stank Beck
Stfb
KG
Howgill Castle
new farm buildings
Stag Inn
P.H.
Low Howgill
Gullom Holme
High Slakes
Low Slakes
Milburn Beck
Grange Moor
Milburn Grange
LONG MARTON 1¾
65
66
67
28
29

Map 5.9

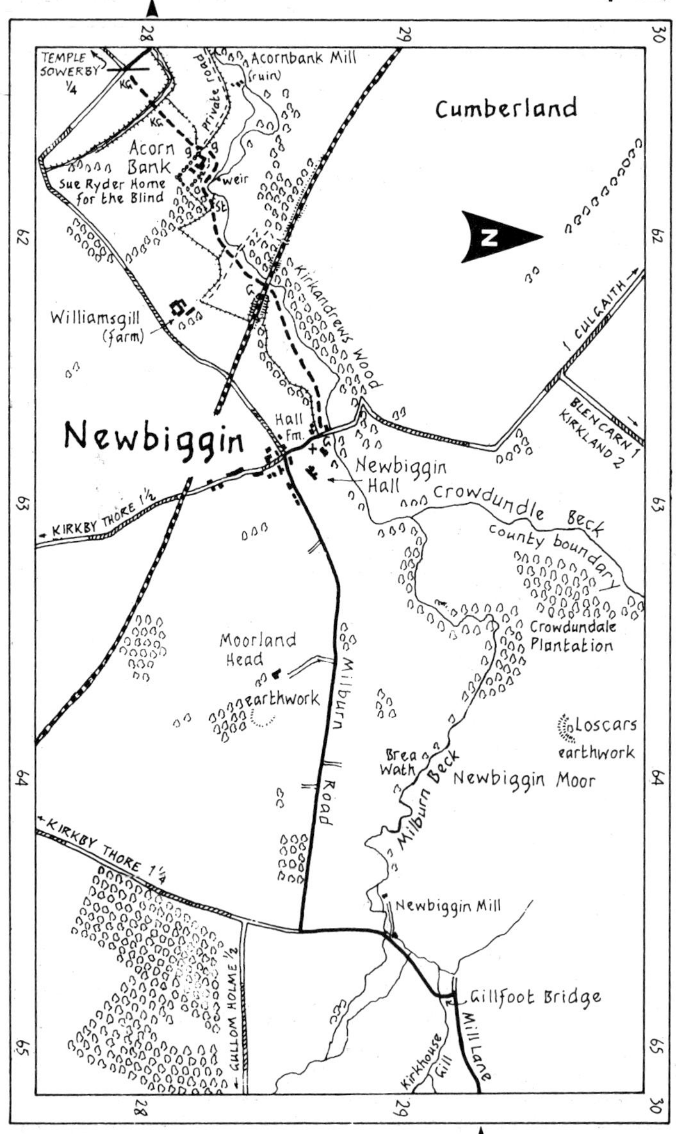
TEMPLE SOWERBY 1/4
KG
KG
Acornbank Mill (ruin)
private road
Acorn Bank
Sue Ryder Home for the Blind
weir
St.
Cumberland
N
Kirkandrews Wood
Williamsgill (farm)
CULGAITH
Newbiggin
Hall Fm.
Newbiggin Hall
BLENCARN 1
KIRKLAND 2
Crowdundle Beck
county boundary
KIRKBY THORE 1½
Crowdundale Plantation
Moorland Head
earthwork
Milburn Road
Loscars earthwork
Brea Wath
Milburn Beck
Newbiggin Moor
KIRKBY THORE 1¼
Newbiggin Mill
GULLOM HOLME ½
Gillfoot Bridge
Mill Lane
Kirkhouse Gill
28
29
30
62
63
64
65

and cottages around a large central green. The only road entrances into the village are narrow ones at each W corner although narrow, easily defended gaps between houses, called 'through-gangs' were other means of entry. The school, at the top end of the village, was established before 1790, and on the village green is a tall maypole set in the base of an old cross. For the Coronation of Queen Elizabeth II in 1953 a new maypole and weathervane were erected, a bus shelter was constructed, and a chestnut tree planted in front of the village school.

A little outside the village to the SW is the plain church of **St. Cuthbert.** Although mostly Norman its interior was completely 'restored' in 1894. It is a single cell church with a S aisle which was extended by one bay in 1605. The gabled bellcote was added when the church was restored, but it incorporates finials from the previous bellcote dated 1665. In the porch is a 13c tomb slab with wheeled cross and shears. The chancel walls are lined with panels from 18c box pews.

Those having walked the Low Level Route from Dufton would have crossed the farm lane to **Howgill Castle.** This H-shaped building dates from the 14c and has 17c buildings standing between huge towers with walls 10ft/3m thick incorporating stairs, passageways and tunnel vaulted basements; measures to keep the cattle safe when the Scots were raiding Westmorland. The barns, byre, wagon sheds and sawmill arranged around the courtyard were added *c.*1880. The sawmill and threshing barn on the N side were powered by an undershot waterwheel, which remains in use.

At Milburn the High Level Route and the Low Level Route come together and follow a common course until we come to Ullswater.

The right-of-way from Milburn church to Newbiggin is blocked in the vicinity of Kirkhouse Gill and Milburn Beck, so our route is obliged to follow the minor road called Mill Lane.

Map 5.9

From Milburn go down Mill Lane, cross Milburn Beck and turn R on the road to Newbiggin.

Newbiggin is almost on the Cumberland border and is now one of three villages in Cumbria sharing the same name. The church of **St. Edmund** was rebuilt in 14c and extensively restored in 1853-4. It has Decorated nave and chancel windows and a panel of the 121st Psalm above the door. In the village is a **Wesleyan Chapel,** 1880, neglected and empty.

Next to the church of St. Edmund is **Newbiggin Hall,** a large house with hipped slate roofs, corniced stone chimneys and embattled parapets, with some 15c and Georgian work but now mostly Victorian.

To the L of centre, on the N side, is a tower, known as The Jerusalem, probably built in the 1460's as a temporary refuge for the Crackenthorpe family who fought on the losing side in the Wars of the Roses. A more permanent tower was added to the rear in the early 16c, two storeys high with corner turrets. Life-size sculpted figures in armour were placed on the ridge but these were removed until 1983 when two were returned to Newbiggin. Soon after the second tower was built Christopher Crackenthorpe built, in 1533, a hall to link The Jerusalem with a third tower. The hall was remodelled in 1569 and a new, oval, dining room was built at first floor level in 1796. The third tower was rebuilt in 1844 by Anthony Salvin and a further wing was added to the N corner *c.* 1890 by C.J.Ferguson.

To the SE of the Hall is a range of contemporary farm buildings. A coach-house and barn form the N range, the groom's quarters form the W range and the labourers' quarters and a byre occupy the E range. To the W of the Hall is a combined hen-house, pig-sty and earth closet. These were built in 1796 and the hen-house still retains its original stone nesting boxes inside. The large kitchen garden has high stone walls, dated 1795, and there is a ha-ha on the NW side of the Hall. The Hall is private property and cannot be visited.

At the crossroads in Newbiggin turn R on the road to Culgaith and just past the Hall and church turn L on a path before you reach the bridge over Crowdundale Beck. The path follows the beck downstream, passes under the Carlisle-Settle railway line and into the grounds of the National Trust property Acorn Bank.

Acorn Bank, formerly Sowerby Manor, was once owned by the Knights Templars but after the suppression of their Order in 1312 their possessions were, by an Act of Parliament, given in 1323 to the Knights of St. John of Jerusalem, otherwise known as the Knights Hospitallers. The property remained with that Order until the Dissolution of religious houses by Henry VIII in 1543. The property was bequeathed to the National Trust in 1950 by Dorothy Una Ratcliffe, the authoress, and it is now a Sue Ryder Home for the Blind.

The central part of the house and its W wing date from *c.* 1600. The E front is symmetrical, three storeys high and nine bays wide and dates from *c.* 1730-50, when the house was remodelled and extended. The present dining room is fully panelled with vine-leaf and Greek-key decoration, and there is an Adam fireplace and overmantle. Other rooms retain 17c and 18c panelling, fireplaces and cornices. The Home is not open for viewing.

To the NW of the house, in the grounds, is Acorn Bank Mill on Crowdundale Beck and an adjoining Miller's House to the SE. Both are of late 18c date. The mill machinery is still in situ and the two cast-iron water wheels survive. The overshot wheel which powered the corn mill and saw mill machinery probably predates the undershot wheel, which was used to power tub haulage by an aerial ropeway in the owners nearby private gypsum mine until the mid-20c. Integral with the mill on the SW side is a four-bay pig-sty and to the S is a bank barn incorporating a cottage and byre. The whole mill building is in ruinous condition, and there are plans to remove the water wheels to a museum in Penrith. The National Trust ought instead preserve this aspect of Westmorland's heritage.

The house has attractive gardens and an outstanding herb garden and wild garden. The gardens are open to the public between 1 April -31 October every day, 1000-1730 hours, but there are, as yet, no facilities for visitors.

The Knights Templars, who were the early owners of the manor of Sowerby, gave their name to nearby Temple Sowerby, often referred to as the 'Queen of Westmorland's Villages'. Its pleasant, hilly central village green lies just off the busy A66 and the 'King's Arms' provides refreshment and accommodation.

Cross the cattle grid at the entrance gates of Acorn Bank and go SW across the field to a beck and the Newbiggin road at a T-junction. Temple Sowerby lies ahead, but we turn R.

Map 5.10

From the T-junction of the Temple Sowerby-Newbiggin-Culgaith roads at Acorn Bank there commences an unavoidable road trog that will be popular with no-one. There are two mile-long stretches of the busy A66 Scotch Corner-Penrith road to be walked, and there are no footways, but these stretches are separated by minor roads and paths, so it is not so unbearable.

From Acorn Bank turn R to the B6412 road (Millrigg Bridge crossing the beck is on the county boundary) then turn L to the A66. Here turn R and go W, crossing the River Eden by the arched Eden Bridge. There are plans to provide Temple Sowerby with a bypass and future road works may affect the A66 in the vicinity of Tollbar Cottage. After about 1 mile take the first road on the R (not the access to Winderwath) to Winderwath Farm and Woodside, then W, parallel to the main road. At the end, at Hornby Gate, turn R, away from the A66.

Map 5.11

From Hornby Gate a RUPP follows an unenclosed farm road to Hornby

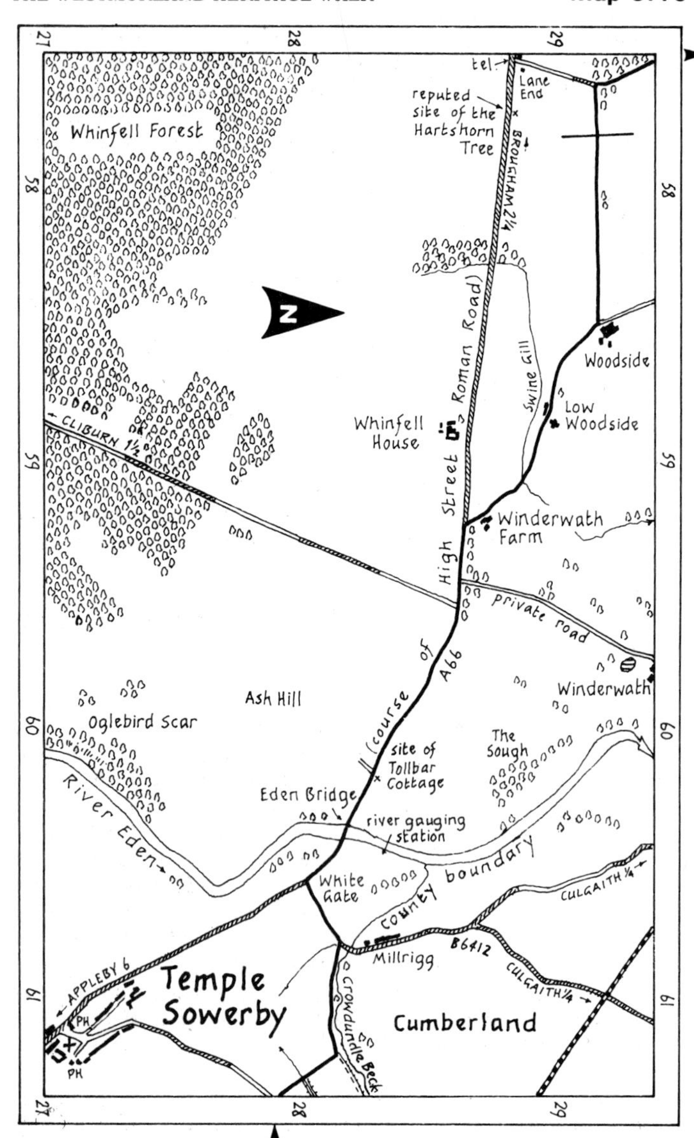
Whinfell Forest
tel.
Lane End
reputed site of the Hartshorn Tree
BROUGHAM 2¼
High Street Roman Road)
Whinfell House
Swine Gill
Woodside
Low Woodside
CLIBURN 1½
Winderwath Farm
Private road
Winderwath
(course of A66
Ash Hill
Oglebird Scar
The Sough
site of Tollbar Cottage
Eden Bridge
River Eden
river gauging station
White Gate
county boundary
CULGAITH ¼
B6412
Millrigg
CULGAITH ¼
APPLEBY 6
Temple Sowerby
PH
PH
Crowdundle Beck
Cumberland
27
28
29
58
59
60
61

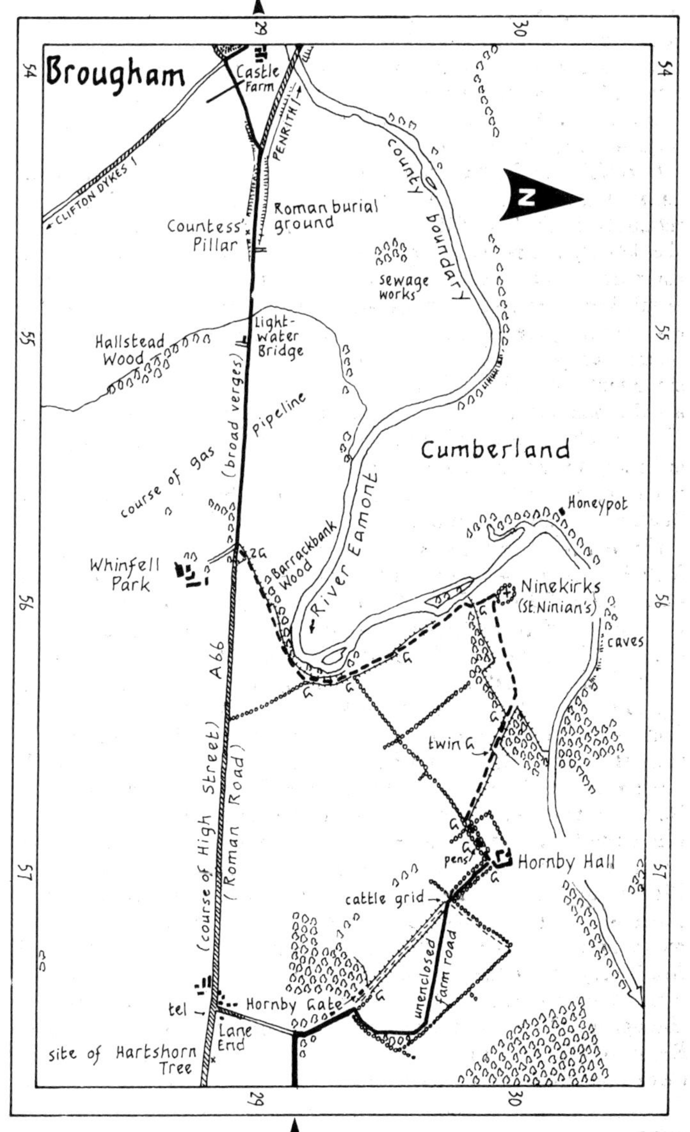
Brougham
Castle Farm
PENRITH
CLIFTON DYKES
Roman burial ground
Countess' Pillar
county boundary
N
sewage works
Hallstead Wood
Light-water Bridge
(broad verges)
pipeline
course of gas
Cumberland
River Eamont
Honeypot
Whinfell Park
2G
Barrackbank Wood
Ninekirks (St.Ninian's)
caves
A66
twin G
(course of High Street)
(Roman Road)
Hornby Hall
pens
cattle grid
unenclosed farm road
tel
Hornby Gate
Lane End
site of Hartshorn Tree
54
55
56
57
29
30

Hall, whereas a sensible alternative (though not a right-of-way) advances directly between fences towards the Hall, cutting off a section of the farm road. Hornby Hall is of red sandstone rubble with a slate roof, on a long rectangular plan. It dates from mid-16c. The three-storeyed gable porch was added c.1584 and has shields of arms on it. A path then goes towards a big bend in the River Eamont, making Ninekirks its objective.

Ninekirks, or **St. Ninian's Chapel,** stands in lonely isolation on the bank of the Eamont. It was built some time before 1393 and was rebuilt by Lady Anne Clifford in 1660 and stands today very much as she left it, a fine example of Gothic Survival. The rood screen, community rail, three-decker pulpit with sounding board, canopied family box pews and oak seats with carved armrests, all in the Jacobean tradition, are all her work of 1660 and are all well preserved. A quaint oak poor box, inside the door, is of 1663 and the local sandstone font is of 1662. In front of the communion rail, under a cover, is a red sandstone grave slab with a floriated cross and sword carving. The church was declared redundant on 1 August 1977 when the parish of Brougham was united with the parish of Clifton. It is still consecrated ground and is now cared for by the Church Commissioners' Redundant Churches Fund.

We have to return to the A66 in order to get to Brougham and another RUPP takes us from Ninekirks by the banks of the delightful river to the main road at Whinfell Park. Broad verges beside the main road provide some kind of refuge from the heavy traffic for the next mile and just past the Countess' Pillar we turn off gratefully L on the B6262 to Brougham.

The **Countess' Pillar** is a 14ft/4.26m high stone octagonal shaft with a pyramid top above a cubic block adorned with the arms of Lady Anne (Clifford and Veteripont) and her mother (Clifford and Russell) and a skull on one face and sundials on each of the other three faces. It was erected by Lady Anne Clifford (the Countess of Pembroke) in 1656 (the date on the face of the pillar is erroneous) to mark the spot where she bade farewell to her mother for the last time, when Anne left nearby Brougham Castle after a visit on 2 April 1616. In March 1985 the monument was repaired and repainted by English Heritage. There is a long inscription on a brass plate on the back of the pillar recording Lady Anne's wish that an annuity of £4 be distributed on 2 April every year to the poor of Brougham, to be handed over at a stone table which stands *c.*10ft/3m E of the Pillar. For three centuries the 'Brougham Dole' has been distributed from this spot: the present Rector of Clifton with Brougham, the Rev. T.W.H.Rutherford, has carried out the ceremony for the last 10 years.

6

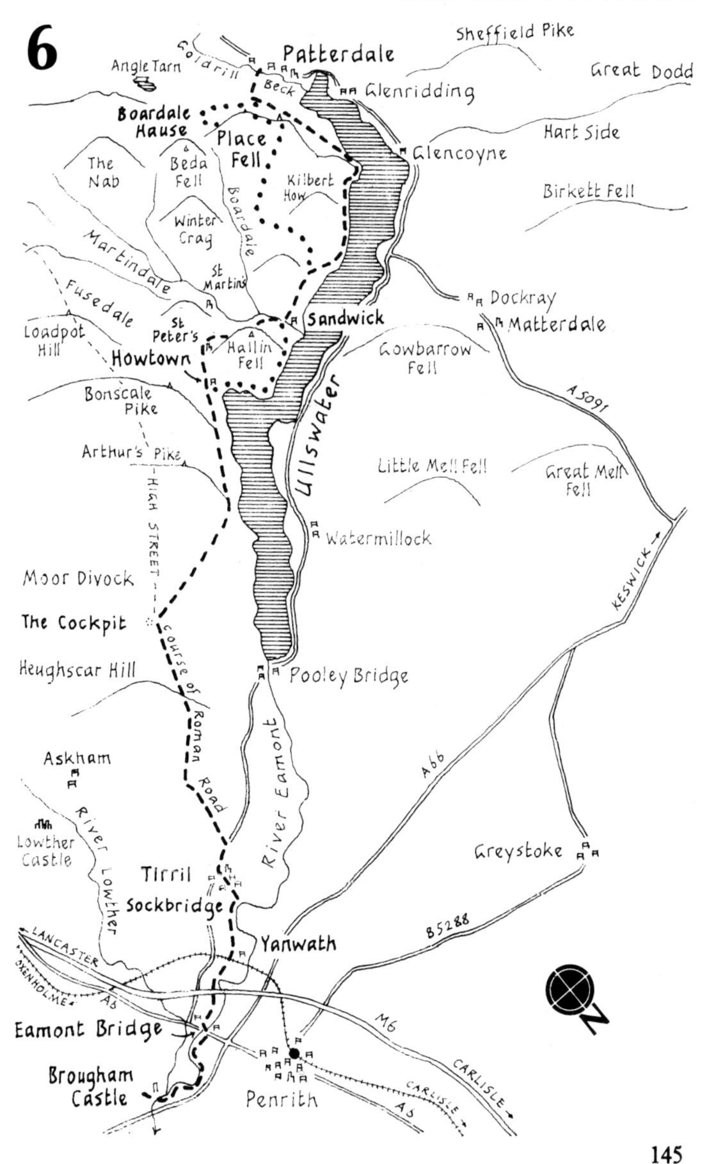
Sheffield Pike
Patterdale
Great Dodd
Angle Tarn
Goldrill
Beck
Glenridding
Boardale
Hause
Place
Fell
Hart Side
Glencoyne
The
Nab
Beda
Fell
Kilbert
How
Birkett Fell
Boardale
Winter
Crag
Martindale
St
Martin's
Dockray
Fusedale
Sandwick
Matterdale
Loadpot
Hill
St
Peter's
Hallin
Fell
Gowbarrow
Fell
Howtown
Bonscale
Pike
A5091
Ullswater
Arthur's Pike
Little Mell Fell
Great Mell
Fell
HIGH STREET
Watermillock
Moor Divock
KESWICK
The Cockpit
Course of Roman Road
Heughscar Hill
Pooley Bridge
River Eamont
Askham
A66
River Lowther
Lowther
Castle
Greystoke
Tirril
Sockbridge
B5288
Yanwath
LANCASTER
OXENHOLME
A6
M6
Eamont Bridge
Brougham
Castle
Penrith
CARLISLE
CARLISLE
A6
N

HORNBY HALL
NINEKIRKS
COUNTESS' PILLAR
108
109
110
111

BROUGHAM CASTLE
EAMONT BRIDGE
YANWATH
112
113
114

SOCKBRIDGE
TIRRIL
CELLERON
WINDER HALL
114
115
116

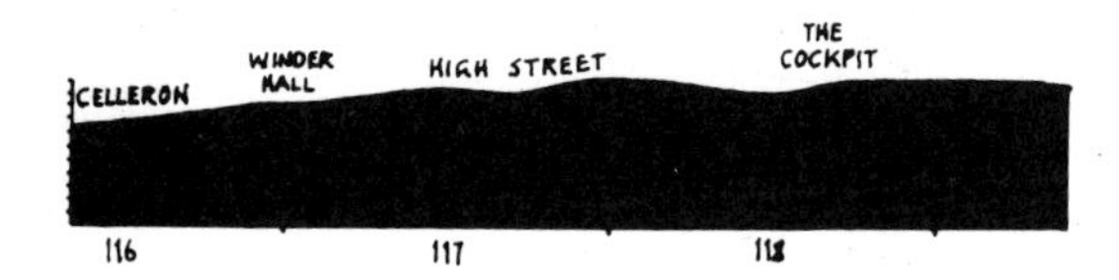
CELLERON
WINDER HALL
HIGH STREET
THE COCKPIT
116
117
118

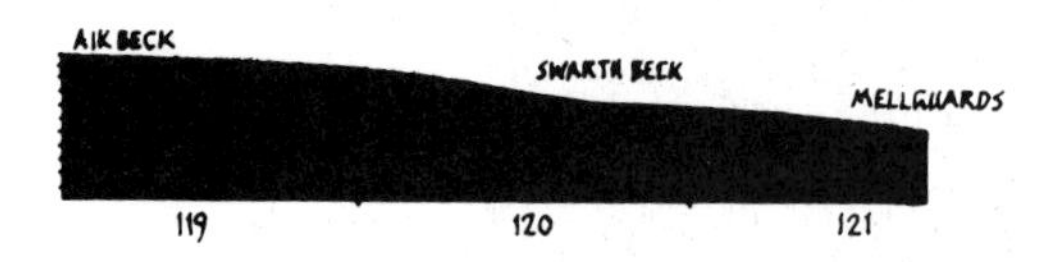
AIK BECK
SWARTH BECK
MELLGUARDS
119
120
121

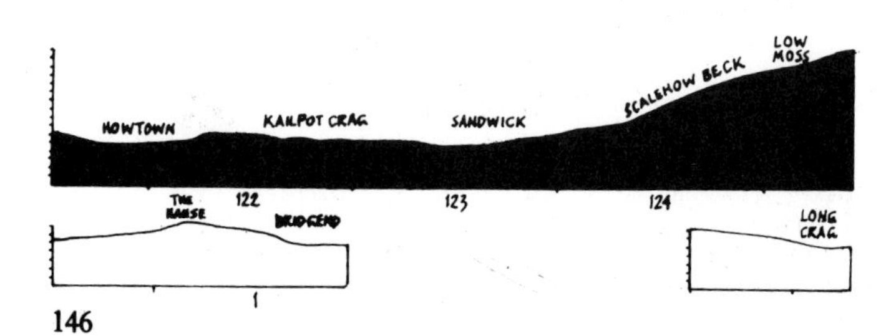
HOWTOWN
KAILPOT CRAG
SANDWICK
SCALEHOW BECK
LOW MOSS
122
123
124
LONG CRAG
1

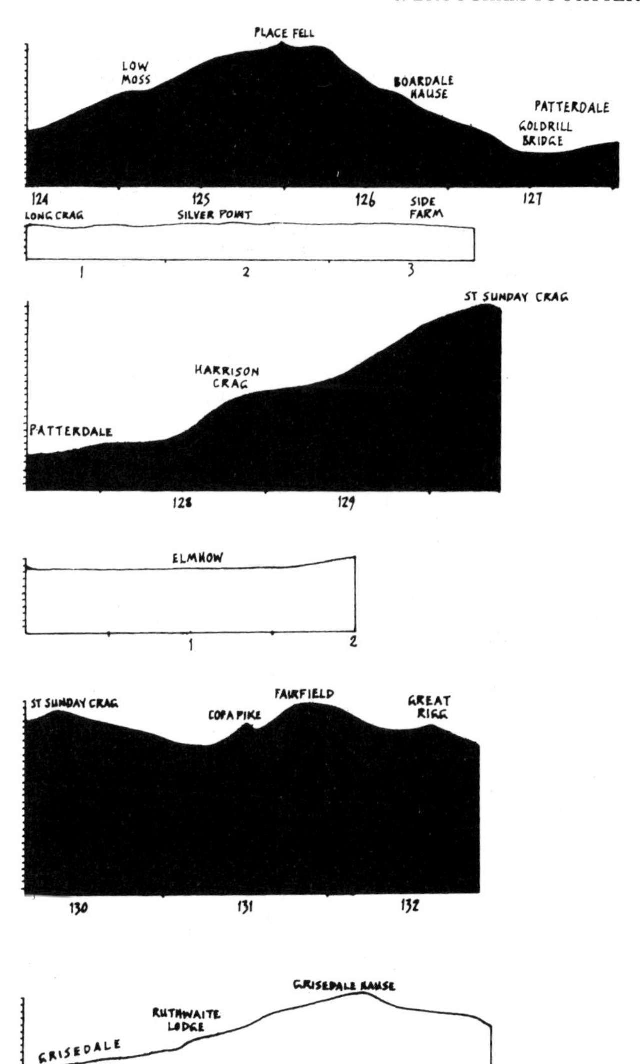
PLACE FELL
LOW MOSS
BOARDALE HAUSE
PATTERDALE
GOLDRILL BRIDGE
124
125
126
SIDE FARM
127
LONG CRAG
SILVER POINT
1
2
3
ST SUNDAY CRAG
HARRISON CRAG
PATTERDALE
128
129
ELMHOW
1
2
ST SUNDAY CRAG
COFA PIKE
FAIRFIELD
GREAT RIGG
130
131
132
GRISEDALE HAUSE
RUTHWAITE LODGE
GRISEDALE
2
3
4

Map 6.1

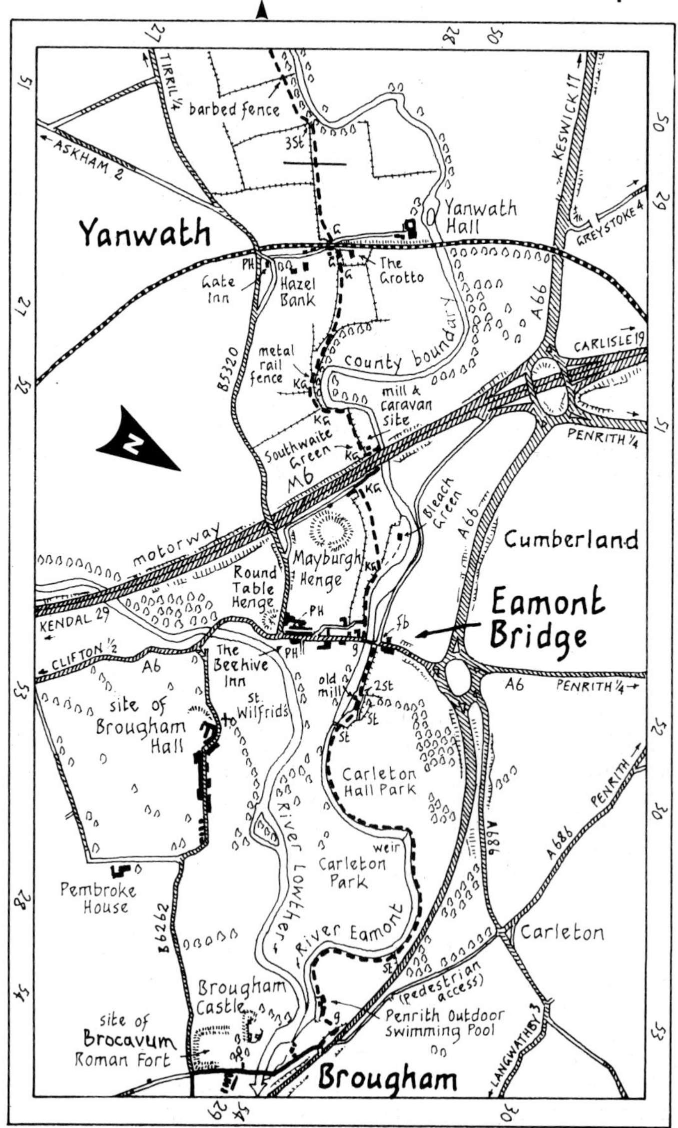

TIRRIL 1/4
barbed fence
3St
ASKHAM 2
Yanwath
Yanwath Hall
KESWICK 17
GREYSTOKE 4
PH
Gate Inn
Hazel Bank
The Grotto
A66
county boundary
CARLISLE 19
metal rail fence
KG
B5320
mill & caravan site
PENRITH 1/4
Southwaite Green
M6
Bleach Green
motorway
Mayburgh Henge
A66
Cumberland
Round Table Henge
Eamont Bridge
KENDAL 29
PH
fb
CLIFTON 1/2
The Beehive Inn
A6
PENRITH 1/4
site of Brougham Hall
old mill
2St
St. Wilfrid's
St
Carleton Hall Park
PENRITH
River Lowther
A686
weir
Carleton Park
Pembroke House
B6262
River Eamont
Carleton
(pedestrian access)
Brougham Castle
site of Brocavum Roman Fort
Penrith Outdoor Swimming Pool
LANGWATHBY 3
Brougham

6. Brougham to Patterdale

At Brougham we are just over half-way round Westmorland. We have left behind the moorland hills of the Howgills, Mallerstang and the Pennines and now we make a significant turn towards the Lakeland fells.

As we turn southwestwards there is a dramatic change in the geology and scenery. The M6 motorway is roughly along the divide between the sandstones of the Eden valley and the Carboniferous limestones which form the foothills that encircle the northern sector of the Lake District in an arc from the Lune valley in the SE round to Whitehaven in the W. We leave these and the Millstone Grits behind as we follow the course of a Roman road up into the fells of the Lake District: fells which between Martindale and Ullswater, are of Borrowdale Volcanics until we get to Ambleside. The pastoral wooded landscapes of the Eden valley give way to the rugged fells and crags of the central Lakeland fells.

From Eamont Bridge to Patterdale is a distance of about 15 miles/ 24km. There is a gradual ascent with views over Ullswater before a final climb up Place Fell: an ideal introduction to the delights to come.

Map 6.1

Brougham was once strategically placed at an important crossroads where the N-S route from Scotland to England met the E-W route from Durham and Yorkshire to Cumberland.

The Roman roads, probably based on earlier British tracks went northwards via Old Penrith and Carlisle (Luguvalium) to Hadrian's Wall; eastwards via Stainmore to York; southwards via Low Borrow Bridge at Tebay and down the Lune to Lancaster and Chester; and westwards over the Lakeland fells via High Street and Ambleside (Galava) to Ravenglass (Glannaventa), the port on the Cumberland coast.

The Romans built a fort at Brougham and there has been evidence of a large, thriving village. Remains of the fort (Brocavum) can be seen in a field to the S of Brougham Castle. **Brocavum** was probably built, or rebuilt, in 2c and was occupied until the late-4c. Its size suggests an occupation of up to 1000 troops and inscriptions indicate that both infantry and cavalry used it, doubtless to patrol the road system.

Picturesquely situated in meadows beside the River Eamont are the impressive remains of **Brougham Castle,** which was built partly over the site of the Roman fort Brocavum. Its moat and banks are well preserved and its massive 12c keep towers over it all.

After the death of David I of Scotland the land hereabouts came into English hands under Henry II and he granted land to Gospatrick, son of Orm, who built the keep *c.*1175. The lordship passed to the Vipont family in the late 12c and to the Cliffords, through marriage, a century later. It remained with the Cliffords until the death of Lady Anne, who restored it in 1651.

The castle is open to the public and you enter it through the gate-house *c.*1300-30 which carries the inscription 'Thys made Roger' -Roger was the fifth Lord Clifford. In the gate-hall beyond an inscript-ion records the repairs made by Lady Anne in 1651. Pass through a small courtyard to the inner gatehouse and keep. The keep is well preserved: it has walls 11ft/3.3m thick and it is *c.*40ft/12m square. It has a dungeon below the guardhouse, and two wells. On one floor is a chapel with two graceful windows and stone seats for priests, and on the third floor is a 13c oratory with a piscina in the wall.

To the E of the keep is the Great Chamber, now completely ruined, but further remains of buildings to the S including hall, kitchen, chapel and lodgings can be seen. The SW tower, The Tower of League, was built in the late 13c by Robert Clifford and still stands to its top, third floor.

There are two other places in Brougham that we should visit but they are not on our route, and they may be more easily visited from Eamont Bridge: **Brougham Hall** and **St. Wilfrid's Chapel** lie to the W of Brougham Castle along the B6262.

Brougham Hall was the seat of a family called Bird from the time of Henry VI to the 18c, and was locally known as 'Bird's Nest'. The last of the family was James Bird who was an eminent lawyer and anti-quary and was for many years land agent and manor steward to the Countess of Pembroke. He died without male heirs and the estate was sold by his granddaughters in 1726 to John Brougham of Scales. He was succeeded by his nephew Henry, grandfather of the First Lord Brougham and Vaux, the most famous of that family, who success-fully defended Queen Caroline against George IV's divorce petition in 1820. He became Chancellor of the Exchequer in 1830, and worked on the Reform Bill of 1832 and the anti-slavery laws. It was during his Chancellorship that he drove about in a carriage specially built for him, which was the forerunner of the closed carriages which bore his name.

The First Lord Brougham lived at Brougham Hall between 1810-68 but he demolished the medieval and Tudor hall *c.*1830-40. His replacement hall was demolished in 1924 and only the first floor and curtain walls are standing. The Army used the site as a wartime base - the nearby new houses are built on the site of the army camp. In December 1942 Churchill, Eisenhower and King George VI all visited Brougham to inspect a prototype tank that had been developed there: it generated 13 million candle power, to blind the enemy - the forerunner of today's laser.

A bridge across the road connected the Hall with the beautiful little chapel of **St. Wilfrid's,** which is well worth a visit. The simple, low building was built in 1658 but Lord William Brougham, Henry's brother, who inherited the estate, 'restored' it in 1840 and 'Normanised' the windows internally, but he also filled it with remarkable medieval Continental woodwork.

The masterpiece of St. Wilfrid's is the triptych or reredos, a remarkable carving dating from *c.* 1490 in three panels and attributed to Albert Durer. The central panel shows the Crucifixion and a group scene set in borders of extraordinarily fine work, and there is a deep canopy above it. The L panel shows Our Lord's presentation in the temple, the circumcision and the bearing of the Cross. The main scene in the R panel is the Descent from the Cross and there are scenes of the Baptism and the Entombment. This altar-piece was removed in 1968 for restoration and it was then exhibited for five years in the Victoria & Albert Museum. When the triptych was returned it was loaned to the Cathedral at Carlisle where it can now be seen. It is considered to be the best example of its type in Europe.

A locker with a magnificent lock and hinges has a vivid carving of the Resurrection on the door, showing Christ rising from the Tomb while the guardians sleep and may also be by Durer. There is also wonderful carved and gilded panelling on the walls of the chapel: one has scenes of the early life of Christ, Cain and Abel, David and Goliath. Another shows St. Martin, St. George, St. Ann and the Virgin, and the Adoration of the Magi. There are also panels in the organcase with carvings of the Entry into Jerusalem, the Madonna and Child, and the Crucifixion.

There is nothing in all Westmorland to surpass these treasures of St. Wilfrid's. Those who make the diversion to view them will be well rewarded. When the door is locked a key is available at Brougham Lodge, which is the house standing at the junction of the B6262 and A6.

Our route from Brougham follows the county boundary along the course of the River Eamont, at first on one bank in Cumberland and then on the other bank in Westmorland.

Cross the River Eamont at Brougham Castle by the by-passed Brougham

Castle Bridge. Where the road makes a junction with the new A66 turn L and follow the river upstream, past Penrith's open-air swimming pool all the way to Eamont Bridge. You reach the A6 by some lights that control traffic over the hump-backed Eamont Bridge, and you turn L to cross the river by a tubular steel footbridge.

The bridge over the river at **Eamont Bridge** is 16c and is very similar to Warcop Bridge over the Eden. It has three segmental arches with triangular cutwaters and has a total span of 120ft/36.5m. It marks the boundary with Cumberland, but ever since King Canute exchanged Cumberland for Lothian in 1032 this has been disputed territory. There have been claims and exchanges over Cumberland until the 1610 Act of Union. It was not until the Papal Intervention of 1237 that the boundary was settled.

On the Cumberland side of the river are two dated houses: one is 1734 and the other has an inscribed lintel 'Wharton 1781 D'uimns in Diem sed Nox venii. Nathan & Elizabeth Coull MMDCCXVII'. The first house in Westmorland is dated 1671 and carries the Latin inscription 'Omne Solum forti patria est' the cry of the exile from Ovid 'Every soil is fatherland to a brave man'. The house is also dated John Hall 1751, and next door is the Post Office, dated 1744. Beyond the Post Office, on the opposite side of the road, is a row of four cottages dated 1719. Further along the main road is the magnificent **Mansion House,** 1686, with five bays and 2½ storeys, a rare example in the N of England of the Anglo-Baroque style which became popular elsewhere in England a little earlier in the 17c. The central porch has quoins and a moulded doorway with enriched and dated lintel, cornice and balustraded top forming a balcony to a first floor window. An incongruous modern extension, 1980, was built when the house was converted into the offices of a credit card holiday company. Further down the road are two pubs: **The Crown Hotel,** dated 'WM Bushby 1770' at the junction of the B5320 road to Pooley Bridge, and opposite it **The Beehive Inn,** 1727, which was once kept by a Jacobite chaplain who turned innkeeper after the failure of the 1745 Rebellion. A rhyme above the door says:

> In this hive we are all alive,
> Good liquor makes us funny;
> If you be dry, step in and try
> The flavour of our honey.

On the opposite side of the A6/B5320 junction from the Crown Hotel is **King Arthur's Round Table,** thought by Scott to be a tilting-ground:

'Penrith's Table Round
For feats of chivalry renowned.'

It is a huge circular monument dating from *c.* 1800BC and was used for religious purposes. Roughly 150ft/45m in diameter, with an external bank 5ft/1.5m high enclosing a quarried ditch, it has two entrances. In 17c two standing stones were recorded outside the N entrance but both stones have now gone, and only the S entrance is visible today. The site was considerably disturbed in 19c and the low mound in the centre probably dates from those amateur excavations.

The henge was named after Arthur as a result of Shakespeare's version of an old ballad of Sir John Falstaff relating how Sir Lancelot du Lac slew the giant Cumberland robber chieftan Tarquin in a single combat, thereby releasing 64 knights of King Arthur's Court whom Tarquin had imprisoned. The 'Giant's Grave' in St. Andrew's churchyard, Penrith, is supposed to be the last resting place of Tarquin.

There is another henge monument at Eamont Bridge, easily seen from our route beside the river and from the M6 motorway. **Mayburgh** dates from *c.* 2000BC. Its roughly circular ramparts measure *c.* 380ft/116m across and 8-15ft/2.4-4.5m high and enclose 1.5 acres/0.6ha. A single stone 9ft/2.7m high stands in the centre of the enclosure. The site is unusual among British henge monuments in that it lacks a ditch. The bank is composed of water-worn cobbles from the River Eamont which makes the digging of an internal quarry ditch unnecessary.

At the crossing of the Eamont Bridge turn immediately R and follow the river again, but this time in Westmorland on a track to Bleach Green past Mayburgh to Southwaite Green Cottages. Turn R, pass under the M6 motorway to Southwaitegreen Mill and the caravan site then keep close to a loop in the river, then cross to pass under the London Euston-Glasgow Central railway to a lane near The Grotto on the approach to Yanwath Hall.

Yanwath is a small village straggling down the cul-de-sac alongside the main railway line. At the bottom of the cul-de-sac, to our R, is **Yanwath Hall**, probably the finest manorial hall in the country, an exceptionally interesting example showing the development of the pele tower into a manor house. The most dominating feature is the large square, three-storeyed pele tower, built by John de Sutton in 1322. It has a cellar with a vaulted roof and its walls, 6ft/1.8 thick, rise up 50ft/15m to a battlemented and turreted top. The Hall itself dates from 15c and is built on three sides of a cobbled courtyard. In it is preserved an oak bedstead in which it is said Mary, Queen of Scotts, slept when on her way from Carlisle to Bolton Castle. It is also said that Queen Elizabeth I visited Yanwath Hall during her tour of the N and slept in the same bed. The Hall passed from the Dudleys to the Lowthers in 1671 and it still forms part of the Lowther estate. It is now a farmhouse.

The Quaker Thomas Wilkinson (1751-1836) was born at Yanwath and lived at **The Grotto,** a short distance from Yanwath Hall. When aged 40, in 1791, he walked from Yanwath via Stainmoor to London in 8 days to attend a Quaker meeting. He was a friend of William Wordsworth and when William and Dorothy and Coleridge went on their Highland tour in 1803 they borrowed Wilkinson's account of his tour and followed his route. Wilkinson delighted in landscape gardening and he designed the rock path beside the River Lowther in Lowther Park and he helped to design the gardens of Tent Lodge, on the N bank of Coniston Water, where Alfred Tennyson spent his honeymoon in 1850. It was to Wilkinson that Wordsworth addressed 'To the Spade of a Friend' (1806). Wilkinson was a staunch Quaker and he helped Clarkson in his work for the abolition of slavery. He was buried in the graveyard of the little Quaker Meeting House at Tirril. Thomas Clarkson lived in Eusemere on the shores of Ullswater at Pooley Bridge.

From Yanwath Hall the right-of-way (signposted 'Romanway') has been altered from the route shown on the OS Outdoor Leisure NE sheet. Firstly it stays on the N side of a hedge to the high bank above the Eamont and crosses three stiles in a very confined space.

Map 6.2

From the three stiles the path goes to cross an unsatisfactory barbed fence, followed by an obscure descent into a very tall patch of wild rhubarb on the bank of the river. This may be a problem spot in times of flood, on which occasions walkers will need to follow the B5320 from The Grotto at Yanwath to Tirril.

The right-of-way continues on the bank of the river across Lady Beck to a footbridge across the river, turning back at an acute angle S towards Sockbridge. This dog's hind leg will inevitably be shortened by those going alongside the Lady Beck direct to Sockbridge.

Sockbridge is the start of the 'Wordsworth Trail': Richard Wordsworth, Receiver-General of Westmorland and grandfather of the poet, was the first of the family to settle in Westmorland and he lived at **Wordsworth House** (built in 1699). He lies buried in the nearby church of Barton. The village is now joined to Tirril by recent development and is a dormitory area for Penrith. **Sockbridge Hall** is a

Map 6.2

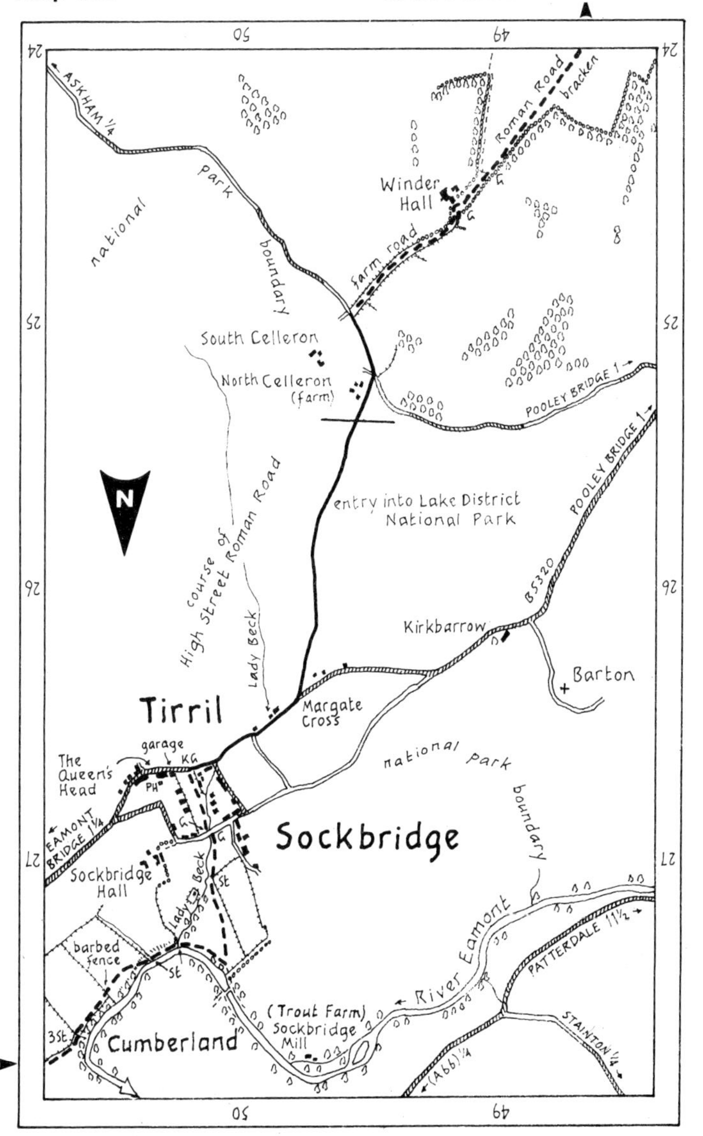
ASKHAM ¼
national park boundary
Roman Road
bracken
Winder Hall
farm road
South Celleron
North Celleron (farm)
POOLEY BRIDGE 1
entry into Lake District National Park
course of High Street Roman Road
Lady Beck
B5320
Kirkbarrow
Barton
Tirril
Margate Cross
garage
KG
The Queen's Head
PH
EAMONT BRIDGE ¼
national park boundary
Sockbridge
Sockbridge Hall
Lady Beck
St
River Eamont
PATTERDALE 1½
barbed fence
3St
(Trout Farm) Sockbridge Mill
Cumberland
STAINTON ¼
(A66) ¼
50
49
24
25
26
27

Map 6.3

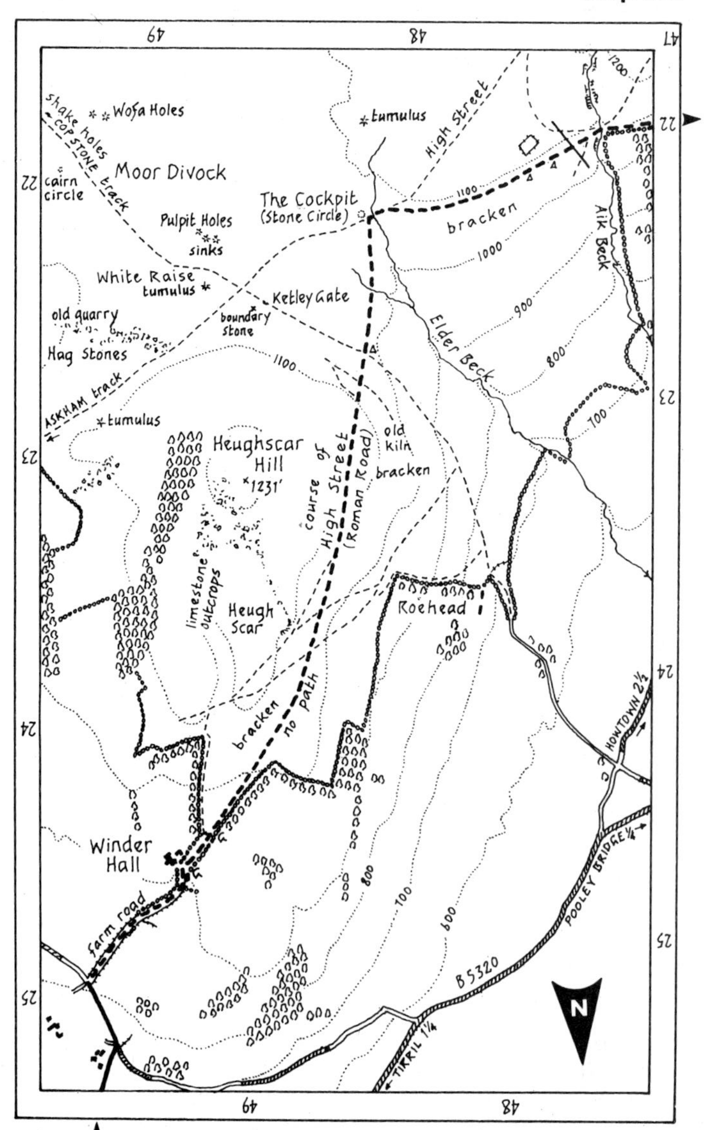
Wofa Holes
Shake holes
COPSTONE track
Moor Divock
cairn circle
tumulus
High Street
The Cockpit (Stone Circle)
Pulpit Holes
sinks
bracken
White Raise tumulus
Ketley Gate
boundary stone
old quarry
Hag Stones
ASKHAM track
tumulus
Elder Beck
Aik Beck
Heughscar Hill 1231'
course of High Street (Roman Road)
old kiln
bracken
limestone outcrops
Heugh Scar
Roehead
bracken
no path
Winder Hall
farm road
HOWTOWN 2½
POOLEY BRIDGE ¼
B5320
TIRRIL 1¼
N
1200
1100
1000
900
800
700
600
49
48
47
22
23
24
25

mid- and late-16c house of scored stucco over stone rubble with a slate roof. Notice the massive central and end chimneys.

Cross the road at Sockbridge, cross the Lady Beck and a field and meet the B5320 Eamont Bridge-Pooley Bridge road at Tirril.

Tirril is an old village on the line of the High Street Roman road. Near the village green is a barn dated 1767 and behind it is a house dated 1735. Another has the date 1765 and the inscription 'To know thyself is a Proof of Wisdom'. The Queen's Head is a long low building of scored stucco over stone, built in 1719 and extended in 1735. Near it is a house of 1712.

At the far end of the village is **The Old Meeting House,** 1733, single storey, the original Quaker Meeting House, later to become a reading room before the present one was built in 1914 on the village green. It is now a cottage. In front is an enclosure which was the Friend's burial ground and here is buried Thomas Wilkinson of Yanwath. It also has the grave of a young man called Charles Gough who was killed on Helvellyn in 1805. Gough's body was not found for three months and had been guarded all that time by his faithful dog. Scott and Wordsworth both used the story. There are now no gravestones in the cemetery: the Gough Memorial on Helvellyn, erected in 1890, honours the dog.

Go W along the B5320 Pooley Bridge road to Broad Ing then fork L at Margate Cross on a minor road to Celleron, entering the Lake District National Park on the way. Turn L at the farms at Celleron on the road to Askham, but after 300m or so turn R on the farm road to Winder Hall. (There is a right-of-way from the Celleron junction direct to the Winder Hall farm access but where it meets this farm access there is no stile. Until one is provided a diversion via the Askham road is necessary.)

We are now on the High Street Roman road.

Map 6.3

The Roman road from the fort at Brougham takes a direct line to Troutbeck near Windermere, reaching a height of 2716ft/828m on the ridge of the fells which take its name. The road goes beyond Winder Hall (built in 1612) as an indistinct track in the bracken below Heugh Scar but as it rises higher across the flank of Heughscar Hill to Moor Divock it becomes clearer, and navigation is obvious all the way to The Cockpit, a small stone circle. Moor Divock is a wild, open area where wild ponies roam, and apart from the stone circle there are cairns and other signs of Iron Age settlement.

Tempting though it is, we are not going to follow High Street any further. At The Cockpit we turn off W, and traverse the hillside after the crossing of the Eller Beck.

Map 6.4

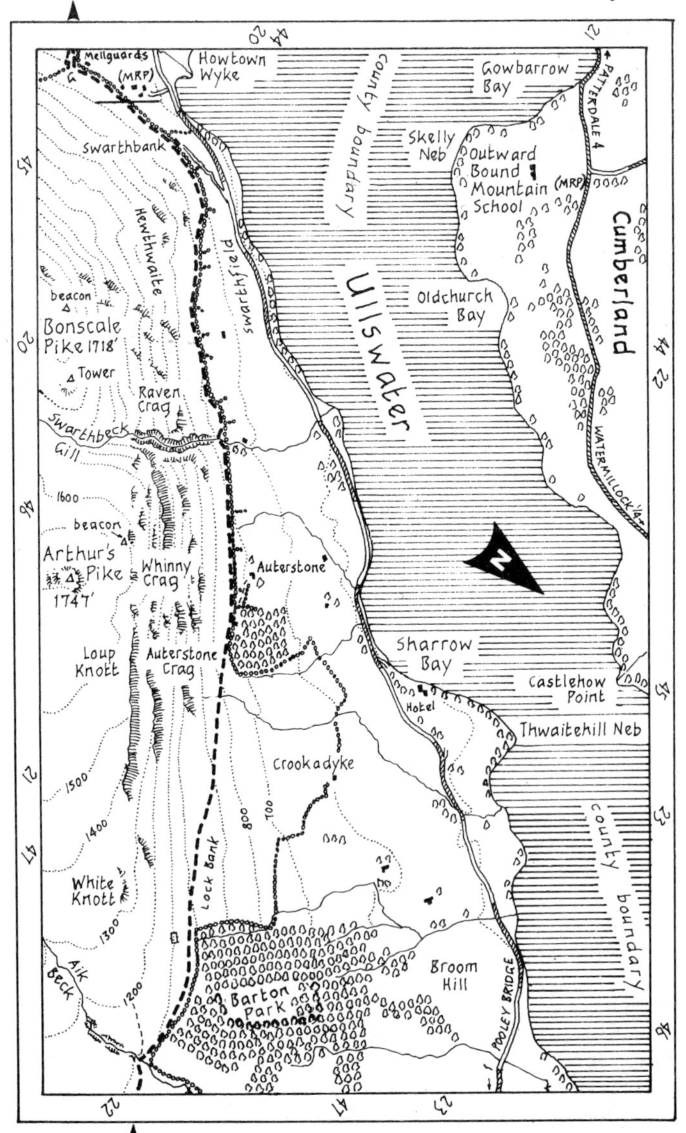

Meilguards
(MRP)
Howtown
Wyke
County boundary
Gowbarrow
Bay
PATTERDALE 4
Swarthbank
Skelly
Neb
Outward
Bound
Mountain
School
(MRP)
Hewthwaite
Swarthfield
Cumberland
beacon
Bonscale
Pike 1718'
Ullswater
Oldchurch
Bay
Tower
Raven
Crag
Swarthbeck
Gill
WATERMILLOCK 1/4
1600
beacon
Arthur's
Pike
1747'
Whinny
Crag
Auterstone
Loup
Knott
Auterstone
Crag
Sharrow
Bay
Castlehow
Point
Hotel
Thwaitehill Neb
Crookadyke
1500
800
700
1400
County boundary
Lock Bank
White
Knott
1300
Aik
Beck
1200
Barton
Park
Broom
Hill
POOLEY BRIDGE

Map 6.4

Our path makes a long gradual descent from Moor Divock below the flanks of Arthur's Pike (1747ft/532m) and Bonscale Pike (1718ft/524m) towards the shores of Ullswater.

Ullswater is the lake of L'Ulf, a Norse settler and is regarded as the Lake District's most beautiful lake. Second only to Windermere in size it is one of the leading lakes for the yachting enthusiast: fortunately motor speed-boating has been banned by the Lake District Special Planning Board.

The lake occupies the course of an Ice Age glacier and its serpentine shape is a result of the varying degrees of resistance of the underlying rock. The lake extends in three reaches from Pooley Bridge in the N to Glenridding and Patterdale in the S, a distance of 7½ miles/12km, and the geological differences of each reach account for the varying types of scenery along the lake's length. The comparatively flat but rich pastoral landscape of the Eamont valley between the Eden and Pooley Bridge is of sandstone and limestone, but wooded Dunmallard Hill is a volcanic outcrop. In the middle reaches the soft Skiddaw Slates provide an undulating landscape on the Cumberland shore, while the hard Borrowdale Volcanics tower above the southern, Westmorland, banks. The Borrowdale Volcanics make the fine mountain scenery at the head of the lake, providing the dramatic fells and austere crags of Helvellyn and Fairfield.

The lake is over 1km across at its widest point and it is at its deepest (over 200ft/60m) off Glencoyne. It is only 50ft/15m deep at its narrowest point, between Geordie's Crag near Howtown and Skelly Nab. The lake contains perch and trout and a whitefish - a freshwater herring called a schelly, from which Skelly Nab gets its name. They were once caught in huge quantities by a net strung across the lake at its narrowest point.

Soon after leaving The Cockpit, at the crossing of the Aik Beck, our path, a bridleway, follows the wall above the Barton Park wood and goes down below the crags of Arthur's Pike to the intake wall of Aughterstone, Swarthbeck and Swarthfield. At Swarthbank do not drop down to the steamer pier in Howtown Wyke, but keep above the intake wall to Mellguards and Howtown.

Map 6.5

Howtown is a small hamlet near the end of the narrow road from Pooley Bridge, which is also served by the Pooley Bridge-Glenridding steamer service. Its church, **St. Peter's,** 1880-2 in the Early English style, is at the top of the pass - Martindale Hause - going over into

Map 6.5

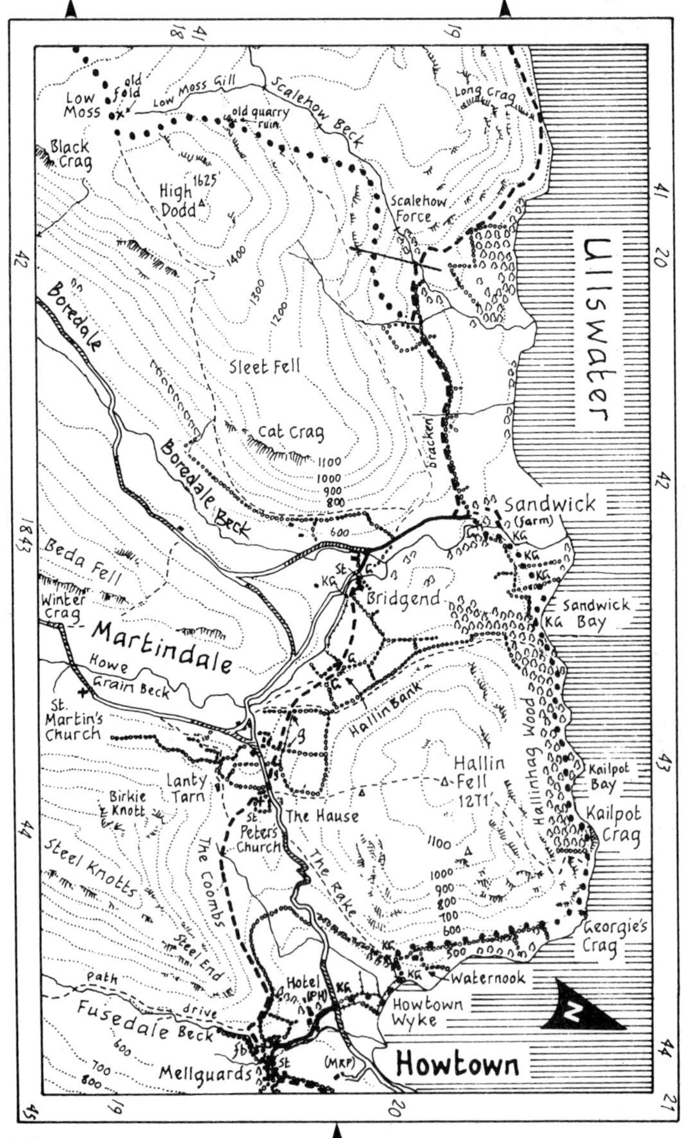
Low Moss
old fold
Low Moss Gill
old quarry ruin
Scalehow Beck
Long Crag
Black Crag
High Dodd
1625'
Scalehow Force
Ullswater
Boredale
Sleet Fell
Cat Crag
Boredale Beck
bracken
Sandwick (farm)
Beda Fell
Winter Crag
Bridgend
Sandwick Bay
Martindale
Howe Grain Beck
Hallin Bank
St. Martin's Church
Hallin Fell
1271'
Hallinhag Wood
Kailpot Bay
Kailpot Crag
Lanty Tarn
Birkie Knott
The Hause
St. Peter's Church
Steel Knotts
The Coombs
The Rake
Steel End
Georgie's Crag
Waternook
Path
Hotel (PH)
Howtown Wyke
drive
Fusedale Beck
Mellguards
Howtown

Martindale. At the far side, in Martindale itself, is **St. Martin's** church, 1633, which is worth a visit. It is starkly simple, a small stone rubble church with nave and chancel all in one and a stone-flagged floor and king post roof. The plain benches are made out of old box pews, the carved reading desk is dated 1634, but there are no stone effigies or memorials. St. Martin's was visited by William and Dorothy Wordsworth, and both recorded their impressions. Dorothy wrote an entralling account when describing their ramble through Boredale and William, in the second book of 'The Excursion', gave a touching description of the old peat gatherer who sheltered from the storm in the roofless chapel. **Martindale** is famed for its important, carefully conserved, herd of red deer which roam freely over the fells between Ullswater and the Shap road.

At **Howtown** we have our fifth High Level/Low Level options, and a little further on, beyond **Sandwick,** we have another set of options. These High Level/Low Level choices on the SE shore of Ullswater are not necessarily because of bad weather ruling out a climb over Place Fell but more particularly to enable you to savour the delights of the path near the lake shore. The Low Level route is one of the finest walks in the district.

Low Level Route

From Mellguards take the lane down to Howtown and the Howtown Hotel and the path to the lake shore at Howtown Wyke. Follow the shore for a short way, then up behind Waternook and around the foot of Hallin Fell, through Hallinhag Wood to Sandwick.

Hallinhag Wood is situated on a steep NW facing slope of Hallin Fell. It is a typical example of a mossy oakwood on rocks of the Borrowdale Volcanic Series, comparable to similar woods in the valleys of the Duddon and, of course, Borrowdale. We shall see similar woods to this in Great and Little Langdale.

The main trees are sessile and pendunculate oaks, but there is also hazel, birch, wych elm, sycamore and holly. What makes Hallinhag Wood so special is its diversity of breeding birds, which include species typical of both woodland and lakeside - birds of prey such as buzzard and kestrel and tree-nesting water birds such as goosander and red-breasted merganser. Other typical woodland species to be found include the redstart, green and great-spotted woodpecker, pied and spotted flycatcher and tree pipit.

At Sandwick turn L up the road then R behind Town Head, keeping above the wall to the footbridge over Scalehow Beck, just below Scalehow Force. The well-wooded shores and steep fellsides provide ever-changing

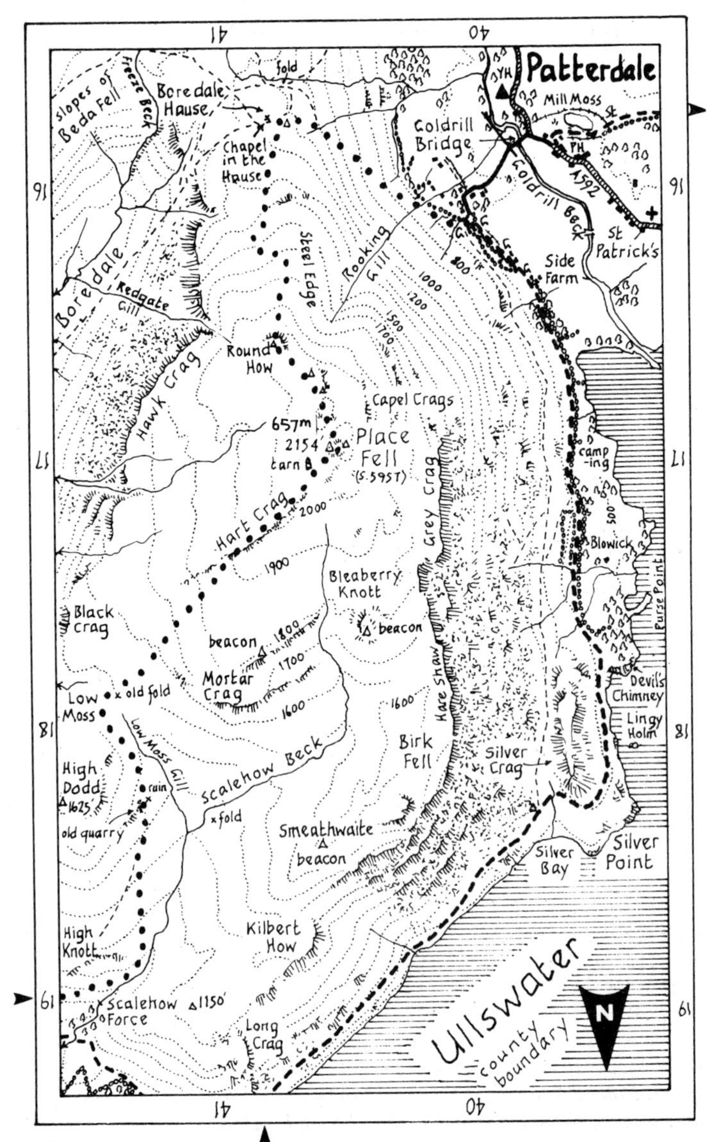
Patterdale
YH
Mill Moss
St
PH
A592
Coldrill Bridge
Coldrill Beck
St Patrick's
Side Farm
slopes of Beda Fell
Freeze Beck
Boredale Hause
fold
Chapel in the Hause
Steel Edge
Rooking Gill
Boredale
Redgate Gill
Round How
Hawk Crag
Capel Crags
657m
2154
Place Fell
tarn
(S.5957)
Hart Crag
2000
1900
1800
1700
1600
1500
1200
1000
800
500
Grey Crag
camp-ing
Blowick
Bleaberry Knott
beacon
Black crag
Mortar Crag
Low Moss
old fold
Low Moss Gill
Hare Shaw
Purse Point
Devil's Chimney
Lingy Holm
High Dodd
1625
ruin
old quarry
Scalehow Beck
fold
Birk Fell
Silver Crag
Smeathwaite
Silver Bay
Silver Point
High Knott
Kilbert How
Scalehow Force
1150
Long Crag
Ullswater
county boundary
N
41
40
91
17
81
61

views, seen in perfection in June greenery or rich October colours.
(Low Level Route continues on Map 6.6)

High Level Route
From Mellguards leave the drive L over a stile and descend to Fusedale Beck to a footbridge. The path rises on the opposite side, initially with a wall for company, on a clear path up The Coombs, branching R at the top to St. Peter's church on The Hause.

(From here the energetic may make a direct, short but steep ascent due N on a path to the summit of Hallin Fell (1271ft/388m) to obtain the superb view of Ullswater's middle reaches and the secretive valleys of Martindale, Boredale, Bannerdale and Fusedale.)

From the top of The Hause a waymarked route takes you past Hallinbank to Bridgend and Dawgreen and a short length of road takes you to Town Head at **Sandwick.** Town Head is partly built into the hillside. Built in 1720 it was extended in 1837. Notice the sheep dipping pen built into the front garden wall.

The High Level/Low Level Routes run together for a short way above the wall, but just before the footbridge over Scalehow Beck the High Level Route strikes up higher ground to the L, following the valleys of Scalehow Beck and Low Moss Gill to a col.
(High Level Route continues on Map 6.6)

Map 6.6

Low Level Route
The walk above the shore of Ullswater is a delight, and is straightforward. At Silver Bay you can take an 'inland' path between Silver Crag and the crag-faced Hare Shaw, but the lower one via Silver Point is probably the more attractive.

Where the NW slopes of Birk Fell fall down to the lake there is an unusually extensive area of vigorous juniper growth, the most extensive in Lakeland and equalling or exceeding that around High Force in Teesdale in size. It grows on leached brown soils of Borrowdale Volcanics and at the base of the slope is a stand of birchwood - we have seen at Hallinghag Wood that such acidic soils would normally be occupied by sessile oak woods.

Both low level paths keep parallel, but unite at Broadhow, a 17c cottage which Wordsworth acquired with the help of Lord Lonsdale, although the poet never lived there. If you take the lower path you will be tempted to turn off at Side Farm on the right-of-way along its access lane, but this short cut avoids Patterdale and its youth hostel and you are not so well placed for the next stage of the journey, unless you like road walking.

Where the two paths unite at the fell gate take the lane down to the bridge over the Goldrill Beck. Turn R here for Patterdale, or turn L for the youth hostel.
(Low Level Route continues on Map 7.1)

High Level Route

Place Fell (2154ft/657m) is a hummocky, steep sided fell, and our High Level Route makes the easiest ascent of it. The views from the top are exhilerating, and you will be torn between making the climb over its top or keeping to its flanks above the shores of Ullswater.

From the col at Low Moss the OS Maps show the path going W above Mortar Crag to cross the headwater of the Scalehow Beck, but the obvious path follows the line of Hart Crag direct for the summit of Place Fell and its OS column. Ignore the line of the path as shown on the OS Outdoor Leisure Map: follow the cairns S to Round How then steeply down to the confusing series of paths at Boredale Hause.

Boredale (or Boardale: the Ordnance Survey spell it both ways on different maps) carries an old pony track route from Howtown to Patterdale. The ruin on the pass of Boredale Hause (1300ft/386m) was once an old chapel - the Chapel in the Hause - which no doubt offered comfort and guidance to those lost in the mist in this bleak place.

From Boredale Hause turn NW on a broad and obvious track - the upper one of the two is the most convenient - joining the Low Level Route at the fell gate near Placefell House, and so to the crossing of the Goldrill Beck and into Patterdale.
(High Level Route continues on Map 7.1)

Ullswater from Birks.

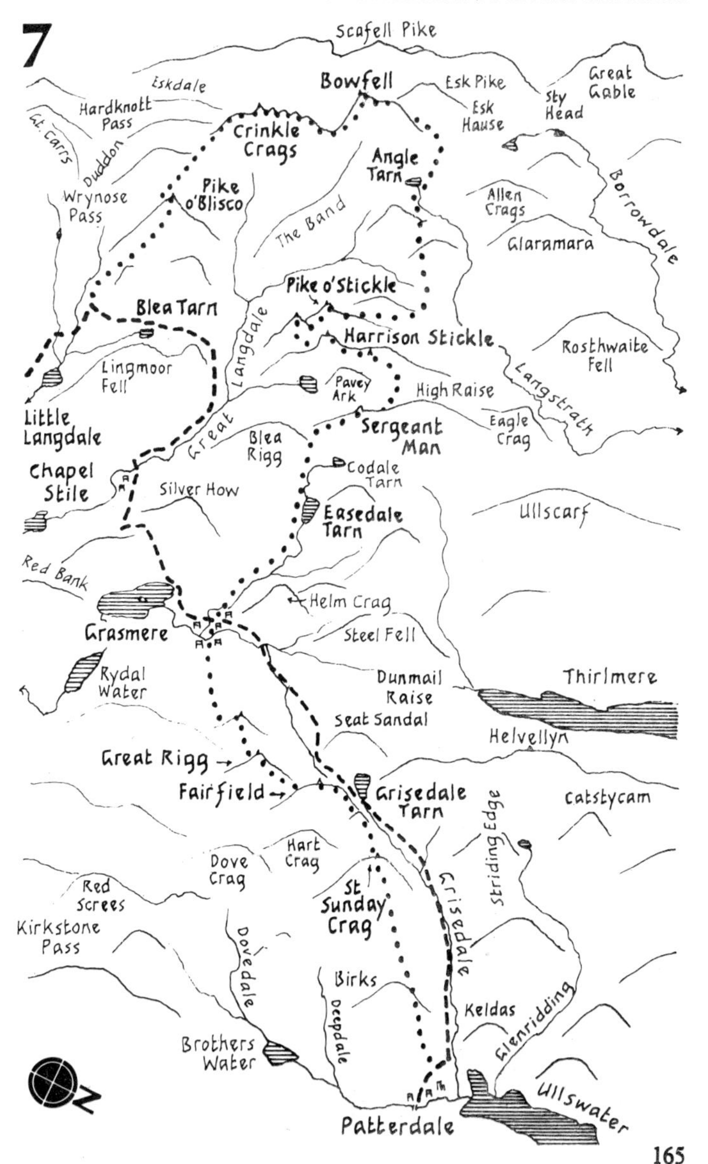
7
Scafell Pike
Eskdale
Bowfell
Esk Pike
Great Gable
Sty Head
Esk Hause
Hardknott Pass
Gt. Carrs
Duddon
Crinkle Crags
Angle Tarn
Borrowdale
Wrynose Pass
Pike o'Blisco
Allen Crags
The Band
Glaramara
Pike o'Stickle
Blea Tarn
Langdale
Harrison Stickle
Rosthwaite Fell
Lingmoor Fell
Pavey Ark
High Raise
Langstrath
Little Langdale
Great
Sergeant Man
Eagle Crag
Blea Rigg
Chapel Stile
Codale Tarn
Silver How
Easedale Tarn
Ullscarf
Red Bank
Helm Crag
Grasmere
Steel Fell
Rydal Water
Dunmail Raise
Thirlmere
Seat Sandal
Helvellyn
Great Rigg
Fairfield
Grisedale Tarn
Catstycam
Striding Edge
Hart Crag
Dove Crag
Red Screes
St Sunday Crag
Grisedale
Kirkstone Pass
Dovedale
Birks
Deepdale
Keldas
Glenridding
Brothers Water
Ullswater
Patterdale

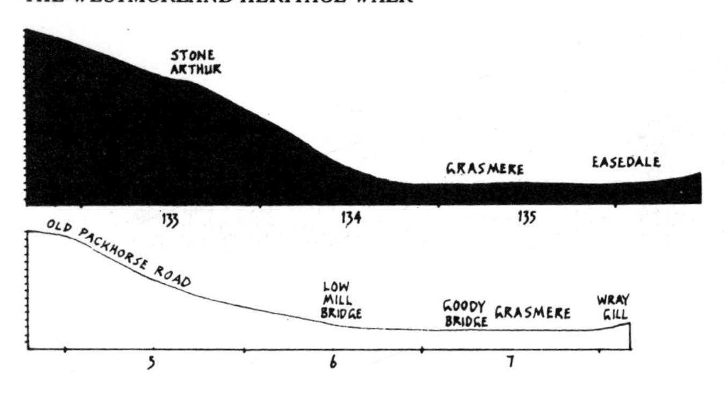
STONE ARTHUR
GRASMERE
EASEDALE
133
134
135
OLD PACKHORSE ROAD
LOW MILL BRIDGE
GOODY BRIDGE
GRASMERE
WRAY GILL
5
6
7

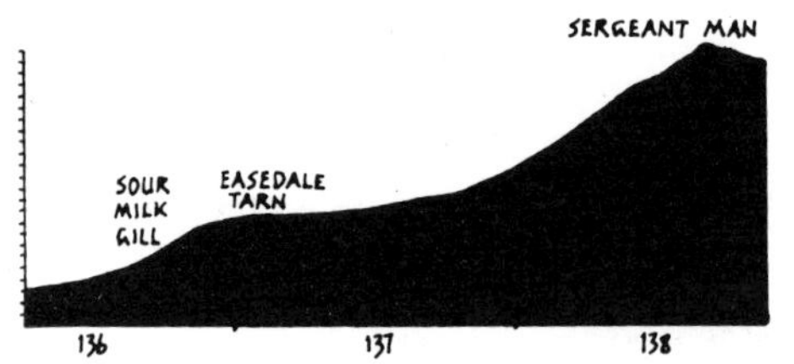
SERGEANT MAN
SOUR MILK GILL
EASEDALE TARN
136
137
138

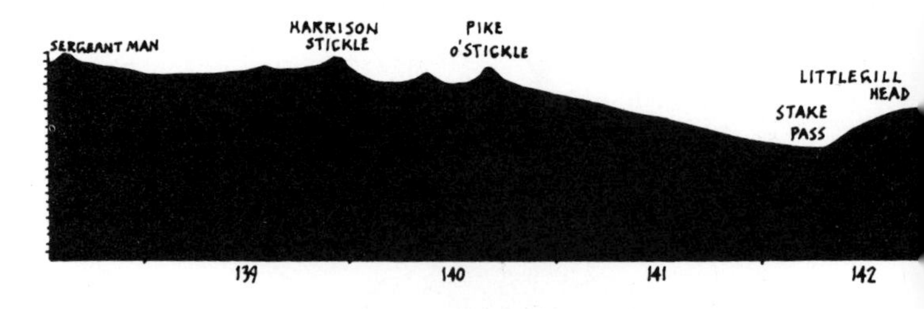
SERGEANT MAN
HARRISON STICKLE
PIKE O'STICKLE
LITTLEGILL HEAD
STAKE PASS
139
140
141
142

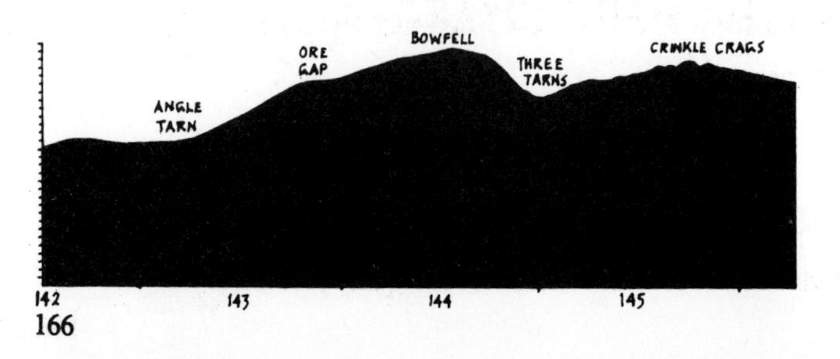
BOWFELL
ORE GAP
THREE TARNS
CRINKLE CRAGS
ANGLE TARN
142
143
144
145

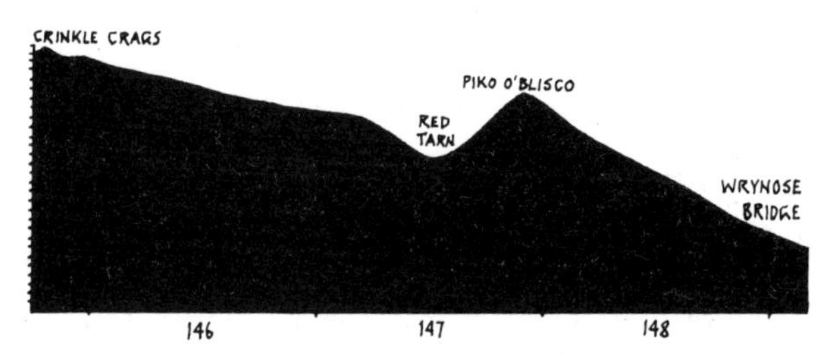
CRINKLE CRAGS
PIKO O'BLISCO
RED TARN
WRYNOSE BRIDGE
146
147
148

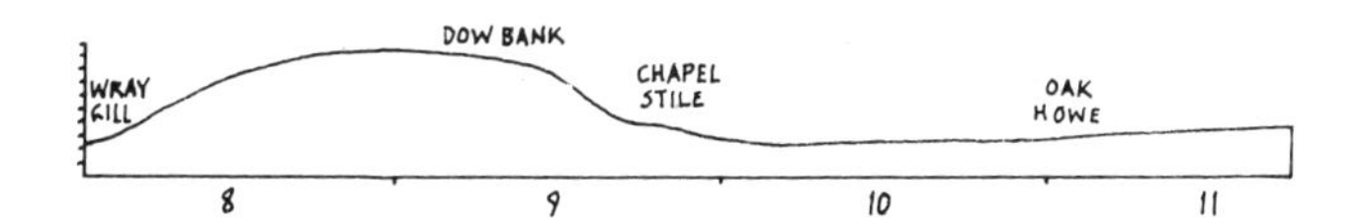
DOW BANK
WRAY GILL
CHAPEL STILE
OAK HOWE
8
9
10
11

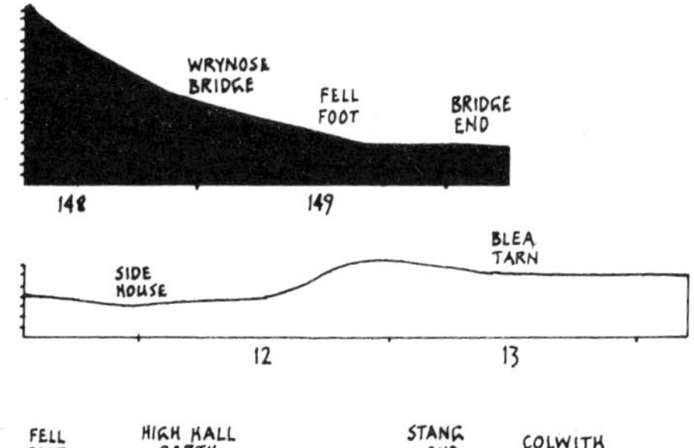
WRYNOSE BRIDGE
FELL FOOT
BRIDGE END
148
149
SIDE HOUSE
BLEA TARN
12
13

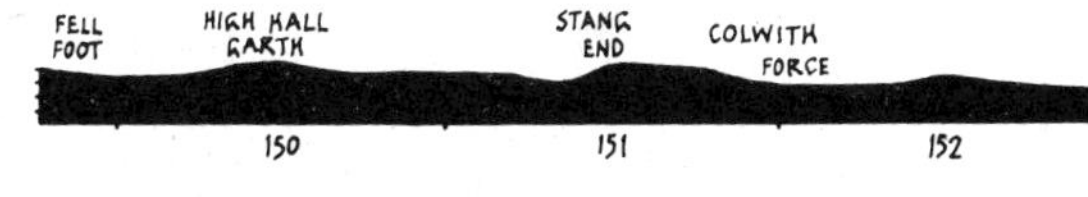
FELL FOOT
HIGH HALL GARTH
STANG END
COLWITH FORCE
150
151
152

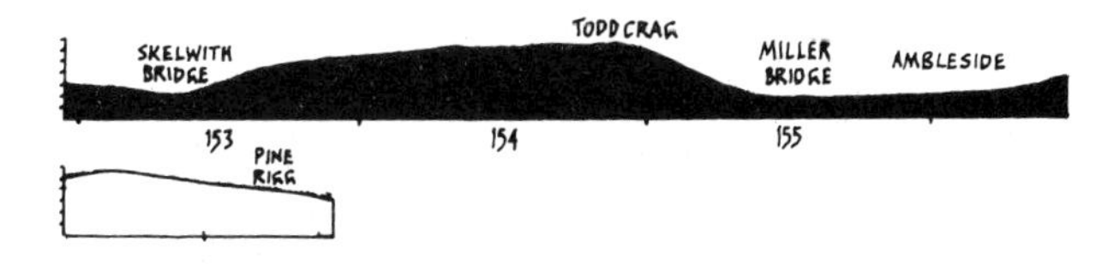
TODD CRAG
SKELWITH BRIDGE
MILLER BRIDGE
AMBLESIDE
153
154
155
PINE RIGG

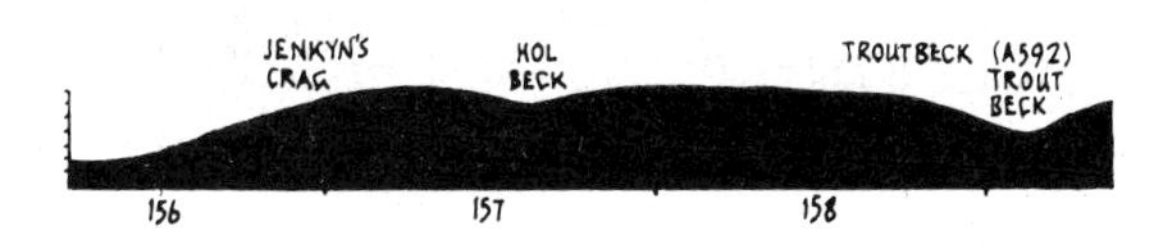
JENKYN'S CRAG
HOL BECK
TROUTBECK (A592)
TROUT BECK
156
157
158

7. Patterdale to Little Langdale

How fortunate for Westmorland to have its county boundary follow the high tops of the magnificent central fells of the Lake District! We take full advantage of this for the traverse along the skyline around the head of Langdale, but recognise that, for a variety of reasons, some walkers may wish to take a low level alternative. On this section, therefore, we have provided two high level and two low level options.

The first of these options is between Patterdale and Grasmere. The **High Level Route** goes over St. Sunday Crag and Fairfield and covers a distance of 8 miles/12.8km. The **Low Level Route** goes up Grisedale and is about 7 miles/11.2km long.

The second option is between Grasmere and Little Langdale. The **High Level Route** covers more high ground than the stretch on the Pennines above Dufton and is a distance of about 14 miles/22.5km. The **Low Level Route** goes by way of Chapel Stile, Great Langdale and Blea Tarn to join the High Level Route in Little Langdale after 7 miles/11.2km. Both routes must then continue down the valley of the Brathay for at least another 4 miles/6.4km before there is much chance of finding overnight accommodation.

Map 7.1

Patterdale is the valley of St. Patrick. It has been claimed that St. Patrick was shipwrecked on Duddon Sands in AD 540 while on his way to Dublin, but he certainly was off course if he walked over to Patterdale and Brampton: both places have churches dedicated to him. **St. Patrick's Church,** 1853, has a curious clock tower in its NE corner with a saddleback roof, but is otherwise unremarkable. **St. Patrick's Well** is beside the road between Patterdale and Glenridding, but there is nothing to indicate what it is. It was once reputed to have healing powers.

Patterdale Hall stands at the head of the lake behind trees, not far from the church, and at the foot of Grisedale. A doorway in its SW range bears the initials and date 'I & DM 1677'. The inscription possibly refers to the Mounseys - the Mounseys were the 'Kings of Patterdale' and the house was known as The Palace. In 1824 John Mounsey sold the house to William Marshall of Leeds, and it is probable that the extensive additions of 1845-50 by Salvin are due to him.

Our route now enters the high country of the central Lakeland fells

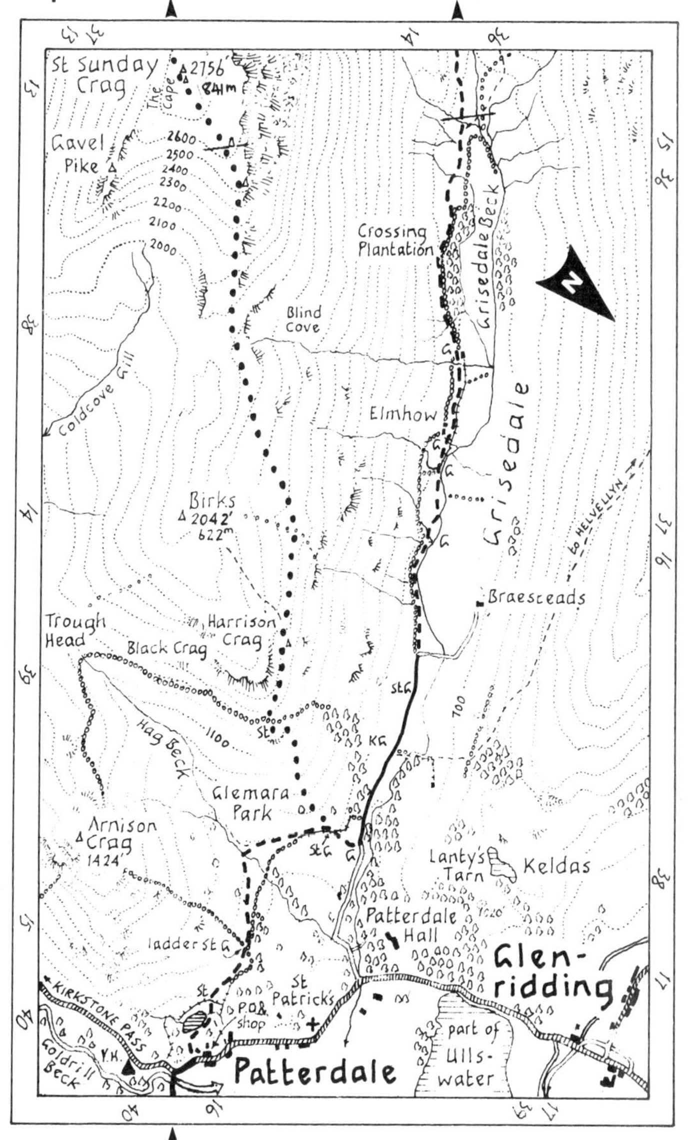
St Sunday Crag
2756'
841m
The Cape
Gavel Pike
2600
2500
2400
2300
2200
2100
2000
Crossing Plantation
Grisedale Beck
Blind Cove
Coldcove Gill
Elmhow
Grisedale
Birks
2042'
622m
to HELVELLYN
Braesteads
Trough Head
Harrison Crag
Black Crag
StG
700
Hag Beck
1100
St
KG
Glemara Park
Arnison Crag
1424'
StG
G
Lanty's Tarn
Keldas
Patterdale Hall
1020'
ladder StG
Glen-ridding
KIRKSTONE PASS
St
St Patrick's
P.O.& shop
Y.H.
Goldrill Beck
part of Ullswater
Patterdale

Map 7.2

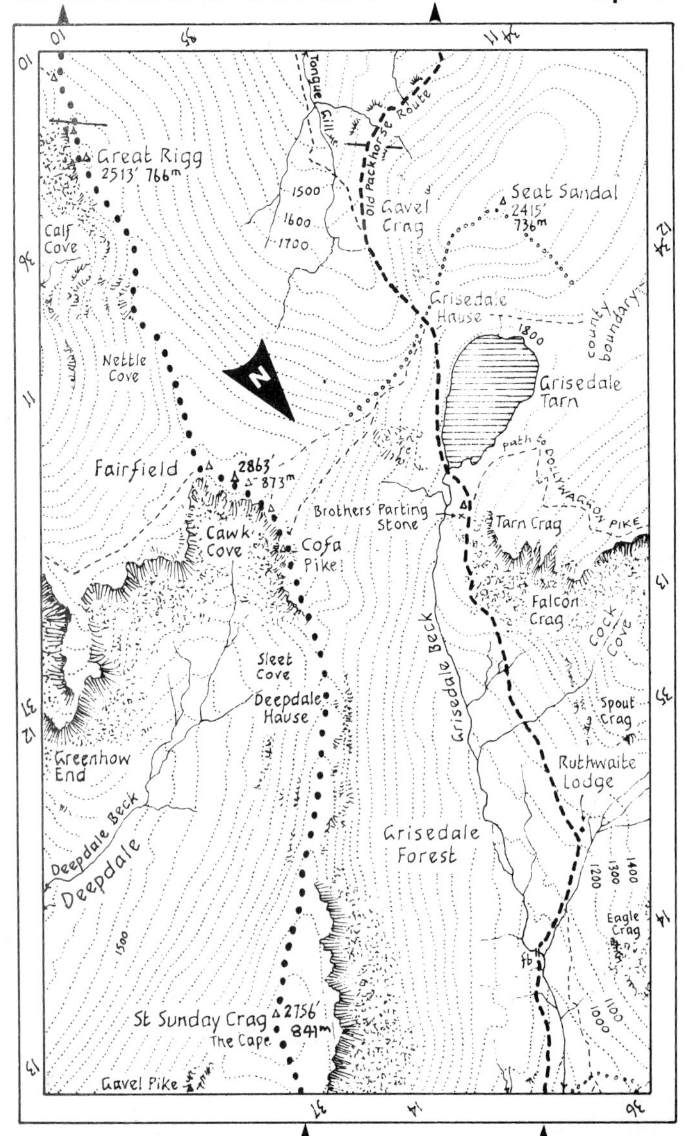

Great Rigg
2513' 766m
Tongue Gill
Old Packhorse Route
1500
1600
1700
Gavel Crag
Seat Sandal
2415'
736m
Calf Cove
Grisedale Hause
county boundary
1800
Nettle Cove
N
Grisedale Tarn
path to DOLLYWAGGON PIKE
Fairfield
2863'
873m
Brothers' Parting Stone
Tarn Crag
Cawk Cove
Cofa Pike
Falcon Crag
Cock Cove
Sleet Cove
Grisedale Beck
Deepdale Hause
Spout Crag
Greenhow End
Ruthwaite Lodge
Deepdale Beck
Grisedale Forest
Deepdale
1200
1300
1400
Eagle Crag
1500
fb
1100
1000
St Sunday Crag
2756'
841m
The Cape
Gavel Pike

and we provide High Level and Low Level options between Patterdale and Grasmere.

The two routes run together into Grisedale, so from the A592 lay-by by the PO and shop in Patterdale take the path up to Mill Moss contouring round Glemara Park and descending to the Grisedale road. Just before the road is reached the High Level Route turns off L.

Low Level Route

The track up Grisedale provides incomparable views of Helvellyn and Fairfield ranged around. The Patterdale-Grasmere track was once a busy pack horse route. Not for nothing is the pub at its end, on the Grasmere side of Dunmail Raise, called The Traveller's Rest.

The route is straightforward. The path follows the lane past the turn-offs to Grassthwaitehow and Braesteads and continues past Elmhow on a good track.

(Low Level Route continues on Map 7.2)

High Level Route

The route makes a steep climb, finding a way between Black Crag and Harrison Crag, passing below Birks and then making a gradual ascent to St. Sunday Crag (2756ft/841m) and its broad grassy top, which is called The Cape.

(High Level Route continues on Map 7.2)

Map 7.2

Low Level Route

The good path climbs up beside the Grisedale Beck crossing over and up to Ruthwaite Lodge (climbing club hut), finely situated below the crags of Dollywaggon Pike. The path climbs higher, and at a cairn meets the path going up to Dollywaggon Pike and Helvellyn, then crosses the outlet of Grisedale Tarn.

Grisedale Tarn is a bleak stretch of water in a windy spot between the folds of Fairfield, Seat Sandal and Dollywaggon Pike. The tarn is reputed to be the resting place of the Golden Crown of King Dunmail. In AD 945 Edmund, King of the Saxons, joined forces with Malcolm, King of Scotland, to do battle with Dunmail, the last King of Cumberland. Most of Dunmail's army was slain, but one of his followers rescued his golden crown and threw it into Grisedale Tarn where, it is said, it lies to this day. Dunmail's remains are supposed to lie buried under the pile of stones at the summit of Dunmail Raise, where the A591 Kendal-Keswick road passes out of Westmorland into Cumberland.

Somewhere alongside the old pack horse route near **Grisedale Tarn** is the spot - you will have to find it for yourself - of the **Brother's Parting.** In 1805 William Wordsworth accompanied his brother John from Grasmere to a point on the Patterdale side of Grisedale Tarn. They bade farewell as John was returning to the command of his ship, the 'Earl of Avergavenny'. They were never to see each other again: John's ship was lost in a storm off the coast of Dorset. To commemorate the sad farewell William carved some lines on a rock near the place of their parting: time has made them illegible, but an engraved plate now marks the spot. Find it if you can!

From Grisedale Tarn a gradual traversing ascent soon brings you to Grisedale Hause (1986ft/600m). The old pack horse route is to be preferred to the more direct route for the descent towards Grasmere.
(Low Level Route continues on Map 7.3)

High Level Route

A lovely easy descent on a narrowing ridge from St. Sunday Crag leads down to Deepdale Hause (about 2230ft/680m), then a stiff but short climb over Cofa Pike soon brings you to the top of Fairfield (2863ft/873m). The plateau summit has a confusing collection of cairns and in bad weather the route off the top down the Great Rigg ridge needs to be followed with care, although cairns mark the route.
(High Level Route continues on Map 7.3)

The high, S-N mountain ridge of Fairfield and Helvellyn is notable for its E facing well-formed corries and arêtes. The crag-girt coves are the habitat of lime-loving mountain flowers which have found refuge on the open faces and rock ledges of the high corries. Nearly four dozen flower species are recorded here and perhaps surprisingly one dozen of these have not been found in the nearby Pennines. One rare flower is the clustered alpine saxifrage while others include the purple saxifrage, mossy saxifrage, moss campion, the bright yellow alpine cinquefoil, the alpine mouse-ear with its daisy-like white flowers and mountain avens, while the alpine lady's mantle is extremely abundant on many cliffs.

Map 7.3

Low Level Route

The old pack horse track is a good path descending beside and then across Little Tongue Gill. It follows the intake wall and goes down to the A591 Kendal-Keswick road on the outskirts of Grasmere. Go down the lane opposite, crossing the infant River Rothay at Low Mill Bridge and continue along the lane below Helm Crag, to a road junction after 1 mile,

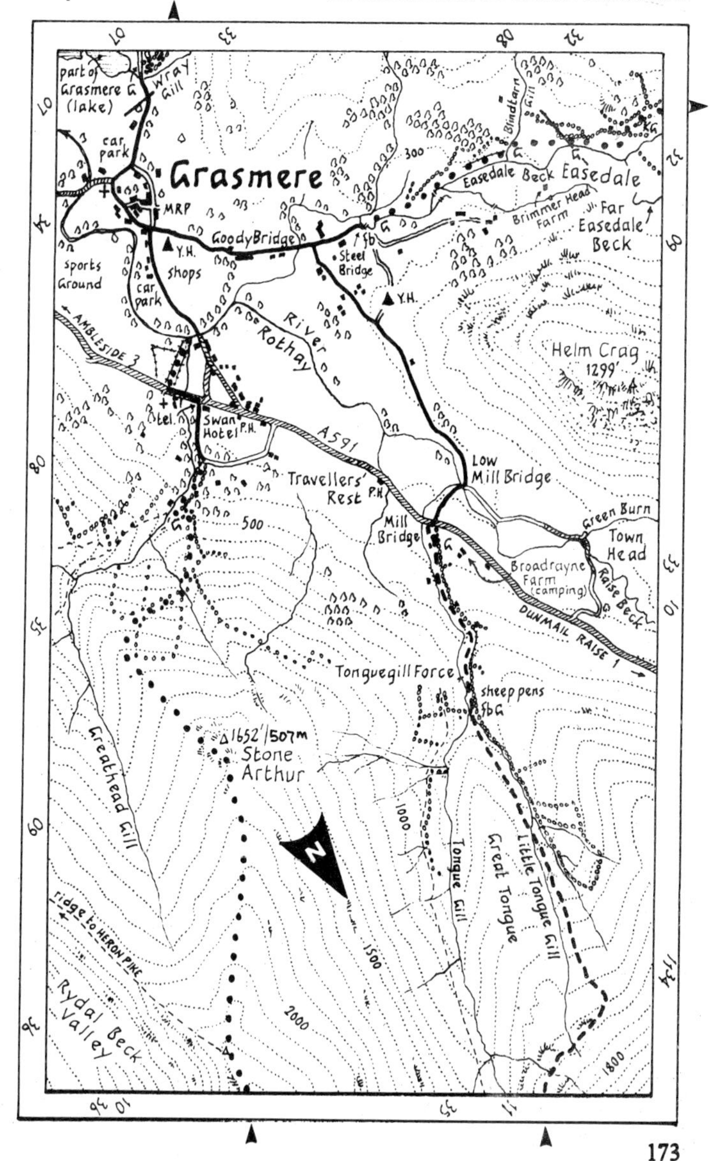

part of Grasmere (lake)
Wray Gill
car park
Grasmere
MRP
Y.H.
shops
Goody Bridge
Sports Ground
car park
Steel Bridge
fb
Y.H.
Easedale Beck
Easedale
Blindtarn Gill
300
Brimmer Head Farm
Far Easedale Beck
River Rothay
AMBLESIDE 3
tel.
Swan Hotel P.H.
A591
Helm Crag 1299'
Low Mill Bridge
Travellers' Rest P.H.
500
Mill Bridge
Green Burn
Town Head
Broadrayne Farm (camping)
Raise Beck
DUNMAIL RAISE 1
Tonguegill Force
sheep pens
fb G
1652'/507m
Stone Arthur
Greathead Gill
1000
N
Tongue Gill
Great Tongue
Little Tongue Gill
ridge to HERON PIKE
1500
2000
Rydal Beck Valley
1800

passing Thorney How YH on your R. Turn L at the T-junction, go over Goody Bridge and into Grasmere.
(Low Level Route continues below, after Grasmere, on page 177.)

High Level Route

Just past the cairn on Great Rigg (2513ft/766m), at another cairn, bear R away from the narrower Heron Pike ridge on a broader ridge SW to Stone Arthur, a prominent group of rocks on the skyline above Grasmere. The imperial OS maps give Stone Arthur a height of 1652ft, which when converted gives 504m. The new metric survey 1:10,000 has elevated the outcrop to 507m, which when converted equals 1663ft.

Descend steeply down to a lane and continue ahead to the Swan Hotel on the A591 Kendal-Keswick road. Here turn L and at the RC Church of 'Our Lady by the Wayside' cross over the road to a footpath opposite, which, when it meets the River Rothay, turn R to the bridge carrying the road from the Swan Hotel. Turn L and walk into the centre of Grasmere.
(High Level Route continues below, after Grasmere)

The combination of lake, village and dale at **Grasmere** is generally thought to be the quintessence of Lakeland landscape. William Wordsworth thought so, and he made the village his home. Grasmere is perhaps the best known of all Westmorland's villages, either because of its own natural beauty, or its Wordsworthian and other Lake Poets connections, or because of its rush bearing ceremony or its annual sports.

The village is geared to accommodate and cater for tourists, with its gift shops, Lakeland perfume, sheepskin and knitwear shops, artists studio's, etc. There are no shops in the village to serve the daily needs of the resident population - they have to rely on travelling shops or go to Keswick or Ambleside. This commercialism, and the caravan rallies in the most prominent part of the dale at the height of the holiday season, are perhaps the only two regrettable features of an otherwise unspoilt village.

Anyone who visits Grasmere without having read Dorothy's Journals or William's poems will miss a lot, because only they can give the close observation and keener appreciation of the natural beauties of the district which they knew intimately. Any tour of Grasmere must therefore begin with a visit to Dove Cottage (Dove Cottage is just off our map, on the E side of the main road A591, about 10 minutes' walk from the village centre: it is signposted).

Dove Cottage and its **Wordsworth Museum** are visited by thousands of pilgrims every summer's day. The cottage was originally a small inn known as 'The Dove & Olive Branch' and was on the main road from Rydal to Grasmere. William took the cottage at a rent of £8 p.a. in December 1799 and his family lived there for 7½ years until they outgrew the place.

William moved here aged 29 with his sister Dorothy and lived a frugal existence, but life had its compensations - the delectable walking country and no shortage of visiting friends, notably Samuel Taylor Coleridge, Thomas de Quincey and Sir Walter Scott.

During his residence here William wrote 'The Prelude', 'Imitations of Immortality', 'Miscellaneous Sonnets', 'Lyrical Ballads' and a number of other poems, including some of the 'Lucy' poems (the chief of which were written in Germany), 'Ode to Beauty', 'To the Cuckoo', 'The Rainbow', 'I Wandered Lonely as a Cloud', and 'The Solitary Reaper'. Meanwhile Dorothy wrote her 'Journals' and gave detailed descriptions of life at Dove Cottage.

A former Earl of Lonsdale had incurred a debt to the Wordsworth family and the discharge of this long-standing account by his successor relieved the financial situation sufficiently to enable William to marry Mary Hutchinson, a childhood friend, on 4 October 1802. He brought her, and her sister, to Dove Cottage, and during their years there Mary bore him three children - John, Dorothy (Dora) and Thomas. When Mary was expecting their fourth child, Catherine, they were forced to look for larger accommodation. Dorothy wrote: 'We are crammed into our little nest edge-full'. In May 1808 they moved to Allan Bank, on the other side of the village.

When the Wordsworth's left the cottage was occupied by Thomas de Quincey (1785-1859). He held the tenancy for 28 years, although he lived there for only 22 years. He married a local girl and became a confirmed opium addict: whether because of her, history doesn't say. De Quincey's life at Dove Cottage is described in his 'Confessions of an English Opium Eater' and he brilliantly portrayed the lives of William Wordsworth and Samuel Taylor Coleridge in his 'Recollections of the Lakes and the Lake Poets' written after he left in 1830. In that year De Quincey went to live at Nab Cottage, overlooking Rydal Water.

Dove Cottage is preserved largely as it was, while a converted barn nearby now serves as a museum. It contains a reconstructed farm kitchen, furnished in the style of the early 19c. On the upper floor Wordsworth devotees can gaze with due reverence at the display of early notes and manuscripts, including those of Dorothy's 'Journals'. There are also some of Coleridge's manuscripts from 'Christobel' and 'Dejection'.

Dove Cottage & Museum: Hours of Admission

April-September	0930-1730	(Sundays 1100-1730)
March & October	1000-1630	(Sundays 1100-1630)

Let's return to the house-moving of William and his family. In 1808 they moved to **Allan Bank** on the Easedale side of the village (the house and its grounds are now owned by the NT, but the house is not open to the public). William did not like Allan Bank, called it a 'temple of abomination' and three years later moved to **The Parsonage.** They were at The Parsonage for two years, and while there lost two of their children - Catherine (3) and Thomas (6). William then secured the post of Distributor of Stamps for Westmorland with a salary of £300, and the family were able to move out to the more accommodating **Rydal Mount,** at Rydal, where William spent his later years (1813-50). Both William and his wife Mary are buried under a simple stone in **St. Oswald's** churchyard (qv).

Wordsworth's other friend (not hitherto mentioned in detail) was Samuel Taylor Coleridge (1772-1834). He moved to the Lakes in 1800 and often took the 5-hour walk from his home in Keswick to visit William. His son, Hartley Coleridge, at one time lived at Rose Cottage, on the opposite corner to Dove Cottage, and also at Allan Bank. For the last eleven years of his life, to his death, aged 52, in 1879, he lived at Nab Cottage. He also lies buried in the churchyard of St. Oswald's.

We therefore naturally progress towards the centre of the village and **St. Oswald's Church,** where William and his family worshipped. It is an unusual church and has changed little since William described it in 'The Excursion':

> '... with pillars crowded, and the roof upheld
> By naked rafters intricately crossed,
> Like leafless underboughs, mind some thick grove,
> All withered by the depth of shade above.'

The oldest visible part of the church dates from 13c and the numerous alterations over the many centuries make it something of an architectural curiosity. Unusual features are its roof and the two-storeyed double nave. The thick encrustation of pebble-dash makes the dating of the exterior impossible.

Until the 19c the floor of the church was earthen and rushes where strewn on the floor in place of a carpet. Each year they were cleared and replaced in a festival that dates back to at least the 16c and probably much earlier. The annual **Rushbearing Festival** takes place on the nearest Saturday to St. Oswald's Day (5 August) and the village children, dressed in their summer best, carry rushes and flowers to the church in a procession proceeded by a band. After the service the children receive the traditional reward of a piece of Grasmere gingerbread. (Beside the northern lychgate is the Grasmere Gingerbread Shop which was, until 1854, the village school.)

In the churchyard, beside the riverside, are the graves of William and Mary Wordsworth, and next to them Dora Quillinan, their daughter. To the N is buried Hartley Coleridge (whom William wished to have buried near him). There is also the grave of Sir John Richardson (1787-1865), the distinguished Arctic explorer, who lived at Lancrigg for seven years writing his classic books on the flora and fauna of the Arctic. Several of the yew trees in the churchyard were planted by William in 1819.

We can't leave Grasmere without mentioning the **Sports.** These are the oldest and most commercial of the annual Lakes sports shows involving hound trails, guide's races and other races, Cumberland and Westmorland wrestling. They take place on the Thursday nearest 20 August.

Low Level Route

From St. Oswald's church go beside a car park and a garden centre on a road towards the head of Grasmere (lake).

(Low Level Route continues on Map 7.8)

High Level Route

From St. Oswald's church go to the green in the village centre and cross over into the road that goes towards Easedale, passing Butharlyp How YH on your R and Allan Bank on your L. A short way beyond Goody Bridge the public road ends. Cross the slate footbridge called Steel Bridge and take the path beside the Easedale Beck into Easedale. The path has been so heavily used and eroded by floods over the years that at times it is like walking in a boulder-filled trench. Across the meadows of the Easedale Beck, below the slopes of Helm Crag, is Brimmer Head Farm, reputedly the oldest house in Grasmere, dating from 1574.

(High Level Route continues on Map 7.4)

Map 7.4

In their early days at Grasmere William and Dorothy called **Easedale** 'the black quarter' because it seemed to them that all the bad weather came from that direction. It still does today!

High Level Route

The well-defined path climbs up alongside the spectacular waterfalls of

Map 7.4

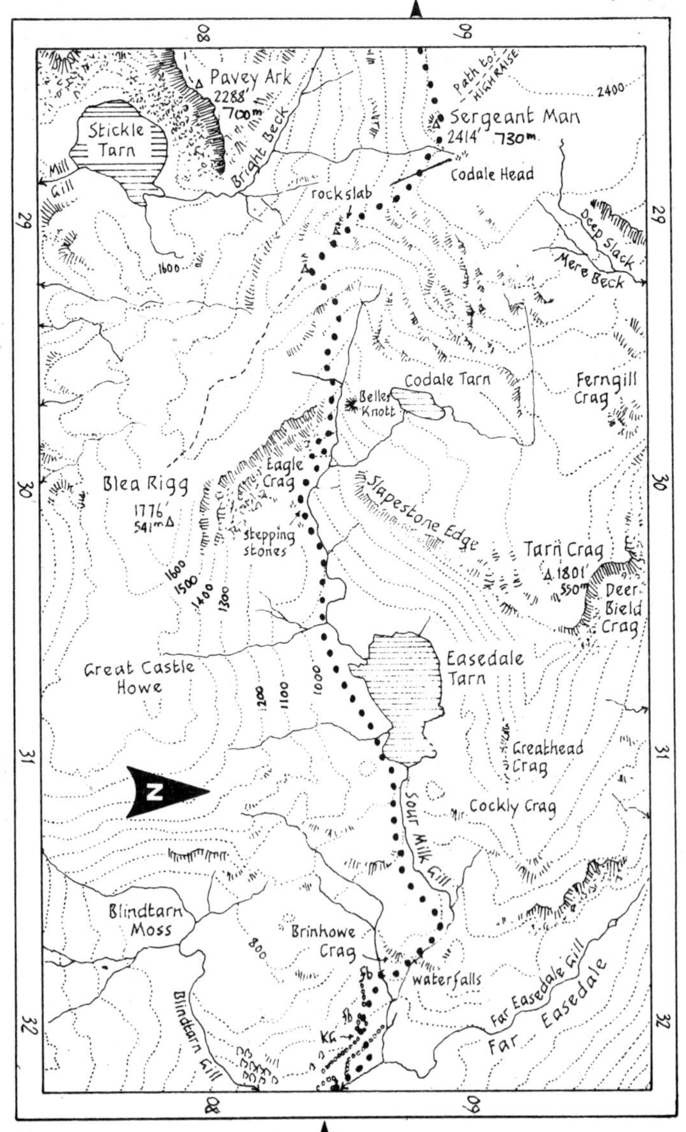

Pavey Ark
2288'
700m
Stickle Tarn
Mill Gill
Bright Beck
path to HIGH RAISE
2400
Sergeant Man
2414' 730m
Codale Head
rockslab
Deep Slack
Mere Beck
1600
Codale Tarn
Belles Knott
Ferngill Crag
Eagle Crag
Blea Rigg
1776'
541m
Slapestone Edge
stepping stones
Tarn Crag
1801'
550m
Deer Bield Crag
1600
1500
1400
1300
Easedale Tarn
Great Castle Howe
1200
1100
1000
Greathead Crag
Cockly Crag
N
Sour Milk Gill
Blindtarn Moss
Brinhowe Crag
800
waterfalls
fb
Far Easedale Gill
Far Easedale
Blindtarn Gill
KG
80
90
29
30
31
32

Sour Milk Gill then by more waterfalls to the outlet of Easedale Tarn, a gem in a wild setting. On the way up there is a good view across the valley to Helm Crag, with the prominent rock formation known as The Old Lady Playing the Organ at the N end of the summit ridge. The Lion and the Lamb is another group of rocks at the S end of the ridge, prominent when viewed from the Swan Hotel at Grasmere.

On the approach to the Tarn there was once a refreshment hut, built in Victorian times, but by the 1960's vandals had wrecked the building and it was subsequently demolished: a windbreak and cairn now mark the spot.

The path beyond the Tarn's outlet goes through a notoriously boggy patch and it may be best to skirt to higher, drier ground, but pass below Eagle Crag and aim for the shapely Belles Knott - the Matterhorn of Easedale. As you climb higher bear slightly L to reach a cairn on the Blea Rigg-Sergeant Man ridge. Turn R, cross a rock slab and where the steep ground levels out avoid the boggy area of Codale Head to gain the summit of Sergeant Man. The imperial OS maps give Sergeant Man a height of 2414ft, which when converted gives 736m. The new metric survey 1:10,000 has reduced the fell to 730m, which when converted equals 2395ft.

The county boundary lies just to the N, having come up from Dunmail Raise over Steel Fell.

(High Level Route continues on Map 7.5)

Map 7.5

The county boundary follows the high ground of the Langdale Horseshoe, on the watershed of the Mickleden Beck and Oxendale Beck and their feeder streams, and our route follows it, or as close to it as possible, all the way from Sergeant Man to Pike o'Blisco.

The upper reaches of the Langdale valley are flanked by magnificent mountains and the walk along the skyline of the Langdale Horseshoe is an exhilerating day's walk (although fell-runners in the annual Langdale Horseshoe Fell Race from the New Dungeon Ghyll Hotel do the 17 miles/27km circuit in 2½ hours!). Most of the valley and its mountains are owned by the NT. Much of the credit for this must go to the historian George Trevelyan who bought Stool End and Wall End farms and the Old Dungeon Ghyll Hotel and presented them to the Trust in 1928. He added further farms in 1944 and his daughter and his old college (Trinity, Cambridge) contributed to further purchases in 1963. In recent years the Trust has been faced with heavy maintenance liabilities, mostly to the footpaths, because of increasing use by visitors, for whom Langdale is one of the most popular valleys in the Lakes.

Map 7.5

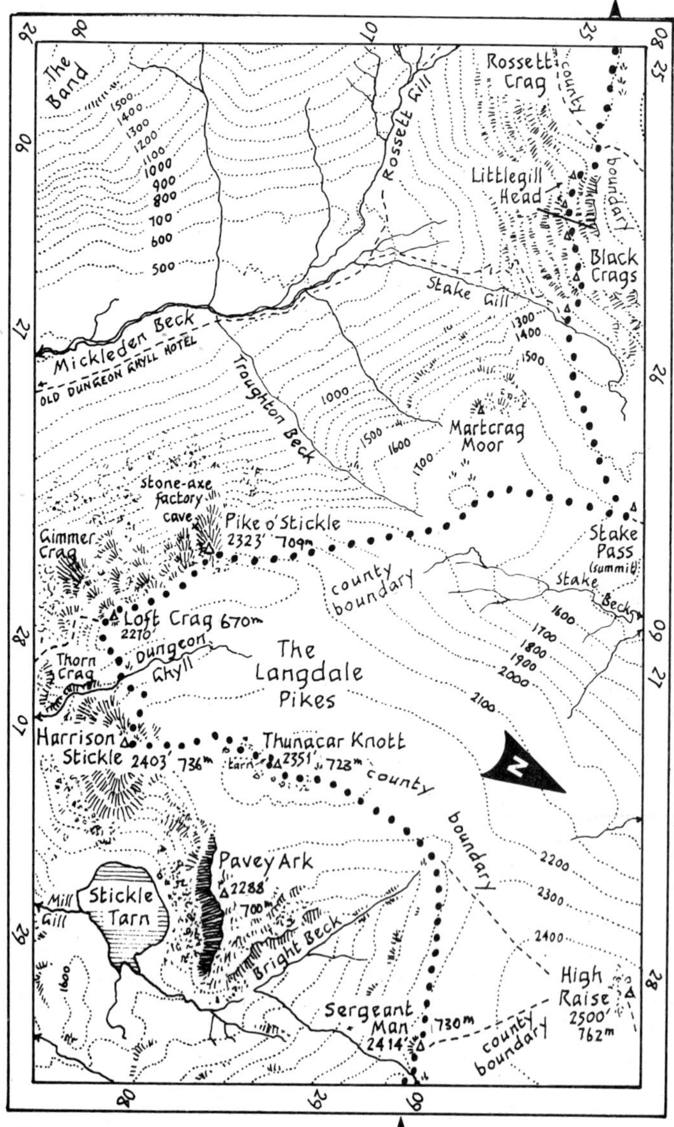
The Band
Rossett Crag
Rossett Gill
Littlegill Head
Black Crags
Stake Gill
Mickleden Beck
OLD DUNGEON GHYLL HOTEL
Troughton Beck
Martcrag Moor
Stone-axe factory cave
Pike o'Stickle 2323' 709m
Gimmer Crag
Stake Pass (summit)
Stake Beck
county boundary
Loft Crag 670m 2270'
Thorn Crag
Dungeon Ghyll
The Langdale Pikes
Harrison Stickle 2403' 736m
Thunacar Knott 2351' 723m
tarn
Pavey Ark 2288' 700m
Mill Gill
Stickle Tarn
Bright Beck
Sergeant Man 2414' 730m
High Raise 2500' 762m
N

High Level Route

From Sergeant Man contour round the valley of the Bright Beck to Thunacar Knott, missing out the featureless plateau of High Raise (2500ft/762m) and passing behind Pavey Ark. The Ordnance Survey have been adding bits and pieces to the fells hereabouts. Their imperial maps give Thunacar Knott a height of 2351ft and Pavey Ark a height of 2288ft. When converted these figures are 717m and 697m respectively. The new metric survey 1:10,000 has elevated Thunacar Knott to 723m and Pavey Ark to 700m, which when converted equals 2372ft and 2296ft respectively.

The rugged cliffs of Pavey Ark rise sheer above the waters of Stickle Tarn, but the cliffs are hidden from view until you get onto Harrison Stickle, from where there is also the best view of Stickle Tarn. The Tarn was dammed in the last century to provide a controllable head of water for the mills in the valley: the gunpowder mills at Chapel Stile and Elterwater were in production from 1824 until the end of World War I. The path down Stickle Gill (Mill Gill) to the New Dungeon Ghyll Hotel is one of the most heavily used and was consequently badly eroded until recent repair work was carried out.

In good weather the route from Thunacar Knott is obvious, but in mist the way is confusing because of the number of paths, depressions in the ground and rocky outcrops, and a compass bearing is advisable. The route is generally S to the summit of Harrison Stickle, the easternmost and highest of the Langdale Pikes. It is isolated from the other pikes by the ravine of the Dungeon Ghyll and our descent from the top crosses the head of the Ghyll. Miss out Thorn Crag (2099ft/640m) to the SW and climb up westwards to Loft Crag and Pike o'Stickle (2323ft/709m), the most impressive of the Pikes. The OS have been having fun and games with our Langdale Pikes! Their imperial maps give Harrison Stickle a height of 2403ft and Loft Crag a height of 2270ft. When converted these figures are 732m and 692m respectively. The new metric survey 1:10,000 maps have elevated Harrison Stickle to 736m and Loft Crag to 670m, which when converted equals 2415ft and 2198ft respectively.

Pike o'Stickle is a conical volcanic boss, with a steep front to the valley of Mickleden. On its E side a steep runnel of scree goes down almost to the valley floor: this used to be a good 'scree-run' line of descent, but erosion and over-use has exposed smooth rocks and it has become an accident blackspot. At the top of the scree-shoot is the site of a 3000-year old Neolithic stone-axe factory, discovered in 1947. The hard volcanic rock flakes when struck and provided an ideal material for axe heads. Axes were roughed out at this site and taken to the coast. A small man-made cave in the crag face was possibly used as a shelter for the axe-makers.

Pike o'Stickle towers over the long green glaciated valley of Mickleden and you can see a series of moraines at its head. Ranged around are the impressive peaks of Rossett Crag, Hanging Knotts and Bowfell, with Crinkle Crags above The Band opposite and Pike o'Blisco further round to the SE.

From Pike o'Stickle a descent NW leads towards Martcrag Moor, then turns slightly N to the head of Stake Pass (1575ft/480m), an important crossing between Langdale and Borrowdale. When in commercial use as a pack-pony route this pass was marked out by stakes.

A path follows the County Boundary W then SW to follow the ridge over Mansey Pike to Rossett Pike, but our path takes a route below the crags, a route that has only become popular since the inception of the Langdale Horseshoe Fell Race. From Stake Pass then, descend SW towards Mickleden, but at the crossing of Stake Gill bear R below Black Crags on a faint but cairned path, climbing up to the col of Littlegill Head, on the ridge to Rossett Pike.

(High Level Route continues on Map 7.6)

Map 7.6
High Level Route

From the col at Littlegill Head you can either follow the County Boundary over the ridge to Rossett Pike (2136ft/651m) - a route to be preferred if it is wet underfoot - or traverse round the back of Rossett Pike to the outlet of Angle Tarn. Angle Tarn is a typical corrie tarn, at a height of 1903ft/580m, backed by the awesome crags of Hanging Knotts on the N face of Bowfell.

You must gird up your loins for the ascent and traverse of Bowfell and Crinkle Crags, the most arduous and most exciting section of our walk around Westmorland. For well-equipped walkers in clear weather it is one of the best ridge walks in the country. At Angle Tarn turn R on the main 'Yak Route' from Langdale to Scafell Pike, but keep with it for only a short way, turning off L up the grassy rake to Ore Gap, the col between Esk Pike and Hanging Knotts. The path here is stained red from a rich deposit or iron ore. The presence of the mineral led to the strongly held belief that compass readings could be seriously affected. However, research has shown that compasses are only affected if a reading is taken in certain places with the instrument lying on the ground.

The path up Bowfell is well-defined, crossing large boulders, and it isn't long before its summit is reached at 2960ft/902m. This is the highest point reached on our walk, and a magnificent one at that. The view is extensive and on a fine day Cross Fell in the Pennines - the second highest peak on our walk at 2930ft/893m - can be seen in the distance. The fell is the true

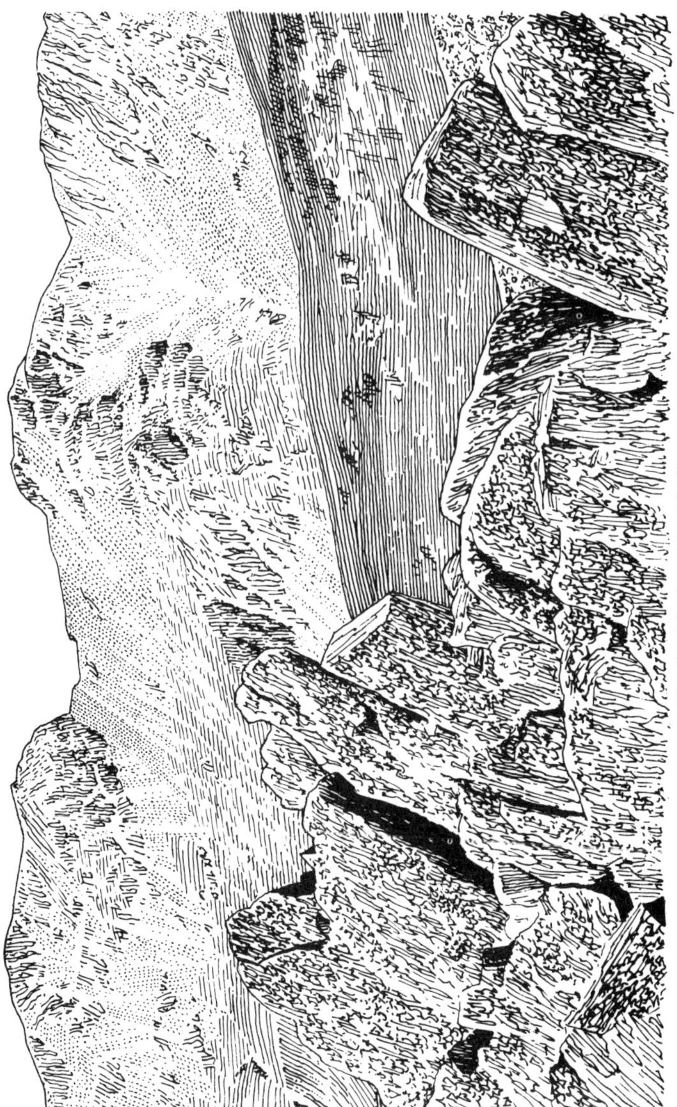

The Scafells from Crinkle Crags

Map 7.6

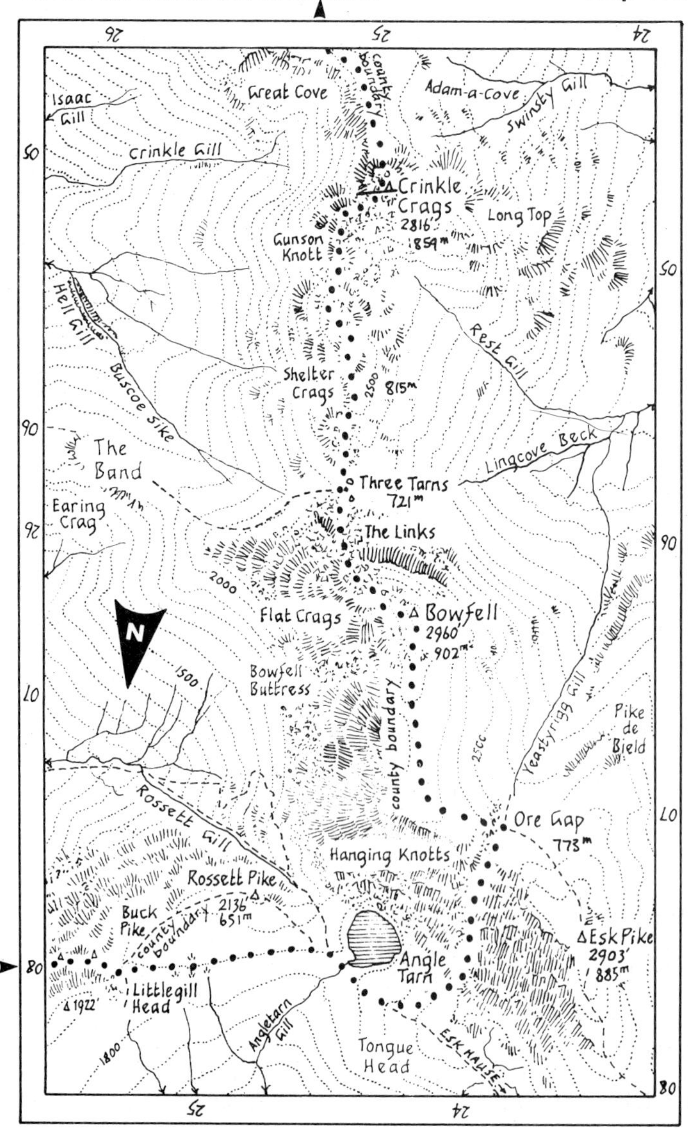
Isaac Gill
Crinkle Gill
Great Cove
county boundary
Adam-a-Cove
Swinsty Gill
Crinkle Crags
2816'
859m
Long Top
Gunson Knott
Hell Gill
Rest Gill
Buscoe Sike
Shelter Crags
2500
815m
The Band
Lingcove Beck
Three Tarns
721m
Earing Crag
The Links
2000
Flat Crags
Bowfell
2960'
902m
N
1500
Bowfell Buttress
county boundary
Yeastyrigg Gill
Pike de Bield
Rossett Gill
Ore Gap
773m
Hanging Knotts
Rossett Pike
2136'
651m
Buck Pike
county boundary
Esk Pike
2903'
885m
Angle Tarn
Littlegill Head
1922'
1800
Angletarn Gill
Tongue Head
Esk Hause

head of Langdale and its summit is a mass of shattered rock and is very rugged.

A steep descent on its S side leads down to Three Tarns - in dry conditions there sometimes aren't any - and a path coming up from Langdale via The Band comes in from the L. Our way continues S, over the knobbly ridge of Shelter Crags to Crinkle Crags (2816ft/859m). When seen from eastern viewpoints the fell presents a serrated ridge of rock rather like a cock's comb at the head of Oxendale. Seen from Langdale there are five 'crinkles'; one on the L and four grouped together. The highest point is the one on the L of the group of four. Walkers frequently lose themselves in poor visibility because the walk along the ridge nowhere follows a straight line.

(High Level Route continues on Map 7.7)

Map 7.7

High Level Route

The descent from Crinkle Crags to Red Tarn is very rough and scrambly but it is gradual and it contours round the head of Great Cove on a good path SE between Great Knott and Cold Pike, crossing the head of Brown Gill and meeting the Wrynose Pass-Oxendale path just to the N of Red Tarn.

An impressive steep ascent direct to the top of Pike o'Blisco beckons, but it doesn't take long. The imperial OS maps give Pike o'Blisco a height of 2304ft, which when converted gives 702m. The new metric survey 1:10,000 map has elevated the fell to 705m, which when converted gives 2313ft. A descent down its eastern side makes an interesting rocky step, and then our path turns away from the Redacre Gill descent to Langdale, going SE down Wrynose Beck to Wrynose Bridge on the Wrynose Pass road.

Wrynose Pass is notorious for its steepness and narrowness, almost matching the conditions of Hardknott Pass, to which it leads. Before 1939 the road was unsurfaced, but because it was so heavily worn by army training during the War it was surfaced, largely with concrete. It now has a tarmacadam covering.

Turn L at Wrynose Bridge and follow the road down to the valley.

(High Level Route continues on Map 7.9)

Map 7.8

Low Level Route

Just as you come up to Grasmere (lake) as you pass out of the village turn R through a gate, go up a stony track and keep the woods on your L as you climb up below Silver How. As you reach the highest point on this path you come to a cairn on the path coming up from the Red Bank road at High Close YH on its way to the Blea Rigg ridge. Turn L and descend towards High Close, but then turn R and go steeply down below Spedding Crag and

Map 7.7

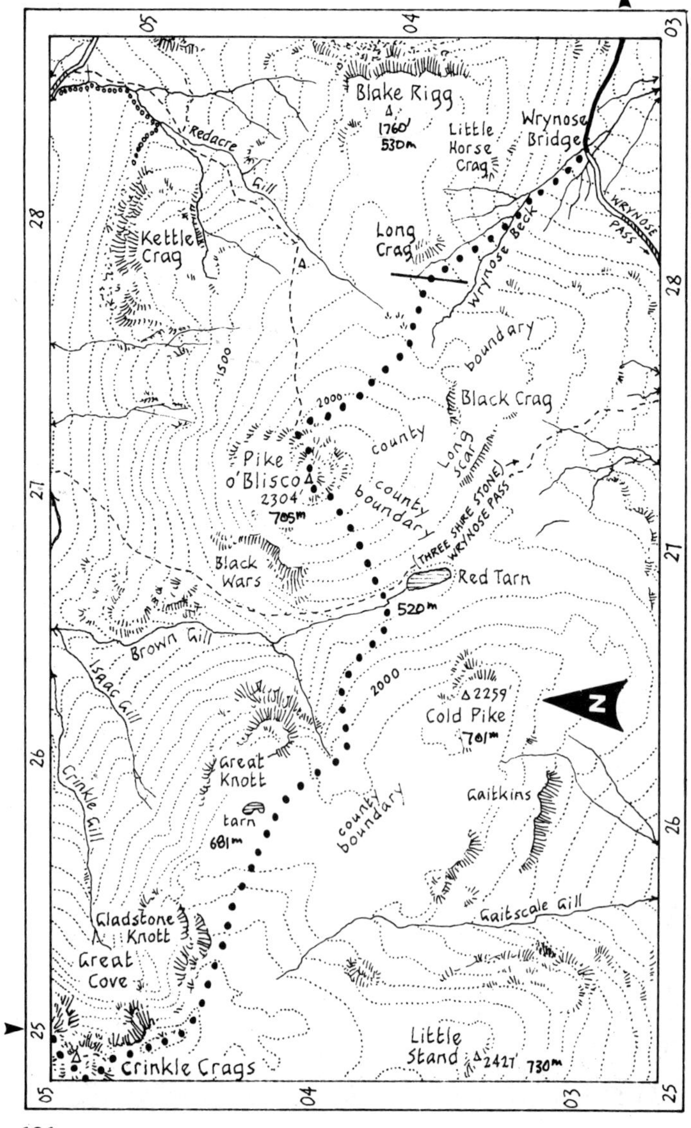
Blake Rigg
1760'
530m
Little
Horse
Crag
Wrynose
Bridge
Redacre
Gill
WRYNOSE
PASS
Kettle
Crag
Long
Crag
Wrynose Beck
boundary
1500
Black Crag
2000
county
Long
scar
Pike
o'Blisco
2304'
705m
county
boundary
(THREE SHIRE STONE)
WRYNOSE PASS
Black
Wars
Red Tarn
520m
Brown Gill
Isaac Gill
2000
2259'
Cold Pike
701m
N
Great
Knott
Crinkle Gill
tarn
681m
county
boundary
Gaitkins
Gaitscale Gill
Gladstone
Knott
Great
Cove
Little
Stand
2427'
730m
Crinkle Crags
05
04
03
28
27
26
25

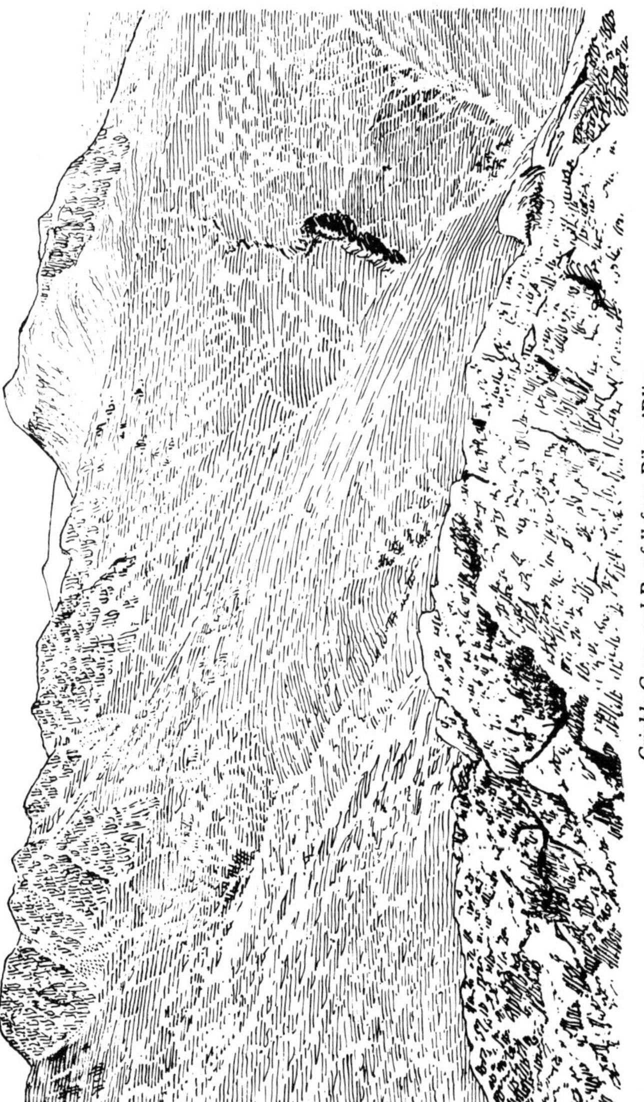

Crinkle Crags and Bowfell from Pike o'Blisco

Raven Crag to Walthwaite and Chapel Stile.

Old **Chapel Stile** is a tightly knit group of grey stone and slate houses that were built mainly to house quarrymen and employees of nearby quarries and the gunpowder works in nearby Elterwater village. Langdale stone and slate from Spout Crag and Elterwater quarries is still worked, and is exported all over the world. Some of the local quarries have been worked out; and one, Thrang Quarry, on the Langdale side of the village, was developed in the mid-1960's for rows of houses of the worst possible design that have attracted much criticism.

The church of **Holy Trinity** was built in 1857 on the site of a pre-Reformation chapel. In its churchyard is a tombstone to Rev. Owen Lloyd, incumbent for 12 years, with an epitaph by Wordsworth.

At the junction in the village by the church turn L to the shops and as you meet the main Langdale road cross over and take the track W. This track passes Thrang and Thrang Farm and goes just S of the Thrang Quarry development, past the old spoil heaps of the quarry and on the farm road to Baysbrown.

Cross New Bridge over the Great Langdale Beck and follow the flood-bank upstream - the path runs along the top of it until the farm track bears away from the crystal-clear beck. A RUPP crosses the beck by a good wooden bridge donated by the Friends of the Lake District and goes up to Oak Howe on a knoll. The right-of-way goes between the house and a barn and between tumbled walls before descending to the beck again, but people have created a short cut on the true R bank of the beck and you can follow this if you wish.

Climb the ladder stile, or go through the gate, and go alongside another broken wall. There are two paths here: our path is **not** *the one beside the beck.*

(Low Level Route continues on Map 7.9)

Map 7.9

High Level Route

Our descent beside the Wrynose Gill meets the Wrynose Pass road at Wrynose Bridge. There is no onward path to the River Brathay so we have to turn L down the road to Fell Foot Farm. This road can be very busy with traffic in summer, so take care.

At Fell Foot Farm the High Level Route joins the Low Level Route and both routes then run together as a common route. The route continues on Map 8.1.

Map 7.8

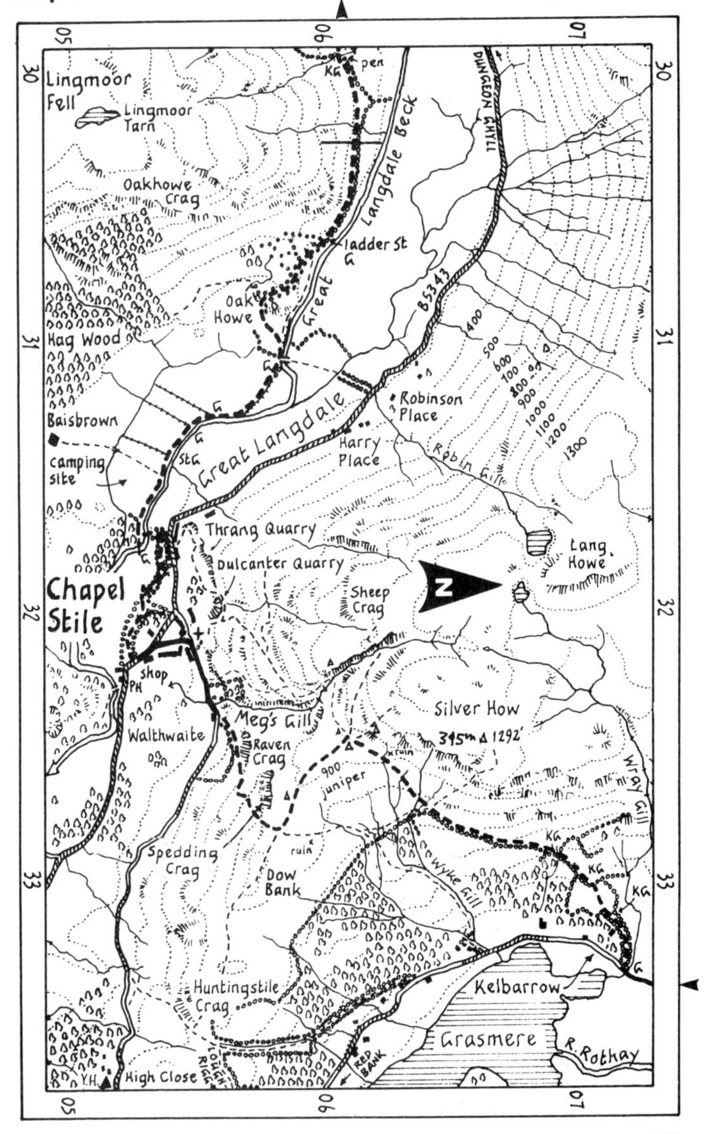
Lingmoor Fell
Lingmoor Tarn
Oakhowe Crag
Hag Wood
Baisbrown
camping site
Chapel Stile
shop
PH
Walthwaite
Spedding Crag
Huntingstile Crag
Y.H.
High Close
LOUGH RIGG
RED BANK
Grasmere
R. Rothay
Kelbarrow
Dow Bank
ruin
juniper
900
Raven Crag
Meg's Gill
Silver How
345m 1292'
Wyke Gill
Wray Gill
KG
Sheep Crag
Dulcanter Quarry
Thrang Quarry
Lang Howe
Robin Gill
Harry Place
Robinson Place
Great Langdale
Oak Howe
ladder St
Great Langdale Beck
DUNGEON GHYLL
B5343
pen
Z
400
500
600
700
800
900
1000
1100
1200
1300
05
06
07
30
31
32
33

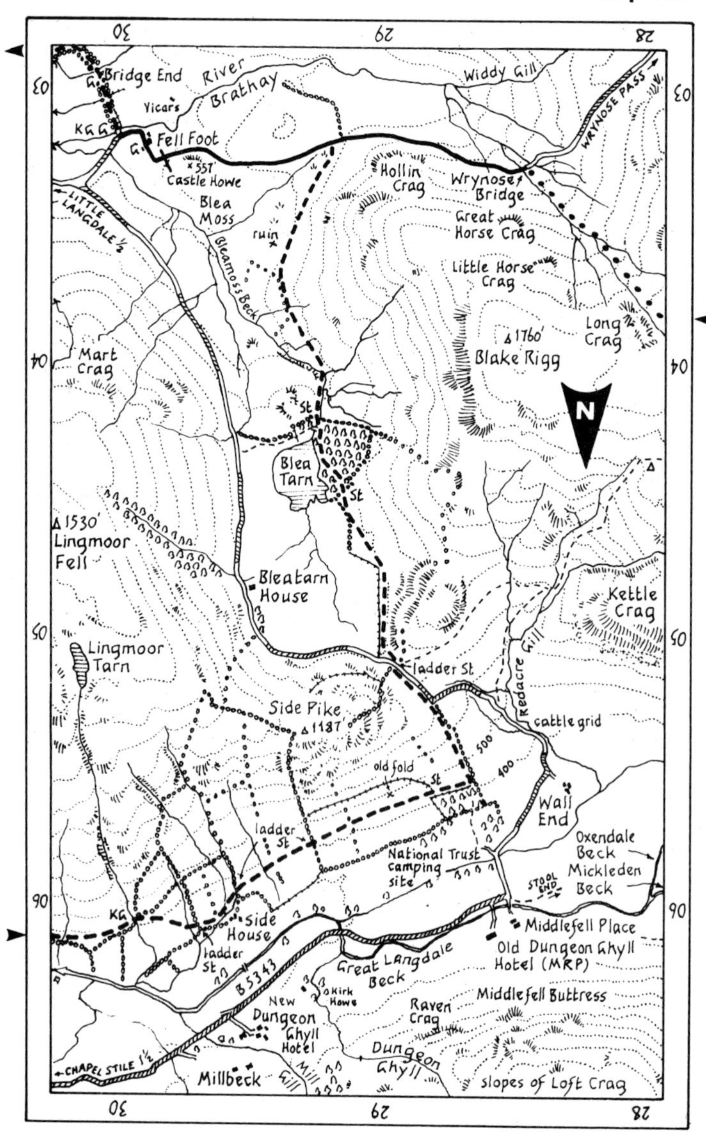
Bridge End
River Brathay
Vicar's
KG
Fell Foot
557'
Castle Howe
Widdy Gill
WRYNOSE PASS
Hollin Crag
Wrynose Bridge
Great Horse Crag
Little Horse Crag
Blea Moss
ruin
Bleamoss Beck
LITTLE LANGDALE ½
Long Crag
1760'
Blake Rigg
N
Mart Crag
St
Blea Tarn
St
1530'
Lingmoor Fell
Bleatarn House
Kettle Crag
Lingmoor Tarn
ladder St
Redacre Gill
cattle grid
Side Pike
1187'
500
400
old fold
St
Wall End
ladder St
National Trust camping site
Oxendale Beck
Mickleden Beck
STOOL END
KG
Side House
Middlefell Place
ladder St
Old Dungeon Ghyll Hotel (MRP)
B5343
Great Langdale Beck
Kirk Howe
New Dungeon Ghyll Hotel
Middlefell Buttress
Raven Crag
CHAPEL STILE 1½
Millbeck
Mill Gill
Dungeon Ghyll
slopes of Loft Crag
30
29
28
03
04
05
90

Low Level Route

The path keeps above the intake wall and at the crossing of the Lingmoor Tarn beck passes through a kissing-gate and begins a descent towards Side House. Keep behind the farm and alongside a beck, cross a plank bridge and over ladder stiles, continuing along the flank of Side Pike at a steady level. Don't be tempted to go too low - don't aim for the gate going into the NT's camp site, unless you intend to camp there: aim for the top corner of the larch plantation. At the corner of the wood with a wall, where a path comes up from the camp site, go steeply up the fellside, keeping the wall on your R, and you soon reach the road coming up out of Great Langdale and going over to Little Langdale. Go through the gate to the cattle grid, which marks the top of Side Gates Pass (735ft/224m).

Cross the road and pass through a gap in the broken wall opposite on a path bearing L beside a fence, going S to Blea Tarn and its plantation. The path through the larches and dense rhododendrons has recently been cleared. You emerge at a delightful spot, the outlet to Blea Tarn running crystal-clear over shingle through short turf.

The view N over **Blea Tarn** gives one of the finest views of the Langdale Pikes and the scene is a favourite one with photographers and artists. Overlooking the Tarn is **Blea Tarn House** in a setting which moved Wordsworth to describe it in 'The Excursion' (II, pp327-48). It was here that his 'Solitary' lived: the seeker of solitude would have to go much further afield in the summer months now!

At the outlet of the Tarn climb the stile beside the beck and follow a good path S passing delightful minor waterfalls. Do not drop down to the ruin but keep to the higher path, heading for a wall corner on the opposite side of the Wrynose Pass road. You may be tempted to cross over to Castle Howe (557ft/170m) by a direct route, but Blea Moss is usually a very boggy place - try to keep high.

At the Wrynose Pass road the Low Level Route joins the High Level Route. Turn L and go down the road to Fell Foot Farm. Both routes now run together as a common route. The route continues on Map 8.1.

Slaters' Bridge, Little Langdale

8

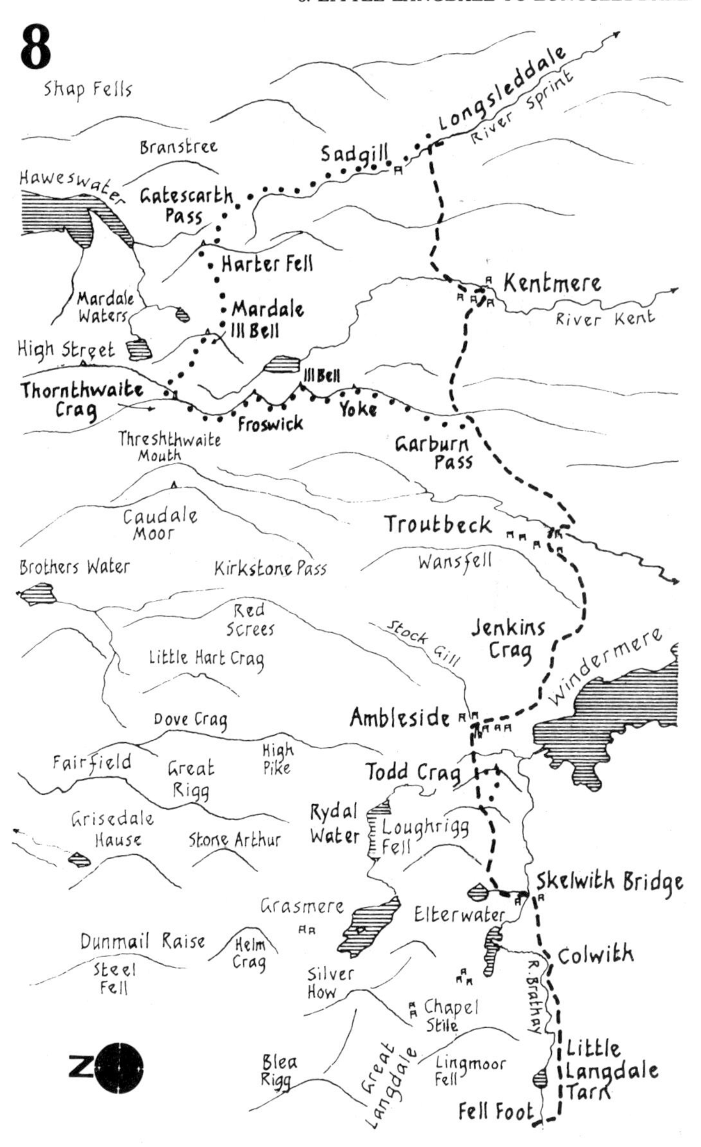
Shap Fells
Longsleddale
River Sprint
Branstree
Sadgill
Haweswater
Gatescarth Pass
Harter Fell
Kentmere
River Kent
Mardale Waters
Mardale Ill Bell
High Street
Ill Bell
Thornthwaite Crag
Froswick
Yoke
Threshthwaite Mouth
Garburn Pass
Caudale Moor
Troutbeck
Wansfell
Brothers Water
Kirkstone Pass
Red Screes
Stock Gill
Jenkins Crag
Little Hart Crag
Windermere
Ambleside
Dove Crag
Fairfield
Great Rigg
High Pike
Todd Crag
Grisedale Hause
Stone Arthur
Rydal Water
Loughrigg Fell
Skelwith Bridge
Grasmere
Elterwater
Dunmail Raise
Helm Crag
Steel Fell
Silver How
Colwith
R. Brathay
Chapel Stile
Blea Rigg
Great Langdale
Lingmoor Fell
Little Langdale Tarn
Fell Foot

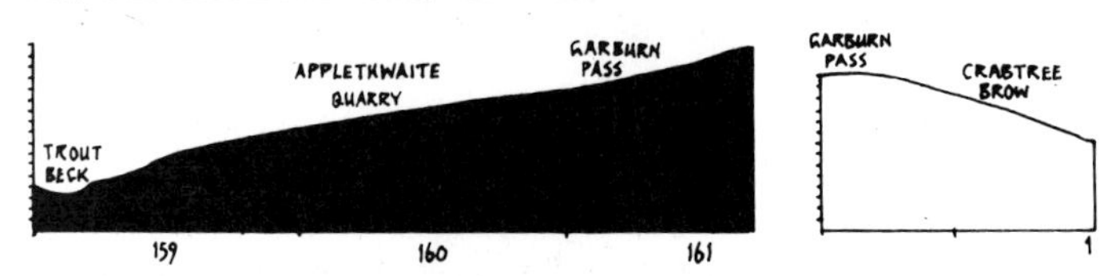
TROUT BECK
APPLETHWAITE QUARRY
GARBURN PASS
159
160
161
GARBURN PASS
CRABTREE BROW
1

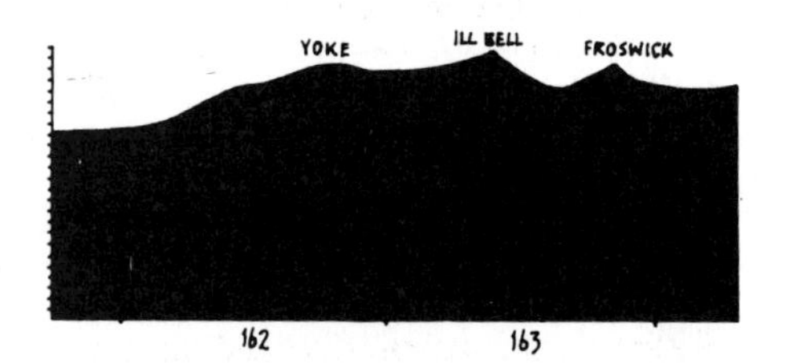
YOKE
ILL BELL
FROSWICK
162
163

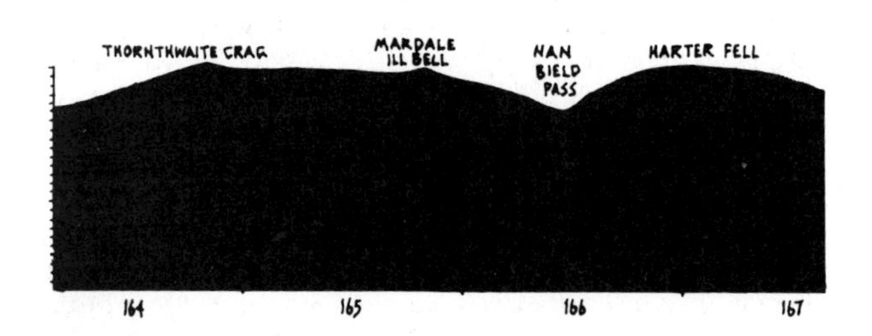
THORNTHWAITE CRAG
MARDALE ILL BELL
NAN BIELD PASS
HARTER FELL
164
165
166
167

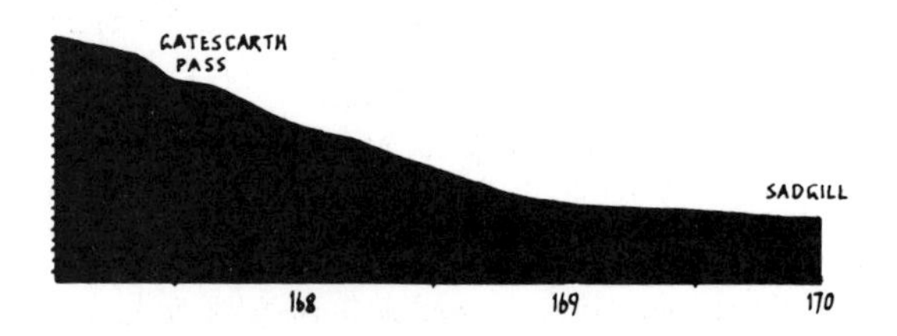
GATESCARTH PASS
SADGILL
168
169
170

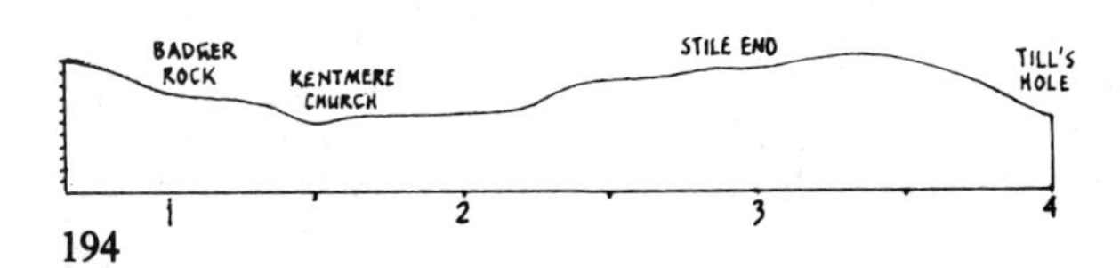
BADGER ROCK
KENTMERE CHURCH
STILE END
TILL'S HOLE
1
2
3
4

8. Little Langdale to Longsleddale

Our route turns eastwards down the valley of the River Brathay, across the head of Windermere and through Ambleside. Although the boundary of Westmorland runs down the eastern shore of Lake Windermere then in a direct line S to the Kent estuary, the route is of no interest for walkers. Instead we go further E to Troutbeck then over two low passes into Kentmere and Longsleddale before turning S and following the River Kent to Kendal then SW to Grange-over-Sands.

From Little Langdale through Ambleside and Troutbeck to the Garburn Pass is a distance of 12 miles/19.3km. The **Low Level Route** continues to Kentmere and Sadgill in Longsleddale for 4 miles/6.4km while the **High Level Route** follows the watershed around the head of Kentmere, past the headwaters of the Rivers Kent and Sprint before descending to Sadgill, a distance of 9 miles/14.4km. It is perhaps best to find accommodation in the village of Troutbeck or Kentmere, because it is another 10 miles/16km down Longsleddale to Kendal, where there is a multiple choice of accommodation.

Map 8.1

At Fell Foot in Little Langdale our High Level and Low Level Routes run together through Ambleside and Troutbeck to the Garburn Pass before splitting again to make a circuit of Kentmere and Longsleddale.

The River Brathay marks the County Boundary between Westmorland and Lancashire but as there is no right-of-way on the Westmorland side, other than the Little Langdale-Wrynose road, we have to cross over into Lancashire as far as Skelwith Bridge.

From Fell Foot Farm go down the road a short way then turn R over the River Brathay on a track to Bridge End, where a bridge crosses the Greenburn Beck. A good track is followed above the intake wall, through gates and E to the cottages at Hall Garth. There is much evidence of former slate mining activity here: the cottages themselves and the high banks of stacked slate waste beside the track. The Slaters' Bridge across the Brathay at the outlet of Little Langdale Tarn is an ancient bridge, a masterpiece of delicate stonework built by the quarrymen to take them from their homes in Little Langdale, Elterwater and Chapel Stile to their work in the Black Hole Quarry. (Those wanting accommodation in Elterwater can go over Slaters' Bridge on a path to High Birk Howe Farm then on a RUPP through the

Map 8.1

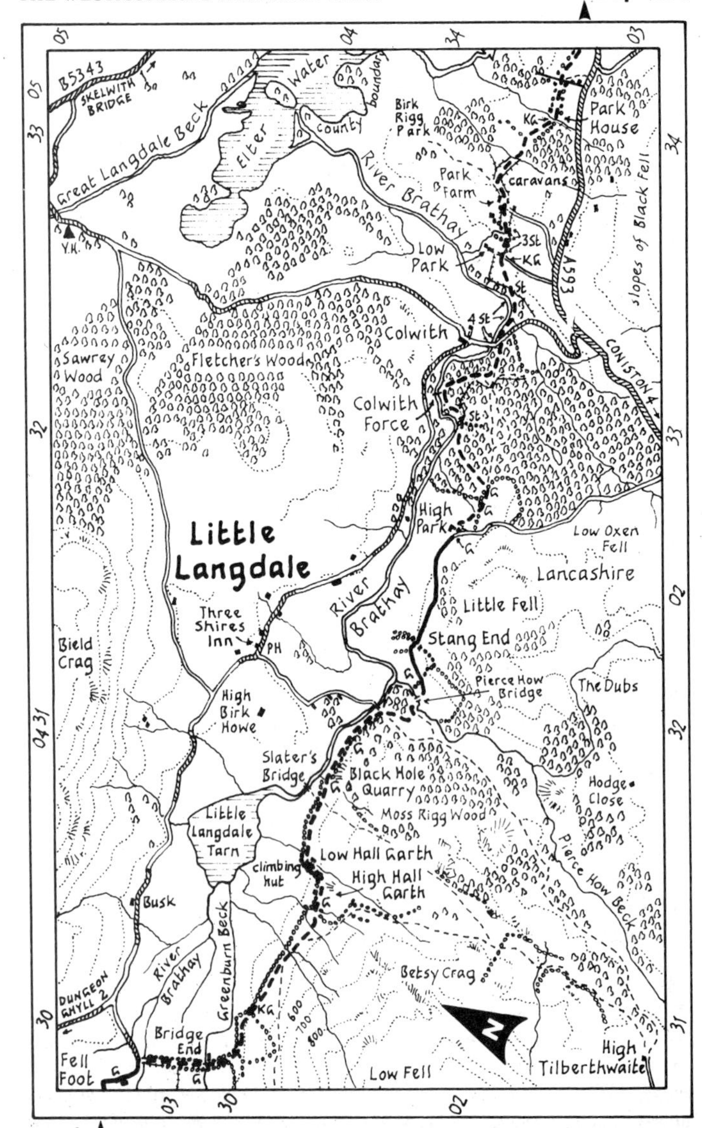
B5343
SKELWITH BRIDGE
Great Langdale Beck
Elter Water
county boundary
Birk Rigg Park
KG
Park House
River Brathay
Park Farm
caravans
slopes of Black Fell
Y.H.
Low Park
3St
KG
A593
St
4 St
Colwith
CONISTON 4
Sawrey Wood
Fletcher's Wood
Colwith Force
St
High Park
Low Oxen Fell
Little Langdale
Lancashire
Little Fell
River Brathay
Three Shires Inn
PH
Stang End
Bield Crag
Pierce How Bridge
The Dubs
High Birk Howe
Slater's Bridge
Black Hole Quarry
Hodge Close
Moss Rigg Wood
Little Langdale Tarn
Low Hall Garth
climbing hut
High Hall Garth
Pierce How Beck
Busk
River Brathay
Greenburn Beck
Betsy Crag
DUNGEON GHYLL 2
KG
600
700
800
Bridge End
Fell Foot
Low Fell
High Tilberthwaite
05
04
34
03
33
32
31
30
02

woods to Elterwater.)

A lane from the Three Shires Inn in Little Langdale comes down to the Brathay and crosses it by a deep ford with a stony bottom: vehicles should take care; pedestrians cross by a footbridge. The track crosses the river and continues southwards towards Tilberthwaite, and you follow this for a short way, bearing L on a track at the foot of a knoll called Pierce How. (Alternatively keep to the bank of the Brathay around the N side of the knoll, and turn S at a bend in the river.) The track crosses a minor beck (Pierce How Beck) by a bridge and becomes a metalled lane, climbing steeply up to Stang End, and then more gradually to High Park.

At High Park our route, a bridleway, leaves the lane and passes between the farm buildings, through a gate in a fence, and then into Tongue Intake Plantation. Immediately on entering the wood leave the bridleway and bear L, downhill, on a path towards the Brathay. You soon arrive at **Colwith Force,** *one of the most charming and neglected of Lakeland waterfalls. It lies in a narrow, tree-lined glen and can be approached with care. The water drops 90ft/27m in two leaps, the upper fall being split into five channels by rocks.*

Our path winds down through the NT woods, keeping the river in earshot, if not in sight, and comes out at the Elterwater road at Colwith Bridge.

The road to the L leads to **Elterwater,** a small village with a few shops, a youth hostel and the Britannia Inn on the village green. A new time-share holiday complex has been built in the grounds of the former gunpowder mill that was in full production from 1824 until 1930.

The lake of **Elterwater** is one of the smallest of Lakeland's lakes. It has a very irregular shape and is strangely elusive, half-hidden by reeds and trees, and occasionally glimpsed from our path.

At Colwith Bridge turn R for a short way along the road, cross over and take the signposted path across the meadow. The path climbs up a steep bank and up to Low Park and Elterwater Park (or Park Farm): note the dates on various farm buildings and the examples of stonemason's lettering. Descend past a motley collection of static holiday caravans and continue E on a rough track through the fields to Park House.

Map 8.2

Take the track from Park House but instead of following it to the A593 Ambleside-Coniston road fork L at the oak tree and continue E on a path, faint at first, parallel to the main road. The path improves as it enters the wood, then meets a few bungalows before it joins the main road. Just beyond a signposted path takes you a short way to the banks of the Brathay

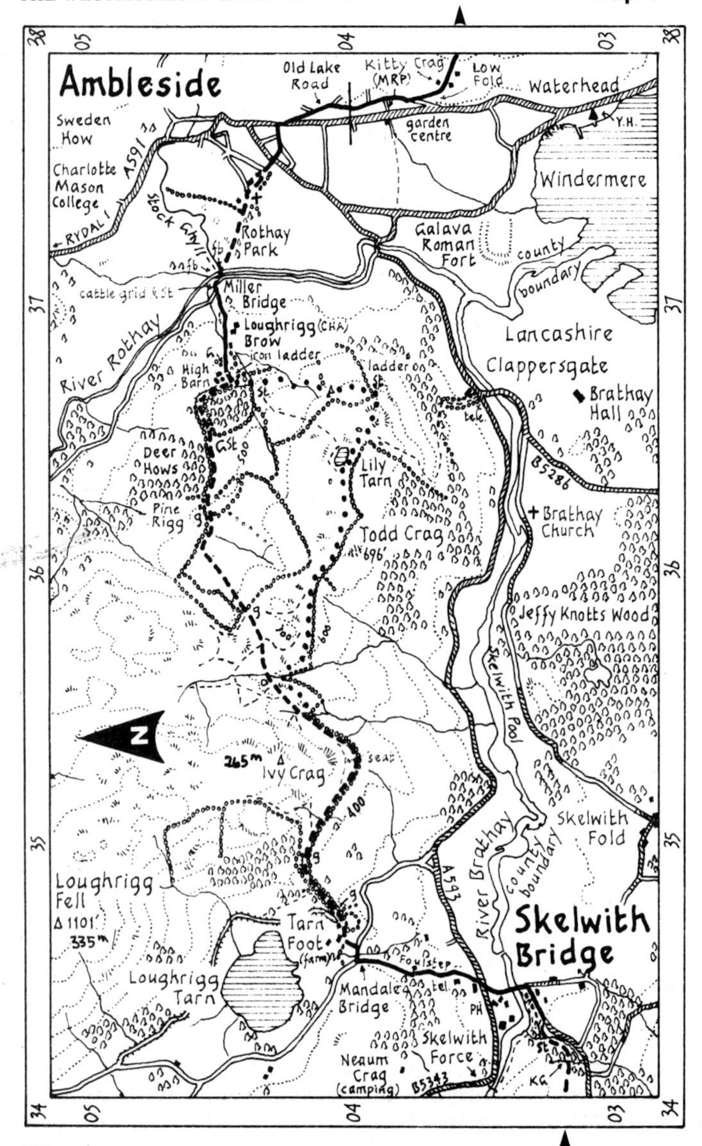
Ambleside
Old Lake Road
Kitty Crag (MRP)
Low Fold
Waterhead
Sweden How
A591
garden centre
Y.H.
Windermere
Charlotte Mason College
RYDAL
Stock Ghyll
Rothay Park
Galava Roman Fort
county boundary
fb
cattle grid & St
Miller Bridge
Loughrigg Brow (CHA)
iron ladder
ladder
High Barn
Lancashire
Clappersgate
River Rothay
Brathay Hall
tele
B5286
Deer Hows
Lily Tarn
Pine Rigg
Brathay Church
Todd Crag
696'
Jeffy Knotts Wood
Skelwith Pool
265m
Ivy Crag
seat
400
Skelwith Fold
Loughrigg Fell
1101'
335m
A593
River Brathay
county boundary
Tarn Foot (farm)
Skelwith Bridge
Loughrigg Tarn
Mandale Bridge
Foulstep
tel.
PH
Skelwith Force
Neaum Crag (camping)
B5343
St
KG
05
04
03
38
37
36
35
34

and the second of its two waterfalls: **Skelwith Force** *is only about 20ft/6m high but it has the greatest volume of water of any in the Lake District.*

Follow the main road as it bears L - take care of traffic: there are no footways - over Skelwith Bridge to the Langdale road B5343 junction. Cross over to the TCB and go up the lane called Foulstep past Neum Crag caravan site to a crossroads. Turn R here, over Mandale Bridge, then L to Tarn Foot (farm) on a bridleway that traverses the S flanks of Loughrigg Fell.

Loughrigg Fell is an unpretentious fell, only 1101ft/335m high, but it has a number of rocky outcrops and several viewpoints. Its biggest attraction is that it overlooks four lakes - Grasmere, Rydal Water, Elterwater and Windermere, and it has its own modest lake, Loughrigg Tarn, for good measure. The Tarn is just behind Tarn Foot, 5 minutes off our route.

Jonathan Otley (1765-1855) was born in Grasmere and went to Keswick as an apprentice basket and swill maker, but he gained lasting fame as a geologist and author of the first reliable guide to the Lakes. In his 'Guide to the Lakes' Otley urged the traveller to walk to the top of Ivy Crag on Loughrigg where 'he will have an instantaneous burst upon a most extraordinary assemblage of landscape beauties'.

Our path goes just below Ivy Crag and although the main bridleway continues in a NE direction and over the old golf course to Miller Brow we urge you to turn R on a minor path alongside the intake wall and over Todd Crag, 696ft/212m, to Lily Tarn, where there is a surprising and pleasant view over Windermere, the Roman fort of Galava, and Ambleside itself.

From Todd Cragg there is a magnificent view of **Windermere,** a blue wide lake stretching away into the distance. More than 10 miles/16km long, a mile/1.6km wide and over 200ft/60m deep, it is the longest natural expanse of fresh water in England. Passenger vessels, rowing boats, motor lunches, countless yachts, speedboats and water-skiers make the lake alive with ever-changing colours and constant noise. Looking down on Waterhead the lake and its shore is a hive of activity.

In Borrans Field, at the head of the lake, beside the outlet of the Rivers Rothay and Brathay, are the remains of **Galava,** a Roman fort sometimes called Borrans Fort, borran being an old local term for a heap of stones. Little remains apart from foundations. The original fort was probably built during Agricola's northern campaign in AD 79 to command the road that led from Brougham over High Street and then over Wrynose Pass and Hardknott Pass to Hardknott Fort and the Roman port at Ravenglass. The fort was later overlaid by another fort in the 2c and measures 298ft x 450ft/91m x 137m. A defensive ditch guards the N and E sides and the Rothay bounded the W side -though the river was much nearer to the fort then - and marshy ground leading down to the lake guarded its S side. Probable landing points and roads from both lake and river have not been found.

The fort was excavated by Prof. R.G.Collingwood and some of the finds may be seen in the Brockhole National Park Centre. A beautiful model of the fort, together with finds and detailed archaeological drawings are on display in the **Armitt Museum** above the library in Ambleside.

Ambleside (from the Norse 'Amal's shielding' or summer pasture) is an old town of many quaint nooks and corners, originally built 1 mile/1.6km from the lake but now grown considerably. We shall visit Ambleside shortly, but while we are on this vantage point on Loughrigg Fell we can look down on the homes of several notables who loved this district. Although Grasmere can claim the Lakes Poets, the Ambleside area can claim more celebrities of later generations.

Below us to the S, at the Hawkshead road junction, is **Clappersgate,** a cluster of houses scarcely big enough to be called a village. The Croft, a large house now converted into flats, was the home of Mr. Branker who often entertained the Lakes Poets. White Craggs has a wonderful rock garden commanding a view of the Rothay and Brathay, created by the late Charles Henry Hough and his family. It has flowers brought from all parts of the world, including rare plants from China and Tibet collected by Reginald Farrer and William Purdom on the expedition described by Farrer in 'The Eaves of the World' and its sequel 'The Rainbow Bridge'. The garden has been open to the public since 1919 and the story of its making, and an account of all the rare plants to be found there is told by Hough in a beautifully illustrated little booklet 'A Westmorland Rock Garden'. Purdom was born just across the road in The Lodge at Brathay Hall and he accompanied Farrer to Tibet in 1913. On his return to Peking in 1915 Purdom was offered and accepted the post of Forestry Expert in the Ministry of Agriculture of the Chinese government. He carried out much important work before his death in 1921.

From Todd Crag and Lily Tarn, or from the main bridleway from Ivy Crag and the old golf course to Miller Brow, our path meets a lane near Loughrigg Brow (former home of the late Canon Bell, vicar of Ambleside and Lakeland poet, now a CHA guest house) and comes out on the 'Under Loughrigg' back road from Rothay Bridge to Rydal Bridge at a cattle grid.

The house opposite the famous stepping stones across the Rothay is where Gordon Wordsworth, the last surviving grandson of the poet, lived until his death and burial in Grasmere churchyard in 1935.

Loughrigg Holme was for a short time the home of Dora Wordsworth and her husband Edward Quillinan.

Cross the River Rothay by the footbridge, cross the Stock Ghyll by another footbridge and go through Rothay Park to the church of St. Mary's and into Ambleside.

St. Mary's was built in 1850-4 by Sir George Gilbert Scott in the Early Decorated style and it aroused a great deal of criticism at the time because its spire, 180ft/54.8m high, was considered to be out of place in this valley. It has memorial windows to William Wordsworth, his sister and his wife, and to Mathew Arnold. (Mathew Arnold was the son of the great Dr. Arnold of Rugby who built his house, Fox How, on the Grasmere side under Loughrigg, in 1833. Dr. Arnold lived at Fox How during his holidays with his family, including his granddaughter, later Mrs. Humphry Ward, the novelist). The Rushbearing Festival takes place in St. Mary's on the first Saturday in July.

The one building in Ambleside which excites most interest is the curious **Bridge House** on the Rydal road. It occupies the whole of a narrow bridge over the Stock Beck, is of only two rooms and has an outside staircase to the first floor. It probably dates from 17c and is said to have been built as a garden house linking the house and gardens of the former Ambleside Hall with its orchards on the other side of the stream, although local legend says that it was the home of a Scotsman who wished to avoid a land tax. Since 1926 it has been in the care of the NT and is now used by them as an information centre.

Nearly opposite Bridge House is a picturesque old water wheel of a former corn mill and a little higher up the Stock Ghyll is Horrax's bobbin mill which attracted the attention of Dickens on his visit in 1857. Further up Stock Ghyll, behind the Salutation Inn, the Stock Ghyll Force falls in a 76ft/23m drop over a rocky ledge in a wooded ravine. Several Victorian viewpoints for the waterfall and its gorge, protected by iron railings, can still be seen.

Just beyond Bridge House on the Rydal Road is The Knoll, the house which Harriet Martineau built in 1845 with money earned from her writings, and in which she lived for 31 years until her death in 1876. Among her many guests were Charlotte Bronte, George Eliot, Mrs. Gaskell, Emerson and Mathew Arnold. Her 'Complete Guide to the English Lakes' (1855) is one of the better-known early guides to the area.

Opposite The Knoll is Green Bank, once the home of Mrs. Dorothy Benson Harrison, the niece of Wordsworth, by whom she was brought up. She came to Green Bank with her husband and family in 1827

Map 8.3

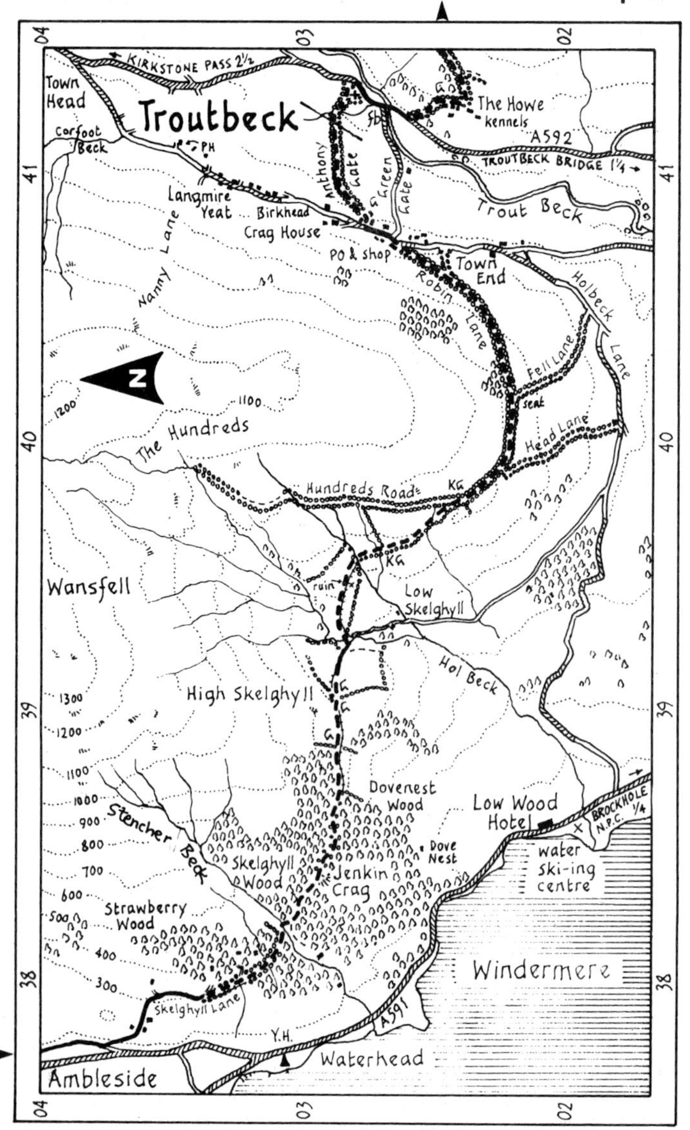

KIRKSTONE PASS 2½
Town Head
Troutbeck
Corfoot Beck
PH
The Howe
kennels
A592
TROUTBECK BRIDGE 1¼
Anthony Gate
Green Gate
Trout Beck
Langmire Yeat
Birkhead
Crag House
Nanny Lane
PO & shop
Town End
Robin Lane
Holbeck Lane
Fell Lane
Seat
Head Lane
N
1200
1100
The Hundreds
Hundreds Road
KG
ruin
Wansfell
Low Skelghyll
Hol Beck
High Skelghyll
1300
1000
900
800
700
600
500
400
300
Stencher Beck
Dovenest Wood
Low Wood Hotel
BROCKHOLE N.P.C. ¼
Dove Nest
Water Ski-ing centre
Skelghyll Wood
Jenkin Crag
Strawberry Wood
Windermere
Skelghyll Lane
A591
Y.H.
Waterhead
Ambleside
04
03
02
41
40
39
38

when the Wordsworths were still living at Rydal Mount, and lived there until 1890. (Green Bank is now known as Scale How, the Charlotte Mason College of Education.)

Beyond Green Bank is Lesketh How, former home of Dr. Davy, brother of Sir Humphry Davy. On the hillside above is Eller How, at the entrance to Scandale, where Anne Jemima Clough, the first Principal of Newnham College lived from 1852-62 and ran a school in Ambleside.

Unless you wish to visit the town centre and its cafes, chippies, gift shops and climbing shops keep St. Mary's church and the putting green on your R, go along the bottom of Compston Road to a crossroads, go across into Kelsick Road and follow this up past the library and Armitt Museum to meet the main Keswick-Kendal road A591.

Go S down this a short way, then cross over and bear L along Old Lake Road: as its name implies, this was the way to Waterhead before the main road was constructed in Victorian times. 'New' Lake Road was built to cater for those who came up the lake by steamer and went on by charabancs to visit the 'shrine' at Grasmere.

Map 8.3

We leave Ambleside by taking the Old Lake Road and then Wansfell Lane steeply uphill and into Skelghyll Wood. This is a delightful mixed woodland and the bridleway passes above Jenkin Crag, a good viewpoint for the activity in the North Lake: the view extends from Waterhead as far S as Belle Isle and Bowness. The area is of interest to geologists and botanists because a narrow band of Coniston Limestone passes through the junction of Borrowdale Volcanics and Coniston Slates. This band of limestone runs through the village of Troutbeck, is worn away to form Garburn Pass, goes through the village of Kentmere and through the pass to Sadgill in Longsleddale - a line followed by our Low Level Route.

Below the woods, on the way down to the lake, is Dove Nest, built in 1780 and home for the summer of 1830 of Mrs. Felicia Hemans (1793-1835) where she entertained Wordsworth and other Lakes Poets. She is remembered, if at all, only for her poem 'The Boy Stood on the Burning Deck'. The house was subsequently improved and occupied by the poet Rev. Robert Percival Graves, who was the minister of the church at Bowness in 1843. Below Dove Nest on the Lake Road is the extensive Low Wood Hotel, an 18c coaching inn used by the Lakes Poets and other writers. Its whitewashed range of buildings form a very prominent landmark on the shore of Lake Windermere when seen from the Langdale and Coniston fells.

A good track passes through gates to High Skelghyll and above Low

Skelghyll, to join the Hundred Road, a walled trackway that curves round from Wansfell. We continue ahead on Robin Lane, ignoring Head Lane and Fell Lane going off to the R, and we soon arrive in Troutbeck village at Town End.

Troutbeck is a picturesque village spread along the fellside looking down on the main Windermere-Penrith road A592 in the valley below. The village buildings are grouped around the springs issuing from Wansfell which provided the communal water supplies for the village. The springs filled water troughs, relics of the coaching days when horses had to be watered before beginning the hard climb over Kirkstone Pass to Patterdale. Kirkstone Pass was one of the few passes in Lakeland when Clarke drew his maps in 1785 but it must have been little more than a cart-track because in 1787 William Gilpin described it as not the 'commodious width of a carriage road'.

There are several old houses and farms along the narrow hilly road - **Town End,** 1626, is a typical statesman-farmer's house with its barn, 1666, across the road. It is the property of the NT and houses a collection of carved furniture and other fascinating implements of the past, collected by the Browne family who lived there for generations until 1944. (The house is open weekday afternoons except Mondays, 1400-1800. Closed Saturdays and Good Friday.)

The main village inn, 1689, is oddly named **The Mortal Man** but was originally The White House. It formerly had an inn-sign painted by the artist Julius Caesar Ibbotson (1759-1817) who once lived at Troutbeck. The sign showed on one side fat, jolly Nat Flemming and on the other side pale, thin Ned Partridge, with the words:

'O mortal man that lives by bread
What is it makes thy nose so red?
Thou silly fool, that looks't so pale,
'Tis drinking Sally Birkett's ale'.

Black's guide of 1841 mentioned the sign as being there 'a few years ago'; the modern sign is a poor imitation of the original.

Almost as soon as you meet the road passing through the village N of Town End a road called Green Gate goes down R into the valley. Do not take this but go a little further then turn R on a bridleway called Anthony Gate. This track passes between buildings at first, then between walls, down to Troutbeck church. A gate takes you into the churchyard and to the church itself.

The **Chapel of Jesus Church** is entered through the W tower, which was built in 1736 when the church was rebuilt. The six oak beams were taken from the original church of 1562 and the Jacobean panelling in the chancel stalls came from Calgarth Hall, Windermere, when the church was re-furnished in 1861. The Royal Arms above the gallery was painted in 1737. It shows the arms of George III, the reigning monarch at the time, and the heraldry of England, Scotland and Ireland, and the lilies of France.

The dominating feature is the beautiful E window which immediately attracts your attention as you enter because it is so large and colourful in such a small and simple church. It was installed in 1873 and is the work of three famous 'Pre-Raphaelite' artists - Sir Edward Burne Jones, Ford Maddox Brown and William Morris. The overall design is by William Morris, who also designed the rich green foliage. All the large figures are by Burne Jones:- the youthful Christ, without beard, flanked by the Virgin Mary and St. Peter on the L and St. John and St. Paul on the R. Burne Jones also did the scenes from the Gospels - Reception of the Children and Appearance in the Garden, and also Noah and St. John the Baptist. The other smaller windows were done by the other two - Maddox Brown did the Appearance at Emmaus and St. Peter's Confession, while Morris did the Baptism and Annunciation.

Opposite the church is the small village school and nearby is the Queen Victoria Jubilee drinking fountain.

Map 8.4

From Troutbeck Church emerge on to the A592 Windermere-Penrith road, turn S on the footway and cross the Trout Beck by Church Bridge. Go S a little further, then turn L up a stony track between stone walls to the Howe, bending NE as the track cuts up across the fellside. This is the Garburn Pass road, a RUPP which we follow over the fell and down into the Kentmere valley.

Two lanes come up from the S and both of these (the first a bridleway, the second a RUPP) and **Garburn Pass** *itself are much used by trail bikes and trials bikes, the old quarry at Applethwaite being a popular place for them to try out their skills. The RUPP is enclosed between walls for most of its way to the Pass, and is rough in places. At the gate near the top the High Level Route strikes off N, marked by cairns, but you can continue to the gate in the wall at the Pass itself, before turning off if you wish, though the official right-of-way is that indicated on our map. The imperial OS map gives Garburn Pass a height of 1475ft, which when converted gives 450m. The new metric survey 1:10,000 has reduced the pass to 447m, which when converted equals 1466ft.*

High Level Route

We have chosen a high level circuit of the western half of the Kentmere fells,

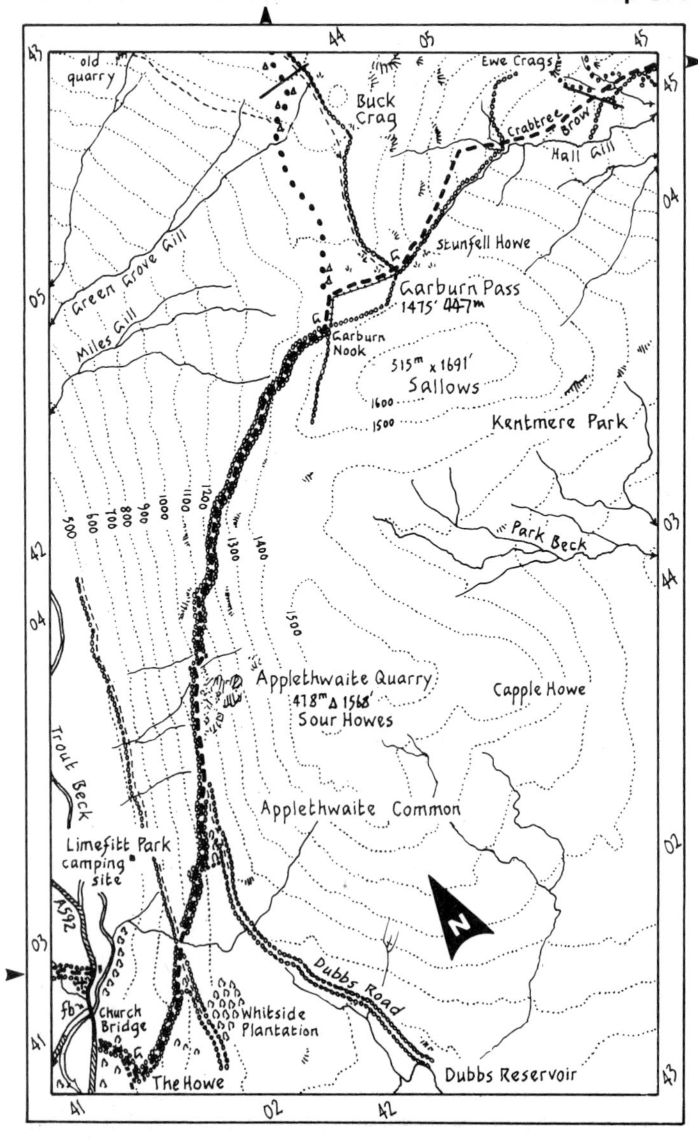
old quarry
Buck Crag
Ewe Crags
Crabtree Brow
Hall Gill
Green Grove Gill
Stunfell Howe
Garburn Pass
1475' 447m
Miles Gill
Garburn Nook
515m x 1691'
Sallows
Kentmere Park
Park Beck
Applethwaite Quarry
478m Δ 1568'
Sour Howes
Capple Howe
Trout Beck
Applethwaite Common
Limefitt Park camping site
A592
Church Bridge
Whitside Plantation
Dubbs Road
Dubbs Reservoir
The Howe

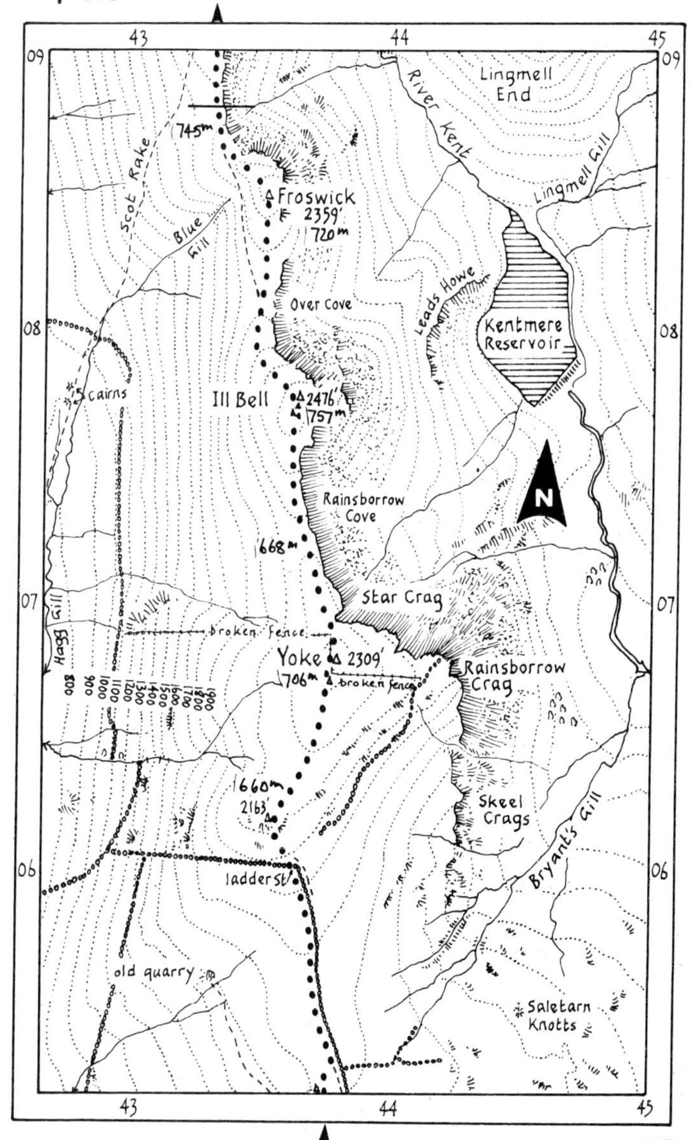
43
44
45
09
08
07
06
Lingmell
End
River Kent
Lingmell Gill
745m
Scot Rake
Froswick
2359'
720m
Blue
Gill
Leads Howe
Kentmere
Reservoir
Over Cove
cairns
Ill Bell
2476'
757m
Rainsborrow
Cove
N
668m
Star Crag
Hagg Gill
broken fence
Yoke
2309'
706m
broken fence
Rainsborrow
Crag
800
900
1000
1100
1200
1300
1400
1500
1600
1700
1800
1900
660m
2163'
Skeel
Crags
Bryant's Gill
ladder st
old quarry
Saletarn
Knotts

known as the Kentmere Horseshoe, as a delightful way of savouring the upper reaches of the valley and for giving us views of some of the ground that we have covered during the past few days.

Aim for the wall and follow it N.

(High Level Route continues on Map 8.5)

Low Level Route

The descent from Garburn Pass, unlike the ascent, is not between walls, but the route is obvious as it descends the valley of Hall Gill towards Kentmere village.

(Low Level Route continues on Map 8.8)

Map 8.5

High Level Route

Follow the wall up the ridge from Buck Crag to a stile in a corner then out on to the open fell. There is a steep climb up to the cairn at 2163ft/660m and then an easier incline to the summit of Yoke, the southernmost of three peaks on the ridge leading to the High Street plateau.

The path keeps to the ridge with the steep cliffs of Rainsborrow Cove below to the R, so don't go too close to the edge in poor visibility. A dip, then a rise up to Ill Bell, the highest top of the three on this ridge, offers the finest views over Windermere. Its top, and that of Froswick to the N are both distinctive peaks when viewed from the SW. A short quick descent then another short climb brings you up to Froswick (although its summit can be by-passed by a path across its W flank). A descent again, then the Roman road High Street comes up from Troutbeck and Hagg Gill to the ridge.

As with the Langdale Pikes, the Ordnance Survey have been adding little bits here and there to the tops around the Kentmere Horseshoe. The old and new heights look something like this:

Fell Top	OS Imperial	Conversion to Metric	OS Metric 1:10,000	Conversion to Imperial
Yoke	*2309*	*704*	*706*	*2316*
Ill Bell	*2476*	*755*	*757*	*2483*
Froswick	*2359*	*719*	*720*	*2362*
Thornthwaite Crag	*2569*	*783*	*784*	*2572*
Harter Fell	*2539*	*774*	*778*	*2552*

Happily High Street and Mardale Ill Bell are unaffected by these changes.

(High Level Route continues on Map 8.6)

Map 8.6

High Level Route

The Roman road joins the ridge just S of the magnificent beacon on the

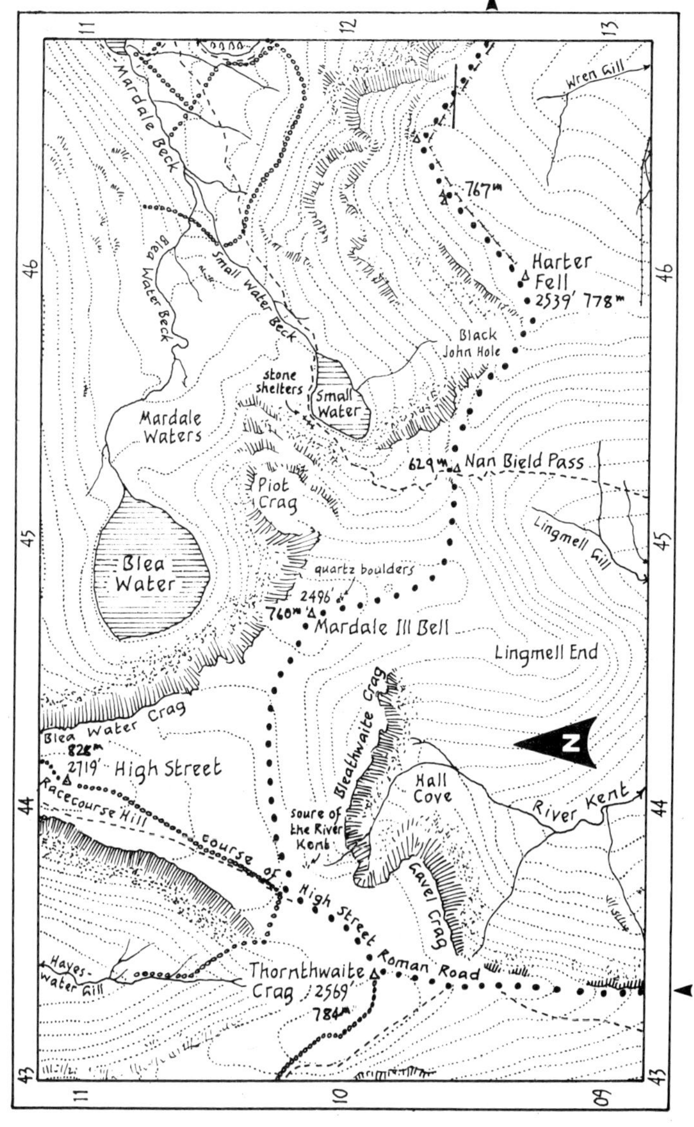
Mardale Beck
Wren Gill
767m
Harter Fell
2539' 778m
Blea Water Beck
Small Water Beck
Black John Hole
stone shelters
Small Water
Mardale Waters
629m Nan Bield Pass
Piot Crag
Lingmell Gill
Blea Water
quartz boulders
2496'
760m Mardale Ill Bell
Lingmell End
Bleathwaite Crag
Blea Water Crag
828m
2719' High Street
Hall Cove
Racecourse Hill
River Kent
soure of the River Kent
course of High Street Roman Road
Gavel Crag
Hayeswater Gill
Thornthwaite Crag 2569'
784m
11
12
13
46
45
44
43
10
09

wall-end of Thornthwaite Crag and although the Roman road makes a direct line towards High Street we divert off it to visit the cairn (and find shelter behind the wall in windy weather!).

The beacon is the most distinctive summit cairn in the Lakes - a stone column 13ft/4m high, commanding a superb view over Troutbeck, Kentmere and Windermere and the fells to the W, N and E.

In Roman times the fell sides were thickly forested and the valleys were boggy and inhospitable and likely places to suffer ambush. The route along the High Street ridge is almost on a direct line from the Roman fort at Brougham to Troutbeck where it is assumed (because there is no evidence) that it met the Roman road from Watercrook Fort at Kendal to the fort of Galava at Ambleside.

High Street (2719ft/828m) is the highest point on the long ridge that carries the Roman road from Ullswater to Troutbeck. The top is grassy and even, in sharp contrast to its craggy eastern face and steep W and S flanks. Until 19c it was an annual meeting place for shepherds, where stray animals could be exchanged and an excuse easily found for revelries. Shepherds from Mardale, Troutbeck, Martindale, Patterdale, Kentmere and Longsleddale took part. There was a fair, casks of ale were consumed and there were games, wrestling and horse-racing: the summit plateau carries the name Racecourse Hill.

The next few hundred yards of the path are tricky in misty conditions as Thornthwaite Beacon stands on the edge of the SW spur of the High Street plateau. If you take a bearing NE from the beacon you should meet a wall at a corner, close to the source of the River Kent, and from here you can take another bearing E below the rim of the High Street plateau leading towards Mardale Ill Bell. The path follows a traversing line and if you find yourself going down steep ground you are heading towards Bleathwaite Crags, and are too low.

On the E side of High Street and Mardale Ill Bell (2496ft/760m) are two hanging valleys beneath craggy heights, occupied by two tarns - **Blea Water** and **Small Water,** the former having the astounding depth of 223ft/68m. Blea Water is one of the best examples of a Lake District corrie lake, intermediate between the arctic/alpine lakes of the Cairngorms and the lower altitude corrie lakes such as Llyn Idwal in Snowdonia. Its very clear and pure water is almost devoid of any flora or fauna. The two tarns and other becks feed into Mardale Beck and the valley of Mardale, now occupied by the **Haweswater Reservoir.**

Thirlmere was not enough to provide Manchester's need for water and in 1929 a dam was constructed to flood the valley, and the village of Mardale was submerged under 95ft/29m of water. During the drought of summer 1984 the water level dropped to its lowest ever

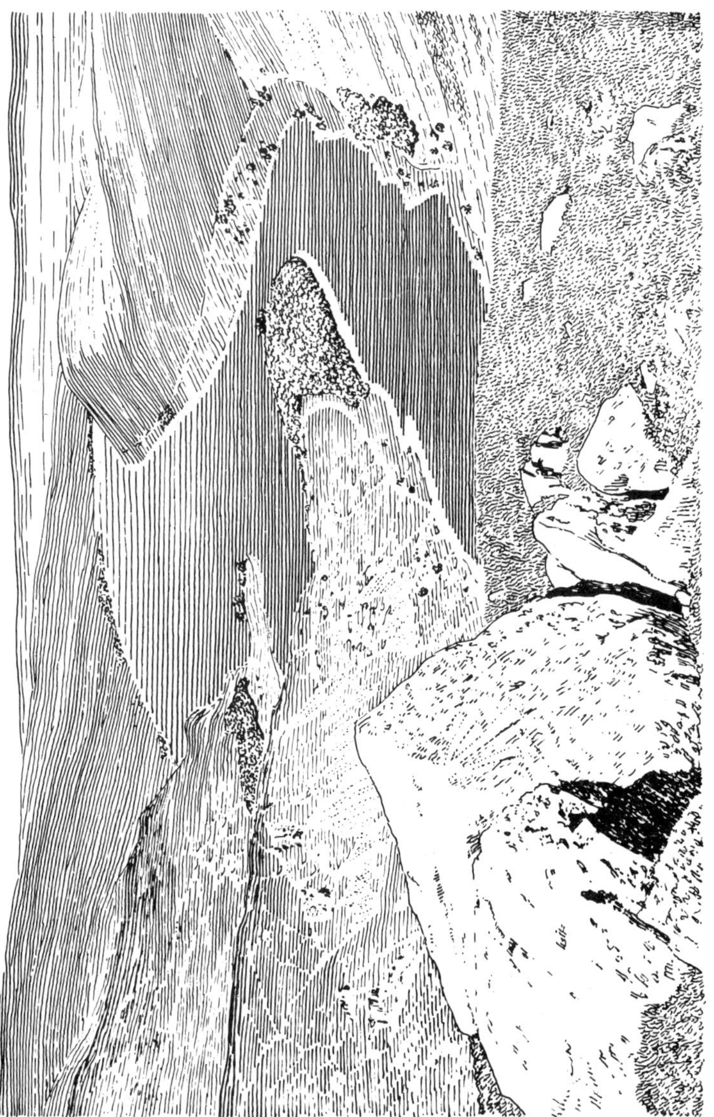

Haweswater from Harter Fell

recorded level, and the drowned village, its packhorse bridge and intake walls were exposed, attracting thousands of tourists who created traffic jams on the long narrow approach road.

Mardale Ill Bell dominates the head of Mardale and a good path goes over its top as you join the path coming SE from the top of High Street. The path descends SE on a narrowing spur and you are soon at the narrow notch of Nan Bield Pass (2063ft/629m). A bridleway comes up from Mardale via Small Water, crosses the Pass and descends to Kentmere: in bad weather escape S, steep at first as the path zig-zags down towards Kentmere Reservoir and the relative shelter and safety of the valley. (The reservoir was created during the last century to provide a constant head of water for the mills in the valley.)

Our path climbs steeply up a rocky spur above Small Water Crag and when the gradient eases off bear E across the dome of Harter Fell to its ugly collection of stones and stakes on its summit. The top of Harter Fell is an elongated plateau pointing NE and we follow the fence, a good guide in mist. The third cairn marks a turn of direction, and is also a good viewpoint for Haweswater and the Cross Fell range of the Pennines.

(High Level Route continues on Map 8.7)

Map 8.7

High Level Route

From the top of Harter Fell follow the line of the fence SE down to Little Harter Fell and Adam Seat, and to the gate in the fence at the col of Gatesgarth Pass.

Gatesgarth Pass is the old route from Mardale to Longsleddale and was the quickest way from the old village to Kendal market. Carts could be taken over the 1890ft/576m pass, but neglect since the Manchester Corporation Water Works submerged the hamlet caused its decline. The path is good all the way though it is a bit boggy on its descent towards the head of Mosedale.

The track coming up from the head of Haweswater is a bridleway and is in Eden District (formerly North Westmorland Rural District). The descent from the gate down into Longsleddale is a RUPP and is in South Lakeland District (formerly South Westmorland Rural District). At some time the rural distict councils must have disagreed over the status of this green lane.

Soon after the Gatesgarth track meets the Mosedale path at some substantial sheep folds it passes through another gate and commences a descent between walls down into Longsleddale, a narrow valley running straight and carrying the River Sprint from its source on Harter Fell down to the Kent and Kendal. The importance of the route is illustrated by the

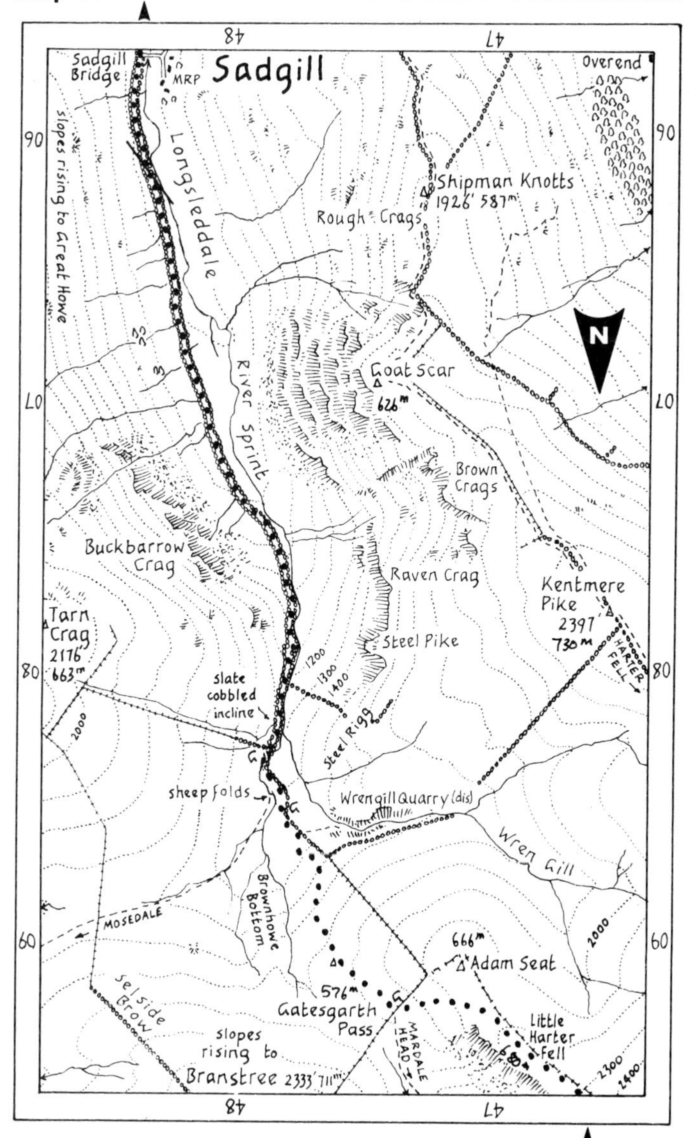
48
47
Sadgill Bridge
MRP
Sadgill
Overend
slopes rising to Great Howe
Longsleddale
Shipman Knotts
1926' 587m
Rough Crags
90
N
Goat Scar
626m
River Sprint
70
Brown Crags
Buckbarrow Crag
Raven Crag
Kentmere Pike
2397
730m
Tarn Crag
2176'
663m
Steel Pike
HARTER FELL
80
slate cobbled incline
1200
1300
1400
2000
Steel Rigg
sheep folds
Wrengill Quarry (dis)
Wren Gill
Brownhowe Bottom
MOSEDALE
60
666m
Adam Seat
2000
576m
Gatesgarth Pass
Selside Brow
slopes rising to
Branstree 2333' 711m
MARDALE HEAD
Little Harter Fell
2300
2400

Map 8.8

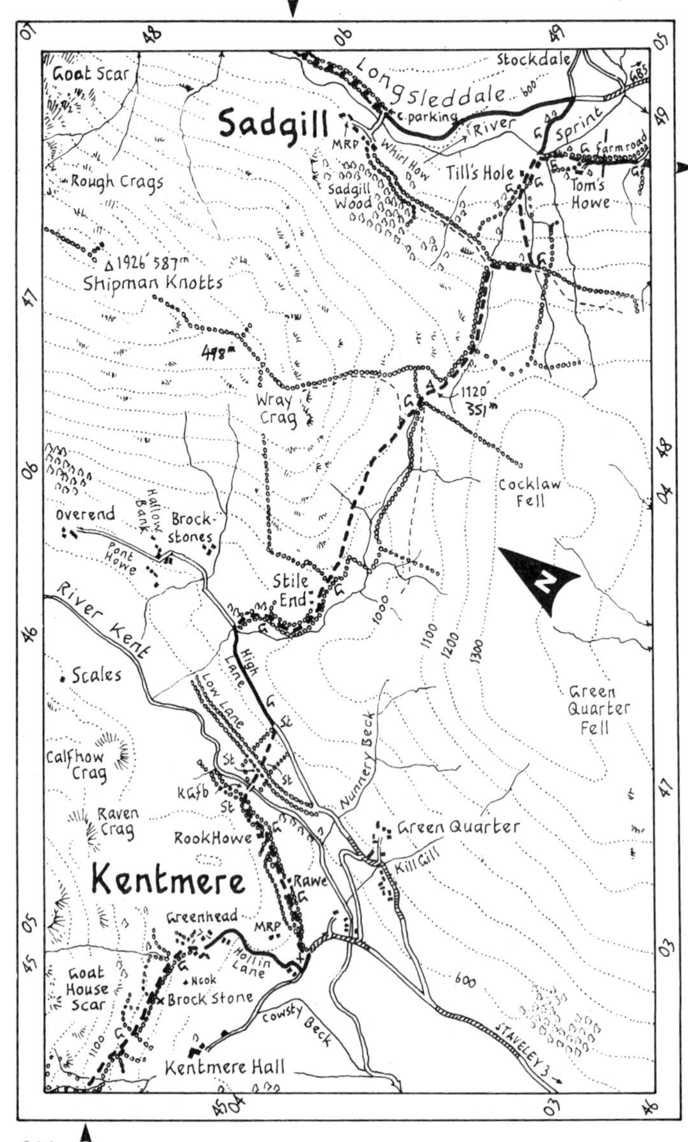

Goat Scar
Stockdale
Longsleddale
Sadgill
parking
River
Sprint
Farmroad
MRP
Whirl How
Till's Hole
Rough Crags
Sadgill Wood
Tom's Howe
1926' 587m
Shipman Knotts
498m
1120' 351m
Wray Crag
Cocklaw Fell
Overend
Hallow Bank
Brock-stones
Pont Howe
Stile End
River Kent
High Lane
Low Lane
Scales
Green Quarter Fell
Nunnery Beck
Calfhow Crag
KGfb
Raven Crag
RookHowe
Green Quarter
Kill Gill
Kentmere
Rawe
Greenhead
MRP
Hollin Lane
Goat House Scar
Ncok
Brock Stone
Cowsty Beck
Kentmere Hall
STAVELEY 3

good cam stones in the bed of the track on a steep incline which must have been a difficult place for traffic using the Wren Gill Quarries. Over one wall is the infant River Sprint, leaping over waterfalls in its race to get down the valley, while over the other wall rises Buckbarrow Crag, the SW flank of Tarn Crag.

A delightful green lane winds down Longsleddale to Sadgill, the first settlement in the valley, and the first we come to after leaving Troutbeck. *(High Level Route continues on Map 8.8)*

Map 8.8

High Level Route

The green lane ends at Sadgill and our route continues down the valley at first on the road but then, after a short way, having passed a prominent glacial mound called Whirl How (marked on OS maps as a tumulus) turns R on the farm track to Till's Hole, where you join the Low Level Route. *(Route continues as Common Route below)*

Low Level Route

The Garburn Pass track descends to the valley of Kentmere and the village of the same name. On reaching the outskirts of the settlements the Brock Stone is seen over the wall on the R and you pass through a gate. Hollin Lane from the upper Kentmere valley comes down from the L, and we turn R and follow it down to the church.

Kentmere is a scattering of farms and houses grouped around its church and hall in the middle of the valley. The church of **St. Cuthbert** is a plain, cement-rendered building which, although it has 16c roof-beams, was rebuilt in 1866 and again renovated in 1950. The nave and chancel are all in one, and the Norman style windows have no stained glass. There is a bronze memorial tablet to Bernard Gilpin which was made in the Art Nouveau style by the Keswick School of Industrial Arts in 1901.

Kentmere Hall is seen on the approach to the village. It is a 15c house attached to a 14c pele tower, a large farm which was the home of the Gilpin family for over 200 years. Bernard Gilpin (1517-83) was born here: a champion of the Reformation he became known as 'The Apostle of the North' and was made Archdeacon of Durham in 1586. His lands were lost in the Civil War through following the cause of Charles I.

Kentmere's lake or 'mere' was drained in the late 19c and dug for diatomite - it was the only source of diatomaceous earth in England. It was used locally in the manufacture of asbestos products, but the mining, and the manufacture, has now ceased. In 1955 a wooden boat was discovered in the lake, probably 1,000 years old. It is now in the National Maritime Museum.

Immediately beyond Kentmere church turn L on a track to Rawe and Rook Howe on a public footpath passing between stone walls and through two gates. At a stile turn R and drop down to a footbridge over the River Kent. Climb up the other side, crossing the Green Quarter-Overend bridleway (called Low Lane) by stiles and up through the pasture to the Kentmere-Hallow Bank lane (called High Lane).

Turn L up High Lane then take the first turn R on the RUPP to Stile End and over the ridge of the fell to Longsleddale. Pass through a gate and pass a cairn that marks the summit of the pass (1152ft/351m). A steep direct descent follows, but instead of following the RUPP N to Sadgill turn R on a bridleway for 100m then turn L through a gate on another bridleway to Till's Hole.

Common Route

At Till's Hole the High Level and the Low Level Routes join, and henceforward both routes run together to the end of our journey at Grange-over-Sands.

There are two ways down Longsleddale - the road keeping to the eastern side and a bridleway down the western side. We keep to the bridleway. *(Route continues on Map 9.1)*

Longsleddale.

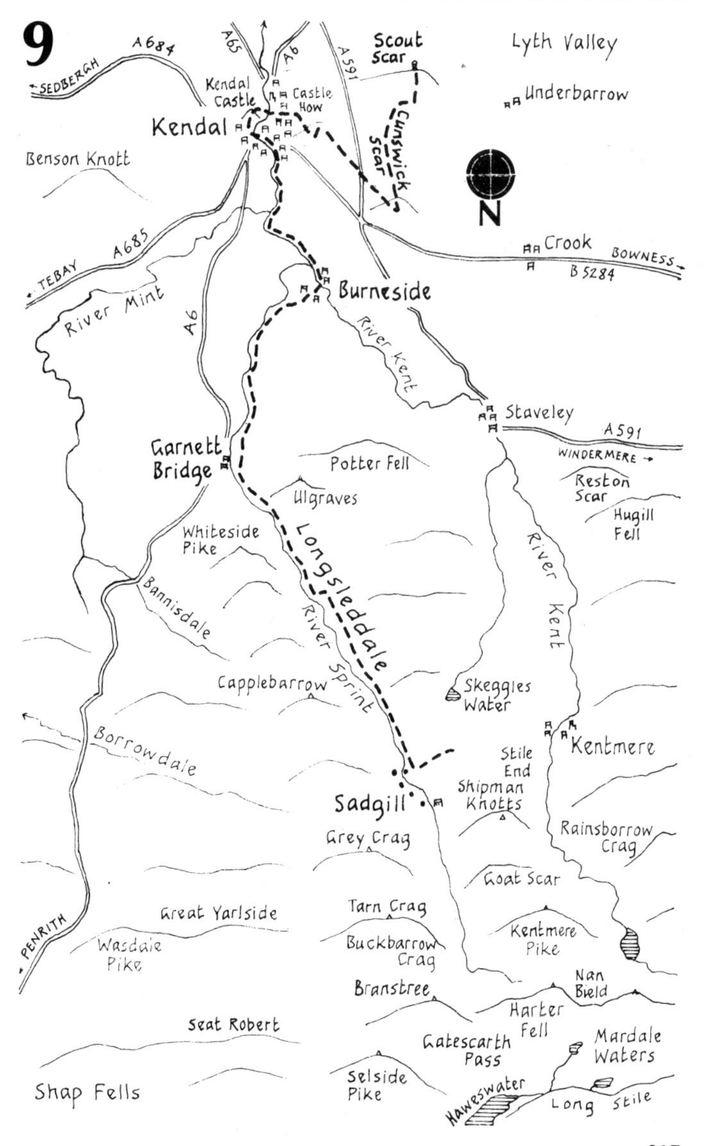
9
A684
SEDBERGH
A65
A6
A591
Scout Scar
Lyth Valley
Kendal Castle
Castle How
Underbarrow
Kendal
Cunswick Scar
Benson Knott
N
A685
TEBAY
Crook
BOWNESS
B5284
Burneside
River Mint
A6
River Kent
Staveley
A591
WINDERMERE
Garnett Bridge
Potter Fell
Reston Scar
Ulgraves
Hugill Fell
Whiteside Pike
Longsleddale
River Kent
Bannisdale
River Sprint
Capplebarrow
Skeggles Water
Borrowdale
Kentmere
Stile End
Shipman Knotts
Sadgill
Grey Crag
Rainsborrow Crag
Goat Scar
Great Yarlside
Tarn Crag
Kentmere Pike
PENRITH
Wasdale Pike
Buckbarrow Crag
Branstree
Nan Bield
Harter Fell
Seat Robert
Gatescarth Pass
Mardale Waters
Selside Pike
Shap Fells
Haweswater
Long Stile

WAD'S HOWE
KILNSTONES
171
172
173

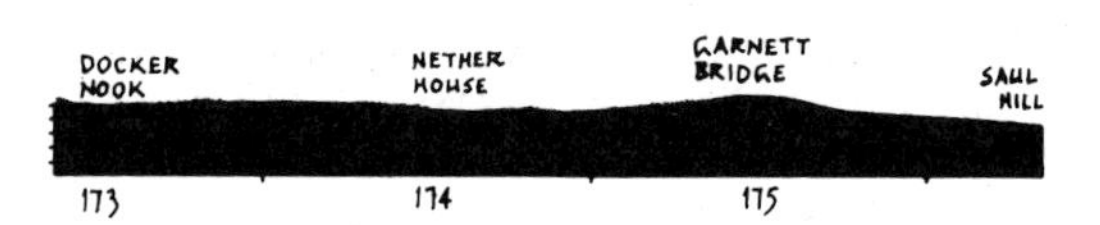
DOCKER NOOK
NETHER HOUSE
GARNETT BRIDGE
SAUL HILL
173
174
175

SAUL HILL
SPRINT MILL
BURNESIDE
RIVER
KENT
KENTRIGG
176
177
178
179

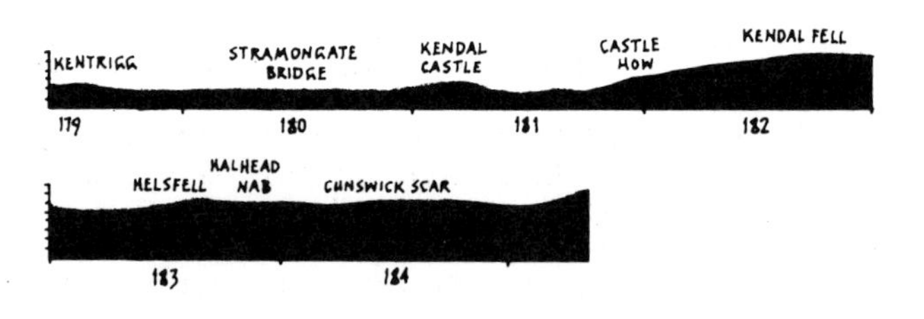
KENTRIGG
STRAMONGATE BRIDGE
KENDAL CASTLE
CASTLE HOW
KENDAL FELL
179
180
181
182
HELSFELL
HALHEAD NAB
CUNSWICK SCAR
183
184

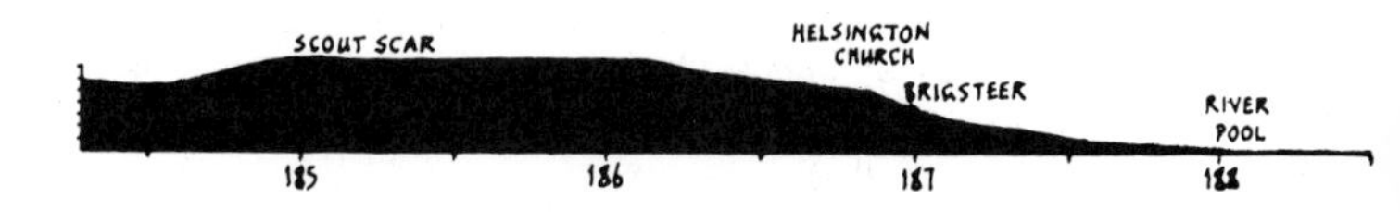
SCOUT SCAR
HELSINGTON CHURCH
BRIGSTEER
RIVER POOL
185
186
187
188

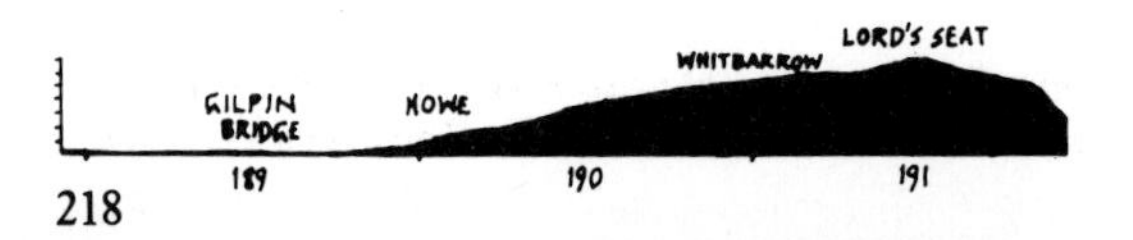
GILPIN BRIDGE
HOWE
WHITBARROW
LORD'S SEAT
189
190
191

9. Longsleddale to Kendal

This section of our walk is the shortest and the most straightforward.

At Sadgill in Longsleddale we leave behind the Borrowdale Volcanics that create the fells and crags of the upper valley and go through a band of shales and limestones, then a broader band of Coniston Grit and finally through an area of the Bannisdale Slates, which occupy most of the SE sector of the Lake District.

We follow the River Sprint down Longsleddale, out of the National Park at Garnett Bridge, but continue following the river until we meet the River Kent at Burneside. We then follow the River Kent, soon joined by the River Mint, and into Kendal. Having taken a Town Trail through Kendal we climb up out of the valley and re-enter the National Park.

From Sadgill to Kendal is a distance of about 10 miles/16km and from the town centre up to Underbarrow Scar is another 4 miles/6.4km.

Map 9.1

Our route follows the delightful River Sprint down the valley, clearly defined all the way on a good bridleway, passing farms and cottages.

In the middle of the dale, just below St. Mary's church, is **Ubarrow Hall** (or Yewbarrow Hall) which, like Kentmere Hall, has a ruined medieval pele tower and an attached 17c house. Botanist John Wilson was born here and in 1744 published a 'Synopsis of British Plants ... and Botanical Dictionary', which was the first systematic account of British plants in English. He died in Kendal in 1751.

Hereabouts are two prominent woods on opposite sides of the valley. Longsleddale Wood - formed by Ubarrow, Bowers, Grubbins and High House Woods - is an ash and oak woodland in a relatively natural state. It forms an interesting contrast with the pure oak woodland formed by Beech Hill, Kilnstones and Docker Nook Woods on the other side of the valley.

Map 9.2

Our route continues down the valley, diverting from its straight course only to keep to the bridleway as it goes into a re-entrant side valley of Docker Nook Gill.

As we reach Garnett Bridge the valley widens out slightly and curves to the S. Where the bridleway meets a lane at Garnett Bridge Gill cross over

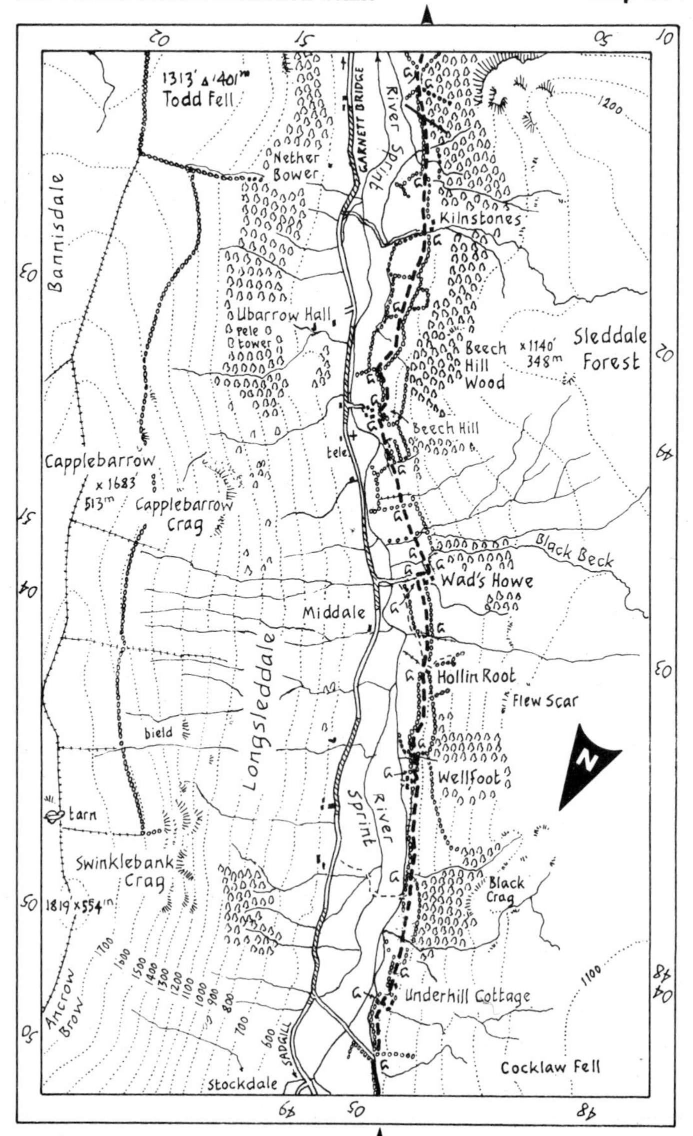
1313' ▵ 401m
Todd Fell
Nether Bower
GARNETT BRIDGE
River Sprint
Kilnstones
Bannisdale
Ubarrow Hall
pele tower
Beech Hill Wood
x1140' 348m
Sleddale Forest
Beech Hill
tele
Capplebarrow
x1683' 513m
Capplebarrow Crag
Black Beck
Wad's Howe
Middale
Longsleddale
Hollin Root
Flew Scar
bield
Wellfoot
tarn
Swinklebank Crag
1819' x 554m
Black Crag
Ancrow Brow
Underhill Cottage
SADGILL
Stockdale
Cocklaw Fell
1200
1100
N

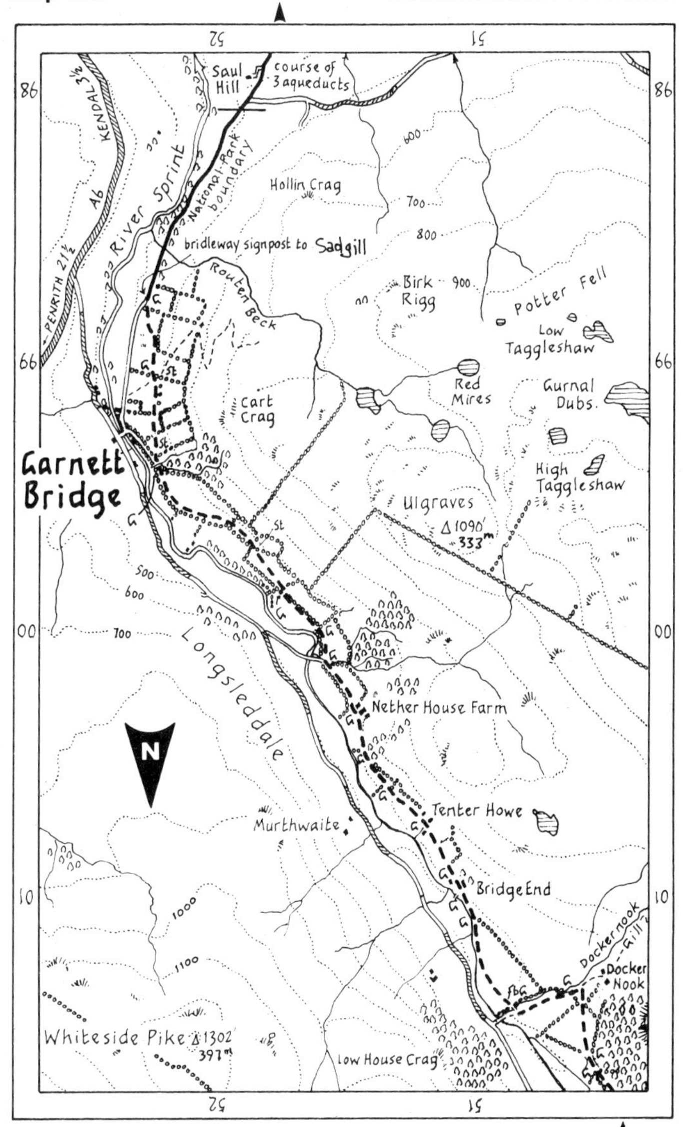

52
51
86
66
00
10
Saul Hill
course of 3 aqueducts
KENDAL 3½
A6
PENRITH 21½
River Sprint
National Park boundary
Hollin Crag
600
700
800
900
bridleway signpost to Sadgill
Routen Beck
Birk Rigg
Potter Fell
Low Taggleshaw
St
Cart Crag
Red Mires
Gurnal Dubs
Garnett Bridge
High Taggleshaw
Ulgraves
Δ1090′
333m
500
600
700
Longsleddale
Nether House Farm
N
Tenter Howe
Murthwaite
Bridge End
1000
1100
Dockernook Gill
Docker Nook
FbG
Whiteside Pike Δ1302′
397m
Low House Crag

and continue slightly up but at the same general level, by-passing the hamlet reaching the Longsleddale-Garnett Bridge-Burneside road at the bridleway signpost for the route we have been following. The Lake District National Park boundary follows the W side of the road as far as Saul Hill then we leave the Park temporarily as we pass through Kendal. At the Saul Hill road junction we pass over the routes of three different parallel aqueducts which carry water from Thirlmere up to the water treatment works at Watchgate on the opposite side of the valley.

Map 9.3

Follow the road, continuing ahead (L) at the fork, past Saul Hill and Hill Farm, and when the road bends R go ahead through a gate on a path down to the River Sprint at Sprint Mill. Bear R of the buildings (do not cross the river) and along the Sprint Mill access track to Sprint Bridge, where the Burneside-Oakbank road crosses the river. The short length of the Sprint Mill access is part of The Dales Way from Ilkley to Bowness, which we met briefly when at Sedbergh. Turn R along the road and follow it as it bends L past Burneside Hall and into Burneside village.

Burneside is a large village by Westmorland standards, serving as a dormitory suburb for Kendal, although quite a number of people are employed at Cropper's Paper Mills. The mill in the village has been making paper since *c.*1833 and was bought as a going concern by James Cropper in 1845. Other mills were upstream at Bowston and Cowen Head, but they have both been closed during the last 20 years.

Contrary to popular belief Burneside does not derive its name from standing beside the rivers, or burns, of the Sprint and Kent, but from the Norse name 'Bronoff's Head'. For centuries the Manor was known as Burneshead and today in its corrupted form is pronounced in three syllables: Burn-e-side.

The Manor of Burneside was originally in the possession of the de Burneshead family and about 1283 the heiress married Richard Bellingham of Tindale in Northumberland. The Bellinghams were one of the most powerful families in the N, both territorially and politically, from 1290 (Edward I) almost continuously until 1690 (William & Mary). The Bellinghams came to live at Burneshead in the reign of Edward II and remained there until the time of Sir Robert Bellingham in the late-16c. Sir Robert's father, Sir Roger Bellingham, who died in 1533 had built the Bellingham Chapel in Kendal's parish church (qv), where he lies buried with his wife. He had been Henry VIII's deputy Warden of the Marches in Northumberland.

The Bellinghams made their home at **Burneside Hall,** which was originally a 14c hall-house with pele tower. In 1585 Sir James Belling-

Map 9.3

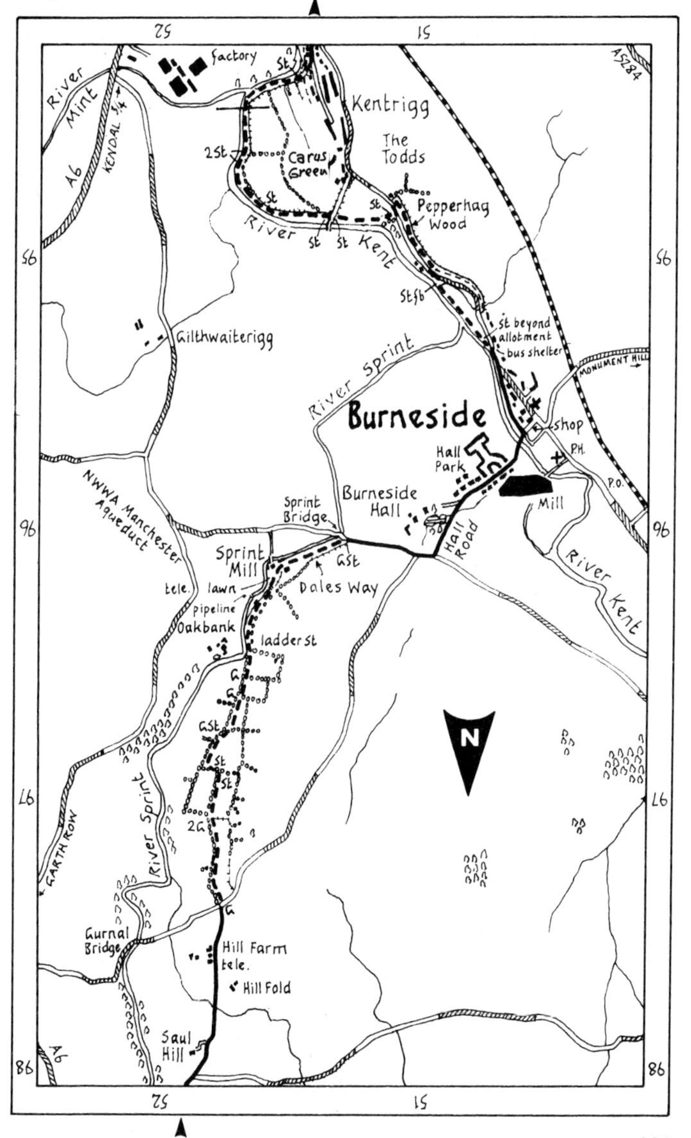

factory
River Mint
KENDAL 1/4
A6
Kentrigg
The Todds
Carus Green
2St
St
Pepperhag Wood
River Kent
StFb
st beyond allotment
bus shelter
A5284
MONUMENT HILL
Gilthwaiterigg
River Sprint
Burneside
shop
Hall Park
P.H.
P.O.
Burneside Hall
Mill
Sprint Bridge
Hall Road
NWWA Manchester Aqueduct
Sprint Mill
GSt
tele.
lawn
Dales Way
pipeline
Oakbank
ladder st
GSt
2G
GARTH ROW
River Sprint
N
Gurnal Bridge
Hill Farm
tele.
Hill Fold
Saul Hill
A6

Map 9.4

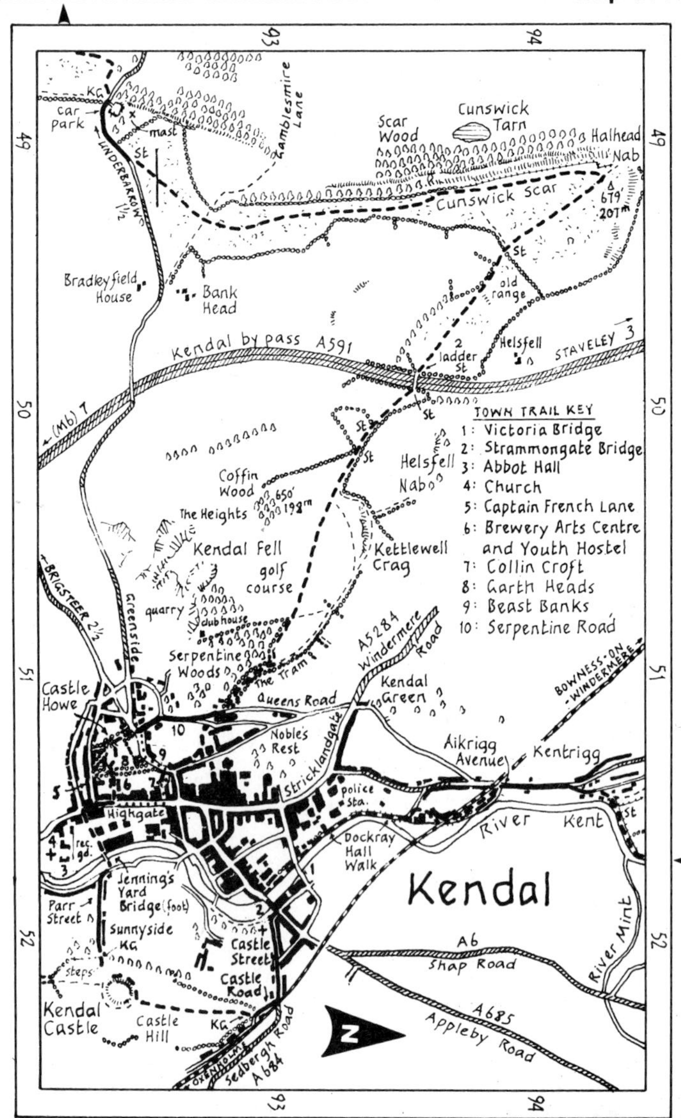

Cunswick Tarn
Scar Wood
Halhead Nab
Cunswick Scar
679'
207m
Gamblesmire Lane
KG
car park
mast
UNDERBARROW 1½
St
Bradleyfield House
Bank Head
old range
Kendal by pass A591
2 ladder St
Helsfell
STAVELEY 3
(M6) 7
TOWN TRAIL KEY
1: Victoria Bridge
2: Strammongate Bridge
3: Abbot Hall
4: Church
5: Captain French Lane
6: Brewery Arts Centre and Youth Hostel
7: Collin Croft
8: Garth Heads
9: Beast Banks
10: Serpentine Road
Coffin Wood
650'
198m
The Heights
Helsfell Nab
Kettlewell Crag
Kendal Fell golf course
BRIGSTEER 2½
Greenside
quarry
club house
Serpentine Woods
The Tram
A5284 Windermere Road
BOWNESS-ON-WINDERMERE
Castle Howe
Queens Road
Kendal Green
Noble's Rest
Stricklandgate
Aikrigg Avenue
Kentrigg
police sta.
Highgate
rec. gd.
Dockray Hall Walk
River Kent
Kendal
Jenning's Yard Bridge (foot)
Parr Street
Sunnyside KG
Castle Street
Castle Road
steps
Kendal Castle
Castle Hill
KG
OXENHOLME
Sedbergh Road A684
A6 Shap Road
A685 Appleby Road
River Mint
N
49
50
51
52
93
94

ham converted it into a splendid Elizabethan mansion, creating a walled courtyard and gatehouse and making an interesting example of a defensive dwelling. Although now much decayed the farmhouse still preserves the banqueting hall, chapel and porter's lodge.

As soon as you have crossed the River Kent in the centre of the village turn L along the back road and just after it meets the main Burneside-Kendal road take a footpath alongside the river, which rejoins the main road shortly after. Cross the road and take the footpath on the other side (a safety measure, to avoid traffic coming round the blind bend ahead). Where the path meets the road go back a short way and take the signposted path opposite around a small spruce plantation and go along the bank of the River Kent again. The River Mint joins the River Kent, and we are soon on the outskirts of Kendal.

Map 9.4

Where the River Mint joins the River Kent we keep to the bank of the river then climb up to the Burneside Road on the Kendal side of Kentrigg.

This area of the mid-Kent valley contains a number of striking hills, rounded grassy mounds dotted throughout the landscape. They are remains from glacial times: Kentrigg is one, and Castle Hill, on which stands Kendal Castle, is another. There are several down the valley, easily seen from the M6, the A6 or the A65.

Go S down Burneside Road and just before the bridge carrying the Oxenholme-Kendal-Windermere railway turn L along Aikrigg Avenue towards the river again. The path follows the leet to the former Dockray Hall Mill, passing under the railway, around and through a small industrial estate, and back to the bank of the river again.

This promenade beside the River Kent - Dockray Hall Walk - is followed, and it gives a delightful prospect of Kendal Castle on its hill above the river, best seen from Victoria Bridge with Stramongate Bridge in the middle foreground. The walk takes you past offices of the County Council to Sandes Avenue, which is carried over the river by Victoria Bridge. Cross over the road and keep to the same side of the river, beside a school playing field and a sock-knitting factory to reach Stramongate Bridge. Stramongate Bridge used to be the bridge that carried the main road to Scotland over the Kent. The original was built in 1379 but it was widened in 1793-4. Today it only carries traffic into Kendal, as part of its notorious one-way system.

Turn L and cross the river by Stramongate Bridge and note the lovely view up to Kendal Castle, our objective. Turn R at the end of the bridge, go past the toilets and follow the road past St. George's Church and Castle Street, a one-way street in our favour. Castle Street meets Sedbergh Road, the A684 (two-way) and we follow this uphill. Just before the road dips under the railway bridge turn R along Castle Road and after a short way pass through a kissing gate on a signposted path up to Kendal Castle. Go straight up the ridge of Castle Hill to the picturesque ruin on the top.

Here we can look over Kendal and consider the development of the town before taking a Kendal Town Trail on the next stage of our journey.

Kendal

Kendal is a fascinating old town and it grew up at a strategic location where the valley of the Kent narrows, forming a natural southern gateway to the Lake District.

The layout of the town is characterised by the narrow **yards** or lanes branching off the main street every few yards at right angles for the entire length of the town. Originally there were 150 of them - some narrow alleys, some widening out into squares, having passages of cobbles or flagstones, or sometimes both, and narrow entrances from the main street through archways under the frontage buildings. Houses were built down one or both sides of the yard and were usually associated with a workshop. The cottages housed the workers in Kendal's 'new' industries - weaving in one yard, cloth and wool dyed in another. (The wool was washed down by the river - steps are still visible on Waterside - and was hung out to dry on the fellside above Beast Banks called Tenter Fell on 'tenterhooks' on iron or wooden posts.) The houses often belonged to the owner of the main house at the top, facing the main street, and his name was given to the yard -e.g. Dr. Manning's Yard, Redmayne's Yard and Wakefield's Yard. A house in Rainbow Yard has a galleried front and houses in several yards have long flights of outside stone stairs to the upper floors. Unfortunately all too many of Kendal's yards were demolished in the 1960's and were replaced by insensitive modern developments, but developments of the 1980's are more sympathetic to the vernacular style of the town.

Kendal was a weaving town at least from the 14c and the town's motto 'Wool is my Bread' is an indication of the importance of the woollen trade. Between 1330-50 Kendal was the leading wool town in England and its trade flourished for 600 years. 'Kendal Green', a heavy cloth, was famous for centuries and Shakespeare, in King Henry IV has Falstaff speak of 'three misbegotten knaves in Kendal Green'. The town's museum has cards of wool showing how the green colour was produced - blue from woad *(Isatis tinctoria)* and yellow from Dyer's broom *(Genista tinctoria)* were mixed together: a shade of bottle green, similar to the school uniform in Kendal of today.

Kendal is today a town of about 23,000 people but although the wool trade has declined in importance there are still carpet-making

Kendal Town Hall

and horse-blanket manufacturing - two trades being reminders of the medieval prosperity of the town. The main business now ranges from shoe-making, to insurance, pumps and Kendal Mint Cake.

Kendal has had its share of famous sons, daughters and scholars, as well as other notables. Perhaps most famous of these was **Katherine Parr** (of whom more later) but others were **James Pennington,** b. Kendal 1777 a leading authority on currency and finance, who was consulted by Sir Robert Peel during the preparation of the Bank Act of 1844. **Ephraim Chambers,** born at Milton, S of Kendal in 1578, was educated at Kendal. He became the first encyclopaedist, which was first published in 1788. **William Hudson,** b. 1730 in the White Lion Inn, where his father was publican, became a famous botanist. He was resident sub-librarian at the British Museum for a year and published his 'Flora Angelica' the year after he was elected a Fellow of the Royal Society. **De Quincey** was on the staff of the Westmorland Gazette from its foundation and was its editor from 1819-20.

After Katherine Parr the next best-known Kendalian was **George Romney** who, although born and buried in Dalton-in-Furness, has many associations with Kendal. Both he and his son married Kendal girls. He lived in a house in Redmayne's Yard, off Stricklandgate, and also in Kirkland where he died - both houses are marked by plaques. When 22 Romney married Mary Abbot and in 1762, when 28, he went to London, leaving his wife, two children and half his savings. In London he made a name for himself, meeting and painting everybody. He exhausted himself with labour - he painted Nelson's Lady Hamilton no fewer than thirty times - and when aged 65, broken in health and mind, he returned home after 37 years to live with his loving wife for the last three years of his life. Tennyson relates those year in 'Romney's Remorse'. Romney died on 15 November 1802 aged 68 and was buried in his home town. His cenotaph in Kendal's parish church was erected by his son. Many of Romney's paintings are on show in the Town Hall and Abbot Hall.

We shall refer to other notable local people as we meet them in our Kendal Town Trail.

Kendal Town Trail

As we are on Castle Hill we shall naturally start our Town Trail at **Kendal Castle.** We shall then descend to the town and walk through it from the S to the centre before climbing up on the opposite fellside to Serpentine Woods. With the help of our street plan (Map 9.4) you should be able to pick out the general route and perhaps some of the buildings of interest we refer to from this vantage point at the castle.

Kendal Castle is of a motte and bailey type, its earthwork dating from 13c and the greater part of the building dating from 14c. The castle was partially destroyed in 1553 and dismantled in 1566. Camden, writing in 1586, described it as 'almost ready to fall down with age'. Poet Gray wrote a description of the castle on his visit in 1769 which West amended in his 'Guide to the Lakes' published in 1779.

The castle is famous as the birthplace of **Katherine Parr,** the last of Henry VIII's wives, and of her brother William who was created Lord Parr and Ross of Kendal in 1539 and Marquis of Northampton in 1543.

Katherine Parr was born in 1512, eldest child of Sir Thomas Parr, Baron of Kendal, Master of the Wards and Controller of the Household to Henry VIII. Because of her father's duties it was inevitable that the Parr family should spend much time in London, in close proximity to Court circles, during Katherine's childhood.

Sir Thomas died when Katherine was only 5 years old, leaving his wife a widow aged 22: Lady Parr never remarried. Katherine was married to Lord Borough (Edward Burgh) at the age of 12. After his death 3 years later she married Lord Latimer (Sir John Neville), a widower with two children.

When he too died, in 1543, he left Katherine a large fortune. In the same year, on 12 July, she married Henry VIII at Hampton Court, and lived with him for 3 years, 6 months and 5 days until he died in 1547. Katherine then married Thomas Seymour, Lord High Admiral of England, Baron of Sudeley, who was brother of Jane Seymour, Henry's third wife who died in 1537. Katherine died of a fever at the age of 36 shortly after the birth of her daughter, her first child, on 5 September 1548, at Sudeley in Gloucestershire, where she lies buried.

From the castle make a steep descent N to a gate at the end of the road called Sunnyside and follow this downhill, over the course of the former Lancaster-Kendal canal. The road is then named Parr Street and runs down to meet Aynam Road, the A65 one-way street. Turn R, against the flow of traffic and just before Katherine Street cross over the road by the pedestrian crossing and then cross the River Kent by Jennings Bridge, a footbridge leading into Abbot Hall Park. Go diagonally L across the park, past the children's play area and bandstand to a bridge over the Blind Beck and into the grounds of Abbot Hall.

Abbot Hall is the finest building in Kendal and was built as a private house in 1759 for Col. George Wilson of Dallam Tower near Milnthorpe. It was designed by John Carr of York and cost £8,000. It is now an art gallery. The ground floor rooms are restored to their 18c decor, with period paintings, furniture and objects d'art. The upper floor galleries house frequently changing exhibitions of contemporary painting, sculpture and crafts.

(Hall open Monday-Fridays, 1030-1730; Saturday and Sunday, 1400-1700.)

In the stable block of the Hall is the **Lakeland Life Museum.** Its displays feature the major aspects of working and social life of the Lake District, and include printing and weaving displays, and traditional urban and rural trades such as those of the blacksmith and wheelwright. Two rooms are furnished in the style of the 1900's, with costumes and household equipment of that period. The museum has expanded into the adjoining **Grammar School** (qv) and is open for the same times as Abbot Hall.

From the grounds of Abbot Hall go S to the adjoining churchyard of Kendal parish church.

The fine church of the **Holy Trinity** was wholly rebuilt or greatly altered in 1201 and restored in 1230 and is in the late-Perpendicular style. It was drastically restored in 1830-32. The church was extended in 14c to accommodate the influx of Flemish weavers who came to Kendal in 1331 and 1345 and it is one of the few churches - perhaps the only one - in the country to possess five aisles. The church is of such splendid proportions that its breadth of 103ft/31m makes it the fifth widest in England and it is only 3ft/1m short of the width of York Minster.

Although the body of the church has been drastically restored the brasses and monuments in the chapels are of considerable interest. The Bellingham Chapel in the N aisle was added in the late-15c and the chapels of the Stricklands and Parrs in the S aisle were added in the early-16c.

The Bellingham Chapel has a fine stalactite ceiling. An altar tomb with a modern brass of Sir Roger Bellingham, d. 1533 and his wife, and good effigies. There is a late-13c coffin lid with a foliated cross, sword and shield, and there is a brass 20ins/510mm long of Alan Bellingham in his armour, who died in 1577. The Parr Chapel has the tomb of Sir William Parr of Kendal Castle, grandfather of Queen Katherine, while the Strickland Chapel has a tomb with two shields of Sir Walter Strickland from Sizergh Castle who died in 1528. Under a flat canopy on four pillars is the effigy of Walter Strickland, d. 1656, son of Sir Thomas, covered in a shroud, with his head on a pillow.

The church is usually approached through its fine wrought iron gates, made in 1822, but an alternative is to take Church Walk on the N side of the churchyard. Here is the **Old Grammar School,** founded in 1525. Note its bank of central round chimneys, thick old slates, wavy bargeboards, carved pinnacle and porch and a well in its garden.

At the churchyard gates Church Walk leads into Kirkland, the oldest part of Kendal, formerly a village centred around the church's Saxon predecessor.

Adjoining the S side of the churchyard is a charming old pub, the **Ring o' Bells,** 1741, and opposite the churchyard gates is **Kirkbarrow Lane,** known locally as 't'crack': in medieval times a track led up this lane from the church to the vicar's fields, the Anchorite and the Kirkbarrow, names echoed in the nearby housing estate.

There are some interesting old buildings in Kirkland and the yards leading off it, then **Chapel Lane** and **Peppercorn Lane** cross Kirkland and lead to Abbot Hall. Just by the zebra crossing, Kirkland crosses **Blind Beck.** The beck rises from the high ground of Kendal Fell and flows for part of its way in an underground channel, so giving its name. For most of the year it is dry, but after heavy rain and melting snow it is a raging torrent. Blind Beck marks the boundary where Kirkland village enters Highgate and Kendal.

Go up **Highgate,** *keeping to the left-hand side, passing the ends of Gillinggate and Captain French Lane, then the old Highgate Hotel and after 50yds/50m turn L into the grounds of The Brewery.*

The Brewery is now an arts centre, converted from buildings which had, until 1947, been the Kendal brewery of Whitwell Mark & Co., but which for 20 years had been used as a storage depot for Vaux breweries. The former Brewery's offices on the Highgate frontage have now been converted into a **Youth Hostel.**

We shall return to **The Brewery** and **Youth Hostel** when we have completed the remainder of our Kendal Town Trail.

Continue towards the town centre and where Highgate narrows at Highgate Brow just beyond the youth hostel cross over and look out for Yard 83, **Dr. Manning's Yard.** In this yard there used to be a ropeworks, a dyeworks, a tannery and a bark mill as well as the house. *Emerge from the yard then cross the road and continue to Sandes Hospital.*

Thomas Sandes was a wealthy tradesman and philanthropist and was Mayor of Kendal in 1647. In 1659 he built a house on Highgate and behind it founded the **Sandes Hospital** for eight widows in 1670. The gatehouse has a lozenge above its entrance with the initials TSK (Thomas Sandes, Kendal) and a coat-of-arms of teasels and wool shears, the heraldic bearings of the Shearman Dyers Company. In the gateway is a collecting box, inscribed 'Remember the Poore' and 'Remember the Poor Widows'. Sandes almshouse was established 'for the maintenance and relief of 8 poor widows to exercise spinning and carding wool and weaving raw pieces of cloth for Kendal Cottons. The widows to be 52 years of age and upwards and of good reputation'. The almshouses behind were rebuilt in 1852 and have a chapel in the centre, while at the top of the yard is the old **Bluecoat School** for boys which he founded 11 years before his death. Sandes lived with his wife Katherine at **Grandy Nook Hall** (qv) on Low Fellside.

Continue along Highgate along the left-hand side and just before you reach the Midland Bank turn L into Colin Croft.

Colin Croft is a cobbled yard with warehouses at the bottom and cottages at the top. Here the yard turns R then L and climbs up the fellside, up steps and under houses. The cobbles and steps and the cottages themselves were restored by the Kendal Civic Society.

Where Colin Croft emerges from under a house on **Beast Banks** *turn R and go downhill, past the end of* **Low Fellside** *and down* **All Hallows Lane,** *with the Town Hall facing you at the crossroads at the bottom.*

Kendal Town Hall consists of two buildings: as you face it the original 'White Hall' is on the R, built in 1825 by Francis Webster, Kendal's first architect of note, while the main hall on the L is an extension of 1893. A musical carillon of tuneful bells mark the passing hours, played every third hour (0900, 1200, 1500, 1800 and 2100) and changing tune for each day of the week. In the 1970's the 0600 chimes were stopped because of complaints from the management of the nearby Kendal Hotel that the chimes were too early for his guests. Now that the hotel no longer functions the early morning chimes ought to be re-introduced!

Almost opposite the Town Hall is **Titus Wilson's** shop, originally of 16c or 17c date, and next along Highgate is the **Fleece Inn,** its first floor overhanging the pavement and supported by pillars. The inn was built in 1656 at a time of the town's growth and prosperity. The lamb on the wrought iron inn sign and the name itself are reminders of the wool trade around which Kendal flourished.

Adjoining the Fleece Inn, and approached through an arch under the building, is the **Old Shambles,** built in 1779 to house butchers' shops. Cottages in the yard have recently been restored and at the top is a handsome building, only one room deep, with an attractive Georgian frontage, which was originally 'The Butchers' Arms'. Worn and twisting steps in the corner on the L lead you up through a pair of narrow stone gate stoops on Low Fellside.

Return down the Old Shambles to the Fleece Inn and keeping on the same side of Highgate as before turn L and go N. Cross Highgate by the pelican crossing and go down **Finkle Street,** *which the local authority is reluctant to pedestrianise. Halfway down the LHS, beside an opticians shop, steps lead up L under an archway into the* **New Shambles** *and into* *the* **Market Place.** *Turn L in the Market Place and then R when you reach the main road by the war memorial. Highgate here becomes* **Stricklandgate** *and you go down the hill keeping to the RHS. Across the road you will see the* **Woolpack Hotel,** *its unusually large arch being a reminder of the days when great wagons piled high with wool were brought to the staplers in the yard.*

Continue down **Stricklandgate** *and notice on the right an estate agent's office.* This building, **Black Hall,** was for centuries the home of the Wilson family. Apart from its huge round chimneys it is distinguished by the model of a large black hog, the sign of the brush company who once used the building as their factory. A few yards further down Stricklandgate, beyond the main Post Office, is No.95, the YWCA. Known as **Prince Charlie's House** it was built in 1724 and during the Rebellion of 1745 Prince Charles lodged here on his way S through the town, and he spent another night here on his retreat.

Carry on down Stricklandgate and at the pelican pedestrian crossing cross over and turn L into **Maude Street.** *At the end go into the public park called* **Noble's Rest** *and follow the path round to the L and up through the wooded bank diagonally L to reach* **Low Fellside.** *Just to the R, on the opposite side of the road, is the whitewashed* **Grandy Nook** *with its upper floor projecting out over the narrow road.* This was the home of Thomas Sandes, who built the hospital at Highgate. Low Fellside is a narrow road linked by cobbled alleyways and stone staircases to the blocks of cottages and tenements terraced on the hillside. Earlier properties used to house weavers, labourers and the poorest people in the town, but the area was cleared in the mid-1960's and replaced by the modern flats.

Turn L in Low Fellside and follow the road S to its junction with Beast Banks and All Hallows Lane, and go L down towards the traffic lights at the main junction beside the Town Hall. Turn R and go along Highgate back towards The Brewery and the youth hostel.

In the grounds of **The Brewery** are two objects of local interest, but unfortunately nothing to tell the visitor what they are or their history. One is the famous clock 'Leyland Motors - For All Time': until 1970 this stood on the main A6 Shap Road near the equally famous, or infamous, Jungle Cafe, but when the M6 motorway opened and heavy goods vehicles stopped going over Shap, Leyland Motors withdrew their sponsorship. The other object is the Victorian drinking fountain and signpost indicator that stood at the junction of roads outside Windermere railway station until road improvements caused its removal.

We begin our departure from Kendal by going up the graceful flight of steps in The Brewery grounds and through the doorway at the top to emerge on a footpath which runs alongside the high boundary wall. This is called Garth Heads, and a turn either L or R leads you to steps which climb the steep slope, under the beech trees to emerge on to a flat open green space. This area is 3.5 acres/1.4ha in extent and is called **Castle Howe** and was the original Kendal Castle. It is a motte and bailey with the remains of its ditch still present in parts. On the top of the steep conical motte 25ft/7.6m above the bailey is **The Monument,** an obelisk erected in 1788 'Sacred to Liberty' by the people of Kendal in memory of the Revolution of 1688, commemorating the arrival in England of the Protestant William of Orange and the abdication of James II. From the top there are views down, over or through the beech trees to the 13c Kendal Castle on the opposite side of the river.

Go behind Castle Howe to its NW corner and emerge onto Beast Banks. Turn R, cross over the road then turn L along another road towards Tenter-fell and Queens Road. Turn R on Queens Road and go N, turning into Serpentine Woods at the first pedestrian entrance on the L or, for our purposes, at the second entrance on the L signposted to a viewpoint on The Heights.

Serpentine Woods were laid out in 1824 and visitors were charged 6p admission to see the fine trees that had been planted in the 18 acres/7.2ha of woodland. In 1849 the woods were opened to the public freely and the paths provide a self-guiding nature trail. Along the N side of the woods is The Tram, an easily graded track following the line of an original horse-drawn tramway, constructed to carry quarried stone down into Kendal from the quarry on Kettlewell Crag.

Kendal to Scout Scar

We have really reached the limit of our Kendal Town Trail now as from here we head out into open countryside again on the next and final stage of our journey.

Leave Queens Road at the signposted footpath alongside Serpentine Wood by The Tram, now tarmacadamed for much of its length. It can be followed all the way to Kettlewell Crag but at the gate, with the corner of Serpentine Wood on your L, follow the wall up to a stile in another wall and then take another footpath across the golf course. The right-of-way may not be clear across the turf of the fairways but head NW to a wall corner and follow the wall down a funnel with another wall to a stile in the corner, and the way becomes clearer.

At the squeeze stile in the wall corner we re-enter the Lake District National park.

Keep the wall on your R and drop down to the footbridge over the cutting which carries the A591 Kendal by-pass. Two ladder stiles follow in quick succession on the far side and a clear path continues through the turf on the limestone in a NW direction across the former rifle range, to another stile in a corner of walls. You may turn L here and keep the wall on your L to make a short cut, but it is only a few minutes further on to the cairn on the top (679ft/207m) where there is a panoramic view of the fells above Kentmere and Windermere that we have recently traversed.

Turn away from the cairn and head S above Cunswick Scar keeping Scar Wood and its boundary wall on your R. Where the path reaches a farm track - Gamblesmire Lane - which crosses your route at right angles the official right-of-way ends and you are supposed to turn L down the farm track to Bank Head. However, an unofficial path - but one which local people, including one of the authors, are claiming a right-of-way after more than 20 years use - continues across the track SW to a crude stile in the wall on the Underbarrow Road just short of the car parking area in some old quarries in the crest of the hill. (One of the authors recalls that there was once a narrow pedestrian gateway where the wall is now blocked up and the rudimentary stile, made by through-stones, has been provided. There are currently plans by the local highway authority and the National Park authority to make this diversion 'official' and provide a proper stile.)

Brewery Arts Centre, Kendal.

10

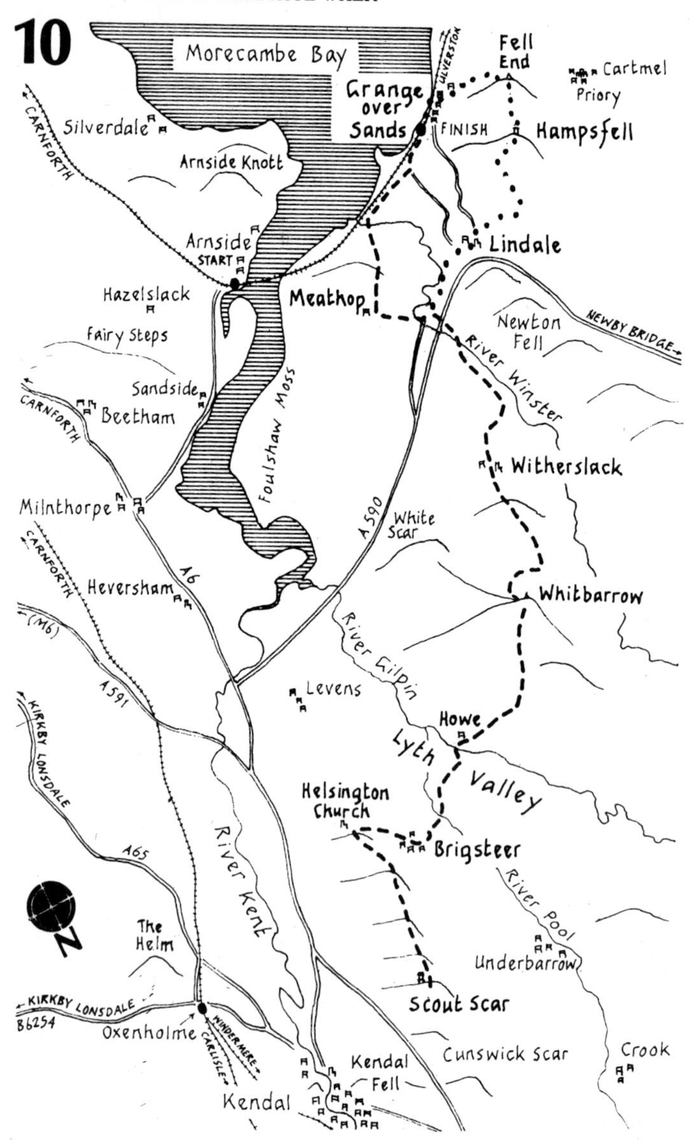

Morecambe Bay
ULVERSTON
Fell End
Cartmel Priory
Grange over Sands
FINISH
Hampsfell
CARNFORTH
Silverdale
Arnside Knott
Arnside
START
Lindale
Hazelslack
Meathop
Newton Fell
NEWBY BRIDGE
Fairy Steps
River Winster
Sandside
CARNFORTH
Beetham
Foulshaw Moss
Witherslack
Milnthorpe
A590
White Scar
CARNFORTH
A6
Heversham
Whitbarrow
(M6)
River Gilpin
A591
Levens
KIRKBY LONSDALE
Howe
Lyth Valley
Helsington Church
Brigsteer
A65
River Kent
River Pool
The Helm
Underbarrow
Scout Scar
KIRKBY LONSDALE
B6254
Oxenholme
WINDERMERE
CARLISLE
Cunswick Scar
Crook
Kendal Fell
Kendal
N

10. Kendal to Grange-over-Sands

A prominent escarpment of Carboniferous limestone W of Kendal looks out over the southern Lake District and the head of Morecambe Bay. Our goal is not far distant but between here and Grange-over-Sands we have to cross three more limestone escarpments - Whitbarrow, Yewbarrow and Hampsfield Fell - interrupted by the alluvial valleys of the Lyth and the Winster.

From Underbarrow Scar to Grange-over-Sands is a distance of about 15 miles/24km, but some 3miles/4.8km less if you take the Low Level Route to Grange railway station in a rush to catch that train home!

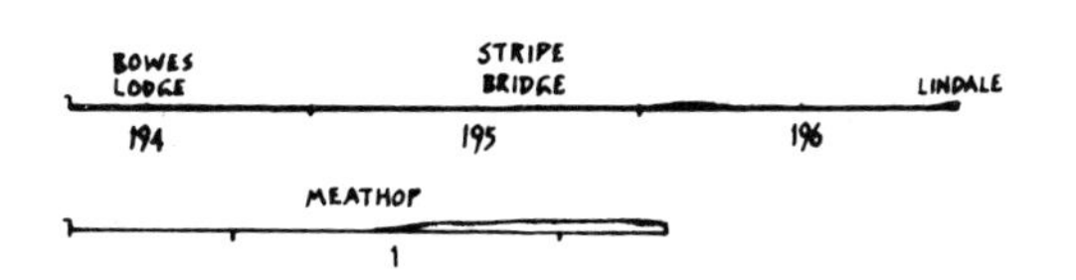

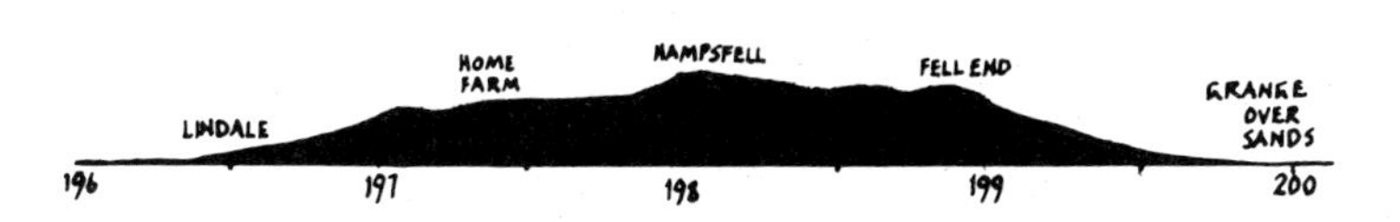

WINSTER BRIDGE
B5277
GRANGE STATION
2
3

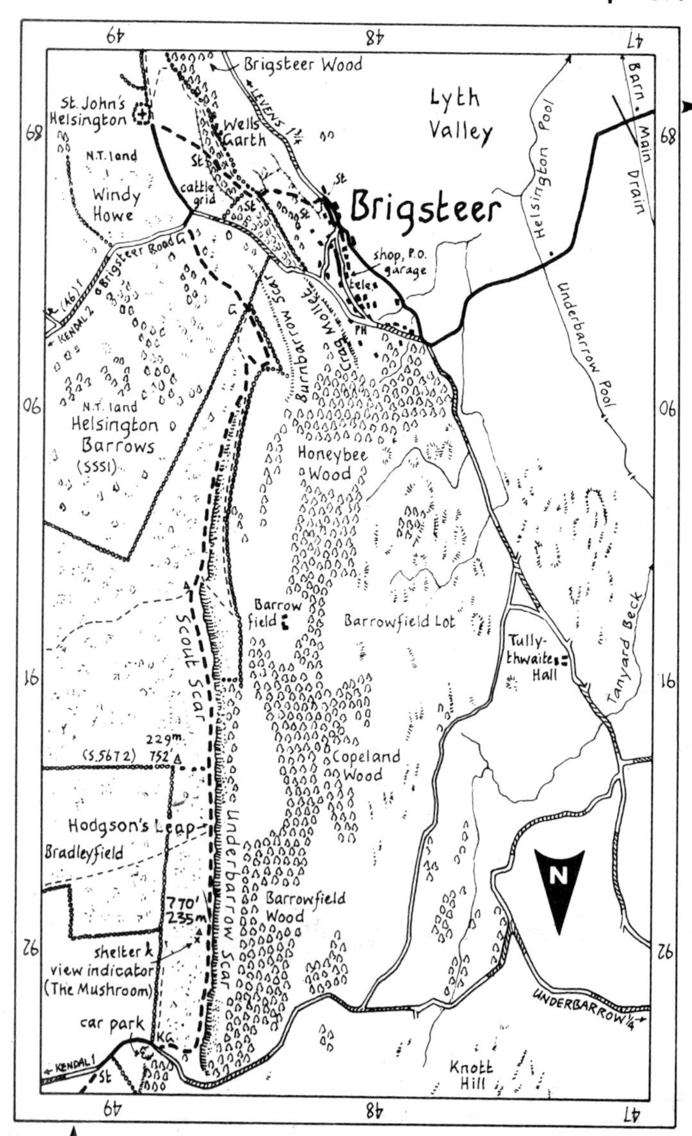
Brigsteer Wood
LEVENS 1½
Lyth Valley
Barn. Main Drain
St. John's Helsington
Wells Garth
N.T. land
Windy Howe
cattle grid
Brigsteer
Helsington Pool
shop, P.O. garage
tele
PH
Brigsteer Road
KENDAL 2
(A6)
Burnbarrow Scar
Crag Mollett
Underbarrow Pool
N.T. land
Helsington Barrows
(SSSI)
Honeybee Wood
Barrow field
Barrowfield Lot
Tully-thwaite Hall
Tanyard Beck
Scout Scar
229m
(S.5672) 752'
Copeland Wood
Hodgson's Leap
Bradleyfield
Underbarrow Scar
770'
235m
Barrowfield Wood
shelter & view indicator (The Mushroom)
car park
KG
KENDAL 1
St
UNDERBARROW ¼
Knott Hill
N
49
48
47
68
06
16
26

Map 10.1

From the Underbarrow Road, just over the crest of the scar on the descent, past an access to a car park in an old quarry on the R, a signposted path on the L passes through an iron kissing gate to the popular viewpoint of The Mushroom above Underbarow Scar (770ft/235m).

Cunswick Scar, Underbarrow Scar and Scout Scar are names for three parts of a Carboniferous limestone escarpment running almost 3 miles/5km W of Kendal on the N-S fault line with the Silurian slates. The limestone outcrops W of the River Kent in Kendal and forms a contrasting backcloth to the town, its dip slope rising gently to 770ft/235m at its highest point before falling in a steep, W-facing scarp.

The main feature of the limestone escarpment is the unimproved calcareous grassland and areas of dry heath scattered with trees and shrubs and extensive areas of loose limestone. The herb-rich grassland is dominated by blue moor grass. Three rare flowers grow here - the hoary rock-rose, spring sandwort and dark red helleborine. Several species of orchid grow, of which the most notable are the lesser butterfly orchid, the fly orchid and the fragrant orchid. The grassland is the habitat of many butterflies such as the small heath, meadow brown and dark green fritillaries.

The cliffs of the scarp are producing a number of short but severe graded rock climbs. Below the steep scree slopes is an ash, oak and hazel woodland, with whitebeam and yew in the dense woodlands below.

The shelter called **The Mushroom** occupies the highest point: although everyone in Kendal calls this viewpoint Scout Scar it is actually Underbarrow Scar, Scout Scar being further S on the escarpment. The Mushroom once had a diagram painted on the inside of its dome-shaped roof indicating the features of the landscape that can be seen from this admirable viewpoint. It was painted over during the hostilities of World War II so as to be unhelpful to landing German parachutists. A poor attempt has been made to recreate the indicator: a panorama in the reference section of Kendal's library shows what it was originally like.

You can walk anywhere on the open fell but limestone stones and whins may cause you to take the delightful turf path above the crest of the scar, undulating slightly as it leads due S. Delightful views over the Lyth Valley to Whitbarrow Scar enable you to plan the next stage of the journey and in the distance you can see the head of the Kent estuary and Arnside and the hills above Grange-over-Sands.

The summit of Scout Scar with its OS survey column (752ft/229m) is

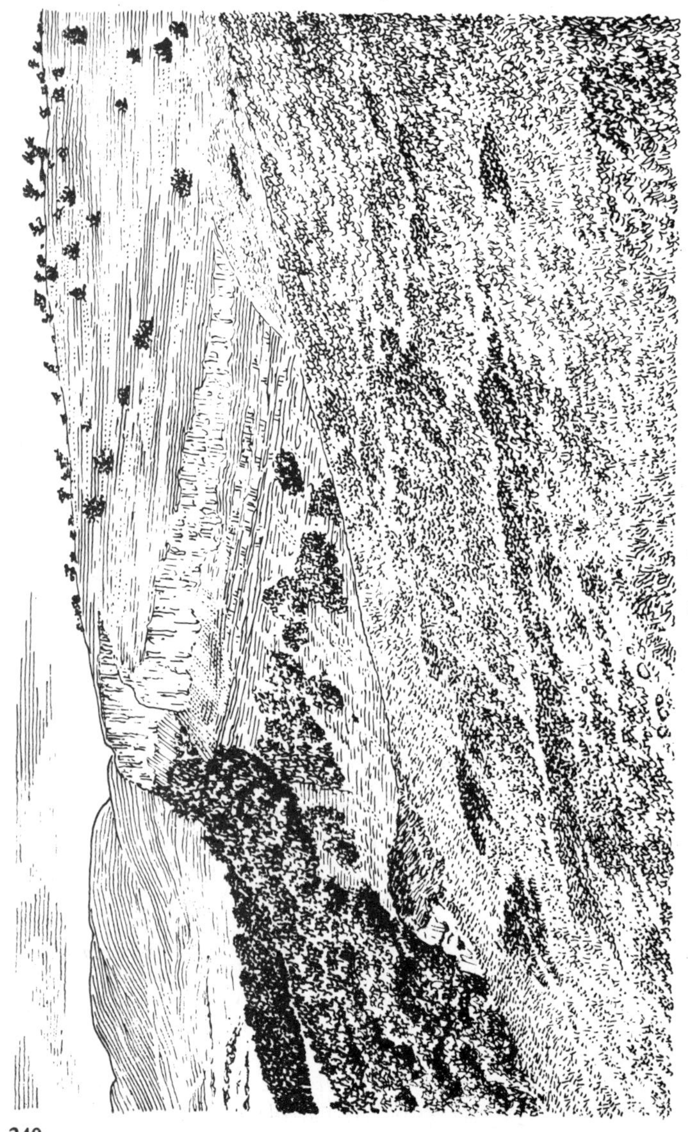

Scout Scar

passed un-noticed, and our path follows the Lake District National Park boundary for a short way. The ridge of the scar is gradually dipping S and when you pass through the first gate it has almost disappeared. At the second gate you reach the Brigsteer Road, so turn R here then first L, over the cattle grid and along the unenclosed road to the isolated church of St. John's, built in 1726. Our path now doubles back, descending the pasture, through woods, and down into Brigsteer village.

Brigsteer is a charming little village, with attractive clusters of cottages on the hillside above the Lyth valley. Brigsteer and the Lyth valley are famous for two things - the delightful Brigsteer Woods, to the S of the village, where lily-of-the-valley and dwarf daffodils grow and Lyth valley damsons. On May weekends crowds flock into the Lyth valley to see the damson blossom. Sheltered between the limestone scars of Underbarrow/Scout and Whitbarrow the valley is well sheltered for the damson orchards; damson jam and damson wine still figure prominently in local fare.

Take the lowest of the roads through the village to a crossroads, then turn L and follow a minor road across the Lyth valley to the A5074 on the far side. There are no footpaths across the valley of the River Gilpin and this narrow road is the only way for us. The drainage channels have been drastically 'canalised' and vandalised by the North West Water Authority in recent years and their natural history value has decreased considerably, but at least the low-lying meadows don't get flooded as much as they used to. En route you will pass an area where peat digging still takes place, the only area in Westmorland now left, but quickly disappearing. Hereabouts you re-enter the Lake District National Park.

Map 10.2

As soon as you have crossed the new (1983) bridge over the River Gilpin 'canal' turn R on a right-of-way between fences to South Low Farm and the A6074. Turn R on the main road and follow it as it bends uphill. Just after the junction with the lane to Draw Well the road bends R and you take the footpath on the L at Low Farm to The Howe, crossing another lane en route.

From The Howe we make the ascent of Whitbarrow Scar, mostly through plantations, though the path reaches open ground on the summit. The signposted path winds up through Township Plantation and passes through a gate in the wall, entering Whitbarrow Plantation. The path heads generally SW and leaves the plantation by climbing a stile over the boundary wall.

Here we reach the open fell and our objective is clear: the cairn on the top of Lord's Seat. The imperial OS maps give Lord's Seat a height of 706ft,

Map 10.2

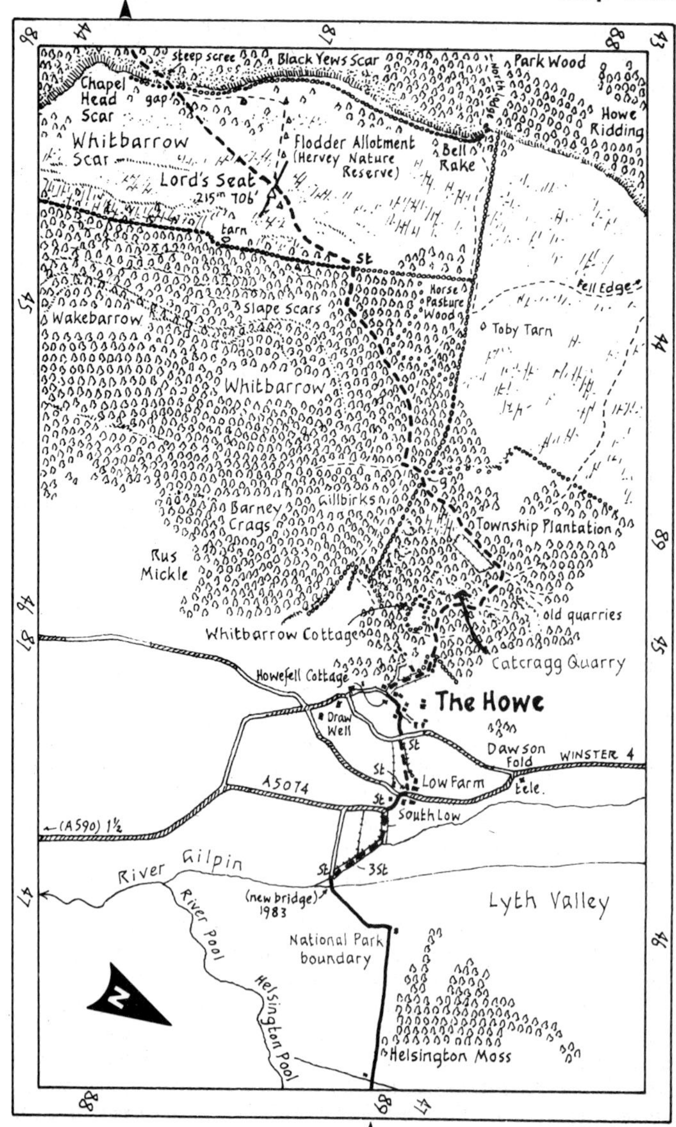

steep scree
Black Yews Scar
Park Wood
Chapel Head Scar
gap
Howe Ridding
Whitbarrow Scar
Flodder Allotment (Hervey Nature Reserve)
Bell Rake
Lord's Seat 215m 706'
tarn
St
Fell Edge
Horse Pasture Wood
Slape Scars
Wakebarrow
Toby Tarn
Whitbarrow
Barney Crags
Gillbirks
Township Plantation
Rus Mickle
old quarries
Whitbarrow Cottage
Catcragg Quarry
Howefell Cottage
The Howe
Draw Well
Dawson Fold
WINSTER 4
A5074
Low Farm
tele.
South Low
← (A590) 1½
River Gilpin
3St
River Pool
(new bridge) 1983
Lyth Valley
National Park boundary
Helsington Pool
Helsington Moss
N

which when converted gives 215m. 215m is the height given on the new (Second Series) Landranger 1:50,000 scale maps, but the 1:10,000 scale maps give the height as 203m, which when converted equals 666ft.

Whitbarrow Scar is a vast area of limestone pavement and has an interesting flora and fauna as well as panoramic views. Lord's Seat, the highest point, carries a memorial cairn to Canon Aidan Hervey, founder of the Lake District Naturalist's Trust which eventually became the present organisation, the Cumbria Trust for Nature Conservation. The 250 acre/101ha Hervey Nature Reserve was acquired in 1969. The reserve has a variety of habitats ranging from open grassland and rocky areas to developing woodland. Breeding birds include the skylark, meadow and tree pipits, cuckoo, willow warbler, various tits and the spotted woodpecker. Nearby there are buzzard, raven and woodcock as well as roe and red deer.

Map 10.3

From the summit of Lord's Seat the public footpath is cairned on a route W towards the edge of the scar, then turns S alongside the wall, but most people take a bee-line SW across the open fell. A gap in the wall marks the descent on a path across steep scree through Park Wood. As it reaches another woodland path at a cairn turn S, then along the edge of the wood and through a gate at a corner of a pasture. The path now turns SW to the former kennels of Witherslack Hall and reaches a road at Witherslack Hall Farm.

As you descend the scarp you pass through woodland of birch, hazel, yew and juniper, then a lower growth of oak and ash, then a belt of pure yew wood. Below this, on the lower slopes of the scarp, are thickets of birch, hazel and ash. At the bottom you are in a slight valley with a forest of mixed sessile oak and ash and then as you rise up to the road at Witherlack Hall the underlying rock changes to Silurian slate and the trees are all oaks - tall, well-grown, ungrazed and uncoppiced, a relatively rare feature in this district where so much of the woodland has been coppiced for charcoal and the furnaces and bobbin mills.

The roof of **Witherslack Hall** can be seen in the woods on the descent from Lord's Seat. It was built in 1874 as Lord Derby's hunting lodge. It is now the Sandford School.

From the gatehouse to Witherslack Hall go NW along the road for a short way, then leave it and fork L on a track, then L again to Lawns House, through a gate and on a track across the pasture to another gate and into Lawns Wood. Keep the wall, and then the fence, on your L, making a gradual climb up to the limestone ridge of Yewbarrow. The wood thins out

Map 10.3

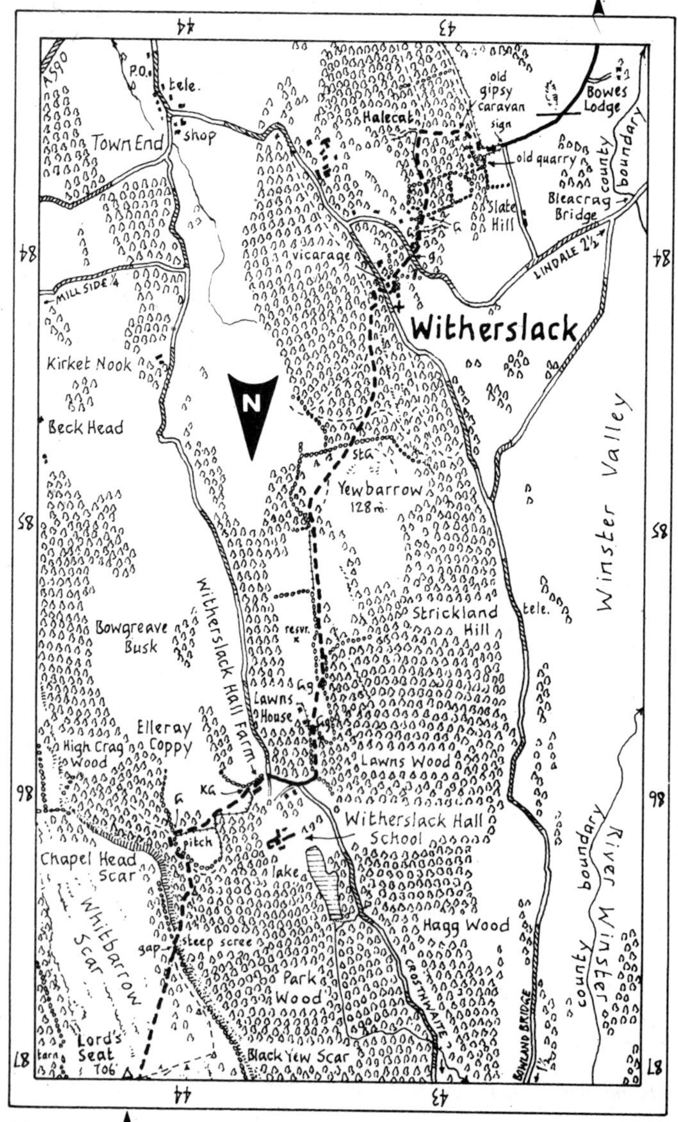
A590
P.O.
tele.
shop
Town End
Halecat
old gipsy caravan
sign
Bowes Lodge
old quarry
county boundary
Bleacrag Bridge
Slate Hill
vicarage
LINDALE 2½
MILL SIDE ¼
Witherslack
Kirket Nook
Beck Head
N
Sta
Yewbarrow 128m
Winster Valley
Witherslack Hall Farm
resvr.
Strickland Hill
tele.
Bowgreave Busk
Lawns House
Lawns Wood
Elleray Coppy
High Crag Wood
KG
Witherslack Hall School
pitch
Chapel Head Scar
lake
Whitbarrow Scar
gap
steep scree
Hagg Wood
Park Wood
CROSTHWAITE
BOWLAND BRIDGE
county boundary
River Winster
Lord's Seat 706
tarn
Black Yew Scar

as you cross the ridge, but then you cross a wall by a stile and enter another plantation and the bridleway drops down to Witherslack. Instead of following the bridleway all the way into the village turn off R and down to the road beside the church and the old vicarage.

Witherslack was the birthplace of the brothers John and Peter Barwick. John (1612-64) was a very loyal and active Royalist and was at one time committed to the Tower of London, where he remained for two years. After the Restoration he was offered the Bishopric of Carlisle, but declined. He eventually became Dean of St. Paul's and was buried there when he died, two years before its destruction in the Great Fire of London. The village church was built under his will. His younger brother Peter (1619-1705) was physician to Charles II. All his life he worked for the poor, without fee. He helped the sick in London during the Plague of 1665 and his house was destroyed in the Great Fire in 1666. He supported William Harvey's discovery of the circulation of the blood.

The church of **St. Paul** was built in 1669 and was consecrated in 1671 when the E window was added. It is an almost perfect example of a plain Gothic church of its period, with a severe white classical interior. The nave and chancel are all in one, although they were heightened in 1768. Inside there are panels bearing the arms of the Barwick brothers, and the Royal Arms are of Queen Anne, 1710. The fine canopied pulpit was once a three-decker of 1670, but the sounding board was removed in 1768. The church tower has a one handed clock, 1768, on its S face. The sundial in the churchyard was erected in 1757 and has the initials J.B. (for John Barwick) and the date 1671 on its dial to commemorate the patron of the church. A plaque on the outside S wall of the church says 'Rev. John Barwick STD, born of this hamlet, late Dean of St. Paul's, Built this Chappell. AD 1664'. (Although this date is not correct. Note also the spelling of 'Chappell'.)

Outside the church gate is **Dean Barwick's School,** founded 1678 and rebuilt 1874. (Although the tablet above the door says Dean Bancroft's School.) Adjoining is the **Masters House.** To the S is the Old Vicarage, now a country house, hotel and licensed restaurant.

Our path passes between the church and the old vicarage and continues SW, crosses another road, then turns slightly S into Halecat Wood. At an obvious crossing of paths turn R (W), passing the rotting remains of an old gypsy caravan and go down to a lane beside an old quarry. You are now out into the open pastures of the Winster valley. Go W on the farm track which curves round to Bowes Lodge, just inside Westmorland as the River Winster marks the county boundary.

Map 10.4

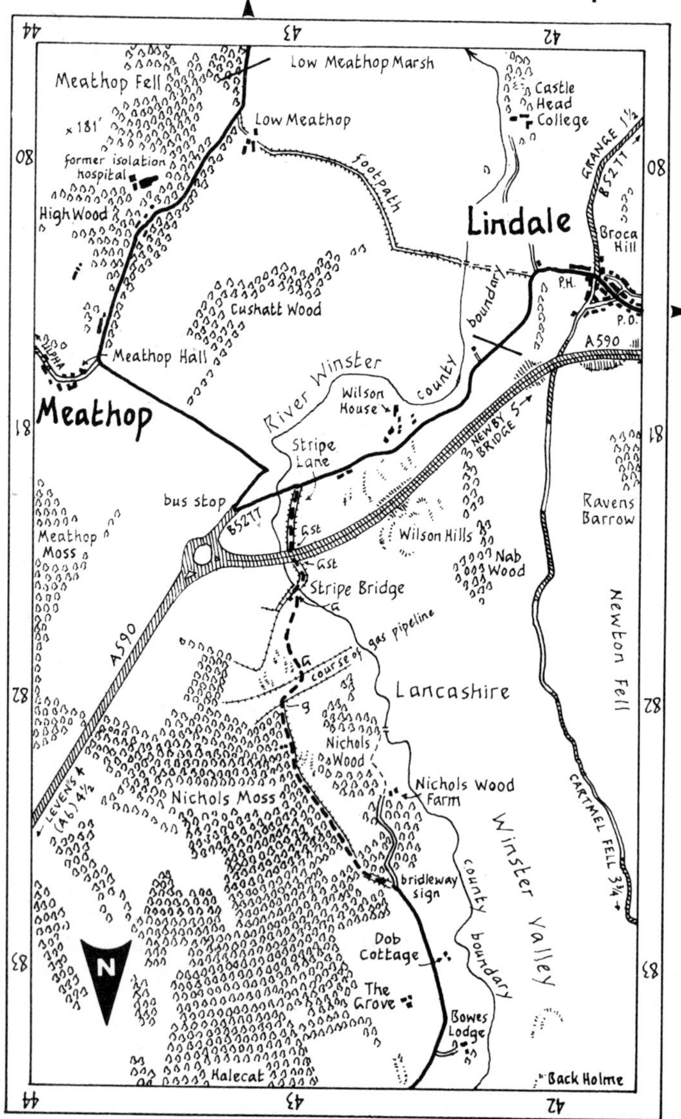

Low Meathop Marsh
Meathop Fell
Castle Head College
Low Meathop
x 181'
former isolation hospital
footpath
GRANGE 1½ B5277
High Wood
Lindale
Broca Hill
P.H.
P.O.
Cushatt Wood
boundary
A590
Meathop Hall
River Winster
county
Wilson House
Meathop
NEWBY BRIDGE 5
Stripe Lane
bus stop
B5277
Ravens Barrow
Meathop Moss
Gst
Wilson Hills
Nab Wood
Stripe Bridge
Newton Fell
gas pipeline
A590
course of
Lancashire
Nichols Wood
Nichols Wood Farm
LEVENS (A6) 4½
Nichols Moss
Winster Valley
CARTMEL FELL 3¾
bridleway sign
county boundary
Dob Cottage
N
The Grove
Bowes Lodge
Halecat
Back Holme

Map 10.4

Keep just inside Westmorland by following the farm track past Bowes Lodge, The Grove and Dob Cottage, but instead of going ahead to Nichols Farm fork L on a bridleway along the edge of a plantation and across Nichols Moss.

Nichols Moss is an area of raised peat bog at the lower end of the Winster valley, a remnant of the estuarine raised bog which was once extensive in the valleys at the head of Morecambe Bay. It is now a nationally rare habitat: the only other example in Westmorland is at Meathop Moss, immediately to the SE, across the A590.

The moss is some 1-2m higher than the surrounding agricultural land to the N and S. On its W side there is the transition to oak woodland over acid Silurian rocks and on its E side is a transition from woodland, scrub and grassland over Carboniferous limestone. Dense Scots pine and birch woodland surround the bog while the E edge is marked by a line of low limestone cliffs with yew, hazel, ash and some sessile oak.

The transition zone between the limestone and peatland has been known for nearly a century for its extensive populations of insects. Over 200 species of butterflies and moths have been recorded on Nichols Moss, including such notable species as the dark tussock moth, the silvery arches, the saxon and argent and sable. The uncommon large heath butterfly has also been recorded here.

Opposite Nichols Moss, on the other side of our footpath, is **Nichols Wood** which has developed on two small steep sided hillocks of Silurian rocks standing above the peat bog. The wood is dominated by sessile oak with birch, yew and rowan, with an understorey of hazel coppice and scattered hawthorn and blackthorn. On the steep SW side facing the river is holly, ash and wych elm. Bluebells and bilberry are characteristic flora of such acid ground conditions.

The path crosses the route of a gas pipeline, carrying natural gas from Morecambe Bay, passes under electricity cables and crosses the county boundary at Stripe Bridge over the Winster just before reaching the A590 dual carriageway of the Lindale by-pass. Cross the dual carriageway and follow the bridleway (Stripe Lane) between fences to the B5277 road.

Here we have the last of our High Level and Low Level options. The Low Level Route isn't required because of any difficulties that might be encountered on the High Level Route: it is simply a quick way of getting to Grange, on the level all the way, and on a road too, so it is somewhat of an anti-climax. The High Level, on the other hand, makes a final climb for a panoramic view over the Kent estuary from Hampsfield Fell before descending to Grange. Beside, the inclusion of the High Level Route makes

Map 10.5

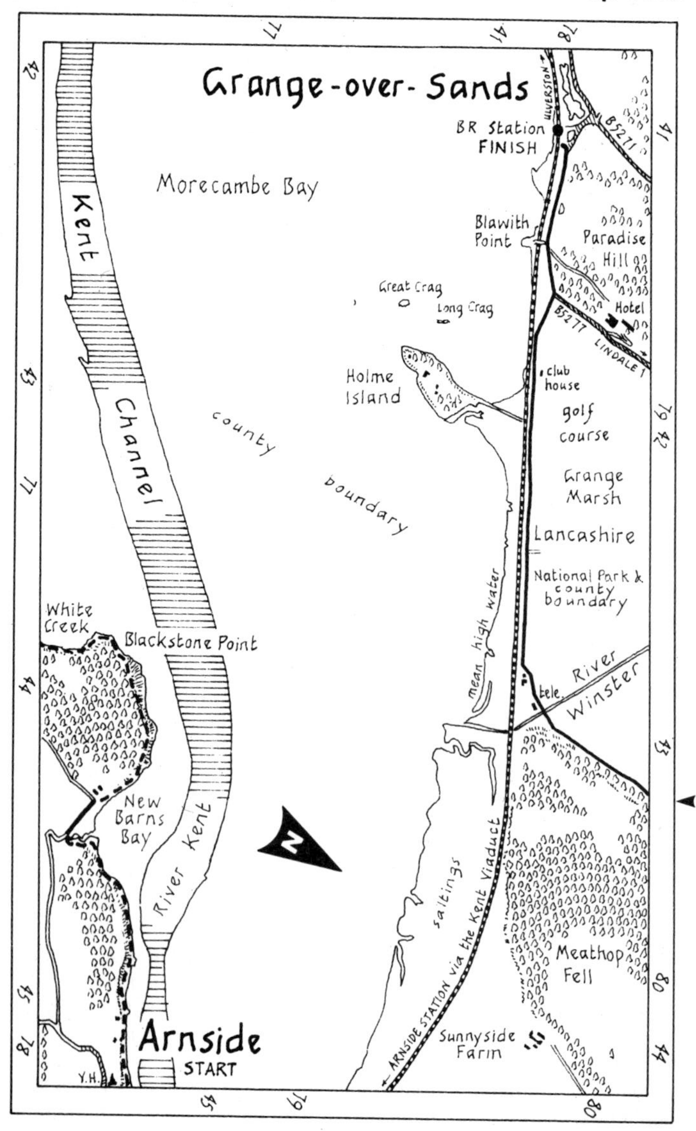

Grange-over-Sands
BR Station
FINISH
ULVERSTON
B5271
Morecambe Bay
Kent
Channel
Blawith Point
Paradise Hill
Great Crag
Long Crag
Hotel
B5277
LINDALE 1
Holme Island
club house
golf course
county
boundary
Grange Marsh
Lancashire
National Park & county boundary
mean high water
River Winster
tele
White Creek
Blackstone Point
New Barns Bay
River Kent
N
saltings
ARNSIDE STATION via the Kent Viaduct
Meathop Fell
Sunnyside Farm
Arnside
START
Y.H.

the walk the magic 200 miles (if you have been following our High Level options all the way throughout this guide).

Low Level Route

When you get to the B5277 turn L (E), cross the River Winster again and go back into Westmorland. At a junction with a minor road, by a bus stop shelter, just before you come to the A590 roundabout, turn R and follow the minor road to Meathop and beyond.

Meathop is a cluster of farms and old grey stone houses near the hospital which was built in 1891 as an isolation hospital for infectious diseases. It is now a convalescent home. The church which serves the hamlet is at Witherslack.

(Low Level Route continues on Map 10.5)

High Level Route

When you get to the B5277 turn R (W) and follow the road into Lindale. Although following a road may not seem to be anything like a high level route this is the only way we have of getting to Hampsfell. The only traffic using this road is that going to Lindale and Grange: fortunately the new by-pass has taken away the heavy traffic going to Barrow.

(High Level Route continues on Map 10.6)

Map 10.5

Low Level Route

The Meathop road runs along the edge of Meathop Marsh below Meathop Fell. It crosses the now canalised River Winster and then follows below the railway embankment: there is no view of the Kent estuary.

Without any ceremony the road crosses the county boundary and leaves Westmorland and the Lake District National Park.

On the L, out of sight behind the railway embankment, is Holme Island, a limestone knoll jutting out into the Kent estuary. In 1832 a city magnate built his summer retreat here. His house was in the Gothic style and in the grounds is a circular temple of *c.* 1850, a coach house, and a lodge at the end of the causeway leading to the island. He must have been annoyed when the railway company came along in 1857 building their high embankment and having noisy, smoky trains carrying tourists to gape down into his seclusion!

The road passes Grange's golf course and reaches the B5277 Grange-Lindale road. Here turn L and in a short distance you reach the railway station and the end of our walk around Westmorland.

As we said, a boring end to the journey. You would have been better served by taking our High Level Route!

Map 10.6

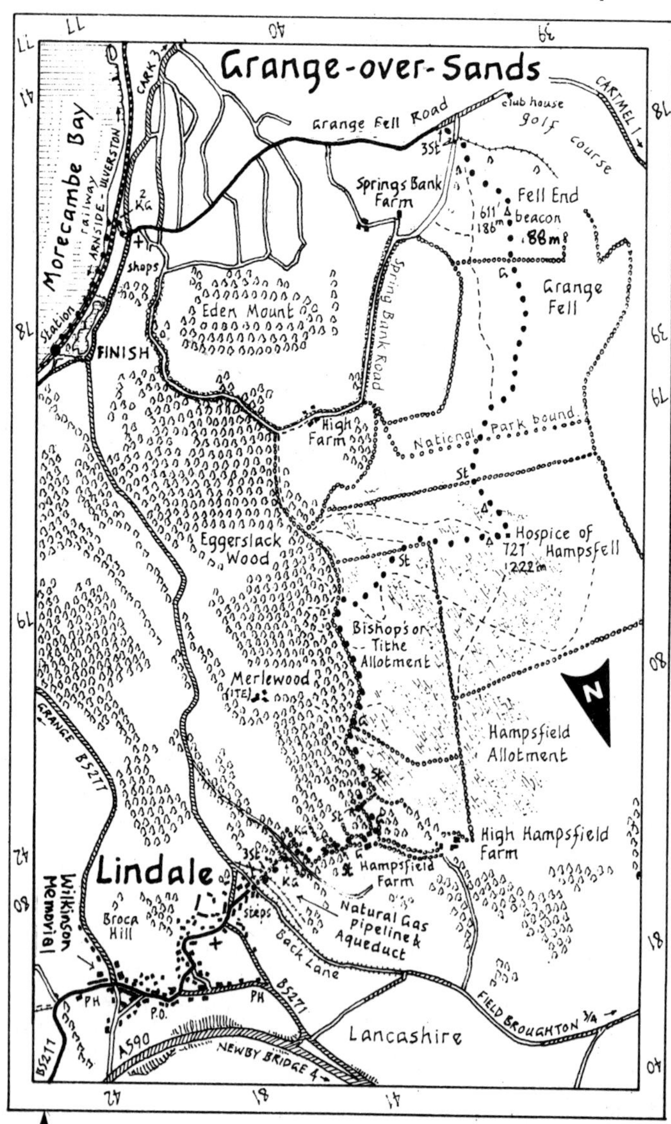

Grange-over-Sands
Morecambe Bay
Grange Fell Road
club house
golf course
CARTMEL 1
CARK 3
railway
ARNSIDE - ULVERSTON
Station
shops
FINISH
Springs Bank Farm
Fell End beacon
Grange Fell
Eden Mount
Spring Bank Road
High Farm
National Park bound.
Hospice of Hampsfell
Eggerslack Wood
Bishop's or Tithe Allotment
Merlewood
Hampsfield Allotment
High Hampsfield Farm
Hampsfield Farm
Natural Gas Pipeline & Aqueduct
Lindale
Broca Hill
Wilkinson Memorial
steps
Back Lane
GRANGE B5277
B5271
FIELD BROUGHTON 3/4
Lancashire
A590
NEWBY BRIDGE 4
P.O.
N

Map 10.6
High Level Route

The most interesting thing in Lindale is the **Wilkinson Monument,** a cast-iron obelisk standing on a mound beside the B5277 where it turns off for Grange. It is in memory of John Wilkinson (1728-1808), the great iron-master, and bears a relief profile of him in a medalion and an inscription in beautiful Trajan lettering.

Wilkinson's father Isaac was a farmer at Clifton, Cumberland, and also foreman of an iron furnace. He moved to Backbarrow, near Haverthwaite, *c.* 1738, where he developed his iron furnaces. In 1748 his son John, aged 20, started an iron furnace at Bilston, then both father and son moved first to Denbighshire, finally settling at Coalbrookdale. In 1779 John cast the parts for the famous and beautiful Coalbrookdale Bridge, the earliest of all iron bridges. The Wilkinsons later moved to Castlehead, SE of Lindale, and in 1786 John launched a cast-iron model of a ship in the local River Winster to prove that iron ships could float. He made a huge iron coffin for himself and also the obelisk to serve as a tomb marker, and directed that he should be buried in his own garden. This was done, but later the family sold Castlehead and the new owners had his remains moved to Lindale church. The obelisk was re-erected in its present position but it was once struck by lightning and lay neglected in the shrubbery for many years before being erected again. In 1983 it was taken away for restoration amidst doubts and arguments as to who should foot the bill for its repair.

Go up Lindale's steep main street, turning L just past the Post Office and then L again past the large village hall with its big clock and past the grey stone village school, 1838, enlarged 1894, with its single bell-cote and bell, and arrive at the church, down in the dell.

The church of **St. Paul,** 1828, was designed by George Webster of Kendal. The chancel was added in 1864, the church enlarged in 1894, and the N aisle added in 1912. The church's predecessor was where George Fox, the Quaker, preached in 1652. The Royal Arms above the door are of George III and there is an interesting carved and painted reredos of Christ flanked by two angels with St. Martin on one side of him and St. Elizabeth of Hungary on the other. On the S wall of the church is a memorial tablet to Mary Wilkinson, wife of John the iron-master, above the spot where he was re-buried. In the churchyard is a massive monument to Webster, who died in 1861. It is in the late-Classical style and at the top is an inscription slab surrounded by cast-iron railings.

At the B5271 turn L, then quickly R on a path with steps leading up to another road called Back Lane. Our path beyond follows a parish boundary, which is the boundary of the Lake District National Park and we cross water aqueducts and gas pipelines on the way as it climbs up to Home Farm, then turns L (S) on a track alongside a wall through Bishop's or Tithe Allotment.

Eggerslack Wood lies below, on the flank of Hampsfield Fell, and the open expanse of Hampsfield Allotment is above. In the woods is **Merlewood,** a large Victorian mansion built for the calico printer Alfred Binyon in 1853. In 1856 it became the home of Eliza Horrocks of the Preston cotton-spinning family in whose family it remained until 1933 when it was sold to the Mutual Holiday Association Ltd. It became the Merlewood Hotel until 1940 when it was requisitioned by the War Office for army training. It reverted to use as a hotel in 1947 and was acquired by The Nature Conservancy Council in 1951 as its first research station in the country. The Institute of Terrestial Ecology was created in 1973 and the two research bodies (NCC and ITE) occupied Merlewood jointly until 1980 when the NCC moved to Blackwell, formerly a girls private school, near Windermere. Perhaps one reason why these organisations were here is because of the wide variety of habitats in this part of southern Lakeland - Silurian slates, Carboniferous limestone, peat moss and salt marsh.

Hampsfield Allotment is an area of limestone pavement, similar to the scars we have walked over since leaving Kendal. On the summit (727ft/222m) is a **Hospice** built by a 'former pastor of Cartmel parish for the shelter and entertainment of wanderers over the fell'. A ground floor room with a fireplace provides the shelter. Projecting stone steps lead up to a flat roof where a direction indicator in the form of a compass, with all points of interest in view named, provides the entertainment. The summit is a superb viewpoint, and a grand climax to our walk.

A confusing number of paths lead up to the Hospice but we take a direct line to a stile in the wall near a corner and we soon reach the summit.

Our path leads away from the Hospice in a southerly direction, over a wall by a stile, and out of the Lake District National Park, then S towards the cairn on Fell End (611ft/188m). A descent off the end leads you down to a road near a junction with Grange Fell Road. Follow Grange Fell Road steeply down into Grange-over-Sands, passing 17c **Hardcragg Hall** *(its sundial is dated 1663) with its Beatrix Potter associations. At the main road stands* **St. Paul's** church, built of limestone in 1853 in the Geometric style. The aisles were added in the 1860's - the S aisle is wider than the N aisle - and the chancel was added in 1932. At the top end of Main Street, below the church and outside the Crown Hotel,

1789, is a tall, square, limestone and sandstone clock tower of 1912. *Cross over The Esplanade and go down to the railway line, then follow the Promenade along to the railway station and the finish of our Westmorland Heritage Walk.*

Alternatively, from the clock tower, go down Main Street towards the station, passing through the busy 'shopping centre' with rows of Victorian shops on both sides dating from the 1860's to the turn of the century. The Victoria Hall is 1898 and designed by the Kendal architect John Hutton. Turn R when you can into the Victorian Park Road Gardens with its ornamental beds of flowers and shrubs and pond with ornamental wildfowl. A gate at the end of the gardens bring you out beside the railway station.

Grange-over-Sands likes to be called the 'Torquay of the North' although it cannot claim the size or range of amusements of the Devonshire resort. Its nickname, however, sufficiently indicates its ambitions and is completely justifiable on the score of its climate, its promenade and sea front gardens - a beautiful setting between sea and mountains.

Grange began to develop as a resort when the Furness Railway arrived in 1857. The large hotels and a Convalescent Home attest to its popularity as a resort and retirement centre. Opposite the railway station the railway company built the **Grange Hotel** in 1866: the driveway up from the road passes the former stable block which was used as a licensed waiting room for horse and coach rides into the countryside. To the E end of the village, out towards Lindale, is the **Grand Hotel,** built in 1877 as a health hydro, and nearby is the **Netherwood Hotel,** 1893, a magnificent mansion in the Tudor style with panelled ceilings, stone fireplaces and other fine Tudor period pieces. At the W end of the village is the very large red brick and white terracotta **Convalescent Home,** built in 1914 and still used as such. The town has a predominantly elderly population and as the hills in the town are a bit too steep for some retired people the local estate agents do a roaring trade in property that is 'a level walk close to the town centre'.

There is a centuries-old coach route across the sands from Grange to Lancaster which saves a 14 mile/22.5km detour round the head of Morecambe Bay and a guide still exists to prove the route through the constant shifting quicksands and waters of the Rivers Kent and Keer and accompany anyone who wishes to approach or leave the Lake District by this route.

The guides were originally appointed and maintained by the Prior of Cartmell and the Abbot of Furness petitioned Edward II for the appointment of a coroner because so many people were drowned in

Arnside Knott from Grange Station

the crossing. When Cartmell Priory was dissolved the Duchy of Lancaster took over the appointment of the guides and to this day part of the guides' salary is paid by the Duchy revenues, although administered by the Charity Commissioners. The guides are also farmers and fishermen. A full and interesting account of the guides and their work, and the ancient industries of fluke fishing, cockling and mussel gathering in Morecambe Bay are given in the books 'The Sands of Morecambe Bay', by Mr.J.Pape and by the current guide Cedric Jackson, 'Sand Pilot of Morecambe Bay'. Turner's painting of 'Lancaster Sands' shows a stagecoach arriving at Hest Bank *c.*1828 after a crossing of the sands from Grange.

Anyone who wishes to cross the sands should get in touch with the guide at Guide House, Cart Lane, Kents Bank, nr. Grange-over-Sands, who will advise on the suitability of crossing.

We, however, suggest that you take a short railway journey alongside the estuary of the River Kent and over the viaduct to bring you back to Arnside and your starting point.

We have tried to show you in this walk around Westmorland part of Westmorland's heritage - upon the natural landscape of bleak moors, lush green valleys, magnificent mountain peaks and sylvan lakes has been introduced farming, settlements by both temporal and spiritual magnates, military training grounds, quarrying and planned and unplanned town development.

Westmorland's heritage is thus a mixed one - a blend formed by differing needs at differing times and one that, set in the most naturally beautiful part of England, we hope you have seen and enjoyed as much as we have.

Hell Gill Force, Mallerstang.